# FOREVER

Other Novels by Judith Gould

*Sins*

*Dazzle*

*Never Too Rich*

The Love-Makers Saga:

*Love-Makers*

*Texas Born*

# Judith Gould

# Forever

A DUTTON BOOK

DUTTON

Published by the Penguin Group
Penguin Books USA Inc., 375 Hudson Street, New York, New York 10014, U.S.A.
Penguin Books Ltd, 27 Wrights Lane, London W8 5TZ, England
Penguin Books Australia Ltd, Ringwood, Victoria, Australia
Penguin Books Canada Ltd, 10 Alcorn Avenue, Toronto, Ontario, Canada M4V 3B2
Penguin Books (N.Z.) Ltd, 182-190 Wairau Road, Auckland 10, New Zealand

Penguin Books Ltd, Registered Offices:
Harmondsworth, Middlesex, England

First published by Dutton, an imprint of New American Library,
a division of Penguin Books USA Inc.
Distributed in Canada by McClelland & Stewart Inc.

ISBN 0–525–93495–2

Printed in the United States of America
Set in Sabon and Shelley Allegro

Designed by Steven N. Stathakis

PUBLISHER'S NOTE

*For*
*Stephen Biegner and Douglas McDougall*
*and*
*Vicky's irrepressible younger sister*
*—the best company on those journeys*
*through the Balkans and the Crimea*

My very special thanks go to the
Irving Paul Lazar Agency & especially
to Alan Nevins
for going a million light years
beyond the call of duty

THE LAST ENEMY THAT SHALL BE
DESTROYED IS DEATH.

—The Second Epistle of
Paul the Apostle
to the Corinthians

MINE IS YESTERDAY, I KNOW TOMORROW.

—Book of the Dead, circa 3500 B.C.

# *Prologue*

The world had never seen anything like it.

From across the sundered nation and beyond, the hordes converged upon the city to pay their last respects to the woman they had loved. By bicycle and train and car and boat they came; a privileged few even arrived at Tempelhof Airport by plane. Many had walked for days, carrying their children on their shoulders. Young and old, male and female, rich and poor, priests and sinners they came.

Lili Schneider was dead. She would sing no more.

She lay in state at Schloss Bellevue like a queen, in a closed, curvaceous black coffin mounted with ormolu. The viewing line stretched around the Tiergarten for nearly three kilometers, and for four days it never grew shorter.

They were drab mourners in that bleak postwar year, but even in death Lili Schneider infused the people with color and filled their hearts with joy. Radios played nothing but her acclaimed recordings of Wagner and Smetana and Beethoven and Schubert. Millions wept from grief, and millions more at the sheer beauty of that matchless voice.

And so they came:

Mothers clutching their hungry babies . . .

Grandmothers who had lost everyone in the war, for whom Lili's songs brought the ghosts momentarily back to life . . .

Soldiers back from distant fronts, who had been given courage and kept homesickness at bay listening to her recordings . . .

Widows whose husbands, in happier times, had once taken them to see Lili in operas and operettas . . .

And now young *fräuleins* holding hands with their GI sweethearts.

Lili Schneider had been an enchantress. A dream-weaver. A siren. She had cast her spell over an entire nation, and even death itself could not break it.

Lili with the face of an angel. Lili with the voice of a nightingale. Lili with the body of a whore.

Men had worshipped her, women had adored her. She had ruled the stages of the greatest opera houses in Europe—not to mention the bedrooms of the most powerful men of her day.

She belonged to Germany. And now, after an absence of five years, she had returned. Inside the oval coffin, her remains were pathetically charred and shriveled. The fire that had engulfed the house in London had destroyed her completely. Gone was her life and her beauty, but her music would live on forever.

Millions wept. And over the airwaves, the entire country tuned in as each radio station played the same thing: Lili's recording of the Brahms Requiem.

Even in those days of scratchy LPs and static-filled airwaves, Lili's voice rose above the flaws. For whatever she sang, she imbued with the magical spark of life itself, giving it shape and volume and emotion and thunder.

Carleton Merlin, a young correspondent for the *Herald-Tribune,* had managed to fight his way to the graveside. There he raised his bulky camera just as Louisette Bielfeld, Lili's even more beautiful sister, lifted her black veils, brushing them back away from her face. Carleton waited as a pallbearer handed her a small silver scoop. He waited as she dug it into the mountain of earth beside the grave. Then, the moment she tossed a symbolic scoopful down into the grave, he clicked the shutter and captured Louisette's soul.

When the film was developed, he was perplexed: Louisette was smiling a smile as enigmatic as the Mona Lisa's. He stared at the photograph and frowned. *Why?* he wondered. *Why is she smiling?*

Although Carleton did not know it at the time, the moment he had pressed the shutter was the moment his life truly began.

And that precise moment, also, would herald the end of his life, many years later.

For Lili Schneider's power was such that even in death it would reach across the years, across the seas—and across the very sands of time itself.

# Book One

# DEATH

# 1

"From the legendary Pharaoh's Palace Resort and Casino here on the world-famous Boardwalk in Atlantic City," boomed the slick professional announcer, "it's the annual, forty-eight-hour Children's Relief Year-Round Aaaaall-Star Telethon! And now, introducing your host and hostess for the first six-hour portion of the CRY telethon, won't you please help me welcome those superstars of stage, screen, and television—heeeeeere are Shanna Parker and Joe Belmotti!"

The live audience in the Cleopatra Auditorium applauded wildly as the first orchestral stanzas of "On the Boardwalk" started up and two spotlights clicked on. Bathed in one, Shanna Parker strode perkily out from stage left, all aglitter in a figure-hugging gown of silver-and-blue sequins. Joe Belmotti, tanned as a nut in his formal black tie, entered smoothly from stage right in the second spot.

"Thank you," Shanna purred into her hand-held microphone. Then, porcelain smiles beaming, she and Joe Belmotti called out, "Hello, America!" in unison while spreading their arms wide to encompass everybody.

"HELLO, SHANNA AND JOE!" the audience roared back, bursting into a fresh round of frenzied applause.

"What a nice audience!" Shanna told them warmly. "Let's hear it for all of you!" And tucking their microphones under their arms, she and Joe began to clap enthusiastically.

"And now, what do you say we hear it for the good cause we're all here for?" Joe Belmotti added once the applause died down.

More wild clapping followed.

"Isn't it wonderful to be here, Joe?" Shanna asked him excitedly. "I wouldn't have missed this for anything in the world! You wouldn't believe the guests we've got lined up! But first, why don't you tell all those viewers out there who are not familiar with CRY what this wonderful organization is all about, and how much good it is doing each and every day?"

Joe Belmotti picked up without missing a beat.

"And wonderful it is, the good CRY is doing, Shanna. Did you know that every single day, millions upon millions of children around the world are going to bed hungry or dying of treatable diseases? That's why CRY—"

"Which stands for Children's Relief Year-Round," Shanna interjected quickly.

"—feeds and clothes millions of children, and sends doctors and nurses out into third-world countries—and even to pockets of poverty right here at home."

"And, since CRY is a nonprofit agency," Shanna added, "it's the pennies, nickels, dimes, quarters, and dollars which *you*, the good sponsors, pledge and send in which finance all these good deeds. Without your tax-deductible contributions, all those millions of innocent children we're helping would suffer. Not only that, but there are so many millions more crying out for help right now."

"You know, Shanna, sometimes I think I can actually hear them."

"So can all of us, if we listen closely enough. Now, why don't we show our friends all across America the pledge room, where the first shift of two hundred and fifty volunteers—who, I might mention, have generously donated their time—are manning the telephones for our toll-free, one-eight-hundred pledge number, which will appear on the screen from time to time?"

And in the pledge room, spurred on by the two celebrities, the switchboard for the 1-800 number suddenly lit up like a Christmas tree.

"God, but that woman has a voice!" Sammy Kafka rhapsodized as the two men let themselves be swept out of the Metropolitan Opera House by the formally dressed crowd. "Like an angel she sings!" He kissed his fingertips noisily. "Ah, but to spend a lifetime with her and be privileged to hear her practice! That would be heaven, dear boy! Sheer blissful heaven!"

"But I thought you didn't like fat women," Carleton Merlin observed with a smile.

"Fat?" Sammy Kafka looked up at his friend sharply. "Who says she's fat? She's zaftig!" He clenched his liver-spotted hands and shook his fists robustly. "*Zaftig!*" he repeated with a boyish gleam in his eye.

Carleton Merlin laughed and clapped Sammy gently on the back. He was long since used to the weaknesses of his oldest and dearest friend. One perfect high C, and Sammy inevitably fell rapturously, instantaneously, head-over-heels in love. It never failed.

"That way," Sammy said quickly, and unerringly pointed to the right. Carleton, much the taller of the two, craned his head and looked. Sure enough, there was an opening in the crowd.

Wisely, Sammy held onto Carleton's arm so they wouldn't get separated. For Sammy Kafka was very, very short, and could easily be swallowed up in a crowd. He was also exquisite—a darling old man with wild tufts of snowy white hair who was forever dapper—a dandy in his late seventies. Carleton had never once seen Sammy looking anything less than perfect—and perfection in Sammy Kafka's case included a fresh red carnation in his lapel, a perfectly tied bow of polka-dot silk at his neck, and a high-gloss shine on his shoes.

Something about Sammy gave an impression of perpetual youth. Perhaps it was the way his crinkly gazelle eyes smiled out at the world in wonder, as if every day was his first. Or it could simply have been his enthusiasm, his sprightly step, or the jaunty, youthful tilt of his head. Whatever the case, he looked so endearingly cute that no matter what eccentricities he displayed, friends and strangers overlooked them—a response not shared by those who worked in the world of music and knew him better. World-class composers, conductors, musicians, singers—even set designers—for them the darling little man meant sheer unmitigated terror.

For Sammy Kafka was the most eminent classical music critic in America. Some said the entire world.

Carleton Merlin was younger than his seventy-seven-year-old friend: he'd recently turned a chipper seventy. But in his own way, he was just as different from the rest of humanity as Sammy Kafka.

People tended to forget that Carleton Merlin had been born in Boston—he looked the very picture of Southern aristocracy, a genial mint julep of a gentleman. Whereas Sammy was tiny, he was tall and imposing; whereas Sammy looked like a gust of wind could blow him away, Carleton wore his paunch with pride. He tended toward white tropical suits, Panama hats, and thin black string ties—which, together with his white goatee and hair, made him a dead ringer for a plantation colonel. His silver-headed cane was no affectation: an accident many years ago had left him with a pronounced limp.

"Just look at them!" Sammy growled. "You'd think King Kong was on the rampage!" He gestured angrily at the crowd, which surged across the Lincoln Center plaza and on down the steps to the street. "Inside, it's all 'Brava! Brava!' and now they have left it all behind them already! Where are they rushing off to in such a hurry? Little egg-carton rooms? After-theater suppers? *People!*" he snorted. "Sometimes they don't deserve the beauty their money buys them." Malevolently he eyed the crowd that still poured by. "*Dilettantes!*" he shouted. In his mind, it was the worst thing he could call anyone.

Carleton had to laugh. Sammy had never borne any patience with people who ate and ran. *And what is opera?* he could almost hear Sammy expound. *Why, it's the finest damn feast on earth—food for the soul! So how can they eat and run, dammit?*

"Come, let's wait for these lemmings to thin out," Carleton said in disgust, and steered his friend to the fountain in the middle of the plaza. It had become a tradition for them to sit there and savor the performance they had just heard—if, indeed, it was justified. Tonight that was happily the case, and they both felt elevated and electrified—too elevated and far too electrified to scurry off into the glittering late spring night. Such a perfectly staged opera deserved to be savored, lingering on the senses like a fine wine singing on the palate.

For long minutes they just sat there by the crashing jets, Sammy, with his head tilted to one side and his hands folded precisely on his lap, Carleton, with his large-boned gnarled hands resting atop the silver knob of his ebony cane.

A shift in the breeze enveloped them in a thin mist of cool spray.

"So . . ." Sammy said. "Are you planning to stay in town long this time?"

Carleton didn't hear him. The "Ombra Leggera" from Meyerbeer's *Dinorah* still filled his mind with the rich, resonant notes of the first-rate soprano.

"I said," Sammy repeated a little testily, "now that you're back, are you planning to stay in town for a while?"

"For the next few days, yes." Carleton nodded. "Then I have to fly back to London, and from there on to Vienna."

"Still researching that damn Schneider biography, I see," Sammy said with a disgruntled grumble. "You and Lili Schneider! You've spent how many years on research now? Two and a half? Three?"

Carleton glanced at him with an amused smile. "Closer to five."

"Five years!" Sammy sighed, and shook his head morosely. "At our age, that could be the remainder of our lifetimes."

Carleton shrugged. "Lili warrants a definitive biography. So far, everything published about her has been either thoroughly sanitized or else totally scandalous."

"And you've found out something new? Something earth-shattering, I suppose?" Sammy was careful to sound cynical and vaguely disinterested. He knew only too well that Carleton guarded his biographical discoveries jealously. Asking him specific questions was the fastest road to nowhere. A roundabout little song-and-dance number would achieve far more.

"Oh, I guess you could say I've been making some progress," Carleton said offhandedly, and nodded.

"That's good," Sammy nodded. "That's good."

"I like to think so." Carleton stared at the five soaring glass arches of the opera house, which, with its modern Sputnik chandeliers and Chagall's dreamy murals, never failed to depress him. The stark modernity made him long for the gilded confections of the grand old opera palaces of Europe.

"And when your research is all said and done," Sammy went on in that same disinterested tone, "we will find out that Lili had a passion for Swiss chocolates, or that she didn't pay her couturier bill on time, or bartered her body in exchange for diamonds or some such?"

"Well ... something to that effect, I suppose," Carleton said solemnly, as though such minutiae weighed heavily on his mind.

"And, judging from your past biographies, I assume you will also wait until right before publication, and then call a press conference where you will announce some earth-shaking information that will jolt the public to its very toes?" His line cast, Sammy squinted sideways at him and waited.

But Carleton didn't bite; he swam blithely past the bait. "A news conference ... hmmm." He frowned thoughtfully and nodded slowly. "Yes. My publisher would like that, I think. A tidbit ... something tasty ... a morsel to whet everyone's appetite ... I must remember that. Tends to sell a lot of copies, you know."

Sammy stifled a growl of disgust. Trying to get solid information out of Carleton could be like prying open a clam that had been welded shut—using one's bare fingers yet.

"And this tidbit you will share with so much fanfare ... I suppose you already know what it is?"

"Well, I have given it some thought," Carleton admitted, "yes."

"And it *will* be earth-shattering?"

"That too." Carleton managed to look bored, as if it was the farthest thing from his mind—a sure indication to Sammy that he was not only holding back, but sitting on a doozie.

*What could it be?* "A lost recording?" Sammy ventured slyly. "A hitherto undiscovered studio tape?"

"I'm always on the lookout for one." Carleton seemed totally blasé. *You're putting me to sleep*, his droopy eyes communicated.

Sammy felt like shaking him and screaming. "You've dug up an illegitimate child?"

But it was as if Carleton hadn't heard. "Of course, I'm leaving no stone unturned. With biographies, one has to dig deep and keep digging. You wouldn't believe the secrets the average human mind harbors. So when it comes to a great dead genius, you can expect the secrets he or she took to the grave to be buried more deeply than most."

"Carleton, you really are a first-class schmuck!" Sammy said in hurt disgust. "Don't forty years of friendship count for anything? You know I can keep a secret. But the way you're carrying on, well ... one would think you'd discovered the cure for cancer!"

Carleton just smiled.

"You know how I hate mysteries." Sammy moped.

"Ah, but this one, my friend, will be well worth waiting for. You shall see."

"If you say so," Sammy said peevishly, knowing it was futile to pry any further.

*Which only proves one thing,* Sammy thought. *Whatever he's discovered, it's big. Really big. But what could it be?*

They sat in silence a while longer. The departing opera buffs had thinned to a mere trickle; the plaza was nearly empty, giving it a slightly perilous, gloomy appearance.

Finally, Sammy sighed. "It's time we got going," he muttered, getting to his feet, "or else we'll make perfect targets for muggers." Looking down at himself, he adjusted the carnation in his lapel.

Leaning on his cane, Carleton pushed himself to his feet, and together, the two friends strolled slowly to the steps and down to where Columbus Avenue crosses Broadway, where they embraced and parted company, promising to call each other soon. With his usual sprightliness, Sammy headed uptown, while Carleton with his usual slow but steady, stately limp, made his way south and east.

He couldn't help but chuckle.

*If only Sammy knew!* But even if he'd told his friend what he was sitting on, Sammy wouldn't have believed him. Nobody would. *Until recently, neither would I,* he reminded himself.

It was a short walk to 205 West Fifty-seventh Street, and his apartment at the Osborne, the second-oldest luxury apartment building in the city. Reddish stone, symmetrically placed bay windows, and the style of a heavily rusticated Renaissance palazzo gave the building a dignity which even its grime and ground-floor storefronts could not entirely mar.

The night doorman greeted him with a smile. "The opera again?" he guessed as he held the door.

Carleton laughed and waved his cane. "You, my friend, should be a detective."

And with a rare dance step which attested to his ebullient mood, Carleton made his way to the elevators doing an ungainly imitation of Fred Astaire.

He was still dancing clumsily when he let himself into the substantial splendor of his apartment. It was enormous for a lone man, especially a man whose wants decreased with every passing year. As far as he was concerned, there were altogether far too many rooms filled with far too many bibelots and dust catchers—a lifetime's accumulation of, well, just *stuff.* Funny, how the older one got, the less material things meant.

*I pity Stephanie the day I kick the bucket,* he thought. *In fact, I pity anybody who has to clean this place out and get rid of all these tschotskes.*

Humming the "Ombra Leggera," he flipped his Panama hat at the coat tree; as usual, it landed perfectly on one of the hooks. Then, leaving his cane by the front door, he limped to the kitchen to rummage through the refrigerator. Eyeing the shelves Pham Van Hau, his housekeeper, kept stocked with food, he decided to build himself a substantial sandwich. Got out the pumpernickel and Pham's specialty, a cold, cholesterol-rich pork roast which would have made his doctor blanch. Cut a two-inch-thick slice, put it between the bread, and added ketchup for good measure. Then, pouring himself a healthy jolt of red table wine, he munched and sipped contentedly as he limped his way to the room in which he spent nearly all of his time.

Like many a person who lived alone, he automatically flipped on the television for company. It happened to be set to one of the local independent stations.

". . . Weren't they wonderful, Joe?" gushed the perky voice onscreen. "And to think they haven't sung as a trio since nineteen sixty-eight! This truly was history in the making! You know, just hearing them again took me right back to the heyday of Motown?"

"It did me, too, Shanna. Weren't those the days? Anyway, on to more serious matters. According to the note I was just handed, would you believe that in the last three hours we've raised a total of . . . twenty . . . three . . . million . . . dollars! Now isn't that something?"

Rousing applause greeted this news.

"It sure is, Joe. But as anyone out there who's been to a supermarket knows, money isn't worth what it used to be . . ."

Carleton set down his sandwich and shot a scowl at the TV set. Then he went into the connecting bathroom, plopped his dentures into a glass, took a blood pressure pill, and limped back out. He was still wide awake, too wide awake to go to sleep just yet. Maybe he'd work on the Schneider biography for a few more hours. *Every hour is precious,* he thought. *And there's still so much to do . . .*

". . . And just so nobody gets the wrong idea, Joe, we've got to make our viewers understand that they shouldn't be fooled by what seems like a lot of money pouring in. It really isn't much, not for what CRY wants to do."

"That's right, Shanna. You know, CRY isn't just the sound of a child weeping, it's—"

"—A call for help," Shanna finished smoothly for him.

"CRY needs help all right!" Carleton snarled, glowering as he snapped off the TV. "Goddamn hypocrites!" he muttered.

Just then, from out in the hallway, he heard the doorbell.

Frowning, he cocked his head. It was nearly midnight.

"Now who the hell can that be?" he muttered to himself, before shuffling painfully off to see.

# 2

"The eighth amendment in the Bill of Rights is the right to bear . . . no. That is the second. The eighth . . ."

Pham Van Hau kept his voice soft as he inserted the key in the last lock and turned it. He was a slim Vietnamese refugee in his early thirties, and his upcoming U.S. citizenship test loomed large and foremost in his mind.

The lock cylinder clicked and he opened the door, slipped into the high-ceilinged reception room with his usual light step, and drew back as the rank smell of corruption abruptly hit him. He crinkled his nose in disgust and waved a slender-fingered hand in front of his face. What on *earth* was that smell? *Spoiled meat?*

"Perhaps he took off traveling again and forgot to put out the trash," he thought as he closed the door and bolted it, set down his Balducci shopping bag, and hung up his lightweight sports jacket on the coat tree. For a moment, he just stood there frowning, his high-cheekboned head cocked to one side.

The apartment was quiet.

"Nobody is at home," he murmured to himself.

He could always tell right away. Empty apartments always had that peculiar lack of sound, that feeling of dead air.

*Well, there was no use loitering. But first things first.*

Moving quickly, he pushed open the door to the double parlor that overlooked the corner of Fifty-seventh and Seventh. He stood in the doorway and looked around the room. No. Nothing here. Crossing the room, he threw open the three bay windows. The sounds of traffic from below drifted in, but Pham paid them no heed. If anything, he welcomed the noise. It made the apartment seem more alive . . . less spooky, somehow.

Sniffing suspiciously, he went in search of the source of that sweetly cloying odor. It did not come from the kitchen. Going from room to room, he raised all the windows to air out that terrible stench.

Miss Stephanie's old bedroom. The smell seemed stronger at this end of the hall. Pham's shiny dark eyes searched the room. No, nothing in here, either. He went into the adjoining bath. "No," he said aloud, and frowned deeply.

Master bedroom. He paused outside the half-open door, hands on his slight hips. It had to be coming from in here, that smell. His ears caught the muted sounds of buzzing, almost like a swarm of bees. *Bees! In the house? In the middle of the city?* Cautiously he pushed on the open door, breathing only through his nose.

Straight ahead, an overturned chair lay on the floor. And, directly in his line of vision, a pair of bare feet dangled slackly above it. He heard a strange whimpering and didn't realize the sound came from within himself.

Trembling, he made his eyes drift up the naked legs, flaccid abdomen with its shriveled privates and white pubic hair, and—oh, Holy Buddha—the lolling, bloated features of . . . Mr. Merlin! A swarm of flies, startled by Pham's arrival, rose up from the corpse and buzzed madly around it like a swirling cyclone.

Pham stood there, frozen in horror. His employer . . . his *former* employer . . . was hanging from the heavy Dutch chandelier, a belt around his swollen neck and festering face. And already, the cyclone swarm was thinning, the body darkening as the flies blatantly alighted to continue their interrupted feast.

Pham overcame his paralysis. Stumbling backward, he clapped a hand over his mouth and then turned and bolted back to the reception room. He fumbled with the bolts, threw open the front door, all the while yelling as loudly as his lungs would permit, which, neighbors could attest, was loud enough to wake the dead.

Only it didn't wake Carleton Merlin.

"You know what, lady?" Jed Savitt, convicted rapist, serial killer, and death-row inmate, held Stephanie Merlin's gaze with eyes like flat gray pebbles. "You're the best piece of tail ever walked through that door."

"Cut," Stephanie Merlin called out wearily to her camera crew.

The floodlights abruptly dimmed. The videocam stopped rolling.

Stephanie pushed a hand through her hair, sighed, and then folded her hands as she leaned across the metal desk. She locked eyes with the killer. "Mr. Savitt." She fought to keep her voice unemotional and professionally clipped. "Must I keep reminding you that we are taping this program for prime time?"

Savitt's chilly eyes seemed to bore straight through her, and she shivered involuntarily. *They're dead eyes,* she thought with a shudder. *Thank God I'm not alone with him.*

Just the idea made her skin crawl.

Besides herself and him, there were six others in the small, airless room on death row. Two uniformed prison guards, the warden, who manned the telephone in case the execution was stayed, and a crew from "Half Hour," Stephanie's syndicated news magazine show, which aired once a week on two hundred independent television stations nationwide.

As usual, she had chosen Rusty Schwartz, her best cameraman, Rob Manelli, who worked magic with the lights, and Ted Warwick, her producer. It was a skeleton crew, but all the space and situation allowed.

Stephanie stared at Savitt and took a deep breath. He was leaning back in his chair, his eyes eating her up. In his early thirties, he was a six-footer with virile good looks. His thick, straw-colored hair, strong chin, and freckles could have made him Mr. American Pie—except for a nose that had once been flattened and one little mental defect. He had a thing about young girls. And baseball bats.

Stephanie found it hard not to let her loathing show.

She told herself that this was all part and parcel of her job. Some job.

Stephanie Merlin was twenty-eight years old and handsome, too big-boned to ever be called exquisite, and too challenging and authoritative to be considered beautiful. She was, however, undeniably striking, and for some reason, camera lenses, even videocams—perhaps the most unkind lenses and cameras ever crafted—tended to emphasize her high cheek-bones and wide-spaced, pale topaz eyes.

She was five feet, nine inches tall, one hundred and twenty-five pounds, with luminous pale ivory skin and strawberry blond, shoulder-length hair. She wore it pulled back, clipped with a large blue bow. Gold earclips in the shape of snail shells and a simple thick gold necklace set off her dark blue suit and white silk blouse.

Jed Savitt wondered what she would look like naked with her hair down. While impaled on two baseball bats.

"Let's get a few things straight before we continue," she told him in her brisk, business voice. "I didn't ask to come down here. Your lawyer called *us* and offered *me* an exclusive interview. See that door?"

She pointed and he nodded.

"You're either going to cooperate, or my crew and I are marching right through it and then it's, *Ciao* baby. *Capishe?* The choice is yours. Now which will it be?"

Savitt looked at her long and hard and then grinned. Rather, his lips grinned; his eyes never came to life. "You know, you're one tough lady," he said admiringly. "Sure you weren't a prison matron once?"

Stephanie started to push back her chair.

"Okay, okay!" America's most notorious serial killer waved at Rusty Schwartz and Rob Manelli. "Tell them to roll."

Schwartz and Manelli looked at her for confirmation.

She nodded. "All right, guys," she said, "you heard the man. Pick up where we left off."

The lights clicked back on, bathing the room in a glaring white flood, and the tape in the videocam began rolling.

Stephanie crossed one leg over the other and continued where they had left off. "Now then, Jed." Her voice sounded appropriately professional. "You have one hour remaining until your scheduled execution. Before you die, is there anything you would like to say to the families of your victims?"

He smiled. "Stephanie," he returned with the easy first-name familiarity of television. "They were not my victims. As you know, I was convicted of the . . . ah . . . crimes, yes. But I still maintain my innocence."

"Then you're saying you did *not* commit the twenty-eight murders?"

"That's precisely what I've been saying these past seven years, but no one would listen." He smiled into the camera, displaying a mouthful of very white and very even teeth.

"Do you feel hostility toward society about your sentence?"

"Hostility?" He blinked his eyelids rapidly. "Why should I feel hostile?"

"If you are innocent, as you claim—"

He shrugged. "Life's a bum rap. But to answer your question: No, I'm not angry. You've got it all wrong. It's not society that wants to electrocute me, Stephanie. It's the stupid prosecutor and that stupid judge. Not to mention all those misguided relatives screaming for blood—anybody's blood."

"Then you don't believe you've received a fair trial by a jury of your peers?"

"Peers? Who are my peers?" he scoffed. "Postal workers?" he asked distastefully. *"Housewives?"*

She was aware that the floodlights, aimed straight at him, turned his stony eyes into silver pinpoints.

"Are *you* my peer, Stephanie?"

There! He's doing it again! Taking control. Asking the questions.

*All right, tough guy!* she thought. *Let's see how you react to this one.*

"Tell me, Jed." She kept her voice deliberately level. "Are you afraid of dying?"

He kept right on smiling at her. "I'd be a liar if I said I wasn't. You see, Stephanie, we're all afraid of dying. Show me one man or woman who doesn't want to live forever, and I'll show you a liar." He paused. "Don't *you* want to live forever, Stephanie?" His voice had dropped to the barest whisper.

The hairs at the nape of her neck rose and tingled.

The silence seemed to hum.

Then the telephone bleated. It sounded like a bomb going off. They all jerked and stared at it—except for Stephanie. She kept her eyes locked on Jed Savitt.

*He thinks it's the governor with a reprieve,* she realized.

The warden, a tall, ruggedly built man with salt-and-pepper hair, picked up the receiver by the second ring. "Warden Woods here." He listened and then snapped, "Goddamn it! Transfer this call to extension one six! And for Chrissakes, don't tie up this goddamn line again!" Angrily he slammed the phone back down.

Stephanie's eyes never left Savitt's; now she saw the hope that had come into them fade, like a light bulb dimming.

"That call's for you, Miss Merlin." Warden Woods's voice intruded. She turned to him. "Who was it?"

"I didn't take the time to ask; we've got to keep this line clear for the governor or a last-minute Supreme Court decision. If you want to take it, the extension phone's out there, in the press room." He nodded toward the riveted steel door.

She shot her producer a look. "Ted, could you please go and see who it is?"

"Right-o." Ted Warwick gave her a mock salute; when the guard unlocked the door and opened it, she could hear the raised rumble of dozens of voices. Then the door quickly clanged shut again and the intense silence returned.

Stephanie folded her hands on the table and looked thoughtful. "So, Jed. During the trial, it came out that you'd been using seven different aliases—"

He smiled and shook his head. "What you mean, Stephanie, is that the prosecution *claimed* I used seven different aliases. There's a difference."

"But they introduced evidence! Drivers' licenses and passports with your photographs in them—"

"Really, Stephanie." He looked disappointed. "And here I was, giving you credit for being such a smart girl!"

"But the drivers' licenses and passports weren't forgeries. They were the real McCoys. And they had your fingerprints all over them! How do you explain that?"

He shrugged.

"Jed," she sighed, "this is strictly off the record. Okay?"

"Yes, Stephanie?" He gave her his full attention.

"Why did you ask for *me* to come and interview you? Your lawyer specifically told everyone that you wouldn't grant any interviews."

"Yes, but did anyone listen? You saw them when you came in here, Stephanie. You heard them just now." He gestured to the door Ted Warwick had gone through. "The press room's full of hungry animals hot on the scent of blood. Do you know how many reporters are out there, Stephanie? Over one hundred and fifty. All waiting to see me die." He chuckled dryly. "Death, it seems, is the ultimate human interest story."

"Maybe. But you still didn't answer my question. Why *me?* They were all camped out here already. You could have had your pick. The

*New York Times,* or 'Sixty Minutes.' Even 'A Current Affair,' if your taste runs in that direction."

He hunched over slightly, folded his arms on the desk, and looked at her with his most sincere expression. "I've wanted to meet you for the longest time, Stephanie—it was my deathbed wish, you might say. You know, like those terminally ill children who get one last wish before they die, and someone takes them to Disneyworld, or an athlete comes to visit them?"

She nodded.

"Well. You made *my* wish come true. You see, *you,* Stephanie Merlin, are *my* Disneyworld. *My* athlete."

Close up, his incisors looked savagely pointy and sharp, and he covered the microphone so that the videocam's sound system couldn't pick up what he said.

"What would you say if I were to tell you that I've been watching your show religiously for over two years now? And not because it's good. But because . . . you fit my feminine ideal?"

She fought the impulse to grimace.

"I see that you're not impressed. But then, I didn't think you would be."

"I'm . . . honored that you should think so highly—"

"No, Stephanie. No, *no.*" He shook his head. "You're not honored. You're frightened!"

She stared at him. He'd hit the nail right on the head.

"Are you afraid I might hurt you? Is that it?" He didn't expect a reply. "Obviously, you'll be as relieved as the rest of them once they strap me into Old Sparky and throw the switch, won't you? You'll think I'll be gone for good then, and you find that comforting."

She stared at him.

"But guess what? I *won't* be gone! You see, I'll be waiting for you on the other side, Stephanie."

The flat gray of his eyes seemed to reach out and touch her physically.

"You do believe in life after death, Stephanie, don't you?"

The air between them seemed charged; she could swear it rippled and distorted.

The door opened again, distantly, as though it were part of a lateral dimension. Again, the multitude of voices outside rose in sound.

"Steph," Ted Warwick called to her. "Could you come to the phone for a minute?"

She waved him off without turning around. "Jot down the number and tell whoever it is that I'll call back."

"It's important, Steph. It's Sammy Kafka. He's calling from New York."

*Sammy!* For a moment her heart stopped. "Ted?" she said weakly.

He gestured her outside.

Jed Savitt watched as she pushed her chair back, rose, and headed for the door.

"Don't stay away too long," the killer called out after her. "My time's running out!"

She was glad when the door clanged shut on his giggles. *Just what I need,* she thought, shaking her head as if to clear it. *A death-row comedian.*

The large room where the press was gathered was a beehive of noise and activity. Thick electrical cables snaked all over the floor.

"Ted," she said firmly. "Please. What's happened?"

He pulled her into a corner, away from curious ears. "It's your grandfather," he said softly.

She grabbed him by the arms, her eyes wide, searching his face.

"Sammy said . . ." He sighed and wished there was some gentler way to break it. "He said it looks like suicide."

"Sui—" The word slammed into her, its punch leaving her reeling. She leaned her head back against the cinderblocks and shut her eyes.

Somewhere, a million miles away, an intercom speaker crackled and a distorted voice came on: *"Ladies and gentlemen, the Supreme Court of the United States has just stayed Mr. Savitt's execution. Mr. Savitt will not be giving interviews and is being returned to his cell at this time. You will be briefed in full shortly. We appreciate your patience."*

The amplified voice made absolutely no impression on Stephanie Merlin. Rivulets of silvery tears coursed down her cheeks. Slowly, she raised her head and opened her eyes. Then a quiet kind of strength shone in her face.

"My grandfather," she told Ted Warwick with quiet conviction, "would never have killed himself. *Never!*"

## 3

*Inflight · New York City*

*S*tephanie stared out the square of scratched Perspex, unaware of the receding lights below as the jet banked and climbed steeply. Her face was pale, and she was hugging herself tightly. She felt so cold, so robotic. *But if I'm a robot, why do I feel such pain?*

She felt a hand gently touching her shoulder. Slowly she raised her tear-streaked face. The cabin attendant was leaning across the businessman in the aisle seat beside her. "Can I get you anything?"

Stephanie shook her head. "No, thank you," she said dully, and started to turn away.

The attendant looked at her a moment longer and then touched her on the shoulder again. "Could you come with me, please?"

Stephanie was too shrouded in grief to question her or refuse. Obediently, she fumbled with the buckle of her seat belt. Her fingers felt numb and awkward, as if she was suddenly all thumbs. As she squeezed past her fellow passenger, it seemed as if her every movement was in slow motion.

Once in the aisle, she looked at the attendant as if to ask, *What now?*

"You look like you could use some privacy," the woman said sympathetically. "Come with me. There's an empty row in the back."

Stephanie nodded. "Thank you," she said gratefully, and followed on unsteady legs. Once settled, she accepted a glass of brandy and drank it all down at once.

"If you need anything else, just press the button," the attendant told her gently. "I'll be happy to get it for you."

*I need my grandfather alive,* Stephanie wanted to tell her. *Can you get him for me?* But politeness won out. She said, "Thank you," once again, and then turned to stare unseeingly out at the flashing light on the wingtip. After a while she closed her eyes wearily and surrendered herself to the pain.

Pain and memories. With death they were one and the same.

Death had taken her grandfather. Had stolen him away from her.

How ironic that death, too, should have thrown them so closely together in the first place . . .

She had been five years old and staying with her long-widowed grandfather when her parents died in a freak accident. Apparently the radar on a light plane had gone out while a blanket of fog was shrouding Mont Blanc. The pilot never knew the tramway up the face of the cliff was directly in his flight path. Even when he crashed into the packed car, his last thought must have been that he'd hit the mountain.

Stephanie often wondered if her parents, aboard the doomed tram, saw the aircraft coming at them in that last split second of horror—and if they'd mercifully died in midair. She could only hope so.

"We've both got to be brave," her grandfather had told her after the funeral. "All we have left now is each other."

Nothing was too good for Carleton Merlin's only living relative. He spoiled his granddaughter shamelessly, hiring a decorator to turn her room at the Osborne into a pink fantasy fit for a princess. He showered her with gifts and bought her so many clothes she couldn't possibly wear them all before outgrowing them.

It was he who insisted she attend Brearley, one of Manhattan's finest and most expensive private schools. And it was he who attended the PTA meetings, who took her to the zoo, which she adored, and the opera, where she fell asleep.

When he crisscrossed the country doing the talk-show circuit each time one of his celebrity biographies was published, he took her with him. In her sophomore year of high school, when she decided she wanted to become a journalist, he paved the way by using his connections to get her a summer job at the *New York Post*. Thanks to him, she spent the summer of her junior year in the newsroom at NBC.

NBC decided her. She loved the excitement of the newsroom. It gave her a sense of participating in history as it was being made. Not surprisingly, she decided to apply to Columbia and take courses in broadcasting and journalism.

"It's a tough field," Carleton Merlin warned her.

She proved herself tougher, spent the summers and semester breaks in various newsrooms, and graduated summa cum laude. Carleton had been as proud as the NBC peacock. "She'll be the next Barbara Walters," he told anybody who would listen.

After spending a year as a news writer at WOR-TV, she was hired to cover the metropolitan beat for "Live at Five." Suddenly, it seemed, she lived with a spiral notebook in one hand and a microphone in the other. Every day brought her a new assignment, a new tragedy, new victims and new heroes. It excited her like nothing she had ever imagined. But increasingly, she became frustrated at the one- and two-minute time slots allotted each story. She wanted to understand the people involved, their motivations and the long-term effects of their tragedies and triumphs.

Together with Ted Warwick, a producer for "Live at Five," she came up with the idea for a weekly newsmagazine show focusing on a single subject. They called it "Half Hour," made a pilot, and pitched it to the networks. The networks all turned it down.

They plunged ahead anyway, quit their jobs, and put their money where their mouths were, deciding to syndicate the show. When their money ran out, it was her grandfather who injected fresh capital. "I'm not doing it for you," he lied to Stephanie. "I'm doing it because I think it's a good investment."

He was right. They sold the show to hundreds of independent stations. "Half Hour" took off like a rocket and propelled Stephanie to instant celebrity. Overnight, she became one of the most visible women on television—and richer than she'd ever dared dream.

She knew that without her grandfather's backing it would never have happened. She owed him everything.

She wiped the tears from her eyes.

The plane was making its final approach to La Guardia, and the fuselage shuddered as they descended into warmer air. The cabin was caught up in that bustle which marks an imminent landing. Muzak was playing, the passengers were livelier, the interior lights brighter. Attendants hurried up and down the aisle, gathering up cups and glasses. Another few minutes and they'd be landing. In the city that never sleeps. Where Carleton Merlin now slept for eternity.

"Grandpa," Stephanie mouthed soundlessly to herself, and her face distorted as the pain inside her grew more intense.

*Why, God?* she demanded in silent rage. *Why couldn't he have lived forever?*

Usually she was among the first passengers off a plane; tonight, she was last. She was in no hurry. There was no Grandpa to call and tell she was back in town. Nothing awaited her but the confrontation with his death. The longer that could be postponed, the better.

Sammy Kafka waited for her at the end of the jetway. He was dressed in a black suit and wore a black tie and an old-fashioned black crepe armband. For the first time in her memory, he was without the trademark carnation in his lapel or a welcoming smile on his face.

Wordlessly, they threw their arms tight around each other. Now that her grandfather was dead, his oldest and dearest friend was the closest thing to family Stephanie had left. She remembered how, when she'd been five and Grandpa had first introduced them, Sammy had squatted down in front of her and, before hugging her fiercely, had said, "Hello, Girlie. I'm your Uncle Sammy."

And she'd been his Girlie, and he her uncle, ever since.

"Tell me this is only a bad dream, Uncle Sammy," she begged softly. She drew back from the embrace and dug her hands into his arms. Her eyes held a mixture of hurt, disbelief, sorrow, and pleading. It was exactly the way the little girl who had lost her parents at the tender age of five had looked. "Please tell me I'll wake up soon, and that he's really here!"

The little man looked up at her with moist brown eyes. "Oh, Girlie, how I wish I could! I'd give anything to be able to make that happen." He handed her a beautifully ironed handkerchief, and she wiped her eyes and dried her face. "Do you have any luggage?" he asked.

She shook her head and sniffled. "I took the first flight I could get on, and there wasn't time to pack. Ted said he would take care of it."

"Good." Sammy nodded approvingly. "Then we don't have to wait around. Let's blow this joint. I've got a car and driver waiting."

During the drive into Manhattan, she stared out the window at the sparse oncoming traffic. *New York won't be the same without Grandpa,* she thought. *It's as if I no longer have any reason to live here.*

They were passing Flushing Meadows and the remnants of the 1964 World's Fair when she turned to Sammy. "The police—" she began, and had to take a deep breath to get the words out. "You said they claim he . . . he killed himself. How?" She swallowed to lubricate her dry throat. "How did it happen?"

He took her slender young hand in his. "There's time enough to learn the details, Girlie," he advised. "Let it rest for now."

Her voice was soft but steely. "Uncle Sammy, I *need* to *know!* Please. Don't try to spare me any pain. It won't help."

He swallowed miserably. "If you insist, Girlie," he said with a sigh. "It was sometime after he and I went to see *Dinorah.* That was last Monday at the Met. Pham left for a week that same day—I think to bone up for his citizenship exam—and when he returned today, he let himself in and found . . ."

"But *how* did he die?"

"Apparently he'd been dead about a week. He . . ." Sammy hesitated a moment. "Are you sure you want to hear this now, Girlie?"

"Uncle Sammy." She used her most obstinate voice.

"All right already!" But he could barely get the words out. "Pham found him hanging from the chandelier in the bedroom."

"Oh, God!" Stephanie shut her eyes.

She could picture that heavy Dutch chandelier as if it were right in front of her, and it occurred to her that she'd never liked it—as if an object she liked would have made a difference somehow.

She said quietly, "There's so much to do . . . so many arrangements to make . . ." Trying to think of little things to occupy her mind.

Sammy squeezed her hand, told her all she didn't have to worry about a thing. He would see to everything.

She squeezed his hand back in thanks.

By the time they hit Manhattan, Stephanie told him she'd decided to spend the night at the Osborne. "But I have to drop by my own place first."

Her building was in the Village, in a converted meat-packing plant at the end of Horatio Street, right by the river. She told Sammy to wait in the car while she ran upstairs. "I'll be back in a few minutes," she promised. "I have to get Waldo. And yes. I'll be all right by myself."

"There's no rush, Girlie," Sammy assured her. "Take your time."

When she let herself into her seventh-floor triplex, she climbed the narrow spiral stairs from the living room up through a well in the two-story rooftop addition. Her plant-filled study led out to a terrace overlooking the Hudson. For once, she did not stop to hit the outdoor floodlights to inspect her lavishly planted fiefdom, which a landscaping firm tended twice weekly. Tonight was a simple mission.

"Steph! Steph!" Waldo's strident voice greeted Stephanie as she came up the stairs. "How are *you*? How are *you*? I love you, Steph!"

Stephanie had never intended having a parrot as a pet. Four years previously, an acquaintance had dropped Waldo off before going out of town, never returning to reclaim him.

So the giant Amazon parrot—named for the Great Waldo Pepper— was hers.

"I love you, Steph! Hiiiii . . . hiiiii . . ."

"If your Steph isn't very responsive today," she murmured, approaching the big brass cage hanging by one of the windows, "it's because she's feeling real low. You'll have to bear with me, Waldo."

Once back outside, Stephanie handed the cage over to the driver. He handled it warily as he deposited it on the rear seat of the car, where it took up half the space. Without being asked, Sammy got out and moved to the front passenger seat.

He twisted around as she climbed into the back, beside the cage. "Girlie, are you sure you want to spend the night uptown? You'll be all alone . . ." He looked worried.

"I won't be alone, Uncle Sammy," she said softly. She strummed the bars of the cage with her fingers. "I'll have Waldo here."

"A parrot." Sammy Kafka rolled his eyes. "She'll have a parrot for company, heaven help us!" Then he got serious again. "Are you sure, Girlie?" He looked at her closely. "Really, really sure?"

"I'm sure, Uncle Sammy." She nodded.

"There'll be a lot of painful memories," he warned her.

"I want them," she said softly.

And thought, *I need them.*

# 4

They hadn't driven a mile before all hell broke loose. One moment the half-deserted streets were peaceful and sunny, and the next, the roar and shrieks and thunderous explosions of bombardment rent the air.

It was as if the skies had suddenly broken open and the apocalypse was at hand. A fusillade of forty simultaneously launched Israeli rockets crashed to earth, five of them smashing into a six-story building not three hundred feet in front of the taxi.

"Allah help us!" the driver shrieked as he slammed on the brakes and yanked the steering wheel abruptly to the left, throwing the battered white Mercedes into a short broadside skid.

In the front passenger seat, Johnny Stone grabbed the dashboard with one hand and the door handle with the other as the balding tires squealed against the locked brakes and the car slid sideways, wedging him against the door. When it came to a halt, they were blocking both lanes.

The building in front of them disintegrated as if in slow motion. The front wall burst out and the roof blew sky-high. A tree was uprooted and sent flying, and tortured pieces of wreckage rained down all around, miraculously falling short of the car. Already, a massive rising cloud of dust and debris was obscuring the destruction.

"Another few seconds," the Arab driver muttered, "and we would have been blown up also. But we are alive. *Insah Allah.*"

"*Insah Allah,*" Johnny Stone agreed, automatically reaching for the Leica which hung from around his neck. It was the professional photographer's instantaneous reaction, and he had to fight against it, forcing himself to leave the camera be. He had taken enough pictures of scenes just like this one. *What good will one more do? What good had any of them done?*

Just then a second fusillade of rockets fell, and orange fireballs mushroomed all around. What sounded like a sonic boom rolled over them, and the street ahead shimmered in the heat wave as furious flames leapt and crackled and devoured.

"We turn around," the driver said, already backing up and putting the Mercedes through a series of deft maneuvers. "I know another way," he said, flicking Johnny a sideways glance. "Allah willing, we will still get you to Damascus in time for your flight."

Johnny twisted around in his seat. His eyes were veiled as he looked out the dusty rear window. All around, fires burned furiously. The cloud of dust was starting to settle, and where the building had stood, he now saw furnished rooms listing like some crazy giant dollhouse.

Lebanon. He sighed wearily.

How he'd loved it, how wonderful had been the energetic clash of East meeting West.

His lips tightened grimly. How he had come to hate it.

But he'd always returned for one more picture, one more documentation of death and destruction and suffering. Well, no more. This time he was off—*arrivederci,* baby!—and for *good.* Nothing could stop him, not high water or hell, not his editor back at *Life,* not all the bombs in the Middle East. Once his mind was made up about something, Johnny Stone was unstoppable. The only drummer he stepped to was his own.

Johnny Stone was an award-winning photographer, a freelancer who dared tread where lesser—or wiser—men refused. He was thirty-five years old, a mixture of Irish and German with black hair, green-blue eyes, and a decidedly cynical cast to his mouth.

He was not handsome, but he was virile: tall and lean and hard-bodied. Women found him devastatingly attractive.

He also had talent, fame, nerves of steel, and an abundance of self-confidence.

And he needed them now. On both sides of the taxi, the buildings were bombed-out ruins, jagged fingers of stone and stucco reaching up into the sky. There was very little glass to be seen: it had been blasted to smithereens. In the distance, mushrooming gray clouds of smoke rose high from behind rooftops before being tattered by the sea breeze. Explosions still reverberated, but grew more distant, like receding thunder.

Johnny Stone was barely aware of it. He was preoccupied with the printout which had come over the AP wire in the bunkerlike press office less than an hour earlier. Every word was engraved in his mind.

NEW YORK, May 22 (AP)—*Carleton Merlin, the world-famous biographer and best-selling author whose unauthorized works have included the lives of Frank Sinatra, Elizabeth Taylor, Jacqueline Kennedy Onassis, Stavros Niarchos, Maria Callas, the Krupp Dynasty, and Pablo Picasso, was found dead in his apartment here, police say.*

*The cause of death was apparently suicide.*

*Mr. Merlin is survived by a granddaughter, Stephanie Merlin,*

*the host and co-founder of the syndicated television show "Half
Hour."*
    *Funeral arrangements have not yet been made.*

Johnny had known Carleton Merlin; liked to think he'd known him well.
And the man he knew would never have committed suicide—not in a million years.

Not Carleton Merlin, whose books had consistently hit the number
one-spot on the world's best-seller lists, whose voracious appetite for details and truth and secrets had made him one of the most widely read,
respected—and yes, *feared*—men in publishing.

Johnny stared out the windshield. They had left the city center behind. The explosions now looked almost like benign puffballs . . . or dirty
wads of cotton. It would not be long before they'd reach the Syrian frontier, and then Damascus. From there it was a hop to Amman via Alia, the
Royal Jordanian airline, and another hop from Amman to Cairo. And
from Cairo to New York was a nonstop breeze.

He smiled wryly to himself. If someone had told him yesterday that
he'd be leaving Sidon today because of Stephanie Merlin, he would have
scoffed. Stephanie was a chapter of his life that was closed. There
wouldn't—couldn't—be any picking up where they had left off.

Some things just weren't meant to be.

Stephanie. She would be—what? Twenty-seven now? No, twenty-
eight: she had been twenty-one when they'd met; twenty-three when
they'd each gone their separate ways.

Had she changed much since then? he wondered. Five years. These
days, a lot could happen in that amount of time.

He stared out at the twisted pines and walled-in gardens flashing
past, and already he was seeing Stephanie again, his mind spinning,
spinning—taking him back into the past—back, back . . .

. . . Back to five years ago, to that fateful Friday of the Memorial Day
weekend. He had jùst returned from Nicaragua after six wretched weeks
spent trampling around in the steaming jungle, documenting another war,
more death and destruction.

He'd called her as soon as he'd gotten in.

"It's me," he'd said from the hotel suite high above Central Park.

"Hello me," she'd replied. He knew from her voice that she was smiling: it surpassed the Seven Wonders of the World, that smile.

"I'm back," he said unnecessarily.

"Obviously." She laughed.

"Miss me?" He was fishing.

"Hmmmm," she said noncommittally.

"Look," he said, "when can we meet? I haven't seen your glorious bod in well over a month and a half now. One more day of deprivation, and I'm liable to regress to wet dreams."

"It'll have to be late."

He rocked on his heels, the telephone in one hand, the receiver in the other. He frowned out across the park. The weather was unseasonably hot, and a shimmering haze enveloped the city. He could barely make out the buildings on the northern end of Central Park. "I was hoping you could make it sooner rather than later."

"I'd like to," she said with a sigh, "but I can't, Johnny. Really. I've got to fill in for one of the regular anchors on the eleven o'clock news." Then her voice brightened. "How about we meet right after? Say . . . about midnight?"

"We also serve who sit and wait," he quoted.

"Waiting will make it all the sweeter," she assured him.

"And me more miserable in the meantime. So where do we set off the fireworks? Your place or mine?"

Hers was the sprawling triplex on Horatio Street.

"That all depends," she murmured thoughtfully. "Where are you?"

"The Essex House."

"Big spender!" There was laughter in her voice. "Tell you what. I like the idea of making it in a hotel. Makes me feel cheap and wanton."

When he hung up, he was feeling ridiculously happy. After six weeks of celibacy, of stumbling through the fetid rainforest, of battling mosquitoes and diarrhea, of eating wretched rations and throwing caution to the winds to document the lives of the rebels, just hearing her voice again was like tuning in to some vibrant, exhilarating frequency. He realized then just how deeply she had slipped into his soul and made a home; what a difference she made in his life.

It had taken him six weeks of separation to realize he was among that fortunate minority who are destined to find the love of their lives.

And so Johnny Stone—stud, ladies' man, and confirmed bachelor—ran straight out and spent over twelve thousand dollars on a diamond engagement ring at Tiffany's. He'd spent the rest of the afternoon ordering a roomful of flowers, arranging a midnight champagne supper complete with violinists, and popped over to Bergdorf's to splurge on a casual but hideously expensive silk shirt and cotton slacks ensemble. He even got his hair cut.

At eleven, he watched her on the tube, eating her up with his eyes and wondering, with irrational jealousy, how many male viewers were doing exactly the same thing at the exact same time. Then he let the violinists in, doused the electric lights, lit the candles, and checked the vintage Dom Pérignon. The bottle was icy cold.

Everything was perfect.

Eleven-thirty rolled around. Then midnight. The violinists waited silently. Twelve-thirty . . .

At one o'clock, he told the fiddlers to pack it in. He was half out of his mind with worry. He called the studio. Her apartment. Her grandfather. He even called missing persons. All to no avail.

One-thirty . . . two.

The candles burned down and sputtered.

Two-thirty. The ice had melted in the champagne bucket and become tepid water.

She never bothered to call until late the next afternoon. "Hope you didn't wait up too long, but a juicy story was breaking," she'd told him without apologizing. "I had to run with it."

He told her that it was okay, that he'd fallen asleep anyway . . .

A few days later, they met for dinner at a little Italian restaurant down on Bleecker Street. He didn't mention the date she'd broken, and she didn't bring it up, either—she was too wrapped up in the story she was still working on.

"It's a major break for me, but I can't talk about it just yet," she'd told him, her eyes bright with ambition. "But this story will make me, Johnny. You just wait and see. It'll *make* me!"

It was while they sipped an after-dinner sambuca that he popped the Tiffany box on her. Trying to act real casual, as though it was a little pin or a charm.

"I got you this," he said, feeling suddenly awkward and gangly and all thumbs. Like a boy on a first date.

"For me? Aw. How sweet . . ." Slowly she lifted the lid. "A diamond!" She was so startled by the engagement ring that she instantly retreated into flippancy. "Girl's best friend, a diamond," she teased.

"I was passing Tiffany's this afternoon when it occurred to me a little rock might offer your story some competition." He kept it cool, not about to make a big deal out of sitting on the ring for days.

"Hmmm," she said, picking it up and looking at it appraisingly. "It's one way to get a girl's attention, I grant you that."

Her heart was racing, and she wanted to hug him and cry, "I do! I do!" But first, she needed to hear him say three magic little words.

"I'd say it's more than just an attention getter," he said stiffly, with annoyance. "It's supposed to say *you're mine.*"

"*Yours?* Like you're putting dibs on me?" She slipped the ring half on, took it off, slipped it half on again. "Has it ever occurred to you that I might not be *anybody's?*" She'd intended it as a playful gibe, but she couldn't help the undercurrent of bitterness in her voice. His total lack of any romantic sensitivity hurt. Where was the champagne? Where were the violins?

For his part, all the wasted effort he'd gone through in order to be romantic—only to be stood up—stung equally. He'd been deflated, wounded. And now he felt the need to wound her back.

"In case you aren't aware of it, I've given you an engagement ring," he said coldly.

She took it off her finger. "And that's it?" She stared at him across the table and waited.

He knew what she wanted to hear, but somehow, her attitude just wouldn't let him come out and say "I love you." Besides, he was waiting, too—to hear her apologize for having stood him up; maybe even put two and two together and come up with four—that if she'd met him at the Essex House as planned, she'd have been knocked off her feet by violins and champagne and the whole perfect, dreamy night he'd planned.

"If you don't want my engagement ring, then fine," Johnny said grimly. "Just say so. Believe you me, it isn't as if I've got to go around begging someone to take it."

It was as if he'd plunged a knife into her. She went absolutely rigid. But like him, Stephanie was never one to show her vulnerable underbelly.

She drew a deep breath. "In that case, *here!*"

She slapped the ring down in front of him, snatched up her purse, and got to her feet. She looked down at him, her every inch quivering with barely controlled anger.

"Give it to one of your admiring hordes," she whispered hoarsely. And then swiftly, before her tears could show, she bit down on her pale lip, turned on her heel, and marched out.

He stared bleakly after her. Good God! What on earth had happened? Wretchedly, he rubbed his face with his hands. How could he have let things get so totally out of hand? Was he insane? He didn't want to hurt her—he loved her, goddammit!

Too late now.

As soon as he'd gotten back to the hotel, he'd tried to set things right. He called her to apologize, but she slammed the phone down the moment she heard his voice. And *that* got him riled up all over again.

The bitch! he'd thought. Well, if that was the way she wanted to play it, then *fine!*

Some things obviously just weren't meant to be.

Johnny looked out the dusty windshield. They were coming out of the Al Jabal Ash Sharqi mountains. Below, Damascus sprawled across the dusty plain. The first leg of the journey back.

But back to what? To a love that had never gotten its chance to bloom? To offer condolences and then slip away quietly and disappear? Or to acrimoniously pretend that what they'd once shared had never been?

God, when he thought about it! The stupidity! The ruffled male pride—that damned wounded ego! He'd given up so easily—returning the ring to Tiffany's first thing the following morning.

He hadn't seen Stephanie again, and she'd never gotten in touch with him, either. Neither of them seemed to realize what was good for them.

But somehow, her grandfather knew. For weeks, Carleton Merlin had called him, urging him not to give up. And, he surmised, the kindly, shrewd old man had been on Stephanie's case, too.

But Carleton Merlin might as well have saved his breath. Neither of them was willing to move first. They were both so intractably, so foolishly, so youthfully stubborn!

And meanwhile, five years had somehow managed to slip past. Five years . . . five of what could have been the best years of both their lives.

And the worst thing was, he still loved her.

# ❦ 5 ❦

*T*hat first night. How endless it seemed. It was as if morning might never come.

Worn out though she was, Stephanie didn't think she would sleep a moment: the ache and loss within her were too great. She left Waldo in the living room, covered the cage with a sheet, and spent the entire night in her grandfather's bedroom, clinging to the belief that she would somehow feel closer to him there.

But without him, the grand, shabby gentility of the high-ceilinged room seemed different . . . bigger . . . empty. With his death the apartment had lost its soul.

She prowled the room in a state of agitation. This bedroom had been his favorite of all the rooms, and as he'd gotten older he'd spent most of his time in here with his favorite pieces of furniture and most-treasured books. Pushed against a wall was the Empire sleigh bed in which he'd slept, and which doubled as a couch. All around were the cornice-topped mahogany bookcases groaning under the weight of thousands of volumes and classical marble busts which looked down with sightless eyes. Here, too, was his mahogany desk, pushed into the three-windowed bay which let the light pour in, and out of which he'd been able to gaze while working. His old, manual Remington typewriter, which he'd refused to part with, was the same one he'd had since he'd been a young man—on it he had written the biographies for which he had become so celebrated. And, scattered all around it, were the paraphernalia of the writer: the piles of notes and manuscript pages, bowls of rubber bands and paper clips, reference books, beakers holding pencils, and little bottles of Liquid Paper. There was the big crystal ashtray she'd always remembered; now it held the dead remnants of a half-smoked cigar: one of his Monte Casinos. If it hadn't been for the sleek red multilined telephone, the state-of-the-art stereo system, and the thirty-six-inch television and VCR, it could have been a stage set for a nineteenth-century gentleman. But Carleton Merlin had not been one to begrudge himself the finest in up-to-the-moment electronics.

"Everything I need is in this one room," he'd told Stephanie not so long ago.

For hours she talked to him as she prowled—as though he sat right there, in his favorite, faded leather swivel chair by the desk, listening to her every word. She told him about Raiford Prison and Jed Savitt, America's most notorious killer. She told him about the kind attendant on the return flight, and Sammy Kafka meeting her at the airport and dropping her off to pick up Waldo. And, in every other sentence, she told him how she couldn't believe for a minute that he'd killed himself.

The night dragged on.

Every so often, she'd stare up at the tarnished brass chandelier—the one her grandfather had supposedly hanged himself from—and tried to imagine him climbing up on a chair, looping a belt around his neck, and kicking the chair out from under him.

But each time, she shook her head. It was no good. No matter how hard she tried to visualize it, the scenario just wouldn't play. She kept thinking: *How could he have managed it with his bad leg? He had barely been able to get out of a chair, or even step up on a curb without relying on his cane.*

On the drive into the city, she had told Uncle Sammy as much.

"The police say that suicides often show unbelievable determination," he had replied.

But no. The suicide verdict just wouldn't play. But how could she prove it?

When she ran out of things to tell him, she puttered around his desk, poking among the piles of papers and scribbled notes. An eight-by-ten color slide caught her attention.

She picked it up, held it against the desk light, studied it for a long time. It was a first-rate photograph of a painting which depicted weary, stooped old people on one side awaiting their turn to step into a fountain, from which they emerged young and straight and beautiful on the other. Not pretty as paintings went, but powerful, and strangely arresting. And its subject matter was unmistakable. The fountain of youth.

Lowering it thoughtfully, Stephanie noticed a stick-on label in the lower lefthand corner of the cardboard frame. It was neatly printed in what she recognized as her grandfather's hand:

Lucas Cranach, the Younger (1472–1553)
*Oil on panel*
*Property of the British Museum*

Setting the slide down, Stephanie's eye wandered to the stack of old, fading black-and-white photographs.

She picked them up, flipped slowly through. The first showed a beautiful young girl of about six standing beside a dog almost as large as she was. The next was of the same girl, at about age twelve, standing beside an even more beautiful girl, obviously her sister. The resemblance was striking. They both had pigtails and wore Bavarian dirndls, and there were rolling meadows and a steep-roofed chalet in the background. Another photograph showed them along an esplanade, flanking ... what? A wizened, ancient dwarf? Obviously a close friend, from the way they hugged each other ...

The next few photographs were even older ... the brown-and-white variety, with sawtooth edges. Were these the parents of the girls? Perhaps. Then came more black-and-whites. A woman walking with both girls *and* the dwarf, all three in First Communion dresses, all three smiling at the camera. One showed the first girl, older now, her arms hooked through those of two young men ... obviously admirers.

Suddenly something raised the hairs on Stephanie's arms; made them stand up straight. She recognized this young woman of sixteen or so. It was Lili Schneider—future world-class opera diva and beauty, whose voice had thrilled millions ... whose very biography her grandfather had been working on!

There were other photographs, as well.

Lili hamming it up with school friends ... Lili standing beside a piano, where a stern-faced woman with swept-back hair sat with her fingers poised over the ivory keys ... an older Lili onstage, bewigged and begowned for *Der Rosenkavalier* ... a smiling Lili on the arms of a handsome Nazi officer ... a whole slew of pictures of Lili with Nazis ...

And Nazis. And more Nazis—

It was too chilling.

Stephanie let the pictures drop.

The stereo caught her eye. She went over to it. *What had Grandpa been listening to last?* she wondered. She turned on the sound system and punched the CD player. The disk drawer slid silently out, the disc shining iridescently in the lamplight. She picked it up to look at the label. But she had already known.

Lili Schneider.

Of course, it would have to be.

She replaced the CD in the disk drawer, punched the PLAY button, and listened to it for some time. They were songs from various light operettas ... Lehár and Strauss and Sieczynsky. But the voice ... Ah, but it was so unearthly clear and sweet ... pitch-perfect and unlike any other ... a voice of such magic that it instantly raised new gooseflesh along her arms and neck and legs.

*A captivating voice,* she thought, *too beautifully sweet for the Nazis ... as if ugly people had to listen to ugly music ...*

Had Grandpa been listening to this when he'd ... died? She wondered. But the stereo hadn't been on when she'd come in. Or had someone shut it off? Pham? The police? Of course, it did not matter. What mattered was that Grandpa was dead and gone and lost to her forever.

Her mind became a kaleidoscope of memories. There were so many of them. She laughed again at the funny ones, smiled at the good ones, and cried. She relived her life with her grandfather . . . relived every emotion . . . all the happinesses and sadnesses of a lifetime condensed into a single night.

It was sometime in the hour before dawn while sitting on the sleigh bed that she finally nodded off.

She jerked awake to brilliant sunshine flooding the bay. From outside, the sounds of the city intruded: car horns honking, urgent sirens screaming, loud bursts of rap issuing forth from a passing car. For a moment she was disoriented. She had been dreaming about Grandpa. He had been sitting in his swivel chair right here, in this very room, enjoying one of his Monte Casinos—smug and mysterious about something he'd dug up for the Schneider biography.

*The cigar!*

She sat bolt upright, wide awake now.

Of course! Why hadn't she thought of it before? The cigar was the key—proof that Grandpa *hadn't* committed suicide! The police would have to listen to her and start an investigation.

Because Grandpa hardly ever smoked. He only allowed himself to enjoy a good cigar on very, very special occasions—when he was feeling exceptionally good about something. And Pham had cleaned house the same day Grandpa and Sammy had gone to see *Dinorah* . . . in other words, he had cleaned house the very *day* her grandfather was suspected of having committed suicide! And Pham was nothing if not thorough. Grandpa had to have smoked it *after* Pham had cleaned—within twelve to twenty-four hours of his death!

*The cigar proved that he must have been feeling* exceptionally *good . . . and people who felt exceptionally good did* not *loop belts around their necks and commit suicide!*

Galvanized, she decided she would talk to the police.

She consulted her wristwatch. It was past seven o'clock.

She got up and stretched. She felt stiff and rumpled and dirty; she'd been wearing the same clothes since yesterday morning. She decided it wouldn't hurt to get cleaned up and look presentable.

She went into her old pink bedroom, where she kept some changes of clothing, and showered in the bathroom that had once been hers. Afterward, she immediately felt more alert and less stiff. The shower had worked some of the kinks out of her joints. From her closet, she chose a white blouse, long red pleated skirt, matching back-pleated jacket, and black, medium-heeled pumps. Applying makeup took a scant few minutes.

She jolted herself even wider awake by making and drinking a potful of coffee. Then she fed Waldo, filled his water dish, and left for the police station.

The morning air was brisk and there was a determination in her every step. She couldn't bring her grandfather back, but she sure as hell could make certain of one thing. She thought: *I'll see to it that his death isn't dismissed as suicide.*

Suddenly she stopped walking as the enormity of her thoughts hit home.

*If it hadn't been suicide, then . . .* She felt a chill. *Could it be possible? Had he been cold-bloodedly* murdered?

Another thought hit her out of the clear blue.

He'd pried. He'd researched people's backgrounds with the doggedness of a bloodhound, unearthing secrets and sniffing out well-hidden facts. Always digging, digging, digging. And when he'd dug deeply and relentlessly enough, he'd sat down and written those secrets into his books.

*Exposing secrets created enemies.*

Shaken, she continued walking, her mind reaching out in all directions.

But *who?*

*Why?*

*And for what?* The current research? Or things he'd dug up for the books he'd written in the past? In one of them, she felt certain, she would find the key.

But in which one?

Her steps quickened. She intended to do her damndest to find out.

## 6

Under the equator, the seasons are reversed. When it's winter above, it's summer below. But in both hemispheres, the names of the months remain the same. In Portuguese, May is *Maio;* it just happens to fall in late autumn.

And autumn in Rio de Janeiro can be decidedly summery. On this particular day, the temperature hit a high of seventy-five degrees and, like a human tide, the skimpily clad sun worshippers descended on the world-famous beaches of Ipanema and Copacabana or the twenty-one less famous ones to soak up the rays and display youthful bronzed flesh.

For the young and carefree, skin cancer is a lifetime away.

A hundred nautical miles to the northeast it is a different story. Although the temperature climbed to seventy-six on the private island of Ilha da Borboleta, the pristine white sand beaches surrounding it were devoid of sun worshippers; the man who lived here took cancer and the effects of ultraviolet rays on the human skin as serious threats to his health. Both he and his beautiful mistress avoided direct sunlight like the plague.

If there is such a thing as Fantasy Island, then Ilha da Borboleta certainly fit the bill. A good portion of its seven square miles of gentle hills and volcanic outcroppings were kept carefully thinned out and pruned back at all times, the shiny green vegetation never rotting and stinking of tropical decay. The manicured lawns were like a blanket of soft fabric mowed in a precise pattern of swaths. Exotic species of palms and rare tropical flowers of all sizes, shapes, and colors grew and thrived in great profusion.

Quinta Santo Anastácio, the blue-and-white tiled *palácio,* had been erected by a rubber baron back in the nineteenth century. The intricate Portuguese tiles which covered its outside walls had weathered beautifully over the last century and a half, and the terra-cotta roofs had been conscientiously restored.

Ilha da Borboleta was the private domain of Ernesto de Veiga, a reclusive billionaire who, it was reported, was one of the three richest men in the world.

The security measures were awesome, as befit a man of his wealth and stature. Around the clock, one of two speedboats equipped with searchlights and sophisticated radar and weaponry patroled offshore, while squads of armed security guards with trained attack dogs were on land duty twenty-four hours a day.

The island was accessible only by seaplane, helicopter, and yacht. Ernesto de Veiga owned several of each.

He was sitting deep in the shade of the bougainvillea-shrouded verandah, a tall craggy man of indeterminate age in a short-sleeved, white cotton shirt and dark trousers. A yellow silk scarf was knotted around his throat. He sat facing outward, so that he could enjoy the view. And indeed, from time to time he would look over the wicker table which held his freshly squeezed vegetable juice and lepidopterist's implements and gaze out past the cascading vines and flowers and spiky palm fronds and across the beautifully kept grounds.

From the shrubbery, giant clouds of butterflies flashed bright rainbow colors. Insects buzzed indolently all around.

He drew his eyes back in and looked at the brilliant emerald-green-and-black butterfly he was holding by its yellow thorax with a pair of tweezers. It was still alive and fluttered its wings in a desperate attempt to escape.

He held it up. "Do you know what this is?" he asked in Portuguese-accented English.

"Of course, senhor," replied Colonel Valerio, U.S. army, retired, who stood off to the side in the military position of at ease. "It's a butterfly."

De Veiga shook his head and smiled. "No, no, no, colonel. This is no mere butterfly! *This* is an *Ornithoptera priamus!* It is found near the coasts of the Moluccas and New Guinea and northern Australia. And, as of now, here! Beautiful, is it not? My first male of this species for my collection! Notice the yellow dots near the costa? Here?" He pointed with an index finger. "It is quite similar to those of the female *Ornithoptera victoriae*. A butterfly's colors," he added, "are a result of its ability to convert its own excreta to pure pigment. Fascinating, no?"

That explained, de Veiga unscrewed the lid of a jar inside which he kept an ether-soaked sponge. Swiftly he plunged the butterfly down into the fumes until its fluttering ceased, then took it back out and replaced the lid tightly. He laid the unconscious insect with its half-closed wings against a six-inch-square wooden rack which had two lateral laths and a cork-lined groove into which to fit the thorax. Then, selecting a tiny pin, he impaled the butterfly with one swift jab. Bending forward, he blew gently on its abdomen, and its jewel-like wings opened wide. He laid a strip of parchment vertically down on each wing, and with a pair of needles mounted on tiny wooden holders, secured them in that position. Then he slid the wooden rack into a larger rectangular container of ether.

"There, my pet," he said softly to the butterfly. "You see? Death can be absolutely painless, and now your beauty will bring joy forever."

After a minute he slid the wooden rack back out of the ether. Now it was just a matter of waiting a week or so for the butterfly to dry. Once that was done, he would remove it from the rack, place it under glass, and carefully label it.

He motioned for Colonel Valerio to roll forward a giant, mesh-enclosed cage mounted on casters which had been pushed away against the wall. Inside it, thousands of live butterflies like the one he had just mounted fluttered and swirled, like a constantly changing kaleidoscope of gemstones.

"Ah!" Ernesto de Veiga looked up at the colonel. "A miracle, is it not?" His eyes were gleaming. "Just yesterday, these were still but chrysalides. And now look at them!" For a long moment he stared into the cage with pride. Then, lifting the lid, he set them free.

Up and out the green butterflies fluttered, rising like a column of living jewels before becoming a cloud of scattering emeralds.

"There." When they had dispersed, de Veiga folded his hands on the wicker tabletop and looked questioningly up at his chief of security. "Now then," he said. "I take it you have good news to report, Colonel?"

"Yes, senhor." Colonel Valerio nodded. He was a tanned, lean man with tiny white crinkles in his leathery skin, dressed in a khaki shirt, web belt, black beret, and khaki trousers which bloused over his jungle boots. He wore a holster on his hip and mirrored aviator shades which rendered his face expressionless. His shirt was damp and clung to him, but if he suffered any discomfiture he did not show it. He was ex-army and had spent a lifetime in the humid tropics. Compared to the steamy jungles of Central America, Ilha da Borboleta was paradise. But then, it was paradise compared to any other place in the world, too.

"The body has been discovered?" de Veiga inquired softly as he sipped his glass of vegetable juice.

"Yes, senhor." Colonel Valerio's voice was clipped. "I have just received word."

"And the cause of death?"

"Suicide by hanging."

"How unfortunate." The billionaire brought his drink thoughtfully to his lips. "What about his research material?"

"Senhor?"

"You mean it is still there?" De Veiga's expression did not change, but his voice conveyed infinite displeasure.

"You never said it should be destroyed, senhor."

De Veiga took another sip of his drink. "See that it is."

Colonel Valerio spun a neat about-face and strode briskly down the verandah and around a corner. As his footsteps receded, a woman of indeterminate age and breathtaking beauty swept out through the French doors. She moved soundlessly on gold sandals, but Ernesto de Veiga was immediately aware of her: even unseen, his mistress exuded an extraordinary presence.

He turned his head to look at her. Today she was wearing a loose jumpsuit of turquoise parachute silk, and her hair was completely hidden by a matching turquoise turban. Her complexion was very pale. Like many South American women, she had on bright red lipstick and a little too much makeup; unlike them, she also wore upswept sunglasses encrusted with genuine diamonds. Her carefully shaped eyebrows were the color of rich honey.

"What did Valerio want?" she asked in Portuguese as she swept toward him in a cloud of jasmine.

"He reported the suicide of that American writer."

"Suicide?" For a moment she lifted her sunglasses and stared at him through the most extraordinary green eyes.

Ernesto de Veiga permitted himself a slight smile. "It seems the poor man hanged himself."

"Ah!" she said with delight. Lowering her glasses, she went to stand behind him. Her strong slender fingers kneaded his shoulders possessively. "He *is* dead then?" she asked, just to make sure.

"Oh, very. Or should I say, unfortunately so?"

Her voice turned suddenly bitter. "You will say nothing of the kind, Ernesto! That meddling old fool! Lili Schneider is long dead and buried. Why didn't he let her rest in peace?"

"Unfortunately for him, he didn't. But do not worry, my butterfly. Her memory is now safe." He reached up, took her by the wrist, and slipped a thirty-carat diamond solitaire on her ring finger. "A present for the most exquisite butterfly of them all," he said, kissing her hand.

"Oh, Ernesto!" She raised her hand and moved it around to admire the brilliant shards of blue, the flashes of pure white light. "You shouldn't have."

"It's D-flawless."

"Of course," she said. She leaned down and touched her soft cheek against his. Then, smiling, she reached into her voluminous sleeve and withdrew a flat clear plastic box. "And I have a present for you also."

He took it from her and looked through the lid. A butterfly. Wings a translucent shade of green and iridescent pearl gray. Speckles of pale violet spots.

He clapped his hands in childlike delight. "A *Salamis parhassus!* My very first!"

She smiled. "I know," she said. "Unfortunately, I couldn't acquire a live caterpillar or a chrysalis. Yet."

Eagerly he opened the box. Barely touching the delicate edge of a wingtip, he murmured, "In death it gives us beauty everlasting."

"Yes," she agreed softly and continued stroking his shoulders. "Indeed it does."

After leaving the police station, Stephanie wandered around midtown. She had no clear destination, and went wherever her feet carried her. She needed time to clear her head and make sense out of everything that had happened. She couldn't shake the feeling that she had wandered through a looking glass—and had been plunged into another, darker world. A nightmare world inhabited by suffering and pain.

There was so much to cope with. So many questions gnawing at her.

And the police had been of no help. They'd insisted her grandfather had committed suicide—showing her his note to prove it, a note typed on the treasured old Remington on which he'd written his best-sellers.

"It's not even signed!" she'd pointed out angrily. "And what kind of sentence is this—'*I cannot bare to live any longer.*' He'd never misspell a word like *bear.*"

"A man under stress would," she'd been told.

Now she suddenly wasn't so sure anymore.

And what if the police were right, and the cigar he'd smoked *had* been the last earthly treat he had permitted himself?

*It wasn't. I have no proof, but I know.*

Perhaps he'd been ill? Suffering from some painful, terminal disease he'd kept secret from her?

The thought was like an explosion in her chest. She practically reeled under the impact.

Suddenly she became aware of where she was—the corner of Park Avenue and Sixty-fifth Street. The very block where her grandfather's doctor had his offices!

She wondered: *Has my subconscious guided me here?*

"Doctor will see you at once, Miss Merlin," the receptionist told her warmly.

Stephanie conveyed her thanks and walked into the doctor's office. She was filled with trepidation. The idea that her grandfather might have been hiding a terrible disease from her was unbearable. *We've always shared everything.*

Lyle Forsyth, M.D., Carleton Merlin's physician, said, "I gave your grandfather a thorough physical not three weeks ago. X-rays, EKG, blood tests, the works. He was in excellent health for his age, Stephanie. That's why I couldn't understand it when I heard he—"

"He *didn't!*" Stephanie cut in vehemently. "I just had to make sure there was no reason he might have wanted to."

Dr. Forsyth's manner was gentle. "Are you holding up all right? Can I prescribe anything for you?"

"Thank you, but no." She shook her head. *I have to feel the hurt,* she thought. *I don't want my bereavement clouded by chemicals.*

She rose from the chair and shook the doctor's hand. "I appreciate your having seen me."

She returned to the Osborne to find Pham puttering around the living room, trying to clean between fits of silent tears. The moment Stephanie came in, the young Vietnamese man opened his arms wide. "Oh, Miss Stephanie," he moaned, clutching her tightly. "I am so sorry."

For a while they clung to each other and shed tears together.

"He was such a fine man," Pham said thickly, shaking his head. "I am going to miss him."

"I know, Pham, I know."

After a while, Pham sniffled, then drew a mantle of dignity around his tender feelings. He said, "By the way, some gentlemen called. The lawyers. Also the accountant. They want to set up meeting with you." His harsh voice made it clear what he thought of business intruding before Carleton Merlin was even laid to rest.

Stephanie nodded. She thought: *I know what they want to discuss. Death and taxes. The two go hand in hand.*

Stephanie sighed and sank into a chair beside Waldo's cage. Pham glided silently back in, set a cup of hot tea and a plate of biscuits down on the gueridon beside her, and slid just as soundlessly back out.

Stephanie sat there numbly.

"Wal-*do!*" the bird squawked, eyeing the biscuits with greedy eyes. He cocked his head sideways. "Waldo wants a crack-*er!* Wal-*do!* I love you, Steph!"

Absently, Stephanie fed him one biscuit after another until they were all gone. She was deep in thought. There was so much to think about, and she already felt so drained. First there was the funeral, during which Grandpa would be rendered unto God; then there was Caesar or, more accurately, Uncle Sam, unto whom were to be rendered other assets, namely taxes. There were so many details to worry about, so many things to take care of. Insurance policies. Bank accounts. Safety deposit boxes. Bills. Personal property to dispose of.

Suddenly it was all too much to take.

*One thing at a time,* she cautioned herself. *Don't try to do everything at once. And don't be afraid to ask for help. That's what friends are for.*

She picked up the phone and called Sammy Kafka at his apartment.

When he answered, Stephanie said thickly, "Uncle Sammy? You said I could call whenever I needed you. Could you please come over?"

"I'm on my way, Girlie," the sweet old man promised.

# 7

*T*homas Andrew Chesterfield III did not appreciate late-night telephone calls. He appreciated even less having to get up at an ungodly hour to run a sleazy errand. The truth of the matter was, he had no choice.

He put down the phone with a sigh and looked at his wife. Katinka lay on her side, facing him, her unlined face in peaceful repose, her black satin hair fanned out over the pillowcases. The ringing of the telephone hadn't awakened her; she'd only rolled over on her side and curled herself into a ball, tucking her knees up against her breasts.

He studied her a while longer. There was something about her sweet youth and otherworldly beauty that hammered home what the phone call had been all about. *Would you be able to dream so peacefully, my darling, if you knew what I was involved in?*

To all outward appearances, Thomas Andrew Chesterfield III was one of Manhattan's chosen few. In every aspect of his life, he seemed to have it made.

He had looks, power, money, and, as though to round off his perfect life, beautiful Katinka, his highly visible social wife (his third), and four attractive grown children (two from each previous marriage).

But Thomas Andrew Chesterfield III had two very pressing problems, neither of which would go away.

The first was Dennis, the younger of his two sons.

The second had come about as a direct result of the first.

Four years previously, handsome young Dennis, then eighteen, had run with a racy, cocaine-tooting crowd. Rough sex had resulted in the death of a beautiful girl, and Dennis had fled the scene, not knowing that one of his acquaintances had set up a video camera in a closet. What was supposed to have been a sex movie made as a prank had turned into a snuff film—starring Dennis.

It was then that the blackmail began.

And Thomas Andrew Chesterfield III, sophisticated legal eagle, had actually believed he could avoid scandal and social ruin by agreeing to pay the blackmailers fifteen thousand dollars a month in perpetuity.

The lawyer who knew all the moves was, for once, absolutely stymied. For if word of Dennis's involvement in a sex murder got out, the family would be ruined—and all because of one rough-and-tumble sex scene gone wrong.

And then one day, the demands for cash suddenly ceased. Instead, a new and even more ominous demand had been made—that as a lawyer he represent a mystery client whose identity he would never try to discover.

One evening, not quite a month ago, just when Chesterfield least expected it, a call had come.

"Mr. Chesterfield?" It hadn't been so much a voice as a genderless whisper. "Do you know who this is?"

"N-no," he'd said shakily.

But of course he knew. Why else did his intestines suddenly twist themselves into strangling knots?

"I think you do, Mr. Chesterfield," the voice had continued smoothly. "Have you ever heard of a man named Carleton Merlin?"

"Yes. Of course."

"Good. Now here's what you have to do. Mr. Merlin has been poking his nose into things best left untouched."

Chesterfield's guts loosened a little. This was more familiar territory. "You want to sue him?" he asked.

The whisperer laughed softly. "Oh no, Mr. Chesterfield. We want him eliminated."

The pain which shot through his abdomen was like a shock. "I beg your pardon?"

"You are to see that he is killed—"

He'd slammed the phone down then and there, and refused to answer its incessant rings. Finally he'd unplugged it. Snuff tape or not, he wasn't about to get involved in murder.

The next day, one copy of the videotape had been messengered to his home, a second to his office, and a third to one of his clubs.

Luckily, neither his wife, secretary, nor anyone at the club had intercepted them.

That evening, the caller telephoned again. "Did you change your mind, Mr. Chesterfield?" the genderless whisper asked.

"I am not a killer and I don't know any killers," he'd whispered wretchedly.

"That doesn't matter. There is a freelance assassin in New York who specializes in 'accidental' deaths. He is known only as The Ghost."

"The Ghost?"

"It seems he is called that because he is invisible. You see, Mr. Chesterfield, no one has ever seen him. At least," the caller added ominously, "no one has lived to talk about him."

Chesterfield's hands were shaking. "H-how do I get hold of him?"

"Rumor has it he's friends with some of the hookers and porno girls on the West Side. You have merely to cruise around and ask."

That was when his forays into the underbelly of the city had begun.

It was a descent into a sewer inhabited by hustlers and hookers, pimps and johns, thieves and con men. He hit all the haunts of the hard-core perverts—the peep shows, porno circuses, topless bars, X-rated movie houses, massage parlors, and dim street corners. Always asking the same question: "Do you know a man by the name of The Ghost?"

It had taken him two weeks to find the hooker on the southwest corner of Thirty-eighth Street and Ninth Avenue, the one who'd leaned into his Jaguar's open window and said, "Yeah. I might've heard of The Ghost. He bad."

Her name was Shanel and she was short and black, with dark shiny eyes, hard little breasts, and tight round wiggly buttocks packaged into a nude-looking body stocking fitted with strategically placed zippers.

"Can you tell me how I can get hold of him?" he asked.

She'd looked pointedly up and down the avenue. "Let's you and me go for a ride," she said, pulling the passenger door open and swinging her hip onto the front seat. "It gonna cost you fifty bucks, though. Okay?"

The hooker had been a conduit. And, through a convoluted method by which the assassin couldn't be traced, The Ghost had gotten in touch with him.

Now Carleton Merlin was history. According to the newspapers, it had been suicide.

Chesterfield breathed a little easier. Naively, he'd dared hope that this was it—that all the copies of the tapes would be returned to him, and the past forgotten.

Wishful thinking.

Tonight another call had come.

"Mr. Chesterfield? It seems Mr. Merlin was working on a book at the time of his, ah . . . suicide. My clients want to see all the research material destroyed."

"But . . . I don't know any burglars!" he'd begun to protest.

"I'm sure The Ghost can be of help to you."

Thomas Andrew Chesterfield III only had to circle the block twice before he saw Shanel on the corner, repairing her lipstick with the aid of the side mirror of a parked hatchback.

He guided the big car into the space right behind it. In the wash of his headlights, she finished painting her mouth in apparent boredom before sashaying nonchalantly back and sticking her head through the open passenger window. "I thought it you," she said when she saw Chesterfield.

He smiled bleakly and kept checking his rearview mirror for patrol cars.

"Chill out and stop being so jumpy," she said, trying the passenger door. It was unlocked, and she scooted in and pulled it shut. "Drive," she instructed concisely.

He waited for a flotilla of empty cabs to sail by and then pulled smoothly away from the curb.

"Pull in over there," Shanel said, after they had been driving a minute. She pointed to the right. Chesterfield nodded and aimed the hood of the Jaguar into the same big empty parking lot she'd directed him to the last time. It was right atop one of the Lincoln Tunnel ramps, and was open to both Thirty-seventh and Thirty-eighth Streets. During the day, it was filled with exhaust-belching commuter buses from Jersey; nights, it was a favorite pitstop for Midtown hookers and their johns.

He left the engine idling and turned to Shanel. She was looking at him in the faint glow of the dash. "Well? What you want this time, man?"

"I need your help, Shanel."

She gave a low laugh. "Everone need my help."

They sat there in silence for a minute. She fiddled in her bag for a cigarette and lit it with a Bic lighter. He pushed a button so all the windows whined down some. Headlights from behind rose and fell as another car pulled into the lot. He kept his eyes on the rearview mirror.

Shanel fixed him with her dark shiny gaze. "You need to contact The Ghost again, or you change your mind and want a blow job?"

"I need to get in touch with The Ghost. I need him to—"

"Unh-unh!" she said quickly, shaking her head. "I just the go-between. I don't wanna know *nothing!*" She looked suddenly scared. "Nothing! You understand?"

He nodded. "Then just let him know that I . . . ah . . . require his services again."

"All right. But that'll cost you."

Sighing, he dug out his wallet, slid out a crisp fifty without letting her see how much he was carrying on him, and held it out to her. She just sat there and shook her head. "A hundred," she said.

He stared at her. "Last time it was only fifty."

"Yeah, I know." Her lips slid up into a tough kind of smile. "But ain't you heard? Inflation, it hit everbody!"

## 8

*T*hese were mean streets, even for a black ghetto dweller.

Especially a lone black *female* ghetto dweller.

Vinette Jones walked briskly through the public housing project as if she couldn't wait to escape. Her fingers clutched her tan vinyl handbag, a reminder that it might be snatched out of her hands at any moment. She had lived here nine years—nine years too long—and had found out the hard way that anything was possible.

Vinette Jones was only twenty-three years old, but she looked thirty-five. Her skin was as cocoa brown as that of her African forebears, her tightly kinked hair was close-cropped, and her bearing was straight and proud. Tall, she was almost gaunt, and just missed being handsome. Nevertheless, she radiated a steely strength and a quiet, don't-fuck-with-me resolve.

Walking with her shoulders squared, she kept her eyes straight ahead, careful to look neither to the left nor to the right, determined to witness nothing that might be dangerous to her health and well-being. Not that she needed to look around to see what was going on. The same things as always. Crack dealing, crack buying, and crack smoking—that and stolen property changing hands and wolfpacks of teens roaming, keeping their deceptively lazy eyes peeled for easy prey.

The ugly project of dirty apartment blocks was one vast supermarket.

Random killings had become commonplace, stray bullets nothing out of the ordinary.

Vinette heard crack vials crunch underfoot; in her peripheral vision, she saw hundreds . . . thousands . . . of the empty, scattered vials glittering in the gutters and on the hard-packed, grassless ground.

She felt a knot tighten in her stomach. This was no place to raise a child. Especially not a child like her own Jowanda.

Tiny, beautiful, innocent Jowanda. Premature child of her womb, flesh of her flesh.

Her eyes misted over. Jowanda. Born when she herself had been strung out on shit. When she'd lived with Vernon, the no-good bum who'd turned her on to drugs, gotten her pregnant, and then run off when she'd been in her ninth month.

Jowanda, born in the delivery room of the CRY Hospital for Unwed

Mothers. Where, right before giving birth, Vinette had gotten a visit from that nice grandmotherly lady who worked at the D.C. affiliate of the CRY orphanage—and where, for fifty dollars cash, she'd signed yet-to-be-born Jowanda over.

"We'll take very good care of her, and once you've straightened your life out and want her back, you only have to come in," the nice lady had told her gently. "You can have her back anytime."

Somehow, the act of selling her baby was what eventually reached something deep inside Vinette, and with it had begun the long road to recovery. It had taken her three interminable years. How she'd suffered! First the DTs and the indescribable craving. The clinics and constant therapy. Slipping and going back on the shit. Then finding Jesus and finally overcoming her drug dependency for good. *To him that overcometh will I give to eat of the tree of life,* it said in the Scriptures, and it was true. Having found Jesus, she felt her whole life suddenly change. She felt herself blossoming. She'd found a new high—a high such as she'd never known from drugs—and she never wanted to touch the damn shit again.

Cleaned out, she had gotten herself a real job—even if it was only as a ladies' washroom attendant in a swanky downtown hotel. So what? It was an honest job where she made an honest dollar. And with the job came self-sufficiency, and with self-sufficiency came a feeling of pride. Finally off the welfare rolls, she was able to hold up her head.

The ache inside her was overwhelming. *Jowanda, baby, where are you?*

Because, after she'd straightened herself out and gone to the CRY orphanage here in D.C., Jowanda was not there, contrary to what the nice grandmotherly lady had promised her, and she'd also discovered that they didn't even have any records on her!

It was as if her baby had never existed.

But the nice grandmotherly lady who'd had her sign the papers in the delivery room *did* exist, and she hadn't been so nice this time. Something hard, like shutters, had come down over her eyes as she insisted she'd never in her life set eyes on either Vinette or Jowanda Jones.

Vinette clutched her handbag even tighter. Well, lies were not good enough for her, not since she'd cleaned herself out and Jesus had entered her life. No sir! Her baby was out there somewhere, waiting for her to reclaim her.

Oh yes, she was going to find her Jowanda, wherever she was. She was determined to get her back. Even if the D.C. CRY orphanage had been a dead end, and all she'd gotten was blank stares and the runaround, she wasn't about to let that stop her. CRY had its headquarters in New York City, and maybe someone there would be able to help her. Surely a big institution like that, with millions of sponsors and children's hospitals and orphanages in countries around the world, had to keep detailed files and records.

So Vinette Jones had scrimped and saved and squirreled away her washroom tips. She even took to walking to work and back instead of taking the city bus, just so she would have enough money to buy a round-trip bus ticket to New York.

She was headed to the bus terminal right now, looking neat as a pin, and wearing her best dress and least-scuffed pair of shoes. Fortified with the strength of the Lord, determination glowing on her face like shining steel.

She breathed a little easier and let her guard down a bit. Her footsteps quickened. Another brisk half-hour of walking, and she'd be at the bus terminal and on her way north. To New York City.

North, to find her baby.

## 9

*W*ith Johnny Stone's arrival, Sammy Kafka and Pham Van Hau conspired to make themselves scarce. Both claimed sudden long errands they needed to run now that Carleton Merlin's funeral was over.

*Errands my ass,* Stephanie thought, wishing they hadn't gone. It didn't take a psychic to figure out the reasoning behind their transparent excuses.

They might as well have saved themselves the trouble. She didn't want Johnny Stone, nor did she want to be alone with him. She hadn't even wanted to let him in, but after he'd explained how he'd come all the way from Sidon, what choice had she had?

So here he was now. Five years later. Live and jet-lagged. Bending over Waldo's cage, scratching his beak and cooing total nonsense.

*And Waldo was eating it up; damn the traitorous bird!*

For a moment, Stephanie stood back and watched her ex-lover through slitted eyes. She had to hand it to him. Johnny Stone knew exactly the right buttons to push.

Some things apparently never changed.

Neither did some others. For instance, he didn't look half bad. No, she had to admit that he looked rather appealing. *Too* damn appealing, in fact.

"I swear this bird missed me," Johnny was saying. "Didn't you, Waldo, old boy?" He turned his face to look at Stephanie, his penetrating eyes fishing—obviously wanting her to say she'd missed him, too.

"Waldo," Stephanie said coldly, "goes crazy over anybody who gives him attention."

"*Anybody?* You mean, I'm not special?" He kept watching her, a flick of a smile on his lips.

She longed for the power to magically wish him away. His condolences had been said, and she'd offered him a drink, which he'd accepted and finished. Was there any reason for him to hang around?

"That's enough for *you,* old boy," he told Waldo. Straightening, he came slowly over to where Stephanie stood, her arms folded in front of her. "You know, despite the tragic circumstances, it really is good to see you again," he said.

She didn't reply, but nodded curtly.

"You must miss your grandfather terribly."

"Yes." Her voice was shaking. "I do." Quickly she turned away, not wanting to share the grief misting her eyes. He followed her.

"Stephanie, I know how hard this must be for you. This place isn't the same without him. It felt different the instant I walked in."

Sniffling, she blinked back her tears, raised her chin, and made her face expressionless. "Thank you for your concern, Johnny, but you don't have to worry about me. I'm fine."

"No, you're not, dammit!" he said softly, the heat of his gaze pouring intently into her. "I know you well enough to know you're keeping all your emotions bottled up."

"Please, Johnny, I . . . I'd like to be alone now."

He placed his hands on her shoulders. "You shouldn't be alone," he said quietly. "Not today of all days."

She shook her head and tried to push him away, but his touch charged her blood, electrified her skin.

*But I don't want him!* something inside her cried.

Her eyes were shadowed pools as she inhaled a massive heaving breath. Somehow she managed a staggering step backward.

"Don't pull away," he urged in a whisper, his hands still on her shoulders. "You need me. That's why I came, darling."

*Darling!* The long-forgotten endearment penetrated her defenses and hit home somewhere deep and hidden within her.

"Don't call me that!" she hissed, the words tearing angrily from her lips. A sudden redness rose from her throat into her face, and despite herself, she could feel the violent trembling of suddenly wobbly legs, could sense the painful thrust of her nipples against the softcup bra under her black silk dress. Then her eyes quickly fell. "I . . . I think it's time for you to go now, Johnny," she whispered huskily.

Gently he chucked a finger under her chin. "Darling, don't look away. Look at *me.*"

She was finding it difficult to breathe. Electricity charged the air, seemed to snap and crackle and spark.

"Stephanie . . ." His hands tightened on her shoulders.

"No!" she whispered, shaking her head. "It's wrong! It—"

"Darling . . ."

Again she shook her head, once more attempting to pull away, but he gently raised her head to his; with his other hand, he cupped the softness of her face from cheekbone to jaw, his touch feather-light, his fingers communicating consolation.

She stared up at him, her head tilted back. For an instant her pupils dilated, and then her expression softened, the breath catching in her throat as she beheld the full force of his gaze. The turquoise of his eyes was uniformly serene, but sparkles of silver winked in their depth, like hypnotic sun dapples on gently shifting water.

Time seemed to telescope, then stood absolutely still.

The longer she stared into those luminous turquoise pools, the more she knew she was gone. It was useless to fight it; senseless to continue contesting the long-suppressed feelings which fluttered and stirred wildly inside her. Almost against her will, she found herself reaching up and covering his warm hand with hers.

He held her gaze. "If only for a short while," he murmured, "I want you to try to forget your loss."

As though possessed, she swallowed hard and nodded, the emotions within her ballooning to choking. Suddenly she wanted so badly for him to grab hold of her and kiss her, to make her feel protected and safe and loved, for the haven of his arms to ensure the reality of living and chase away the suffocating cloud of death.

As though he had read her mind, both his hands cupped the satin smoothness of her face. "Stephanie . . ." he breathed, his thumbs caressing her cheeks, "my Stephanie . . ."

A mild, damp breeze blowing in from the open windows ruffled her dress and tugged at the black velvet ribbon which held her hair at the nape of her neck.

"Stephanie . . ." he whispered again.

"Johnny . . ." she returned, her own voice a hoarse whisper. But before she could say more, he shushed her and bent toward her, his mouth pressing against hers.

Slowly, the tip of his tongue teased her lips before worming between her teeth to dance and dart and probe.

She shut her eyes and let herself go. She felt as if she were drowning. Swirling wondrously down and down. Down to endless depths.

So many sensations this kiss aroused! So many feelings it opened up and released. Delicious, the paralyzing heat which spread from her mouth, filling her with a sweet pliant languor which seeped through her entire body.

How she loved it. How she needed it. How much she'd missed it. It was useless, now, to attempt resistance any longer. There was nothing to do but press herself tightly against him, slip one arm around him, place the other hand behind his head, and draw his face even closer into hers.

She inhaled the masculine scent of his skin, feasted on the sweetness of his breath.

His lips left hers, and it was as if a part of her was suddenly missing, a sweet stolen from between her very lips. Her eyes abruptly flew open.

"Don't stop!" she whispered, clutching him fiercely and staring into his eyes. "Please don't stop!"

In reply, he silently bowed his head even lower, his lips now tracing a moist path down her chin and neck, until he found the throbbing, rapidly beating pulse in her throat.

He closed his mouth around it and licked gently.

Her entire body arched. It was almost more than she could bear. Everything inside her longed for him, cried out to possess him.

She closed her eyes as she felt him unbuttoning the buttons at the back of her dress, gasped as he slid it down over her shoulders and unhooked her brassiere. The sudden rush of air was cool against her naked torso.

And all the while, his lips were still at her throat, as though taking communion from her speeding pulse.

She mewed softly as his caressing hands slowly slid back up her spine, then deliberately traced the curve of her shoulders. She barely felt him reach behind her neck to untie the black velvet ribbon which kept her hair pulled back.

Thick blond cascades, freed of their restraints, were suddenly released and came tumbling down. Sweeping the tops of her shoulders. Softly framing her flushed face.

His lips left her throat, and he raised his head to eat her up with his eyes.

"Stephanie," he whispered huskily in her ear. "Beautiful, beautiful Stephanie." He glided his hands through her hair, feeling the cornsilk texture, his fingers alternately kneading and stroking and massaging.

She let her head move limply in whatever direction his fingers dictated, yielding herself to pure undiluted sensation. The unhurried deliberation with which he proceeded was delicious, and yet at the same time maddening.

Then she felt his palms smoothing their way down, past her face and shoulders, until they slid over the curvaceous silken contours of her breasts. Cupping a hand under each, he lifted the satiny weights, his thumbs and forefingers teasing the aroused, jutting strawberry nipples.

Only after what seemed an eternity did he dip his head and solemnly lower his mouth, first to one nipple, around which he licked light little whorls, before giving equal attention to the other.

She moaned and trembled violently. It was all she could do to endure the exquisite thrills of pleasure, all she could do not to cry out for him to take her, here, this very instant, and fill her to bursting!

She cradled his head in her hands, drawing his face closer into her breasts.

Such luxury, this passion. How had she managed to do without for so long?

Without warning, his arms gathered her up and in one effortless movement swooped her off her feet. She let out a little cry of surprise and clung to his neck as he carried her toward the door, Waldo watching quietly from the cage, his head cocked.

Once again, he proved himself almost psychic as he unerringly chose the neutral territory of the guest room, the one room in the entire apartment that was completely devoid of ghosts and memories for her.

Reverently he laid her down on the cool spread of ivory lace and old, crocheted cushions. From the ceiling above the headboard, a sweep of fringe-bordered white muslin curved down from a corona. A faded, tattered garden of old needlepoint cushioned the floor.

It was like being in another time, another century. Another dimension entirely.

She lay back, luxuriously naked, watching as he removed his shoes, peeled his trousers down lean muscled thighs, and discarded his jacket and shirt. They dropped soundlessly to the floor.

Her eyes feasted.

He seemed carved in that half light, a chiaroscuro Praxiteles sculpture come to life, his shaft engorged and swollen, like a gleaming sword of flesh. Such a perfect specimen of manhood; his chest broad and powerful, his arms corded. Absolutely sublime: a muscled ying to her softly voluptuous yang.

He slid onto the bed and stretched out atop her, his weight upon her, but evenly distributed, so as not to crush. His skin felt satin smooth against hers, and his manhood was trapped between their bellies. Like something live and hard straining to be freed.

He kissed her again, his fingertips feathering her face and arms, sides and hips, breasts and belly.

Gentle, gentle. Butterfly brush strokes.

She watched, quivering, as he moved slowly down her body, a symphony of lips and hands. Moaned as he drilled his tongue into her navel. Gasped as he hugged her buttocks and pressed his face into the triangle of soft blond curls between her legs.

She nearly levitated from sheer pleasure.

Oh, the ecstasy of his warm tongue upon the radiant liquid of her womanhood! The sheer torture of his lips closing around her secret of secrets, gently nibbling and sucking. Then the overwhelming loss when he stopped, like being deprived of life-giving sustenance.

But not for long. He spread her legs apart, driving her even wilder by kissing and nuzzling and stroking her inner thighs.

Stephanie gasped. She could actually feel the beginning of orgasmic pleasure coming on!

She dug her elbows into the mattress and half sat up. "Put it inside me!" she whispered. "I can't wait any longer! Love me! Please, Johnny! *Now!*"

"No," he whispered, "not yet. Lie back and enjoy it. You don't have to do anything . . ."

Tenderly, he slid a finger up inside her moistness.

"Johnny!" she screamed, as her back arched. Her head bore into the cushions, and her rib cage stood out like bold latticework. "Oh, oh my Go-*od! Please,* Johnny. Now!"

He glanced up at her, his eyes glowing in the near dark. There was an intent expression on his face, a kind of purpose and power shining from within him.

"Not yet, Sweet," he whispered. "All in good time." His eyes seemed to reach into hers. "Trust me. Okay?"

She went into whimpering spasms as he kept up with the teasing, bringing her to the verge of orgasm, only to stop the moment before the tide could fully engulf her. The impatience she felt was almost palpable. And still he teased, his tongue setting off little fires, his lips searching out secrets.

The tide threatened her again.

And again he sensed it and backed off.

Suddenly she could bear it no longer. Without warning, she lunged forward and grabbed his head. Then her legs jackknifed, her pelvis rose, and she thrust herself at him, rubbing herself obscenely in his face.

Grabbing her ankles, he forced her legs apart and buried his face even deeper in the pungent sweetness of her. Suddenly the heat blasting at him was too much. In a frenzy, he tore his face away from between her splayed legs, forced them down flat, and changed position.

Now he was kneeling over her, one leg straddling each of her thighs. He looked down into her face.

She was staring up at him, her eyes glazed with a mixture of greed and triumph.

"You want it?" he whispered.

"God, yes!" she moaned.

As he grabbed hold of her hips and lifted them to meet his, the thundering pulse within her roared and deafened, and the rushing blood sped to a screaming crescendo. This was the moment! she knew. His weapon of flesh was poised and ready, in the air right in front of her.

"*Johnny!*" she cried.

For a moment longer he seemed to hover in midair, seemingly held there by some unseen force. Then she cried out his name again and the straining erection lowered and drove down into her.

It was as if the earth moved and the heavens split asunder. Scissoring her legs around his waist, she dug fierce fingers into his flesh and slammed herself against him as if to swallow him whole.

A look of rapt, almost beatific concentration came over her as he slowly began to thrust. Closing her eyes, she joined his movements, rocking forward and backward, forward and backward, timing it so that they moved together in a perfectly synchronized dance of flesh.

Forgotten, for the moment, was the grim reality of the day. The funeral and the burial belonged to another time ... another lifetime entirely. This ... this lovemaking was a celebration of life. A conquest of death. A reaffirmation, a rebirth.

As he began to pump faster, her moans came like supercharged breaths. "Fas-ter!" she urged him on. Then she began to moan and scream and twist and writhe as the first full wave of orgasm came rolling over her.

Wildly her head flopped from side to side, and she dug her nails so fiercely into his back that he cried out in pain.

She barely heard his bellow, so powerful was the thunder reverberating within her. Her head whipped back and forth in a frenzy, her thrusts increasing in fury to keep up with his. And all the while, his eyes stayed on her. On her face, screwed up in agony and ecstasy, where her mouth was gaping and gasping, as though her insatiable passion was fed from the very air itself.

The thrashing of her gleaming body fueled his hunger, and his moans and grunts merged with hers. He drew his lips back in a kind of snarl. His heart was jackhammering as a torrent began to rise from deep inside him.

Faster, faster, faster they slammed into each other. Ravenously, like things possessed. Harder, harder, harder! Smashing against each other as if for dear life itself.

Harder now, he squeezed her breasts. She shouted and raked his back. He was too caught up in the engulfing heat to even cry out. Again, he squeezed her nipples, and despite her sudden tears, a blasting shudder seized her in its spasms and her entire body began to quake.

Her pupils froze and she stared wildly into his eyes as the apocalyptic climaxes tore through her, drowning him in a torrent of juices.

Her screams and levitations triggered the explosion within him. He shouted, cursed, and grabbed her almost cruelly, rearing up like an untamed bronco. Sensing him coming, she contracted as tightly as she could.

The seed flew wildly out of him even as he reared and bellowed, and together, the two of them tumbled over the edge of the earth and out into the far reaches of time and space and the darkness and dazzling light beyond.

For a long moment, they clung to each other, still joined, their bodies shuddering with aftershocks. After a while they slowly returned to reality, and she went slack and rolled away.

She lay on her back, gasping for breath. Finally she could feel her breathing returning to normal. She turned her head to look at him. "I don't believe it!" she whispered. "I feel like I've been reborn!"

He grinned. "If this is what rebirth feels like, I want to be born again. And again."

She reached for his phallus and squeezed it, gently milking it of its last drop. "You know," she whispered, staring sideways up at him, "it's true what they say. Making love *is* a reaffirmation of life."

Then the bedside phone shrilled.

He could feel her tense.

"Damn!" she swore, pulling back from him.

His arms tightened around her. "Let it ring," he advised softly, stroking her hair. "If it's important, whoever it is will call back."

But the old-fashioned, rotary dial phone kept on ringing shrilly. Twice. Three times. Four. Five.

With a growl of frustration, she yanked herself out of his arms and snatched up the receiver. "Yes?" she snapped into the mouthpiece in the middle of the sixth ring.

A man's voice asked, "Ms. Merlin?"

"Y-yes," she said, her voice suddenly cautious.

"My name's Rubin," the caller said. "Irv Rubin. I'm a friend of Johnny Stone's. He left a message that he was back in town and could be reached there."

"Would you like to—"

"In a moment," he interrupted smoothly. "I know this is a bad time for you, Ms. Merlin, but we're doing a cover story on your grandfather here at *New York* magazine? Naturally, we were wondering if you could—"

Suddenly she felt more than a little annoyance; she was downright furious. "You're damn right this is a bad time!" she snapped, cutting him off in midsentence. "In case you don't know it, my grandfather was just buried this afternoon. Good-*bye!*" She slammed the receiver down and closed her eyes for a moment. When she opened them, something hard and cold had come into them.

Johnny was looking at her with furrowed brows. "What was that all about?" he asked.

She turned to him slowly, her fury increasing. So that was why he had come. To give one of his journalist buddies a direct line to her.

"You bastard!" she hissed softly, her voice taking on a venomous edge. "You lowlife, sneaky, dirty rotten bastard!"

"Stephanie! What *is* it?" He reached for her, but she flinched and rolled away and jumped off the bed before he could touch her. She stood at the foot of it, arms hugging herself. "Get out," she said quietly.

He was stunned. After the beautiful love they'd just made, she was acting as if he were poison!

"Stephanie, if I've done something, I'd like to know what it is."

Even his voice now seemed to induce the completion of some electrical circuit inside her—disappointment, betrayal, violation, *opportunism*—so that all the rapture she'd felt was gone, and only hurt and disillusionment remained. Her heart felt hollow, and her body threatened to collapse inward.

He stared at her. "Do you mind telling me what I've done?" he asked quietly.

She glared at him. "Why don't you figure that out for yourself, Mr. Casanova?" she said bitterly.

"If that's the way you want it," he said tightly.

She flashed him a look which would have withered a cast-iron penis, and which, she noticed with more than a modicum of gratification, had its desired effect. Then, raising her head coldly, and without speaking another word, she turned and walked out of the room with dignity, her back straight and proud.

For a moment he just stared after her, wondering what had gotten into her. Then, remembering all too well how icily stubborn she could be, he got out of bed and began stalking around the room, snatching his clothing from where it lay scattered on the floor. Fuming, he got dressed.

She was waiting for him out in the reception room, wearing a robe, hand on the front doorknob. Without a word, she opened it wide.

Without a word, he stalked past her.

Without a word, she shut the door softly and threw the deadbolt home. Then alone again, she wandered into the living room and flopped down into a chair.

Wearily, she rubbed her face with her hands. *How could I have been so goddamn stupid?* she demanded of herself. *Rebirth*, hell! *Who was I kidding?*

## 🌿 *10* 🌿

*New York City · Walnut Creek, California ·*
*Ilha da Borboleta, Brazil*

*V*isitors getting off the high-speed elevators found themselves in a vast expanse of windowless space, the decor of which was sleekly corporate. Halfway between the elevators and the reception desk, and flooded from invisible spotlights, stood a larger-than-life, carved marble statue of a stylized, genderless child with upraised arms as though beseeching—or preparing to take flight.

Along the far wall, multicolored askew letters, contrived to look like child's print, jutted eight inches out from the plush carpeted walls. They read:

### CHILDREN'S RELIEF YEAR-ROUND, INC.
a-not-for-profit-corporation

In keeping with CRY's polished image, the receptionist was a cool, poised young brunette with pulled-back hair and red-framed glasses. At the moment, she was frowning over her steepled, red-lacquered fingernails. "I'm sorry," she said as Vinette finished explaining about Jowanda, "but that matter should be taken up with your regional CRY office."

"I know, but they wouldn't help me! That's why I'm here. Don't you see, ma'am? They lost my baby!"

"Let me assure you, Ms.—" She paused, eyebrows raised.

"Jones," Vinette supplied.

The receptionist lowered her hands to the desktop, folded them, and smiled tolerantly. "Let me assure you, Ms. Jones, that CRY does not *lose* children. CRY is dedicated to *caring* for them."

"Well, they lost my Jowanda!" Vinette declared. "Why else can't they find her?"

"Then there must be a computer mixup. Why don't you go back to your regional CRY office? I'm sure they'll straighten this out."

But Vinette hadn't come all this way for nothing. "I want to see somebody *here*," she said stubbornly.

"I'm sorry," the receptionist said firmly, "but in order to do that you need an appointment."

Vinette's heart sank. "But I don't even know *who* I'd have to see!" she pleaded desperately. "Please, ma'am! I came here all the way from Washington, D.C.! There must be *somebody* who can help—"

The telephone on the reception desk bleeped softly. "Excuse me," the receptionist said, lifting the receiver. "Reception, good afternoon."

She listened for a moment and her attitude immediately changed.

"Oh, Mr. Crandall!" she gushed. "Why yes, *sir!* I'll call you the moment they arrive! Of course I'll ask them to wait so that you can meet them out here personally . . . Why, thank *you*, Mr. Crandall!" She hung up looking inordinately pleased, and self-consciously smoothed her hair.

Vinette waited for a moment before clearing her throat.

Startled, the receptionist looked up. She had already dismissed Vinette from her mind.

Vinette drew a deep breath. "I would like to set up an appointment."

"Fine." The receptionist reached for a memo pad. "And who would you like it with?"

Vinette squared her shoulders. "Mr. Crandall."

The receptionist laughed and shook her head. "Good try, lady, but no dice." She pushed the memo pad aside. "Mr. Crandall's our CEO and only concerns himself with the overall picture."

Vinette stood there, her mind racing. She asked, "In that case, could I kindly borrow a sheet of paper and a pen?"

The receptionist sighed again, but could see no harm in the request. She reached into a drawer and handed Vinette a pen and a sheet of paper.

"I thank you," Vinette said politely, and headed for one of the conversation areas. Sitting down, she hunched over the low glass table and hurriedly began to print five neat, large words on the paper. When she was done, she traced the letters over and over in order to make them thick and dark so that they could be read from a distance. While she worked, she kept glancing anxiously toward the elevators.

*Ping!*

The automatic doors slid open and a couple emerged.

The man was middle-aged and distinguished-looking; he held himself with the kind of self-assurance only great wealth and power can bestow.

The woman was immaculately groomed, with perfectly coiffed silver hair, and was expensively dressed. In the subdued lighting, diamonds flashed brilliantly from her tapered fingers.

Vinette was acutely aware of her own cheap clothes, her lack of jewelry and sophistication, the mean project from whence she hailed. She watched as the couple went to the reception desk to announce themselves.

"Mr. and Mrs. Hammacher!" the receptionist gushed warmly. "How nice to see you! Mr. Crandall's expecting you. He'll be right out to give you a personal tour. Please, do have a seat—" Smiling, she indicated the conversation groupings with a sweep of a hand and immediately picked up the telephone.

The couple approached where Vinette was sitting.

Vinette's heart was thumping madly. Offering up a silent prayer, she waited for the couple to come a little closer. Then she held up the sheet of paper. The thick, neatly printed block letters read: CRY—WHERE IS MY BABY?!

Mrs. Hammacher tensed, laying a hand on her husband's arm.

"I'm sure there's nothing to worry about, dear." Mr. Hammacher cupped a hand under his wife's elbow and changed direction, giving Vinette a wide berth. Even so, he cast her a worried glance over his shoulder.

The receptionist, suddenly aware of what Vinette was up to, glared across the room and instantly telephoned Security.

Vinette sat there with quiet dignity. Her eyes unwavering. Her sign accusing.

Within moments, two burly, baby-faced men from Security hurried out, closely followed by a craggy-faced, white-haired executive who exuded power and charm. His face hardened as he looked around. "What the hell is going on here?" he demanded quietly of the receptionist.

"I'm terribly sorry, Mr. Crandall!" She rose from behind her desk. "But this woman"—she pointed a trembling finger in Vinette's direction—"is making a nuisance of herself. She refuses to leave!"

The men from Security moved toward Vinette.

The white-haired executive held up a hand. "Hold it right there, boys," he told them authoritatively. He turned apologetically to the Hammachers, who were standing off to one side. "I'm sorry for this disturbance. This won't take but a minute." Then he strode toward Vinette and regarded her with speculative amusement. "Well, ma'am, you've certainly got my attention. Now, what seems to be the problem?"

Vinette shut her eyes and took a deep breath. She had rehearsed her speech over and over. And sure enough, the entire story spilled out in such a concise, easy-to-follow nutshell that it surprised even herself.

When she was done, she said, "I'm appealing to you for help, Mr. Crandall. I don't know where else to go, who else to turn to."

Hugh Crandall smiled. "If you ask me, I'd say you've come to the right place, done the right thing, and talked to exactly the right person. Now, let's see about finding your baby, eh?"

He helped her to her feet and led her over to the receptionist. His smile was still in place, but his eyes had suddenly turned cold and hard.

"Get Aaron Kleinfelder to take care of Ms. Jones *at once*," he told the receptionist. "If he can't get this problem sorted out by quitting time, I want Ms. Jones put up in a hotel room at our expense. I expect every courtesy to be extended to her."

He turned once more to Vinette, a twinkle in his eyes. "I will say one thing for you, Ms. Jones," he told her admiringly. "You certainly know how to get things done."

"No, Mr. Crandall." Vinette shook her head, and there was something about her which shone like polished steel. "I just put my faith in Jesus. It's Him gets everything done, praise the Lord!"

Aaron Kleinfelder was a cherubic man with laugh-crinkled eyes, wiry frizzy gray hair, and an imposing belly of Pickwickian proportions. Once Vinette was seated, he offered her a sugar biscuit out of a tin.

She shook her head. "Thank you, but no," she said quietly, although she hadn't eaten a bite all day and her stomach was rumbling. "I don't want no cookies. All I want is to find my baby."

"In that case," he assured her cheerfully, "we'll just have to find her, won't we?" He helped himself to a handful of biscuits, but kept the tin within Vinette's reach. "You see, Miss Jones, *this* baby"—he rolled his chair sideways and tapped the top of his computer terminal—"will help us to find *your* baby."

Vinette smiled tentatively for the first time that day. "May I?" Shyly, she gestured to the open tin of biscuits.

"Help yourself," he invited, and pushed it toward her.

"I thank you." She took a biscuit and bit into it delicately.

"Now then," Aaron Kleinfelder continued. "First, I've got to call up the correct file. Do you happen to know whether your baby was put into one of the orphanages? Or into a CRY foster care program?"

"Orphanage." Vinette nodded definitely. "Least, that's what the lady back in D.C. told me."

He nodded. "Then we'll start from there." Spinning around on his chair, he flicked on the screen and typed CRY ORPH CODE on the keyboard.

Like magic, the gray screen literally exploded with green letters: ENTER YOUR PERSONAL ACCESS NUMBER.

He tapped the keyboard in a flurry. Then the screen went blank and changed yet again in the blink of an eye:

CRY ORPHANAGE-PLACED PERSONS

01  AFRICA
02  AMERICA-CENTRAL
03  AMERICA-NORTH
04  AMERICA-SOUTH
05  ASIA
06  AUSTRALIA
07  EUROPE

SELECT ONE:

Aaron Kleinfelder punched in 03. The screen read:

> CRY ORPHANAGE-PLACED PERSONS
> AMERICA-NORTH
>
> 1.00   CANADA
> 2.00   UNITED STATES
>
> SELECT ONE:

He tapped in the code for the United States. Then the screen immediately flashed up:

> SUPPLY NAME OF STATE OR UNITED STATES TERRITORY

"Dis . . . trict . . . of . . . Co . . . lum . . . bi . . . a," Aaron Kleinfelder said in slow syllables as he typed it in. "There." He sat back, and within four seconds, the letters changed to:

> 1.000   PERSONS CONSIDERED FOR CRY
> 1.001   PERSONS REJECTED BY CRY
> 1.002   PERSONS CURRENTLY IN CRY-ORPH PROG

He immediately typed in 1.002. There was a pause, then:

> PERSONS CURRENTLY IN CRY-ORPH PROG
>
> 01   CRY IDENTIFICATION NUMBER
> 02   SOCIAL SECURITY NUMBER
> 03   NAME OF PERSON

He glanced at Vinette. "You wouldn't happen to have a CRY identification number for your child, would you?"

She shook her head.

"Then I'll need your child's full name," he said. "Jones is her last name?"

She nodded. "Her first name's Jowanda. Middle name Daneece." She spelled the names slowly.

He typed JONES, JOWANDA DANEECE.

The screen replied: REFER FILE CRY ORPH TS IO NA CD 748300099440001.

Aaron Kleinfelder punched in that file, and after another moment's pause, the screen suddenly began to flash: ACCESS DENIED ENTER OPUS NUMBER.

* * *

In the subterranean, two-thousand-square-foot computer room of Scientifique Cosmeceuticals, Inc.'s research and development facility in Walnut Creek, California, a shrill alarm bell was assaulting the eardrums.

"Code Red! Code Red!" shouted one of the dozens of computer operators seated at rows of white Formica work stations. "Someone's trying to enter the OPUS File!"

The department head strode out of her glassed-in office and came to stand behind the young black man who had raised the cry. "All right, Bobby," she said coolly, her hands in the pockets of her starched white lab coat, "let's find out who it is." She stared down at his computer screen. "With all the industrial espionage going on, I wouldn't be surprised if it's a hacker for the competition. But who knows? It could even be an accidental entry."

"Doubt that," Bobby said, looking back over his shoulder and glancing up at her. "But we'll know soon enough. I put the automatic trace on." He grinned. "The other guy can switch off, but we'll *still* be hooked into *him*. Nice, huh?"

She nodded, her eyes never straying from the constantly changing screen.

"What's in the OPUS file that's so important, anyway?" he asked.

His superior shrugged. "Beats me," she murmured, "but one thing I know for sure." She kept staring at the screen. "That program has more safeguards than the Pentagon."

ACCESS DENIED ENTER OPUS NUMBER.
Aaron Kleinfelder stared at the continually flashing words in disbelief. "Now what the hell?" he murmured, and immediately looked contrite. "Pardon my French," he said, glancing at Vinette.

She smiled. "It's nothing I haven't heard before."

He nodded absently, reached for another biscuit, and chewed it reflectively. He'd never been denied access to any CRY file—ever—nor did he know what the devil an OPUS NUMBER was supposed to be.

He frowned and scratched his chin. "I'd say this is very curious," he murmured to himself. "Most definitely curious . . ."

"What is?" Vinette looked at him anxiously. "Is something wrong?"

He gestured toward the screen. "My baby won't give us any info on your baby. That's what's wrong."

"So what do we do now?" Vinette's voice had risen sharply.

Aaron popped another biscuit into his mouth and pulled up his shirt sleeves. "Now," he said, "I start being creative." He looked at Vinette. "But I've got to warn you, this might take a long time."

Vinette looked directly into his eyes. "I have plenty of time, Mr. Kleinfelder," she said, sitting ramrod straight. "That is, if you do, too? I wouldn't want to keep you from your family—"

"Nah." He flapped a hand. "Kids are all grown, and the wife's divorced me. Told me it wouldn't be so bad if I was seeing another woman, but how could she compete with my love for work?" He smiled wryly. "So voilà! I've got all the time in the world. But it's going to take a lot of intense concentration. I don't mean to offend you, but I'll work faster and better if I'm by myself."

Vinette nodded. "I understand perfectly, Mr. Kleinfelder," she said quietly, already pushing back her chair.

There was a knock on the door, and Aaron's administrative assistant popped her head in. She looked like a grown-up Orphan Annie: red frizzy hair and little round granny glasses. "It's five-thirty, boss," she said. "Okay if I cut out now? Or do you need anything else?"

Aaron glanced over at her. "I need something, Lisa. Could you find Ms. Jones a hotel room close by and settle her in as a guest of this company?"

"Right-o, boss." Lisa smiled and sketched a British style salute, the palm of her hand facing outward.

Aaron chuckled, but his eyes were distracted. Already, he was a million miles away, his mind consumed with bytes and chips and bits of data.

In his spartan office on Ilha da Borboleta, Colonel Valerio listened to the faraway voice at the other end of the telephone and said, "You're sure it's the same woman who raised the stink in the Washington office?" He was seated on a gray vinyl swivel chair, his jungle-booted feet resting atop his gray metal desk.

"Absolutely, sir. But here, there's no fobbing her off. They're actually listening to her."

"I see." Valerio tapped an unfiltered cigarette out of a pack of Camels. "Where is she now?"

"They put her up at the Grand Hyatt. I wasn't sure if it was important, but—"

"It isn't, but you did right in calling me." Valerio hung up. He checked his black-dialed, stainless steel chronometer watch and then punched the number of the exclusive Union Club in New York.

"The Union Club, good evening," answered a John Gielgud kind of a voice. "May I help you?"

"Yes," Colonel Valerio said, "I believe you can." His Zippo lighter flared like a torch as he lit his cigarette. "I would like to speak to Mr. Thomas Andrew Chesterfield the third. He should be having cocktails right about now."

## 11

tephanie brooded and Lili sang. For once, even Waldo was quiet as the glorious Schneider voice rippled and trilled and dipped and soared. Something alive had been released from the speakers and was flying freely, filling the room with a commanding virtuosity and the very essence of vocal beauty.

Stephanie didn't know what had compelled her to slip that particular disc into the CD player, but the "Er weidet seine Herde" from Handel's *Messiah* had never sounded clearer, or more gracefully melodic and spiritually uplifting.

Unfortunately, it didn't lift her spirits any. Nothing could—not after her grandfather's funeral and, as though to add insult to injury, being taken for a ride by Johnny Stone. Oh yes, and a ride it had been, too; he had literally *ridden* her—*humped* her like some cheap piece of female flesh—just so some hack journalist could interview her!

The goddamn son of a bitch!

Abruptly disgusted with everything—him, herself, death, and life in general—she got up and switched the music off. The sudden silence in the double parlor was almost unearthly.

There. At least now she could lick her wounds in supposedly golden silence. Perhaps a long soak in the tub would soothe? She considered the curative properties of a nice, steamy hot soak and a tall cool drink.

The telephone bleated intrusively.

"Oh, *damn!*" She glared across the room at the offending instrument. Then, with a sigh, she started to cross the carpet, but the bleating stopped and a perfect duplication of her own voice said: " 'Lo? Uh-huh . . . yeah . . . uh-huh . . ."

Despite her funereal mood, she couldn't help but laugh as she backtracked to the sofa and plopped herself down. She'd almost been fooled that time: Waldo had the beeping of microwave ovens, the bleating of telephones, and her own harried phone voice so down pat it was positively eerie.

"Damn bird," Stephanie swore affectionately.

Waldo climbed up and down the bars of the cage, shrieking happy laughter.

The telephone bleated again—on top of Waldo's cries. This call was real. Stephanie stared hesitantly across the room. For all she knew, it was that bastard Johnny Stone, calling to offer a smooth apology—as if she'd fall for his crap again.

She picked up on the fourth ring. But it wasn't Johnny. It was Ted Warwick, her producer. "How're you holding up?" he wanted to know.

"All right," Stephanie said. "You don't need to worry about me, Ted. Really."

Call waiting clicked. *Maybe* that *was Johnny calling* ...

"Hold on a minute, Ted, would you?" She put him on hold and depressed the cradle. " 'Lo?"

This caller wasn't Johnny, either, but a male stranger. "Ms. Merlin?"

"Y-yes?" Caution had crept into her voice. "Who is this?" The last thing she needed was journalists. Or crazies calling out of the clear blue.

"I hope I'm not disturbing you, Ms. Merlin," the caller said. "You don't know me, but I was acquainted with your grandfather. My name is Alan Pepperberg."

Stephanie frowned as she speed-searched through her mental files, but the name Pepperberg didn't ring any bells.

"Can you please hold," she said, "I'm on the other line." She switched back to Ted, told him she had to run, then switched back. "Mr. Pepperberg?" she said. "If you could hold another half a minute, I'd appreciate it."

"That's fine," he said.

Putting down the receiver, she hurried down the hall to her grandfather's study. The swollen, worn Rolodex was on his desk, atop a towering stack of reference books. Picking it up, she quickly flipped through the Ps. *No Pepperberg.*

She picked up the study extension. "I'm sorry, Mr. Pepperberg. Your name and number are not among my grandfather's addresses."

"That's not surprising," he said. "He and I had just recently crossed paths—actually, we only spoke on the telephone—and I was supposed to get back to him. Then I read that he'd died."

She waited for him to explain.

"The reason I contacted him initially was because of a Lili Schneider recording I have," he said. "He expressed interest in hearing it."

"Mr. Pepperberg," she said wearily, "I believe he had every Lili Schneider recording ever made. Why would he want to listen to another copy of what he already had?"

"This particular recording is not a copy, Ms. Merlin. It has never been released. It's an unauthorized recording."

Stephanie caught sight of her blank face in a mirror across the room. "I think you've lost me."

"I'll gladly explain it all. Is it possible for us to meet and discuss this in person? Over lunch, perhaps?"

She suppressed a sigh. "Mr. Pepperberg," she said as patiently as she could, "the Schneider biography died along with my grandfather."

"Ms. Merlin," he said softly, "did you know that your grandfather was on the verge of his greatest discovery?"

Stephanie's head was spinning now. Instantly her suspicions about angry sources and subjects rushed back.

"Ms. Merlin? Are you still there?"

She was clenching the receiver so tightly that her knuckles were white. "Yes," she managed.

"There's one more thing." He hesitated.

"And what's that?"

"I don't care what the newspapers reported. Your grandfather had absolutely no reason to commit suicide, Ms. Merlin. No reason under the sun. Not with what I had for him."

"And if my grandfather did not commit suicide?" she half whispered. "What would you call it then?"

His voice was hushed. "I think you already know the answer to that, Ms. Merlin."

Stephanie drew a sharp breath. Hadn't she herself expressed that very sentiment to the police only three short days ago? But yet, hearing a total stranger put her own suspicions into words was like having a knife twisted inside a wound.

She thought quickly. She had to go downtown to her apartment in the morning, if only to sort through her mail and take Waldo home. "I-I tell you what, Mr. Pepperberg. I have to be down in the Village tomorrow, and there's a place called the Corner Bistro. It's at the triangle where Eighth Avenue, West Fourth, and Jane Streets meet. Do you think you can find it?"

It was an instinctive choice. *I'll meet him on neutral ground,* she thought. *Surrounded by people. One can never be too careful . . .*

"The Corner Bistro," he repeated. "I'll be there, Ms. Merlin."

"Say . . . noonish?"

"Around noon it is."

Slowly, Stephanie replaced the receiver. For a moment, she stood there, hugging herself with her arms. She frowned thoughtfully. Did Alan Pepperberg really know something she didn't?

*A wild goose chase,* she cautioned herself. *That's probably all it is. I better not hope for too much. For all I know, he might not even show up.*

## 12

*New York City*

$\mathcal{R}$eminiscent of a grand Parisian boulevard, Park Avenue, that exceptionally wide thoroughfare with its greenery-planted median, cuts
an impressive swath up the East Side of Manhattan. Lined with some of
the grandest and most expensive apartment buildings in the world, it is a
stronghold of New York's oldest, richest, and most powerful families. It is
no accident that it is also home to the city's oldest, most exclusive, and se-
lective clubs. Charted 154 years ago, the terribly sedate, terribly conserv-
ative, and terribly, terribly snobbish Union Club is the granddaddy of
them all.

At a quarter to six that evening, Thomas Andrew Chesterfield III was
in the subterranean South Room of the club, where he was playing host
to Theodore F. Hallingby, chairman of a major television network whose
business he was trying to woo for the law firm of Hathaway, Mooney,
Buchsbaum, Chesterfield, and Gardini. To help oil the process, Chesterfield had broken out a bottle of one-hundred-year-old Armagnac from his
private liquor compartment in the wall.

He poured it gently into the giant snifters himself, not trusting the
steward with the eight-hundred-dollar bottle. "I've been saving this little
vintage for years," he told Hallingby with a little smile. "No time like the
present to see how it's aged, eh?"

Hallingby went through the ritual of swirling, sniffing, and sipping.
Then he sat back, an appreciative, rosy glow coloring his face. "Ah," he
murmured approvingly. "Excellent, excellent."

"Older than I am," Chesterfield grinned.

Hallingby looked around wistfully. "You know, I sort of like this
club," he said, his matter-of-fact voice belying his envy. "Long waiting list
for new members?"

Chesterfield looked at him. "Actually," he said, "the waiting list isn't
such a problem. Not, that is," he added softly, "if the right member sponsors you."

There. The tantalizing bait dangled.

"That so?" Hallingby said, lifting his snifter to the light, ostensibly to
study the amber liquid.

Chesterfield nodded. "If you're interested in taking a look around, I
can give you a tour."

"Mmmm," Hallingby said noncommittally, not wanting to appear too anxious. He took another sip and exhaled as the fragrant brandy filled him with a sense of well-being. "Might take you up on that offer sometime. Might just do that."

Neither of the men needed to elaborate any further. Both of them understood perfectly. Chesterfield would sponsor Hallingby for membership, and Hallingby would throw his network's business Chesterfield's way.

A steward approached the table and discreetly cleared his throat. "Mr. Chesterfield, sir?"

Chesterfield looked up.

"There's a telephone call for you. The caller says it's urgent."

*Damn!* Chesterfield thought. *I would* be interrupted just as the most important account I've ever snagged is nearly in the bag. But he kept his face devoid of expression. "Fine," he said. "I'll take it here."

Chesterfield waited until the man had gone before he punched the PHONE button on the receiver. "Chesterfield here," he said neutrally.

There was a pause, and then that genderless, sibilant whisper which filled him with such dread.

"I was just watching your son's snuff film once again, Mr. Chesterfield," the voice began. "I must say. The video quality really is quite superb."

Chesterfield flinched and went stone cold inside. For one long, terrifying moment he was almost certain that his heart had stopped. Then, when it resumed its rapid beating, he fought the urge to mop his suddenly sweating brow. Only the sight of Hallingby frowning at him stilled his hand.

Chesterfield gestured that the call was of no consequence, and smiled weakly. But along with shock, he felt fury—and violation, as if he were being raped.

"Mr. Chesterfield!" the voice hissed. "It appears that we once more require the services of our friend, The Ghost."

Chesterfield felt his sphincter contract, and a sharp pain shooting through his bowels.

"Now then," the caller hissed, "the services we need rendered this time are immediate. Do you understand, Mr. Chesterfield?"

Chesterfield sat there numbly, hunched over to conceal his voice and expression. Aware of Hallingby watching him with increasing wariness. "Yes!" Chesterfield whispered hoarsely.

"Then I suggest you don't even finish your drink. Go! Contact The Ghost. Now!"

Chesterfield's face went white. He was barely conscious of Hallingby's deepening frown. All he could see with a terrible clarity were snatches of that accursed video whirling through his mind. The memory was so loathsomely real that, without his realizing it, Chesterfield's fingers tightened around the brandy balloon with viselike force. There was a sharp crack as the glass suddenly shattered in his hand. Shards flew; Armagnac leapt into midair. Hallingby drew back to avoid getting splattered, but Chesterfield seemed unaware of what he had done. He didn't even notice the blood pouring from his hand.

"Who?" he whispered wretchedly into the phone. "Who is it to be this time?"

"Her name is Vinette Jones and she's staying at the Grand Hyatt," the whisperer informed him. "A black woman. Don't worry, no one will miss her."

Chesterfield slammed the phone down on raspy laughter, as yet unaware of his bleeding hand. His breathing was coming in great shuddering gasps. Then the steward, alerted by Hallingby's raised hand, came scurrying with a linen napkin and a towel. "I'll get a bandage at once, Mr. Chesterfield," the man said solicitously, but Chesterfield shook his head.

"No, no. I'll be fine." He raised his bleeding hand and stared at it in dreamy puzzlement, and then he suddenly snapped out of it. "Christ!" he exclaimed, repulsed by the sight of his hand. He snatched the linen napkin the steward proffered and wound it around his palm. "I better go and get this taken care of." He forced a smile. The lies flowed glibly now. "So sorry, old chap. A little family problem's come up, that's all. Have to run. Hate to leave you in the lurch—"

"I'll drive you," Hallingby offered.

"No, no," Chesterfield assured him. "Stay and finish your drink. I'm fine. Just fine."

Then he rushed out. He wasn't fine. And the worst part of it was, he knew that by contacting The Ghost again, all he was doing was buying time.

# 13

Aaron Kleinfelder was a man in his element. He had his Walkman tuned to his favorite jazz station, his beloved computer to tinker with, two desk drawers full of junk food, and access to the soda vending machine out in the hall—for him, the equivalent of all the comforts of home. Except for the cleaning people, the office building was quiet, and he could concentrate fully on his work without being interrupted. To make certain of that, he'd hung a DO NOT DISTURB sign on the door—a little souvenir he'd lifted from Caesar's Palace during last year's computer convention in Las Vegas.

Munching on a pretzel stick, he eyed his computer screen thoughtfully and then typed: DISTRICT OF COLUMBIA = CRY-ORPH PROG MENU.

He hit the SEARCH button and scanned the green, cathode-ray letters filling his computer screen. Then he typed in the code he wanted and reached for another pretzel stick, munching it as he watched his screen change to:

1.010  PARENTS OF CRY-ORPH PERSONS

001  MOTHER
002  FATHER

SELECT ONE:

"Mama, here we come," he said softly, and keyed it in. He glanced at the new information glowing on his screen, and decided to give Vinette's social security number a try. Referring to the information she'd left him, he typed it in. And once again, Aaron watched his screen print:

REFER FILE CRY ORPH TS IO NA CD 748300099440001.

So he entered: CRY ORPH TS IO NA CD 748300099440001.
And then, lo and behold! Once again, the screen began to flash: AC-CESS DENIED ENTER OPUS NUMBER.

*There it was again!* That damned OPUS NUMBER—whatever the hell it was! *Now* what?

"Holy cow!" Bobby, the computer operator in Walnut Creek, California, exclaimed. "Look at that! Someone's at it *again!* Wonder if it's the same dude."

"We'll see soon enough," his superior said crisply.

Bobby's screen was twitching with rapid-fire readout. Then suddenly one flashing number remained in place while all the rest of the numbers and letters kept changing.

"Aha!" he said unnecessarily. "We're closing in on him. Another minute or so, and then we'll have him."

A second flashing digit fell into place even as he talked.

Aaron Kleinfelder was becoming increasingly bemused. Since Vinette's social security number came up with a dead end, he'd punched in her name. And got—what else? REFER FILE CRY ORPH TS IO NA CD 748300099 440001.

Next, he'd tried Jowanda's father, Vernon Merrill West. At this point, he would have been surprised if the reply hadn't been: REFER FILE CRY ORPH TS IO NA CD 748300099440001.

He would have been even more surprised if that instruction hadn't led to: ACCESS DENIED ENTER OPUS NUMBER.

"There is," he murmured darkly to himself, "something definitely fishy going on in the State of Denmark."

The only trouble was, he didn't know what—or even how to begin looking for it. Not without that damn OPUS number.

In the computer room of Scientifique Cosmeceuticals in Walnut Creek, Bobby let out a cry. "Gotcha!" he crowed. Then he whistled softly. "Well, I'll be damned!" he near-whispered. "Same dude."

His superior leaned down over his shoulder and frowned as she read the printout on his screen. "Children's Relief Year-Round? I just don't get it. Aren't they—"

"—the nonprofit group with the godparents program," Bobby completed for her, nodding his head. He swiveled around in his chair and stared up at her in puzzlement. "What I don't understand is, why would somebody *there* be trying to access our files *here?*"

"I don't know," his boss replied, "but print out the data and bring it into my office." Her face was expressionless. "In the meantime, I've got to report this."

Low heels clicking on the white ceramic-tiled floor, she hurried back into her glassed-in office, picked up her telephone, and punched the button of one of the preprogrammed numbers. There was a series of clicks, a wait, and another series of clicks, giving her the impression the call was being routed from line to line. Finally, after a series of yet more clicks and short waits, she heard soft, faraway rings. Then a male voice answered tersely, "Security."

"Yes," she said. "This is Sharon Walker in the Walnut Creek facility. Someone is attempting to access the OPUS files for the second time."

"Did you do a trace?"

"Yes, we have."

"And?"

She glanced out of her glassed-in office. Bobby was letting out a whoop and fisting the air in triumph. Quickly she punched some keys on her own computer.

"Trace complete," she said. "Subject is at terminal one-three-two at the New York headquarters of Children's Relief Year-Round. It just doesn't make sense. They're not connected with us in any way."

"Forget it," she was told. "It was probably some sort of foul-up or a hacker. But you did right in calling. If it happens again, follow the prescribed protocol, just as you have done now."

"I will," she said.

"Who, besides you," the terse voice asked, "is aware of the attempted intrusion?"

"Robert Lubbock," she said, glancing through the glass wall at Bobby, who was in the process of printing out the information.

"I commend you both. Your vigilance will certainly not go unnoticed. In order to ensure mention of it in your personnel files, could you please spell both of your names?"

She did so.

"You did well," he told her again.

"We were only doing our jobs," she said, trying not to sound pleased.

But she was speaking into a deaf receiver; the man at the other end of the line had already hung up.

Deep in the Brazilian rainforest at Sítto da Veiga, Colonel Valerio, U.S. army, retired, booted up his own computer. The screen glowed:

CRY TERM. 132
KLEINFELDER, AARON M.

That was followed by the man's entire history. Professional as well as personal. Home address, unlisted telephone number, bank balances, the works.

*I'm Big Brother,* he thought with satisfaction, *and I'm watching . . .*

# 14

## New York City

"What you come around for this time, huh-*neeeey?*"

Shanel took a long, deliberate drag on her cigarette. Blew the car full of smoke.

Thomas Andrew Chesterfield III stared straight ahead. Out the windshield. Watching a car crawl along Thirty-eighth Street. Another flesh shopper on the prowl.

"I need to contact The Ghost again," he said quietly.

Unexpectedly, Shanel burst into laughter. "Man," she said, slapping a bare thigh, "you sure must have a lot of enemies. The rate you going, The Ghost gonna be one rich ass dude." She drew on the last of her cigarette.

Chesterfield was still staring out the windshield. "This time I need his services right away," he said.

She fiddled with the door panel until she found the window button. With a soft whir, the glass slid down and she flicked the glowing cigarette butt out into the night, watching the sparks scatter. "What you mean, 'right away'?" She turned to look at him again.

His voice was a near whisper. "I need him to do a job *tonight*. Tomorrow morning at the latest!"

Shanel rummaged in her bag for another cigarette and stuck it in her mouth. Her lighter clicked and flared briefly, casting a soft Rembrandt glow on her features. "You know the setup. Money talks, bullshit walks." She drew deeply on her cigarette and exhaled slowly, drawing twin streamers of smoke up into her nostrils. "Cash in advance."

"My bank doesn't open until nine! By then it might be too late."

She considered that in silence. "Well, that is none o' my business. That up to The Ghost. Who knows? Maybe I can't even get hold of him tonight."

"Please!" He grabbed her arm and squeezed. "You must try!"

"Hey! You hurtin' me! Watch it, will ya?"

He released her arm. "I'm sorry. I don't know what got into me. But I need your help!"

"Okay," she said placatingly, "okay . . . take it easy. But I'm making no promises, mind."

He nodded.

She said, "When you leave here, go to the usual bar and wait. If I get in touch with him, he call you. If I don't . . ." She shrugged.

"I understand. But if you *do* talk to him, emphasize that the job *has* to be done tonight or by early tomorrow morning at the latest. Tell him I'm good for the money."

She gave him a strange look. "The Ghost, he know if you are. Just don't double-cross him, that's all. 'Cause, baby, I'm tellin' you one thing. The Ghost, he one baaaaadass dude! He know things."

"What do you mean?" Chesterfield looked alarmed.

"He know things like where you *live*. He know where you *work*." Her voice dropped to a shuddering whisper. "See, The Ghost, he invisible. You can't see him but he *there*. And he always like to know who hire him. It's like—you know. Taking out an insurance policy?"

Chesterfield's bowels contracted painfully. Fear, true paralyzing fear, blasted through his body. His voice trembled. "You mean . . . he's *followed* me?"

"How the hell should *I* know?" Shanel dragged nervously on the cigarette, making the ash glow bright orange. She let the smoke out quickly. "Wouldn't surprise me, though. With The Ghost, you never know." She gave him a quick sideways glance. "So you just be careful, hear?"

The Ansonia, on Broadway between Seventy-third and Seventy-fourth Streets, is a monstrously large, voluptuous Belle Epoque wedding cake of a building. From the outside, it is an epidemic of ornate turrets and balconies, mansard roofs and bulbous domes. Inside, what were once some of the most distinctive apartments ever contained in a single building have long since been brutally carved up into smaller units.

Sammy Kafka's fourteenth-floor apartment, which included a corner turret, was one of the few exceptions. Having had only one previous tenant, it had never been altered. There was an oval reception hall, a round parlor with three tall French doors surrounded by a balcony, a giant, old-fashioned kitchen, and six other good-sized rooms. Sammy had lived there for over forty years now and vowed he wouldn't move unless they carried him out.

Now he turned away from one of the French doors as the urgent wails of sirens, New York's constant song, rose up from among the sounds of traffic rushing by far below. He looked over at Johnny, slumped on a faded green sofa, gazing down into the empty cut-glass tumbler in his hand.

The little man sighed. "Staring into your drink isn't going to get you anywhere, *bubbele*," he said gently.

With a start, Johnny raised his head and looked over at Sammy.

As always, the dapper, ageless dandy was neat as a pin. He was wearing an old-fashioned paisley smoking jacket with burgundy trim, a canary yellow ascot with a pattern of tiny red fleur-de-lys, black velvet trousers, and elegant red slippers with embroidered gold-and-silver crests on the vamps.

Sammy gestured at Johnny's glass. "Another one?"

Johnny sighed. "Sure. What the hell."

He handed the glass to Sammy and watched the old man take it to the imposing, Egyptian Revival buffet, where a silver tray held decanters, crystal, a carafe of water, and a silver ice bucket.

Sammy's fingers were as nimble as his step was jaunty. He expertly used sterling tongs to fish ice cubes out of the sweating bucket. Then he picked up a Waterford decanter which had a sterling label spelling BOUR-BON hanging around its neck, unstoppered it, poured generously, and stoppered it again without a clink. With a glass swizel stick he stirred the drink vigorously and then brought it back to Johnny with a napkin and a flourish. "Voilà!" he said.

Johnny nodded gratefully, said, "Thanks," and belted down a third of it. He sat back, brooding. He was beginning to wonder whether he should even have come up here. He was feeling hurt and depressed and more than a little sorry for himself. Maybe it would have been better if he'd crept off to lick his wounds in private?

But it was too late now. He was here, and had already poured his heart out. And there was no disgrace in that. Not really. He had damn good reason for feeling wounded—hadn't he traveled six thousand miles, give or take a few? And for what? Just so *he,* the good Samaritan, could metaphorically get kicked out on his ass?

Angrily he belted down another third of his drink.

"Before you make any hasty decisions, why don't you wait a day or two until you've both had some time to cool down?" Sammy suggested.

Johnny glared at him. "What for?" he asked belligerently. "To give her the pleasure of having a second go at kicking me out?"

"She's going through a tough time," Sammy sighed. "You know that."

"Yeah." Johnny barked an ugly laugh. "Life's a bitch and then you die. Well, I can tell you one thing. I've had it with her. Up to *here!*"

He sliced a karate chop across the front of his throat, and then slumped back on the sofa, staring morosely into his glass some more.

The old man looked at him for a long moment. Then, suppressing another sigh, he crossed back to the French door and held aside the lace curtain to look down at the sidewalk on the other side of the street. "Just look at them!"

Sammy's half-angry, half-wistful voice made Johnny glance up.

"Rushing from here to there like the world is on fire! Never stopping or slowing down to enjoy life. Forty-two years ago, when I first moved in here, people *strolled.* Lovers sat on the benches in that median down there. They kissed furtively and exchanged shy glances, as if their love was a secret. But now? Now it's all rush rush rush! Nobody takes the time to lift a hat in greeting. Nobody offers a lady a seat on the bus. Nobody *communicates.*" Sammy let the curtain fall back in place and turned around to look at Johnny. "Nobody *listens!*"

"Why tell me?" Johnny smiled grimly at him. "I tried to communicate. Hell, I came all the way from fucking Lebanon to *communicate!*"

"But did you *listen?* I mean, really listen?" Sammy shook his head doubtfully. "I wonder."

Johnny exploded. "Did I *listen!* Goddamn it! I just got through telling you that *she* was the one who wouldn't listen! Wouldn't even let me explain, dammit!" He looked at his glass in disgust and then hurled it across the room.

It crashed against the wall and exploded, shards and ice cubes ricocheting.

Sammy didn't so much as blink an eyelash.

"It was a mistake, goddamn it!" Johnny yelled hotly, jumping to his feet. "Jesus H. Christ! I didn't put Irv Rubin up to calling!" He clenched his fists and shook them. "If I'd known he was going to ask her for an interview, do you *think* I would have let him know where I was?" He paused, the cords standing out on his neck. "Well? *Do you?*"

Sammy went over to him. "*Bubbele, bubbele,*" he soothed, gently pushing Johnny back down into the sofa. "I know you didn't."

Johnny stared up at him. Then, suddenly overwhelmed by his emotions, he hunched forward, buried his face in his hands, and shook his head in despair.

Sammy sat down next to him. "Maybe," he said softly, "I can be of some help. That is, if you don't mind taking a little advice from someone who's older and perhaps wiser?"

Slowly Johnny lowered his hands.

Sammy didn't mince words. "You see, Johnny, you're like me when I was young. Did you know that? Of course you didn't; why should you? But you're a fool, just as I was. A big, egotistical, macho fool. But then, I suppose most men are."

Johnny didn't speak.

"The way I heard it," Sammy continued, "the last time you and Stephanie had a falling out, you just gave up. Thinking that was it, eh?" He cocked a white eyebrow.

"It was!" Johnny insisted.

Sammy smiled sagely. "No, my boy. It wasn't."

"But she—"

"Yes. And you listened with your ears instead of your heart. That's what I meant when I said no one *listens* anymore!"

Johnny heaved a sigh. "I just don't get it! You know?" He made a gesture of frustration. "If someone tells you they don't want you, and they *do* want you, then why do they tell you they don't?"

"That," said Sammy, "is one of the many delicious mysteries of women." He chuckled. "You see, Johnny, women and love are like war. They both have to be fought for and won. It's the same way with everything worthwhile in life." He smiled. "I know you love Stephanie. I also know that Stephanie never loved anyone else but you."

"Well, she sure as hell has funny ways of showing it," Johnny retorted testily.

"Not really," the little man said. "Why do you think she's still available? Not for lack of suitors, I assure you." He patted Johnny's knee affectionately. "You young idiot! You never realized, did you?"

"Realized what?"

"That all this time . . . how long's it been? Five years? She's been waiting for you!"

Johnny was speechless.

Sammy nodded. "You want my advice, go to your hotel. Stay there a few days. Take in some shows. Browse the museums and galleries. But give Stephanie time to heal." His eyes became moist and took on a faraway look. "She needs time, Johnny. Time to sort things out in her head."

"You'd think she had plenty of time to do that already!" Johnny said hotly.

Now Sammy's voice was edged with anger. "Young man," he snapped, "wake up and hear the music! In life, you have to learn to bend with the wind. Don't you realize that by giving up now, you might be throwing away your last and only chance at true love and happiness?"

Johnny scoffed. "True love! That's for romance novels and tearjerker movies!"

Sammy grasped Johnny's arm. "You're a nice boy, Johnny Stone," he said quietly. "A real *meshugahneh,* but nice. But grow up already!" The old man's eyes blazed fire. "Don't throw away your only chance at happiness—only to regret it once it's too late!"

# *15*

New York City

*V*inette Jones carefully marked her place in the Revelation of St. John the Divine with a thin red satin ribbon. Then she closed the red, vinyl-bound Bible, her most precious earthly possession (next to Jowanda, of course), and one she carried with her wherever she went. Putting it down on the coffee table, she got up from the armchair and walked to the window of the sitting room of her hotel suite. The draperies were open, and along with the spectacular view from this, the thirty-fourth floor, she could see her own reflection in the sheet of glass, as though her image had somehow been magically superimposed upon the glittering city.

Vinette could only shake her head in wonder, marveling at the night-time panorama of high rises that stretched as far as the eye could see.

And this suite!

She turned around, her wide eyes sweeping the sitting room. It was so large! So profligately luxurious!

*This is much too good for someone the likes of me,* she thought. But then she smiled, and her face lit up and shone with love. *But it's not too good for my Jowanda,* she thought. *Lord, no. Nothing is too good for my beloved lost baby.*

Thinking of Jowanda brought tears to Vinette's eyes. Sniffing, she turned away from the window and crossed over to the sofa, on which she'd dropped her handbag. She unsnapped it and rummaged through it for a tissue with which to dry her eyes.

It was then that she came across the thick, engraved business card which that nice old gentleman in Washington, the one who'd been hustled out of the CRY building there, had given her. Hadn't he told her that he'd help her if she needed it . . . that what he was looking into could possibly be tied in with the disappearance of Jowanda? Yes, that he had.

A hint of a frown crossed Vinette's face. *Would it be rude to telephone him?* she wondered.

She considered a while, and then came to a decision. *It wouldn't be rude to call,* she thought. *On the contrary. It would be bad manners not to. Yes. She'd telephone and tell him how much she appreciated his offer of help, but that it really wasn't necessary, praise Jesus! And she would share with him the good news that CRY was seriously looking for*

*Jowanda ... that it was only a matter of time before the two of them would be reunited ...*

Walking purposefully over to the telephone, she picked up the receiver, dialed for an outside line, and squinted her eyes to read the telephone number on the card.

The bedside phone shrilled, reaching down through the layers of sleep. Momentarily disoriented, Stephanie blinked awake and automatically groped for the receiver. " 'Lo?" she mumbled into it.

A woman's voice came on the line. "May I speak to Mr. Merlin, please?"

Stephanie drew an annoyed breath, wondering if this was somebody's idea of a cruel joke and for a moment almost snapped that there were no telephones in coffins—not unless you were Mary Baker Eddy. But something stifled her tart reply. Perhaps it was the shyness of the woman's voice? The solemnity of her tone? Or the extraordinary, soft-spoken politeness? Whatever it was, she found herself asking, "Who is this?"

"My name is Vinette Jones," the woman said quietly, "and I happen to be in town for a day or so. Mr. Merlin and I recently met at the CRY facility down in Washington, D.C."

"The what?" Stephanie asked, frowning, and thought: *What on earth is this woman talking about?*

"You know," Vinette said, "Children's Relief Year-Round?"

"Oooooh ..." Stephanie said.

"Anyway, Mr. Merlin was down there doing some sort of research or other," Vinette was explaining, "and I was trying to find my baby, which CRY apparently'd lost. That's how we met. If you could kindly tell him that, I'm sure he'll remember me."

Stephanie rubbed her eyes, willing her fuzzy brain to uncloud. "Ms. Jones," she said slowly, "you wouldn't, by any chance, happen to know what he was doing at the CRY facility in Washington, would you?"

"No," Vinette said, "I'm afraid not. When I asked him, Mr. Merlin says, 'I'm researching a project I'm working on.' That's all he said."

"I see." Stephanie struggled to concentrate. What she really needed, she knew, was a good, long, uninterrupted sleep, a rejuvenating sleep that would clear the cobwebs in her mind and let her think sharply and concisely. The kind of sleep she hadn't gotten in days. "Let me get this straight, Ms. Jones," she said curiously. "You did say that you were there because they'd ... *lost* ... your baby?"

"Yes, ma'am!" Vinette's voice turned indignant. "And neither Mr. Merlin nor me was getting to base one, which is what got us to talking in the first place ... You know how it is when people wait in a long supermarket checkout line with a slow cashier? Or in a gov'ment office where you have to wait for hours?"

Stephanie said she did.

"Anyhow, that's how we got started talking. And Mr. Merlin, he was kind enough to give me his card. He says, 'If you get much more of a runaround, maybe I can be of some help, or at least steer you to someone who can.' I thanked him kindly, and he said, 'Feel free to call anytime.' "

"And that's all he told you?" Stephanie pressed, switching on the bedside lamp and blinking against the sudden brightness.

"Let me see," Vinette said, pausing to search her mind. "We talked about the runaround we were both getting, how it was raining cats and dogs, how drugs was ruining D.C. He bought me a cup of coffee . . . Oh. Come to think of it," she said reflectively, "he did mention something about how his research and their losing my baby might somehow be connected."

Stephanie, feeling a quickening of her pulse, asked, "Did he happen to say how?"

"No, he didn't. And see, I didn't think to ask, because at the time I was so upset, them losing my baby, and all."

Suddenly, despite her fatigue, Stephanie snapped wide awake. First, foremost, and always a journalist, her professional antennae had gone on full alert. She couldn't say what, precisely, had triggered it—it was more of an instinctive feeling, a mere ripple of an intuition—but she got the distinct feeling that there was more . . . much, much more to this than met the eye. It was the kind of feeling she'd long ago learned to put her trust in, and more often than not, had resulted in her breaking the biggest stories of her career.

But this time, what galvanized her was not a potential story, but something far closer to her heart: the need to discover what had *really* happened to her grandfather.

Why had his research taken him, of all places, to Children's Relief Year-Round? He wasn't—*hadn't been,* she corrected herself, having to get used to the idea of thinking of him in past tense—an investigative reporter. No. Her grandfather had been a biographer. Specifically, he'd been researching the life of one Lili Schneider.

Which brought her to the sixty-four-thousand-dollar question. *What in the world,* she wondered, *could a long-dead soprano and an organization like CRY have in common?*

In her hotel suite, Vinette curled the coils of the telephone cord nervously around her index finger. "The reason I'm calling," she was telling Stephanie, "is I wanted to thank Mr. Merlin personally for offering his help, even though I won't be needing it now, praise the Lord. What CRY's doing, they're finding Jowanda by computer. Imagine!" She added meekly, "I'm not catching Mr. Merlin at a bad moment, am I?"

"I can assure you that you're not." Stephanie's voice held more than a hint of dry irony.

Vinette didn't catch it. "Oh, I'm so glad," she said with audible relief. "If you'll pardon my asking, you don't happen to be Mrs. Merlin?"

"No. I'm his granddaughter. Stephanie."

Vinette said warmly, "You sound like a very nice young lady, Ms. Mer—" Suddenly she stopped in midsentence and cocked her head.

"Ms. Jones?" Stephanie was asking.

Vinette glanced over her shoulder toward the door. She said, "I'm sorry. Could you hold on a minute? I think somebody's at the door. I better go check and see who it is. It could be about my baby."

"Sure," Stephanie told her, "go right ahead."

Vinette put down the receiver and smoothed her dress as she hurried to the door. The knocking came again, this time a little louder.

She wondered who it might be. Mr. Kleinfelder, perhaps? Or . . . *Good heavens!* she thought, her heart starting to pump madly. *It might even be somebody bringing me my darling Jowanda! My own little baby could be right outside in the hall, waiting in somebody's arms—*

Swiftly she unlocked the door and yanked it wide.

Instantly, her shining face dulled. It wasn't Mr. Kleinfelder, nor was it someone with Jowanda. It was a uniformed hotel employee with one of those small room service carts with drop leaves which fold out into tables. Its white draped surface was laid with a place setting for one.

"Y-yes?" Vinette asked in confusion.

The employee smiled. "Room service, ma'am."

"There must be some mistake. I didn't order—"

"Compliments of the management, ma'am."

"Oh!" Flustered, Vinette stepped aside. "I'm sorry. Please." She gestured. "Do come on in."

"Thank you, ma'am," said The Ghost.

## 16

*New York City*

The Ghost rolled the cart carefully into the suite and closed the door, surreptitiously locking it so that Vinette had no inkling she had suddenly become a prisoner.

"Ma'am. How about if I set the table up right here, by the sofa? That all right with you?"

Startled, Vinette half turned and bobbed her head. "That'll be just fine," she said. She was standing back, out of the way, uncomfortably watching the efficient dinner preparations and fidgeting as if—as if she felt she should be doing the serving!

Flipping up the drop leaves, The Ghost caught sight of Vinette glancing at the telephone receiver lying on the end table. Obviously she'd been on the horn and had somebody waiting.

Eyewitnesses were one thing; The Ghost avoided them like the plague. But sharing a kill with someone who *wasn't* present—especially someone who didn't have an inkling as to what was going on—added a delicious kind of spice.

"Be out of your hair in a moment, ma'am." The Ghost only said that to keep Vinette from picking up the receiver and talking to whoever she had on hold. "I hope *blanquette de veau* is to your liking?" The Ghost was looking at her with an arched brow, one hand on the handle of the largest of two domed lids.

"Oh, I'm sure it will be!" Vinette said.

"Please, ma'am. If you'll just take a look, then I can be on my way."

Vinette came over to the table and, quick as lightning, The Ghost slid a .44 Magnum out from under the lid and brought it up, the muzzle of the perforated silencer pressing against her forehead.

Vinette let out a surprised cry, as if a rabbit had been produced out of a hat.

"Easy, little mama. Eeeeeasy does it . . ."

The surprise left Vinette's face, to be replaced by dawning horror. She let out a moan as the hammer was cocked.

"Hope you not gonna be stupid, little mama. Don't want to have to pull this trigger unless I have to. Sure'd make a mess if I did. See, this baby'll take out a truck engine. Or blow your head apart like a water-melon."

The smile broadened, displaying perfect white Chiclets.

Waiting for Vinette to come back on the line, Stephanie could hear faint snatches of muted conversation, but it was too distant and indistinct for her to make out what was being said. Then she thought she heard—

What *had* it been? A cry? A ... *sob?*

Stephanie frowned. "Ms. Jones?" she said tentatively.

There was no reply.

Gripping the receiver with her hand, she said louder, "Ms. Jones? Are you there? Is everything all right?"

But her queries were met by silence.

—W—*what ... ?*

For a moment, Vinette's mind simply blanked out. The room, the city, the entire universe seemed suddenly compacted, condensed into the few cubic feet of atoms their two bodies occupied. She was conscious of nothing but the here and now: the gun, the assailant, and the chill steel pressing against her skull; conscious, too, of the sheer fragility of life, of how easily it could be snuffed out.

Cold sweat drenched her, made her reek of her own fear. She could feel herself losing it. Coming apart at the seams like a sweater when you pull at a piece of wool and it just keeps on unraveling and unraveling. Vinette sensed more than saw The Ghost's other hand moving.

Without stirring a muscle of her shock-frozen body, she lowered her gaze, following the hand. Watching. Waiting. Not daring to breathe as the second domed lid was lifted.

She let out a sharp cry.

On the platter, laid out with surgical precision, were all the accoutrements of—a junkie!

The length of rubber, the bent, flame-blackened spoon, the syringe and matches, the tiny foil packet.

Now fear loosened her bladder, but she was barely conscious of the urine soaking her panties and trickling down her thighs. She was praying silently but feverishly, beseeching God to deliver her from this evil, *from every evil!*—and all the while, her mind was shrieking the same outraged question over and over—*Why ... ? Whywhywhywhywhy ... ?*

Stephanie listened intently.

She could hear her own breathing echoing off the mouthpiece and then the hairs at the nape of her neck rose, and shivery tingles swept up and down her arms, legs, and spine.

Something was not right. She could sense it. She hadn't been able to make out any of Vinette's words, but even across the open telephone line, danger reared its ugly head. Seemed to hiss and growl and snap its jaws.

"Ms. Jones?" Stephanie called urgently into the receiver. "Ms. Jones? If you can hear me, tell me where you are! Please! I can send for help!"

But the silence crackled malevolently.

The Ghost was standing behind her, oblivious to the squawks emitted by the telephone.

Vinette was seated now, rigid on the straight-backed chair which had been brought out from the bedroom. Her left sleeve was rolled up, and her trembling forearm rested on the tabletop. The crook of her elbow was facing up in the junkie's classic shoot-up position.

Sobbing, trying to see what she was doing through a blur of tears, she fumbled with the length of rubber, holding one end of it between her teeth, and the other in her right hand. Winding it around her left wrist. Trying to find a vein in her *hand,* because those in her arms had all collapsed from years of shooting up, before finding Jesus.

"Well?" The Ghost's voice, coming from behind her, was a sibilant hiss. "You waitin' for Christmas?" She felt the silencer thump lightly against the back of her skull. "Rather I blow your head all to pieces? Kill you like that?"

Vinette shook her head desperately. Tried to hurry, yanking the end of the rubber with her teeth. Tightening the tourniquet, cutting off the circulation.

On the back of her hand, the veins popped out in bold relief.

Sweat and tears rolled down her face, dripping onto her arm. This was the single hardest thing she'd ever had to do. Harder, even, than going *off* the shit cold turkey. Because after she'd been weaned off it, she'd vowed to Jesus she'd never touch it again.

*But I don't have any choice right now,* she told herself. *If Jesus looks down and sees that gun pointed at my head, He'll understand. I know He will. I don't have any choice—*

"Now pick up the needle!"

Vinette swallowed. Reached out as if for a snake and picked up the prepared syringe with shaking fingers. The long thin needle quivered, catching the light and glinting, the plastic tube and plunger filled with— better she didn't ask; she didn't even want to know.

Suddenly she became aware of squawks coming from across the room. She turned toward the sound. The telephone receiver was still off the hook! In her terror, she'd forgotten all about it. If only she could—

"Now, forget that phone and get real nice and *high,* know what I mean, little mama?"

Vinette's insides were thumping, and she forced herself to clench and unclench her left fist. Making the veins pop out even further.

"Now inject yourself."

"P-please!" Vinette half-turned her head and looked up, her eyes pleading. "I-I don't take drugs!"

The Ghost smirked. "That ain't the way your arms look."

"That's from long ago! I've *quit!*"

More squawks were coming from the telephone receiver.

"Now do it." The Ghost's voice was quiet.

Vinette hesitated, looking into The Ghost's implacable eyes, merciless and without a shred of pity. Biting her lip, she looked back down at her hand and slowly turned the needle toward herself. And thought, *Maybe . . . just maybe . . . I could use it as a weapon?* She slid a sideways look at The Ghost.

"Don't even think about it, little mama!"

It was then that Vinette resigned herself and shut her eyes in silent prayer. When she opened them again, a kind of quiet strength shone through. Bowing her head, she said calmly, "Forgive me, Lord." Then she pictured her dear sweet Jowanda, fruit of her womb.

"I love you, Jowanda honey," she whispered, feeling her heart begin to swell inside her. And sitting straight and tall, with a proud kind of dignity, she neatly slid the needle into a vein and swiftly pushed the plunger.

The effect was instantaneous. Vinette thinking she'd never felt so gooooood . . . She sighed in contentment, feeling suddenly sleepy . . . too sleepy to withdraw the needle. She let it stick in her hand as her breathing slowed. Then she slowly keeled sideways and tumbled off the chair.

She lay sprawled on the carpet. Eyes open. Mouth shut. Lips turning blue.

The needle had snapped when she'd fallen, and half of it was still embedded in her hand.

"Sweet dreams, little mama." The Ghost squatted down, feeling Vinette's neck for a pulse.

She was already dead. The speedball had done its work.

From across the room, urgent squawks were still coming from the telephone.

Rising, The Ghost went over and picked up the receiver without a sound. Just listened to Stephanie's desperate shouts. Then smiled and hung up. Fished the red rose out of the bud vase on the cart, put it in Vinette's hand, and closed the pliable fingers around it.

Thinking, *Yeah, it's checkout time.*

At the Osborne, Stephanie was left holding a dead phone.

# 17

The following day, Stephanie returned with Waldo to her Horatio Street apartment. She snap-locked the front door by giving it a good push with her buttocks, carried the oversize cage down the hall to the loftlike living room, and set it on a table by the spiral stairs. She whisked the cover off it. "Here we are, Waldo!" she announced. "Home sweet home!"

Waldo cocked his head sideways and stared up at her with one eye. "Wal-*do!*" the bird shrieked suddenly, pacing back and forth on the wooden bar in excitement. "Wal-*do!* Waldo wants a crack*er!*"

"Ah, the potential willowy authentic lemon dish returns," a familiar voice offered from somewhere above. "Served, perhaps, with a splendiferous array of lotus stems, straw mushrooms, and special fish sauce?"

Stephanie tilted her head back and looked up. "Pham! What are you doing here?" she asked in surprise. "You're supposed to be studying! I thought your citizenship exam was tomorrow."

Pham sprightly tripped down the narrow spiral steps from the second floor of the triplex.

There was an air of dignified affront. "I am doing what I usually do this day of the week. Try to make your home habitable and clean squeaky. Aieee, the dust!" Pham ran an index finger along the railing and eyed his finger narrowly.

"You know you don't have to do it today," Stephanie told him. "Go home and study."

"I am studying." Pham slipped a stack of three-by-five index cards out of his pocket and held them out to her. "I study while I clean. Here. Ask me question," he said proudly. "Any question."

She took the cards and shuffled them. "All right," she said, choosing one. "Who was the twenty-eighth president of the United States?"

He didn't hesitate. "Woody Wilson."

For the first time in a week, she burst out laughing.

He blushed bright red. "Pham *wrong?*" he asked in mortification.

"No, no, no," she assured him quickly. "Woody is a diminutive of Woodrow."

"Then what so funny?"

"It's hard to explain."

Suddenly she looked concerned. "By the way, what time is it? I overslept and was in such a hurry to get down here I left my watch uptown."

Pham looked at his, which he wore on the underside of his wrist. "One minute until the hour of twelve noon."

"Noon!" Stephanie exclaimed. "I'm running late!" Her lunch meeting with Alan Pepperberg was ... well, not at noon, exactly, but noon*ish*. Still, if she didn't hurry, she'd keep him waiting. "I've got to run, Pham!" she said quickly. "Listen, could you do me a giant favor? Fill Waldo's container with water?"

Pham eyed the cage suspiciously. "You know that bird not like me. Like to peck off my fingers every time I get close to it!"

"Please?" Stephanie wheedled. "I've really got to run."

"Okay. I give it water," Pham said reluctantly.

"You're an angel." Swiftly Stephanie kissed Pham on the cheek. "Well, I'd better dash. See you later! And *study!*"

Breezing into the Corner Bistro ten minutes later, Stephanie stopped just inside the door and looked around the dim interior. All the tables along the windows of the narrow front room were occupied by couples, trios, and foursomes. At none of them sat a lone man. Speculatively, she eyed the backs of the heads of the men hunched over the bar.

The bartender noticed her and gestured her over. "Someone's waiting for you in back, Steph," he rasped, pointing. "Last booth on the left."

She smiled. "Thanks, Jer."

Stephanie nodded approvingly to herself as she strode toward the back. Apparently, Alan Pepperberg believed discretion to be the better part of valor. Either he had arrived very, very early, or else he had managed to use some sort of guile to get the most private table in the joint.

She found him sitting in the tall black-painted plywood booth facing away from everybody else, his view restricted to a dirty little window looking out onto Jane Street. A half-finished caramel-colored drink was on the table in front of him.

"Mr. Pepperberg?" she said softly as she approached from behind.

Startled, he looked up. Then, resting his hands, one of which held a cigarette, flat on the tabletop, he rose to an awkward, half-standing, half-sitting position.

Stephanie appraised him in one experienced journalist's glance. He was much younger than she'd expected—early twenties at the most. Thin, with a slightly manic look, very energetic darting blue eyes, big Adam's apple, and a snow-white Billy Idol peroxide crew cut. He was definitely a Downtown type. Wore six gold ear studs *and* a three-inch silver sword dangling from his left ear. But he was clean and punky, not at all seedy. And clearly not at all what she'd anticipated. He had a creative bent, of that she was absolutely certain—just as she was certain his punk look was a carefully cultivated style.

She held out her hand. "Hi. I'm Stephanie Merlin."

"I know," he said. Carefully, he put his cigarette in the overflowing ashtray, evidence that he'd been saving the booth for quite some time. His grip was surprisingly firm. "I recognize you from TV," he added, a touch sheepishly.

She smiled to put him at ease. "I hope I didn't keep you waiting too long, Mr. Pepperberg?"

"Alan. Call me Alan."

"Alan, then. And I'm Stephanie."

She swung her shoulder bag on the bench opposite his, slid in after it, and placed her elbows on the tabletop. It had decades' worth of names, dates, initials, hearts, and the odd four-letter word carved into its scarred surface.

The moment she was seated, he sat back down and picked up his half-smoked cigarette. He drew on it nervously. "You don't mind?" he asked, turning his head to blow the smoke away from the table.

She shook her head. "No. Go right ahead."

Alan smiled gratefully. He took another nervous drag and toyed with his glass, making the ice cubes tinkle.

"I'm glad you agreed to meet," he said, looking down into his drink. "Especially considering how I called, out of the blue." He looked up and smiled uneasily. "I was afraid you were going to dismiss me as a nut case. But then, opera fanatics usually are weird. Or at least, a breed apart."

Stephanie's expression was one of bewilderment. "*You're* an opera fan?"

He grinned disarmingly. "Mainly, I'm a collector. And what I collect are opera recordings." He glanced over at her. "Just like other people collect art, or Hummel figurines, or spoons?"

Stephanie nodded encouragingly.

"I guess I must have collected, oh, over fifteen thousand old records by now . . . forty-fives, seventy-eights, thirty-threes . . . about another four thousand reel-to-reels . . . probably close on six thousand cassettes. Lost count of the exact number of compact discs, though."

Stephanie stared at him. "My God! Where do you live? Tower Records?"

He grinned. "Well, in a loft, but it is beginning to look like a record store. Anyway, last month?" His voice dropped to a conspiratorial whisper. "I managed to get hold of the master reel of a recording of Callas singing live in Mexico City! *Imagine!*" His eyes gleamed like a religious fanatic's. "The recording was unauthorized. You know. Someone had a recorder and a microphone hidden somewhere in the audience? All in all, it's pretty dreadful as far as sound quality goes." He smiled. "But I had to have it. *Had* to!" He clenched a fist for emphasis. "Shelled out ten grand for it, too."

Stephanie was shocked. "Ten *thousand?* You mean *dollars?*"

He waved his hand dismissively. "It was nothing. Not for one of the crown jewels in my collection. Why, it would have been a bargain at ten times that price! Do you have any idea how *rare* something like this is?"

"Well, one thing's for sure," Stephanie observed dryly, "you obviously aren't a starving artist."

"N-no . . ." He looked a little uncomfortable. "My . . . uh . . . grandfather. He left me a small trust fund, you see . . ."

And suddenly a light bulb lit up inside her head. "The Pepperberg Guaranty Trust Pepperbergs!" she exclaimed. "You're one of them, aren't you?"

He winced. "Guilty." Then he smiled shamefacedly. "I'm the black sheep who refused to go into banking."

Small wonder he could shell out ten thousand dollars on a poor-quality recording! The Pepperbergs were right up there with the Annenbergs and the Rockefellers and the Mellons.

"Tell me something, Stephanie," he said, abruptly changing the subject. "Have you heard of Boris Guberoff?"

"Of course!" She laughed. "Hasn't every schoolchild?"

"He was—for me still *is!*—the world's *greatest* pianist!" He clenched a fist passionately and shook it. "The *greatest!*"

She allowed herself a tolerant, amused little smile. "Greater than all the others, Horowitz, Rubenstein, Feltsman?"

He snorted derisively and made as though to shoo away flies. "Before he came down with arthritis, Guberoff could play the pants off them all! Still can, probably," he said. "He was known as a pianist's pianist. Do you understand how *good* that makes him?"

"Alan," she said directly, "please. Let's get to the point? I didn't come here to play Trivial Pursuit or Jeopardy."

"I know. I'm trying to establish my credibility. I know my classical music. I want to make sure you don't get the wrong impression about me."

She looked puzzled. "Why should I?"

"Because what I'm about to tell you sounds so far-fetched and off-the-wall you're liable to think my elevator doesn't go all the way up."

She stared at him.

"Can you keep an open mind?" he asked softly.

Something in his voice made her nod. "All right, Alan," she said. "Whatever your story is, I'll give you the benefit of the doubt. But that's the best I can promise. Okay?"

He seemed satisfied. "Okay." He downed the remainder of his drink, looked around as though for eavesdroppers, and leaned across the table. "How familiar are you with the project your grandfather was working on?" he half-whispered.

Stephanie shrugged. "Only that it was supposed to be the definitive Schneider biography." She frowned. "Why?"

He answered her question with one of his own. "But you are acquainted with her voice?"

Stephanie nodded. "Definitely," she said.

"In that case," Alan said with a little smile, "I have a little something for your ears." From beside him on the bench he picked up a Sony Walkman and placed it on the table. "Here," he told her, pushing it toward her. "Put on the headphones."

She looped them over her ears while he produced two cassettes. After looking at their handwritten labels, he selected one, fed it into the Walkman, and punched the PLAY button.

Accompanied solely by a piano, that familiar, crystal clear soprano filled Stephanie's ears to bursting—at once sweet and delicate, yet soaringly heroic and muscular—so hauntingly beautiful she could feel gooseflesh rising along her arms. As Lili Schneider rippled and trilled and let go with the powerful instrument that was her voice, Stephanie was so captivated that she barely noticed the wretched quality of the recording, the constant hisses and crackles, the faint voice talking constantly in the background.

All she had ears for was the Schubert song:

*Was ist Silvia, saget an,*
*Dass sie die weite Flur preist?*
*Schön und zart seh' ich sie nah'n,*
*Auf Himmels Gunst und Spur weist,*
*Dass ihr alles untertan . . .*

Abruptly Alan punched the OFF button.

Stephanie's eyes opened, and she removed the earphones. "It's so beautiful!" she whispered.

He smiled, but his voice was hushed. "Stephanie, do you have any idea when this recording was made?"

She shook her head. "No. Why should I?"

"Well, I didn't, either. But I have a friend who's a sound engineer for Virgin Records, and as a favor to me, he used professional studio equipment to fiddle around with this recording. Now, the cassette I'm about to load is the exact same one you just listened to . . . *the* . . . *exact* . . . *same!* Remember that. The only difference is that the singing in the foreground has been quieted, while the talking in the background has been amplified."

"All right." She nodded.

He ejected the cassette that was in the Walkman and popped in the other. "Now, I want you to listen carefully to the conversation."

She put the earphones back on and waited for him to punch the PLAY button.

First, she heard only loud crackles and the rustling, rushing sounds of static. And then, suddenly, she could hear the same song and piano again, but muted, almost as though the singing and playing came from somewhere very, very distant.

When it came, the sudden blare of the voice was so loud and distorted that she jumped. It sounded like a conversation bellowed through a bullhorn. Squawk, squawks, squawking—a single male voice, speaking English with a foreign accent, overriding the distant music. It sounded like a cultured voice, obviously rejecting some advice, something to do with *"a joint venture . . . opening an . . . office . . . setting up a . . . network"*? But only that one voice . . . he was using a telephone, perhaps? It seemed the only explanation for the one-sided conversation.

Stephanie screwed up her face in concentration, struggling to glean information from distorted words, phrases, sentences. *" . . . an agreement in principle . . . reunification has opened vast new markets . . . a capitalist frontier!"*

Alan smoked in silence, his eyes alert to her every reaction. Trying to gauge her responses. Anticipate her questions.

She closed her eyes, shutting him out. Wanting to listen intently, without any visual distractions.

For a few moments, the quality of the recording magically cleared. The piano and singing came crisper now, and the voice gained clarity. *" . . . bringing Western know-how . . . training capabilities and quality control . . . hundred million . . . three, four hundred branches . . . Dresden . . ."*

Then the recording quality became poorer, squawkier again, the words less distinguishable. Despite high technology, the singing now overpowered the speaking voice.

The voice was like crystal chiming true, like an angel's voice swirling in up- and downdrafts, like the sweetest nightingale that had ever sung. Stephanie had trouble disregarding the song as snatches of phrases abruptly became clearer again. *" . . . cashing in . . . negotiating . . . rapid speed, rapid! . . . Staatsbank . . ."* She cupped her hands over the earphones, struggling to catch it all. Determined not to let one syllable of sound escape. *" . . . elections prove . . . don't need analysts to tell me! . . . are you listening? . . . stupidity . . . stupidity! . . ."* Obvious orders overrode whoever was on the listening end—yes, it *had* to be someone speaking on a telephone. *" . . . Dresden . . ."* The man's voice suddenly clear again, as though—*yes!* As though he were pacing while talking, moving restlessly in and out of range of the microphone, a thick carpet muffling his footsteps. *" . . . the headquarters for the entire . . . no, no, no . . . not Leipzig . . . tell them Dresden, or there is no deal . . ."*

And meanwhile, the singing in the background continued smoothly, segueing with the rippling piano chords into the last verse of the *Lied*:

*Darum Silvia tön, O Sang,*
*Der holden Silvia Ehren;*
*Jeden Reiz besiegt sie lang.*
*Den Erde kann gewähr—*

The man's voice suddenly calling out, possibly holding a hand over the receiver. Silencing the singer. "*Liebchen! It is done!*" The pianist caught unawares, and tinkling four last notes before stopping. "*One billion deutsche marks will gain us control of all the pharmaceutical concerns in what was the DDR. We have done it! Do you hear? We have done it! And . . .*" A pause. "*. . . the corporation, it will be headquartered in—no. You must guess where!*" From the consistent, clear quality of his voice, he had obviously stopped his pacing. Stephanie pictured him standing still near the microphone, could sense his quivering excitement at the dramatic suspense he had contrived. And then came *her* voice, faint but unmistakable, as though from offstage: "*I cannot begin to guess, Ernesto!*" Lili Schneider . . . sounding just like the late actress, Lili Palmer, when she spoke. "*Please, Ernesto. Bitte, mein Schatz! Do not torture me like this!*" And he saying, "*Then I shall have to tell you, Liebchen, since you know I cannot bear to see you tortured.*" A dramatic pause. Then: "*Dresden!*" And in the background, a sudden crack—hands clapping together in delight? "*Ernesto! Ernesto? Is it possible? After all these years . . . Dresden, where I gave some of my greatest performances!*"

The cassette abruptly stopped with a snap. Stephanie stared across at Alan, who had punched the Walkman off. Slowly, she lowered her hands, which she held cupped over her ears to shield her from hearing the restaurant's noise. Bits and pieces of conversation still echoed inside her head, bounding around like trapped radio signals seeking escape.

Her mental gears were whirling. What *had* she heard? Lili Schneider singing, and someone, a man named Ernesto, making a business deal involving pharmaceuticals in . . . Dresden? In *East* Germany? No. It was impossible. *Impossible!* One hadn't been *able* to do business with East Germany back when Lili Schneider had still been alive. The Russians had seen to that. And, five years before her death—before the Russians, before Germany had surrendered to the Allies—there hadn't even *been* an East Germany. There had only been *one* Germany. One *Reich*. The currency hadn't even been deutsche marks, but *reichsmarks*!

Stephanie shifted uncomfortably in her seat. Yet there had been no mistaking the word she had caught: "reunification." She *had* heard it. Which meant . . . which *had* to mean . . . that this recording had been made in—but it was impossible!—Lili Schneider had been dead and buried for decades!—*in 1990 or 1991!*

"Alan . . . ?" Her voice was shaky and she was momentarily nauseous, the room too hot, too confining, as though she had been poisoned by the information the cassette had spewed into her ears.

Common sense told her to forget it. Disregard it. To get up and leave. But her professional instincts were not guided by common sense. They were aroused, smelling a story even while rejecting it as fiction—as some con artist's scam, some high-tech flimflam man's ultimate con.

"When?" she asked hoarsely, and wondered: *If it's fiction, then why am I finding it so difficult to speak?* "Alan? The tape. Is . . . ?" She swallowed to lubricate her suddenly parched throat, demanding: "Is . . . it . . . real . . . ? You've got to tell me—"

"—If the tape's genuine?" Both his voice and eyes mocked her. "Yes, Stephanie, it's genuine."

"But . . . it . . . " she stammered. "It can't be! Alan! Schneider's been dead for forty-three years!"

He smiled with the kind of infinite patience one usually reserves for the very, very young or the very, very old and infirm. "Then how do you explain the singing?" he asked. "Hmmm?"

"An old record." She nodded swiftly, definitely, as though it would add credence. "Has to be."

He shook his head. "No, Stephanie. That wouldn't account for the conversation. Nor for the way the singing *and* the piano playing abruptly stop in midsong."

"Someone could have . . . put on a record! Recorded that on tape . . . and have switched it off at a certain point! And then . . . then they'd have . . . dubbed in a few extra piano chords! And added the conversa—"

"You're reaching," he told her gently.

"Yes, dammit!" she growled. "I'm reaching because I have to. There's no way on God's earth—"

He interrupted her. "Oh yes, there is," he said. "Because you see, Stephanie, this is not some sound engineer's trick recording."

"Oh?" Her eyes were challenging. "Then what, pray tell, *is* it?"

His voice was suddenly frosty. "I thought you specifically told me you would keep an open mind."

"And I have! But . . . the dead coming to life?" There was a note of incredulity in her voice. "Really, Alan!" She shook her head.

"But what if she never died?" he asked softly.

"Of course she died. My God! Her funeral was a worldwide event!"

"Rather convenient, her body being burned beyond recognition, don't you think?"

"Now *you're* reaching," she told him.

"Maybe. But how would you explain the pianist?"

Her brow furrowed. "I . . . I don't understand."

"Stephanie, every pianist has a style all his own, as individual as your signature or my fingerprints."

"So?" But she was looking at him cautiously.

"*So?* Don't you realize who was accompanying her on that song?"

She shook her head.

"Boris Guberoff."

"And what's that supposed to prove? He *is* still alive, isn't he? And he's been playing since when? The thirties? The forties?"

"Stephanie," he sighed, "if you know your music, you'll hear that he played that number *too slowly.* Also, that he played awkwardly. He couldn't reach certain keys because of his arthritis, dammit! He had to make *substitutions!* And his arthritis only got bad two years ago!"

She took a deep breath, feeling dizzy, as though she'd somehow stepped into the Twilight Zone. "Alan," she asked shakily, "what are you trying to tell me?" Although deep down inside, she already knew.

"Don't you see, Stephanie?" Alan's voice intruded, sizzled with excitement. "What you were listening to was Schneider singing, with Guberoff accompanying her on the piano! *After* he retired two years ago! *After* his arthritis got so bad he could no longer perform or record!"

Inwardly, she quailed, wishing she could make him disappear, or at least come up with some eminently more reasonable solution.

"Stephanie!" Alan was leaning as far across the table as he could, his voice the barest of whispers. "After I got hold of this tape and realized what I had, what should I happen to read but your grandfather's article on Lili Schneider in *Opera Now.*" He paused. "Have you read it?"

She shook her head. "I know the magazine, but it isn't exactly my cup of tea."

"Anyway, he didn't come up with anything earth-shattering in the article, but he *did* hint that he would in the biography of her that he was in the process of completing. So I called him, Stephanie! I called and told him about this tape! And do you know what he said?"

She shook her head, unable to speak.

"He said, and I quote, 'If that tape is the genuine article, then it just may be the key I'm looking for.' " He stared at her. "Obviously, proof for what he had already discovered for himself, but couldn't yet back up!"

"And what is it he was supposed to have discovered?"

"You know very well," he whispered. "That Lili Schneider is alive and well."

She sat statue-still, staring into his eyes.

"Think about it, Stephanie," he added softly. "What better motive is there for murder, than for the dead not to want resurrection?"

## *18*

*New York City*

"W̵here—?"

The word hung in the air between them, hovering above the table like a threatening cloud. The other patrons seemed to diminish, as though vanishing to some spirit plane, perhaps, their voices and movements reduced to nothing more than distant shadows and distorted whispers. Alan Pepperberg hunched forward on his elbows, as if the two of them were co-conspirators in an up-and-coming revolution.

Despite her dry throat, Stephanie hadn't so much as touched the schnapps he'd ordered for her, nor the club soda which she'd ordered herself. Both drinks sat forgotten in front of her—window dressing. She had nodded her thanks to the waiter and then watched as Alan picked up his glass and polished it off in a single swallow.

"Where?" she repeated inexorably. "Alan, I've got to know where that recording came from!" Her eyes bore into his. "I think you not only know how that recording came about, I think you also know *who* made it."

He expelled a noisy breath and paled. Then he nodded slowly. "Yes," he said cautiously. Something wary came into his eyes. "First, I need your word of honor that you won't tell a soul—and I mean *nobody*—where you got this information."

"Hey!" She spread her hands and grinned disarmingly. "Haven't you heard? Journalists never reveal their sources."

He looked at her stonily. "For your sake *and* mine, I hope to God you don't. Especially after what happened to your grandfather."

It was a physical blow. Despite the warmth in the restaurant, she could feel a sudden cold chill, as if something evil was crawling across her skin.

Alan lit another cigarette before, finally, he said, "Okay." He raked a hand nervously through his spiky platinum hair and glanced over his shoulder. "I got hold of it last month. From the same person who sold me the Callas recording I told you about earlier."

"The one illegally taped in Mexico City?"

"Yes." He nodded. "That one."

She got a pad and pen out of her bag. "I'll need to know this person's name," she said, flipping the spiral pad open. "Also, how to contact him or her."

"Unh-unh." He laughed shortly. "No way, José."

"Why not? All I want to do is talk to him."

"So do a lot of people whose copyrights he's violated."

"Alan, I already told you. I never reveal my sources."

"Stephanie," he said, shaking his head, "you don't understand. *No* one in this pirate recording business wants *any* attention. I mean, drug dealers aren't half as secretive. Would you believe, there are just a handful of unauthorized recording dealers like him in the entire world?"

"I didn't know that."

"Now you do. And they're not exactly listed in the Yellow Pages, believe me."

Without hesitation, she urged, "Then recommend me to yours, Alan. Please?"

"No way." He shook his head adamantly. "The moment they find out who you are, I'll be blacklisted from here all the way to Macao. Not one of them will ever do business with me again."

She sat forward. "Then just supply me with a *name,*" she pleaded. "All I'm asking is for you to point me in the right direction."

He looked at her through a cloud of smoke. "Hell, Stephanie, even if I could, I don't know whether the name my guy goes by is his real name or not. He's very clever, very cagey. There's no known address for him. No telephone number. No post office box. No nothing." He paused for a moment. "When he has a recording he thinks I might be interested in, he calls me, and we take it from there. Usually we meet in a hotel somewhere."

She drummed her fingernails on the tabletop and looked thoughtful. "All right. Since that's a dead end, let's try to approach this from another angle. How, exactly, did you get hold of the Schneider tape? I take it your dealer called you about it?"

"Well, he called me about the Callas tape, and naturally, my ears perked up since I'm a Callas freak from way back when. And, bad as the recording was, I just had to have it!" He smiled wanly. "Anyway, I told him that ten grand sounded a little steep, and he said he'd throw in a recent recording of Guberoff's to sweeten the deal."

He tapped a length of cigarette ash into the ashtray. "Anyway, I didn't get around to playing it for some time. Then, a couple weeks back, I sat down and listened to it. You can imagine my shock when—"

"—you recognized Lili Schneider's voice!" she finished softly for him.

"That's right." He nodded. "There's no mistaking it."

"And your dealer? You mean to say he had no idea at all of what he was giving away?" Her face held a look of disbelief.

"Apparently not. But then, why should he? Listen, Schneider's supposed to have been dead for—what?—over four decades now?" Suddenly a faint thoughtful frown crossed his face. "Come to think of it," he said, rubbing his chin, "I do remember him mentioning how he got hold of it. Apparently there was no great need for secrecy, or else he would never have uttered a word."

Stephanie waited for him to go on.

"Although he didn't give me a name, he did say it was from someone onboard the *Chrysalis*. It seems Boris Guberoff was on a cruise of the Yucatán peninsula, and was secretly taped while playing the piano onboard."

"The *Chrysalis?*" Stephanie searched her mind. "Is that a new cruise ship?"

Alan laughed. "It might as well be, big as it is. It's a yacht. A megayacht. Or, to be more precise, the de Veiga yacht. But whether the tape was made by a guest or a crew member, my dealer wouldn't say."

Stephanie frowned. "De Veiga . . . de Veiga . . ." she repeated under her breath. "Now where have I heard that name before?"

"Ernesto de Veiga," Alan supplied, "the Brazilian multizillionaire. One of the richest—if not *the* richest—men in the world. Tin, lumber, banking, pharmaceuticals. You name it, his fingers are in it."

She nodded slowly, thinking to herself: *So he must be the man named Ernesto on the tape!*

Alan exhaled a streamer of smoke. "So don't say I didn't point you in any direction." His eyes met hers. "Now you've got two places to start."

She nodded. "Guberoff and de Veiga," she said softly.

"And remember. You don't know me. You never even heard of me."

She watched as he punched the EJECT button of the Walkman and took the cassette out. He slid it across the table at her, his face expressionless, and placed the unengineered tape on top of it.

"These are just copies," he said. "I've got the originals."

She stared quizzically down at the tapes and then over at him.

"They're yours," he said, gesturing. "You can do what you like with them."

She looked surprised. "Thanks!" she said. "I owe you one."

He dragged silently on the cigarette.

She dug in her purse for a business card and scribbled her private home phone number on the back. "If you need to get hold of me for any reason," she told him, "any reason at all, don't hesitate to call me at this number. If you get my answering machine, leave a message. I'll get back to you."

Alan nodded and stubbed out his cigarette. "Just remember," he warned softly. "At the risk of repeating myself, you never heard of me. And while we're on that subject, don't be offended if I give you a friendly piece of advice. Okay?"

"Okay. Shoot."

"If you decide to play detective, exercise extreme caution. Do it quietly. Above all, don't do what your grandfather did, and announce an upcoming Schneider scoop. His *Opera Now* article could very well have led to his death."

She nodded soberly. "I'll bear that in mind," she promised.

She got out her wallet to pay for the drinks, but he motioned her money away. "My treat," he said.

When they were back outside in the bright sunshine, she and Alan parted company. "I'm catching a cab," she offered. "Can I drop you off somewhere?"

He shook his head. "No, thanks. It's not far, and I like to walk."

They shook hands, and she stood on the corner, watching him stride off in leathery, metallic glitter, the studs on the back of his jacket spelling CLEAN UP OR DIE. She couldn't help smiling. Definitely an ecologically minded punker, Alan Pepperberg.

An approaching taxi caught her eye and she started to raise her arm to hail it. Then she decided against it. No. She would walk, too. She could use the exercise and fresh air. Besides, it wasn't that far up to the Osborne. Forty-three blocks. At a brisk pace, she could walk it in about three-quarters of an hour, stoplights included.

She could use the cleansing qualities of crisp fresh air and bright sunshine, the invigorating activity of leg muscles in motion. She did some of her best thinking on foot. And, come to think of it, while she was at it, she would stop at the first electronics store she passed. Buy herself a Walkman.

So she could listen to the two cassettes along the way.

## 19

Johnny Stone prowled the sidewalk restlessly, unaware of the throngs of people brushing past him. He had tried, unsuccessfully, to banish Stephanie from his mind. Now his strong, unshaven jaw was set in obstinate determination as he kept a longing, melancholy eye peeled on the Osborne, across the street. Countless times, he'd almost begun to go over and see if Stephanie was in, but each time, Sammy's advice held him back.

*"Give Stephanie a little time to heal ... to sort things out in her head ..."*

But good advice couldn't keep him away completely, hadn't managed to deter him from his vigil. Moving along the sidewalk with the crowd, then turning on his heel and backtracking the way he'd come, he must have stalked the length of the stately building a hundred times already, never once taking his eyes off the windows of the fifth-floor corner apartment.

He wondered if maybe, just maybe, he shouldn't dismiss Sammy's good-intentioned advice? Perhaps he should get it over with and confront Stephanie *now*, instead of waiting.

Meanwhile, the windows of the apartment across the street remained blank, gave no inkling of occupancy. Only once had he seen—*imagined?*—a hand pull the end of one of the heavy curtains aside, as though to peek out unobserved. It was such a surreptitious movement he couldn't be sure he'd actually really seen it. Perhaps it was his imagination playing tricks? Responding to his need to conjure her up? But no hands drew aside the closed draperies to let the sun shine in, no windows were thrown open. It was as if the apartment itself were wearing the bleak joyless shrouds of mourning.

He could imagine her up there, wandering around alone in the dim rooms, with only the screeching bird and memories for company.

He was so involved with staring at the windows across the street that he missed Stephanie entirely—breezing up Seventh Avenue amid a swirl of pedestrians and crossing Fifty-seventh Street with the horde, earphones on and in a world of her own.

And so involved was Stephanie in listening to the Schneider/de Veiga tape, that, although she had passed within ten feet of Johnny, she hadn't

noticed him, either, not even when the ever-shifting crowd had created a momentary void, displaying him clearly.

In the spacious cool lobby, Stephanie found Pham, index cards in hand, pressing the elevator call button.

"The Continental Congress adopted the Declaration of Independence in seventeen seventy-six," he murmured under his breath. "The delegation which drafted it was headed by Thomas Jefferson ..."

Hearing the approach of briskly clicking heels, he turned his slim face toward its source. Instantly his studious visage underwent a miraculous transformation.

"Miss Stephanie!" he greeted in delight. Then, remembering the hours he'd just spent downtown at the triplex, Pham's voice brightened even further.

"Your apartment shine and polish, just like you. Neat as a pin. Now you can have visitors and entertain. The house gods—happy."

The elevator door sighed open. Pham waited politely for Stephanie to precede him. Then he got on and punched the buttons labeled 5 and CLOSE DOOR. "Apartment here will be nice and quiet," he said as the door slid shut. "No bird screaming. Nice change after downtown."

Stephanie hid her smile as they rode up at a stately pace. "That's precisely why I left Waldo at home," she said with mock solemnity, "just so you wouldn't be tempted to cook him, like you're always threatening."

"Parrot great delicacy."

The elevator doors slid open on the fifth floor and they got out, turning immediately left, and there was the apartment door.

Stephanie dug in her bag for her keys. She looked at Pham questioningly as she stuck a key in the first of several locks. "You've been working your fingers to the bone. And now you're back up here to work some more! Really, Pham. There's no reason to keep cleaning and straightening this place up now." There was a catch in her voice as she added huskily, "It's not as if anybody lives here anymore."

Pham drew himself up. "Just because Mr. Merlin dead does not mean standards have to slip," he declared, the indignant toss of his head, which lifted his silky black hair, intended to detract from the tears welling up in his eyes.

Stephanie turned the key of the last lock and pushed the front door open. "Then I tell you what," she said, swiftly stepping into the doorway to block it. She turned around to face Pham, putting one hand on each jamb. "What do you say we make a deal?"

"A deal?" he asked dubiously.

"It's very simple. I'll just go fetch my watch from my old room, and then I'll head on back home." She grinned. "But I'll only go home if *you* call it a day and go on home, too."

Pham stood there, eyes narrowed. "Maybe you wait out here, Miss Stephanie, and I go in and fetch your watch. Otherwise, perhaps you lock me out and stay here and start doing things."

Stephanie stood her ground. "Unh-unh." She shook her head. "If *I* wait out here, then *you're* liable to lock *me* out," she said. "I may be a little, well, contrary every now and then, but you're sly as a fox, Pham. So *I'll* go get my watch," she said with finality, "and *you* wait out here. Besides," she added with irrefutable logic, "it's my watch."

Pham threw up his hands, knowing better than to argue, and shaking his head, watched from out in the elevator vestibule as Stephanie turned around, hurried through the high-ceilinged reception room and made a left to head down the long hall on her way to her old bedroom at the very far end. Oblivious to the fresh, long-stemmed red rose lying on the floor.

Johnny stood on the corner of Fifty-seventh and Seventh. He'd stopped his pretense of moving along with the crowd and stared, piningly, up at the three-windowed bay and the two regular windows which made up the double parlor of the Merlin apartment.

"Stephanie!" he breathed as one of the parlor curtains in the bay was drawn aside. His heart thudded inside his chest. Any moment now, she would throw up the windows and then he would glimpse—

A horde of passersby elbowed him, causing him to half-turn pliantly in the other direction. For a moment, he felt himself swept along with the crowd's momentum, before planting his feet solidly and turning back around to face the building, forcing the crush of pedestrians to surge around him like a school of unruly fish.

He saw another of the parlor curtains being drawn aside. His eyes were riveted as he waited for that precious glimpse of her, his mind a constant tug of war. *Should I go up there? Or should I heed Sammy's advice and give her more time?*

As he stood there, debating with himself, a great flash suddenly lit up all the windows of the Merlin apartment.

The explosion which followed was like a sonic boom. All the windows blasted outward in a shower of glass, sending pedestrians screeching and running for cover. Orange fireballs billowed out of the gaping holes where the windows had been, and swelled into giant chrysanthemum blooms.

Even from across the street, Johnny could feel the heat wave hit him, was aware of a sliver of flying glass shooting into his forearm, piercing his leather sleeve to embed itself deeply in his flesh.

He didn't hesitate. Oblivious to his own safety, he tore across Fifty-seventh Street, squeezing around the bumpers of angrily honking cars, and leaping onto the hoods of those which barricaded his way completely.

## 20

*Sítto da Veiga, Brazil · New York City*

The de Veiga Pharmaceuticals and Genetic Engineering Research Center was located deep in the Amazon rainforest. A small self-sustaining city unto itself, it even had a name, Sítto da Veiga. The main building was a ten-story pyramid sheathed with solar mirrors, which, on clear days, and in the reflection of the equatorial sun, sent a brilliant square shaft of light up into the sky. Clustered around this central monument, like minor temples, were various geometrically shaped, mirror-sheathed research buildings, toxicology laboratories, storage and drug manufacturing facilities, apartments for the small army of resident chemists, biochemists, pathologists, and parasitologists, a power plant, a hospital, a school, a gym, and even a mini-mall, all connected by tentacles of enclosed, air-conditioned solar-glass walkways. A single paved road ended a mile away at a private airstrip with a runway long enough to accommodate jumbo jets.

There was nothing else but impenetrable jungle for hundreds of miles around.

Yet despite Sítto da Veiga's remote location and inaccessibility, the security precautions were reminiscent of a top-secret military base. Nothing had been left to chance. Two electrified chain-link fences, the insides of which were constantly patrolled by armed guards with attack dogs, surrounded the hundred-odd acres tamed from the jungle.

These guards and dogs were housed in the outermost of the complex of buildings. Here, Colonel Valerio presided over a permanent garrison composed of forty-eight security personnel. His position as vice president of security for the entire multibillion-dollar de Veiga empire notwithstanding, his office here, like his office on Ilha da Borboleta, was by choice spartan. It gleamed, however, with the spit-and-polish befitting a former military officer, just as his quasi-uniform of starched khakis, web belt, and jungle boots suited his cropped military haircut and ramrod straight posture. The sole luxury he allowed himself—air-conditioning—was turned all the way up, giving the cell-like office a walk-in freezer chill.

Colonel Valerio, hands clasped behind his back, was staring out the wall of windows at the giant mirrored pyramid that rose from among the sprawl of lower buildings. Behind it, in the distance, he could see a big four-engine jet descending to the airfield. He knew it was one of the thrice-daily supply flights, and paid it no heed.

Other, more urgent matters, occupied his attention.

One Aaron Kleinfelder, vice president, Data Division, of Children's Relief Year-Round, was still trying to break the OPUS file.

Colonel Valerio asked himself now: should he report Kleinfelder's persistence to Ernesto de Veiga at once? Or could it wait?

Unclasping his hands, he cocked his arm to glance at his wristwatch.

It would have to wait. It was nearly three o'clock, and he couldn't bother the bossman for a little over half an hour yet. Only an earthshaking emergency was allowed to intrude upon the daily hour of medical therapy Dr. Vassiltchikov prescribed for Ernesto de Veiga and Zarah Böhm—and on the de Veiga scale, this emergency rated no more than a 4.5. Alarming, but definitely not a life-or-death crisis. In the meantime, any additional tremors could easily be contained by arranging for the CRY computer to go down. *That should stymie Mr. Kleinfelder and his busy little fingers for a while.*

For an instant, Colonel Valerio's eyes became curiously focused. Aaron Kleinfelder. The man had all the makings of a worthy foe. How unfortunate that this was no game in which worthy foes were prized or respected. On the contrary. Far too much was at stake.

Colonel Valerio did a smart about-face, marched briskly to his gray metal desk, and picked up his remote telephone. It was time to activate The Ghost. Again.

At CRY headquarters in New York, Lisa Osborne hung up the phone and went into her boss's office. "Boss," she said, "you're not going to believe this."

Aaron grunted and looked up from his keyboard. "Believe what?"

Lisa shut the door. "The police just called." She paused and held his gaze. "They want me to come in."

"*You?*" Aaron sat up straight. "What would the police want to talk to you about?" He stared at her. "You haven't done anything, have you?"

"No, but I checked Vinette Jones into the hotel last night," she said softly. "Remember?"

"Ah, yes. Ms. Jones. Did you get hold of her yet?"

Lisa, hugging herself, walked slowly over to the desk. "She's dead, Aaron." Her voice was hushed. "*Dead!*" she repeated.

He inhaled a sharp breath and let the air out slowly. "What happened?"

She shrugged. "The cops say she ODed."

"No." He shook his head. "She couldn't have. She struck me as a God-fearing, Christian sort of woman."

"That's not what the cops seem to think. The one I talked to?" She waited for him to nod. "He said all the veins in her arms had collapsed from shooting up so much."

"I'll be damned."

Lisa sighed. "Well, I might as well mosey along. If I have to identify the body, I want to get it over and done with."

He nodded. "Take the rest of the afternoon off."

"Thanks. Well, see you later." She turned and started for the door.

Aaron swiveled around in his chair and stared out the window. *Does this mean I should stop searching for the child?* he wondered. Then he shook his head. *This makes the mystery only that much more tantalizing. If I have to, I'll continue the search on my own time.*

That decided, he swiveled back around. "Damn!" he muttered.

Now the computers were down.

They were still down by the time four o'clock rolled around, so Aaron decided to call it an early day. It was a long way home on foot—he lived at Eighty-first and Riverside Drive—but all the better. The weather was perfect, and God knew he could use the exercise.

When he reached Riverside Drive and Eighty-first Street, Aaron looked around with pleasure, soaking in the peace and quiet. The swell of the midtown crowds had thinned out to near nothing; this was a quiet residential neighborhood, one where birds sang in the trees and squirrels leaped from branch to branch and you could actually hear yourself think. With a little stretch of the imagination, it wasn't difficult to believe that this elegant parkside street was part of another, smaller and gentler, city.

The pedestrian light was red. On the opposite side of the intersection, a well-dressed young woman with a perambulator was waiting for it to change; an older couple beside Aaron, coming home from the supermarket with plastic shopping bags in hand, were exclaiming in outrage over the price of groceries. Then the traffic light changed and they all started to cross.

Aaron was in the middle of the intersection when he heard the roar of an engine being gunned. He stopped walking and looked to his right. A brown UPS delivery van was bearing down on him, hurtling forward at full speed.

It took a moment for the situation to register, and when it did, it was too late. The windshield and the grille loomed larger and larger, he heard the woman with the perambulator shout a warning, and at the last moment, Aaron lifted an arm to shield his face. He screamed at the moment of impact, and it was as if a giant metal fist had smashed into his body. Then mercifully, everything went black.

A red rose, tossed out the van's window, landed beside him on the pavement.

# *21*

Thomas Andrew Chesterfield III was seated in his office, hanging up the telephone. He was stunned by the news. It was the last thing he had expected to hear from the whisperer who filled him with such dread.

"You have been of great service, Mr. Chesterfield," the whisperer had told him. "You have done well. But before we terminate our relationship completely, we have one last request to make of you. After that, you will receive the original and all the copies of your son's film in existence."

He had listened with growing disbelief, thinking, I'm dreaming!

The whisperer said, "Now then, Mr. Chesterfield. I'm going to give you a telephone number. Please memorize it carefully and pass it on to The Ghost. Tell him that a client wishes to retain his exclusive services, and that, in return, one million dollars will be deposited into any Swiss or Cayman bank account of his choosing. Also, that the client will pay an additional one hundred thousand dollars per job. Up front. The Ghost is to deal directly with us."

"I'll try and pass on your message this evening."

"Good. And one more thing, Mr. Chesterfield? I advise you to forget the telephone number as soon as you have given it to The Ghost. Please. Do yourself a favor. Forget it, and don't pry."

Chesterfield's voice was shaky. "And . . . that's it?"

"Why, yes, Mr. Chesterfield. That's it. After this, you will be out of the picture completely."

Can this be for real? Chesterfield kept wondering. All he had to do was fulfill this one last request, and he would be off the hook *forever?*

He kept staring at the telephone, afraid that the whisperer would call back to tell him it was all a mistake . . .

But the telephone remained blessedly silent.

And for once, he couldn't wait until nightfall.

After dark, he cruised along Ninth Avenue for the last time.

His eyes searched the hen party on the corner. There she was! Wearing a little gold bralike thing, gold hot pants, and six-inch gold spike heels. He saw her turn her head and recognize his car. Then she sashayed over to him, one hand twirling a tiny gold purse on a long thin chain. Making it blur like a propeller.

She ducked her head in through the open window. "It you again."

He swallowed almost painfully and nodded.

Slowly she slid the pink tip of her tongue across her upper lip. On the corner, the girls jabbered like magpies and then fell quiet. From down Thirty-eighth Street, a fire truck pulled out of the firehouse, emergency lights flashing.

"You miss me?" she asked.

He nodded, not speaking as ear-shattering klaxons added to the scream of the sirens, and then the truck roared past and was gone, its cacophony fading.

"Well?" she asked when the noise started to die away. "You going to ask me in?"

He nodded and she pulled her head back out the window, tried the door, and waited until he unlocked it from the instrument panel. Then she pulled it open and slid in.

"Drive," she said. "You know the way."

He pulled carefully out into the traffic, made a right turn, and then another right into the by-now familiar parking lot.

"How much?"

"One-fifty to pass on the message," Shanel said.

He forked it over. She counted it, unsnapped her purse, and crumpled the bills inside before snapping it shut again.

"Now, what you want me to pass on?" she asked.

He told her how someone wanted to deal with The Ghost without going through him, and that he had a phone number in case The Ghost was interested.

"How much they paying?" she asked. "Not that I care."

He told her.

She shrugged; his reply didn't surprise her in the least. "I'll call and tell him. But you better write the phone number down on a piece a paper. I don't remember numbers. Every time I try, they just slip right outta my head. You know?"

He used a notepad and pen he kept in the glove compartment. After he jotted it down, he tore the sheet off the pad and handed it to her.

She palmed it and stuck it in her little gold bag.

He dropped her off at her corner for the last time.

Without her hooker drag, Shanel would have been unrecognizable to her clients. She looked positively chic wearing a sedate white-and-beige striped blouse with the top two buttons open, a silk Hermès scarf tied loosely around her neck, a canary yellow vest, and tobacco-colored cotton slacks. Her lace-up shoes were flat and brown and expensive, and her London

Fog raincoat was tan. She wore it unbuttoned. She had a big Vuitton shoulder bag wedged under her arm.

She closed her umbrella and shook the rain off it. Then she walked into the airlines ticket offices opposite Grand Central Station, looked around, and followed the signs to the escalator. When she got to the second floor, she headed for the pay phones.

She chose the one at the farthest end because it afforded the most privacy. Then, setting down the Vuitton bag, she rummaged around inside it. Kleenex, compact, wallet . . . there it was: the paper with the telephone number the white dude had given her. She dug around in the jumble some more. Mace, panty hose, roll of stamps . . . lipsticks, tampons, more lipsticks—right *on!* The MCI card she'd lifted from an obnoxious john while giving him head. Looking at it made her smile; running up *his* bill would give her immense pleasure.

She hummed to herself as she lifted the receiver, inserted a quarter in the phone, and followed the instructions printed on the back of the card. First she punched 950-1022 for the MCI long distance line. Then, when she heard the tone, she pushed 0 and the Los Angeles number the dude had written down. And after she got a dial tone, she still had to press the fourteen-digit customer code printed on the front of the card, all those numbers making her feel like she was dialing outer space.

Then she waited.

First, there was a series of clicks and pauses, as if the call was being rerouted; then more clicks and more pauses, like it was being rerouted some more. Finally, she could make out the sound of distant rings.

A guarded voice answered, saying, "Yes?"

Shanel said, "I'm supposed to give you a message from The Ghost?"

The voice said, "I'm listening."

She took a deep breath. "Well, The Ghost say . . . lemme see . . . it was something to do about accepting a business arrangement your man proposed. Un-huh. And The Ghost also say, soon as the money, it deposited in his account? That he work exclusively for you then." She paused and asked tentatively, "You want me to give you the bank account number and stuff?"

"Please," the voice said dryly.

She cradled the receiver between her shoulder and ear and burrowed around inside her bag. "Here it is!" she said into the phone, and read off the information.

The voice at the other end of the line repeated it, and added, "I will need a telephone number where The Ghost can be reached at all times."

"Let me see . . ."

She had to search in the bag for another scrap of paper. She read off the number.

"It's an answering service," she explained. "You can leave messages there around the clock, seven days a week. The Ghost checks in daily. When he hear from you, he call. Okay?"

"Yes. You can inform him that the money will be wired to his account within the hour, along with the fee for the first job."

She glanced surreptitiously over both shoulders and lowered her voice. "You need him for a job *already?*"

"Just pass on the information."

And the line went dead.

The next afternoon, Thomas Andrew Chesterfield III bounded down the steps of the Fulton Street subway station, a spring in his step and a whistle on his lips. He had just left his office, and he, like a veritable horde of well-to-do Upper East Siders, took the train simply because it was the fastest way to get uptown from downtown during rush hour.

Christ, but he felt good! Better than he had in years. Because suddenly, everything had changed. Life was sunny once again. Just an hour earlier, a messenger had dropped off a giant Jiffy bag addressed to him. It was marked PERSONAL.

As promised, it contained eight VHS videocassettes.

Heart thumping, he'd told his secretary that under no circumstances was he to be disturbed. Then he'd shut his door, dashed back behind his desk, and began prying the cassettes open with a pair of shears. He not only unraveled the tapes, but snipped them into useless pieces.

When he was done, he stuffed his handiwork into his wastebasket and smiled. There. Now there was no way anybody could salvage them. Each tape was as good as shredded.

At last, he could breathe easier. No more blackmail. No more whispering phone calls at odd hours.

His token ready, he breezed through the turnstile, swinging his briefcase jauntily. Once downstairs, he took up position at the edge of the crowded subway platform, slid the folded-up *Wall Street Journal* from under his arm, snapped it half open, and began reading.

It wasn't long before the train roared out from the maw of the tunnel and into the station, its headlight shining like a Cyclops's eye. Chesterfield refolded his newspaper, tucked it back under his arm, and waited. Unnoticed by him, someone slid a red rose between the pages of newsprint.

The roar turned into thunder as the train approached, and just as its brakes screeched their ear-piercing squeal, Chesterfield was shoved violently from behind.

Arms flailing, he went flying through the air—wanting to shout that this was all wrong! But before he could open his mouth, his body hit the third rail. He thrashed about wildly and screamed, thousands of volts frying him, and then, as if death by electrocution was not enough, the train crashed into him, dismembering him as well.

In the ensuing panic and confusion, The Ghost strolled calmly off the platform, unseen and unheard. Thinking: *At this rate, I'll be able to retire within a year. As long as these jobs keep right on coming . . .*

With no lights save the glow emitted by the banks of television monitors, computer terminals, and fiber-optic readout, Dr. Vassiltchikov was a strange, vivid shade of green. Like something out of a sci-fi movie.

At consoles angling off in front of her sat her two young assistants, one male, one female. Both young enough to be her grandchildren, which they were not; both glowing the same iridescent shade of green as the tiny doctor, who paced incessantly back and forth like a luminous green phantom.

"Body temperature of Subject Number One." Her voice was clipped and had a thick, eastern-European accent.

"Fahrenheit 97.152," the female assistant rattled off.

"And Subject Number Two?"

"Fahrenheit 97.380," the male assistant supplied.

"Good, good." In Dr. Vassiltchikov's murmur was an edge of excitement, and she permitted herself one of her very rare smiles. Warm satisfaction glowed in her like fragrant, heady wine, but now was not the time to bask in self-congratulation. Reward enough that her theory had been proven, that her efforts at lowering the body temperatures of both Ernesto de Veiga and Zarah Böhm another fraction of a degree had been successful. More important, the lowered temperatures had remained at those precise levels for weeks now. *Weeks!* And never had her two subjects been healthier!

Abruptly a faint bitterness crossed her lips, the bright joy of her achievement rapidly diminishing. How it rankled, not being able to publish her findings! How it soured everything, this inability to trumpet her hard-won achievements to the world!

And to think she had always believed herself to be above such petty human vanities! For years, love of science and research, and working for the sheer satisfaction of it alone, had been enough. But now . . .

Now, in her eighties, with time swiftly running out, she found herself yearning for those sweet tangible fruits which should have been hanging abundantly from the tree of her labors—receiving her due from her peers; perhaps being nominated for a Nobel Prize; above all, knowing that other scientists would forever use her discoveries as reference points in their own work, thus perpetuating what she had begun, their footnotes ensuring her the one, the true, the only real immortality!

But enough. Why harp on the impossible? Going public with her discovery was out of the question, and for a multitude of reasons.

There was the need to keep her subjects—her benefactors—utterly secret; there was the controversial methodology involved; there was also the smallness of most people's minds to consider.

Her anger and contempt for the rest of mankind flared up, burned ulcerously. And as if those were not obstacles enough, then there was always the question of her past . . .

Now the walls, crammed to capacity with state-of-the-art electronics, seemed to mock; the super-sensitive microphones, which amplified the sounds of steady breathing from inside the treatment room, seemed to emit a chorus of raspy jeers. Everything—the LED readouts, which, from the probes attached to both subjects provided instant information on such essentials as body temperature, blood pressure, pulse, EEG, and the like; the dozens of computer screens capable of calling up a staggering encyclopedia of medical and physiological information—all this was suddenly reduced to insignificance.

For how *could* any of it be significant if no one ever learned of it?

The irony of the situation did not escape her. She, who had discovered the fountain of youth, would herself soon die, growing older, more feeble, and looking more like a prune as she turned back the clock for her benefactors.

Meanwhile, Zarah imagined herself weightless, floating in the womb whence she came. The womb to which, daily, like clockwork, she eagerly returned.

Eyes shut, and lying absolutely still, she imagined the various monitors and probes attached to her naked body to be the deliciously sexy reproductive organs of some alien creature to whom she was bonded by its thread-thin tentacles.

It was almost obscene, the well-being she felt, and her mood was due to a variety of factors:

The earphones she wore, through which the newly digitalized, compact disc release of Lili Schneider's "Dov' è l'Indiana bruna?" filled her ears with Delibes's glorious *Lakmé*, scratchily recorded back in 1946, but technically flawless and pure now. *Oh, but how pure and perfect!*

The plastic catheter of the IV to which she was hooked up, which steadily dripped its solution of youth-prolonging hormones, cells, and mutated DNA proteins into her bloodstream, along with, on this day, the thrice-weekly additive of growth hormone.

And, above all, her well-being stemmed from the secure knowledge that she was as beautiful, as young, as unlined and as body-perfect as ever—and would remain that way for decades to come.

The windowless treatment room in which she and Ernesto reclined was by no means stark and sterile. It was luxuriously soothing. Thickly carpeted, with track lights aimed at gilt-framed Gauguins and Picassos glowing from the mulberry-colored walls. There was not a gurney or a hospital bed in sight: she and Ernesto reclined on gray leather lounges which had been custom-molded to fit each of their bodies.

And it was in this simple but lush room, with its computer-regulated environment, where not only the climate, but the very air itself was electronically controlled so that it was constantly oxygen enriched, that Zarah felt most at peace. From where the world seemed perfect in almost every way.

Nothing to speed her pulse, nothing to raise the pressure of her blood. Reduced to this state of sheer mental bliss, her corporeal body seemed for the time being, at least, to cease to exist. For she was in her own, her very own, very safe, and very, very nurturing cocoon . . .

Eyes shut, Ernesto felt himself floating, his body one entity; his mind, uncooped from its earthly cares, another entity entirely, as capable of swooping and soaring—of reaching out to the furthermost stars in a milli-second—as it was of drifting indolently, like a lazy butterfly on a breeze-less day, scant inches above the carapace from whence it had been freed.

How utterly ironic that this daily hour, spent shackled to the IV, should be when he felt his greatest freedom. Nothing—no amount of worldwide travel, of crossing any country's borders with the privileges ac-corded a VIP of his stature, not his staggering wealth or the fleets of air-planes and limousines at his disposal—nothing could generate such a feeling of unadulterated liberation.

For only here, with unseen video cameras trained on him, and elec-tronic probes on wires or in the form of microchip skin patches attached to various parts of his body, so that his every breath and beat of his heart was monitored, could he put his mind at rest and indulge in the flights of fancies he so yearned for.

He didn't think it the least bit odd that some of his best ideas came to him while he lay motionless, the IV dripping its youth-prolonging solu-tion of cells and hormones and mutated DNA proteins into his blood-stream.

Gradually, the lights brightened. Ernesto sighed to himself. The IVs were empty. An hour had passed. Reality was reasserting itself.

With a hiss, the stainless steel air-locks slid apart and Dr. Vassiltchikov marched in, her stride purposeful and authoritative, her face raisinlike in the unflattering bright lights. Deftly she slid the catheter nee-dles out of the backs of Zarah's and Ernesto's hands, tugged on the tub-ing, and let go. Automatically, the two catheters rose up into the ceiling and disappeared.

"I will have the monitors and probes off you in no time," she said as she worked. "Then, when you are both dressed, I want to take you on a short tour. That way, you can see our latest research results for yourselves. I think you will both be quite excited by the progress we have made!"

# 22

"Gene-cloning, growth hormone replacement, and now caloric-restricted diets," Dr. Vassiltchikov said, ticking off each item on her fingers.

The three of them were marching side by side, the little doctor in the middle, along the glass-enclosed walkway which connected the central, ten-story solar-glass pyramid with the biochemical laboratories housed in the separate, sealed-off, four-story cube.

"When you think about it, we have made thousands of years of progress since the so-called 'dark ages' of placental implants and ewe cell injections. *Thousands!* But then"—Dr. Vassiltchikov permitted herself a smile, "I do not need to tell the two of *you* that, do I?"

They stopped at a set of brushed steel doors which had neither handles, knobs, nor locks. On each, a large yellow decal with black lettering had been affixed. The one on the left warned:

**CAUTION**
**Biological Hazard**
Restricted Area
Authorized Personnel Only

And on the right:

**DANGER**
**Carcinogenic Contaminants**
**Teratogenic Substances and**
**Radioactive Isotopes in Use**

Producing her plastic identification card, Dr. Vassiltchikov slid it into a slot, a green light glowed, and the doors hissed apart.

They walked through and the doors hissed shut behind them. Now they were in the first of three separate airlocks, whose function it was to completely seal off the laboratory in case of contamination. Twice more, Dr. Vassiltchikov slipped her ID card into an electronic slot, and at last they entered the biochemical laboratory.

The fluorescent lighting was bright, the recirculated air chilled. A king's ransom in up-to-the-moment scientific and technical equipment only added to the unwelcomingly cold, and unpleasantly sterile, atmosphere. Determinedly high-tech with its exposed blue anodized girders and red anodized struts, it was, thought Zarah as she followed the doctor and Ernesto through the huge windowless main room, as ugly and utilitarian a place as could possibly exist.

Along both walls of the sixty-by-forty-foot room were lab stations, each equipped with machinery outfitted with various dials, intricate glass tubing, electrical connectors, computer terminals, monitors, and stainless-steel ventilator hoods. At each, a technician in a white lab coat was busy doing unfathomable things.

Unlike Zarah, Ernesto found it all fascinating. For him, nothing was too complex or perplexing. Nothing sickened or repelled, and he wanted to know everything, going out of his way to peer through every microscope in use, asking to have everything explained to him. He regarded the four new Cray Y-MP2E supercomputers, which ran the entire facility, as he would the Holy Grail.

Zarah stirred restlessly and made moues of impatience, but Dr. Vassiltchikov indulged Ernesto his thirst for knowledge—in part because she knew which side of the laboratory's bread was buttered—but also in part because of the sheer delight he took in everything.

On they moved, until at last they had worked their way to the far end of the room. Here, six different doors branched off to other, more specialized, biochemical labs. Dr. Vassiltchikov chose the left-most door. This particular one warned:

TOP SECRET AREA
CAUTION
BIOLOGICAL AND RADIOACTIVE
AREA
Strictest Radiological and Genetic
Protocols Must Be Observed

First Dr. Vassiltchikov reached into a wall-mounted wire basket and handed them each a plastic badge which measured radioactivity. They pinned them to their breast pockets and only then did she unlock this door with her card.

Now they were in another glass-enclosed walkway, one which led to the outermost perimeter of the biochemical laboratories. Then came another steel door. And another. And another. Three separate airlocks protected against possible contaminants leaking out.

Finally, they found themselves in the first of a series of smaller top-secret laboratories, each of which required a higher security clearance than the one before it.

The first of these was bathed in green light and was unbearably warm and humid. Ignoring the visitors, the six lab technicians on duty concentrated on their work: pulling trays of agar plates out of incubators, using glass pipettes to transfer tissue samples onto slides, bending over the lenses of electron microscopes.

"This is one of the things I wanted to show you," Dr. Vassiltchikov said with evident pride. She led the way to one of the workstations. "May I?" she asked a plain, middle-aged woman whose white lab smock glowed Day-Glo green in the light.

"Why, of course, doctor." The woman slid off her swivel stool and at once stepped aside.

Dr. Vassiltchikov stood on tiptoe, bent over the microscope, and peered down through the twin lenses. "Amazing," she murmured.

Dr. Vassiltchikov turned to Zarah and Ernesto. "When you look through that microscope, what you will see at the exact center is a single—I repeat—*single!*—diaphanous strand of human DNA magnified *one hundred thousand times!* The other identical strands crowding around it are its self-replicated clones!"

She gestured for Ernesto to look, which he did with alacrity.

"That particular bit of tissue," Dr. Vassiltchikov explained, "should have lost its ability to replicate itself weeks ago! But, as you could see for yourself, it is continuing to divide and divide, thus spinning off perfect, identical copies of itself." The little doctor looked around; then, with both arms, she shepherded the two of them away, out of anybody's earshot. "We are on the verge of another major biochemical breakthrough!" she whispered with soft intensity. "Soon, we shall no longer *need* our sacrificial angels! We shall be able to produce your medication right here—in the laboratory! Imagine how much safer that will be for all concerned! And, once our technique is perfected, think of the staggering possibilities: through mere replication, *one* single strand of the Methuselah DNA will give us *centuries* worth of fresh medication!"

Ernesto's voice was hushed. "My God! You really have made breakthroughs! By when do you think you can have this technique perfected?"

Dr. Vassiltchikov shrugged. "Alas," she sighed, "that is difficult to predict. At least, we now know one thing: it is not a matter of *if* it will be possible, but rather, *when*. Now then. If you will come along, there is still more I wish to show you. I'm certain you will find our restricted diet results equally as exciting."

Dr. Vassiltchikov led the way to a set of doors marked LIVE SPECIMENS and got out her electronic card. They stepped into yet another airlock. The door behind them slid shut, their ears popped as the pressure changed, and then the door in front of them slid open.

They were in a dark, curving tunnel, much like the viewing area of an aquarium or the reptile house at a zoo. But instead of fish or snakes, be-

hind the brightly lit, wire-embedded glass were a variety of animals rang-
ing from the simplest one-cell creatures all the way up the zoological ladder to rats, cats, dogs, and apes.

"You remember our Ark room?" Dr. Vassiltchikov asked as she gestured around.

"So-named because there are two of every creature," Ernesto replied,
smiling.

Zarah did not join them, but loitered by the entrance. Producing a
handkerchief, she held it delicately in front of her nose. She hated the
combined smells of animals, feces, and urine; loathed all things that
squirmed, crept, crawled, slithered, swam, flew—with the exception of
butterflies, of course. She loved those.

Dr. Vassiltchikov left her by the door and joined Ernesto at the first
window. Beyond the glass were two double-barreled microscopes, each
hooked up to a special television camera. She punched a glowing button
under the window and instantly, two high-resolution color video screens
popped on.

Each showed a single protozoa magnified a hundred thousand times,
and both were identical in every way but one.

"As you can see," Dr. Vassiltchikov pointed out, "the one on the right
is not moving because it is already dead. Fed an ordinary protozoan diet,
it lived for fourteen days, one day short of its normal maximum life span
of fifteen. That was a week ago. However, the healthy specimen here on
the left"—she tapped on the glass with the tips of her fingernails—"has
been restricted to a low-calorie diet through which it has received a minimum of protein, but enough vitamins and minerals to prevent malnutri-
tion. It has been thriving for twenty-one days already. In other words—"

"—its life span has nearly been doubled!" exclaimed Ernesto.

They moved on to the next window, behind which two other cameras, also mounted on stereo microscopes, were hooked up to video
screens.

"The lowly water flea," Dr. Vassiltchikov said, pressing the button to
activate the screens. "Again, the one on the right, fed its normal diet, has
died within the parameters of its ordinary life span, which is a maximum
of forty-two days. Yet the one at the left, born at exactly the same moment, has been kept on a calorie-restricted diet. Judging by past tests, it
should enjoy a total life span of approximately sixty-one days."

"Remarkable," Ernesto murmured. "Truly remarkable."

"And now to the rats," Dr. Vassiltchikov said. "The one on the right
has enjoyed a normal diet for the past thirty months. Notice how its white
coat has turned gray and oily. From daily examinations, we know it is succumbing to a variety of diseases—destruction of the heart muscle, kidney
disease, diabetes, cataracts, a general failing of the immune system. If one
of those doesn't finish it off soon, tumors will."

Ernesto now eyed the rat on the left side of the divided window. "But that one is still all white!" he said in astonishment.

"Yes." Dr. Vassiltchikov looked pleased. "And healthy as the proverbial horse. Remarkably, each batch we have tested came up with the exact same results. Those on a calorie-restricted diet almost never contracted heart or kidney diseases. And, while many do go on to develop eventual cancers, they can live up to fifty months—a third of a lifetime longer!—all because their food intake has been restricted."

Ernesto rubbed his chin. "Then you have no doubt but that a restricted diet leads to longevity?"

"No doubt whatsoever. But before we get too excited, we must bear in mind that these are all lower species, with relatively short life spans. It could very well be that longevity has been triggered by a built-in mechanism which lets them survive famine years in order to reproduce."

Ernesto asked, "But how, specifically, will Zarah and I benefit from these various avenues of research? Are they really necessary? I thought we are, and will continue to be, in a state of geriatric arrestation."

"And you will be, so long as you continue your daily treatments." She looked at Ernesto directly. "There is no doubt but that without the benefits of the Methuselah DNA, you and Zarah would both be your real, instead of your current, geriatric ages."

"I realize that," Ernesto said. "And while I understand the results of these treatments, they seem almost redundant."

Dr. Vassiltchikov smiled and led the way back to the entrance, where Zarah was waiting, handkerchief to her nose. "And then again," she said softly, "who can tell? Perhaps every little battle helps win the war. You and Zarah have both been on reduced dietary intake for several years now. I am counting on caloric reduction to at least lower your chances of developing tumors or other forms of cancers."

Ernesto nodded slowly. "And the growth hormones?"

"They help you shed body fat, and convert half that fat into healthier lean body mass. Also, growth hormones stimulate the body's production of Growth Factor-One, which is an extremely powerful, insulinlike protein. It helps maintain general organ health and spurs the growth of tissue. Conclusive tests have shown that six months of growth hormone treatment can cut almost *two decades* of age-induced changes off any human body. Also, you must not forget that aging affects the heart, kidneys, gastrointestinal tract, and even the bones of the spine. All of these shrink as the years pass. Fortunately, Growth Factor-One can combat that shrinkage." She watched his eyes closely. "It would be ironic, would it not, if the Methuselah DNA gave you life everlasting, only to have your vital organs and bones shrivel to nothing because of a stupid oversight?"

"I see that you are covering all the bases." Ernesto nodded approvingly as they reached Zarah.

"I like to think so." Dr. Vassiltchikov sighed. She looked sternly from him to Zarah and then back to him again. "Above all," she warned, "there is one thing none of us must ever forget."

"And what is that?" Ernesto asked quietly.

The doctor took a deep breath. "There is a wild card in every game."

"A wild card?" whispered Zarah, slowly lowering the handkerchief from her nose.

"There are many wild cards," Dr. Vassiltchikov explained flatly, gesturing with her hand. "Accidents. Tumors. Storms. Infections. An unanticipated chunk of concrete falling off a building. A car's brakes failing—"

Zarah was aghast. "*Hör' auf damit!*" she hissed in German. "*Lass das bleiben!* You are frightening me!"

Dr. Vassiltchikov kept her voice soft. "Wild cards, or acts of God, if you will, are a fact of life. You must learn to live with them. No matter how successfully we can retard aging, who is to say something else might not occur? Something entirely beyond our control?"

Zarah was shivering. "*Ich will nichts davon hören!*" Her breathing sounded like that of some small, trapped animal. With a sob, Zarah flung herself into Ernesto's arms and buried her face in his chest. "I'll never get used to dying!" Her voice was muffled by his chest.

"Ssssh," he soothed, smoothing her hair, giving her arms and shoulders and back little pats, placing kisses all over the top of her head. "There is no need to be frightened, none at all . . . ssssh." He luxuriated in her helplessness and dependence upon him. "There, there. Nobody is going to let you die . . . nobody is going to let you grow old . . ."

"I'm sorry," she murmured after a while. "Something always seems to be frightening me. Sometimes it is the fear of dying—and if not that, the prospect of living forever and watching everyone around me die . . . I don't think I'll ever get used to that!"

Dr. Vassiltchikov had been observing her in silence. Now she smiled gently. "Zarah, Zarah," she chided softly, clucking her tongue. "How often must I tell you? Of course you will get used to it." She reached out to stroke the soft young face almost lovingly. "Because so long as you are *vorsichtig*—careful—you will have all the time in the world to get used to it. *Endlose Zeit*, Zarah . . . do you hear? All the time in the world . . ."

# ❦ 23 ❦

## New York City

The memorial service was held at Town Hall. All the orchestra seats and most in the mezzanine were filled. Banks of pale pink peonies and branches of fragrant lilac, heavy with blossoms, were artfully arranged across the stage.

The entire production crew from "Half Hour" had turned out to eulogize Stephanie, as had representatives from many of the two hundred independent television stations that carried the show. Ted Warwick, "Half Hour"'s producer, sat in the front row. On his immediate left was a grim-faced Johnny Stone; on his right, Christy Mason, a beautiful redhead from Kansas City with a high sincerity quotient and a low recognition ratio. She looked nervous and had every reason to be: it wouldn't be easy to fill Stephanie's shoes as the show's new anchor.

Sammy Kafka was onstage, dwarfed by the profusion of flowers, his chin barely reaching above the polished oak lectern as he looked out at the somber sea of upturned faces. How could he be expected to express, in a string of mere sentences, the sunshine Stephanie's presence had brought into his life? Or the fighting spirit, which had always been such an integral part of her character, which he'd so admired? Or the love they'd shared, so toasty warm and secure it had never needed verbalizing, which made him feel like he really had been her uncle, and she his very own favorite niece?

Words, his sole means of expressing all this, seemed so insufficient. But they needed to be said, and the audience was waiting. So he cleared his throat, adjusted his bow tie, and recalled his favorite anecdotes. Trying to flesh out his Girlie that way.

His eyes were moist. He was saying, as he fingered away the tears, ". . . she had her whole life ahead of her. God only knows what she might have accomplished. What happiness she could have found. What a marvelous mother she would have made—" And then his voice cracked, and for a moment, he couldn't continue.

In the front row, Johnny couldn't bear hearing another word. Abruptly, he jumped up from his seat and lurched blindly along the aisle to the rear of the auditorium, his heart on fire, his raging lungs demanding air. He nearly howled aloud, so great was his anguish.

Outside, on the sidewalk, he gnashed his teeth in painful frustration, turning small, aimless circles, to all appearances a drunk on a binge. But he was cold sober, his drunkenness rooted in primeval despair.

Because if only he'd listened to his heart and not taken Sammy's well-intentioned advice; if only he'd gone up to see Stephanie instead of pacing indecisively opposite the building, then she might not have been inside the apartment when the explosion occurred—that terrible explosion which had destroyed everything, her included; that massive explosion which had left no real human remains behind . . .

In the mezzanine, one of many anonymous faces took the opportunity to slip out unnoticed.

The Ghost was holding a red rose and twirling it. Feeling satisfaction and thinking: *People may think it's easy to kill and do a first-rate job. But I know differently. It takes a special talent to be the angel of death . . .*

# ❦ Book Two ❦

# LIFE

# 1

Traffic was thin but slow; a zipper of lightning rent the sky ahead. Inside the Lincoln Town Car, the closed windows were half misted over; outside, relentless rain lashed the windshield. The arcing wipers, working overtime, swished and thudded metronomically, barely managing to keep up with the deluge.

The car had stayed in the slow right lane of I-684, its headlights on. At Brewster, New York, it had swung onto I-84 and had crossed the state line into Connecticut. Now, after Danbury, it left the interstate and slowly commenced north along the Housatonic on the small, twisting country road that was Route 7. The downpour cut down on visibility, the shroud it created isolating the car and shutting it off into an eerie world of its own. Quaint townships with Anglican names came and went—New Milford, Boardmans Bridge, Gaylordsville, Kent, Cornwall Bridge . . .

Just before West Cornwall, the Town Car turned left onto a narrower and even more remote country road, drove sedately along for two winding miles, and then slowed to a crawl. It made a sharp left turn into a steeply graded, uphill gravel drive, both sides of which were meadows of wildflowers being thrashed flat by the rain. A quarter of a mile farther the drive ended at that most incongruous of structures in this decidedly Yankee setting—a small Palladian villa.

The car stopped and the driver twisted around in his seat. "Here we are," he said cheerfully.

Sammy Kafka squinted at him from the mouse-colored velour of the backseat. "Since when," he demanded, "do I need to be told I've arrived where I've asked to be driven? Eh? Eyes I've got, and a nursemaid I don't need."

"That's for sure," the curly-haired young driver laughed. He chucked open his door, popped a huge black mushroom of an umbrella, and was quickly out to hold the rear door. But he stood well back, knowing better than to help the old man.

Sammy slid out from the seat and carefully held onto the door as he tested his land legs. They felt stiff from sitting for so long, but were steady enough. That confirmed, he reached inside the car for his own ivory-handled English umbrella and opened it without haste. Then, while the driver went to unload the luggage from the trunk, Sammy, with a stab of nostalgia, gazed at Carleton Merlin's country house.

The mere sight of the shuttered villa released a potent flood of memories, brought a lump into his throat. The beautifully proportioned folly was such an anomaly amid the Currier and Ives landscape, that he'd always loved it all the more. Constructed of gray-stuccoed brick, it was one story and authentically proportioned. The perfect symmetry delighted the eye: two identical pilastered wings with tall French windows extending from a central pedimented portico. To soften what would otherwise have been a mausoleumlike austerity, creepers—wisteria and ivy—had been left to their own devices and allowed to run riot, clinging thickly to the walls. A procession of stately stone urns marched across the top of the roof cornice, and there were two chimneys.

But despite its having been beautifully maintained, the house now had that forlorn aura of uninhabited buildings, its green shutters closed to the world. One was loose and flapped, banging in the wind. To Sammy, the noise sounded plaintive, as though the building were alive and wailing for someone—anyone—to come open it up and breathe life into it once again.

Shaking his head mournfully, he climbed the shallow broad steps to the sheltered portico, closed the umbrella, and shook off the excess water. His eyes misted as he unlocked the double doors, turned off the alarm system, and stepped into the foyer. Sighing heavily, he stuck his umbrella in the familiar blue-and-white umbrella stand just inside the front door and switched on the lights. Then, while waiting for his suitcases to be brought up from the car, he looked around.

It was almost eerie, he thought. Absolutely nothing had changed since his best friend's death: the impressive foyer was exactly as it always had been, a testament to Carleton's exceptional taste and indulgence for luxury. Suitably grand, and furnished in an exuberant melange of periods— English Regency, Imperial Russian, Neoclassical, the odd touch of Napoleon III. A blue-striped fabric from Madeleine Castaing covered the walls, and gilt-framed portraits of noblemen, hanging one above the other, made the fourteen-foot ceiling seem to soar even higher.

"There. That's it." The driver deposited the fifth and last of Sammy's brown, 1920s-alligator suitcases inside the door. "Should I carry them to some particular room?"

"Just leave them right there, Mendel," Sammy told him. "I can take care of them from here on. I'll telephone when I need you to come and pick me up. It will probably be in a day or two."

Sammy waited until the car was out of sight. Then, satisfied that he was alone, he closed and locked the front doors, and plucked his umbrella back out of the blue-and-white stand. Quickly now, he pushed aside another door and passed into the dark living room, flipping a light switch as he went.

Instantly, the giant Directoire billiard lamp above the center table clicked on, flooding the porphyry urn with its masses of dried hydrangeas and the stacks of books, arranged to radiate outward from its hub, with two soft pools of light. But Sammy didn't waste a moment admiring the splendid tableau or anything else in the beautiful oval room. Marble, mirrors, carpets, paintings, memories: for the time being, he shelved them all, darting past antique chairs and treasure-laden tables to his destination, one of the three sets of French doors on the curving opposite wall.

With practiced flicks of his wrist, he yanked aside two pairs of blue brocade curtains, unlatched the French doors at both top and bottom, pulled them open, and unhooked the dark-green shutters. He shoved them wide.

Weak gray daylight and the soppy, wet sounds of rain filtered into the room. A leaking drainpipe poured a thin waterfall.

Snapping open his umbrella, he held it high and started jauntily off, looking up at his destination.

There it was. A hundred yards uphill, set slightly back. Eerily misted, and paled to the point of looking mysteriously washed-out by the rain.

It had been Carleton Merlin's pride and joy, the one-room library-cum-guest-house up there—a larger but otherwise authentically detailed replica of the Treasury of the Athenians at Delphi. Complete with pediment, Doric pillars, and triglyph.

Sammy hiked uphill through the long sodden grass, low-hanging leafy branches whipping at his umbrella. It was a short but rather steep climb which, despite his incredible health and vigor, never failed to make him aware of every one of his seventy-seven years.

His handsewn shoes, silk socks, and trouser legs were soaked through when he had reached the portico. He slowly went up the three steps and in its shelter stamped his feet and shook his umbrella out vigorously.

Just as he turned to the front door, it opened soundlessly from within and a single cobalt blue eye stared suspiciously out through the three-inch crack.

"Your driver's gone?" a voice whispered. "You're alone?"

Sammy nodded. The door closed, he could hear the clink of the safety chain being removed, and a woman opened the door wide.

He could only stare.

"What's the matter?" asked the dark-haired young woman with the silky Louise Brooks cut. "This is the third time you've reacted to me in this way. The third time!"

"That, Girlie," he said gently, reaching out and touching her cheek tenderly with his fingertips, "is because I still can't get used to this new you. But for your voice . . ."

"What about it?"

He sighed sadly. "I could have passed you on the street and never even recognized you."

"Well?" demanded Stephanie Merlin, her gaze and voice so implacably level, and her smile so emotionless and bleak, that he felt thoroughly chilled. "Isn't that the whole point?"

Then she grabbed him by the arm and yanked him forward.

"Now hurry up and get *in* here!" she hissed. "You're late and we've got work to do!"

Just then Waldo's shrill, demanding squawks started up, and suddenly everything was back to normal.

Her voice softened and she even sounded like her old self. "But first, you'd better get out of those wet clothes, Uncle Sammy," she said huskily, bending down and planting a noisy kiss on the top of his head. "If you don't, you're liable to come down with a nasty cold."

"That'll be a dollar thirty." The waitress set down a plastic cup of coffee and a powdered jelly donut wrapped in a sheet of grease-proof paper.

"Here. Keep the change." The Ghost put a couple of dollars on the counter, picked up the coffee, blew on it, and turned to glance out the window. The rain was blasting down from gunmetal clouds, hitting the plate glass like pellets and distorting the flashing BURLESK and GIRLS GIRLS GIRLS neons across Eighth Avenue. Wet gusts blew in through the door with every arriving customer.

Turning away from the window, The Ghost set down the disposable cup and opened the *New York Post*.

As usual, the tabloid did not disappoint. WEALTHY L.I. TYCOON MURDERED. BOMB BLAST NEAR TURKISH NATO BASE. TV STAR SUICIDE ATTEMPT. STATE DEFICIT CRISIS DEEPENING. CITY TAX HIKE IMMINENT.

*Fools gotta learn about cash business,* The Ghost thought smugly. *That way you don't pay no taxes . . .*

OFF-DUTY COP STABBED IN BROOKLYN MUGGING. MORE LAYOFFS LOOM IN BUSINESS WORLD. And, shunted to page 18, a two-column headline: HIT-AND-RUN COMA VICTIM IDENTIFIED.

Swiftly The Ghost began to read:

> Police yesterday identified last Thursday's hit-and-run victim, whose identity had been withheld pending notification of next-of-kin, as Aaron W. Kleinfelder, 49, of Riverside Drive.
>
> Witnesses said the victim, a computer programming specialist, was crossing the intersection to his apartment building at

Riverside Drive and West 81st Street at 4:30 P.M. when he was
run down by a stolen delivery van.

    EMS paramedics took Kleinfelder to St. Luke's Hospital.
Doctors interviewed last night said he was still in a coma but de-
clined to speculate on the possibility of complete recovery.

The Ghost closed the newspaper and stared off into space. *Damn!*
Why didn't I read last Friday's paper or call the hospital? A week after the
fact's a fine time to discover the mark's still alive. Christ. Talk about
fucking up!

The Ghost expected to catch some flak, but the client was full of surprises.
There wasn't a word of complaint, nor a single curse or threat, just that
crisp authoritative voice over the telephone saying, "You did right in letting us know."

    "How you want me to handle this? I can either finish him off in
the hospital, or wait and see if he dies anyway. I'll leave that up to
you."

    There was a pause. Then: "Don't do anything yet, but keep tabs on
his condition. Who knows? Could be, he'll be out of it for seven days or
seven years. Could even be, he'll die before he ever wakes up. But if he
does come out of his coma, take care of him immediately. On the other
hand, as long as he doesn't, I don't see why there's any need to attract undue attention."

    "I'll check in with the hospital daily. That way we won't have any
more unpleasant surprises."

    "Good, and don't forget to keep me posted." And with that, the cli-
ent rang off.

    After hanging up, The Ghost deposited a quarter, punched 411
for information, and asked for the number for St. Luke's. Called the
hospital and said, "Yeah. Need to find out about a patient's condition?"

## 2

Stephanie was waiting for Sammy with a giant snifter of brandy when he came out of the bathroom. He was wearing a borrowed white bathrobe and carried his carefully folded jacket over one arm.

Stephanie proffered the snifter with all the solemnity of a sacrament. "Here. Drink."

Sammy swooped the snifter out of her hand and took an appreciative sip. A moment later, he was smacking his lips noisily. His face glowed and he positively beamed.

"Brrrrrandy!" He rolled the word lavishly on his tongue. "An elixir to feed the muses and warm the cockles of me heart! Soon ye'll have me spoutin' off the old poet's—"

"Wal-*do!*" The screeches coming from the brass cage at the far end of the room cut him off. "Wal-*do! Waldo wants a crack*er!"

Sammy dropped the brogue. "Do you think, Girlie," he suggested hopefully, "that a shot of brandy in his water might . . . ah . . . shut him up?"

Stephanie stiffened. "You will do nothing of the kind. Now then. We've got a lot of things to discuss. Did you bring them?" She looked at him questioningly.

"I have them right here, Girlie." He lifted his jacket.

"Good. Why don't we get comfy and sit over there?"

Briskly she led the way, picking an unerring path between all the furniture.

Empty, the grandly proportioned, high-ceilinged room with its bookcases built into architectural niches probably looked like some archbishop's crypt. But happily, Carleton's eclectic mixture of lavish furnishings and the gee-gaws he'd picked up on his travels made it delightfully comfortable, extravagantly cluttered, and utterly pleasing to the eye as well as to all the other senses.

The sheer profusion of *things* staggered the imagination.

The thousands of leather-bound books, many first editions, bursting from the recessed shelves. The brilliant palatial Turkey carpet glowing, like the rose window of a great cathedral, on every square inch of the floor. The shimmering blue-and-gold Lyonnaise silk curtains, lavishly swagged and heavily tasseled, which were drawn across the tall windows and which, back in the eighteenth century, had graced a Hapsburg's palace. And last, but certainly not least, there was the splendid pair of identical *lits à la Polonnaise,* both draped in antique yellow silk and sprouting tattered ostrich plumes from their coronas. They had come from the state bedchamber of a château.

Stephanie dropped herself down on one and indicated for Sammy to take the other.

A low table between the two beds held brass lamps which spilled soft pools of light on tall stacks of paper, each one consisting of hundreds of Xerox pages held together with pink rubber bands. From the looks of it, they had all presumably been read and carefully sorted into categories: manuscript, transcribed interviews, copies of articles, documents, and God only knew what else.

Sammy turned to Stephanie in amazement. "Don't tell me, Girlie," he said in astonishment. "You've gone through *everything?*"

She nodded, tugging off the black wig as she talked. "Gone through it, sorted it, studied it, you name it." Tossing the wig aside, she shook out her own strawberry blond hair and used her fingertips to fluff it.

"But in just the past week?" Sammy looked incredulous.

"What can I tell you? I'm a fast study."

Sammy watched as she carefully removed first one blue-tinted contact, and then the other. She put the lenses in their plastic container and snapped it shut. Then she looked over at him with her normal topaz gaze.

"Besides," she demanded, "what else is there to do up here? Watch weeds grow? So—voilà! I busied my hands and occupied my mind. You're now looking at *the* expert on the life and times of Lili Schneider."

Again Sammy glanced at the stacks of paper. "You know," he said quietly, with a sorrowful little shake of his head, "when you consider the years of work that represents, and you realize how easily it could all have been destroyed—"

"Yes, and it almost *was* destroyed. Thank God for Grandpa's almost pathological phobia of material getting lost or a fire breaking out. Otherwise, he'd never have kept copies of everything up here."

Suddenly a veil seemed to shroud Stephanie's eyes, and her voice grew hushed. "It's ironic, Uncle Sammy, isn't it? Grandpa's fear wasn't a phobia after all. It . . . it's almost as if he'd had a premonition."

"Well, I only hope you'll be even more careful than he was."

"I intend to be." She stared at Sammy. "Why do you think I have to remain 'dead' for the time being? Not for the fun of it, believe me." She paused. "Now then. Can I see the passports?"

Sammy slid a buff-colored, business-size envelope out of his jacket and reached it across to her.

"You followed my instructions?"

"To the letter," he replied, nodding. "All are names of girls who died within a week or two after birth in the same year you were born. I got their names out of the Bergen, Putnam, Dutchess, and Suffolk county newspaper obits of the time. Then I got copies of their birth certificates from the respective courthouses. Finally, I used them, and the pictures we took of you, for the passport applications."

"Good."

She untucked the flap of the envelope, extracted the brand-new passports, and fanned them out on the bed like playing cards. Selecting one at random, she opened it and inspected the photo closely. Then she slowly flipped through the others, carefully studying each one. Herself with dark brown hair. Red hair. Black hair and blond. The redhead wore wire rims; the one with the long black hair, Nana Mouskouri glasses.

She nodded to herself with satisfaction. None of the pictures looked remotely like herself.

They'd better not, she thought. Because Stephanie Merlin is dead. And as long as she remains dead, I'll be alive.

"May I ask you something, Girlie?"

"Fire away."

"All right." He steepled his hands and pressed the tips of his fingers against his lips. "I asked myself, 'Sammy, why would your darling Stephanie need *four* different identities instead of one?' So I thought about it and thought about it. I racked my brains. And can you guess what conclusion I kept coming to?" He leaned forward. "That you don't need four passports just to lay low. No. You wanted *four*, Girlie, because you've decided to play gumshoe." His voice dropped to a hoarser octave. "Please, for my sake and yours, tell me I'm not right, Girlie."

She shrugged, a lazy feline gesture of immense contradiction, one which gave away nothing, and yet confirmed everything.

Feeling frailer than he had in a long, long time, Sammy got up and went over to sit beside her. He took one of her hands and raised it to his lips. "Please, Girlie. I beg of you. Let the authorities investigate this?"

"The authorities!" she sneered, and yanked her hand back as if it had been scorched. "For crying out loud, Uncle Sammy! Get *real!* If they didn't do anything about this before, why would they do something now?"

Her sudden fury discombobulated him, and his face suffused with color. "Well, with Carleton's manuscript . . . and these, these notes . . ." he stammered. "All this *evidence* to back you up—"

"Come on, Uncle Sammy. Isn't it time you stopped fooling yourself? You yourself told me the fire department attributed that explosion to a gas leak. Remember?" She laughed softly, bitterly. "Only, there was no gas. I would have smelled it, and so would Pham."

He sighed again.

"Either that bomb—and it *had* to have been a bomb, Uncle Sammy, it couldn't have been anything else—was meant for Grandpa's research material and manuscript, or for me. Most likely, it was meant to kill two birds with one stone: his work *and* me." Her eyes suddenly shone with tears. "But instead of getting me," she moaned, "it got Pham!"

"Girlie . . ." He put a hand on her arm.

"I know, Uncle Sammy! I *know!*" She knuckled away her tears and sniffled. "You're going to say I shouldn't be blaming myself. But Pham went in there because of *me,*" she said guiltily, "because I left my watch behind!" Her tears coursed in rivulets down her cheeks now. "Oh God! Why *did* he have to be so stubborn? I started to go in, but then the wire of my Walkman snagged on a doorknob and he sailed right past me, calling out that I should wait out in the vestibule for him."

Sammy's voice was gentle. "How many times do I have to tell you, Girlie? What happened to Pham isn't your fault."

But it was as if she hadn't heard.

"It was horrible, Uncle Sammy! Horrible! I was right outside the parlor when . . . when it happened!" Suddenly she flung her arms around his neck and clung to him for dear life.

He held her, for once helpless, not knowing what words of comfort to murmur. Her body heaved with sobs, and he could feel her tears on his neck. "It's all right," he soothed, patting her convulsively shuddering back. "There . . . there now, Girlie . . ."

"It . . . it was like . . . a huge fireball!" She sniffed and swallowed hard. "It . . . blossomed right out into the hall at me! If I hadn't raced out to the vestibule—" A cry rose in her throat and her voice faltered.

Still patting her back with one hand, Sammy stroked her hair with the other, forehead to neck, forehead to neck. "You needn't go into it again, darling," he soothed. "The important thing is, you escaped harm."

Stephanie pulled away from him. "But Pham didn't!" she cried wretchedly.

"No," he said quietly, "that he did not."

Stephanie's eyes became flat round mirrors. "I want the bastards who killed Grandpa and Pham!" she whispered. "I want those murderers!"

"Darling, darling Stephanie." Head tilted, Sammy looked at her sorrowfully. "Why do you *insist* it had to have been a bomb? It could very well have been an accident. Yes, an accident . . ."

She shook her head. "I'm telling you, it *wasn't!*" Her earnest young face was waiflike, haunted, stubborn.

"But how can you be so sure?"

She drew a deep breath. "Because Grandpa told me why he was murdered!"

"He—*what!*" Sammy stared at her.

She nodded. "He told me the motive," she insisted. When he remained silent, she said, "His notes? When I went through them?"

"Yes?" he asked. "And what did you find?"

"Well, they . . . they explained a lot, Uncle Sammy. You see, he'd already finished researching the Schneider biography, and was nearly done with the second draft of the manuscript when he discovered he'd only told *half* the story."

He frowned thoughtfully. "You know, Girlie . . ." he said slowly. "Come to think of it, the last time he and I spoke he . . . he did say he'd uncovered something. He didn't disagree when I said that it was no doubt earthshaking."

"And it is, too," she said softly. "Because you see, Uncle Sammy, he discovered that Lili Schneider isn't dead."

"You can't possibly mean—"

"I *do,* Uncle Sammy!" Her voice was excited. "That's *exactly* what I'm saying! Lili Schneider is very much alive and breathing!"

"But . . . the funeral! The body! If Lili isn't buried in that crypt, then who is?"

"That," said Stephanie with quiet conviction, "is just one mystery among many that I intend to clear up."

"And where will your investigation take you?"

"Wherever it dictates. I'm going to start at the beginning and work my way forward through time." Her voice suddenly took on a steely resolve. "And no one had better try and stop me," she added, setting her determined chin firmly. "And when I say no one, I mean *no one.*"

## 3

They were still at it long after dark. Stephanie had Spagoed-up two frozen, plain, Mama Celeste pizzas with olive oil, sliced red onion, smoked salmon, sour cream, fresh dill, and caviar—all of which Sammy had stocked the refrigerator with earlier in the week, and which she whipped up in the kitchenette. She'd also scared up a bottle of '82 Belair Lussac which went down like liquid velvet.

"Uncle Sammy, would you believe at this point in time I know more about Lili Schneider than I know about you?" she asked, cutting a bite-sized portion of pizza by candlelight.

"In that case, why don't you fill me in on what you've learned? Hm?"

"All right." Stephanie took a sip of wine. "Lili Theresa Bielfeld was born May twenty-second, nineteen ten, in Neunkirchen, a small Austro-Hungarian town which is now part of Austria. She was the second of three sisters. The eldest, Louisette Erzebeth Bielfeld, was born ten months earlier; the third, Liselotte Elisabeth Bielfeld, was born a year later. Their father, Gerhard Franz Bielfeld, was a railroad engineer; their mother, Valerie, nee Szoke, was from Budapest, and was an amateur pianist and *hausfrau.*"

She paused a moment, not knowing whether to continue.

Sammy said, "Go on."

"Well, apparently the three births brought with them both a tragedy and a blessing. The tragedy came in the form of Liselotte's illness, which manifested itself early on."

"Which was?"

"Geromorphism. It's a horrible condition which results in premature decrepitude and senility. As a child of five, she already must have looked middle-aged. At fifteen, she probably looked like a wizened old woman—with the mind and body to match." Stephanie stared at Sammy. "Do you have any idea of what it must have been *like* to see a younger sister wasting away and turning into an old woman?"

"No, I can't. But about the blessing you mentioned?"

"Lili's talent, which also surfaced at an early age. When she was five, her mother arranged for her to start taking singing lessons—not that Neunkirchen had anything more to offer than a small-town music teacher. Anyway, the lessons continued for two years, as did Liselotte's frequent trips to specialists in Vienna and Budapest and stays at various spas—not that any of it helped. There's still no cure for geromorphism today. Then, when the sisters were five, six, and seven, their father died from complications arising from an ulcer operation. To make ends meet, the piano had to be sold and the singing lessons stopped—along with Liselotte's visits to the specialists and spas."

Stephanie looked at Sammy for confirmation.

"Um," he said noncommittally.

"Finally, when things really got down to the wire, their mother decided to move back to her native Budapest, where she and the girls shared a five-room cold-water flat with her brother and his family of six. An astute move, it turned out, since Budapest had more than its share of spas and doctors—and even more so because it was the brother who truly recognized Lili's voice for the exceptional instrument that it was. In fact, he took it upon himself to find a second job so that Lili could be provided with the best vocal coach Budapest had to offer.

"The city being one of Austria-Hungary's two great cultural centers, it's not surprising that Lili's tutor turned out to be none other than the internationally renowned and very, very expensive Madame Milena Szekely. Between Liselotte's medical bills and Lili's lessons, it must have cost the poor uncle everything he could lay his hands on—and more. The doctors weren't known for their charity, nor was Madame Szekely. 'If you want the lessons badly enough, you will somehow scrape up the money,' was her motto. Apparently, Lili's uncle did, and thus Madame Szekely, a human monster of a perfectionist, became the single biggest influence in young Lili's life."

Sammy nodded slowly, signifying both agreement and encouragement that Stephanie continue.

"As time passed," she went on, "Liselotte became older- and more shriveled-looking while, ironically, Lili and Louisette turned into great beauties. Everywhere the two of them went, heads turned. Louisette was the more classically beautiful, but only Lili was blessed—or cursed, depending upon which way you want to look at it—with The Voice, the consensus being that Louisette was absolutely tone-deaf." Stephanie looked at Sammy. She asked, "Still want me to continue?"

"By all means." He motioned with his fork, on which he had speared another bite of pizza.

"In that case," she said, pushing back her chair and getting to her feet, "I'll need to wet my whistle with something other than wine. It's dehydrating me. And after the solitude of the last week, my vocal cords aren't quite up to snuff." She looked down at him. "Can I get you something else while I'm up?"

"Well, maybe a hair more of that excellent Château Belair Lussac?"

"I'll go fetch another one," she said and went off, quickly returning with a bottle and a corkscrew for him and a glass of club soda with ice for herself. Then she sat back down and there was a pop as Sammy pulled the cork.

"Ah," he said, swirling his replenished glass under his nose and inhaling ostentatiously. "Ambrosia." He took a sip. "Now then," he said, putting the glass down and smacking his lips. "Why don't you go on with Lili."

"Yes, well, sometime in nineteen twenty-five, Madame Szekely came to the conclusion that her star pupil really did have the stuff of which world-class divas were made. She decided that Lili should devote— 'sacrifice,' I believe the old dragon liked to call it—her life to music. Ergo, Madame Szekely pulled the appropriate strings and our Lili was accepted by Budapest's Franz Liszt Academy, one of the finest, and, at the time, probably most prestigious music schools in the world."

"And?" Sammy prompted her.

"And . . ." Stephanie took another quick sip of soda. "She studied there under various teachers for several years—and naturally with Madame S., who wasn't about to relinquish her best paying student, on the side. Then, in nineteen twenty-seven, it seems our Lili finally got fed up with having dragon breath constantly puffed down her neck. Going behind her teacher's back, she auditioned for, and was accepted by, the chorus of the Budapest State Opera. Madame S. was apoplectic. She kept screaming at Lili that it was too soon, that she wasn't ready yet. Things like that. But Lili was stagestruck—and intractable. Having tasted of freedom, she was determined never to be shackled again. Teacher and pupil parted acrimoniously, and within the year, besides singing supporting roles, Lili became the leading understudy for resident sopranos. Hers was definitely a star on the rise."

Stephanie paused and frowned deeply.

"Here things get rather vague. I've been over both drafts of the manuscript and all the research material time and again, but dammit! Try as I might, I *still* haven't managed to piece together exactly what happened!"

"Then tell me what you do know," Sammy suggested.

"All right. But it's just bits and pieces," she warned, "and I'm whistling in the dark. I was thinking that Lili perhaps showed too much talent, or maybe was a tad too aggressive and ambitious. She could have upstaged a diva. Who knows?" Stephanie shrugged and brooded. "The possibilities are endless when you start thinking about it. I mean, there's a reason prima donnas are called prima donnas—right?"

Sammy made noises of agreement.

"All I do know is that I've been through everything with a fine-tooth comb, and there's nothing, absolutely *nothing*, to suggest what might have happened. But it must have been a real doozie. Why else would a promising young starlet of the Budapest State Opera suddenly be booted out, finding herself persona non grata? Hmm?"

"And that's all you've got?" Sammy asked neutrally.

"That's all." She nodded in the flickering candlelight. "Why?" she asked slowly, cocking her head to one side. "Do *you* know something I don't know?"

He said, "I'll tell you what I know later. Just continue, Girlie. You're doing splendidly." He smiled. "Really you are."

"If you say so." She gave him an oblique look and broke off a little piece of pizza crust and popped it into her mouth. She chewed it reflectively and patted her lips fastidiously with her napkin. "Anyway," she said, once she'd swallowed, "the next events are well documented, and occurred a scant week later. That was when Lili's mother, her ill sister, Liselotte, her uncle, and his entire family died in a train derailment when the coach they were riding in jumped the tracks and plunged into the Danube."

"Tragic," Sammy said, nodding his head. "But at least there was one small mercy. For poor Liselotte, the suffering was over."

"Yes. Luckily for Lili and Louisette, though, neither of them was on that train. Louisette had come down with the flu, and Lili'd insisted upon staying at home with her. Lucky on the one hand, but unlucky on the other. They escaped almost certain death, but their safety net—the uncle—was dead. Suddenly on their own, they found themselves unemployed—and without a living relative or friend in the world."

"They did have it rough, those two," Sammy said.

She cut another tiny bite of pizza and nibbled it off the fork, pearly teeth flashing. "You know," she said, "Lili must have known her chances of being rehired by the opera were slim. That's probably why she and Louisette lost no time packing their bags, leaving Budapest, and popping up in Vienna."

"Where, unfortunately, Lili's reputation must have preceded her, since the Wiener Staatsoper had extremely close ties to Budapest's," Sammy said, nodding.

Stephanie drank some more soda. "Anyway, the Bielfeld sisters continued on to Berlin, where times proved tough. Without a sponsor or references, Lili wasn't even able to get an audition for the Berliner Staatsoper. So, until an opportunity presented itself, and so she could continue the expensive vocal coaching her voice required, both girls moved in with, and worked for, an 'aunt.' "

"An aunt?" said Sammy. "Didn't you just get through telling me they didn't have any living relatives?"

"Yes, Uncle Sammy. But by 'aunt,' read 'madam.' And by 'work,' read 'prostitution.' "

"Prosti*tu*tion!" Sammy exclaimed. "Lili? Let me get this straight,

Girlie." He looked at Stephanie with inquisitive narrowed eyes. "You're sure?"

"Oh, most definitely yes." Stephanie nodded again. "I've got a Xerox copy of an old group photo of the brothel's girls. The original was destroyed in the explosion, but even in the photocopy there's no mistaking Lili and Louisette. It's in one of those stacks over by the bed. Want to see it?"

"I'll look at it later. Now do continue, Girlie! Quite frankly, some of this is news to me. I find it fascinating!"

Stephanie smiled. "So do I. Anyway, let me see. Where was I?" She picked at a piece of pizza crust.

"Berlin," Sammy prompted.

"Right. Berlin." She nibbled on the bit of crust. "It took a while, but sacrificing their bodies to pay for Lili's vocal coach finally paid off. Her new teacher helped her arrange an audition with the Berliner Staatsoper, and she was hired on the spot. From then on, things happened in quick succession. Barely a few months went by before—*bingo!* She got her Big Break. The year was nineteen thirty-two and the operetta was—what else?—that ever-popular pastiche *Der Rosenkavalier.* What happened is your typical corny success story. On opening night, the leading soprano had an accident on her way to the theater and her understudy, in this case, Lili, had to go on in her stead. Needless to say, she wowed 'em with a drop-dead performance, got a thirty-minute standing ovation, and a star was born. Hollywood couldn't have plotted it better."

Sammy opened his mouth to say something, but checked himself and took a sip of wine instead.

Stephanie considered him without haste. He was suddenly poker-faced, and while she didn't have an inkling as to what was going on in his mind, she was convinced that he knew something she should know.

"All right, Uncle Sammy," she said at last. "Out with it. Now's not the time to hold out on me."

He pushed his chair back. "Why don't we take our drinks and go sit over there on the beds?" he suggested, getting to his feet and picking up his wineglass and the bottle of Belair Lussac. "This will take a while, and we might as well get comfortable."

"Might as well," she agreed, scarfing one last, big bite of pizza as she got up.

Sammy said, "Think Budapest all over again."

"Budapest?" Stephanie repeated blankly. She was lying sideways on one of the *lits à la Polonnaise,* head propped up on an elbow. "Budapest . . . Budapest . . . now what . . . ? Of *course!*" Suddenly she sat up straight. "The reason Lili got fired from the opera!"

Sammy laughed. "Like in Berlin, this incident also happened on opening night, but, on stage—during the season premiere of *La Rondine,* no less. Anyway, what should fall open as the star soprano came on, but a trapdoor, right where the poor woman should have been standing?"

"Good God!" Stephanie stared at him. "You're kidding!"

"I kid you not, Girlie. Had the near-sighted lady been standing in the spot the stage directions required, she would undoubtedly have been seriously injured. Maybe even killed. Certainly put out of commission."

"Nasty, our Lili," murmured Stephanie.

"Oh, yes." Sammy nodded. "Definitely not one to bide her time or leave anything to chance. But she learned a powerful lesson. You see, she was caught red-handed, and by no less than three eyewitnesses. Still clutching the lever of the trapdoor, apparently saying something like, 'Oops! I just leaned against this! I hope it wasn't anything important?' "

"That's . . . awful!"

"When you think about it, she really did have the luck of the devil. Instead of being fired, she could have had criminal charges brought against her. And justifiably so."

"What I want to know," Stephanie said, "is since *you* knew all this, why didn't you tell Grandpa? There isn't anything about this in his manuscript, nor in his notes."

"Why?" Sammy snorted. "For the simple reason that Carleton never asked me, that's why. He kept his research such a secret, you'd have thought he was guarding the gold at Fort Knox. You see, Girlie, if he didn't tell me what he *did* know, how was I supposed to guess what he *didn't?*" He added dryly, "I may be many things, but psychic I'm not."

"No, of course not," Stephanie murmured, "and no one expects you to be. Now then . . . in Berlin . . . I take it Lili got antsy waiting in the wings? And once again tried her old incapacitate-the-diva trick?"

"Yes, but she'd learned an important lesson in Budapest. Subsequently, this 'accident' occurred far from the opera premises, and she had an alibi—she was in a meeting with the theater director at the time."

"How did she manage that?"

"Easily. She simply arranged for some friends to do it instead of getting her own hands dirty."

"Friends?"

"Brownshirts, actually. You see, Lili'd become thick as thieves with a group of them. At any rate, as you already know, they succeeded at doing in Berlin what she had failed miserably at in Budapest. The story handed out at the time was that the soprano, who was an Austrian Catholic, was mistaken for a Jew."

Stephanie could see Sammy's wineglass shaking in his angrily trembling hand.

"Can you believe that?" he asked hoarsely. "Saying it was all right to beat a woman half senseless merely because she'd been labeled a Jew?"

Stephanie could only shudder. It was all too easy to imagine the ghastly scene . . . the gang of young ruffians . . . an innocent, defenseless woman attacked and kicked and beaten . . . An act not only condoned, but, in those years, probably applauded.

It was too awful to contemplate, that world gone mad.

Too awful, too, that a singer of Lili Schneider's caliber should have resorted to such abhorrent means to justify her ends.

"Anyway, continue with your story, Girlie. Perhaps I can be of help and fill in some more gaps for you."

Stephanie nodded gratefully. She polished off the rest of her soda, put the glass down, and tucked her legs under her, sitting in the Lotus position. "Back in Lili's days," she said, "the Berliner Staatsoper was under the direction of Detlef von Ohlendorf—"

"*That* unrepentant Nazi!" Sammy swore in a soft explosion of breath.

"He's still around," she said, "isn't he?"

"Oh yes, and riding a crest of popularity, yet," Sammy said sourly. "He must be well into his eighties, and he's so in demand he flies from one opera house to another in his private jet, conducting the Stuttgarter Philharmonic one day, and the Melbourne Opera the next. It's unbelievable, the way his past has been forgiven."

"According to Grandpa's manuscript, Lili and von Ohlendorf—or should I say, 'The Maestro'?—became like *this*." Stephanie held up a hand, two fingers crossed.

"Quite true," said Sammy.

"He also wrote that they were like Fred Astaire and Ginger Rogers—they were that perfectly attuned to each other's creative juices."

"That's true also. Whether or not I personally despise the man—and make no mistake about it, Girlie, I loathe him—the fact remains that no matter what he directed Lili in, the result was utter magic. It all started with their first Bregenzer Festspiele, where they knocked 'em dead with their *Fidelio*."

"After which," she added, "their *Così Fan Tutte* made history at the Salzburger Festspiele, and their *Rienzi*, by Wagner, became the hit at Bayreuth."

"You have done your homework," he said, sounding impressed.

"Well, not surprisingly, an invitation to visit Hitler at Berchtesgaden soon followed, during which the Führer confided to Lili that he was her greatest fan. Naturally, propaganda minister Goebbels was on hand, and promptly trumpeted the news in the papers and over the airwaves, after which our Lili could do absolutely no wrong. Oh, and one more thing. Contrary to popular belief, it was *not* Goebbels, but von Ohlendorf, who actually came up with the idea for Lili's Sunday afternoon radio broadcasts."

"The ones which made her the Third Reich's number one soprano," murmured Sammy, half to himself.

"*And* the hottest thing to hit the German airwaves since Hitler's speeches." Stephanie was silent for a moment. "I wonder. What was it? That crystal-clear voice? Her incredible range? Or her ability to embrace the entire repertoire from light operetta to heavy-duty Wagner?"

"Most likely," Sammy said dryly, "she just struck a deep Teutonic chord in the Germans of the time."

"Yes. That does make more sense," Stephanie said. "But whatever it was, she sure had the country eating out of her hand. Lili fever suddenly gripped Germany. Every Sunday, millions of Germans and Austrians gathered around their radios to tune in and hear her sing. Uncle Sammy, did you know that in one week alone—one ... single ... week!—over *four hundred* baby girls were named Lili?" She stared at him. "Or that a street in virtually every major city was named in honor of her?"

"No, but it doesn't surprise me."

"And then, what should happen? All those Bielfeldstrasse signs were barely up, when they all had to come down again and be changed!"

"Because of Friedrich Wilhelm Schneider."

"That's right." Stephanie nodded. "The SA Gruppenführer of Berlin, and SA Chief of Staff Ernst Röhm's righthand man. Apparently, Gruppenführer Schneider was one of those ironies of the Third Reich: a convicted murderer, known homosexual, and opera groupie, all rolled into one. At any rate, he looked like Hitler's Aryan ideal: blond hair, blue eyes, pale Nordic skin, freckles. Plus a somewhat pretty face on a muscle-bound body. According to Grandpa's manuscript, he was also one of Röhm's favorite gay playmates."

"Now that," said Sammy mildly, "I have heard."

"Which brings us to the next big event in Lili's life," Stephanie went on. "Her wedding to Gruppenführer Schneider in May of nineteen thirty-three. The ceremony was held—where else?—in the Berliner Staatsoper, and was—what else?—broadcast all over Germany. The Berliner Philharmonic played; the opera chorus sang. There was an SA honor guard *and* an SS honor guard. Hitler, Himmler, Goering—you name them, they all attended. It was a civil ceremony, mind you, but staged by Albert Speer with all the pomp and circumstance worthy of a Wagnerian coronation."

"Or," Sammy interjected drily, "a Nuremberg rally."

"That too," she said. "But do you know what I still can't understand, Uncle Sammy?"

"And what, my darling, is that?"

"*Why* they got married, what with their respective careers—not to mention *his* sexual proclivities. I mean, it could hardly be called a match made in heaven."

"No," Sammy said, "that it certainly couldn't. It was an arrangement made right here on earth."

"But for what reason?"

"The question you want to ask, Girlie, is: arranged by whom?"

"In that case, uncle dearest, who *was* it arranged by?"

"*Numero uno.*"

"You can't mean—"

"That's right, Girlie, I do. Schikelgruber himself."

Her mouth actually fell open. "Hitler!" she whispered, tugging at her ear and staring at him. "But . . . *why?*"

"Because, my darling, although the Führer detested his friend's sexual proclivities, personally he really *liked* Friedrich Wilhelm Schneider. The two of them went way back, all the way to the trenches of World War One."

She sat there, digesting this new information in silence. "I . . . see," she said slowly after a moment. "Hitler tried to . . . to change him. To steer him straight."

"Precisely! And, since the Gruppenführer was such an opera buff, Hitler used Lili as bait. But the marriage didn't make the gay man straight, nor did it quell the rumors about his continuing relationship with Röhm and his boys. If anything, the gossip only intensified, now that Lili's spotlight included poor Friedrich."

Stephanie's face shone with a sharp, rapt beauty, her precision-tuned mind assimilating what amounted to having struck a bonanza in pure gold. After a moment, she said, "Yes, Uncle Sammy, yes! Knowing it was Hitler who arranged the marriage suddenly makes everything fall into place! My God! It explains, for instance, why Lili should have been in the process of getting an annulment when, what should happen—"

"June of 'thirty-four?" Sammy suggested.

"Exactly! When Röhm's merry band bought it on the Tegernsee, all slaughtered for so-called 'treason'—Gruppenführer Schneider included!" Stephanie shook her head in bemusement. "And here I was, ready to swear on a stack of Bibles that Lili was either psychic, or else must have possessed an uncanny knack for survival."

"Which she did, Girlie. Make no mistake about it."

"Oh, believe me, I'm not. But in *this* instance, her survival instincts had nothing to do with it. Uncle Sammy! Don't you see?" Stephanie sat forward, eyes gleaming, bolts of excitement streaking through her like live charges of electricity. "Lili must have been *forewarned* about what was going down! My God! Think of what this means! She was probably told . . . even ordered . . . to distance herself from her husband . . . maybe by the *Führer* himself!" After a moment she murmured, "Small wonder she rose above the stink like a helium balloon."

"And," Sammy added, his lips twisting in irony, "in the process came out smelling like the proverbial rose."

Stephanie nodded. "Anyway, afterward, she and von Ohlendorf left on a whirlwind world tour. First stop, the Paris Opera, where everyone went bananas over Lili. The second, her Covent Garden triumph in London, where she was pelted with flowers during every performance. Then it was on across the Atlantic to the old Metropolitan Opera House in New York, where both Lili and von Ohlendorf were offered contracts for astronomical sums of money—which, being the good Nazis that they were, they graciously turned down. Then it was on to Mexico City, Buenos Aires, Montevideo, Rio, and finally back across the Atlantic. Everywhere they went, word of their previous triumphs preceded them, and resulted in sold-out performances and mob scenes. Lisbon . . . Madrid . . . the Teatro Grande in Brescia . . . La Scala in Milan—Lili packed them in. And then came the highlight of the tour, when, at the request of the pope, she sang a special high mass at St. Peter's Basilica in Rome."

"As a matter of fact, Girlie, I remember that from my youth. You couldn't pick up a newspaper or a magazine without seeing the front-page pictures of Lili kneeling and kissing His Holiness's ring."

"What a joke!" she said. "Lili was . . . probably still is, since I'm convinced she's alive . . . the consummate, ruthless, power-hungry bitch. Everything points toward it. After returning to Berlin, what did she do? Why, she consolidated her power base by having a series of affairs with high-ranking Nazis—each more powerful than the last. And then, when she ran out of conquests? Why, she simply arranged for her maestro, Detlef von Ohlendorf, to take over the *Vienna* opera—and joined him there, the two of them practically running the cultural life of that city while she set up housekeeping with the head Nazi there."

"Some would call her the last of the great courtesans."

Stephanie bristled. "Courtesan indeed!" she sniffed. "Uncle Sammy, courtesans don't play musical beds the way Lili did. First, mistress of the most powerful Nazis—plural—in Berlin? And then the most powerful Nazi—singular—in Vienna? After which, during the Allied Occupation of Austria, what does she do? Mmm? If I remember correctly, she seduced the commander of the Russian occupying forces."

"Yes, him." Sammy nodded.

"But—surprise, surprise!" Stephanie's voice dripped sarcasm. "Frau Schneider found out there was a price to pay for having been such a highly visible—and *vocal*—member of the Nazi party. Suddenly her career was down the tubes, since the Allies wouldn't let her perform, record, or broadcast in either Austria *or* Germany."

Stephanie sat forward, half raising herself from the bed.

"But did she let that stop her? No, it damn well did not! Our Frau Schneider, who had screwed every powerful man from Berlin to Vienna, hired herself a *dueña;* for Chrissakes—a *dueña!*—and started running around London as if she were some helpless, cooing teenage virgin!"

"Yes," Sammy said quietly. "But, Girlie, you must admit it worked, don't you? She did catch Sir Kenneth Hughes-Coxe."

"Who just so happened to be the chairman of Heavenly Records, and the single most powerful classical record producer in the entire world to boot! He not only made her *Lady* Hughes-Coxe, if you please, but a British subject—free of the Allies' shackles and welcome to sing anywhere on earth—Austria *and* Germany included!" Stephanie sat back and brooded. "Which brings us back to square one . . ." Her voice trailed off as she frowned.

"And what square is that, my darling?" Sammy prodded gently.

She stared at him. "Lili had everything at this point in her life, and I mean *everything.* The past was behind her. She had wealth beyond compare. Worldwide fame. Immense power. Even a title, for God's sake!"

"So what are you saying, Girlie?"

"What I'm saying is, *why* would she manufacture herself a convenient death and disappear? I mean, think about it, Uncle Sammy." Her voice dropped to a whisper. "What could disappearing get her that all the money and power in the world couldn't?"

# 4

"I'm sorry, Uncle Sammy," Stephanie said. "The answer's still no."
The two of them were sitting in the rear of the dark blue
stretch limousine, cocooned from prying eyes by gray-tinted one-way
glass.

Stephanie, wearing the Nana Mouskouri glasses, black contacts, and
long, glossy black wig, possessed a high-style urban chic. She had on
bright yellow culottes over opaque black tights and bumblebee shoes with
bold black-and-yellow stripes and moderate heels. Her loose shirt was of
vertically striped yellow-and-black silk, and the lightweight, outsized yellow blazer had an embroidered crest on the pocket.

She couldn't be missed from a mile away—which was the whole
point.

"It's far too attention-grabbing an outfit for me to be anything but on
the up-and-up," she'd explained to Sammy earlier, when he'd registered
his surprise.

"Nothing better than to hide in plain sight," he'd agreed, nodding.

Now, she opened her yellow-and-black shoulder bag and checked the
contents to see if she'd forgotten anything. The right passport and visa.
Makeup. Tissues. Wallet. Traveler's checks.

"I do wish you'd reconsider, Girlie?" said Sammy wistfully.

"I already told you." She snapped open a compact and eyed herself
critically in the little round mirror, moving it this way and that. "It's much
safer if I do this on my own." Stephanie frowned at her dark and exotic
complexion. Carefully, she daubed a bit more bronze powder onto her
cheeks, expertly fluffing away the excess. As she worked, she flicked him
a disapproving sideways glance.

"But you really could use my help, you know." He crossed his legs
jauntily and clasped his hands around his knee. "In case you've forgotten,
my dear, classical music is my forte. I know my operas and musicians and
composers and singers backward and forward."

He paused to gauge her reaction, but she was busy painting her lips.

"Not to mention," he went on, "I speak Italian fluently, German
quite well, Hungarian passably, and French . . . well, French like a for-
eigner, what else? But I would come in very, very handy in Europe. Especially," he added slyly, "in Eastern Europe?"

"Nice try, but no cigar," Stephanie said flatly, putting the lipstick away. She closed the compact with a loud snap of finality.

Pouting, he sat back, folded his arms, and tucked his hands up into his armpits.

"Be that way," she said unconcernedly. Humming to herself, she dropped the compact into her bag and buckled it shut. Then she put her elbow on the armrest, rested her chin in her hand, and stared out the tinted window at the other lanes. The traffic was bumper to bumper, moving along at a snail's pace.

They rode along in silence for a while. She watched a rusty, clattering station wagon in the next lane with surfboards sticking out the back. It was full of happy kids in their late teens.

The silence in the back of the limo grew longer. Finally, knowing it was time to placate, she turned and faced Sammy. The little man had his back turned to her, and was staring out the other window.

She tapped him gently on the shoulder. "Uncle Sammy?" she ventured softly.

He slid her a miffed, tight-lipped little sideways look.

"Oh, come on, Uncle Sammy," she pleaded. "Please try to understand. The only reason I don't want you along is because you're far too famous a music critic not to attract undue attention. Now, you *know* that!" She waited. "So we're going to part like this, are we?"

He cackled unexpectedly. "Almost had you that time!"

"I'll say you did. Then there are no hard feelings?"

He reached for her hand and laced fingers with her. "How could there be?" he asked solemnly. "You're my Girlie."

"And you are my Uncle Sammy." She flashed him a lovely smile and planted a noisy kiss on his forehead.

"Now then," he said. "There's just one last little thing."

"I know," Stephanie said intuitively. She sighed and slumped in the seat. "Johnny."

"Yes, Johnny." Sammy nodded. "He's still in town, you know. A day doesn't pass when he doesn't visit or call." The old man paused. "He's shattered, Girlie. With your 'death,' his whole world has collapsed."

She drew a deep breath and let it out noisily. The cheerful youths in the battered station wagon were now bopping up and down in their seats to the beat of '50s rock and roll. For a moment, she shut her eyes. Then she turned back to Sammy.

"Finding Grandpa and Pham's killers has to take priority," she said.

"And Johnny?" he asked. "What about how all this affects him? He's hurting. You can't know what witnessing that explosion did to him, Girlie. He blames himself for your 'death,' you know."

She nodded.

"I guess what it comes down to is, it's really not fair to continue letting him believe you're dead. No, Girlie, not fair at all."

"I *know,*" she said miserably. Then she shook her head. "No, Uncle Sammy," she said slowly, "much as I'd like to let Johnny in on it, it will be safer for all three of us if he still believes me dead."

Sammy looked at her sadly, but didn't press the point. He kept holding her hand. He was still holding it when they pulled up in front of the Pan Am terminal at Kennedy Airport.

The driver stopped in the NO STANDING zone, got out, opened the rear door, and went around to get her luggage out of the trunk.

"You'd better not go in with me," Stephanie told Sammy in the car.

"I understand. But I'll be beside you in spirit all the way."

"I know you will!"

They gave each other a fierce hug.

"You'll take good care of Waldo?"

"Don't worry, Girlie, don't worry. Much as I hate him, I'll take care of that bird."

She hugged him again. "Just to ease your mind, I'll check in regularly. Okay?" She looked at her new watch. "Yikes! I'd better be off. It won't do to miss my flight."

She touched her lips with her fingertips and then gently touched his lips with them. "Bye, Uncle Sammy," she said huskily.

"Bye-bye, Girlie," he said. "Hope to see you soon."

Stephanie let a porter grab her three suitcases.

"Up, up, and away!" she said brightly.

Three clicks of her heels, and the automatic doors swallowed her up.

# ❧ 5 ❧

*H*e moved stealthily on sure feet, guided by instinct rather than sight, like a hunter, or a foraging creature on the prowl.

Like the night, which offered him haven, he was clad entirely in black: turtleneck, pants, gloves, and black sneakers with thick black rubber soles. Prudently, his canvas carryall, which held his implements, was matt black and fitted with nonreflective zippers.

He moved through the woods with the furtive ease of a ghost, the night his uncertain ally. He knew it could as easily become his deadliest enemy, too.

He had left his car, camouflaged with branches, half a mile down the road in an unused, overgrown forestry access road. Now, going the rest of the way on foot, he slipped soundlessly through the murmuring forest and dense brush, ducking under branches and skirting obstacles with an almost psychic ease.

Suddenly his ears caught the distant sound of an approaching car. He froze, making himself one shadow among many and stood there, head lowered, eyes half-closed, so that neither his face nor his eyes would reflect light, but he would still be able to see.

Before long, a halo of light appeared from around a curve. It grew brighter and brighter, and then the brilliant burst of blinding headlights swept directly at him like searchlights, emphasizing his fragile vulnerability.

He sensed, rather than saw, the Martian light on the roof of the car. Moments later, his worst suspicions were confirmed when he heard the crackling chatter of the police-band radio drifting out its open windows.

*Holy mother of God!* he thought. *A patrol car!*

He could hear the blood rushing madly around inside his head and, breath held, mentally counted off the passing seconds: *One and two and three and . . .*

The cops drove by without slowing down, the chatter of their radio fading, their red taillights receding before disappearing around yet another bend.

He relaxed but forced himself to remain in place a few minutes longer. Waiting for his night vision to readjust and to make absolutely certain his presence hadn't been suspected and the police wouldn't return to investigate. Then, and only then, did he resume his stealthy prowl.

W-what—?

The wildlife preserve ended so abruptly that he'd stumbled out of the trees before he'd even realized it. Swiftly he drew back into their protective cover, and without rush, studied the terrain.

He was at the edge of a meadow, fifty feet from the west side of the main house. Up in back of it and to his left was the ghostly Greek temple he correctly assumed was the guest house. Below, to the right, the ribbon of dark country road was without traffic.

All was dark at the main house. All was quiet at the temple. Nothing stirred but the shrill nocturnal insects.

Keeping in a low crouch, he crept through the sloping meadow toward the house. Once he reached it, he flattened himself against the wall and listened intently. Nothing.

Staying close to the building, he made a complete circumference, his ears keen, alert to the slightest sounds coming from within. There were none.

Still, better safe than sorry. At the front entrance, he did the obvious. Rang the buzzer several times and waited in the shadows.

Nothing barked; no one came to answer the door. It was as he had thought: There was nobody at home.

He returned to the back of the house and chose one of the French doors. A ghostly decal on a pane of glass warned of an ADT alarm—as if that would scare him off.

He unzipped his canvas carryall, took out a penlight, and shone it along the window frame. Aha. There it was—a small square on the door, and another on the door frame. A vibration sensor alarm, for guarding against vandals and untrained thieves.

He smiled. Talk about a piece a cake, he thought.

Working swiftly and with confidence, he held the penlight in his mouth and took two magnetized Slim Jims, a small pair of wire cutters, and a short length of wire with an alligator clip attached to each end out of the carryall.

He put the cutters and the length of wire down on the top step. One of the Slim Jims he stuck between the two square alarm units. He used the other to jimmy the lock.

It didn't take but minutes. There was a click as the tumblers turned.

Now came the trickier part. Still holding the magnetized Slim Jim between the two units, he used his other hand to pick up the wire cutters, snipped the alarm wire, and swiftly attached an alligator clip to each of the cut ends.

There. Now for the moment of reckoning.

Despite his self-confidence and the simplicity of the alarm system, his heart sped up as he slid the Slim Jim out of the door. He was prepared for the piercing alarm—which was probably hooked up to the local police station—to go off and send him scurrying back into the safety of the woods.

But there was no sound. Only silence. And the silence was very, very sweet.

Putting his tools back in the carryall, he zipped it closed, picked it up, and opened the door. After feeling his way through the blue brocade curtains, he stepped into the living room, shut the door behind him, and locked it from the inside.

He played the penlight around the grand, high-ceilinged room, illuminating part of a treasure-laden table here, the fine veneer of an antique chair there. Gilt-framed mirrors reflected the blinding pinpoint of light right back at him.

Quickly he went from room to room, but he didn't bother to stop and search them. He knew instantly that would be a waste of time. He wouldn't find anything here. He could sense that the house had been unused for weeks; months, even: it was pervaded by that closed-up, stifling smell that is the hallmark of places in which no one has lived for a time.

Returning to the living room, he pushed his way through the heavy curtains, went back outside, and pulled the French door shut. He disconnected the alligator clips, reconnected the alarm, and returned the tools to the carryall. Then he stood up, his eyes sweeping the hill.

The ghostly pillared portico of the temple was just visible in the night, like something ethereal and otherworldly hovering in midair.

He hiked briskly but unhurriedly up the steep incline, going the long way around in order to remain in the shelter of the trees. He approached the building from the rear, sprinted toward it in a crouch, and squatted below the nearest window. Putting the carryall down on the ground, he placed his hands on the sill and carefully inched up to have a look-see.

The place was dark, and without using his flashlight, he couldn't tell whether it was occupied or not.

Keeping close to the building, he continued moving in a crouch along one of the side walls, stopping again to peer into another window.

There was still no sign of habitation, but he knew that didn't prove it was *un*inhabited, either. In the country, people went to bed early, and someone could very well be asleep in there.

He climbed the shallow steps to the portico and knocked loudly on the front door. Waited. Knocked again. Waited some more.

It was just as he had thought. There was no one here.

He switched on his penlight and moved it around the door. Saw that it was thick and sturdy, made of solid oak and fitted with good Medeco locks.

*Well, there's more than one way to skin a cat,* he thought. Suppressing a grin, he went back to the side of the house, where he ran the penlight beam along a window.

As with the main building below, it was fitted with vibration sensor alarms—just as he'd expected. And the locks were child's play—as he'd expected, also.

He shook his head at the folly of homeowners. It never failed. People barricaded themselves behind expensive front doors and felt deceptively safe while the hardware on their windows was cheap and flimsy.

Humming to himself, he stuck the penlight in his mouth, unzipped the carryall, and got busy. Inside of three minutes, he had the window open and was inside, playing the thin beam of light around the huge library/guestroom.

"Well, well, well!" he said to himself. "What do you know . . ."

Because there was no one here now, but there had been recently. The lingering smells of food and perfume still hung faintly in the air.

This time, he decided to risk turning on the lights. After making sure all the curtains were tightly drawn, he found a wall switch and flipped it on.

Setting his carryall down, he looked around and let out an impressed whistle. Everything, from the two lavishly canopied beds on down to the smallest bibelot, looked as though it belonged in a museum. *There's a fortune here,* he thought. *Luckily for the owner, I'm not a thief. I'm just tracking somebody who's supposed to be dead . . .*

Save for the green hills and onion-domed churches of Mitteleuropa, there is something distinctly Parisian about Budapest, which, until 1872, had been three independent communities—Buda and Obuda on the west bank of the Danube, and Pest on the east. On this early afternoon the sky was cloudless, but the air pollution was so bad that the horizon was obscured, and grayish-blue haze shrouded the imperial architecture, grand monuments, boulevards, and verdigris bridges.

It was nearing two in the afternoon when the taxi dropped Stephanie in front of the elegant rococo façade of a six-story, turn-of-the-century apartment house on the Buda side of the city. Once elegant, the riverside building had long since gone to seed, a sad, grimy remnant of the grand and splendid past.

Standing on the bristly second-floor doormat, she reached up and wound the old-fashioned brass bell. It emitted a grating noise, more like an old bicycle bell than chimes. She waited. There were slow footsteps and the tap of a cane on the other side of the door, and then she was aware of an eye surveying her through the peephole.

She stepped back and smiled reassuringly to show that she was harmless. After a few seconds, locks turned, and then the paneled door creaked open about six inches.

"*Igen?*" said an ancient woman, surveying Stephanie suspiciously.

Stephanie took a deep breath. *"Beszél angolul?"* she asked haltingly. The woman frowned. *"Sajnálom,"* she said. *"Nem értem."* She started to close the door.

"Wait wait wait!" Stephanie cried quickly in English, and then enunciated slowly: "Bae ... sayl *on* ... gaw ... lool?"

Now the enormous eyes lit up with understanding. "Ah! *Beszél angolul!"* The woman laughed and opened the door wider. "Of course," she said with an unmistakable pride in her voice, "I speak the English."

*I should have known,* Stephanie thought wryly. *Instead of making an ass out of myself by butchering a few simple words of Hungarian, I might as well have started off by speaking my native tongue.* Then she held out her hand and introduced herself. "My name is Amanda Smith, and I've come from the United States to see Madame Balász."

"I am Madame Balász." The woman stepped aside and indicated with a gesture that Stephanie should enter.

"This way. Please." Leaning on her cane, the short old lady led the way down the hallway, which was quite grand, if rather shabby and stifling—hot, dim, airless, and stuffy—and pervaded by that peculiarly sour smell of being inhabited by a person of extremely old age.

At the far end of the hall, Madame Balász pushed open an etched glass door and stepped aside. "Please," she invited, gesturing Stephanie inside a gloomy formal salon, which, upon first glance, was missing only the decaying wedding cake; otherwise, Miss Havisham would have felt right at home. "You will make yourself comfortable. I will return back in some moments."

Left alone, Stephanie looked around. The room looked like it hadn't been used in years. The walls were covered in a faded, once-rich blue damask which showed stains from multiple leaks; above the cornice, the ornate plaster ceiling was a road map of cracks. On an old Bösendorfer grand piano were displayed dozens of old photographs in enamel and ormolu and tarnished silver frames. One of the pictures caught her eye. Drawn toward it, she picked it up and used her palm to wipe the thick layer of dust off the glass.

Holding it up to the little light there was, she studied it closely.

The faded, cracked photograph showed two young women in obvious operetta regalia: lavish gowns with hooped underskirts, elbow-length gloves, fans, tons of costume jewelry, and towering white wigs sprouting ostrich plumes.

One was a woman she had never seen before; the other was a very beautiful and very, very young Lili Schneider.

"Ahem!" Someone in the doorway cleared a throat noisily.

Startled, Stephanie guiltily put the frame back down and turned around. The old lady, leaning on her cane, stood there. "Now, then," she said. "About what did you wish to see me?"

# 6

*M*adame Balász was the most peculiar woman Stephanie had ever seen. Short, thin, and, to say the very least, more than a bit eccentric, she was determined to make up for her eighty-three years by projecting an imperious strength and a formidable, almost aggressively French sense of style.

From a distance and in dim lighting, she could have passed for no more than forty. She wore a snappy red military-style tunic with gold braid and buttons and big epaulets, along with tight black pants, red shoes, and bright red leather gloves which hid her aged hands. Her head of thick, youthful brown hair was cut in bangs and she had giant Betty Boop stars for eyes.

The starry eyes were the result of spidery, black-mascaraed false lashes she'd glued to both the upper and the lower lids, and the youthful hair was—what else?—a wig, unabashedly anchored in place by a thick black rubber band under her chin, which did double duty as a kind of surgery-free facelift, and thus left her features miraculously devoid of deep wrinkles.

They sat outside, on rusty green bistro chairs on the balcony overlooking the Danube, sipping Aszu wine. A fat, black Persian cat purred contentedly on Madame's lap, its eyes sleepy slits as its mistress stroked her with a red-gloved hand; another black Persian lay curled at her feet, delicately licking its privates.

"Cats," Madame Balász said, "such marvelous animals! So graceful and affectionate, and yet so aloof and independent. Take Aïda here." She regarded the cat on her lap with particular affection. "She looks like a princess, does she not? And Othello there." She nodded at her feet. "It is not difficult to see why the Egyptians worshipped them." She watched Stephanie closely from between her spidery lashes. "It is said that they have nine lives and that curiosity kills them. But then, curiosity can kill any of us, don't you think?"

Stephanie wondered if she should construe this as some kind of warning, or at least a hint? She really had no way of knowing. It was, she considered, most likely just part and parcel of Madame Balász's ongoing repertoire—nothing more than a morsel dropped while flitting from one subject to another. She had been at it for over three hours already, filling

Stephanie's ear with all sorts of fascinating details, stories, and bits and pieces of information, the last concerning the time she had been dining alone in a restaurant, and a total stranger at the next table had bitten her neck. "He was short and ugly, with eyes like a bug's. Can you imagine! A hideous little thing looking like Peter Lorre jumping up, biting you on your neck, and then running out?"

"Perhaps he thought of himself as a vampire," Stephanie suggested.

The old lady digested this in silence and then nodded her head thoughtfully. "Perhaps you are right. Transylvania is not far from here, you know."

Stephanie didn't know quite what to think, so she prudently kept her mouth shut. She had a sip of wine.

"Now then," the old lady said, continuing to stroke the purring black fluff on her lap, "to get back to the subject you are most interested in. Lili."

Stephanie smiled. "Don't tell me she was a vampire."

Madame Balász did not return her smile. "Lili, you know, was fascinated by the stories of the vampires."

"Really? But why?"

Madame Balász sighed. "Lili," she said, "absolutely abhorred the very idea of aging and death. You see, Ms. Smith, it was her dream to live forever."

"Really?" Stephanie's voice was hushed. "Was she searching for the fountain of youth, then?"

The chic old woman in her Marschallin tunic sat back and smiled, her eyes returning to normal. She tilted her head and regarded Stephanie. "Aren't we all?"

Stephanie shook her head.

"*Igen.* And Lili had more reason than anyone to want to find the secret of eternal youth. Consider, for a moment, how tragic her early life was. Death and aging surrounded her."

"I know." Stephanie nodded. "First her father dying when she was so young . . . and her sister, Liselotte, being born a geromorph . . ."

"A tragedy, that! Enough to chill one's blood! *Igen.* I knew Liselotte, the poor thing. It was impossible to believe she could be Lili and Louisette's sister. She . . . she looked like the girls' grandmother! Imagine. And so young!" Madame Balász shuddered at the memory, clutching her tunic at the neck, as though she felt a sudden chill. The cat on her lap opened its eyes and meowed plaintively. "There, there, my sweet," she soothed.

Stephanie's voice was thoughtful. "It must have affected Lili deeply, seeing her sister turning old so quickly."

"*Igen, igen.* That it did." The old lady shook her head pityingly.

"And then to think that that tragedy had to be compounded by yet more tragedy!"

"You mean the railroad disaster."

"It occurred north of here, at a bend in the Danube." Madame Balász nodded and made sympathetic clucking noises with her tongue. "It proves one must never underestimate gypsy curses."

"Why?" Stephanie stared intently at her. "Was there a curse on the Bielfeld family?"

"*Nem tudom.* Who can tell? But shortly before Liselotte's death, Lili took her to see a gypsy whose hands were said to have healing powers. This was after all the doctors and specialists had given up, you must understand. They asked me to go with them, and I did. Louisette stayed at home. She was always a little superstitious, and gypsies frightened her. Also, Louisette was one of those who did not want to see what lay in her future. Some more wine?"

"No, thank you, I still have some."

Madame Balász asked: "Have you ever had your fortune read?"

"No. Once or twice I was tempted, but in the end I decided against it."

Madame narrowed her eyes and it was like two spiders drawing their legs together. "Perhaps it is just as well. Knowing too much can be as dangerous as knowing too little." She nodded.

"Now, about this gypsy with the healing powers. She was Romanian; all the very best gypsies are, you know. A lovely woman, with beautiful features. I could instantly tell she could see into the future. 'You will be alone with one other who is not here,' she told Lili. Those were her precise words: 'You will be alone with one other . . . and as for you,' she told Liselotte, 'I cannot heal you, nor can anyone else. But take heart, child. Soon you will need suffer no more. You shall pass to the other side, where everything and everyone are beautiful.' " Madame Balász's eyes gleamed darkly. "And she was right, wasn't she?"

Stephanie blinked.

"The train wreck!" Madame Balász hissed. "Do you not see? It occurred the following week!"

"Oh. Yes, I . . . I do see." Stephanie felt strangely disquieted. All this disturbing talk of vampires and geromorphs, healers and curses, had suddenly ceased to be fascinating. The deceptively serene Danube view, the lengthening afternoon shadows, and the very fact that she was in Eastern Europe, land of strange myths and stranger legends . . . It was as if she were mired in a dream which had taken a turn she didn't much care for—but was unable to wake up from.

"Now for the most surprising part. Do you know who the gypsy was truly drawn to? I myself was flabbergasted."

"Who?" Stephanie felt it only polite to ask.

"Not poor Liselotte, which is why we had gone to see her in the first place. *Nem.* It was to *Lili* that the gypsy gravitated! I remember she told her, 'I know your wish is to live forever.' Imagine! She had never even *met* Lili. Nor had she ever laid eyes on any one of us. It was truly frightening. I wanted to flee, but despite myself, I was fascinated. And then I heard her tell Lili: 'The secret you search for exists, and if anyone finds it, it shall be you. Then, for years, you may bloom with the beauty of everlasting youth. But beware, my child! Beware! In the end, all living things must rest at peace.' Such cryptic words! For the longest time, I myself did not understand what she was telling Lili. But then, years later, I was enlightened by what I saw. You see, my own eyes could not deceive me."

"If you'll pardon my saying so," Stephanie interrupted politely, "I'm slightly confused."

"I shall explain." With a flutter, a sparrow landed on the balcony next door and began chirping its little heart out. On Madame's lap, Aïda's sleepy yellow eyes opened, but the regal cat remained quiet as its mistress's gloved hand continued to stroke gently, gently . . .

"Ah! Just listen!" The old lady tilted her head and smiled. "Do you hear how marvelously it sings? How joyful it is to be alive?"

"Yes. It's quite beautiful."

"The bird reminds me: Lili and I, though we studied separately, had the same teacher. Did you know that?"

"You mean, Madame Szekely?"

"*Igen.*" Madame Balász nodded. "Also, we attended the Franz Liszt Academy together. I remember one day in particular. Madame Szekely had arranged for Lili and me to sing together. Do you know 'Le Rossignol'? 'The Nightingale,' by Delibes?"

Stephanie shook her head.

"A pity it is not performed more often: it is achingly beautiful. Almost impossible to sing. You see, it calls for just three instruments: flute, piano, and mezzo-soprano. All three must be virtuosos, you understand: the song demands it. On this occasion, we had only the piano, which is the way Madame Szekely had planned it. I sang the vocal part, and Lili sang the part of the flute—without words, naturally, just vocal intonations. It was exquisite. *Exquisite!* More heartrending than that sparrow . . ."

The little bird flew off and Madame sang a few lines, her voice surprisingly strong, rising and trilling and swooping delicately, and Stephanie understood once and for all that a voice was truly an instrument. Then the old lady let the song trail off and fell silent, smiling at some pleasant distant memories in her past.

Stephanie said: "You were going to explain what the gypsy meant when she spoke so mysteriously to Lili."

"Very well." Madame Balász sighed, clearly annoyed at being jerked so abruptly from her reveries. "After Lili left Budapest, it was quite some years before we saw each other again. But then, of course, I was under contract to the Staatsoper here, while she was quite famous around the world. I remember when she returned—Budapest was the last stop of her world tour. She was to star in several operas. *Tosca, Madama Butterfly, Der Rosenkavalier*—I believe they were—as well as to give some solo performances. Having been if not exactly old friends, then at least good acquaintances, she insisted I get a large role in each of the operas. I was, naturally, honored, delighted, and extremely grateful—for nothing, as it turned out! Lili left here without singing a single note in public. Her revenge upon Budapest for her inauspicious beginnings here, I suspect. But that is another story entirely. The point I am making, Ms. Smith, is that I *knew* Lili. Do you understand? *I . . . knew . . . her!* And, we were the *same* age and, of course, *looked* the same age!" She paused and eyed Stephanie speculatively. "Do you follow me?"

"I . . . think so," Stephanie said slowly, although she wondered where in heaven this could be leading.

"I have a photograph from back then. It is inside"—Madame Balász gestured fluidly toward the open French doors—"atop the Bösendorfer."

"The large one," Stephanie asked, "where you are both wearing powdered white wigs and gowns?"

"*Igen.* You saw it, then. It was taken during dress rehearsals, shortly before Lili canceled all the performances and left." Madame Balász still stroked Aïda, each movement of her hand identical to the last, and her eyes seemed to have glazed over with memories. "It was many years before my path crossed Lili's again. The next and last time was during a trip I took to London, not long before her death. Nineteen forty-nine, I think it was. *Igen.* Nineteen forty-nine. She was Lady Hughes-Coxe then, and gave a small *intime* dinner party for me. Her husband was there. And Maria Callas came with her husband, the little Italian doctor."

"Meneghini . . ."

"*Igen.* Dr. Meneghini. Go inside. On the piano is a small Fabergé frame. It is in the back of the others. You cannot miss it: the frame is of raspberry enamel. Bring it out here."

Stephanie put down her wineglass, went inside, and found the exquisite frame where Madame Balász said it would be. She first blew and then wiped the coat of dust off it, went back outside, and held it out.

The old lady shook her head. "*Nem,*" she said. "I am quite familiar with it. Go ahead. You. *You* look at it!"

Something in her tone caused Stephanie to hesitate, made the fine downy hairs on her arms and at the nape of her neck rise, as though they were the hackles of a threatened cat.

"Well?" Madame demanded impatiently. "What are you waiting for? Look. *Look!*"

Stephanie held the photo up to the light. It was black-and-white, faded and cracked. It was easy to date it by the wide-shouldered fashions of the time. There, on the left, was Madame Balász at about age forty. And beside her—an incredulous expression came over Stephanie's face—a beautiful young Lili Schneider, who looked twenty-nine or thirty at most.

"Well?" Madame Balász demanded in a sibilant whisper. "Do you see?"

"Yes, but some people age differently."

"Now you have closed your mind." Madame Balász sighed with disappointment. "We were born the same year, Lili and I. She was Gemini, I am Capricorn. Yes, Ms. Smith." The old lady sat abruptly forward, her eyes bulging like the bloated abdomens of black widow spiders. *"Both of us were the exact same age when this picture was taken!* Both *of us were thirty-nine!"*

"But . . . what about makeup . . . skin care . . . the different ways people age?"

"You are making excuses. I do not see why. Tell me, Ms. Smith. Don't I *look* thirty-nine in the picture?"

"Y-yes . . ." Stephanie admitted cautiously.

"And Lili? How old does she look?"

"Twenty-nine . . . no more than thirty."

"Exactly!" The wide-open spidery lashes were perfectly still. "You see, Ms. Smith, the beautiful gypsy was right, wasn't she? Lili *had* found the fountain of youth. What else could have accounted for it? And why else, before the dinner guests arrived on the day this picture was taken, did Lili *beg* me not to let anyone know that we were the same age? Mmm? Of course you know why. Even if you do not want to admit it. Because she was *frightened* that people would discover her secret and demand to share it!"

Stephanie stared down at the sluggish river on which a long, low white excursion steamer, all giant black windows, glided soundlessly downstream, ugly as a stretch limousine. For a moment she shut her eyes. For all the normalcy of the scene, things were *not* normal, were far, far from normal. Or so the old lady claimed. Yet there *had* to be a simple, innocent, *logical* explanation for the photograph. Yes. Cosmetic surgery, at the time still in its infancy . . . experimental sheep cell injections . . . something like that. Yes.

Because, believing Lili Schneider to be alive, perhaps well preserved but definitely an old, *old* woman could be . . . yes, logically and easily explained; someone else might have burned to death in her house, and that person might be buried in her tomb. But that Lili, still alive, could, at age eighty-three, still be a beautiful *young* woman even today? No. Logic, common sense, even science defied the very idea. There *was* no fountain of youth. It was a fairy tale, a legend, a castle in the air.

The thought persisted: *But what if it does exist . . . ?*

Straightening her spine, Stephanie turned to the old lady. "Madame Balász," she asked softly, "after your trip to England. Did you ever see Lili again?"

Madame Balász shook her head. "*Nem.* The following year was that terrible fire. A horrendous tragedy."

"And you are certain that Lili died in it?"

"Of course she died in it! Lili was only human. Why do you ask?" The false lashes blinked rapidly.

Stephanie frowned. "Then you don't believe there's a possibility, however remote, that she's still alive somewhere?"

"Lili? Of course not! How would such a thing be possible?"

"Well, perhaps she wasn't in the house when the fire broke out," Stephanie suggested.

"She had to have been. True, she was burned beyond recognition, but she died. Her dental charts proved it. And the funeral was a worldwide event."

"I wonder . . ." Stephanie murmured half to herself.

"But what are you saying?" The old lady's voice quavered. "That Lili did *not* burn to death?"

"I really don't know," Stephanie said slowly. "Somebody died, that much is clear. But if Lili was frightened because her secret—if it indeed existed—"

"It *did!*" Madame Balász insisted. "I saw the results with my own two eyes!"

"Then she surely knew that since she didn't age like her contemporaries, word of her perpetual youth would soon leak out. Think about it. If she'd *really* wanted to guard it, wouldn't she have *had* to disappear and go into hiding?"

Madame Balász blanched. "Stop this at once!" she demanded, her voice rising shrilly. "You are frightening me! Lili is dead and buried. Do you hear? Dead . . . and . . . buried!"

"But is she?" Stephanie whispered.

"Why can you not let her rest in peace? Was her life not tragic enough without you trying to resurrect her ghost? Now please. You have outstayed your welcome. Leave, Ms. Smith, and do not return. Leave Lili in peace! Leave *me* in peace! Go. *Go!*"

Stephanie didn't move. "If she did indeed die," she asked softly, "what happened to her secret?"

Madame Balász's polite façade suddenly cracked and all her pent-up rage for Lili blazed through. "She took it to her grave with her, the bitch!" she spewed, spittle flying. "What do you think happened to it?"

Stephanie was taken aback by the woman's violent reaction. "You're . . . sure?"

"Of course I'm sure!" The thick starry lashes narrowed. "Oh, how I *begged* her to share her secret with me—for old time's sake, for money— anything she wanted! *Anything!* But did she? Oh, no! She refused me! *Refused!* She had to keep it for herself, that stingy Nazi wretch! And look at me now! Ancient! Decrepit!"

Weeping openly, the old lady yanked off her red gloves and tossed them wearily aside. Tears streamed down her face as she slid the rubber band out from under her chin and pulled off the wig. Her stretched features suddenly sagged; flesh hung in folds like wattles. Her head had but a few meager wisps of white hair.

She raised her ancient hands. "Look at me!" she moaned. "Oh, look at me, look at me! I'm hideous! *Old!* On death's very doorstep! And to think I could still have had the first flush of youth! If Lili had only *shared* her secret, I'd still have my entire life ahead of me!"

Stephanie, transfixed, could only stare. It was frightening but fascinating, the woman's transformation. Without the props, all the aggressive style and remarkable chic were gone; left in their place was the brittle shell of just another old woman with incongruous, clownish false eyelashes. *Or an aged drag queen,* Stephanie thought.

After a moment, Madame Balász became aware of Stephanie's gaze. She raised her head, body taut, a viper about to strike.

"*Out!*" she shrieked suddenly in such a piercing banshee screech that Aïda leapt off her lap and fled inside with Othello—two howling, blurry black streaks seeking escape.

*Like me,* Stephanie thought, wishing she was already gone. She got to her feet and stood there, her jaw tightening, about to say something. Then she thought better of it, turned on her heel, and marched quickly inside. She started to set the photograph back down on the piano, but on impulse, she slipped it inside her purse. *I'm not stealing it,* she told herself. *I'm merely borrowing it. Who knows? It might come in handy.* Then she looked back out.

On the balcony, Madame Balász was once again singing Delibes's "Nightingale," but instead of her voice rising joyfully and soaring freely, there was something fettered about it: something hauntingly sad, excruciatingly dirgelike. And as she sang, the weeping old woman, hands clasped in her lap, was still twisting her torso from side to side, the song rising to a lament.

Yes, she was just another very old, old woman. Even her voice sounded weak now. Ancient, strained, scratchy, cracked.

Before she let herself quietly out, Stephanie looked over her shoulder one last time. At a shriveled, slowly dying nightingale. Practicing its swan song.

Madame knew nothing, that much was clear.

"Strike one," Stephanie said softly to herself.

# 7

*Salzburg, Austria · Budapest, Hungary*

When Holly Fischer landed at the Salzburg airport, the hotel's car and driver were already waiting for her. The car was a big blue Mercedes and the driver was a blond young man named Rolf. He deposited her luggage in the trunk, and they were soon underway.

Rolf explained why he wouldn't be able to drive her right up to the hotel entrance. "The Goldener Hirsch hotel is located in the old town," he said, in an Arnold Schwarzenegger voice, "in a section which is strictly pedestrian. All vehicular traffic is forbidden. We will have to park in one of the Festival Hall parking garages and make the rest of the way on foot."

"That's fine," Holly Fischer told him, and turned back to the view outside the tinted glass: purple mountains, the city gathered around the foot of the hill atop which the ancient fortress hulked broodingly, the shallow Salzach River spanned with bridges, the domes and spires of baroque churches. Salzburg. Birthplace of Mozart and site of the world-renowned Glockenspiel and the even more renowned music festival.

Holly Fischer wore her blond hair severely pulled back, and had on a rust-colored, belted silk jacquard dress and a matching Mad Hatter's hat—both from Christian Lacroix—and rust-red Ferragamo sling-back heels. From the rearview mirror, Rolf calculated that she had at least twelve thousand dollars on her back; her Vuitton purse and three Vuitton suitcases, he reckoned, had surely set her back another four thousand dollars—and *Gott* alone only knew how many tens—perhaps even hundreds—of thousands of dollars in clothes and jewels she had packed.

After parking the car in the garage, he whipped the three suitcases out of the trunk and led the way.

The Goldener Hirsch hotel had been going strong for eight hundred years. Ideally located between the Getreidegasse, Mozart's birthplace and now a crowded pedestrian street of whimsically crooked houses with gilded, wrought-iron shop signs hanging over the entrances of expensive boutiques, and the Festival Hall, where the annual world-famous Salzburger Festivals are held, it is enchanting, elegant, and picturesque.

"If you need a car and chauffeur during your stay, I would be delighted to be of service," Rolf told her as he surrendered her luggage to a hotel porter. "Just ask for me. Rolf." Glancing around, he lowered his voice discreetly. "And if you ... er ... need anything ... anything at all ..." He grinned knowingly, leaving the hint dangling.

"Thank you, I'll keep that in mind." Then, dismissing him with a chilly smile, she swept out of his life and into the hotel.

It was as though she'd stepped backward in time—or had mistakenly wandered onstage during the production of an operetta. All that was missing was the singing. For not only did the lobby *look* like a stage set, but the staff even *dressed* accordingly—costumed entirely in local loden. The overall atmosphere was, however, charming and luxurious, without being cloyingly sweet or hopelessly provincial.

The desk clerk took one look at her and fell all over himself to be helpful. Within minutes, Stephanie was ensconced in the privacy of her suite.

The first thing she did after taking off the Mad Hatter's hat, kicking off her shoes, and unpacking was to place a local telephone call. That done, she rang the front desk. "This is Miss Fischer," she began, "in suite—"

"*Ja, gnädiges Fräulein?*" the concierge inquired smoothly. "I hope everysink ist in order?"

"Oh, yes," Stephanie assured him. "But I need your help. I'd like a car and driver to take me to St. Wolfgang tomorrow." She paused and added: "I'm to see Herr Detlef von Ohlendorf."

There was a gasp of awe, a momentary silence, and then a gush of spontaneous enthusiasm. "Certainly, *gnädiges Fräulein!* Ve are honored to be of service to anyone who visits our esteemed maestro!"

"You had a marvelous driver pick me up from the airport this afternoon. Rolf, I believe his name was?"

"Rolf Schalk. *Ja.* You vould like him again, *gnädiges Fräulein?*"

"Well ... n-nooooo," Stephanie said slowly.

"Vas there a problem?"

"On the contrary. I was quite impressed with him. It's just that I won't be here for very long, so I'd like to take the opportunity to meet all the Austrians I can."

"A vise decision, to be sure! I quite understand, *gnädiges Fräulein!* Vhen would you like the car?"

"I am sorry, sir," sniffed the assistant manager of the Gellert Hotel in Budapest. "It is absolutely forbidden to give out the information you request. Our guests demand the strictest confidentiality."

"But this is a special circumstance!" the new arrival insisted.

"I am sorry. I cannot make any exceptions." The assistant manager buried his nose in the guest book.

"In that case," the young man said, "I would like to speak to the manager, please." The words were polite and softly spoken, but there was no mistaking the threatening undertone.

The assistant manager sighed and shut the ledger. "As you wish." He sniffed disdainfully and glided off.

The new arrival waited, a twitching muscle in his eyelid the sole indication of his impatience. After some minutes, the assistant manager appeared with an older man. He was a sleek, middle-aged Hungarian with a balding pate and a subdued, self-important presence.

"I am the managing director." The man's manner was deferential but not unctuous. "How may I be of assistance?"

"I'm supposed to meet a friend here, and I've been told she checked out."

"Ah." The manager clasped his hands in front of him. "And who, sir," he inquired concernedly, "might that be?"

"A Ms. Smith. Ms. Amanda Smith?"

"A lovely young lady!"

"Then you remember her?"

The manager bristled. "A guest as beautiful and polite as Ms. Smith is always fondly remembered," he declared staunchly. "We would treasure her as a regular guest."

"Good. Then I take it you can help me?"

The manager eyed the questioner warily. "That, sir," he said carefully, "would depend upon the . . . ah . . . kind of help you require."

"I'd like to know where Ms. Smith went after she checked out. You see, she was supposed to meet me here. Surely she must have left me a letter? Or at least a note?"

"I am sorry to say that she has left neither. Perhaps she . . . forgot?"

"Then it's imperative I find her."

The manager sighed painfully. "Regrettably, our policy does not allow us to give out that kind of information."

"Look, it's very important. I really do have to find her!"

"Presumably it is a matter of life and death," the manager said with a little smile.

"As a matter of fact, yes. It is. Her father is very ill, and I didn't want to send a cable or have to tell her over the telephone."

The manager's smile disappeared and he sucked in his cheeks. "I see," he said gravely. "In that case, sir, I think I can make an exception. But I am not sure it will help you."

"I'd appreciate anything."

"Very well. She said she was checking out to stay with some friends here in Budapest."

"Friends? Here? Did she say who?"

A sad shake of the balding head. "Unfortunately, sir, she did not. She did, however, ask us to arrange an airline reservation for another friend of hers."

"Oh?" And he thought wryly: *Amanda Smith seems to have no end of friends.* "You wouldn't happen to remember his name, by any chance? Perhaps if I can catch up with him—"

"It is not a he, sir, but a she. Perhaps you even know her. A Miss Holly Fischer, I believe her name was."

"Holly . . . Holly . . . oh, I know! She and Amanda went to school together. And where did Miss . . . er . . . Holly wish to fly?"

"To Salzburg, sir. I hope this information will be of some assistance?"

"Undoubtedly it will. I can't thank you enough."

Two and a half hours later, he was onboard a Malem jet for the hop to Vienna, where he'd catch a connecting AUA flight to Salzburg.

Not surprisingly, he was in an uncommonly good mood. *And why shouldn't I be?* he asked himself. *For all her efforts, she's leaving a trail a blind man could follow.*

Which, he thought smugly, was exactly the way he liked to track somebody. Nice and easy . . .

## 8

*In* the morning, she was jarred awake by the simultaneous ringing of the travel alarm clock and the telephone. Stephanie punched off the alarm and fumbled with the phone.

" 'Lo?" she mumbled sleepily.

"Really, Girlie." It was Sammy Kafka. "It's all I can do to keep up with these aliases of yours—"

"Uncle Sammy! Do you realize what time it is?"

"Nine o'clock Central European, three A.M. Eastern Standard." He chuckled. "Rise 'n' shine, Fräulein Fischer!"

"How can anyone be cheerful at this ungodly hour?" she growled.

"If you like, I can call you back? Give you time to order from room service?"

"No. No," she sighed, "Fräulein's awake now." She tossed the pillow away and sat up groggily.

"So tell me, Girlie. How did things go on the Eastern front?"

Instantly she flashed upon Madame Balász, the cats, and the strange conversation on the balcony overlooking the Danube.

"Would you believe, strangely?"

"Mmm. Yes, as a matter of fact, I would."

"But here's the kicker, Uncle Sammy. Assuming that Lili Schneider really is alive, according to Madame Balász we may—and I stress the word *may*—not be looking for an old lady."

"Say that again?"

"According to the Madwoman of Budapest, Lili found the fountain of youth sometime back in the forties."

There was silence on the other end.

"Also," Stephanie said, "Balász hates Lili with a passion for not sharing the formula with her." She paused and added quietly, "You know, she really had me believing it exists."

"Let things fall into place," he suggested. "Try to keep an open mind."

"Believe me, I'm trying."

"By the way, you know how I never finish reading the newspaper, and when I finally get to it, I always read last week's news—or the week's before?"

"Y-yes?" she asked cautiously.

"Remember that woman you told me about, Vinette Jones? The one who called you?"

"What about her?"

"If it's the same Vinette Jones, she died the same night she called you."

"*What!*" Stephanie was sitting up straight now. "What happened?"

"An apparent intravenous drug overdose."

"Oh, Jesus. She sounded straight as an arrow to me."

"Well, I'm just telling you what the newspapers reported. I called the police and they said the same thing."

She felt ripples of fear, like a chill breeze, crawling up and down her spine. Her voice was shaky and hushed. "Uncle Sammy? Do you think it's possible that someone shot her up? Purposely? To kill her, I mean?"

He remained silent.

"Because I remember . . . while I was holding? She—she cried out! And then, before the phone on her end was hung up, I could swear somebody different was on the line. The . . . the breathing just didn't sound like hers!"

Sammy sighed. "Who knows, Girlie, who knows? All I can say is: be careful. Very careful!"

"You know, Uncle Sammy, Vinette Jones told me she met Grandpa at the D.C. branch of CRY—you know, Children's Relief Year-Round? The one with the Godparents program?"

"Yes?"

"Well, Ms. Jones said his research had brought him there, just as her missing baby had brought her. And yet there's nothing in Grandpa's manuscript about CRY, nor is there a mention of it in his notes. Believe me, I would have caught it. But if his research took him down there, there's nothing to indicate why."

"Perhaps," said Sammy, "his visit there had nothing to do with the Schneider biography."

"It had to have. You know what a one-track mind he had." She paused. "Ms. Jones mentioned someone who works at the New York CRY headquarters. What *is* his name? Something like the title of that new opera."

"Klinghoffer?"

"No. Kleinfelder. Could you give him a call and find out what he knows?"

"With pleasure, Girlie. Sherlock here will get on it right away," he promised.

"Well," she said, "I'd better get up and start making movements. At noon's my interview with the musical Führer of the Third Reich."

The three-story, steep-roofed chalet commanded a scenic hilltop above the picturesque village of St. Wolfgang and the Wolfgang See, a placid, deep blue Alpine lake. The chalet's enviable location aside, it seemed to have been positioned expressly to flaunt its superiority, as though rising above all else. There were four cars parked in the gravel driveway—two dark blue Mercedes sedans, a black BMW, and a white Opel stationwagon.

As she ducked out of her hired car, Stephanie couldn't help but show her surprise. The house, while large, was surprisingly modest for a man whose recordings sold in the hundreds of millions of copies, and who enjoyed a ballpark income of six to seven million dollars a year from record sales and conducting fees. She had expected something far grander— something more along the lines of a renovated *Schloss*. Instead, Detlef von Ohlendorf's chalet, with its geranium-laden windowboxes and two tiers of wooden fretwork balconies, was quaintly beautiful.

"Yodel-oh-hee-hee," Stephanie said under her breath as she clipped smartly along the geranium-lined flagstones to the front door.

Everything about her was brisk and efficient—she had dressed to convey the businesslike air of a stylish but successful magazine writer, and was wearing a nubby, wide-lapeled colorful tweed suit, ocher silk blouse, and a pair of half-glasses on the tip of her nose. Her hair was pulled back in a kind of Bavarian twist—a bow to the locale—and she carried a serious brown leather briefcase and a notebook. She'd stuck a gold pen above her right ear.

The unsmiling, unblinking woman who answered the door had a long face and hard blue eyes. A mass of writhing blond coils was wrapped around her head like thick sausages—or well-fed snakes. She had a jutting chin with a large mole on it, from which sprouted a single long hair, and she wore a dirndl with a lace-edged sweetheart neckline and a tight, red-patterned bodice which pushed up her breasts into mighty mounds.

She didn't so much look at Stephanie as case her, and Stephanie returned the look boldly. "My name is Holly Fischer," she said in English. "I'm scheduled to interview Herr von Ohlendorf?"

"Ah. Fräulein Fischer. We talked on the telephone. I am Frau Ludwig." The woman's English was thickly accented but fluent, her smile brief and unwelcoming. She opened the door further and motioned Stephanie inside. "Please come in. Maestro is expecting you."

Frau Ludwig led Stephanie briskly down a long pine-paneled hallway to the back of the house, where she stopped at a glass-paned door. Fingers curled around the door handle, she turned to Stephanie. "As I told you on the telephone, Fräulein Fischer, Maestro is a very busy man. You will have to make it short. A half hour, that is all he can spare. *Ja?*"

Frau Ludwig opened the door, and they stepped out onto an enormous stone-flagged terrace. Stephanie gasped at the breathtaking view—the tiny village and the sapphire blue of the lake below, and the pine-covered green mountains rising high all around. There were white tables and chairs with yellow sunshades, and unoccupied cushioned lounges.

"There is Maestro!" Frau Ludwig said unnecessarily.

Old photographs of Detlef von Ohlendorf invariably showed a thin, tall, stern man with strong cheekbones, pale hair, and an intense authoritarian air. Now, confronted with him in person, she was slightly amazed by his actual physical presence, for like many a living legend, he was much smaller in reality than his pictures or reputation had led her to believe. Only five feet eight inches tall, he nevertheless managed to exude a force field of electrifying energy which, combined with his well-preserved looks, made him seem far younger than his eighty-three years. His face was still virilely handsome, his posture schoolboy straight, and he had about him that distinguished aura of command only great wealth and power can bestow.

"Ah!" he exclaimed, stepping forward to meet her halfway. "You must be Fräulein Fischer." He swooped up Stephanie's hand and raised her fingertips gallantly to his lips, his sharp, pale blue eyes openly appraising.

"It is good of you to see me, Maestro," Stephanie murmured.

"Ah, but surely the pleasure is mine. It is not every day I meet such a beautiful young woman!"

She laughed at his obvious flirting. His hand lingered on hers, and she could feel his eyes shamelessly undressing her. After an awkward moment, she cleared her throat and took a step backward.

"Please," he said, letting go of her hand. "Let us sit." And placing a hand under Stephanie's elbow, he guided her toward the nearest table with the same famous elegance with which he conducted the great orchestras of the world. After he pulled out a cushioned chair and she was seated, he sat down across from her.

Too late, she realized that she had already been cleverly manipulated—and to her severe disadvantage. For he had seated her so that she faced directly into the sun. Any nuance of expression she might have hoped to catch would be lost. She reminded herself to take care.

"Could I offer you a cup of coffee?" he inquired pleasantly, ever the charming host.

"Thank you, yes," Stephanie said. She was trying hard not to squint against the sun's glare.

He turned to Frau Ludwig. "Two coffees, Frau Ludwig."

"Yes, Maestro. At once." She turned and marched efficiently back into the house.

With deliberate slowness, Detlef von Ohlendorf casually crossed his legs. "Now then, Fräulein," he suggested gently, velvet gloves hiding iron fists. "Shall we begin?"

The coffee was rich and strong and made from freshly ground beans. Stephanie took hers black and it tasted, she reflected, more like a good rich Turkish brew than anything remotely Viennese. She set her cup down, dabbed her lips with a small square linen napkin. The most famous conductor in the world was still sipping delicately from his china cup, a man rendered featureless by the corona of blinding glare. On the table between them, the plate of assorted pastries Frau Ludwig had brought out with the coffee remained untouched. Only a determined fly, attracted by the sticky glaze of sugar on the tiny *Zwetschkenflecken,* and the sweet filling of the slices of *Mohnstrudel,* showed a sweet tooth.

"The last time I saw Lili," he said, "was in nineteen forty-nine." His cup clinked into his saucer.

"You're certain?" Stephanie asked.

"Of course I'm certain. Lili was Lady Hughes-Coxe by then, and her husband was very powerful. You see, Fräulein Fischer, after the war, the Allies forbade me to conduct for an indefinite period of time. It was Sir Kenneth who arranged things with them and gave me my first postwar job. That was in nineteen forty-seven." He paused. "It would be hard not to remember everything about Sir Kenneth and Lili. I owe them everything I enjoy today. The power. The prestige. The wealth." He gestured around. "Everything. I am totally beholden to them."

"Beholden enough," she asked softly, "to help Lili disappear?"

"I beg your pardon? I'm afraid I do not grasp your meaning, Fräulein."

"Then you don't believe she's still alive, or that her death was faked?"

His cup and saucer rattled as he set them down. He sat forward and leaned across the table.

"Just what are you suggesting, Fräulein?" he demanded softly.

"I'm not suggesting anything. I'm merely asking whether you have had any contact with Lili Schneider after nineteen forty-nine, that's all."

He folded his arms on the table. She could hear his breathing. It sounded suddenly quick and heavy.

"Are you saying . . . no, you cannot be. Lili is dead and buried. I attended her funeral. Why are you hinting that she is still alive?"

"Because I have come across some evidence—"

"Evidence!" he interrupted, snorting derisively and throwing up his hands. "My God! Don't you realize I would be the first to know it if she *were* still alive? Don't you understand that Lili and I were the best of friends? That the way we worked together made us closer than *lovers?*" He sat back, staring at her. "Neither of us ever did anything without the other's approval, Fräulein. Ever! And you sit there and talk of *evidence?*"

Stephanie did not reply. She put down her pen and notebook and reached for her briefcase. Swinging it onto her lap, she unlatched it and took out a gray portable cassette recorder.

"Please, Fräulein." He waved it away. "I believe it was understood that this interview was not to be recorded."

"And I respect your request, Maestro," she assured him quickly. "I only want you to listen to my evidence."

"Very well." He nodded.

She could feel his condescending smile, and flushed. Then she poised her finger on the PLAY button and punched it.

First there was silence; then that was followed by faint hisses and crackles. They gave way to undefinable voices in the background, and then the first gentle notes of the piano began smoothly. After six seconds, Stephanie pressed the STOP button.

Her voice was soft. "Well, Maestro? Do you recognize the pianist?"

"Yes, yes," he said with irritation. "Guberoff. It has to be: the style is his. If you are acquainted with it, you can tell that he is having difficulty because of his arthritis."

"Bravo, Maestro!" she whispered.

"Fräulein, what is the point of all this?" he asked testily.

"You will see in a moment, I promise."

The lively gentle piano started up again. And suddenly, that hauntingly crystalline voice, pure as the driven snow, rang out powerfully:

*Was ist Silvia, saget an*
*Dass sie die weite Flur preist?*

"Lili?" von Ohlendorf whispered hoarsely. "Can it be?"

Stephanie watched the conductor closely. He was sitting rigidly now. She could well imagine the color draining from his face, could almost feel the wave of shock hitting him like a physical blow. But she was not prepared for what happened next.

His hand suddenly lashed out. All she could see was a blur, and then the recorder went flying off the table.

She tried to make a grab for it, but her reactions were too slow. It went crashing down to the flagstones, still continuing to play:

*—Dass ihr alles untertan.*
*Ist sie schön und gut dazu?*
*Reiz labt wie milde Kindheit ...*

He got to his feet so suddenly that his chair toppled over backward. "Stop it!" he whispered. "My God, stop it! Stop it stop it stop it!" He clapped his hands over his ears to drown out that heavenly voice.

Stephanie stared at him. "Is it?" she asked. *"Is it Lili?"*

*"Turn . . . the . . . verdamtes . . . zeug . . . off!"* he screamed.

Stephanie shrank back in her chair. Now that he had moved away from the sun she could see his face clearly—and it was frightening to behold. All flushed and contorted. Crimson with rage.

"You are demented!" he shouted. Then something within him snapped, and in a fit of wrath, he swung his foot back and brought it swiftly forward, kicking the recorder. It tumbled end-on-end across the flagstones like a football, but the Sony kept on playing, as if to provoke him further.

"She is dead!" The cords on his neck stood out like taut wires. *"Warum haben Sie*—why did you bring this trick tape to me? I demand that you tell me! Have I not suffered enough?" he raged maniacally. "Must you raise the dead, also? It is part of . . . of . . ." Suddenly his eyes bulged even further and he let out a strangled cry. Like a marionette whose wires had gone slack, he took one staggering step backward, and then another, and another. His pale, elegant hands jerked to his throat, the index fingers and thumbs working desperately to loosen the collar.

*"Heiss!"* he whispered in horror. *"Mir . . . ist . . . es . . . so . . . heiss!"*

"Maestro!" Stephanie jumped to her feet.

And all the while, the incredibly sweet song and its piano accompaniment continued to issue forth from the recorder, mockingly beautiful and serene, as though nothing at all untoward was happening.

Von Ohlendorf suddenly pitched forward and Stephanie quickly caught him. Gently, she lowered him down to the cool flagstones. His face was contorted with what seemed an unendurable effort.

*Oh God! He's dying, dying . . .* "Frau Ludwig!" Stephanie yelled. Then, turning back to the old conductor, she said gently, "It's all right, you're going to be fine." She loosened his collar while she spoke. "There," she soothed, "that's better, isn't it?"

A door crashed, then swift clacking footsteps approached in a run. "Maestro!" Frau Ludwig cried. *"Ach Du lieber Gott!"* She dropped to her knees on the other side of the prone man and stared at Stephanie. "It must be his angina!" she said. "The medicine! Quickly! It is in one of his pockets!"

They searched his clothes until Stephanie found the little container of nitroglycerine in an inside breast pocket. "Is this it?"

Frau Ludwig snatched it from her. She opened it with shaking hands, extracted a tiny pill, and placed it under his tongue.

*"Es ist schon gut,* Maestro," she murmured to the gasping man, cradling his head in her hands as if he were a child in need of comfort.

*God, he can't die!* Stephanie thought. *I'll never forgive myself if he does.*

"Look! he is calming down already." Frau Ludwig heaved a sigh of relief and sketched a quick sign of the cross with her thumb. *"Gott sei*

*Dank!"* she said fervently. Then, obviously shielding the old man's head with her arm, she turned slowly to Stephanie. "What did you say to make him so upset?"

Stephanie could feel her face breaking out in a prickly flush. "I . . . we . . . just talked . . ." she supplied lamely.

*"Er hat ein schwaches Herz*—a weak heart."

"I . . . didn't know . . ."

"You didn't know?" Now that it looked as if he might pull through, Frau Ludwig's anxiety converted itself into rage. Her face was hard, glazed, accusing. "You nearly killed him!" she hissed from between her teeth.

"We . . . were just talking about the past," Stephanie said tightly. "And then I put on that tape—"

But Frau Ludwig's mind was already made up. "You are a trouble-maker!" she decreed triumphantly. "I knew it from the first instant I set eyes on you!" Her face had a crimson shine to it. "Well, you have made your trouble. You can be happy and go home. Just leave poor Maestro in peace!"

Stephanie knew it was pointless to argue with this ogre of a woman, and she watched in disturbed fascination as Frau Ludwig lovingly moved von Ohlendorf's head to her lap.

"Well?" Frau Ludwig demanded. "Do you intend to stay here forever? Go! *Verschwinden Sie!"*

Stephanie got to her feet and looked down at her. "Despite what you may wish to think," she said with supreme dignity, "I did not come here to make him ill."

"No? Well—you almost succeeded in murdering him!"

That said, Frau Ludwig dismissed Stephanie's presence and luxuriated in giving the old man all the benefit of her unrequited love. She rocked his head gently in her arms.

*"Ist schon gut,* Maestro," she cooed softly in a singsong nursery voice. *"Sie geht schon weg.* She is leaving . . ."

Stephanie gathered up her briefcase and notebook and walked over to where the cracked cassette recorder was hissing static. She picked it up, punched the OFF button, and cut around the side of the house to the parking lot. But before she turned the corner, she paused beneath the flower-laden fretwork balcony and turned her head to have one last look.

Frau Ludwig and her Maestro were still in the pietà pose—the very picture of worshipful suffering and love.

Stephanie nodded to herself. There was nothing more to be learned from him. "Strike two," she said to herself, and disappeared around the corner.

# 𝟫

*R*oom service brought her a steaming pot of coffee, two crescent rolls with butter and jam and, best of all, the *International Herald-Tribune*. Stephanie pulled open the curtains. The pale morning sunlight spilling across the carpet dispelled the remnants of last night's gloom.

Now, blowing on the cup of hot coffee she'd poured herself, she sat and sipped it slowly, catching up on the news.

She found it impossible to concentrate on reading, and frowned thoughtfully into space. Yesterday's telephone conversation with Sammy kept nagging at her.

It just didn't make sense. According to Uncle Sammy, Vinette Jones had died of a drug overdose. *Yet the woman I spoke to didn't sound at all like a junkie,* she thought.

Impatiently, troubledly, she got to her feet and paced the room. She clasped her hands in front of her, playing that old child's game with her fingers. Here's the church and here's the steeple. Open the door and see the—

People! The congregation! Men, women, children—babies.

*Babies!*

She unlaced her fingers and snapped them. *Now* she was cooking! Only, it wasn't babies. No. It had something to do with—

*Missing* babies!

Unconsciously, she paced even faster, her mind whirling like a dervish.

Vinette Jones had been searching for her baby—a baby the CRY orphanage in Washington, D.C. had ostensibly "lost"!

Excitement swelled Stephanie's chest to bursting, caused her blood to tingle with effervescence. She felt nearly manic with triumph. Eyes alight, she raked a hand through her hair as she strode back and forth along the length of the room like a tigress.

Vinette Jones had been searching for her baby.

Vinette Jones had been *murdered*. Not only that. She'd been *silenced!*

"Holy Moses!" Stephanie exclaimed, suddenly standing stock-still. As though to help her think, she pressed a thumb and index finger against her forehead.

But *why* had Vinette Jones been silenced? Because of the missing child? Or had the woman been shaking the bushes too hard?

She continued her rapid prowl across the room, every journalist's instinct telling her that with Vinette's death, at least, she'd hit the nail right on the head. No matter how she played it in her mind, she was unable to shoot it down. The scenario played, and played well.

Now all she needed was irrefutable proof—which was easier thought than done. Not to mention the two whoppers which were still waiting to be solved.

First: What on earth had directed her grandfather to CRY?

It was a question she'd been agonizing over ever since the night Vinette had telephoned, and she still hadn't been able to come up with a satisfactory answer. There had been nothing in her grandfather's notes about CRY, not so much as a word. Was it because whatever lead he had was still so fresh he hadn't even gotten a chance to write it down?

She wondered now: had he, like Vinette Jones, been silenced: and if so, for what? Discovering that Lili Schneider was still alive? Or for snooping around CRY?

Which led her to the second whopper of a question: *How were CRY and Lili Schneider connected?*

For in Stephanie's mind, they had to be. She, better than anyone, had known her grandfather's work habits. He had been a one-project-at-a-time man, doggedly pursuing whatever he was working on.

Somehow the diva and the nonprofit agency were connected. Had to be! But how? How and *why?*

The telephone rang, startling her. When she picked up, it was Sammy. "How's my Girlie?"

"To tell the truth, wide awake."

She carried the telephone over to the armchair, whipped the cord around, and plopped herself sideways into the seat, her legs dangling over one of the upholstered arms. "By the way," she said, "I got to thinking."

"About Vinette Jones?"

"Yes. For some reason, she just didn't strike me as the type to have shot herself up with dope."

"My thinking exactly, Girlie."

"So what I figure," Stephanie said, "is this. Vinette had to have been murdered . . . or silenced, if you will . . . for stirring up too much interest in her 'lost' baby."

"Could be," Sammy remarked carefully.

Stephanie got to her feet and carried the telephone over to the open window and looked out. Across the picturesque orange rooftops, distant church bells were pealing and sunshine bathed aged ocher walls. Below, in the narrow street, the tourists were already out in full force, armed with cameras and videocams and pocketfuls of currency.

"And, if you ask me," she continued, "in Vinette's case, drugs, instead of bullets, were the weapon of choice. Not only to kill her, but to throw the police off the scent so they wouldn't investigate her death as murder." She paused. "How am I doing?"

Sammy was momentarily silent. "Much as I hate to say it, Girlie," he said quietly, "I think you've got something there."

"Yes," she sighed. "The only trouble is, I can't for the life of me figure out how Lili Schneider, Grandpa, CRY, Vinette, and a missing baby are connected. But somehow, they've got to be! They've simply got to!" She paused and her voice dropped an octave. "I was thinking, Uncle Sammy . . ."

"Yes, my darling?"

The sun was starting to creep higher into the sky, and she walked away from the window and went back to her chair.

"It might not be such a bad idea if you had a talk with this Mr. Kleinfelder. The one Ms. Jones mentioned to me worked at CRY?"

"Really, Girlie, give me *some* credit!"

"Then you've already been to see him?" she asked excitedly.

"No, but I called him at work yesterday. He is, I was told, not in his office, nor is he expected to come in anytime in the near future."

"Oh, no!" She took a deep breath. "Oh, Christ no! Uncle Sammy, is he—?"

"No, Girlie," Sammy told her gently, "he is not dead. He *is*, however, in critical condition at St. Luke's."

She felt a wave of relief wash over her. "Then he will be all right?" she asked hopefully.

"According to his doctors, it's still too early to tell."

"What happened?"

"The poor man's in a coma, and he may never come out of it. That's the bottom line. He was apparently the victim of a particularly nasty hit-and-run."

The news was like a blow to her stomach. "Aw . . . *shit!*" she gloomed. "All right," she said wearily. "You might as well give it to me straight."

"You aren't going to like it," he warned.

"So tell me something I don't already know."

"Okay," he said, drawing a deep breath. "But it's not pleasant. According to the police report, it happened at Riverside Drive and West Eighty-first Street. Mr. Kleinfelder, on foot, had the green light and was in the middle of the street, walking north. Eyewitnesses agree that the driver of a delivery van not only seemed to be taking aim at him, but must have stepped on the gas. At the last moment, Kleinfelder turned, saw what was happening, and apparently threw his arms up in front of his face to protect himself. Not that it helped any. He was hit head-on and thrown about twenty feet. Then, brakes squealing, the van careened around the corner and took off."

"Did they catch the driver?" she asked, although in her heart she already knew the answer.

"No. But they found the van right away. It was parked in a No Stopping zone not two blocks from the scene of the crime. It had been reported stolen. If you ask me, it was a very neat and professional job."

The pain in Stephanie's gut burned like indigestion. *Another innocent victim silenced,* she thought, shivering. *And once again there's a CRY connection; Kleinfelder had worked for them. But what could he have discovered that had warranted his death?*

"I suppose," she muttered bitterly, "that unless Mr. Kleinfelder comes out of his coma, we have nothing to go on?"

Sammy sighed in reluctant agreement. "I'm afraid not, my darling." He paused and added, "Oh, and before I forget: one last thing. I saw in the papers—it was either in Liz or Suzy or William Norwich, I forget which column, exactly, but the de Veiga yacht? The *Chrysalis?* The one on which that pirated recording was allegedly made?"

"What about it?"

"It's arrived in Marbella with the reclusive Ernesto de Veiga and his equally reclusive mistress onboard. Eduardo, their son, is supposed to join them either today or tomorrow."

"Mmm," she said slowly, "I wonder how difficult it will be to crash that party."

"Girlie, you wouldn't!"

"You know me better than that, Uncle Sammy! Of course I would!"

# 10

*I*n Rome, the jet had barely crept to its final halt when Stephanie sprang to her feet from her strategic first-row seat. Even as the exit door was still being opened, she slid past the cabin attendant and strode hurriedly off onto the jetway, unclasping the flap of her shoulder bag as she walked. Her Holly Fischer passport in hand, she reached the nearest immigration booth and smiled.

The inspector took her passport and frowned as he compared the un-flattering mug shot with the challenging reality of the young woman poised breathlessly before him. Still frowning, he thumbed through the un-stamped pages. Then, with a total lack of expression, he put her opened passport down on the counter in front of him and allowed her to pass.

Enlisting the aid of a porter, she led the way in search of a bank of twenty-four-hour coin-operated luggage lockers. When she came across some, she tipped the porter and deposited the appropriate coins into the slot. She heaved two of the suitcases inside, locked the door, and pocketed the key.

Left with the bulkiest but lightest of the three Vuitton cases, she picked it up and followed the signs to the nearest ladies' room. Along the way, she stopped and checked the departure monitors. The next flight to Milan, she noted, would take off in just under an hour. If she hurried, and was lucky enough to get a seat, she would be able to make it in time.

Footsteps quickening, she headed into the washroom and locked her-self into a booth. She remained there for twenty minutes, but if anyone had been following her, she would have appeared to have vanished into thin air.

For the Stephanie Merlin who had entered the washroom was a head-turning, perfectly made-up blond with blue eyes, pink lips, and a sassy strut.

But the Stephanie who strode back out was a reasonably attractive, harried businesswoman with curly red hair and green eyes—the result of colored contact lenses and a wig—who wore a minimum of makeup and conveyed an air of brisk, authoritarian efficiency.

Stephanie had assumed the identity of Virginia Wesson. To complete the disguise, she now wore round gold-rimmed glasses and dark red lipstick, and she'd changed from the rust-colored jacquard dress into a severely tailored gray silk business suit.

Collecting her two suitcases from the luggage locker, she briskly clicked her way to the nearest ticket counter, purchased a round-trip ticket, and checked her three suitcases. Then she hurried to the gate, where her flight was already boarding.

Fifteen minutes later, the sleek Airbus A320 swept off the runway and climbed steeply into the sky. Jetting her north.

North to Milan, and a date with an unsuspecting pianist named Boris Guberoff.

His name was Manfred Löbl, and he was a stately man: Loden-suited, silver-haired, courtly. And so buffed he practically *shone*. He had his manicured hands clasped in front of him and was shaking his head regretfully at the man standing opposite him.

"It is a most unusual request, sir," he was saying. "Please, you must understand. Discretion is our watchword. Our clientele expects it—indeed, *demands* it! As managing director of the Goldener Hirsch, I am duty-bound to continue the tradition of maintaining our exacting standards."

The man with the black briefcase was silent.

"Of course, if Fräulein Fischer had specified that we were free to divulge her itinerary . . ." Herr Löbl parted his hands helplessly and sighed. "Unfortunately, she did not. Therefore, I must assume she wishes to safeguard her privacy. Much as I would like to help you, my hands are regrettably tied." He paused and then inquired. "You did say you are Fräulein Fischer's attorney?"

"No," the man said with a thin smile, "I'm one of her attorney's assistants." He fidgeted with his striped tie and looked morosely down at the pointed silk end. "I just don't know what to do." He looked back up and held Herr Löbl's gaze. "As I said, it's imperative I get Ms. Fischer's signature on these documents. The deadline is midnight tomorrow. If it's missed . . ." He lowered his voice. "I really shouldn't be telling you this, Mr. . . . ?"

"Löbl."

"Mr. Löbl. If the papers are not signed on time, not only will I be to blame, but Ms. Fischer stands to lose millions. *Millions!*" he repeated miserably.

Herr Löbl stood there, twined fingers in front of him, his face thoughtful. "Mmm. Well, we are not unreasonable people. In this one special instance, we can perhaps bend the rules a little, eh?"

"I'd really appreciate anything you can do, Mr. Löbl. Anything. You may well save me my job—and our most important client a fortune!"

"We always try to be of help," the managing director soothed, and gestured. "Please. If you will take a seat, I will go and find out what I can."

The man sat down in one of the upholstered chairs, put the briefcase on his lap, and watched Herr Löbl's dignified stride across the lobby. Then he waited, scanning the constantly shifting mosaic of quiet activity, the continuous comings and goings of well-heeled tourists and businessmen.

Presently he saw Herr Löbl approach and jumped to his feet and moved across the lobby to meet him halfway. "Did you manage to find out anything?" he blurted anxiously.

Herr Löbl said calmly: "Only that Fräulein Fischer was scheduled to fly to Rome this morning. The concierge booked the flight and arranged for her ground transportation at this end."

"*Damn!*" the man whispered. Then he said, "Sorry." He sounded as if he meant it. "It's just that I know I'm going to get sacked!" His expression was bleak.

"Perhaps all is not lost," said Herr Löbl.

"How's that?"

"I asked the head switchboard operator to pull Fräulein Fischer's telephone bills, and I have a record of her calls. Here they are."

He handed over a sheet of computer printout on which two lines, one near the top and one near the bottom, had been boldly circled in black ink.

"As you can see, Fräulein Fischer telephoned New York once. The number she called is printed next to the time of the calls, its duration, and the cost. At the bottom, you will see that she placed another, shorter call, this one to Milan, Italy. The number she called is also there."

"I can't thank you enough." The man looked around. "Could you tell me where the telephones are located?"

"This way, please." Herr Löbl gestured and led him to the telephone booths. "Is there anything else I might assist you with?" he asked.

The man shook his head. "No. I really do appreciate your help. I know you went beyond the call of duty."

At the telephone booth, the man waited until Herr Löbl was out of earshot. Then he called the number in Milan.

There were soft distant rings and then the rapid-fire voice of a female operator: "Grand Hotel et de Milan. *Buon giorno.*"

*Ah! So she had called a hotel! For reservations, naturally—what else?*

"Ms. Fischer's room, please," he said.

"One moment, *per favore.*"

Cradling the receiver between his right ear and shoulder, the man turned around and whistled softly to himself as he waited.

After a moment, the operator came back on the line. "I am sorry, *signore,*" she said. "I have checked with the front desk. There is no one registered by that name."

*So . . .* he thought *. . . she has switched identities yet again!* No matter. He knew where she was staying. That was enough.

And he hung up, smiling with satisfaction.

The centrally located Grand Hotel et de Milan is on the Via Manzoni and has an agreeable, down-at-the-heels kind of charm. Stephanie had chosen it expressly because she had been to Milan several times, but had never stayed there before; she would be in no danger of being recognized by any of the staff.

After freshening up in her old-fashioned double room, she changed into a loose-fitting, doe-colored silk pantsuit, snapped gray sun lenses over her glasses, and went shopping.

Leaving the hotel, she crossed the street and turned left, walking past La Scala, indisputably the single most famous opera house on earth, and momentarily stopped in front of it, looking over at the incomparable visual feast which was the Duomo, the great white wedding cake of a cathedral with its forest of 135 spires. Then she continued on, past the glass-roofed Galleria, possibly the oldest, and definitely the most beautiful, shopping mall in the entire world, and wandered the spiderweb of streets and alleys which compose the historical city center. It was not long before she found what she was looking for.

On the Villa Madonnina, at a shop called Cashmere Cotton and Silk, she bought an outrageously expensive silk scarf which glowed with all the exquisite colors of Byzantium.

And at the nearby Centro Botanico on the Via dell'Orso, a fragrant toiletry shop with grand frescoed ceilings, she purchased a bottle of organic lavender perfume.

After she returned to the hotel, she used her cuticle scissors to cut the label off the scarf. Then she sprinkled it with a few droplets of lavender and used it like wrapping paper—carefully folding up in it the framed photograph of Lili Schneider and Madame Balász which she'd "borrowed" in Budapest.

Done, she set the package down on a little table by the door thinking, *There. The trap is baited. Very sweetly baited, indeed . . .*

## 11

The next morning, Stephanie appraised the building from the sidewalk across the street.

It was nearly a century old, with a façade of red sun-bathed brick, three and a half stories, Italianate, palazzolike, substantial. The front windows were narrow double arches with fanciful Gothic tops. As with many buildings of its kind, she suspected its street front would be deceptive, and she was right. Two long wings stretched far back around a central courtyard garden, making it much larger than it first appeared.

Stately and well preserved, it was a living shrine, testament to Milan's most famous, gifted, and best-loved son: the opera composer Giuseppe Verdi.

Out front on an island of green grass was a Giuseppe Verdi bronze on a pedestal. Right inside the large, darkish cool lobby: another bronze Verdi, this one seated, as Stephanie came in through the glass-paned front doors. And he was on the walls: numerous framed portraits of the composer, with his luxuriant moustache and carefully trimmed beard, staring watchfully out from stretched canvas.

His ghost seemed to haunt this place, not only in spirit, but in body: he was entombed on these premises in a beautiful crypt with blue sky and gold stars on the vaulted ceiling and murals of neoclassical figures to keep him company.

A female staff member with an engagingly ugly face and a kind of short, pared-down nun's veil intercepted Stephanie.

"I am here to visit Signore Guberoff," Stephanie told her in English. The woman nodded. "Please," she said, "if you will follow me?"

She led Stephanie into a clubby-looking room. All dark wood paneling, frosted etched glass, red leather chairs, polished parquet. It was obviously some sort of lounge.

"If you will take a seat," she said, "I will inform Dottore Feltrinelli that you wish to visit the Signore. The Dottore," she emphasized with hushed gravity, "is our esteemed director!"

Stephanie smiled politely. "*Grazie,*" she said, and the woman hurried out, leaving the door half open. Stephanie unslung her shoulder bag, lowered it down on the seat of one chair, and sat down in another. She crossed her legs and waited.

After a few moments, a man entered and regarded her with interest. He was smallish and looked to be on the other side of middle age and had silver hair and a prominent nose and glasses with black rims which refracted glints of light. He wore a beautifully tailored, double-breasted blue suit with a fine chalk pinstripe in it and a yellow silk tie. A matching yellow silk handkerchief showed in his breast pocket.

"You must be the English lady visiting Signore Guberoff," he said.

Stephanie got up. "American," she corrected, extending her hand. "Virginia Wesson." She smiled her very best smile.

"I am Dr. Feltrinelli, the director of the Casa di Riposo." He shook her hand and beamed. "You are a friend of the Signore's?" he inquired politely.

Stephanie shook her head. "No, I'm afraid not," she said. "I'm a . . . friend of a friend. I'm just here to pass along greetings and a gift."

"I see." He tilted his silver head. "I am delighted that you have come! Signore Guberoff does not get many visitors, you know." He added warmly, "I myself will show you upstairs to his room!"

"Why?" Stephanie asked anxiously with a flush of guilt, "is he ill?"

"Oh, no, no, no," the director assured her as they left the lounge together and headed for a staircase. "Ill is too strong a word. Signore Guberoff's health is overall quite well. His arthritis is getting worse, of course, but then . . ." He sighed and parted his hands eloquently. "At such extremely old age, deterioration is to be expected? No?"

She nodded. "A pity it had to affect his hands, though."

"A tragedy, that! The Signore had the touch of an angel. However, aging has affected the talents of everyone here. But not, thank God, their spirits! Listen!"

So saying, Dr. Feltrinelli stopped walking and cocked his head. Stephanie followed his example and listened carefully.

A tenor was singing in the distance. But soon, he was nearly drowned out by a powerful soprano with a still achingly beautiful voice.

A battle of the vocal cords was in progress. The louder she sang, the more exuberantly he belted. The higher her notes and the longer she held them, the more gusto and volume he put behind his.

And then, from elsewhere yet, came an altogether different sound: a piano rippling, skipping, dancing, swirling, pounding—

Dr. Feltrinelli smiled at Stephanie. *"Meraviglioso!"* he whispered. *"Bèllo!"*

"Yes," she said softly, *"bèllo!"* After a moment, she asked, "Is it always like this?"

"Always," he said as they continued walking. "This building has as its soul the very essence of music—or, as I personally like to put it—'One heart and many voices.' " He smiled and then glanced at her. "Yes. A living legacy for musical flowers in their last bloom." He lowered his voice.

"Most, of course, were not stars, but members of the chorus. But try telling them that!"

He chuckled softly as they clicked down the inlaid floor of one of the second-story wings, windows to their right, doors to individual rooms on their left.

Every so often, Stephanie would notice one of the doors on her left opening. Catching glimpses of the rooms beyond the faces, she was surprised. The rooms were real: untidy and cluttered and overflowing with a lifetime's cherished treasures and mementos. They weren't, she realized, so much rooms in a rest home as they were *real homes*.

"Did you know," Dr. Feltrinelli continued as they walked, "Verdi was so beloved by the people of this city that as he lay dying in his hotel room on the Via Manzoni, they actually laid straw on the cobblestones outside his window so that passing carriages would not disturb him?"

"How lovely!"

The words were barely out of her mouth when Dr. Feltrinelli stopped at a door.

"This is the Signore's room," he said, and knocked.

"Meneghini left me that chair," Boris Guberoff remarked, pride and fondness evident in his voice. "It was in her Paris apartment, and I always used to admire it. 'Then I shall leave it to you!' she blurted on one occasion. And she did." He frowned. "Onassis gave it to her, I believe."

The chair in question was a creaky stately throne: genuine Louis quatorze, all ornately carved walnut arms and legs. Like everything else in the cluttered room, it was coated with dust, which rose in silent little puffs when disturbed.

Dust dulled the glass of the framed concert posters which covered every square inch of wall space. Dust cloaked the glossy black sheen of the concert grand and the treasures vying for space on its cluttered top. Awards, engraved gifts, framed photographs: Guberoff with Scriabin's daughter, with Tchaikovsky's great-niece, with more presidents, prime ministers, kings and queens than one could shake a stick at.

"You're sure it's all right for me to sit down in it?" Stephanie asked anxiously, perching on the edge of the precious chair and not daring to put her entire weight on it. Every protesting creak of the ancient wood frightened her. "I don't want to damage it."

Guberoff, swallowed up in the Victorian tatters of what she guessed was his habitual chair, merely shrugged; all he had eyes for was the scented scarf-enfolded package on his lap. It enthralled him completely. Lovingly he began to trace—slowly continued to trace—the elaborate Aubusson-like pattern of the silk with a fingertip.

She held her breath and sat back slowly and cautiously. She placed her hands lightly on the grandly carved arms in order to distribute her weight more evenly.

As the old man continued to trail his finger around on the silk, Stephanie studied him overtly. He wore an old-fashioned, wide-lapeled gray suit with a bright blue vest, white shirt, and a big red-and-green bow tie. A lilac silk handkerchief stuck out of his breast pocket like the petals of an exotic flower; his left lapel had several tiny medals pinned to it, and his cufflinks were gold and shaped like minuscule grand pianos.

He murmured, half to himself, "But what can be wrapped in Lili's beautiful scarf? What could she have sent me!"

Boris Guberoff, born in Kiev in 1904, might have left Mother Russia in 1926, but he had never lost his Russian accent. His English was as thick as ever with rolling Rs and harsh throaty consonants. He looked to be every one of his eighty-nine years.

He was thin and had the profile of an emaciated hawk. Thinning white hair combed straight back over his ears, a balding pate, and a jaw that was almost simian. His dark, watery eyes were heavily hooded, and an age spot, the size of a quarter, stained the right side of his forehead. Smaller age spots splotched his face and hands like the coloring on a bird's egg.

Like many people his age, he had the look of being perpetually surprised—perhaps because he still found himself alive and somewhat kicking.

"Tell me." His acquisitive gaze was still upon the silk package, his fingertip reluctant to stop its tracing. "How is Lili? Is she well?"

Stephanie thought she had prepared herself for the question, but now that it was posed she was appalled that the practiced phrases rose to her tongue but were smothered, as though her mouth were filled with a thick sticky syrup. Quickly she cleared her throat. "She . . . she's younger than ever," she managed dryly.

"Lili—*young?*" He frowned down into his lap and, in the intervening silence, Stephanie could hear the distant tenor and soprano still battling for vocal supremacy. After a moment, Guberoff laughed softly. "Oh, you mean she *looks* young." He sighed and his voice tightened. "Yes, Lili has found the forbidden tree of knowledge and tasted of its fruit. But it is dangerous knowledge! I warned her, you know."

Stephanie's heart skipped a beat; shivers crackled up and down her spine; chills lifted the fine downy hairs on her arms and the nape of her neck.

*So Lili is alive!* she thought with exultation. *Alive and young!*

Her folded hands trembled on her lap; her mind was doing quantum leaps. It was the discovery of the millennium! The biggest story she—or anyone else—had ever, or would ever, investigate in a lifetime!

"Y-you warned her?" she prompted the old man, barely trusting her-

self to speak. Subdued excitement quavered in her voice and she tried, fu-
tilely, to quell it. "Wh-what did you warn her about? What did you think
she had to fear?"

But he was silent—enraptured now with unfolding the square of silk.
Slowly, neatly, he lifted one corner at a time, smoothing that triangular
section with the withered palms of his hands before lifting another and
smoothing it: north, south, east, west. His progress was so slow Stephanie
was tempted to snap at him to hurry.

And then he gasped and his reaction was everything she'd hoped
for—and more.

The "gift" she'd brought him—the photograph of Lili Schneider pos-
ing with Madame Balász, still in its exquisite Fabergé frame—gleamed
richly on its bed of silk like a priceless crown jewel.

He clapped his hands together in delight and stared, mesmerized,
down at the photograph. After a moment, his eyes misted over and a wet
sob, like a rapidly rising bubble, burst up out of his chest. "For *me!*" he
whispered torturously, and sniffled. "For *me* . . ."

To regain rapport, Stephanie leaned suddenly forward. "A memento,"
she supplied softly.

"A memento," he repeated in his frail old man's voice, and nodded.
"Yes, a memento . . ."

"Lili wanted you to have it," she said huskily. "When I told her I was
coming to Milan, she untied the scarf she was wearing—that . . . very . . .
scarf—quickly wrapped the picture in it, and instructed me to bring it to
you. So here it is!"

The words were barely out of her mouth when his fingers seized the
scarf, the sudden movement making it flow magically, as though the colors
were liquid. He lifted it to his face, pressed his nose into the soft whispering folds, and inhaled deeply of the faint lingering remnants of perfume.

"Lili!" he whispered longingly in a strangled voice. "Lili . . ."

Stephanie, feeling like a peeping Tom, had to will herself not to look
away. Guberoff's pathetic, lovesick display agitated her guilt. It was a
cheap, sordid trick she'd pulled. And yet . . . she'd *had* to play on the old
man's emotions; she'd really had no other choice. It was the only surefire
method she'd been able to think of with which to successfully breach his
defenses.

And breach them it had. All it had taken was a scarf and a few drops
of lavender—she'd read in her grandfather's manuscript how Lili had always favored that scent.

Like it or not, she would—*must!*—continue to use any means
necessary—no matter how calculating or contemptible—in order to get the
information she required. Three people had already lost their lives; she
couldn't start worrying about wounding an old man's feelings now. No. If

she hurt him, then she was sorry; she didn't intend to. But in this case, the end more than justified the means.

"Lavender!" Boris Guberoff's voice was muffled by the scarf he was still holding to his face. "I can actually smell her!"

She felt a bracing jolt of adrenaline.

*Now* was the moment for her to use the door she'd wedged open in his mind; *now*, she knew, was the perfect opportunity to trick him into confiding too much!

"Lili said . . ." she began quietly. She glanced momentarily down at her folded hands and then back up at him. "She said she would like to see you again very soon. Of course, she did mention that she doesn't get to see any of her friends as often as she'd like—"

"Well?" he said testily, "she can't very well expect to, can she?"

With a sigh, he let the hand clutching the scarf drop to his lap, and his ancient eyes, unblinking as a lizard's, were moist with tears.

"I warned her in the beginning that the key to life eternal was a secret she would have to keep at all costs . . . that she would end up sacrificing everything for it! And do you know what she did?" His voice trembled. "She laughed into my face! Into *my* face! She said she didn't care what it cost her—career, friends, fame, her own identity—nothing mattered, so long as she lived forever!"

How his emotions tugged her. So pathetic, they were, so misguided, and yet so sweet. Damp trails, like tadpoles, meandered down his papery sunken cheeks.

Her voice was gentle. "Still, you are one of the only people in the world Lili really trusts. You know that." She was appalled by how easily and smoothly the lie slid off her tongue.

"Lili and I . . . we go a long way back," he said simply. Another strangled wet sob came from the depths of his throat. "A long way back."

"Why, you're in love with her!" Stephanie exclaimed softly.

"No!" he cried. Then he shut his eyes as though against unendurable pain. "Yes, God help me!" he croaked, his fingers twisting the scarf in agony. "But how could we ever love each other as a man and a woman? She perpetually young . . . me aging into this shrunken, shriveled old husk!"

He averted his face to hide his overwhelming misery. Her eyes moved away to give him privacy, and she looked around the room, at the posters displayed with such pride, at the young, exceedingly handsome face which had, once upon a time, been his. Now the photographs of his long-lost youth seemed to mock, as though berating him for aging.

"Lili was telling me how much your playing meant to her," she said after a while. "Especially when she sang along. 'Was ist Silvia.' She loved that!"

His head twisted sharply at her, his face shadowed by memories. "Yes, but does *he* care! Oh, no! Business, business! That is all *he* ever thinks about—business and *money!*" He rolled the word distastefully off his tongue, as if ridding himself of something particularly vile and disgusting. "He talked all during our little impromptu concert! He never even listened to us!" The words were accusing, stinging, his expression that of a petulant child.

Her mind flew. Who was the "he" Guberoff was referring to? *The background voice on the tape?* Ernesto de Veiga? It had to be! But what had he been talking about? What . . . ? And then suddenly she remembered.

"But the markets in the East were just opening up," she said. "He had to take advantage—"

The way he stared at her. She could see the slack remnants of muscle tense in his cheeks. And his eyes, they seemed to have clouded over and had suddenly become frighteningly remote.

The lengthening silence made her uneasy, and the ticking of the ormolu clock on the bureau seemed amplified, as if the metronomic *tick-tocks* were getting louder and *louder*.

He leaned toward her. "But how would you know what he'd been talking about?" he whispered. "You were not even there!"

"On the cruise aboard the *Chrysalis*, you mean? Of course I wasn't there." Stephanie forced a laugh. "You know I wasn't."

"Then . . . how? How . . . did . . . you . . . know . . . ?"

"About his conversation? Why . . . I'm sure Lili must have told me! Yes. How else would I have known about it?"

Something shrewd shone in his face. "But Lili does not talk! Lili . . . never talks!"

Speechless, stunned at the speed with which the tables had turned, Stephanie sat staring at him.

"You are no friend of Lili's!" he whispered, aghast. "Lili did not send you here!"

Her mind was racing, trying to figure out a way to salvage the situation. She watched him slowly lower his head and stare in horror down at his lap.

"These . . . these gifts are not from her!"

She flinched as he abruptly flung the picture and scarf to the floor. "Who are you?" he demanded in a shrill, rising voice.

"I told you, I'm a friend of—"

"You are *not!*" He keened suddenly, like an animal in its death throes. "You tricked me!" he moaned. "You've tricked me to find out about *her!*"

Floods of tears were wriggling down his face unchecked now.

Stephanie sat there in miserable silence. She watched him cry, recover his composure, and finally wipe his eyes with his fleshless palms. Then he tugged the square of silk out of his breast pocket and honked noisily into it. With a dignity that was almost painful to see, he raised his head.

"How can you just sit there?" he whispered, his eyes accusing. "Have you no shame? Go! *Go!*"

Never in her entire life had she felt so guilty and cheap. And yet she remained seated. It was as though she had been glued to the fragile chair which had once belonged to Maria Meneghini Callas.

Now he was pale and sweating. With a trembling hand he dabbed his upper lip with the handkerchief. "For the love of heaven, won't you just go?" he cried. "Forget the ramblings of a crazy old man and go!"

She rose carefully to her feet, the creaking of the prized armchair reflecting the wretchedness inside her. Then she bent down and retrieved the scarf and Madame Balász's photograph from the floor.

She gave the priceless Fabergé frame a cursory check. Miraculously, it seemed undamaged; she would mail it back to Budapest without feeling more guilt than already burdened her. She wrapped it in the scarf and stuffed the silken packet inside her bag. Then she slung the bag over her shoulder and hesitated. She looked down at him, but he pointedly turned away, refusing to meet her eye.

She decided against any parting comment. Her face stretched taut, she walked stiffly over to the door.

"Bitch!" she heard him swear under his breath.

The word cut into her like the blade of a knife, and she felt its sharp pain. Quickly, she pushed down on the cool smooth handle, opened the door, and made her escape. She closed the door quietly behind her and slumped wearily against a column in the corridor outside.

She was quivering with shame and indignation. For a moment, she shut her eyes. She deserved his contempt; it had been a despicable thing to do. Inexcusable—

No, *excusable*, she told herself savagely. It had been the only way. And it had succeeded—hadn't it?

"Home run," she said to herself.

But she felt no triumph. Victory had not been sweet. Instead, a filthy aftertaste lingered in her mouth.

## 𝓗 12 𝓗

𝓗e was waiting for her.

Outside, on the grassy island in the middle of the street. Leaning casually against the pedestal of the Verdi bronze, to all appearances engrossed in his newspaper. He could have been a businessman on his lunch break, or a man waiting for his lover.

Stephanie didn't notice him when she came out of the arched entrance of the Casa di Riposo. But then, she hadn't noticed him earlier, when he'd followed her here from the hotel, either.

But he noticed her, and he waited patiently until she had a thirty-yard head start. Then he folded the newspaper, tucked it under his arm, and followed her along the sidewalk at a leisurely pace. All the way back to her hotel.

He watched from a chair in the lobby as she settled her bill at the front desk.

He was waiting in a rental car across the street when she came out, a porter carrying her three suitcases, and watched as she climbed into a taxi.

He followed the taxi to the airport, where he abandoned his car in the NO PARKING zone in front of the terminal.

And he followed her, invisible as a ghost, to the Iberia counter, where she purchased a ticket and checked her luggage.

Luckily there was no one in line. As soon as she was gone, he walked up to the counter.

"Excuse me," he said to the ticket agent. "I need your help."

Francesca Maggi was a romantic Italian first, and an airline ticket agent second. Which was why, as she listened to the man who was inquiring about the female passenger she'd just helped, her heart melted. Francesca knew that the fierce passions aroused by *amore* were all part of the human condition.

"I cannot sell you a ticket to Marbella," she was explaining to the forlorn-looking man, "for the simple reason that there's no airport in Marbella."

"But you told me that that's where she wanted to go."

She smiled. "That's where she *wanted* to go, but that's not where she's going to *land*. I really shouldn't be telling you this, but . . . well, since you have such an honest face . . ." She glanced around and lowered her voice. "She is flying to Malaga! It's the closest airport to Marbella!"

"I see . . ." He frowned. "Is she on a nonstop flight?"

She shook her head. "Her flight lands in Barcelona, where she has to change planes." She looked thoughtful. "She specifically requested a six-hour layover in Barcelona."

He thought, *She's going to change identities again!*

"If you like," she said helpfully, "I can put you on a flight that gets you to Malaga ahead of hers. That way"—she smiled knowingly—"you can be waiting for her at the other end. Doesn't that sound romantic?"

"I don't know how to thank you enough," he said.

After Stephanie landed in Barcelona, she went through customs and repeated her by-now familiar procedure. She checked two of the suitcases in a baggage locker and changed personas in the washroom. Off came the red wig and glasses; for now, she was back to being a strawberry blond. She tore the passports of her last three personas into little pieces and flushed them down the toilet. Then she checked the large suitcase in yet another baggage locker and, unencumbered by luggage, took a cab into the city.

An hour later, she was seated in the chair of an exclusive beauty salon, stoically ignoring the pleas of the hairdresser.

"But you have such marvelous thick hair!" the stylist protested. "It would be criminal to cut it short!"

Stephanie stared at the hairdresser's reflection in the mirror. "I'm bored with it," she said implacably. "Cut it like . . ." She twisted around, her eyes scanning the framed photographs of various hairstyles on the wall. She pointed at a head with short dark Louise Brooks-style bangs. "Like that."

"If you are certain . . ." The man sniffed.

"I am. Oh, and one more thing."

"Señorita?"

Stephanie's voice was weary. "Dye it brown. Dark brown."

## 13

From a distance, it could have been mistaken for a blinding white island. Or, at closer range, some rakish, sharp-prowed intergalactic voyager which had, for mysterious purposes, put down on water.

Perhaps intending to drain the planet dry.

It was the megayacht M.Y. *Chrysalis*, riding at anchor half a mile offshore, stately and unperturbed, as though aloof to the skipping whitecaps and challenging the sea to whip up something worthy of its attention. A smartly uniformed, permanent crew of fifty was onboard to dance constant attendance upon the owner and his guests.

This, the de Veiga yacht, out-Trumped them all. It was rakishly streamlined, two hundred and eighty-nine feet long, and had electric propellers in pods that could rotate three hundred and sixty degrees. With five decks and sixty thousand square feet of indoor/outdoor deck space, it easily carried its burden of auxiliary craft: a Bell Jet Ranger helicopter, two Riva speedboats, an Admiral, a Boston Whaler, and, in a wetberth on its afterdeck, the *Larva*, a sixty-foot Magnum Marine muscle boat.

As befitted the miniship of one of the world's richest men, *Chrysalis*'s interior was stupendously opulent. There was the three-story circular atrium with crystal columns trimmed in gold; the main salon, which was eighty feet long and the entire width of the yacht: forty-four feet; an elevator, a garage, and a discotheque complete with strobes, disc jockey booth, and glass dance floor. And that didn't take into account the revolving sky lounge, gymnasium, health clinic, operating theater, and, since price had been no object, and every conceivable eventuality was anticipated, a morgue.

Besides the two owners' apartments on the fourth deck—his included a panoramic office, hers a complete beauty salon—there were eight haremlike guest suites below, each with marble bathrooms, Jacuzzis, and gold fixtures. Genies, in the persons of crew members, could be summoned at the push of a button or the pull of a tasseled cord.

And, since no true megayacht is without one, on the topmost deck—for privacy's sake tucked between the twin funnels—there was the small freshwater swimming pool. Shaped like a butterfly and tiled with lapis lazuli. Two wide waterfalls, one from each funnel, splashed down into it.

*Chrysalis* had been designed to be a completely self-contained resort on the move, a recluse's paradise from which one could see the world without ever having to set foot off one's own jealously guarded domain. Unless, of course, one chose to.

On this clear and wind-whipped afternoon in June, the helicopter was gone, and they were all up there. On the sundeck, five stories above the sea. By the lapis lazuli pool, the electronically controlled, plexiglass windscreens protecting it from the buffeting warm gusts.

Ernesto de Veiga, seated at a portable desk inside a peaked white silk tent on the port side, its panels tied back with thick silk ropes. Busy at a portable computer that linked him to all the financial capitals of the world.

Zarah Böhm, also in the tent, swathed in a voluminous caftan intricately worked with gold and silver threads, a tight-fitting helmet of snowy feathers completely hiding her hair. Sitting up on a silk-cushioned lounge, chin on her knees, carefully painting her toenails silver.

Eduardo, their sleek Adonis of a son. Swimming in place against the artificial 5.5-mile per hour current in the lapis pool.

And, in an identical silk tent on the starboard side, her back to the others so that she faced shore, an elderly infirm confined to a wheelchair. She had just turned eighty-four, and in her prime must have been a great beauty. Still was in many ways, despite her soft wrinkled skin, watery eyes, and garishly dyed red hair. She wore a lilac silk dress, a matching wide-brimmed hat, and lilac silk slippers. Double strands of opera-length pearls and a pair of Zeiss Ikon binoculars hung from around her neck.

All but ignored by the four of them was the buffet table. Like an altar dedicated to food, it had been heaped with glittering ice, in each cube of which a butterfly had been frozen, keeping chill the al fresco lunch. Crisp baby lettuce greens. Slivers of crudités. Mounds of beluga and sevruga and osietra. Hard-boiled quails' eggs. Succulent pink prawns the size of small lobsters. And, since food was a feast for the eye as well as the taste buds, raw oysters in perfectly butterflied shells, each decorated with a precious black pearl and a single strand of seaweed. Plus there were assorted tropical fruits flown in fresh that very morning from halfway around the world, and pastries baked but hours ago in Vienna and Bad Ischl.

At the poolside, and in both tents, vintage Cristal champagne waited in sweating coolers.

But only the old woman was drinking. Drinking and peering through the binoculars at the thatch-roofed poolhouse, white towers, stucco walls, and pink umbrellas of the Marbella Club. The sky was absolutely cloudless and swept clean by the wind, almost cobalt, so blue was it, the air so crystalline and intense everything looked razor sharp. She felt she could reach out and actually touch it all: the purple coastal mountains, palmfringed tan beaches, the white-washed, bougainvillea-draped villas and apartment complexes.

Sip, spy. Sip, spy. The old lady was in a pleasantly bleary fog, now peering through the binoculars, now sipping her champagne, now lifting the binoculars to her eyes once again, the glass on the table beside her constantly replenished by a steward with a talent for rarely being seen and never, ever, being heard.

Ah, the sheer extravagance, the sweet languor!

Zarah Böhm, toenails completed, began smoothing a light foundation on her face. She glanced across the deck to the other tent, and saw that the old woman was sitting forward, her binoculars once again trained on the coast. "What do you see, *Mutti?*" she called out in German.

The old woman didn't bother to turn around. "What do you think I see?" she snapped back in the same language. "Shore."

"Mother can be so trying at times," murmured an unfazed Zarah. She picked up a gold hand mirror and eyed herself critically. Brought it in close, tilting it *this way and that*. Placed a finger at the corner of her left eye and pulled the taut skin *this way and that*. Was that the beginning of a crow's foot she'd seen? Relieved to see that it wasn't, she continued putting on her face.

In the pool, her son lunged sideways and slapped the button to halt the artificial current. He launched himself across the pool, and with a noisy surge of water, climbed out. Not using the gold-plated ladder, but athletically, doing a neat push-up.

Zarah watched with swelling pride as he leapt to his feet, water sluicing off his honey-tanned body. She smiled at the way he pulled higher his spandex briefs; the noble way he waved away the steward who came running with a fresh towel, a grand seigneur in the making; the way he scooped up the used towel from his poolside lounge and flipped it casually around his neck. "Ah!" he exclaimed in Portuguese. "That was refreshing!" He used both hands to sleek back his wet, jet black hair.

"Eduardo," Zarah said almost reproachfully, now switching to Portuguese. She extended a slender hand, palm up, the fingers curled as though beseeching. "Darling, do come and give your mother a kiss."

Dripping a trail of water on the teak deck, he strode over to her, a tall, lithe heartbreaker of twenty-four. He ducked into the tent and, with mock solemnity, simultaneously lowered his head and raised her beautifully manicured fingers to his lips.

She smiled up at him and touched his face tenderly with her fingertips. What a beautiful young man he was! she thought admiringly. No wonder he had women everywhere eating out of his hand. Lean and darkly tanned, with those thick-lashed eyes, lightning-bolt cheekbones, that hungry mouth. Oh yes, she could understand his attraction. And he was so extraordinarily fit, without a gram of excess fat; with each movement he made she could see the muscles shift and tense and ripple just beneath the surface of his skin.

Someone's shadow momentarily darkened the tent. They both half-turned.

It was Colonel Valerio, mirrored sunglasses reflecting two blinding coronas of sun. He was in his lightweight summer uniform of starched khakis: short-sleeved shirt, knife-creased trousers, sand-colored deck shoes.

Zarah raised her eyebrows questioningly.

Coming to parade rest, he said, in English, "Dr. Vassiltchikov called to say the helicopter just left the airport in Malaga. It will put down in"—as though executing a salute, he cocked his left arm smartly and consulted his watch—"approximately fourteen minutes."

"Thank you, Colonel," Zarah replied in English, and watched him turn on his heel and stride off.

She lay back and sighed. A mere fourteen more minutes of rest. Then an hour of treatment.

Remaining young really demanded so much effort. But not quite too much . . .

Ashore at the Marbella Club, lunch was in progress.

As if drawn by a magnet, everyone had gathered around the pool to eat, splash, and bake their bodies a fierce nutty brown. For a crowd mostly dressed in briefs and bikinis, members of both sexes wore an inordinate amount of jewelry. Gold chains and huge Rolex watches on the men. Diamonds at throat, wrist, and ears on the women.

They were really quite ordinary birds trying awfully hard to emulate an exotic species which, apparently unknown to them, had become extinct in the mid-seventies. Never mind. They were happily pretending this was the same, the very same sizzling Marbella of many years earlier, at the height of Jet Set chic.

In the purple shadows of the umbrellas and thick-trunked palms, very young, jewelry- and bikini-clad beauties sat opposite men old enough to be their fathers, and in some cases well-preserved grandfathers. In the pool, a hopeful Cinecitta blonde with twin peaks of silicone and two strips of pink spandex, floated on a clear plastic air mattress, trying, in vain, to get Noticed by someone Very Very Rich. And from a round table of eight, a female voice drawled, "Prick," but the burst of laughter which followed barely enlivened the almost sanitoriumlike atmosphere. Yet the cushioned, white wooden chaises were all filled, and there were more young people than old.

Where were the spontaneous conga lines of yesteryear? The gypsy fortune tellers? The spur-of-the-moment parties and wild shrieks of hilarity that marked pure reckless fun? Even the waiters seemed to have run out of steam, and dispensed desultory gloom along with the famous veal snout cake and glasses of less-famous Andalusian wine.

Away from the others, in the blazing sun on the beach, a young brunette with a pageboy haircut was just raising a shapely leg to apply sunscreen to her calf when a masculine voice behind her said, "Marrakesh."

Leg still in the air, Stephanie half-twisted around, pulling her Jackie-O-style sunglasses down her nose to peer up at him.

He swaggered into view, at first glance a young bronzed demigod sprayed into bikini briefs. He had dark curly hair and a body belonging to a Greek statue's. But a longer, slightly harder look showed a good-looking man trying desperately to retain his youth. And losing.

From his curly chest sprouted spirals of gray. And the capped or bonded teeth—or were they dentures?—were too brilliantly white not to be artificial.

*Aging gigolos don't die,* she thought. *They come to Marbella and pounce on young women.*

"Marrakesh," he repeated, smiling his factory-enameled smile. "In North Africa."

"The last I heard, it still is." Stephanie pushed the glasses back up on her nose and, ignoring him, lowered the one leg, squeezed sunscreen out of a plastic tube, and raised the other. She began applying lotion to that calf.

"Last summer, wasn't it?" he persisted. "At the duchesa de Fornacetti's palace in Marrakesh."

"Oh, really!" Stephanie groaned. "*Do* give me some credit. That must be the oldest opening gambit in the world!"

"You are English?" he guessed.

She lowered her head and looked up at him from over the rims of her glasses. "Try American."

"Of course." He smiled. "That would explain your abruptness. The English are far more . . . shall we say . . . polite?"

"Either that, or they're possessed of incurable patience. Unlike myself." Her voice turned hard. "Scram, gigolo." And turning her back on him, she rolled over on her belly.

Unexpectedly, he began to laugh. "So you think that's what I am? A gigolo?"

She didn't reply.

"And you?" he asked. "What are you? A husband-hunting gold digger?"

Her head snapped in his direction. "What makes you say that?"

"Because," he said, "you have been here for three days, and for those entire three days you have had your eye on one thing only."

"Oh? And what does that happen to be?"

"The yacht." He gestured with his chin. "Out there. The *Chrysalis.*"

"So?"

"A word of well-intentioned advice, Miss Williams—"

She whipped off her glasses. "How do you know my name?" she demanded. Her eyes had become dangerous slits.

He shrugged. "I have friends at the club. They saw your passport."

"Then I suggest you take *my* well-intentioned advice, Mr. Whoever-
You-Are. Mind your *own* business."

She started to turn away again, but he squatted down, took her by
the arm, and turned her roughly around. "Listen to me, Miss Williams,"
he said, his voice low, almost menacing. "If you are a gold digger, and
your sights are set on that yacht, forget it."

She tried to shake his arm off, but his fingers were too strong.

"What's it to you, anyway?"

"Perhaps I like women and do not wish to see them come to harm.
Or perhaps"—his eyes darkened and flashed—"perhaps us old-timers
have been around long enough to know when not to play with fire. And
perhaps we like to warn others about the dangers."

"What dangers?"

"Here in Marbella, and elsewhere along this coast, we do not speak
of it, we pretend not to see."

"Pretend not to see . . . *what?*"

A veil seemed to come down over his eyes. Then he let go of her arm
and strode away, toward the peaked, thatch-roofed poolhouse.

Slowly she turned in the other direction. And stared out at the sleek,
massive white yacht anchored offshore.

## 14

*Marbella, Spain*

*M*orning. The terrace of the club. The night had been cool, but the day already had all the makings of a scorcher.

The first thing Stephanie did was look out toward sea. She felt relieved. It was still there: majestic, rakish, and blinding white.

As she stood gazing out at it, M.Y. *Chrysalis* dwarfed a multimillion-dollar hundred-footer surging past it. Seemed to take as its due the homage accorded it by the flotilla of colorful small craft bobbing on the water: sunfish, sailboards, motorboats, jetskis, speedboats pulling skiers throwing up rooster tails of spray.

Abruptly she hurried back inside, heading straight for the concierge's desk.

"Good morning, Miss Williams," greeted the thin Spaniard manning the counter.

"Good morning. It's a lovely day out."

"Oh yes, Miss Williams. Very lovely. The sea is perfect."

"Which is why I would like to hire a boat."

"Certainly, Miss Williams. A wise request, to be sure. May I suggest a sailfish? There is just enough wind for beginners. Or perhaps you are familiar with sailing and wish to have something larger?"

Stephanie shook her head. "No, I don't like sailing," she said firmly. "I prefer a speedboat. I wish to have it all day."

She waited until midday, when the sun was highest in the sky, and the daily provision runs from shore to yacht would be starting to wind down.

The sun was burning hot. Wisely, she wore a straw hat and a loose, long-sleeved silk shirt over her black, one-piece Kamali swimsuit. Flat open-backed sandals. And carried a few provisions in a colorful straw bag.

The red, sixteen-foot Riva was waiting at the end of the wooden jetty. And so was the over-the-hill gigolo. Wearing micro briefs, with four gold neck chains *and* a gold medallion hanging between his well-preserved pecs. "Ah," he exclaimed half-mockingly. "The beautiful brave American, Miss Monica Williams."

Pointedly ignoring him, she dropped the straw bag down into the boat and squatted, starting to untie the rope from the cleat. It was thick and stiff and unwieldy. She broke a fingernail on the rough fibers. "Damn!" she swore under her breath and jerked her hand back.

He bent down and took over. Flipped the rope expertly loose. "Perhaps it's a sign that the lamb should not run off to the slaughterhouse?"

"Oh, why don't you just leave me alone!" she snapped testily. "Who are you, anyway? The Jiminy Cricket of Marbella?"

He blinked. "The Jiminy . . . ? I am sorry. I do not understand."

She smiled bitterly. "The conscience of Marbella? Is that what you are? The conscience of a conscienceless resort?"

"Perhaps," he said softly, "I am merely trying to be a friend." He stood there, holding the rope taut.

"Then you're wasting your time." She hopped down into the boat and looked up at him. "I have no friends, Mr. No Name."

"All the more reason to listen, Miss Williams. You see, there are certain people in this world who are not, how do you say? Savory?"

"Oh, really?" She locked eyes with him, conscious of the fact that her face was level with his skimpy briefs. "Are you speaking from experience?"

"What I am saying is this. The rich are different, Miss Williams. And the very, very rich . . ." He gazed past her, at the big yacht. "They are a breed . . ." he murmured, "a law . . . unto themselves."

"Just throw me the rope and shut up."

"Very well." He tossed it down to her and got to his feet. "But I advise you to tread softly, Miss Williams. Very softly and very, very careful—"

At that moment, the whine of a nearby helicopter starting up carried across the water. Both of them turned to look toward the yacht. The whine increased in pitch, and then, like a giant metal mosquito, the Bell Jet Ranger rose smoothly up off the sundeck, hovered for an instant, and turned in the air before nosing sharply down the coast, the whine of its engines and the *whup-whup-whup* of its rotors gradually receding.

Stephanie glanced at her watch. Twelve noon on the dot. She nodded to herself. The punctuality on that ship was positively Germanic.

"Miss Williams—"

She fired the ignition. The rumble of the powerful twin engines and the water thrashing at the stern drowned him out.

"Miss Williams!" he shouted.

"*Adiós, amigo!*" she yelled over her shoulder, and gave the boat gas. The engines roared and it surged forward, the wind tugging at her straw hat and sending it flying. She banked the speedboat into a wide sweeping curve and looked back. He had caught her hat and was standing on the jetty, waving it.

As though to flip him a birdie, she really opened up. The bow lifted high and she kept it at a sixty-degree angle. She grinned to herself. Time she got down to business.

"Fool!" hissed the man as he yanked the Spaniard into the cultivated jungle of succulents and fan palms. "Why did you let her *go?*"

"Stop it!" the gigolo gasped, fingers clawing at the forearm around his neck. "You are strangling me!"

Abruptly, the man let go and pushed him away. The big Spaniard, gasping for breath, stumbled over a spiky, razor-sharp cactus. His eyes blazed with anger.

The man didn't seem to care. He ground his teeth and clenched his fists in a rage of impotence. Then he took a series of deep breaths to calm himself. "You had specific instructions, goddammit!"

"She would not listen," the Spaniard rasped, rubbing his throat tenderly. "The woman is stubborn. Beautiful and stubborn."

*"Shit!"*

The Spaniard drew himself up with dignity. "Now that you have no further need of me, I shall be going."

"Not so fast! Wait!"

"You are *loco!*" the Spaniard pronounced, rubbing his reddening neck, and then suddenly looked stricken. "My chain!" he exclaimed.

"What chain?"

"One of my gold neck chains! You broke! Is gone!"

"Quiet down!" the man hissed. "They'll be able to hear you all the way to North Africa!"

The Spaniard dropped into a squat, eyes and fingers frantically searching the ground.

"*Forget* the chain!"

"Forget—" The Spaniard looked up, furious. "Twenty-two-karat gold, that chain is! You know how much it *cost?*"

"Here," the man said, taking a roll of money out of his pocket. "Go buy yourself another male menopause ornament." He began peeling off bills.

The Spaniard watched greedily. They were all one hundred U.S. dollar bills. Swiftly he calculated.

The American stopped at five and held them out. "This should more than take care of it."

The Spaniard shook his head. "It was a thick chain. Big links. Like so." He held two fingers apart. "Nine hundred dollars it cost."

"Here's another five. And five more for future services."

The Spaniard's eyes lit up. "Then you still have use for me?" He snatched the money and it disappeared inside his briefs.

"That's right, buddy." The man draped a comradely arm around his shoulder. "We still got some work cut out for us."

"Work—cut? I do not understand."

"You will, buddy, you will. Meanwhile, why don't you go work on your skin cancer? Huh? Me, I need some time to *think!*"

There. Straight ahead. Growing larger, ever larger, filling her entire field of vision, the massive yacht. It towered majestically and seemed to defy all rules governing gravity and flotation. The noonday sun flashed off gold-plated hardware, expanses of bronze reflective windows, blinding white paint accented with blue Awlgrip trim.

Stephanie stared in growing disbelief as she hurtled toward it, unaware of the salt spray stinging her eyes. She felt dwarfed, shrunken to insignificance. The sheer enormousness of this vessel! The money it represented! It suddenly sank in and gave her serious pause.

She forced herself to continue breathing, willed herself to hang onto the shreds of rapidly dwindling courage, somehow found the determination to keep up the Riva's speed.

The stranger's voice echoed inside her head. *The rich are different, Miss Williams. And the very, very rich . . . They are a breed . . . a law . . . unto themselves.*

Sudden darkness. The sun completely blocked out now, her little speedboat swallowed up in deep cool shadow. Was she imagining the chill? Or did the yacht give off a sinister aura that conjured up mephitic, Gothic fears?

Stephanie glanced up briefly, her eyes scanning the sheer cliff of decks. Her approach had engendered a flurry of activity: white-uniformed crew members running about, their mouths wide open, obviously shouting down at her.

She wondered, *What are they thinking? That I'm stupid enough to ram them?*

Just when it looked like she would, she braced herself and cramped the wheel hard to the right, hauling the Riva into a tight skidding turn across the yacht's transom.

Crew members were gesticulating wildly as she swept past, mere feet from where the huge Magnum nestled in its dark, cavelike wet berth. On the deck extending out above it, the name *CHRYSALIS*, and under it, its home port, *Rio de Janeiro*, all in gold letters. She caught a glimpse of what, at first, appeared to be an American flag, but no, just a variation of it: the single star and stripes of that maritime convenience, Liberia.

The boat deck under the blue, tautly stretched canvas awning.

Like a serious outdoor fitness club, it was equipped with weights, benchpresses, incline boards, four-person Jacuzzi, and adjoining saunas.

Zarah and Ernesto were naked, lying face-down on side-by-side massage tables, plush blue velour bath sheets draped over their buttocks.

Their skin glowed as their bodies were brutally kneaded, pummeled, slapped, punched, pounded. Hers by a stout cruel-fingered Swedish masseuse with sausages of yellow braids coiled on either side of her head, his by a black former Mr. Universe with twenty-one-inch biceps.

Eduardo was nearby, working out with weights. Curling giant chrome dumbbells. Expelling breaths like air puffed out of a bellows.

From hidden speakers, the muted, elegant strains of a Mozartean ensemble melded with the rhythmic slaps and thumps of massaging hands and clanking weights.

And then, without warning, all hell suddenly broke loose. There was the approaching roar of a speedboat; the shouts of the crew; Colonel Valerio racing past, yelling, "Stay out of sight, everyone! An unknown boat is headed this way!"

Gasping, Zarah jerked up into a kneeling position. "Oh, my *God!*" she whispered. She pressed a blue towel against her bare breasts. "Ernesto!" Her eyes were wide and frightened as she stared imploringly over at him.

"Whoever it is will not get onboard," Ernesto assured her with a smile of calm certainty. He dismissed the masseurs with a flick of a hand, sat up, tied a towel around his waist, and slid off the table. He glanced over at his son as Eduardo, with a loud clang, set his dumbbells down and bounded across the deck, where he grasped hold of the railing and bent far over to see what was transpiring.

"Ernesto!" Zarah whispered again, the fear growing in her eyes.

He stroked her cheek gently and smiled. "Haven't I always provided privacy and security?"

She started to nod, but gripped his arms fiercely as a disembodied voice, speaking English, boomed out over the yacht's powerful bullhorn speakers.

"Attention, unidentified vessel." The crackling words, amplified to the verge of distortion, were loud enough to be heard above the din of any engine and carried far across the water in every direction. "This is Captain Falcão of the motoryacht *Chrysalis*. Please move to a minimum of one hundred meters from this ship. If you remain where you are, your presence will be construed as an act of piracy and severe repercussions will result. I repeat. This is a warning. For your own safety, move at once to a minimum of one hundred meters from this yacht."

The message was repeated in Spanish; French, German, Italian, and Portuguese would follow.

"Who can it be?" Zarah whispered. Her entire body had tensed.

"Probably just a curious tourist," Ernesto soothed, "or, at worst, a nosy journalist. Who knows?" He shrugged and smiled. "Oh, come now! It was just a little joke. Don't worry so much, my beautiful butterfly. Colonel Valerio won't permit anyone to board."

* * *

Having reached the far end of the *Chrysalis*'s transom, Stephanie burst out from the shadows and back into bright sunlight. The bullhorns boomed, but she paid them no heed. At a terrifying speed, she hurled the Riva into a tight left turn and shot forward, parallel with the sunny side of the yacht.

Dark egg-shaped portholes trimmed in chrome flew past in a rushing blur, and the yacht's gleaming white length stretched before her, seemingly without end. The hull, like some sleek, futuristic cliff, rose to flare out high above like an enormous white overhang. Glancing up, she could see crew members leaning over the lip and shouting down—a continuous chorus line of heads dipping into view exactly twenty feet ahead of her.

How comical they looked! And how truly thrilling this was! Never before had she felt quite so magically juvenile, so totally madcap!

Suddenly she threw back her head and roared laughter into the wind. Now that she was back in the sunshine, all the silly fears had vanished. Invincible, she felt. And to think she had let the yacht's sheer size intimidate her, the mere shadow of it frighten her!

Giving the Riva even more gas, she made the bow rise, higher, higher, higher up out of the water until the boat was at a steep seventy-degree angle. Keeping it there, she raced forward atop a boiling cauldron of wake.

White-faced with anger, Colonel Valerio barked a dozen orders as he ran along the *Chrysalis*'s main deck, two stories above the Riva. Here and there he took short cuts so that he would be in place, waiting for her by the time she crossed the bow.

He unsnapped his hip holster as he ran. Brought up the weapon he was carrying, a dark, oily MAC-10 machine pistol.

If the warnings reverberating from the bullhorn speakers didn't scare her off, he knew what would.

From the corner of her eye, Stephanie was aware of the *Chrysalis*'s bow coming up. It was almost time for another turn.

She let the Riva slow enough so that the bow began to descend. Just ahead, she caught sight of a huge indented square in the yacht's hull—*with a massive taut chain angling down into the water*!

Her heart began to pound. *The anchor chain! My God!* It was right in front of her—the speedboat leaping toward it! *Quick!* Right—*right*!

Frantically, she spun the steering wheel as far to the right as it would go, praying that she could somehow avoid smashing into that chain—

As she watched, the gap between speedboat and anchor chain narrowed, the huge heavy links growing larger and larger in front of her horrified eyes. Now she could clearly see the rough rusty surface of once-smooth steel, calculated the gap . . . fifteen feet, twelve, ten, seven

. . . the chain was looming, the Riva still speeding toward it. It was too late. She would crash.

Her breathing had stopped and her body tensed as she waited for the shrill screech of fiberglass on metal, the smashing of the hull—

*Five feet . . . four . . . three . . .* then the world was reduced to a single foot-long link frozen in her mind. She threw her arms protectively up in front of her when the Riva, just beginning to turn, slewed into the chain, the impact shattering the hull and throwing her high into the air and tossing her overboard like a lifeless limp rag doll.

But God was merciful. The world went black before she hit the water.

*"Eduardo!"* screamed Zarah. "What do you think you are *doing?"*

He turned toward her, precariously balancing himself on the middle railing with bare toes. "I have to help her, Mother. I'm going to dive down."

"No!" Zarah shouted. *"No!* For the love of God, I forbid it!" Violently shoving Ernesto aside, she ran over to her son.

"I have to, Mother. She could be drowning!"

"Then let her!" Zarah reached out and grabbed him around the thighs, tugging him off the railing with arms like steel. Her face was a hideously contorted mask. "You fool!" she hissed. "Don't you see? This woman—" She glared at him. "It's exactly what she wants! To come *onboard!"*

He tried to pull away from her, but she held tight. "Mother!" he blurted. "Let go of me!"

"No!" she hissed shrilly. "You cannot rescue her. I forbid it. Eduardo, you will not. I do not care if she dies. *No one* gets aboard this yacht. Do you hear me?" She shook him violently. *"No one!"*

## At Sea

The blackness became a gray fog, and the fog a white shroud of mist. And then that, too, dissipated, and the first thing Stephanie laid eyes on was the most handsome young man she had ever seen. He was staring down at her, smiling gently.

"I kissed you," he said softly. "Just like in the fairy tales. And you woke up."

"Are you an angel?" she whispered.

He laughed softly. "No, I'm afraid not." His English was perfect, tinged with a mere hint of an accent.

"Then I'm not dead?"

"Oh no, definitely not." He smiled again. "I dove into the sea and heroically fished you out. So you see, if it is heaven you're seeking, you're going to have to try harder the next time."

Slowly Stephanie moved her head on the pillow, using the excuse of looking around to break his intense eye contact—and realized, with a start, that she had never been in this room before! It certainly didn't belong in a hospital—it was far too luxurious and ultramodern for that. All silvery-blue-lacquered walls, padded white leather ceiling, seamless black-and-white wall-to-wall carpeting.

Everything, she noticed, was silvery blue highlighted with black and chalky white—from the round king-size bed she was in, with its curved padded head- and footboards and built-in nightstands trimmed with silver, to the round platform it was centered upon; from the low, sleek leather couches accented with gold lamé pillows in the far corner, to the silk festoon blinds drawn over the large windows.

Slowly she turned her head and stared up at him. "Where—where on earth am I?" she whispered hoarsely.

"In good hands," he replied soothingly, reaching out and gently rearranging her bangs over her forehead. "You have absolutely nothing to worry about. Everything is all right now. You are going to be fine." He smiled and repeated, "Just fine. You were very lucky, you know."

And then it all came rushing back to her. The *Chrysalis*, the Riva, the accident.

God, how could she have been so stupid! What had gotten *into* her? She could so easily have killed herself . . . almost had, as a matter of fact.

Small wonder that she ached all over, that she felt as if she had been beaten to within an inch of her life.

A sudden thought occurred to her. "Have I been here for long?" she asked tremulously.

He tilted his head. "Oh, not too long."

Something about his evasiveness caused a fear to clutch at her insides. "How long?" she demanded sharply.

He gestured dismissively. "Only two days."

"What!" Stephanie exclaimed, and abruptly tried to sit up. She regretted it instantly; a thousand splinters of pain shot through every part of her body. Slowly, she lay back down and sighed wearily. "Two whole days . . ." she whispered. "Two entire days . . . gone . . . just like that . . ."

He stared at her. "What is two days when you have your *life!* Remember, you were in quite a bad accident. Dr. Vassiltchikov says it is a miracle you are even alive. But what we all find even more miraculous is that your X rays do not show a single broken bone. Not a one!" He held her gaze. "I would say you were born under a very, very lucky star."

She looked at him steadily. "You're right," she said. "I'm being highly ungrateful. I owe you my life."

He shook his head. "I was merely on hand."

Suddenly her eyes filled with tears. "It was so stupid of me! I don't know what got into me!"

He reached for her hand and held it. "Forget it. Just thank God you are in one piece, which is more than can be said for the Riva."

"The Riva! Oh, shit." She shut her eyes momentarily. "They're going to love me at the Club," she added, wincing.

"Don't worry, I have already taken care of it. They were very understanding and asked me to convey their best wishes. Also, they let me collect your things. Your clothes are in the wardrobe over there, your toiletries are in the bathroom, and your passport is in the nightstand beside you."

Her eyes widened. "But . . . in that case . . . where *am* I?"

"Oh, I would guess approximately sixty miles west of the Bay of Naples."

"But . . . but I was just in Spain!" she sputtered. "In Marbella!" Her eyes were wide. "Where am I! Where is this room!" She stared around uncomprehendingly.

"Hmm, I suppose it did slip my mind to mention that."

"I'll say it did," she snapped tartly, a spirited kind of anger flashing in her eyes.

"Nor have we been introduced yet," he went on smoothly, "a circumstance in which I certainly have the advantage over you. From your passport, I know that you are Ms. Monica Williams from the United States." He was still holding her hand, and now raised it to his lips. "To remedy the advantage," he said softly, his lips a mere breath on her fingertips, "let me introduce myself. I am Eduardo Aloísio Collor de Veiga."

"De Veiga! Then I'm—"

He nodded. "That's right. An honored guest aboard the motoryacht *Chrysalis.*" He chuckled. "Though I will say, your arrival made more of a splash than most guest's, if you will pardon the pun?"

Despite herself, she smiled weakly.

He let go of her hand and gently tucked the sheet up around her neck. "Now, try and get some more rest. According to Dr. Vassiltchikov, it's the best medicine under the circumstances. If you need anything, no matter how minute, do not hesitate. Simply press the appropriate button on the nightstands. They are all labeled, see?" He showed her. "Steward, maid, doctor, cook . . . you can summon any of them with the touch of a finger. And these operate the curtains, lights, door lock, and bath water."

"Like magic." A ghost of a smile hovered on her lips. "Maybe I *have* gone to heaven."

He smiled. "I certainly hope you will think so," he said, his words and gaze conveying unmistakable meaning. "And now I will leave you to rest."

She watched him cross the carpet to the door and open it, his every movement reminding her of a big lean jungle cat.

She struggled to sit up. "Eduardo?" she called out softly.

Holding the door handle, he turned his head and looked questioningly over at her.

She caught her breath. He was bathed in the light of a recessed spot, and, if anything, it only seemed to accentuate his sculptural good looks.

She suspected such handsomeness often spelled trouble for him.

*And, if I'm not cautious, it can just as easily spell trouble for me.*

"Yes?" he asked softly.

For a long moment she could only hold her breath and stare back at him. Finally, she averted her eyes, shook her head, and murmured very softly, "Thank you." Then she lowered her head to the pillow and shut her eyes. Pretending to drift off to sleep.

He looked at her a moment longer and then stepped out, quietly shutting the door behind him.

After he was gone, she opened her eyes and lay there, staring up at the creamy leather ceiling.

But it was not padded leather or the sunburst pattern of gold metal molding, echoing the shape of her round bed which she saw. No. She saw him. Eduardo. Saw his white silk shirt open to the waist, showing hairless dark skin and sinewy muscle. Saw his oblique expression and luminous, penetrating gaze, which stirred something powerful within her. Saw the lithe, barely subdued animal way he had of moving, as if he were a predator constantly on the prowl.

*Enough!* she told herself. *I'm letting my fantasies run away with me.*

Maybe . . . if she got up . . . went out on deck . . . She smiled to herself. He really was awfully good-looking—too good-looking to waste time languishing in here.

Stiffly, slowly, she made herself sit up, swung her sore legs out over the bed, and inched her body up until she was standing. Then she gingerly slipped out of the Egyptian cotton nightshirt someone had dressed her in, and which certainly wasn't part of *her* wardrobe, and dropped it on the bed.

A series of rapid, unexpected knocks on the door startled her. She was elated. *He's back already!* she thought happily, suddenly feeling no pain. *He can't stay away from me!*

Grabbing the top bedsheet, she held it in front of her nude body and called out, "Yes?"

The door opened.

"Eduardo told me you were awake," announced the short bird of a woman with a stethoscope, like giant forceps, hanging from around her neck. "I," she said, "am Dr. Vassiltchikov."

Stephanie swore she sounded just like Dr. Ruth, and she was just about as tiny. But there the resemblance stopped. Dr. Vassiltchikov was thin and fine-boned and wore her gray-and-black hair in a youthful pageboy cut. She also wore half-glasses, the Ben Franklin kind, and looked about as old as Ben Franklin, too.

"May I come in?"

Stephanie tried to think of a good reason to say no, but came up empty. "Why not?" She shrugged.

The little doctor nodded curtly, came in, and shut the door behind her. Crossing the carpet, she beamed up at Stephanie and wagged an admonishing finger. "Since you are getting up, we better first check to see if you have the concussion. *Ja?*"

Stephanie sighed, but nodded.

"First, you must sit back down," the doctor ordered, automatically sticking the earpieces of the stethoscope into her ears. "And drop that silly sheet. I'm sure yours is not the first naked body I have ever seen, *ja?*"

She even giggled like Dr. Ruth.

"Mother?"

Hearing his voice, Zarah smiled brilliantly and closed the French edition of *Vogue*. She was lounging sideways on one of the curved shaded banquettes which were built in all around the covered aft deck, the floor of which comprised the overhanging roof of the Magnum's wet berth, directly below.

Even for morning, Zarah was exceedingly well-turned-out. Wore very bright makeup, expertly applied. Loose, aqua silk lounging pajamas with a loose, pink silk top. Her hair was up, wrapped with an aqua turban which left a yard of excess silk hanging down the right side. Her high-heeled sandals were aqua, and so, too, were the lenses of the big, diamond-studded, butterfly-shaped sunglasses she was wearing.

"We haven't seen you all morning, Eduardo," she chided in Portuguese, holding up a cheek.

He bent down to kiss it.

"You even missed breakfast."

"I know, Mother. I'm sorry."

Reading the expression on her son's face, she said, "Ah. You were with her." She sighed. "Like a moth to a flame, so you are drawn to her!"

He laughed. "She woke up, Mother!" he said excitedly. There was a joy in his eyes she had never before seen. "I talked to her!"

Zarah raised her eyebrows. "Good. The sooner she is better, then the sooner she can leave. Perhaps as early as Naples, even."

Seeing his sudden stormy expression, she took off her sunglasses. "I know, Eduardo," she said quietly, "I know. You are mesmerized by your Sleeping Beauty. I cannot say I blame you."

He did not speak.

"But you must trust me," she continued. "Anyone capable of contriving such a dangerous stunt in order to get onboard surely has an ulterior motive, wouldn't you say?" When he still did not speak, she sighed and held up her thin-fingered hands. "Believe me, my darling. The sooner she is gone, the better—the *safer!*—it is for all of us!"

His eyes narrowed. "How can you say that, Mother?" he asked tightly. "You don't even know her!"

"No, I do not." She stared at him levelly. "Nor do you."

"No, not really," he admitted readily. Shoving his hands into his trouser pockets, he rocked from tiptoe to heel to tiptoe, momentarily staring past her out at the receding wake. Then he drew his eyes back in and let his heels drop flat. "But I like her, Mother," he said softly, looking down at her. "I like her . . . instinctively. I want to give her the benefit of the doubt."

Zarah's eyes flashed coldly. "You fool!" she hissed at him. "You are like all men! Happily led by your cock, no matter to what treachery it may lead!"

"That's not true!" he blurted angrily.

"Oh? Isn't it?" She arched her eyebrows and stretched out on her side, letting one arm drape over the back of the banquette.

"No, it isn't!" he responded in a tight, angry voice. "And even if it were, I still don't see any harm in having her onboard."

"Darling." She slid her glasses back on, the earpieces outside the turban. "You know how reclusive your father and I both are."

He laughed bitterly. "Don't I just! The only thing I can never figure out is who or what you are both hiding from!"

"Perhaps the world?" she suggested quietly.

"Why does that worry you so much, Mother? I mean . . . you don't even have to see her. I'll keep her away from the two of you, if that's the way you want it. God knows, this boat is big enough to get lost on."

"Keeping her away from us will only rouse her interest all the more," Zarah stated flatly. "Especially if she turns out to be a journalist or a paparazza. Worse yet, who knows? She could even be a spy working for our competitors."

"A spy!" He stared at her.

"An industrial spy," she nodded. "Word may have leaked out about Dr. Vassiltchikov's breakthroughs."

"You and your Dr. Vassiltchikov!" he said in disgust. "That's all you care about, isn't it?"

Her facial muscles tensed and her voice went cold with contempt. "Perhaps it's only money that she's after." There was an interminable pause as she shifted position, her movements smooth and feline. "But then again," she added softly, "perhaps it's you."

"Me? How could it be me, Mother? She's never even seen me before!"

She shrugged delicately. "Surely she knows who you are. I'd willingly bet she knew exactly who you were before she staged that . . . that convenient little accident?"

"Do you think she's stupid enough to risk her life in order to get to us?"

"Considering the stakes? Yes, I do." Zarah paused. "But I don't for a moment think she's stupid, Eduardo. Oh, no. She's clever. Exceedingly clever."

Without speaking, he resumed rocking on his heels.

"Darling, please!" She reached for his hand and squeezed his fingers. "Try to be sensible! There really is no need to be so glum! It isn't as if she's that special. Why, you can have your pick of any woman in the world! You know that!"

"Yes," he said grimly, "I know that." His movements stilled, and he withdrew his hand from hers. "But it's her I want," he half whispered, staring out at something beyond the horizon.

"But darling! You don't even know her!"

"In my heart I do."

"Love at first sight?" Zarah clapped her hands together and trilled musical laughter. "My, my, but we must be smitten!"

"You don't have to make fun of it!" The words tore angrily from his lips. "If you want to know, I think I'm in love with her."

"In love with *her!* From *what?* Sitting at her bedside for two days?

Really, darling. I know you dove in and saved her, but does that make for *love?* And she being so . . ." She searched for the appropriate word, and finding none, settled for, ". . . so common?"

"How would you know she's 'common,' Mother?"

Zarah didn't reply. Instead, she sailed smoothly ahead, her voice now a purr. "What you need, Eduardo, is someone of your own *kind.*"

He laughed bitterly. "So tell me, Mother. Is there *any* family in the world truly good enough for Eduardo de Veiga?"

"Truthfully?" she asked. "No. And how could there be?" She whipped off her sunglasses and stared at him. "Although your father is known to be one of the wealthiest men in the world, he manages to keep the true extent of his wealth a secret." Her voice dropped to a whisper. "But you and I, Eduardo, we *know!* We know he is the wealthiest man alive! Wealthier than the Saudi king, the sultan of Brunei, the English queen, and all the *nouveau riche* trash combined!"

Gesticulating wildly, he stomped angry circles in front of her. "Mother, I am not going to jump every time you say 'jump,' or come running whenever you call. I'm not going to seek your permission or blessings for everyone I meet." He whirled at her and leaned close. "Waste your own life hiding away like some crazy hermit! That's your business." His eyes blazed and his breathing came rapidly. "But don't," he warned in a shaky whisper, ". . . don't ever try to live my life for me!"

"Eduardo!"

They were interrupted by the soft *ping!* signaling that the automatic glass doors to the salon were sliding open.

Both fell instantly silent, warily eyeing each other like two combatants forced by the referee to take a break between rounds—the older one with experience on her side, tenaciously battling to keep the younger one, who was showing newfound independence and muscle, in line—neither of them willing to drop it and come to terms, each determined to have his way; both knowing that winning this particular fight would forever change the structure of power between them.

They were still glaring at one another when Colonel Valerio snapped to, hands locked in the small of his back, staring into space as he waited to be acknowledged.

At last Zarah broke eye contact with her son and looked up at the security officer. Her voice was still sharp. "What news, Colonel?"

"It's about the passport I faxed to Washington, ma'am."

"What about it?" she demanded.

"I just received word from the Department of State, ma'am. The passport's genuine and in order."

A sudden knowledge came to Eduardo. "You're talking about Monica Williams's passport," he said softly, his fists clenched at his sides.

"Yes, sir." Colonel Valerio continued to stare off into space.

"Christ!" Eduardo swore, and stared narrowly at Zarah. "I should have known! Here you were, Mother, talking about Monica spying on *us*. And what were *you* doing in the meantime? Trying to dig up dirt on her!"

"Not dirt, Eduardo," his mother corrected crisply. "The truth."

"The *truth!*" he sneered. "What would you know about the truth? My God, you make me sick!"

Throwing up his hands in disgust, he stomped off.

"Eduardo, come back!" Zarah called after him, reaching out beseechingly, as though her fingers could draw him back. "Eduardo!"

But he was already gone.

Zarah let her hand drop. For a moment, she sat there thoughtfully. Then she raised her head.

"Continue digging, Colonel," she commanded softly. "Dig quietly but dig deeply. Everyone leaves traces in their wake. You know that better than I. And if nothing turns up on our unwelcome guest, then so much more suspect she will be."

"Consider it done," Colonel Valerio promised. "Ma'am!" He spun an about-face and marched off.

Zarah picked up the French *Vogue* and continued flipping through it, every now and then licking her index finger to facilitate turning the pages.

But nothing in the magazine registered, and she tossed it aside.

Her thoughts were consumed by the mystery woman her son had pulled out of the sea, the woman who now occupied one of the lavish staterooms on the deck below.

Oh yes, that young, attractive face and youthful body surely held a multitude of secrets—all of which could, and would, be used against her. It would only take ferreting them out. And nobody could ferret out secrets like Colonel Valerio and his network of ex-CIA operatives.

She stretched languorously, like a cat. *Eduardo really is so naive,* she thought. *He may have won the battle, but he's not won the war. Oh, most definitely not.*

After all, he was still so young and callow. And she . . . well, she already had a lifetime's experience behind her.

Dr. Vassiltchikov dropped the penlight into the righthand pocket of her lab coat, shoved the blood pressure cuff in the left, and removed the stethoscope from her ears, letting it hang loose from around her neck. "Your heart, pulse, and blood pressure are normal," she said. "Amazingly, you show no signs of a concussion."

Stephanie grinned. "Does that mean you're giving me a clean bill of health?"

The doctor nodded. "There is nothing wrong with you that rest and aspirin will not cure. Considering your accident, I would say you are one very, very lucky young lady."

"You are the second person to tell me that," Stephanie said. "Soon I might end up believing it."

The doctor gave her a long hard look. *"Believe it,"* she said.

Captain Falcão left the first mate at the computerized helm, walked into the captain's cabin aft of the wheelhouse, and shut the door. Picking up his interyacht telephone, he dialed Ernesto's study.

*"Sim?"* The tycoon's clipped voice sounded hollow from a speaker phone at the other end.

"I hope I am not disturbing you, sir. But the vessel on the radar screen which followed us from Marbella?"

There was a brief pause. *"Que há de novo?"*

The captain said, "Nothing, sir. It is still eighteen kilometers behind us."

"I see."

"Should I take evasive action? We can launch the *Larva* to confuse his radar. Perhaps whoever it is will follow the wrong signal. Or I could send the helicopter back to take a look—"

*"Não,* captain," Ernesto said. "At this point, I do not think any of that will be necessary."

"Very well, sir."

"However, continue to keep me informed and let me know if the vessel changes course or gains on."

In his study, Ernesto rose from behind his sleek massive desk with its built-in computer terminals and walked to the sliding glass doors overlooking the stern. He stood there, gazing thoughtfully out past the polished rails and stanchions to the bubbling wake and the hazy horizon beyond.

*Interesting,* he thought. *Beyond that blue horizon, keeping its distance, but definitely tailing the* Chrysalis, *was another craft. Why?* he wondered. *Who could it be? Paparazzi, ever on the alert for photographs of the rich and their multimillion-dollar toys? No. Paparazzi would keep the yacht within sight of their telephoto lenses. Curiosity seekers, then? Perhaps. Or . . .*

*. . . Or did it have something to do with the mysterious passenger?*

# ❧ *16* ❧

## At Sea

*I*n the bathroom adjoining her stateroom, Stephanie leaned into the mirror over the malachite sink. The multiple reflections which stared back were surprisingly pleasing.

Yes, she thought, both Eduardo and Dr. Vassiltchikov had been right. She did have everything to be thankful for.

Suddenly feeling a thousand percent better, she decided it was time to put in an appearance on deck. She hoped her red-and-white-striped silk crepe slip dress and red tennis shoes would suffice. If not, she could always change. She found her extra pair of sunglasses, the ones with red-and-white-striped frames, slipped them on, and started to leave.

But first things first. This wasn't supposed to be a vacation, she reminded herself. She was working undercover, had gotten aboard this floating palace with a distinct purpose in mind. It was time, high time, to set to work. But first, she would need her—*camera*.

Abruptly she frowned, slowly placed her hands on her hips, and let her puzzled eyes drift around the ultraluxurious stateroom. Funny, she thought, that I haven't come across it. I know I had it in my room back in Marbella, and Eduardo said everything had been packed and brought onboard . . .

Taking off her sunglasses, she spent the next ten minutes searching the stateroom from top to bottom.

It was an exercise in futility. She found everything else—from her freshly laundered and dry-cleaned clothes to her passport, right down to the purse-size packages of Kleenex and tampons and a partial roll of Tums. What she did *not* find was what she was looking for.

Her camera was missing—along with all ten rolls of blank, high-speed film.

Stephanie stood there, mulling it over. Three scenarios popped instantly to mind, and all three seemed highly plausible.

*One:* Her camera had been stolen from her hotel room before her luggage had been packed and collected.

*Two:* Whoever had been sent to collect her luggage had made off with her camera.

*Three:* Someone aboard this yacht had decided she would be better off without it.

The possibility that her possessions had been so closely scrutinized made her glad she had mailed the tape of Lili and Guberoff back to Sammy—whether thieves or more sinister forces were responsible for her camera's disappearance.

Well, whichever it was, she would find out soon enough. Meanwhile, she would do what she'd done in New York with her American Express card and everything else which had Stephanie Merlin's name or initials on it: She would leave her stateroom without it.

Slipping her sunglasses back on, she crossed the room, opened the lacquered, louvered door, and went outside. She found herself in a wide corridor with red-lacquered walls and deep-pile white carpeting cut with a sculptured swath of swirls. She looked around in amazement. She'd never seen a corridor quite like it—anywhere. Not on land and never at sea.

Around the ceiling, gold trim shone like King Solomon's mines, and recessed, glassed-in showcases displayed priceless Far Eastern antiquities—multiple-armed goddesses and flaking, serenely squatting figurines. From a mirrored niche, a four-foot-tall black-and-gold Buddha floated on Plexiglas, smiling benignly.

Her eyes were everywhere at once. This wasn't a floating palace! It was a floating museum! Good Lord! She didn't even want to know the insurance premiums. One year's was probably enough to feed, clothe, and house a small town in perpetuity.

The corridor and glassed-in showcases stretched, seemingly, to infinity.

For a moment she paused, debating which direction she should take. She glanced over her shoulder and then straight ahead again. Both ends of the hall looked almost identical. It only stood to reason that all she had to do was follow her nose. Eventually she would come to a staircase or a door; from there, it would only be a matter of going up a deck or two or three.

Purposefully, now, she walked faster. The antiquities in their glowing showcases had changed to vertigreed bronzes, but she would look at them later. The thing now was to find her way around, get her bearings, and fix on landmarks such as the big Buddha.

Without looking left or right she breezed past an intersecting corridor and nearly collided with an incredibly beautiful woman in aqua silk lounging pajamas who was closely followed by a crew-cut man wearing mirrored aviator shades. "Whoops!" she heard herself say, "so sorry," and was about to continue when the woman's words stopped her.

"Miss Williams!" The voice was cultured, foreign-accented, and musically soft.

That voice! It hung in the air like an exquisite musical note.

It raised the hairs at the nape of Stephanie's neck and sent chills, like something live and multilegged, crawling up and down her spine and along her arms and legs. She'd know that voice anywhere.

Time did the impossible, telescoping elastically for what seemed an eternity before standing absolutely still. Stephanie felt herself losing her grip on reality. Her heart pounded like an amplified bass beat, and she could actually hear the blood rushing wildly through her veins and arteries.

Stephanie fought to still her rubbery, quivering legs and turned around slowly, saying, "Y-yes?"

Zarah Böhm's lips smiled, but her eyes were cool. "How serendipitous! We haven't met yet, but it's time we became acquainted. I am Eduardo's mother. Come." She held out an elegant hand, her sleeves rustling with the slippery sound of silk, aquamarines and pink coral bracelets clinking softly. "I will show you up to the aft deck myself." She smiled, her hand on Stephanie's arm now, gently but firmly forcing her to change direction.

Stephanie reflexively recoiled, her body caught in an involuntary shudder. So cold, that hand! So icy, almost reptilian, the flesh, as though it were . . . well, not exactly dead, but not truly alive, either.

And still time continued to stand still—for the simple reason that time *had* been stayed—or, at least, the passage of years had been slowed!

Stephanie felt the queasiness of sudden vertigo, of her mouth salivating faster than her throat could swallow. It could not be! This woman had to be an uncannily close and much younger facsimile—

*Why can't you believe your eyes? Look at the delicate facial bones! Those are unmistakably Lili's. And her height! Good God, she* is *exactly Lili's height. And what about that singularly pronounced presence and regal deportment?*

Why, she hardly looked ten years older than she had in Madame Balász's old photograph!

Stephanie tried to concentrate. The woman was saying something, but the words went in one ear and right out the other. She could only stare, knew she should stop staring, that it would arouse suspicion. The musical voice turned sharper, and still Stephanie stared, and then—

"*Monica!*" The sudden shout came from far down the corridor, and the spell was broken.

Both women's heads swiveled in the direction of the voice.

It was Eduardo. Running barefoot toward them, clad only in his spandex swimming briefs. The regularly spaced, lit-up showcases glowed briefly on him as he passed each one, tinting his torso in beautiful pinkish light before casting him in shade again.

"Quickly!" hissed Zarah, her fingers digging painfully into Stephanie's arm. "This way!" She began to pull her into the bisecting corridor.

"Monica!" Eduardo bellowed mutinously.

There was a moment of confusion. *This way.* Then Eduardo's bray. Stephanie glanced at Zarah, then over her shoulder at Eduardo again, who was gaining. Who was she to obey?

"Quickly!" Zarah urged.

*"Wait!"* Eduardo yelled. *"Stay there!"*

*This way! Wait!* Stephanie heard Zarah's sharp intake of breath at her son's insurrection, but the woman's features were arranged in a blank regal mask. As though awaiting orders, the man in the aviator shades stood on the sidelines, legs spread, hands clasped in the small of his back at parade rest.

Stephanie found something surreal about being caught in this tableau. The frozen, mannequin-perfect woman clutching her arm; the tan-uniformed man with the aviator shades, lenses reflecting tiny fisheye images of herself; and Eduardo, at one moment distant and the next so close, hurtling toward them as if his life depended upon it.

*Ping!* The sound was a musical note rather than an intrusion, and Stephanie automatically turned toward it. Peculiarly enough, she didn't find it at all strange that two wall panels parted to reveal a hidden elevator. Inside it, an old lady all in yellow was seated in her motorized wheelchair, complete with yellow picture hat, furled parasol, and matching slippers. Only the high-powered binoculars hanging from around her neck were black. With a whir, she rode forward to complete the bizarre tableau.

And then Eduardo, sweat-sheened and breathless, burst upon them, his tautly muscled chest heaving from exertion. And with his arrival, everything snapped back to razor-sharp reality. Staring at Stephanie, he reached out and took her free hand in his.

His touch had the effect of an electrical shock. Stephanie could feel the leanness of him—the moist warmth of his palm, the racing of his pulse; could see the lupine rakishness of his grin; could catch a whiff of the faint masculine scent emanating off his perfectly proportioned, near-naked body.

And all the while, his shiny onyx eyes leaped into her. Leaped and seared and delved.

Never before had she felt a gaze so hypnotically powerful or ravenous. Yet it wasn't merely sexually predatory, his gaze. It was far more calculating and seemed—yes!—to *assess.* And—she was struck by yet another physical shock—she could actually *feel* him probing her physical longings as well as her intellect, almost as though he could actually see, and was coolly appraising, her hidden-most secrets.

She stood perfectly still, not daring to breathe, sheer willpower all that kept her legs from buckling.

"Stay," he managed to gasp between taking deep lungfuls of air. "Onboard. For the rest. Of the. Cruise."

He ignored his mother's head snapping in his direction, Colonel Valerio's disapproving frown, the old woman's cry of delight. It was as if he and Stephanie were the only flesh-and-blood people in the corridor; the others had been reduced to phantoms.

"Please. I'm formally. Inviting you." His breaths were starting to lengthen, and though he was still only grasping her hand, he might as well have been holding her face in his hands and kissing her—his gaze was that intensely intimate. "Just say . . . please say yes!"

"But Eduardo!" Zarah's silver voice chided. "*Querido,* have you considered that Miss Williams might have other plans?"

"Stay out of this—*Mother!*" He twisted his head savagely in her direction and felt barbarously pleased to see her flinch. Then, turning back to Stephanie, his expression gentled. He repeated, with soft urgency, "Please?"

"Well, I . . ." Stephanie began tremulously, and nearly cried aloud as Zarah's nails dug brutally into her other arm.

"You see, *querido?*" Zarah's smile became victorious. "Invitations like this require planning on a guest's part. Surely you are embarrassing Miss Williams! She may well be employed and have a job to return to, or she might not have packed the right things, or—"

"Who cares what she packed?" His eyes blazed. "For God's sake, Mother, this isn't a cruise ship! Dress-up isn't required." Then he turned back to Stephanie, his eyes soft and pleading. "Please, Monica? It's only for ten more days."

"Well, I . . ." Stephanie began hesitantly.

She was unsettled by Zarah's obvious dislike, and loathed those sharp talons squeezing her arm. But she had risked life and limb in order to get onboard, and now that she had, she must stay and see her investigation through. The tape of Boris Guberoff and Lili Schneider had allegedly been recorded aboard this yacht; now her every journalist's instinct told her that this was the place where she had to dig for the truth. Besides, in her heart of hearts, she knew she had found Lili. Now all she had to do was come up with irrefutable, concrete proof. Yes. She really had no choice. This was her great opportunity. On top of which, there was an unexpected bonus—Eduardo.

"This really is so sudden," she said weakly, with what she hoped was just the right amount of vacillation.

"Too sudden, surely!" Zarah interjected, seizing the advantage and forming a caustic smile.

"But still," Stephanie blurted before she realized the impact of her own words, "I'd love to accept!"

Stifling a moan, Zarah let go of her; Eduardo's face broke into a sunny grin. "Wonderful!" he exclaimed.

For what seemed an interminable moment, Zarah stared coldly at her son. Then her gaze switched to Stephanie. "Welcome aboard, Miss Williams," she said tightly from between clenched teeth. And in a furious, whipping blaze of aqua and pink, she turned angrily on her spiky heels and strode off.

As though answering some telepathic summons, Colonel Valerio executed a smart about-face and marched after her.

The old lady soundlessly clapped her liver-spotted hands in approval. "Good for both of you!" she whispered, her watery blue eyes sparkling. Then she extended a fragile, blue-veined hand to Stephanie. "Welcome aboard, child!" she said warmly, and laughed with sheer delight. "I am Eduardo's grandmother, but everyone calls me Zaza. You must, too. Now, I'm sure you both have better things to do than to fuss over an old woman. Go. *Go!*"

Stephanie and Eduardo stood there, smiling at each other as though they shared a delicious conspiracy.

Zaza clapped her hands sharply.

They both turned to her.

Zaza made shooing gestures. "Go, show her around the yacht, Eduardo," she commanded. And then, slashing the air with her furled parasol, she called out after him: "But don't you dare break her heart! You hear me?"

# ❧ *17* ❧

## At Sea

*H*ere she was on the world's most luxurious private yacht. Never before had Stephanie seen such staggering profligacy, such unabashed hedonism, and she doubted she ever would again. And how utterly discombobulating, that such luxury should be lavished upon a giant machine whose only criteria for existence was to move a very select few in what was surely the highest fuel-consumption-per-passenger-ratio this side of Cape Canaveral.

Never before had boats or ships interested her in the least. The odd speedboat, a jetski she'd tried once or twice at Key West, an overbooked cruise ship teeming with a thousand obnoxious tourists in the Caribbean—that had been the extent of her seagoing experiences.

But this! Surely it was beyond the imaginings of mortal men—this gigantic vessel the size of a hotel, with its museum-quality artworks in hermetically sealed glass cases and frames; its three-story engine room which looked like a giant restaurant kitchen, so sparkling clean was it, and crewed not by grease monkeys, but crewmen in starched whites tending the four spit-shined, tractor-trailer-size MTY 7,340-horsepower engines.

How to absorb the circular atrium surrounded by twenty-eight-foot-tall crystal columns, and its Plexiglas roof, which could be opened to the skies at the mere press of a button; the integrated closed-circuit television system with sixty-three TV receivers; the custom wall-to-wall carpets woven on specially built, computerized looms so that their forty-foot widths would be absolutely seamless? And what of the small movie theater, with its wide screen, pearlized turquoise leather chaises, and its film library stocked with more than five thousand titles? Or the banister rails on the staircase, electroplated in 18-karat gold; or the grand salon with its ceiling a mosaic of marble and mirrors, not to mention the two water fountains and a three-sided view of the sea?

Stephanie was overwhelmed. And totally fascinated. She wanted to see everything in this obscene paradise of a floating amusement park. Eagerly she rushed around, tugging at Eduardo's hand, asking him to explain this and that. Like a delighted child let loose in a candy store, she touched and stared and greedily digested, and her wonder and enthusiasm were infectious. Soon *he* was tugging *her*, wanting to share every nook and cranny of this yacht which he had never been particularly fond of, because sharing it with her was somehow different—she made it pure, unadulterated fun.

Below the bottom-most of the five decks he showed her the pristine seven-foot-high hold, divided by watertight doors, where the fuel and water tanks and refrigerated stores were located. He had a crew member unlock one of the gigantic walk-in freezers, and hugging herself against the chill, she marveled at the rows of whole oxen hanging from butcher's hooks, the hundreds of yards of stainless steel shelving devoted to various fowl: chickens, capons, game hens, guinea hens, partridges, pheasants, quail. Another freezer was devoted exclusively to seafood: shrimp, loup, salmon, tuna, tilefish. The drygoods stores were worthy of a small supermarket.

They explored for hours, and she never wanted that magical morning to end. He showed her around the crew's quarters with its own large lounge, galley, and dining room, pointing out how even the lowliest deckhand shared a double outside cabin with lower berths and private bath.

"Better than what most cruise ships offer their passengers," she murmured, and he was inordinately pleased.

He had the head chef give them a whirlwind tour of the enormous stainless steel kitchen, and the sommelier took them into the temperature-controlled wine "cellar," with its gimbaled shelves and one thousand carefully stored vintages. Captain Falcão himself showed her around the wheelhouse, with its gray padded consoles, computerized navigation systems, and state-of-the-art electronics.

In the radio room they saw the communications system, which would have done a space center proud. Hélio, the young technician on duty, was delighted to receive a visit from a striking woman, and took off his headset so Stephanie could listen and showed her what was involved in making a satellite telephone call.

From one deck to the next, Eduardo whisked her. He made sure she knew of the saunas which were kept baking hot twenty-four hours a day, and which she must use while she was onboard. He pointed out the priceless Art Deco panels in the dining salon; they had come from the great liner *Normandie*. And he told her of the formidable electronic security systems, including underwater sonar, to protect from potential pirates or frogmen or saboteurs.

Above all, he was content just to watch her interact with the crew, her natural enthusiasm and ease winning them over so that in no time at all she had them gladly eating out of her hand. Her sparkling inquisitiveness, her instant rapport, and her radiant and ready smile were unexpected gifts, and he sensed that while she was hardly regal like his mother, or fear-inspiring like his father, she instantly gained a healthy respect through sheer joy and intelligence.

On the deck on which her suite was located, he showed her the other empty guest suites, and pointed out how all of them were named after various butterflies. Now that he mentioned it, she noticed that, inset in each of the doors to the suites, was a glass-mounted sample of that particular suite's namesake, as well as a discreet gold plaque engraved with both its scientific and common names. Needless to say, the colors used in each decor corresponded with its namesake's markings: The *Brintesia* suite was black, white, and gray; the *Callophrys,* green; the *Deilephila,* pink and olive; the *Libythea,* blue-gray and orange.

"You," he announced, "are in the *Lysandra* suite."

"Silvery blue, black, and white," she murmured.

"That is correct."

"And yours?" she asked. "Which butterfly is it named after?"

"Mine," he laughed, "does not have a name, thank God! Nor is there a single butterfly motif in it. You see, butterflies are my father's passion," he explained with an apologetic smile, "not mine."

"Then *that's* why this yacht is called *Chrysalis?*" She gave him a sidelong look. "Because of your father's interest in butterflies?"

"I am afraid so." He grinned sheepishly. "And the Magnum in the wetberth?"

"You mean that giant muscle boat?"

"Yes." He smiled. "It is named *Larva.*"

"*Larva?*" She made a face. "You mean—as in *egg?*"

"Yes. You see, when it is launched, it does rather look as if the *Chrysalis* is giving birth."

She laughed. "I'm sure it looks terribly obscene!"

"Oh, very!" he assured her merrily.

They sped to the library, where they lingered among the built-in, railed mahogany shelves which kept the thousands of volumes from spilling out in even the most severe of storms, and he showed her how the various categories were arranged—leather-bound classics, the latest in mass market fiction, hundreds of volumes devoted exclusively to lepidoptery.

"Did you know," he said, "that in the chrysalis stage, butterflies can actually *choose* when to begin their limited life spans?"

"No." She stared at him. "But how utterly fascinating!"

"Of course, they cannot prolong their life spans indefinitely in this way; Mother Nature does set her limit."

"And these?" she asked, running her finger along the spines of some intimidatingly fat medical tomes. "Why are all these here?"

"Oh, those," he said offhandedly. "They all have to do with gerontology. That is Dr. Vassiltchikov's specialized field."

"Gerontology . . ." Frowning, she glanced at him. "Isn't that the study of aging?"

"Yes." He nodded.

Her heart pumped and her spine tingled. *Oh yes!* she thought. *I've certainly come to the right place.*

She was barely aware of him hurrying her to see the yacht's compact but enviously equipped hospital, barely registered his run-through of the major facilities. The lead-shielded X-ray machine. The EKG unit. CAT scan, pharmacy, blood bank—*that* shocked her back to reality. The freezer he'd opened was—she recoiled—stocked with bags of Eduardo's, his father's, and his mother's frozen blood!

Swiftly she turned away, feeling the bile rise to her throat. The ghoulish eventualities which had been anticipated made her queasy; reminded her of her own mortality and finite life span.

He noticed how pale she'd become. "Are you all right?" he asked.

Hugging herself with her arms, Stephanie nodded. "Y-yes," she said, without turning around. "It's just . . ."

Then she changed the subject by gesturing at the opaque curved acrylic door she was facing. Red OFF LIMITS decals in five different languages were affixed to it.

She asked, "What's in there—the Holy Grail?"

"No." He came to stand beside her. "That is Dr. Vassiltchikov's domain."

"Could I see it?" she asked, giving him a sideways glance.

He shook his head. "Sorry. No one is allowed in there without the doctor's express permission. And that includes my parents and myself."

Stephanie stared at the futuristic door. Dr. Vassiltchikov's apparent power over his parents gave her pause. Surely there must be compelling reasons why no one was permitted to arbitrarily walk through that door?

"And in there?" She was pointing at another futuristic door, identically marked OFF LIMITS. Next to it were a computer console, and three rows of built-in video monitors, none of which were switched on. "What's through there?"

"Special treatment rooms."

Stephanie eyed the door with longing. What she wouldn't give to have the opportunity to snoop around in there! "I suppose we need the doctor's permission to go in there, too?" she murmured with a little sigh.

He laughed. "How did you guess?" Then he took her by the arm and gently turned her toward the door through which they had come in. "I think we have had enough of the hospital for now. Besides, I believe it is time you saw *my* area of expertise."

She looked at him. Was she imagining it? Or was he evading further questioning by spiriting her smoothly out of here to other, less touchy distractions?

A number of doors and one flight of steps later, he said, "Here we are!"

Stephanie looked around. They were standing in a cylindrical stainless steel anteroom approximately six feet in diameter, where a curved, hatchlike door had ABSOLUTELY NO SMOKING decals affixed in five languages. Both the ceiling and the floor were made of a metal-plastic alloy grating.

"Through here," he said, patting the hatch with his palm, "are my pride and passion." Then he gestured around at the stainless steel walls. "This chamber is an airlock. That is to ensure that no corrosive salt air can get in to harm my collection."

She watched him punch the buttons of an electronic combination lock. There was a short wait, then the door behind them automatically slid shut. She heard a *clank,* followed by a hissing sound. Then she felt cool air being forced down from hidden vents above, while a vacuum under the floor sucked the old air out. She shivered with the sudden drop in temperature and swallowed against the change in air pressure.

After sixty seconds or so, the forced air stopped blowing and the vacuum shut itself off. The sudden silence was almost eerie. Then there was another faint hiss, and the hatch in front of them slid soundlessly aside.

"Now we can go in," Eduardo said, helping her step into the pitch-black space.

She could smell gasoline and oil. Rubber, varnish, waxes . . .

He flipped a switch in reply and fluorescents blinked on.

She gasped at the sight in front of her. Never before had she seen anything like it, and it was almost too much to believe, this testament to the awesome power of wealth. The huge space was . . . *a seagoing garage?* . . . *a museum?* . . . *both?* For parked on the embossed black rubber deck was a collection of the shiniest cars she had ever seen.

But what cars they were! To call them exotic or antique would be an understatement! They were a select collection of the very finest and rarest four-wheeled vehicles ever built. One-of-a-kind orchids all.

He took her in his arms and before she knew what was happening, he was suddenly drawing her close to his chest. Head tilted back, she stared up at him: he was bending his face down and then his mouth covered hers.

It was like receiving an electric shock. She could feel the scorch of his thighs pressing against her; could feel his hardness and her own engulfing, dizzying heat.

Her eyes widened and she clutched his arms. *But I hardly even know him!*

And yet, it didn't matter. Her entire body longed to succumb. She wanted—*needed*—his kisses on her lips, neck, throat, breasts—

With an almost superhuman effort, she pushed him away and took a staggering step backward. She could scarcely breathe, and her face was flushed. Everything inside her pounded rapidly.

Swiftly she turned away. She felt betrayed by her physical reaction to him, by the torrent of passion his touch had released within her.

How she wanted him! But she could not allow it. Succumbing to him was wrong. Whatever she did, she must do nothing to lead him on. She was a fraud; there was no Monica Williams. If she allowed him to seduce her, sooner or later they would both get hurt by the shaky façade of lies she had constructed.

"Why did you pull away, Monica?" he inquired softly. "Did you not like it? Or are you afraid of me?"

He touched her on the arm, but she quickly took another step away. Everything inside her was in a sudden turmoil. How could she explain to him that she wanted him . . . *needed him!* . . . but that she was here for an ulterior motive—in order to sleuth and spy and perhaps even destroy?

"Is there someone else?" he asked in a wounded voice.

He had come up quietly beside her and turned her around to face him. She let out a sharp little cry as he took her hand, lifted it to his lips, and kissed the tips of her fingers.

"Don't!" she whispered.

"Monica," he said softly.

She was trembling. "Eduardo, *please.*" She looked at him imploringly.

"Why not?" His eyes held hers and reached down, down, down into that deep secret spot inside her where they had reached earlier, in the corridor.

"I am not a naif," he continued quietly. "I know that a special young woman like yourself must already share a relationship with some very lucky man. But I respect that, Monica. I really do."

She drew a deep breath. *Oh, God!* she thought in anguish. *Why can't he just stop?*

He said, "I know we have only just met . . . but you do see, do you not? All I am asking is that you give the two of us a chance."

Her knees were wobbly, and she found the air suddenly stifling.

"Is it asking for too much?" he repeated quietly.

"N-no . . . it's just . . ." She frowned, struggling for an adequate excuse, and then she was saved by the noise: from somewhere outside came the distraction of a thundering engine starting up. She glanced around at the vibrating futuristic door and computer consoles and video monitors, as though the clatter could be pinpointed there, somewhere.

"It is only the helicopter," he said.

"Twelve o'clock high . . ." she murmured.

"Why, yes," he said in surprise. "How did you know?"

"Oh, just by my stomach," she lied quickly. "It always starts to growl at twelve noon on the dot. You could set your clock by it."

And she thought, *Damn! How stupid can I be? If I'm not careful, he'll know I've been watching the yacht and am familiar with the helicopter's daily flights!*

"If your stomach says it is time to eat," he laughed, "then who are we to deprive it?"

"Good. I'm starving!"

"But first . . ." he said softly, and surprised her by drawing her into his arms and kissing her again.

At first she tried to push him away, but his arms tightened around her and she found her resolve weakening. Another shock went through her as his tongue darted into her mouth to probe and explore. Her initial reluctance gave way to eager response.

She stifled a cry as he gently pulled himself back and held her at arm's length. His eyes were wide and luminous.

"We best go and have lunch," he whispered, "before we do something neither of us will regret."

"Yes," she whispered shakily and nodded. "We best go and have lunch."

# 18

## At Sea

*L*unch was al fresco, served at a round, silk-draped table inside one of the silken tents. Off butterfly-shaped plates. While they sat on antique carved Venetian grotto chairs.

Zarah. All in silver: loose, low-cut crocheted sweater of silver rayon, short silver ankle boots with spiky heels, silver turban with a feather sticking straight up the front à la Theda Bara. Plus metallic silver tights that made her legs look as if they were liquid mercury. She had barely nibbled at a few artful crudités and a scant teaspoon of caviar, and had fished a Sterling Silver rose out of its vase. Now she was holding it by its long, thornless stem, stroking the bud languorously across her cheeks, into her bosom, and against her nose and mouth.

Head tilted sideways, Zaza was slumped in her wheelchair, where she had contentedly nodded off in the midst of eating. She was snoring quietly.

Eduardo, seated opposite Stephanie, was devouring a stuffed lobster—while surreptitiously playing footsie with her under the table.

And Stephanie, struggling to maintain a straight face, feigned interest listening to Ernesto de Veiga as he fastidiously ate caviar with a teaspoon and no garnishings, and kept up a steady stream of conversation.

"We do not entertain much anymore," he was saying, smiling charmingly at her and ignoring Zarah's sharp eyes flashing in his direction as he added, "especially such a beautiful young guest as yourself. We have become quite reclusive, too busy with our own interests. Of course, we do attend the occasional opera or philharmonic. But, all in all, our social lives are not what they used to be, no, not at all . . ."

He paused to eat a spoonful of caviar, biting delicately into it to release the flavor slowly upon his palate.

After he swallowed, he gestured with his spoon and said, "Why don't you tell us something about yourself?"

"Oh, but there's really very little to tell."

"On the contrary!" Ernesto smiled at her. "I'm sure there is very much to tell! For instance, do you like opera? Or do you prefer the music of your own . . . ah . . . more youthful generation?"

Stephanie nibbled at a bit of lobster. "To tell you the truth," she lied, "I hardly know the first thing about classical music." She tilted her head and arranged her features into a thoughtful expression. "You don't suppose it's because one develops a taste for it as one gets older?"

Ernesto looked at her from under his hooded eyes and nodded. "You are quite right. Opera, like fine wine, requires a connoisseur. Both improve with one's maturity and experience."

He reached for his glass, swirled the wine around in it, and inhaled its bouquet.

"I still find a fragrant, full-bodied vintage quite impossible to pass up," he said, taking a sip, and setting the glass down. "Much as I find it impossible to pass up any of Richard Wagner's operas, I suppose."

"I've always found Wagner ponderous and rather depressing," Stephanie said.

"Really?" Ernesto looked surprised. "Wagner? Depressing?" He frowned. "To me he has always been extremely rousing and uplifting, much in the way a church service can be."

"I'm afraid I'm not very religious," Stephanie admitted.

"But you do agree that religion has its uses?" Ernesto inquired. He ate another spoonful of caviar.

"You mean as Karl Marx is to have said? As an opiate for the masses?"

"Oh dear me, heavens no!" He chuckled. "I meant—as a *catalyst*. Hasn't religion, over the centuries, been an inspiration for all the best artists and composers? Raphael, Brahms, Michelangelo, Handel . . . even Dali. Tell me, Ms. Williams." He looked at her questioningly. "Do you like Dali?"

"Well . . ." Stephanie said slowly, "I never really gave it much thought. But I suppose he was an awfully good technician."

"Critics have always launched attacks upon technical perfection," Ernesto replied. "Really, it is an outrage, if you ask me! Tomorrow," he said, "we are flying to Milan. Mirella Freni is singing *Madama Butterfly* at La Scala. We have a permanent box there. Would you like to join us?"

Stephanie's pulse had sped up and she could feel her face flush. "Milan . . .?" she murmured, suddenly remembering her all-too-recent visit with Boris Guberoff.

"A family box at La Scala," Eduardo explained, "is the ultimate status symbol in Milan. Especially if it is on the first tier."

"Really?"

He nodded. "Mother loves La Scala," he went on. "Perhaps it is because she has an old friend in Milan. They always go to see the performances together."

"Oh?" It was all Stephanie could think of to say.

"Yes. He's a former pianist."

Stephanie's heart stopped beating altogether, as if the timer on a bomb had ceased ticking. And then, when her heartbeat continued, it was rapid and arrhythmic.

"Who is he?" she forced herself to ask, although in her heart she already knew.

Ernesto smiled, "He is quite well known really. His name is Boris Guberoff. Surely you have heard of him?"

"Only by name." Stephanie quickly dipped her nose into her wine. It was far too late to wish she'd put off visiting Boris Guberoff: that was water under the bridge. Still, what she wouldn't give for the opportunity to see Zarah, Ernesto, and Guberoff together! God only knew what she might learn! However, of one thing she was absolutely certain—she didn't dare let the old pianist see her in present company. He had been too traumatized by her visit to ever forget her, and could be too sharp-eyed not to make the connection between "Monica Williams" and "Virginia Wesson." No. A new hairdo and a name change might not be enough of a disguise. The possibility existed that he'd see through it right away. She also knew, intuitively and positively, that he would have no compunction about trumpeting the fact that she was a fraud. On the contrary: he'd delight in getting back at her.

Eduardo said to his father, "Of course, if Monica prefers, she and I could always explore Capri together while you and Mother are in Milan." He turned to Stephanie with questioningly raised eyebrows.

Stephanie felt giddy with relief. "I've never been to Capri," she said quickly, her eyes glowing. "Do you think I'll like it?"

Ernesto said, "Everyone loves Capri."

"Mmm . . ." Stephanie tried not to appear too eager. "Capri does sound rather enticing. But then, so does La Scala." Pretending to have to think it over, she dipped her forefinger into her wine and ran it slowly around the rim of the glass, making it vibrate and chime. Finally she sighed and sat back. "Well. The weather *is* perfect . . . and with the promise of sea and sun . . ."

"We'll take the Magnum!" Eduardo was delighted. "Good! Then that is settled!"

From the distance came the sound of the approaching helicopter. Ernesto took it as a signal to push back his chair and got to his feet. He held out his hand to Zarah.

"Yes, yes. I hear it." Sighing, she plucked the last petal off the rose and let it flutter to the table. Then she took his hand and rose to her feet. She stood there looking down at her son. "We will see you at dinner?"

Eduardo nodded. "Yes."

"Good." Zarah turned to Stephanie and inclined her head slightly. "Ms. Williams," she said expressionlessly.

"Good-bye," Stephanie said politely. "And thank you so much for the lunch. It was lovely."

Zarah nodded abstractedly, and Stephanie watched as the two of them, still holding hands, walked aft to the helipad. When they reached it, Colonel Valerio joined them, and she saw all three of them making sun visors of their hands while they scanned the sky.

*What are they waiting for?* Stephanie asked herself as Colonel Valerio pointed. *Who—or what?—can the helicopter be bringing?*

And then the Bell Jet Ranger roared in overhead, blotting out the sun and casting a huge shadow. Stephanie ducked her head out of the tent and looked up. The metal mosquito was a hundred feet in the air, hovering and turning on its axis.

To her left, Zaza awoke with a start and let out a little cry, and blinked. "Oh!" she said, disconcerted, and looked around. "Why, I must have been dreaming—"

But it was impossible to hear anything more. Swooping down on its underbelly, the helicopter descended like a hawk, creating great warm gusts of wind which tore any conversation to shreds. The tent flapped furiously, the water in the pool churned, and the Plexiglas wind screens quivered in their tracks. Stephanie had to squint against the blast of air, and back by the helipad, she saw Zarah bending over, clutching her turban to her head.

It was a masterful landing, executed on the proverbial dime. As soon as the skids touched down in the center of the big letter H on the deck, the *whup-whup-whup* of the rotors decreased and the engine noise began to fade into a dying whine.

Ducking down, Colonel Valerio ran to open the passenger door. From inside, someone passed him a red-and-white molded plastic container, much like an oversized thermos fitted with a handle. Holding it in one hand, he used his other to help a small woman in a white lab coat climb out. Then, while the pilot shut his machine down, the four of them, leaning forward to avoid the rotor wash, quickly made their way to the nearest stairs and disappeared.

Stephanie looked across the table at Eduardo.

"That was Dr. Vassiltchikov," she said thoughtfully.

Eduardo didn't have to turn around to look. "Yes," he said.

Stephanie frowned. "She was carrying something, like a thermos. What's in it?"

"Medication."

"But what for?"

"Long ago," he explained, "on a trip through the Amazon, my mother and father caught a very rare opportunistic infection. It is incurable."

"Incurable!"

He nodded. "Incurable and deadly. Luckily, Dr. Vassiltchikov was with them, and formulated their medication. Unfortunately, without their daily doses, they could die." He added softly, "Now you know why we have the hospital facilities with the treatment rooms aboard."

"And the medication has to be flown in?"

"Each and every day." He nodded.

"But . . . surely they must have enough of it stockpiled!"

Eduardo shook his head. "You do not understand. It has to be manufactured fresh daily, and used within a twelve-hour period. Otherwise, it loses its potency."

And Stephanie thought: *Medication? Or the elixir of eternal youth? I wonder . . . which is it?* But instead of asking Eduardo further questions, she said, "Oh-oh."

"What's the matter?"

She pushed back her chair and smiled sheepishly. "I have to use the powder room. I'll be right back. You don't have to get up."

But he proved himself a gentleman all the same, only sitting back down as Stephanie drifted aft. Once certain she was out of his sight, her footsteps quickened purposefully. Hurrying inside, she gripped the gold banister and went down the stairs which Zarah, Ernesto, Colonel Valerio, and Dr. Vassiltchikov had just used. From the deck below, she could hear fragments of their receding conversation.

Grateful for the thick carpeting which muffled her footsteps, she hurried after them. When she reached the deck below, she could see them walking down a corridor toward a flood of refracted brilliant white light which was shot through with rainbows.

She recognized the source of that splintering light at once. It had to come from the midship atrium: the effect of its soaring crystal columns and skylight was unmistakable. Then, seeing Colonel Valerio turning to look back, she quickly ducked around the corner and flattened herself against the paneled bulkhead.

She counted to fifteen, then edged her head around the corner for another peek. The foursome was descending the atrium's curving staircase now, the little doctor in the lead and Colonel Valerio, carrying the container, bringing up the rear.

Stephanie waited until his head disappeared from sight, and then strode briskly forward. *Now, if only I don't run across anyone,* she thought hopefully, speeding up again until she reached the octagonal, light-flooded atrium.

Now her pace slowed and she approached with caution. Turned a full 360-degree circle, eyes sweeping every direction.

There was no one in sight, but from below drifted the faint murmur of receding voices. Best she hurry lest she lose sight of them.

Silently she trotted down the wide, carpeted stairs. She found the massive, fluted crystal columns intimidating rather than stately. When she reached the deck below, Stephanie's eyes ticked here and there, systematically checking corridor, doorways, rounded corners. She was relieved to find no one in sight—and herself suddenly in familiar territory. She had been here earlier with Eduardo, and knew exactly where she was.

This corridor was short, and at the end of it was a set of swinging double doors with glass inserts.

The entrance to the shipboard hospital.

She hesitated, all her senses on high alert. If she remembered correctly, the hospital only had that one set of double doors; she could not recall having seen any other entrances or exits. At least, that had been her impression. Perhaps there was another way in and out—possibly through Dr. Vassiltchikov's forbidden laboratory?

Stephanie's heart stuttered and tension, like sharp little pinches, twitched in her arms.

She stared at the doors. Dare she slip in and spy on whatever they were doing? And what if she was discovered keeping her reluctant hosts under surveillance—what then?

She told herself that some things were better left unanswered. Still, she couldn't help but cast a longing glance up the thickly carpeted stairs: the urge to turn around and flee right up them was overwhelming. Then, as her eyes flicked back to the double doors, her heart really started to jump. Through the inset glass, she could see someone approaching the door from inside.

Someone was leaving the hospital! Would see her when he or she came out—perhaps had seen her already!

Like lightning, she darted back out of sight, flattening herself behind the fluted rainbow distortions of the nearest crystal column. She held her breath, aware of her clammy hands, the nervous tic of her fingers. Would she be seen? Or would the clear, dazzling column of icy light protect?

Tense seconds ticked by with excruciating slowness. Nothing . . . nothing—and then she heard the hospital doors swing open and flap shut again, and moments later she saw—

Colonel Valerio! Striding past her and starting up the stairs. So close she could have reached around the column and tapped him on the shoulder, could smell his spicy aftershave lotion. Surely he must see her! Smell her! Somehow sense her presence—!

But he continued climbing the shallow stairs with that ramrod military bearing of his.

Relief was painful and swollen in her chest. The instant he disappeared from sight, she slid out from behind the column and swiftly tiptoed down the corridor to the hospital. Just outside the doors, she stopped and flattened herself against the wall. Then, cautiously, she peered in through one of the glass insets.

The coast was . . . *clear?* Could it be? Well, it was—at least as far as she could see from here.

She drew a deep breath, gently pushed one door open, and stuck her head inside. Quickly she glanced around in all directions.

Incredible! The coast really *was* clear!

She slipped inside on mouse feet, careful to let the door shut without so much as a whisper. Through a half-open doorway she could hear voices conversing softly. Like the proverbial moth drawn to the flame, so too Stephanie was drawn to that door. She peered through the crack between the hinges with one eye.

She saw Zarah and Ernesto waiting by the hatch leading to the treatment room while Dr. Vassiltchikov was bent over the computer console, busy punching keys, the red-and-white thermos container on the counter beside her. As the little doctor's scarlet-tipped fingers darted over the keyboard, the color video monitors built into the wall came on, one by one, like orderly screens in an electronics emporium—or mission control at NASA.

Stephanie held her breath, her attention riveted. Each twenty-seven-inch, high-definition screen—three rows of six, eighteen in all—showed a different angle of the same . . .

*Treatment room? Art gallery? Which* was *it?*

Stephanie's eyes scanned the monitors—top row, left to right; center, right to left; bottom, left to right—seeing eighteen views of the same streamlined, monochromatic cocoon. Soft glowing pools of light. Beige, geometrically sheared seamless carpet. Two side-by-side gray leather chaises, each slightly different, contoured to a specific human form. She could not help but notice how flawlessly everything had been put together, so that an almost Oriental kind of serenity had been conjured from the hardest surfaces and roughest textures: lacquer, leather, bronze, steel. And hanging on the textured beige walls, art. Major art. Museum of Modern Art-type art. A de Kooning, a large Helen Frankenthaler, a Hans Hofmann, and a very long and narrow Kenneth Nolan.

Strangely, it was not the living trio but the televised, closed-circuit pictures which held Stephanie in thrall—perhaps, she thought, because she was subconsciously using the familiarity of television to still her agitation, her fear of discovery?

Suddenly a voice caught her attention and her eyes abandoned the monitors, flicked down toward Dr. Vassiltchikov, who was saying something—in Portuguese or German, Stephanie couldn't be sure which. She saw Ernesto turn slightly to murmur a reply, and then heard the musical scale of Zarah's soft glissando laughter.

With all the flourish of a concert pianist hitting the final note, Dr. Vassiltchikov tapped one last key and picked up the plastic thermos by its handle. Leaving the video monitors switched on, she joined Zarah and Ernesto at the hatch, where she took a piece of plastic, like a credit card, out of her lab coat pocket and fed it into a slot by the door. There was a moment's wait, then came a stanza of soft electronic beeps, a yellow light blinked on, then a green and—lo and behold!—the hatch slid aside.

Dr. Vassiltchikov waited, hand extended, until her card slid back out and she pocketed it and led the way in, stepping over the sill of the open hatch on thin, birdlike legs. Stephanie glanced at the monitors, but the hatch obviously did not lead directly into that room. Her gaze flicked back to the hatch. Zarah was tugging off her silver turban, shaking out her rich head of honey blond hair. Ernesto took her hand, helped her step through the hatch, and then followed. To Stephanie's surprise, the hatch did not automatically close, but remained open.

Relaxing slightly, she moved away from behind the half-open door and peered around it, her eyes instinctively sweeping the walls and ceiling for security cameras. Seeing none, she took a deep breath, swiftly made up her mind, and hurried inside. She stopped right in front of the video monitors, close enough to make out the smallest details on the high-definition pictures. She listened intently, but the voices she heard coming from the hatch were receding, seemed far away now. She glanced back at the monitors. Still nothing but an empty room.

Perhaps she was wasting her time? Imagining a mountain when she was seeing a molehill?

A sudden movement on the video monitors caught her attention. The trio was entering the room, all eighteen images transmitted from different heights and angles, so that with the sound turned off, Stephanie had the peculiar feeling that she was watching a silent movie shot with eighteen different cameras.

Every movement—Dr. Vassiltchikov setting down the thermos on a sleek brushed steel table, Zarah and Ernesto casually starting to get undressed, all the while keeping up a conversation Stephanie couldn't hear, the way Zarah picked up a set of headphones, pressed one foam cup against an ear and frowned slightly until she was satisfied with what she was hearing—everything, every last movement and gesture, had that air of routine, of having been performed many hundreds, possibly thousands, even tens of thousands of times before. Even the way Dr. Vassiltchikov handled the thermos, as if she were some priestess performing an oft-repeated ritual.

Abruptly, one of the screens began malfunctioning so that it blinked and sent the picture into oscillating waves. Stephanie did her best to ignore the flashes, and kept her eyes on a close-up of the thermos.

Not that it was a thermos, really. She could tell now that it was shaped differently from the usual container; it was fatter and had been molded so that it bulged outward at the center. Also, it had a built-in combination lock centered on the top of the lid. Still, it looked almost ridiculously ordinary and insignificant. Yet Dr. Vassiltchikov was handling it as reverently as if it contained the relics of some saint. She spun the combination lock to the left, then the right, then the left again, and with a practiced twist of the wrist, had the lid unscrewed and lifted it.

Swirls of vapor escaped . . . cold. Freezing cold.

Stephanie was spellbound. If only the screen above would stop oscillating! It really was maddening, the way it impinged upon her concentration! And just as Dr. Vassiltchikov was extracting something from within!

Using her right hand as a visor, Stephanie shielded her eyes from the flashes and drew instinctively closer to the monitor, her attention riveted by a round, wire mesh basket which had been suspended inside the container. After the doctor had lifted it out, Stephanie noticed two sealed glass tubes, like bulb basters without the bulb, nestled within the plastic-coated mesh. Holding the basket up to the light, the doctor inspected the tubes visually, nodded to herself, and set it back down. Then, pulling out a drawer outfitted with a control panel, she pressed one of a row of buttons and glanced up at the ceiling.

Almost instantly, two identical robotic arms, all shiny futuristic steel and taut cables and smooth sprockets, descended into view from overhead. Stephanie could almost hear the soft whir of motor drive; she was oblivious now to the malfunctioning monitor.

The high-tech arms came to a stop, the wrenchlike grips within a foot of the table.

Utmost caution now . . . Dr. Vassiltchikov lifting one glass tube from its nest and carefully placing it, thin funnel-end up, in one of the robotic grips. Again, Stephanie had the impression of soft whirs as the finely calibrated wrench tightened, holding the fragile tube without crushing it.

Her gaze swung to another monitor, opened her perspective to a wide angle. She viewed Dr. Vassiltchikov sideways now, carefully lifting the second tube from the basket and placing it into the grip of the other wrench. Stephanie marveled at the delicacy with which the steel claw tightened around it. Watched the doctor hit another button—

Thin, clear plastic tubing. Nodding to herself, Stephanie thought she understood. It was some sort of IV hookup.

She was proven right when the little doctor opened another drawer, took out a thin packet, and broke the sterile wrapper. She used a hypodermic needle to puncture the funnel end of each glass container before breaking the sterile packaging around the openings of the thin tubes. Then deftly, she fitted the end of each tube over one of the pierced funnels.

More button tapping. The robotic arms swiftly rose now, retracting, pulling the tubes up with them. Up, up, higher, higher, not quite out of sight. Dr. Vassiltchikov switched to two small levers, moved them in tandem as if operating a radio-controlled toy car.

The robotic arms obeyed, glided inaudibly across the room, past the splatter of the de Kooning and the raggedy-edged colors of the

Frankenthaler. In a single neat maneuver, the doctor parked one directly over each chaise.

Stephanie switched her attention to yet another monitor. Zarah was naked now. Her body, thin and bony—downright scrawny except for the high firm breasts!—seemed as if it were viewed through a funhouse mirror; so gaunt it appeared distorted, angular, unreal. Stephanie saw the tensing and untensing of the woman's ribs and tight belly with every breath that she took, the slightest movement magnified by the silence.

*What's wrong with her?* she wondered. *Is it cancer? Anorexia? Vanity? Perhaps she's one of those fashion victims who gladly starves herself to be the perfect clothes hanger? Unless . . . her lack of body bulk was the result of illness, medication, or—*

*Immortality!*

Quickly her eyes skimmed from one monitor to the next to appraise Ernesto from various angles. Front. Back. Sides. He, too, was utterly naked and shockingly, unappetizingly emaciated for his build! But most amazing of all, despite the couple's nudity, and perhaps *because* of their very gauntness, there was nothing at all sexual about their naked states. If anything, they both seemed curiously *asexual;* somehow strangely androgynous.

Onscreen, Zarah took Ernesto's hand in hers. Together, the couple walked between the two narrow chaises, their lips moving, saying something—

What? Words of endearment, encouragement, *intrigue?*

Stephanie felt like a voyeur, like some sleazy rear window peeping Tom. *Which is exactly what I am,* she thought, helpless to tear her eyes away as Ernesto helped Zarah up onto the smaller of the two chaises. She lay down on her back, stretched luxuriously, reached for the headphones. He said something to her and she smiled and touched his arm affectionately before slipping on the headphones. Then he got on the other chaise and reclined on his back, scooting up and down a little to get comfortable.

Stephanie flashed upon human sacrifices atop pagan altars.

Abruptly Dr. Vassiltchikov passed in the forefront of the screen, startling Stephanie, who did an eyesweep of the other monitors, avoiding the malfunctioning one. After glancing at them all, she concentrated on the top row, second screen from the right: Zarah, headphones on, lying peacefully with her eyes closed, a forefinger conducting a rhapsody only she could hear.

Stephanie's eyes snapped to the screen beside it: Ernesto fiddling with electronic controls on the side of his chaise, making it move in three sections, like a hospital bed.

And, on a monitor diagonally below, Dr. Vassiltchikov. Head tilted back, arms outstretched as though orchestrating the slowly descending robotic arms, which stopped two feet above the chaises, where the wrench grips automatically rotated in their sprockets until the glass containers were upside down. Stephanie watched as the doctor pulled down the plastic tubing of Zarah's IV, tore open another sterile needle packet, and inserted a long hypodermic to the end of the tube. She started the IV flow to clear it of trapped air, gently lifted Zarah's arm, and—

"Ouch!" Stephanie vicariously felt the pain in the crook of her own elbow.

Curiosity, morbid fascination, and now repulsion—all kept Stephanie glued to the screen, like a willing spectator at a horror movie, at once recoiling, yet at the same time unable to tear her eyes away. Her face mirrored her personal distaste as clearly as her voice had involuntarily expressed the stab of pain in Zarah's arm.

On another screen the little doctor repeated the IV ritual with Ernesto. The IVs dripped slowly . . . the doctor went back and forth, adjusting the flow . . . the lights in the room slowly dimmed until only the paintings were awash with light . . . and the two patients lay there, cosseted by luxury even while undergoing medical treatment, even as intravenous tubes fed them—*what*—?

But now was not the time to ponder or loiter: on the monitors, Stephanie saw Dr. Vassiltchikov heading for the door.

Prudently taking her cue, Stephanie left as mouselike as she had come. Only once she reached the staircase with its crystal columns did she permit herself to rush. Eduardo was waiting, and she really had no idea how long she had been gone. Too long, surely, to use going to the bathroom as an excuse? *I'd better think up something fast,* she told herself.

The call came to the yacht's hospital as Dr. Vassiltchikov was on her way out. She picked up the remote telephone. "Vassiltchikov." She listened for a moment. "One moment, Captain," she said, and punched the *hold* button. "It is for you." She brought the remote over to Ernesto.

He took it from her. "Thank you, doctor."

Dr. Vassiltchikov nodded briskly and left the treatment chamber and went out to her workstation at the video monitors.

Ernesto released the *hold* button. "Sim, Capitão?"

"It concerns the vessel which is following us," Captain Falcão informed him.

"And?"

"Our radar shows it is still eighteen kilometers behind us. Is there anything you would like me to do?"

"One moment, Capitão." Ernesto turned his head and looked at Zarah. She was lying back, eyes closed, listening to her favorite music over the headphones: her own recently digitalized recording of "Der Freischütz," from 1949. She was in a world of her own.

"*Não,* Capitão," he said softly into the telephone. "I still do not think it necessary to do anything." He flicked a glance at Zarah, who was too involved with her music to overhear. "But let us keep this matter between ourselves, shall we? There is no need to cause anyone undue alarm."

When Stephanie returned to the sundeck, Zaza and the wheelchair were gone; so, too, were the dirty dishes and the buffet. All evidence of lunch had been cleared away.

Eduardo rose from inside the tent as she approached. "I was ready to send out a search party," he said, grinning.

She thought, *Merlin's law: If a lie is called for, one might as well make it a useful one.*

"I stopped in my stateroom to fetch my camera," she said, "but I couldn't find it anywhere. It seems to be missing." She sat down. "You don't think it was left behind in Marbella, do you?"

He cleared his throat. "I see that I must have forgotten to tell you."

"Forgotten to tell me?" She frowned. "Tell me what?"

His gaze became distant. "My parents are very protective of their privacy. I am afraid they are almost pathologically camera shy."

She stared at him. "So what are you telling me?"

"Colonel Valerio always collects our guests' cameras when they first board." He smiled and shrugged helplessly. "Obviously, since you crashed into our midst the way you did, he was unable to inform you of this. He must have taken it upon himself to lock it away for safekeeping."

"I see," she said.

He reached out, took both her hands in his, and looked at her with concern. A passing breeze lifted her hair, raising the sharp slices of bangs into a raven's wings. "I hope you are not upset."

"No," she said. "Now that you've explained it, how could I be?"

"Good. And I am glad you returned in time."

"Why?" She tilted her head. "Was I about to miss out on something?"

He let go of one of her hands, kept holding the other, and pulled her up and led her over to the port side of the deck. A push of a button, and the Plexiglas windscreens slid soundlessly aside in their motorized tracks.

He leaned over the deck railing and pointed forward. "That," he said, and turned to look at her, the breeze ruffling his hair. "You almost missed that."

Now she leaned out over the railing. And there, near the horizon, something hazy and bluish rose dramatically out of the sea.

He stepped back and slid an arm around her waist. Hugging her close, he said softly, "Capri! Just think! It is all ours to discover!"

# 19

*Capri*

It had been the island of Augustus and Tiberius, this rough-cut gem of precipitous cliffs, olive trees, holm oaks, tall pines, wild poppies, and fragrant broom and wild sage. And it was still as magical today, this limestone Eden in a peacock-blue sea, as it had been twenty centuries earlier when it was the playground of the Roman emperors. If ever a romantic paradise for lovers existed, it was Capri.

Stephanie found it impossible not to fall under its sunny spell.

She wondered: *Is it the island which so bewitches? Or Eduardo?*

They had started out at dawn, just the two of them, long before the ferries and hydrofoils from Naples began shuttling the hordes of daytrippers over from the mainland.

Now, with the sun at its noonday height, they were anchored off the needlelike rocks of the Faraglioni, the sea as reflective as crumpled aluminum foil.

After the *Chrysalis*, the sleek sixty-foot muscle boat, with its low rakish hull, wraparound windscreen, and massive cushioned sunning area, seemed wonderfully intimate somehow—their own plush island moored a stone's throw from the paleolithic cliffs.

Sighing contentedly, Stephanie slipped off the spaghetti straps of her bikini top and rolled over onto her stomach to bake.

She smiled with bleary pleasure.

Eduardo was lying on his side next to her, feasting on iced Dom Pérignon, Beluga caviar, and her. "More champagne?" he asked.

"Mmm." She reached for her glass and held it out for a refill. Then she held it to her nose, enjoying the sensation of the popping bubbles. She stretched luxuriously. *Just the two of us!* she thought warmly.

Sipping her champagne, she reflected dreamily upon the last six hours.

The magic had started early. "We'll explore what we can before all the tourists arrive," he'd told her on the ride from the *Chrysalis* to shore. "Then we'll find some wonderful, deserted spot and drop anchor, swim, and have lunch. We can explore the island some more after the hordes have departed . . . perhaps enjoy a late dinner at Al Grottino."

"It sounds lovely," she'd told him.

And it was. She had never experienced a place quite so beautiful and enchanting. She said to him, "One feels one is in the Garden of Eden."

He smiled. "And this early, it is easy to imagine us as Adam and Eve."

They walked for nearly an hour to the Villa Jovis, and the breathtaking view more than compensated for the hike.

"This used to be the palace of Tiberius," Eduardo explained as they strolled the villa's promenades, terraces, gardens, and stairways. "Like all the most beautiful spots on Capri, it is accessible only on foot."

The sun was growing steadily stronger, but there were delicious breezes and much cool shade, thanks to the arbors of flowering trellises overhead. And the scents and colors! Everywhere she looked, flowers spilled over walls and rocks like floral lava. This was truly a hanging garden of an island, with geraniums, lilies, bougainvillea, honeysuckle, and roses, and trees such as laburnum, dwarf pine, and aromatic lime. On their way back to the town, Eduardo showed her where, on the Via Camarelle, the view of the Carthusian monastery was framed entirely with blooms.

She had the sensation of always climbing either up or down—much of Capri being vertical, paths would suddenly turn into winding flights of steps bordered by flowering hedgerows, orchards, bucolic tiny vineyards, views of sugar-cube houses hugging the mountainsides.

"While we are here," Eduardo told her, "the gardens of Augustus are a must. They are but a few minutes' walk . . ."

And so they ventured there, and she was glad they did. There was every imaginable kind of tree and shrub and flower, many of them species she did not recognize, and the exotic colors were stunning to behold. He told her that eight hundred and fifty different kinds of flowers alone grew on the island, and then he steered her to the terraces.

The view was so breathtakingly dramatic that words would have been redundant, and so they admired it in silence. There were the impressive western cliffs and, offshore, the fantastical, needlelike rocks of the Faraglioni rising from the dazzlingly silver-flecked expanse of sea.

And now they were anchored offshore in the blazing noonday sun, on the seaward side of those very same needles. Totally hidden from sight by the Faraglioni. Content to let time and reality drift lazily by.

After a while, Eduardo got up. "What do you say we take a swim?"

She was still lying face-down on the cushions. "Mmm." She yawned and stirred. "You go on ahead. I've got to put my top back on."

"Here. Let me."

Kneeling down beside her, he helped her back into it, and she moaned softly as his touch sent electric currents rippling though her body. He could see the delicate muscles shifting and tensing under the smooth surface of her skin, and encouraged by her reaction, he slowly, ever-so-lightly, traced a fingertip along the ridge of her spine.

Her back arched, and he heard her sharp intake of breath.

Then he turned her around and hungrily clamped his lips over hers, capturing her mouth.

His raging passion sent meteors of fire streaking to the very core of her being, jolting her every nerve. She sensed the big boat whirling about, the sea thrashing, the cliffs roaring.

"My love," he murmured into her mouth, "my love."

Perhaps it was those all-important magic little words. Or the aphrodisiacal climate and the romantic morning. Or it might even have been all the champagne. Whatever the reason, she felt herself melt and greedily now, her slim arms entwined his neck and her lips returned his hunger in kind.

They were consuming one another, two starved cannibals savagely tasting the sweetness of each other's flesh.

He rolled over on his back, pulling her with him.

She gasped when she felt him loosening her bikini top. It was as if his mere touch aroused her, made her drunk with desire, and caused crackling static, like live sparks, to jump from her skin.

And then he slipped the constraining fabric off her and her breasts leaped free, full and strong, the swollen nipples jutting imperiously from the violet areolae.

For a moment he could only stare, his eyes raking the sleek perfect curves of her body. And then his hands explored. Cupped her breasts. Smoothed her latticed rib cage. Followed the firm flat belly that rose and fell with every breath she took.

She cried aloud as he pushed her bikini briefs down the curvaceous flare of her hips and off her legs. Totally naked she was, her recently dyed pubis a soft dark arrowhead, inviting and mysterious. Her thighs gleamed moistly.

Now it was her turn to undress him. Like a supplicant, she knelt before him and peeled his briefs down his legs. Two inches of electric-blue spandex gleamed in her fingers and then his phallus sprang free. So long, it looked, hard and thick and bold; so clean he smelled and masculine. She bent her head solemnly until her lips touched it, and he reached under her chin with his hand and raised her head with the tip of his finger.

Looking solemnly up into his eyes, she kissed his phallus.

The red glans throbbed and waved, as though it had a life of its own.

Still looking up at him, she gently tightened her hand around it. Tentatively flicked a snakelike tongue over it.

Now his hands blurred and he grabbed hold of her, the suddenness of the movement taking her by surprise. But gently he lowered her down to the cushions, and then lay atop her, flesh against flesh, life against life.

She shivered deliciously. So utterly perfect was this moment. So thrilling, to feel his nakedness against hers under the perfect dome of this vast blue sky. Body and soul she wanted to offer him.

"I love you," he whispered into her mouth.

She did not reply, but stared at him with a wild kind of abandon.

Fierce now became their embrace. Like combatants they dueled. Over and over they rolled, fueling each other's passion.

Stephanie reveled in his strength. Eduardo was so powerful, had such might contained in his tightly muscled body and swollen manhood. Such urgency and power held barely at bay.

Then he caught her hands and forced her down flat. Frantically she bucked to free herself, but his tender lips calmed her and she gave herself up to him.

Sounds. The world was reduced to moist little suckling noises. His mouth was exploring her breasts, his tongue trailing delicate little vortexes first around one nipple, and then the other.

She luxuriated in just lying there, her face tilted up to the sun like a sacrifice on a pagan altar as his lips paid unspeakable devotions. The sun dazzled, the heaving sea was her bed, and the needle spires of rocks her silent witnesses—earth, wind, and water bestowing blessings—and he was fire.

After a while, she imagined she was floating deliriously higher, ever higher. He was nibbling on a nipple now, rolling it gently between his teeth, and he let go of her right hand so that he could use it on her other nipple.

She squirmed beneath him as he squeezed it. Waves of pleasure and pain washed through her; a muffled cry escaped her lips.

Her nipple still in his mouth, he looked up into her face, but it held an expression of rapt concentration, her eyes fixed upon a point in the sky overhead. Again he squeezed. And again she cried out. But now her eyes were shut and her mouth was wide open in rasping ecstasy, as if she were drawing pleasure from the very air itself.

Slowly he moved his head down, down, down to her navel . . . his tongue kissing it . . . his lips sucking on it. Heavy shudders that nearly approached orgasms wracked her entire body and made her cry out even louder.

And then he slid even further down, grabbed her by the buttocks, and buried his face in her lap. Her body arched. Her buttocks rose off the cushions. She ground her groin into his face, her hands holding his head captive as she cried: "I can't stand it! Oh Eduardo, I can't stand it! I can't! I *can't!*" And her body spasmed and her breath rushed out in an explosive gasp as she came to orgasm.

Feeling his own torrent rise, he threw himself atop her. She was wet and ready and screamed in a delirium as he guided himself in, and then they were locked together in that immortal embrace from which all life stemmed.

Slowly began his thrusts; steadily they increased in tempo. Beneath him, she moaned and writhed, her hips rising ravenously up to meet him.

Deeper, deeper, deeper! The blood roared deafeningly in his ears, his heart pounded to a crescendo, and everything was reduced to the sensations of the groin. He tossed back his head and clenched his teeth. He could feel her firm muscles closing around him, clamping tight.

Faster, faster, faster! Here between her legs where she writhed like a vixen beneath him. Where they were joined by the umbilical of sex and there was nothing on this earth to tear them asunder.

And then her body arched and spasmed yet again as her second orgasm swept her away.

"Eduardo!" she screamed. "Oh, Eduardo! I'm dying! *I'm dying—!*"

Cruelly now, he assaulted her with the ride of her life. Grabbing her buttocks, he raised her hips high. In he plunged, and out again, and back in and then out! Her quivering screams rose to the skies and echoed from the rocks and traveled far across the water.

And finally, he could bear to hold back no more. His own scream merged with hers and the juices of life spewed forth just as a fresh wave of convulsions wracked her body.

His hips twitched one last time and then he slumped. Panting now, he let go of her, and the two of them collapsed on the cushions, still joined. Stephanie clung to him, her fingers still digging into his arms as she sobbed, "I love you, Eduardo. I love you . . ."

# 20

## Capri

The day-tourists had gone back to the mainland and Al Grottino was packed. Wineglass in hand, Stephanie looked around the vaulted, whitewashed room. The restaurant was located on the Via Longano, one of the tunnel-like *viuzzi* which passed for streets, and its devoted clientele were locals, guests from hotels on the island, part-time residents whose villas were their second, third, or fourth homes, and expatriates who had found paradise and stayed.

Setting down her glass, she smiled across the table at Eduardo. Everything about her was radiant: her heightened color, her eyes glowing with fulfillment. "This place is wonderful," she said softly, plucking a crisp matchstick of fried zucchini off her plate and biting off half. She munched it slowly, savoring the taste, and on impulse reached across the table and finger-fed him the other half.

His lips sucked in zucchini, fingertips, and all.

"Eduardo!" she laughed, feigning embarrassment. "What are people going to think?"

"That we're lovers?" He grinned raffishly. "I know I should behave myself, but"—he confided in a stage whisper—"the truth of the matter is, I cannot help myself! You see, it is all due to an ancient curse which is handed down through the men of my family!"

"*I* see," she said, making her eyes appropriately round and wide. "Genetic, is it? Just like thirsting for other people's blood?"

"And baying at the moon." He nodded definitely. "That is exactly what it is like!"

She rested her chin in the palm of her hand and smiled. Curious, how she felt as though they were the only two people in this restaurant . . . on this entire earth.

Eduardo smiled back at her. "What are you thinking?"

Her eyes were wide. "Would you believe—about how happy I am?" she whispered softly. "About how magical today has been?"

"Which is exactly what I have been thinking," he said.

She gave a wistful little sigh. "Why do I wish that today would never end!"

"Today does not have to end."

She frowned at him. "I—I don't understand."

He stared intently at her. "When the cruise is over, come back to Brazil with us!" His dark gaze was like a live spark reaching out to her. "That way, you and I can be together."

"Eduardo!" Her mouth actually dropped open. "Have you taken leave of your senses?"

He smiled. "I have never felt saner or happier in my entire life." He was silent for a moment. "Well? What do you say?"

She stared at him and then slowly shook her head. "You and I both know it's impossible."

He reached across the table and took both her hands in his. Lifting first one, and then the other, he soundlessly kissed each finger of both.

"And why should our dreams not come true?" he asked her quietly.

"But we have only just met! You know nothing about me!"

"On the contrary," he said solemnly, "I know everything which I believe to be important."

She shook her head and glanced down, studying the tablecloth. "No, Eduardo," she said in a strained whisper, "you don't."

He smiled. "But why let that bother you, if it does not bother me?"

"Because . . ." She took a deep breath and the blood rose up to her face. "Because what you don't know now could very well hurt you in the future!" she blurted.

He laughed indulgently. "Oh, Monica, will you stop being so melodramatic! My God! I know I fished you out of the sea like a mermaid, but you really do make it sound as if you are hiding the most sordid past!"

She was silent.

"Then, if you refuse to come to Brazil with me, I demand to know why."

"Well . . . for one thing I . . . I don't speak a word of Portuguese!"

He smiled. "I daresay you will pick that up quickly enough. And besides, it really is not necessary to speak it, you know. Most people you will come into contact with are quite fluent in English."

She said, "Eduardo, this is all so sudden! I mean . . . how would I support myself? I refuse to be kept, and I won't have a job waiting, so—"

He waved a hand negligibly. "That can all be arranged in the blink of an eye. You can have the job of your choice." There was irony in his grin, as well as humor. "Grupo da Veiga S.A. *is* Brazil, you know."

"But . . . you don't even know my area of expertise!" she protested.

He laughed. "I am sure we can fit you in somewhere. Shipping, lumber, mining, real estate, genetics, software, petroleum, garment manufacturing, pharmaceuticals, an airline . . . you name it, we own it. So voilà!" He flicked a finger at the rim of his glass, producing a clear treble chime. "You will have the pick of a career in the business of your choice!"

"Like magic," she murmured wryly.

"Like magic!" he agreed, and grinned. "Now, then," he said, placing both index fingers against his smiling lips, "tell me. Can you think up any more excuses why you should not come to Brazil?"

Stephanie had a quick sip of wine. "In time, I'm sure I'll be able to. But at the moment . . . er . . . n—" She stopped in midword, spilling wine on the tablecloth as a high-pitched squeal rang out, silencing her and the entire restaurant.

Her head snapped in the direction of the front entrance. She could see the source of the commotion now. A waiter had caught an urchin by the scruff of the collar and was lifting him until his kicking feet treaded air.

"*Aiuto!*" The flailing urchin howled like a wounded animal. "*Aiuto! Aiuto!*"

He was skinny and curly-haired and cute in a ragamuffin sort of way. Stephanie guessed that he couldn't be more than seven or eight years old. He had on shorts and dingy tennis shoes two sizes too big and a faded Bon Jovi T-shirt.

"How cruel!" she exclaimed pityingly. "What does that waiter think he's doing? He's hurting that little boy!"

Eduardo, too, had twisted around in his chair to see what the fuss was about. He turned back to her. "Little boy? Local pickpocket is probably more like it."

Stephanie was outraged by what she took to be Eduardo's blatant callousness. Her eyes flashed angrily. "Perhaps the poor thing's hungry!" she countered heatedly. "Have you given any thought to that?"

But before Eduardo could respond, a loud grunt issued forth from the waiter, and the man's eyes bulged comically. Doubling over in pain, he let go of the kid, who had obviously kneed him in the groin.

The urchin didn't hesitate. Now that he was free, he darted like quicksilver between a row of tables.

And the chase was on.

Two other waiters leapt forward to intercept him in the narrow aisle, but to no avail. Agile as a tadpole, the wily kid dropped down on all fours and quick-crawled under a table.

"Quick-witted little bugger!" Stephanie said admiringly. "Slippery, too. Look at the way he can move!"

Even as she said it, she saw his little head pop up from the other side of the table to scout the territory. Seeing yet another waiter advancing, the child prudently dove back out of sight—only to reemerge two tables away—straight into a waiting pair of arms.

The boy made one last valiant effort. Twisting half around, he shouted something in rapid-fire Italian and pointed directly across the low-ceilinged room at—

Eduardo.

Stephanie frowned.

"*Aspettare!*" Eduardo called out and gestured for the waiter to bring the boy over.

When the urchin was standing by their table, Eduardo spoke to him in fluent Italian, and the boy rattled off a quick staccato reply.

"*Quando? Che?*" Eduardo asked.

The boy replied something, and Eduardo turned to Stephanie. "Could you excuse me for a little while?" he asked quietly, pushing back his chair.

Stephanie had a sudden sense of foreboding. "What's happened?"

"It seems," Eduardo said quietly, "that another vessel has rammed the Magnum. I'm going down to the marina to check on the damage."

She let go of his arm and started to get up. "I'm coming with you."

He shook his head. "Please, Monica. Do us both a favor and stay here. I can get this matter settled much quicker by myself."

"If you're sure . . ." she said doubtfully.

"I am positive," he replied. "I shall take the funicular both ways. You will see. I will not be gone any time."

She nodded and watched in silence as he reached for his wallet, counted out some bills, and handed them to the urchin, who palmed them as expertly as a Las Vegas bookie.

Eduardo looked at her and hesitated. "You will wait for me?"

Stephanie nodded. "You know I will," she replied huskily.

He bent down and kissed her cheek and then, following the urchin, threaded his way between the tables.

She nursed her wine and waited. Eduardo was barely out of sight, and already she felt his absence like a physical pain. Every passing minute seemed like torturous hours, and each time she heard someone arrive, her heart would give a hopeful leap and her eyes would jump to the entrance.

But it was always a stranger—never Eduardo.

"Signorina?" The voice was soft and apologetic.

Startled, Stephanie glanced up. "Y-yes?"

It was the waiter. "The *monèllo*," he said, pointing across the room to the entrance. "The boy. He has returned."

She looked across the sea of heads to the front door. Sure enough, there he was again. The smudged urchin in the Bon Jovi T-shirt, impatiently shifting his weight from one foot to the other.

"Did he say what he wants?" She looked at the waiter questioningly.

The man nodded. "*Si.* He said the signore needs you urgently."

A thousand terrible scenarios suddenly flashed through her mind.

There was an accident with the funicular and Eduardo was mangled in the wreckage. And the owner of the boat that rammed the Magnum was hot-tempered and armed with a gun. And he's been jumped by a gang of knife-wielding thugs on the waterfront, and they've stabbed him and he's leaking precious blood.

Stephanie's face had turned deathly pale. It was so easy to imagine Eduardo lying injured somewhere—perhaps even dying. But she pulled herself together. "Thank you, signor," she said. *"Grazie."*

Carefully, she scraped back her chair and got to her feet. When she was outside, she breathed deeply of the bracing fresh night air. Darkness had long since fallen, and after the warm glow of the restaurant, the *viuzzi* was chilly; gloomy, mysterious, and vaguely threatening—more claustrophobic cave than picturesque tunnel-like street.

"Signorina?"

She looked down. It was the urchin, his pale face shining in the dim lamplight. Then she felt his hand on hers and he tugged urgently on it.

Holding onto her young guide's hand, she allowed herself to be led, stumbling after him, her feet tripping on the uneven cobblestones, the tunnel swallowing up her hollow, echoing footsteps. Deep threatening shadows were everywhere. These deserted, backstreet *viuzzi* were a dank maze, and now in the dark she immediately lost her bearings. She could hear water dripping; sniffed distastefully the sharp odor of cat feces; cried out in shock as her shoe splashed in a puddle.

On he led her, and on.

*"Sostare!"* The boy had stopped so suddenly that she nearly collided with him. In silence, she looked around and then let out a sharp gasp.

As if by its own volition, a thick door was creaking slowly open until it banged back against the ancient weathered stone wall. The rectangle of electric light was empty of human form, and spilled brightly down the narrow front stoop, casting the boy's and her own huge, distorted shadows high on the opposite wall. Somewhere, two fighting cats yeowled.

The urchin let go of her hand. *"Salire!"* He was motioning her up the narrow steps.

Stephanie stood undecided for a moment. Everything inside her had gone stone cold. *So Eduardo hadn't even made it down to the Marina Grande,* she thought with a sinking feeling. *He must have fallen, or been attacked, or have met with some other kind of accident.*

*"Qui!"* The boy gestured up the steps. *"Qui!"*

She looked around. The *viuzzi* was deserted, without even a stray cat in sight. A moth fluttered in the light, drawn to the door.

And, heart pounding, she followed it, rushing up the steps and bursting through the doorway, calling, "Eduardo! Eduar—"

Then the room was plunged into darkness.

"Ed . . . uar . . . do . . . ?" she whispered falteringly, looking around but unable to make out anything in the pitch blackness.

And then a hand was clapped over her mouth, stifling the scream before it could rise in her throat.

## ✍ *21* ✍

*New York City · Capri*

*I*t was 9:02 P.M. in Capri; 3:02 P.M. Eastern Standard Time in New York.

At the Ansonia, the telephone exploded into shrill urgent rings.

Sammy Kafka, a great believer in afternoon naps, grumpily snatched up the receiver on the second ring. "So all right already!" he mumbled sleepily into the mouthpiece. "If it makes you happy, I'm awake. Now talk. Talk!"

There was a hesitant pause at the other end. Then a woman's voice meekly said, "Mr. Kafka?"

"Yes, yes? Who is this?"

"Chartrice Franklin at St. Luke's Hospital? You remember me? The day nurse? You always give me a carnation whenever you visit Mr. Kleinfelder?"

*Oy gevalt!* Sammy scratched his head. Now how was he supposed to remember who he gave carnations to at that nurses' station? As a matter of chivalry, he handed one to whomever happened to be on duty, day or night.

*Chartrice Franklin* . . . he thought, struggling to get his fuzzy brain functioning. And then a light bulb glowed in his head. *Of course! The handsome black woman in ICU with the orange-tinted hair.*

Sammy said, "I apologize, Ms. Franklin," his voice suddenly courtly. "If I sounded a little crabby, it's just that you caught me napping."

"I'm sorry. I didn't mean to wake you. But I remembered, you asked to be notified the instant the patient came out of his coma?"

Now *that* jump-started Sammy's gray cells all right. Any remnants of sleep fell away like brittle husks.

"Has he?" he whispered hoarsely, the receiver trembling in his hand.

"Not fifteen minutes ago!" Chartrice told him happily. "I was seeing to another patient, and Betty, the other day nurse? Well, suddenly she starts screaming like a stuck pig, so I drop what I'm doing and run over to see what it is?" She paused. "Mr. Kleinfelder was comatose one minute and then sat up and goosed her the next!"

Sammy felt like doing somersaults—not that his body had permitted him such youthfully strenuous exercises for more decades than he cared to remember. He said, "May I ask you a question, Ms. Franklin?"

"Of course, Mr. Kafka."

"If I kiss you, will you marry me?"

"Oh, *you!*" she scoffed in mock exasperation. "I should've known!" And laughing, she hung up.

Sammy tossed the receiver into its cradle and leapt out of bed and for one of the rare instances in his life—possibly the *only* instance—the dapper dandy took absolutely no care in dressing. He jumped into a pair of trousers, snatched up whatever clothes were the handiest, and dashed out of the apartment.

*Trap!*

Stephanie clawed desperately at the hand clamped over her mouth. She couldn't get enough air, and the only sounds she could manage were muffled whines of terror. Too late, she realized her foolhardiness.

"Hmmmmmuuuhhh!" she managed again, her fingers yanking furiously at the large strong hand, but the grip was too powerful and relentless and would not loosen. Even as she struggled, she felt herself being pulled steadily backward into deeper darkness.

"Hmmmphfug!" Her jaw felt numb from attempting to scream, her eyes were wide as saucers, and the shock of fear was greater than any she had ever experienced. Remembering the explosion at the Osborne which had killed Pham, Stephanie's blood ran cold. *So I was right!* she thought wildly. *That blast had been meant for me!*

Every instinct urged her to free herself and flee.

But how? *How—?*

*Fight!* shrieked the Furies inside her head. *Fight tooth and nail! Struggle! Maim or cripple or at least temporarily wound your abductor! Trick him! Resist! Go limp! Try anything—so long as it gives you a few precious seconds. A tiny headstart is all you need!*

But before she could act upon any of these strategies, she was pulled into another room, and the door slammed shut with finality. Unexpectedly, a naked overhead light bulb went on. After the darkness, she squinted against the sudden wash of raw light. Her eyes darted suspiciously about. Three rough, whitewashed walls glared brightly in her field of vision. A utilitarian room, sparsely furnished.

Abruptly, the hand released her mouth and she was suddenly shoved forward—not with enough force for her to lose her balance or fall, but enough for her captor to be out of reach of flailing arms and scratching talons.

Stephanie's heart began to pound even more wildly. *This is it!* she thought. *My chance for escape!*

She whirled around to face the door. And found the way blocked.

"Forget about it," the man standing in front of it advised. "You're not going *anywhere*."

\* \* \*

"Pen!" rasped Aaron Kleinfelder, his hoarseness the result of unused vocal cords, dehydration, and physical debilitation. His bed was in a semi-upright position, he was still attached to all his IVs and monitors, and a breathing tube was clipped to his nostrils.

"Here you go," Sammy Kafka said gently, placing a pad on Aaron's lap. He took the cap off a felt-tip pen and put the writing instrument in the man's shaky hand. Gently he closed Aaron's feeble fingers around it. "And don't worry about neatness. I can decipher your chicken scratching later. All right?"

Aaron gave a slight nod. Then slowly, weakly he began to scrawl.

"You . . . you . . . you *bastard!*" Stephanie paced the wooden floor wildly, furiously. "You sneaky, conniving, untrusting *bastard!* I can't believe you've been following me!"

She raised both hands in the air and held them there a moment before letting them drop to her sides in disgust.

"You followed us all over Capri this morning!" she accused, whirling on him.

Arms folded in front of his chest, Johnny Stone was leaning casually against the heavy door, his face expressionless, his eyes hooded. "Guilty." He inclined his head.

"And now you've lured me here!" She drew a reedy breath as a lot of things suddenly fell neatly into place. "There was no accident down at the Marina Grande!" she exclaimed with dawning realization. "That was just a ruse to get Eduardo out of the way!"

"And you here." Johnny inclined his head a second time. "Guilty again."

"And you . . . you had the nerve, the . . . the unmitigated *gall* . . . to follow the yacht here all the way from Marbella!"

"Not the most pleasant of voyages aboard a small cabin cruiser, let me assure you. Hardly like the luxurious seagoing *Chrysalis.*" His voice was heavy on the irony, but his face was still devoid of any expression. "But to answer your accusation: I once again plead guilty."

"For Chrissakes!" she shouted. "Will you stop using that word!"

Johnny's eyelids flickered. "What word? Oh. You mean—'guilty'?"

Her nostrils flared as she drew a deep breath. Then, hugging herself with her arms, she cupped her elbows in her hands and looked away.

He laughed shortly. "Come on, now! My professions of guilt could hardly be impinging upon *your* conscience!"

She spun at him, eyes blazing like lasers. "And what's that supposed to mean?"

"What do you think it's supposed to mean?" He eyed her with the easy insolence of one who has the most intimate knowledge of his antagonist and feels no compunction using it as a weapon. "Considering the fact that you're obviously without conscience—"

"Without . . . without *what!*" she sputtered, staring at him in open-mouthed incredulity. *How dared he!* she thought. *Oh, how dared he! What nerve! Accusing me of having no conscience! Has he forgotten what happened to Grandpa? Has he forgotten the explosion at the Osborne? Good Lord—Johnny can't honestly believe I'd be safe traipsing around as Stephanie Merlin after that close call, can he?*

"What's the matter?" he taunted smugly. "Cat got your tongue?"

"The hell it has!" she objected, ardent in her fury. "You've got some nerve—"

"No, Stephanie," he corrected her quietly, "I'm not the one with nerve. I suggest you listen to me, and listen well. Because, you see, *you* are the one with nerve—"

"*Me!*" she cried violently, quivering from head to toe with potent, indignant affront. "How *dare* you!"

"I'll tell you how I dare." He was still leaning against the door in a deceptively casual pose, his body impassive and relaxed, but his voice was cold. "I dare because I didn't fake my own death and let my friends and acquaintances mourn and bury me. I dare because I wasn't hiding out in Connecticut while someone who cared deeply about me cried and drank himself into stupors."

Prickles of heat stung her cheeks, and in her forehead, a vein pulsated uncontrollably. "Do you think I had any choice?" Her voice trembled. "Do you think I did it for the *fun* of it? For the mere *thrill?*"

He stared at her. "To tell you the truth," he said softly, "I really don't know what to think anymore."

"Then think what you will!" she snapped angrily. "Jump to your own conclusions! That's what you've done already, isn't it?"

"No," he said quietly, "as a matter of fact, it isn't. But I do know one thing, Stephanie. You've got a lot of explaining to do."

"Like hell I do!" She raked him with scathing eyes, sweeping him from head to toe and back up again. "I don't owe you anything. And besides." She tossed her head. "I've had about all of this I can take. Step aside?"

When he didn't move, she started to push past him, but he gripped her arm and pulled her toward him.

"Not so fast," he said softly into her surprised, upturned face. "Like I was saying, you owe me some explanations."

"And like *I* was saying," she spat, eyes flashing, "I don't have to explain anything to you! You're not my keeper!"

"Perhaps not," he admitted, his gaze unblinking. "But I was your lover."

"At least you've got something right! 'Was' *is* the operative verb!"

He held onto her a moment longer, and then he released her and stepped aside. "Very well," he said disgustedly. "Have it your way. Go."

"Why, I thank you kindly, sir!" she said sarcastically before pushing open the door.

"One piece of advice before you leave." His voice followed her out into the other room. "If you're not in the States the next few days, I suggest you have a friend videotape your rival TV shows."

She froze in her tracks, her back still turned, and when she spoke her voice was hushed. "And why's that, might I ask?"

With a deceptively slow, catlike grace, he turned around and leaned against the doorframe. "Because," he improvised softly to her unmoving back, "I don't think you'd want to miss out on the big hullaballoo."

"Hullaballoo?" Her voice trembled. "What hullaballoo?"

"Why, the one over the tabloid story of the year! Of the decade!"

Her spine stiffened, but she did not turn around.

" 'Hard Copy' . . ." He began to reel off some of the names. " 'Current Affair' . . . even 'Entertainment Tonight.' None of them will be able to resist pulling out all the stops when it comes to a modern-day Lazarus, will they?"

She did not speak, but her torso jerked painfully with each mention of a rival show, as if the spoken names alone were slings and arrows with but one purpose, to mortally wound.

"Oh," he continued, "did I forget to mention the print media? Mmm?"

Her voice was faint. "The . . . the print media? What do they have to do with this?" She turned around slowly, her face white.

"Let's see . . ." he went on inexorably, "who is there?" He made a production of pausing and pretending to think while rubbing his chin. "Well, for starters I guess there's always that good old standby—the *Enquirer?*"

"The . . . *National Enquirer?*" she squeaked, in alarm.

"The only *Enquirer* I know of. Just think, Stephanie! For once, they won't even have to defend themselves against a lawsuit." He smiled smugly.

She was fuming in choked silence. She would kill him! Yes! She would kill him as slowly and painfully as humanly possible! Drawing and quartering was much too merciful. But a nice, very slow, very leisurely death . . .

"And then, of course," he continued, "it goes without saying that the *Star* and the *Globe* and the *Examiner* can't be left out. I mean, with a story of this magnitude—"

Stephanie's breasts heaved dangerously and a muffled sound of disbelief escaped her lips. "So help me, Johnny Stone!" she cried. "If you leak so much as a single word . . . I'll . . ." She was stuttering with such fury that she had to stop talking and concentrate fiercely on breathing.

He looked at her in amusement, one eyebrow cocked. "You'll do what?" he asked.

"I'll strangle you with my own two bare hands!"

Johnny merely waved a hand airily. "Stop and imagine, Stephanie, the field day *Weekly World News* will have with you." He sketched an imaginary rectangle in the air. "Can't you see the headlines already? Hell, you'll be on the front page for weeks—maybe months! Let me see . . . what *would* the headlines say?" He ran his finger along imaginary print. "TV CELEBRITY KIDNAPPED BY ALIENS. Mmm." He glanced at her. "You must admit it has a certain ring to it."

Stephanie thrust her jaw forward. "Very funny!" she said.

"But *simple*. All it takes is one phone call to the editor along with a photo or two, which, incidentally, I took with a telephoto lens this morning and—*presto!*" He clicked his fingers. "Your resurrection is worldwide news!"

Stephanie caught her breath, and her calculating eyes darkened and rounded and then narrowed almost at once. "You wouldn't!"

"Ah, but that's a chance you cannot afford to take, now is it?" Johnny's white teeth gleamed. "Of course, if you don't believe me, go ahead. Call my bluff."

Her face turned crimson, and her clenched fists trembled at her sides. "Of all—" she began furiously, then stopped to compose herself by taking several deep lungfuls of air. When she spoke again, her voice was soft and wobbly but carefully measured. "Of all people, Johnny, I never, ever dreamed *you* would resort to something as . . . as cheap and . . . as . . . as low-down and nasty as blackmail! Not you!"

He pretended to look troubled and rubbed his chin some more and frowned down at the floor and then turned on his bright smile for her again. "Come on, Stephanie. Surely blackmail's too strong a word? Why don't you think of it as, ah, a form of preventive persuasion?"

She stared at him. His smile dazzled, but she could see no mercy in those hard, unrelenting eyes. Nor, she knew, could she expect any.

"All right, Johnny," she agreed softly. "Perhaps it's just as well we had a talk."

"Well?" said Johnny Stone with a smile, "I'm all ears."

# ❧ *22* ❧

*Milan, Italy*

*T*eatro alla Scala, the shrine of Italian opera, reigns in a class unto itself. Not only is it Milan's most sacred and enduring institution, but "La Scala," as it is fondly called, is to opera what Dom Pérignon is to champagne or Mount Everest to mountains. Each year, from December 7 through July, millions of music lovers the world over pass through its grand portals to partake of an unmatched audiovisual feast, and they rarely, if ever, leave disappointed. For, unlike the other great opera houses of the world, including New York's Metropolitan Opera and London's Covent Garden, La Scala is not a place where new talent is allowed to surface, or where an understudy steps in for an ill diva and shows such promise and talent that, overnight, a star is born. Quite the contrary: La Scala is the opera house for musical geniuses who have *arrived*, true stars at the peaks of their talent and performance careers.

Of course, it has not always been this way; no legendary monument is created without its growing pains. In the 1700s, La Scala served as both opera house and gambling casino, and it was the games of chance, rather than the musical productions, which lured patrons to its doors. And in the nineteenth century, during the so-called Golden Age of Opera, productions at La Scala were so sloppy, and the audiences so rowdy, that its productions elevated opera-bashing to a high art. Indeed, things got so bad that even Milan's most famous son, Giuseppe Verdi, boycotted his hometown opera house for forty years.

But then came 1898, when a young conductor named Arturo Toscanini arrived on the scene and became La Scala's musical director. He not only saved the opera house from oblivion, but when he left, in 1929, he left behind a legend, and the rest, as they say, is history.

To this day, attending a performance at the *teatro* is to step through a magic doorway and back in time to a lost world of overwhelming beauty, drama, glamour, and pageantry. The interior is decorated all in red, white, and gold, and the show actually begins in the colonnaded foyer before the curtain ever rises. For this is where the crème de la crème of Milanese society gathers and mingles, to see and be seen.

And always, there is a kind of aloof blaséness in evidence, for these are not your average theatergoers all atwitter and abuzz with excitement. No, these are the hard-core, the chosen few, and even before the first chord of the overture is played, or the first musical note is sung, they know they can sit back in utter tranquility, so confident are they in the knowledge that they are about to enjoy the very finest musical performances the entire world has to offer on this, or any other, given night.

On this particular balmy early summer evening, the curtain coming down on act 1 of *Madama Butterfly* was followed by rousing applause. The lights came up gradually in the globe lamps, mounted at intervals around the auditorium in clusters of five, and as the applause died, the audience began to buzz like a very, very lively beehive. Everywhere, people were starting to get up from their red velvet seats and stretch their legs during the intermission.

In the private red damask box to stage right, on the first tier between two massive Corinthian columns trimmed in gilt, Zarah was seated well back in the shadows. As soon as the lights had come up, she had quickly popped her upswept sunglasses back on. In front of her, to her left, sat Ernesto; to her right, also in front, sat Boris Guberoff. Behind her, his arms crossed in the small of his back at parade rest, Colonel Valerio stood guard at the door, his formal attire doing little to lessen his unmistakable military bearing.

As Ernesto stopped clapping, he leaned sideways to say something in Guberoff's ear, but the old pianist, not expecting a sudden voice, practically jumped out of his skin.

Zarah, always keen to the slightest change in someone's demeanor, frowned, pulled her glasses down an inch on her nose, and eyed Guberoff reflectively.

*There's something wrong,* she thought, *he's been acting strange and out-of-sorts all evening.* Earlier, during dinner, his ebullient conversation had struck her almost as forced, and he had eaten furtively, guiltily, as though he had something to hide. And his laughter had sounded false and contrived . . . unusual to say the least. But even more worrisome for her, throughout act 1 he had drummed his fingers—*drummed them like a fidgety, bored schoolchild!*—on the damask ledge of the box!

She stared at the back of his head, at the thinning white hair with patches of liver-spotted pink skull showing through.

*Or was there a good reason he should be so agitated? But what can that reason be? Something to do with . . . me?*

The box was suddenly stifling; already, she could feel the threatening presence of something malignant and unknown growing in the shadows, towering high as the ceiling. With trembling fingers, she took off her sunglasses and held them by one earpiece. "Boris!" she said.

At the sound of his name, Guberoff jerked, then turned half around, his eyes sliding in her direction.

"Boris, you must tell us what is wrong!"

The arthritic old pianist drew a deep breath, dug out his handkerchief, patted his glistening brow.

"Boris . . . !" Her whisper was urgent, panicked.

He let out a bursting sob, and, to Zarah's embarrassment, his composure crumbled. "It was the *lavender!*" he moaned, the wattle at his neck quivering. "I would never have been fooled otherwise!"

Lavender . . . fooled? For one long, horrible moment, the opera house seemed to tilt, seemed on the very verge of collapse. "Boris? What are you talking about?"

Zarah moved forward, sitting on the edge of one of the delicate chairs she herself had chosen for this box—when? Thirty years ago? Forty?

"The woman!" Guberoff blurted, his hooded dark eyes leaking tears. "The one who came to visit me!"

"*What* woman?"

Guberoff sniffed, dabbed his eyes, tried to compose himself. "The American who brought me the picture of you," he whispered miserably. "It was in a genuine Fabergé frame, and she told me you had sent her with it as a gift!" His wattle quivered, shook like a gelatinous membrane. "It was in a scarf dabbed with *lavender!* Don't you see?"

"But . . . I didn't send you anything!" The glasses slipped through Zarah's fingers, fell soundlessly to the carpet at her feet. *An American woman—? Monica Williams, perhaps?*

"Boris!" Groaning, she reached out and clutched his arm. "*Per amor di Dio!*" she whispered, giving him a shake. "What did you *tell* her?"

"I . . . I don't remember . . ." He was sobbing quietly, his face screwed up in pain and self-pity.

"Boris. You must—!"

"She called you *Lili!*" The words burst forth miserably, like a lanced boil. "She knew all *about* you—"

"*What?*" Zarah uttered an appalled gasp and let go of his arm as if she'd been scalded.

"She even knew about the time I was on the yacht," he whined, "when I played 'Was ist Silvia,' and you sang." His voice sounded accusing now, as if he was trying to transfer the blame.

"But how can she have known?" Zarah's bejeweled fingers scrabbled at her throat, diamonds flashing. "Boris! Who told her? You . . . ?"

"*No.* I swear it wasn't me! I don't know how she found out!"

She stared at the old man in disgust. *No, not man,* she corrected herself, *that is pushing it; the pathetic, shriveled, old facsimile of one is more like it!* The frail chair creaked as she slumped back, trying to distance herself from the sour smell of old age which emanated off him. *How could I ever have considered him a real friend?* she wondered.

And now he had told, or had at least confirmed, someone's suspicions. But whose? Monica Williams's?

She gazed out past him, beyond the luxuriously draped confines of the cosseting plush red box. Directly opposite, across the proscenium on stage left, someone raised opera glasses in her direction; in the center aisle, a cluster of people huddled in conversation all seemed to turn and look up at her. The magnificently swagged and tasselled maroon stage curtain billowed malevolently, as though someone—or something?—was moving stealthily behind it, coming closer, closer . . . Zarah shuddered and rubbed her arms briskly. Menace was everywhere she looked—and nowhere as apparent as in the Judas sitting before her.

"Boris." She clasped her hands in her lap. "I think you had better start at the beginning. You must tell us everything!"

"Yes, yes!" he said, eagerly grasping the thin thread of confession as though the severed umbilical cord of their friendship could still be salvaged. And in a whiny voice that taunted her patience, he told her about the visitor he'd received, about the woman who called herself Virginia Wesson . . .

Zarah listened in silence. How she despised his sudden puppyish eagerness to make amends, his pleading eyes which begged for absolution, as though she was his confessing priestess. Oh yes, it was so easy to despise him—so easy to despise everything about him! That simian jaw of his—a *monkey's!* His Russian accent, which once she had found exotic and amusing, now grated in her ears and on her nerves. His affectations— those silly gold cufflinks shaped like grand pianos, those tiny medals he wore proudly pinned to his lapel—as if having been a virtuoso pianist was not proof enough of his accomplishments. How could she have endured his friendship for so long? He was pathetic—*pathetic!* Zarah looked away in revulsion, unable to bear the sight of him any longer.

" . . . took the picture and the scarf and left . . ." Finally finished, Guberoff fell silent.

Now Zarah snapped questions at him:

*What color was Virginia Wesson's hair? What color her eyes? How tall was she?*

He blurted the replies, then cried: "You must believe me, Zarah! She already knew everything! I didn't tell her anything she didn't already—"

"Yes, but you confirmed my existence, Boris," she whispered, sounding all the more theatrical for the nearby stage. "How could you do it, Boris—how could you?"

"Zarah—" he sobbed, and reached out beseechingly, touching her sleeve as though it were the hem of a saint's tunic.

By reflex, she snarled and pulled away, snatched the tulle from between his desperate fingers.

He began to cry again. "Don't hold this against me! Please, Zarah—"

Zarah's lips lifted in a sneer and she raked him with her eyes, taking satisfaction in his misery, gloating over how he seemed even more shriveled and shrunken than before, as if in the last few minutes he'd grown even smaller, even older inside his baggy tuxedo. Then, reestablishing her regal composure, she turned to Ernesto and effortlessly switched from perfect Italian to perfect Portuguese. "If this Virginia Wesson and Monica Williams are one and the same . . ."

"But you heard him," Ernesto murmured reassuringly. "Her hair, her eyes—they do not match."

"Those can easily be changed, Ernesto. No one knows that better than us." She communicated the rest through her eyes and a bitter smile. "We must get back to the yacht at once. Yes. We must find out whether Ms. Williams and Ms. Wesson are one and the same." She felt beside her for her jeweled, butterfly-shaped minaudiere and started to rise.

Calmly Ernesto took her wrist, made her sit back down. "Wait until intermission is over. That way, we do not have to fight our way through the crowds." He twisted around in his seat and switched to English. "Colonel."

"Sir!" Colonel Valerio stepped forward.

"Use the cellular telephone to call the chauffeur. I want the car waiting outside. And call the pilot. Tell him to stand by for immediate take-off."

"Where . . . are you going?" Guberoff whined.

"*We,*" Zarah snapped. "*We* are going, and you are coming with us. There is a woman aboard the yacht, an American. We need to know whether she is this Virginia Wesson who visited you." The sneer was back on her lips. "You do not find that inconvenient, I hope?"

Ten minutes later, they were in the black limousine, hurtling through the dark streets, headed for the airport.

# 23

*Capri*

Johnny Stone was one hell of an SOB—and that, Stephanie concluded, not for the first time, was being kind. She had almost forgotten about his smug air of superiority and that infuriating habit he had of thinking he was always right. Now, reminded of it once again, she fumed, pained at having to share her hard-earned information with him. So she retaliated the only way she could under the circumstances: by being icily aloof and maddeningly, haughtily evasive.

"Getting anything out of you," he said at one point, "is like pulling goddamn teeth!"

She had tossed her head and retorted with cold dignity, "Thanks! I'll accept that as a goddamn compliment!"

And they'd glared at each other like nose-to-nose drill sergeants.

Johnny backed down first. He could see no sense in making an already uphill battle even steeper; things were quite bad enough.

"All I want to know," Stephanie demanded after he'd coaxed another few morsels of information out of her, "is how you found out I was alive and kicking."

He smiled sardonically. "Thought you covered your tracks pretty well, huh?"

"Oh, cut the crap, Johnny!" she said testily. "In case you've forgotten, I've got to leave in a few minutes."

"Okay, okay," he said placatingly, and his voice became soft. "Sammy gave you away."

Sparks practically scattered from under her feet as she whirled on him. "Uncle *Sammy*, did you say? *My* Uncle Sammy?"

"He didn't mean to," Johnny admitted. "He put on a good show, but he just wasn't devastated enough to convince me of your, ah, 'demise.' "

"Should've guessed," she said, glaring at him. "Always luck out, don't you?"

"Yeah," Johnny drawled. "Got the luck of the devil, the two of us. Think that's why we love each other so much?"

She turned her back on him.

With all the verbal slings and arrows flying, it was a miracle that they managed to fill the other in on what each had been up to.

Grudgingly, Stephanie gave Johnny a rundown on Vinette Jones and the baby she claimed the CRY orphanage had lost, and Vinette's subsequent OD and Aaron Kleinfelder's hit-and-run "accident." She recapped her visits to Madame Balász and Detlef von Ohlendorf and Boris Guberoff.

Johnny, in turn, told her how he'd tracked her first to Budapest, and then to Salzburg and Milan and Marbella.

"In Milan, I even followed you on foot from the Casa di Riposo all the way back to your hotel." His voice was filled with a triumph so self-complacent and absolute that it took every vestige of her self-control not to smack him resoundingly across the face. "Just think, Stephanie!" he crowed, rubbing salt into an already smarting wound. "If you'd have turned around, we could have waved to each other!"

"Bastard!" she hissed from between clenched teeth.

It was as if he hadn't heard. "But what I can't understand," he continued thoughtfully, "is the de Veiga connection. How do they figure into all of this? And what steered you to the *Chrysalis* in the first place?"

"Would you believe," murmured Stephanie hopefully, "it all came to me in . . . in a dream?"

"Give me the truth, you devious lying bitch! Out with it!" He grabbed her arms and gave her a good shake.

She stared up at him. "I don't know why you won't believe me," she groused. Then, sniffling virtuously, she gave a deep sigh and yanked her arms out of his hands and glumly explained about Alan Pepperberg and the Schneider-Guberoff recording, and how it had allegedly been recorded aboard the yacht. She ended up telling Johnny nearly everything, withholding only a single and, she told herself, very, very *mundane* detail . . . a little tidbit of a thing he really had no need knowing—Lili's search for the fountain of youth and the possibility of its existence.

"So you think Lili Schneider is alive?" he asked.

"Don't you?" she replied, deflecting the question with a question, and feeling more determined than ever to hoard and protect her precious nugget.

He was frowning. "But you think her being alive is motive enough to get people killed?"

"Well, can you think of a better motive?"

"Do you always answer a question with a question?"

"Do I do that?" she murmured, frowning prettily.

And so it went. Stephanie was an expert at evading questions and deflecting directions of inquiry, and Johnny had a worthy opponent on his hands. Stephanie knew better than to let her guard down. From experience, she was wise to Johnny's repertoire of tricks. But had she been able to read his mind, she would have rested a little less easily.

For Johnny was thinking: *She's holding back. She knows something she's not telling.* Not that it surprised him: After all, the first rule of jour-

nalism was never to exchange more information than was absolutely necessary.

"Now, if there's nothing else—" Stephanie began.

"There *is* one more thing." Johnny cut her off.

She sighed.

"Stephanie." Johnny pinched the bridge of his nose with his thumb
and forefinger. "I want to give you a piece of advice. Whether or not you
heed it is up to you."

"Oh, blow it out your—"

"Just this once, will you *listen?*" he said sharply. "For God's sake!
Hasn't it occurred to you that whatever you're mixed up in, you might be
in over your head?"

"Gee! Thanks for the vote of confidence, mister! But in case you
haven't figured it out already, *Sherlock,* I'm perfectly capable of taking
care of myself."

"Well, I hope to God you're better at it than your grandfather," he
said softly.

"And what's that supposed to mean?"

"Well, it's obvious, isn't it? He must have stirred up a hornet's nest."

"Y-yes . . . ?" she murmured encouragingly. "Do go on . . ."

"Well, you don't think it's *smart* to go undercover without a backup,
do you?"

Her eyes locked onto his. "What are you trying to say, Johnny?"

"Just that you shouldn't be going this alone," he replied calmly. "You
need . . . help."

"By that, I presume you mean *your* help?"

"That's right," he said, giving a nod.

She shook her head. "No, Johnny," she said firmly. "I neither want it
nor need it. And that's final."

"You might not *want* having an outside contact you can trust, but
you're going to *need* one," he said reasonably. "Take a minute and think
about it, Stephanie. What if you need research or legwork done? You
won't be able to do it all yourself, not right under the de Veigas' noses.
They may be rich and reclusive, but they're not stupid."

"If I need help," she sniffed with dignity, "I'll call Uncle Sammy."

*"Sammy!"* Johnny exclaimed incredulously. "You're counting on
someone thousands of miles away?"

"Go ahead and scoff!" she said angrily. "For your information, Uncle
Sammy and I got this far without any help from you!"

"Yeah. And you left a trail a three-year-old could follow!"

Stephanie's face flushed and her breasts heaved, but she did not
speak.

"And besides, Sammy can't do everything or be everywhere. Sure, he's
in marvelous shape for a guy his age. But he's no spring chicken,

Stephanie. What if things get physical? What's Sammy supposed to do? Dart between some ruffian's legs?"

Stephanie wished he would just shut up and give up. Hadn't things gone swimmingly without him? Indeed, they had. The last, the very last thing she needed now was for a doomsayer to come along and point out every potential pitfall. She was tempted to say, *Oh, bug off,* knew it would only make him that much more persistent, and tried another tack.

"All right, Johnny," she said reluctantly. "I promise I'll think about what you've said."

"I'm glad," he said, smiling wryly. "Despite the way you feel about me, I still care deeply about you. You know that, Stephanie, don't you?"

She nodded wordlessly.

"Then perhaps you'll also understand that if something happened to you, I'd never be able to forgive myself. Not if it's something I could have helped prevent."

She stood silently for a moment, then took a deep breath. "Like I said, Johnny, I'll think it over." Her voice was quiet, but there was no mistaking the steel in it. "However, don't mistake that for a yes, because it's not. I refuse to make any commitments I can't keep."

She waited and watched warily as Johnny pursed his lips and thrust his hands back into his trouser pockets and jingled some change. Standing there, the glare of the naked bulb throwing the shadow of his nose across his handsome, strong-featured face, she thought of how attractive he was, and how he would make some woman—some *other* woman—very happy.

After a moment, she saw him nod. "Fair enough," he said.

She held his gaze. "Then stay in touch with Uncle Sammy. If I agree to work with you—and that's a big 'if'—I'll tell him, and he'll pass the message along to you. If I decide I *don't* want your help, I'll have him pass that on, too." She paused and added huskily, "But if I were you, Johnny, I really wouldn't get my hopes up."

"All I asked," he repeated, his voice level, "is that you think about it."

"I know." There was a tightness in her throat. "Which brings me to one last thing."

"Which is?"

Her heavy-lidded eyes watched him closely. "Which is: What if I refuse your help? What happens then, Johnny?" Her voice was hushed. "Are you going to blow the whistle on me and tell the whole world I'm alive?"

He looked at her for a long moment and then shook his head. "No," he said quietly. "You know I would never do anything to jeopardize your safety."

She nodded, feeling some of the tension inside her dissipate.

He drew a deep breath.

"Don't make it so hard for us," she said in a husky voice, and on impulse, she hopped up on tiptoe and brushed his cheek with her lips. "Good-bye, Johnny. I'll see myself out."

Then she stepped away; he could hear her swift footsteps receding, and the front door creaked open.

And she was gone.

Stephanie hurried through the dark *viuzzi*, grappling with the pros and cons of being allied with Johnny: *He's capable and a quick thinker and he never bores. He's had Special Forces training. He doesn't scare easily, and isn't afraid to use his fists—just the person I'd want along on a safari or in a bad inner-city neighborhood. He's as good with a gun as he is with a camera, yet put a coat and tie on him, and he's more than presentable. He even knows which fork is for salad and which knife is for fish. And, he's one hell of a lover.*

Those were the pros.

She sighed to herself.

Now for the cons.

*There probably isn't a man alive who's more egotistical or chauvinistic or cocksure than Johnny Stone. Maybe it's a hangover from his Special Forces days, but he fancies himself a born leader. Whatever the situation, he'll inevitably try to control it—without regard to the feet he steps on in the process. Infuriating, that take-charge attitude, and demeaning, too. As if he were more capable than any man, and far superior to all women!*

Stephanie gnashed her teeth in fury. *I really can't bear having him around! Who does he think he is, anyway—Rambo? This is MY war, MY investigation!*

Her face screwed up in thought, she hurried purposefully on, stopping only to get her bearings in that maze of shadowy, tunnel-like streets.

*There has to be some way I can shake him off my tail,* she thought. *Some way I can disappear into thin air, without leaving a trail . . .*

By the time she reached the restaurant, she had figured out how.

## ☙ 24 ❧

*S*ammy leaned forward in his chair, totally absorbed in Aaron Kleinfelder's scribbling. The slight hiss of the oxygen apparatus, the steady bleeps of the monitors, the medicinal hospital odors, the soft squeak of the felt pen and crepe-soled nurses' shoes . . . for Sammy, all had receded from reality as Aaron's information unfolded on the note pad:

*Where are the children? How can there be missing children?*

*That's right, my friend,* Sammy projected silently as Aaron kept writing. *Keep it up . . . just hang in there until you've finished.*

Not surprisingly, Sammy's main concern was Aaron's strength. Twice already, the man's feeble fingers had let go of the felt pen, and twice Sammy had retrieved it and put it back into Aaron's hand, gently curling the fingers around it.

But what surprised Sammy the most was that he had little trouble deciphering Aaron's messy scribbles:

*Why were CRY's computers down? It was too convenient. Everything was fine the day before. Then suddenly—poof! The next day, nothing.*

Frowning, Sammy said, "Let me get this straight. What do you mean by 'the next day'?"

Aaron's felt pen scratched:

*Day of my "accident"!!*

Sammy frowned. "Why did you put quotation marks around 'accident'?"

*It was no accident.*

Sammy took a deep breath. "Are you implying that someone tried to kill you?"

Without hesitation, Aaron scribbled:

*Yes. The van aimed for me.*

"But who would want to kill you?" Sammy asked. "Do you have any idea?"

Aaron wrote:

*No. But it's strange it should happen after I tried to enter a secret file that shouldn't have existed!*

Sammy half rose and flipped the pad to a clean page and sat back down on the edge of his chair. "So you think," Sammy said, "the reason for the attempted murder is your discovering the existence of that file?"

Aaron wrote:

*Has to be! The program must have some kind of built-in trace system. How else would anyone have known it was me who'd tried to break in?*

"Yes, but I don't see how a machine could tell anyone that," said Sammy, whose experience with computers was next to nil and, if he had his say, would happily remain exactly that way till the end of his days.

Aaron quickly jotted:

*I used my access number and password to enter the program. Like a bank machine PIN number, every password is different.*

"That," Sammy said, "I understand."

Aaron wrote:

*With an automatic trace, finding out it was me through my access number and password, or at the very least, the terminal I was using, would be child's play. Do you understand?*

"Now that you've explained it that way," Sammy said, starting to flip to another blank page, "yes. I believe I do." He had to wait: Aaron's pen moved again:

*I need your help!*

Sammy looked startled. *"My help?"* he said.

"Yes," Aaron rasped. *"Your help!"*

Sammy looked at him and shook an admonishing finger. "Please, my friend. Save your voice and energy."

Aaron nodded weakly and let out a reedy sigh. Then he scrawled:

*I really do need your help. The children need it!*

"But . . . I know bupkes from computers!" Sammy protested.

Aaron wrote:

*So? I'll help you. But until I'm released from here, I need someone to be my eyes, hands, and ears. I'd like it to be you.*

Sammy sighed. "Well, so long as you understand that I'm not in the least bit technically inclined."

Aaron smiled slightly and scribbled:

*Understood. You'll do fine.*

"If you say so," Sammy said dubiously, leaning forward and flipping to a new page.

Aaron wrote:

*Somehow, you'll have to get into the computer file at CRY. The one I couldn't enter. Each time I punched in Jowanda Daneece Jones, I'd get a request to punch in the OPUS number. Damned if I ever heard of it before.*

"Opus?" said Sammy, as though testing the word. "That refers to a musical composition."

Aaron wrote:

*Or a book.*

"That too," Sammy said gloomily. "That too . . ."

Pen moving quickly, Aaron wrote:

*I think it contains information on missing children.*

Sammy sighed. "So what good does that do us," he groused, resignation in his voice, "if we cannot gain entry to the file?"

Aaron's pen slashed almost savagely:

*We WILL gain entry! I just don't know how—yet. If my access number and password still work, we can start from there. The number's 099/3cd. The password's COOKIE.*

"I take it you chose 'cookie' because you have a sweet tooth?" guessed Sammy.

Aaron chuckled as he scribbled:

*Guilty.*

"In that case," Sammy promised, "when I come to visit tomorrow, I'll bring you some. Do you have any particular favorites?"

Aaron wrote:

*Mrs. Field's chocolate chip macadamia, but Oreos will do. Perhaps when you return I'll have thought of a way for us to enter the OPUS file.*

"Get some rest," Sammy advised. "You're no good to us ill or dead." And Aaron wrote:

*Neither are you. Take extreme care—okay?*

A chill ran up Sammy's spine. He stared at Aaron, and once again, he was aware of the bleeping of the monitors and the faint hiss of oxygen.

Aaron was lying back now, obviously tired out, his fingers loosening from around the pen. Slowly he turned his head sideways on the pillow, his eyes emphasizing the seriousness of his message.

Sammy stared back at him. "*Oy vey,*" he sighed, tearing the scribbled pages out of Aaron's notebook and carefully folding and pocketing them. "*Oy vey.*"

"Can say that again," Aaron rasped.

# 25

*U*ncontrollable tempests raged and shrieked inside her, whipped themselves into ferocious typhoons. Fed her hatred. Fueled her fears.

Where the devil *was* Monica Williams! It was past eleven P.M. already! *Where has Eduardo taken her? How much longer do I need to wait until I know, until I can toss away that pathetic old man, that bundle of brittle bones?*

The *Chrysalis* floated placidly on an oily mirror of sea, the twinkling lights of Capri so high above they looked like an uncharted constellation.

Zarah thought, *It's outrageous that the sea can be so calm while such storms rage within me!*

Eduardo was pacing back and forth outside the entrance of Al Grottino. He had already telephoned the yacht four times, but Monica Williams had not shown up there, either. What at first had been frustration and irritation was fast turning into alarm.

Hearing hollow footfalls echoing, he turned around. And saw her!

"Monica!" he shouted and raced toward her.

Stephanie raised a hand and waved and rushed forward on her long legs.

"Thank God!" he breathed as he took her in his arms and swept her right off her feet—*just like a leading man in one of those 1940s movies,* she thought. "You had me so worried! The waiter told me you'd gone off with that boy—"

"I'm fine," she assured him softly, returning his embrace. As he set her back down, she drew back and looked into his eyes. "What happened down at the marina?"

"Would you believe—nothing? The boat is fine. It was all a prank!" And holding her face in his hands, he kissed her deeply.

The touch of his lips sent a jolt of pleasure coursing through her, and her tongue darted around his.

"Where did the delinquent take you?" he murmured, loathe to take his lips from hers.

"I—I don't know," she managed to murmur, her eyes bright as he nibbled gently at her upper lip.

"Did you check your purse?"

"Ummm . . . yes," she lied, shivering deliciously. His tongue was laving her lower lip. "Nothing's been stolen."

"Good. You have to watch these urchins." His mouth left hers to trail moist heat down her chin to her throat, where he kissed her wildly beating pulse. "You were gone such a long time . . ." Now his mouth moved even farther down, his tongue exploring the hollow cleft at the base of her throat. "I was certain something must have happened to you."

The warmth of his breath tickled her breasts, raised goosebumps on her skin, caused her to shudder involuntarily. "I got lost. You know how—confusing these *viuzzi* are."

"I was so worried—"

"At least it gave me a chance to . . . to think." A warm tingling had started up in the hollow of her belly and her legs began to tremble. She could feel the insides of her thighs getting moist. "So much has happened so fast . . . I—I needed a little time by myself to . . . sort things out."

He bowed his head over her breasts. "And did you . . . ?" His tongue now twirled lazily along the neckline of her blouse, at the very, very boundary of public decency. ". . . Sort things out?"

"Yes!" she whispered, and quickly glanced around. "Eduardo!" she hissed. "Someone might—"

"Sssh!" He pulled her into the shadows of the nearest doorway and sucked of her soft flesh. "And what," he inquired, "did you sort out?" Without moving his lips, he glanced up at her, his inquisitive eyes shining.

"I—I made up my mind!"

"About what?" His tongue continued working and her body spasmed and arched.

"You," she said tremulously. "Me. Brazil!"

"And?" His tongue stopped making concentric wet little whorls, and he watched her intently.

She took a deep shuddering breath. "If your offer still stands," she said huskily, staring into his eyes, "I'd be delighted to accompany you there!"

Offshore, the generators on the *Chrysalis* were working overtime.

Like on a carnival ship, every light except those in the wheelhouse glowed brightly, so that the effect was one of two mirror images, one *Chrysalis* floating atop the smooth water, the other upside down in it.

From where she stood outside on the aft deck, Zarah thought she could detect the throb of the Magnum's muscular engines carrying across the water. Her breathing quickened as she listened. Yes, it was the Magnum! The sound was unmistakable!

Feeling a surge of anticipation, she hurried across the deck to the port side, where she could see the approaching running lights. Judging from their size, the powerboat was still more than a quarter of a mile away, but closing rapidly. "Soon," she said softly to herself, "soon we shall see whether two birds can be hit with one stone!"

She watched the distant lights a moment longer, then turned on her heel, her opera gown, a fantasy of an après-ballet tutu as interpreted by Christian Lacroix, rustling with malevolent static.

Colonel Valerio was coming out the automatic sliding glass doors as she was set to march in.

"I was just coming to tell you, ma'am. The Magnum is on its way."

"I know, Colonel. I heard the engines." Zarah frowned momentarily. "As soon as it is docked, send Ms. Williams in to see me. And Colonel: make certain she is alone. *Without* my son!"

Roaring past the port side of the *Chrysalis*, Eduardo spun the wheel and expertly put the Magnum into a tight twenty-degree turn. The big boat responded beautifully, skidding around on a dime and throwing up a rooster tail of spray. He cut the speed, the engine's roar became a throbbing, domesticated purr, and the beast wallowed in its own wake.

Stephanie, holding onto the opulently padded dash, looked forward through the giant windscreen, beyond the bow. He had lined up the muscle boat's pointy nose on the first try with the exact center of the yacht's stern—no mean feat.

"Now for the lights," he said, hitting a remote control switch which activated the underwater "runway" lights in the *Chrysalis*'s wet berth. The row of water-tight halogen bulbs, built into the U-shaped bay, clicked on almost instantaneously, giving the water a bright greenish-yellow glow.

Stephanie didn't need to be told what to do. As he steered straight for that bright watery tunnel, she scrabbled around the windshield as surefooted as an old deckhand and trotted along the expanse of narrowing fiberglass to the bow, where she uncoiled the heavy white mooring rope. Holding a length of it, she walked out onto the bow pulpit, propped her hips snugly back into the semicircular railing, and waited, marveling at how Eduardo managed to dock the big boat as effortlessly as a veteran trucker pulling his eighteen-wheeler into a loading dock. She tossed the rope down to a waiting crew member, who started looping it around a cleat, and made her way back to the cockpit.

Eduardo switched off the engines, left the Magnum in the capable hands of the crewmen, and took Stephanie's hand. Together, they stepped over onto the mother ship. Arms wrapped around each other's waists, they walked forward and up a wide companionway to the next deck.

"That was *nice!*" she breathed, leaning her head against his shoulder and luxuriating in the salty sea smell of him.

"What was nice? My docking?"

"Silly." She nudged an elbow gently into his ribs. "Everything. Morning . . . noon . . . night . . ."

"Ms. Williams?" The lazy drawl came out of the shadows in front of them.

"Yes?" She and Eduardo stopped walking.

Colonel Valerio slid out from the shadows of the lifeboat hull against which he'd been casually leaning. "Ms. Böhm requests the pleasure of your company."

Stephanie's head suddenly began to spin, the stitch in her side an almost coronary pain.

Eduardo said, "They're back from La Scala? Already?" He sounded surprised.

The Colonel's voice was neutral. "Guess they decided to leave early."

Stephanie felt the headlong rush of panic. *They've returned early! From Milan—where they've seen Guberoff!* Stephanie struggled to retain her crumbling composure, fought to keep her voice steady and the words from cracking. "Is it possible for me to take a raincheck? I'm really quite exhausted—"

"I'm sure Ms. Böhm is aware of that." Colonel Valerio smiled with his teeth. "I don't think this will take long."

"Whatever it is Mother wants," Eduardo suggested, "why not get it over with? Besides, I should at least step in and say good-night to her."

Colonel Valerio cleared his throat. "Your mother, sir, asked to see Ms. Williams in private."

"Really?" Eduardo frowned. "Did she say what she wanted?"

"No, sir."

Eduardo looked at Stephanie, made a face, and shrugged with resigned reasonableness. He said, "I shall wait for you here?"

She nodded. "I—I'd like that," she said quietly, and followed the Colonel.

Outside the main salon, he stepped in front of the seeing eye which controlled the automatic doors and they sighed open. He stepped aside, gesturing for her to enter. "Ma'am?"

Stephanie went in, surprised that he didn't follow. The doors slid silently shut behind her.

Now she looked around the sprawling eighty-by-forty-four-foot space, her head tucked slightly forward, her eyes scouting the territory guiltily. She knew her posture, her reluctant sluggishness, must surely look as furtive as she felt . . .

*An American, a young woman* . . . she could almost hear the accusing, thick Russian accent . . . *came with a package wrapped in a scented scarf! Lavender, it was.* Your *scent, Lili* . . .

"Ah. Ms. Williams." That silvery musical voice reached through

Stephanie's thoughts, brought her back to reality with a jolt. "How good of you to come."

Then Zarah—*Lili*—was floating toward her, all frothed up in layer upon layer of lace and tulle. *The ballerina from hell!* Stephanie thought uncharitably, unable to understand how a woman could consciously choose to wear an outfit so obviously uncomfortable and frivolously crushable; wondered, too, how on earth one laundered it, and simultaneously cursed the parched scratchiness she felt at the back of her own throat. She was tempted to lubricate it by swallowing, but feared the movement of her neck muscles would betray her.

"Colonel Valerio said you wished to see me?" Stephanie was surprised by how clear, how miraculously level her voice came out.

Zarah said smoothly, lying through her teeth, "I hope I am not inconveniencing you?"

"Not at all," Stephanie replied, just as untruthfully.

"Good, because I have a little surprise for you!" Zarah laughed gaily, slid an arm through Stephanie's and, as if they were old friends from way back when, pulled her too close while steering her toward one of the six distinctly separate seating areas, this one at the far front of the salon.

Stephanie's eyes, wary and alert, darted about, not knowing what to look for until suddenly, the coronarylike stitch under her heart stabbed sharper. For, half-hidden behind one of the overscaled table lamps, she now saw the back of a white-haired head.

*Dear God!* she thought. *It can't be! Surely they haven't flown the old Russian here from Milan just to confront me!*

Stephanie's steps became more sluggish and she heard, but did not register, Zarah's . . . *Lili's* . . . inanely cheerful, one-sided prattle, each syllable crystalline, like a pure musical note. All she could think of, the way her pulse and heartbeat were pounding, was that Zarah must surely *hear* that percussive beat right through her arm.

But no. Zarah chattered on, leading her around a shagreen sofa table which held a pair of outrageously large lamps. And there Boris Guberoff was, in front of them.

*I mustn't allow my shock to show!* Stephanie heard herself thinking, knowing full well that her face, with its furrowed brow, bewildered expression of utter stupidity, eyes blank with shock, surely *had* to betray her, *must* be a dead giveaway!

Like an aged bloodhound sniffing, the old man slowly raised his head, his hawklike nose twitching, until he was staring directly up at Stephanie.

And Zarah said in a voice so triumphant, so dramatic, and so evil, that it was anticlimactic, "Here's your little surprise—an old friend of yours, I believe, Ms. Williams . . . Ms. Williams?" Zarah let go of her arm and frowned slightly, perplexed by the blankness in Stephanie's stare.

Stephanie felt the force of the old man's gaze. *Was that recognition glinting in the watery hooded eyes?* she wondered, the passing seconds expanding into an unbearable eternity. She could already anticipate his words. *The hair color and hairstyle . . . well, those are different, of course . . . the eye color, also . . . but it is her . . . oh yes,* she's *the one who tricked me!*

Stephanie steeled herself, actually forgot to breathe. And time continued to telescope, the seconds drawing out longer, longer, the silence growing and making room for the sounds beneath the sounds . . . the electricity humming, the hull creaking, the circulating forced air whispering, whispering . . .

"*Yes?*" Zarah snapped, her impatient voice sharp, slicing through the sounds beneath the sounds and sending them scattering.

The old man opened his mouth, then clicked it shut again, his slack jaw working loosely, as though massaging his dentures.

"Well?" Zarah prodded.

He sighed heavily, shook his head, and looked helplessly at Zarah. "I've never seen this woman before in my life. I'm sorry, Lili—"

He gasped, his face purpling at his blunder.

Zarah exploded. "*Imbecille!*" she hissed in Italian, her eyes catching the light of the lamp and throwing off malevolent shards.

Stephanie couldn't believe her ears. *Lili! He had actually called Zarah "Lili"!*

Zarah turned to Stephanie, barely able to manage civility much longer. "I'm sorry, Ms. Williams. I was led to believe you were a friend of his . . . an old man's mistake, surely . . ."

And to Stephanie's astonishment, Zarah—*Lili!*—took her arm and hustled her swiftly away, whisking her out of the old fool's presence before—

Yes! Before more damage could be done!

Stephanie joined Eduardo out on deck. "That was fast," he said. "What did Mother want?"

"Oh, she just asked if I knew a friend of hers," Stephanie said in a contrived, bored tone of voice, when in truth she was still so high on relief, and so painfully stunned by her reprieve, that she thought she knew how Jed Savitt must have felt when the Supreme Court had stayed his execution.

"And did you?" Eduardo asked, "know her friend?"

She shook her head and put her hands in her pockets as they walked along the deck.

"Who was it?"

Stephanie looked at him. "She really didn't say," she replied truthfully, yet at the same time knowing she *was* telling yet another lie—for it was a lie, she thought, if only by virtue of omission.

"The idiot! The idiot!"

Zarah's savage pacing quickened, each layer of her gown rustling angrily with her every feverish move. Abruptly she spun at the wall and hammered her fists on the glossy paneling until her knuckles stung, her rage mushrooming, threatening to consume her and everything within sight.

*Bad enough that I brought the old fool here! But did he* have *to call me by my real name? Did he?*

Colonel Valerio, standing off to the side, waited for her rage to subside.

She whirled around, clawed hands raised and talons flashing. She was magnificent in her fury—Medea come to glorious life.

Still breathing rapidly, she seemed to become aware of her raised crablike hands, looked at them in surprise and forced them down to her sides.

She turned to Colonel Valerio. "Get that sorry excuse of a man off this yacht at once!" she snapped. "Do you hear me? At once!"

"Ma'am! Anything specific you want done with him?"

"*Yes!*" Rage swarmed around her like a dense cloud of killer bees. "*Kill him! Mutilate him! Chop him into little pieces!*" she screamed. Then she regained a measure of control. "No." She sighed so heavily her entire body shook. "Perhaps this Virginia Wesson will try to contact him again. Have your Italian operatives watch him around the clock. Perhaps one or two of them can get a job in that . . . that geriatric hellhole where I hope to God he soon dies!"

Only once Stephanie was alone in her suite, and the sound of the departing helicopter faded, did the accumulation of fear, tension, and, ultimately, relief, make her shudder uncontrollably. It was a full five minutes before she got a grip on herself, and only then did the irony of it all hit her.

She couldn't help but smile, and the smile became a giggle, and the giggle soon turned into such hysterical laughter that she dove to her bed and buried her head under the pillows to mask the sound.

Her laughter grew louder and wilder, and was soon accompanied by tears and kicking feet.

It really was too, too absurdly delicious, too funny for words! *Zarah brought Guberoff back from Milan expressly to identify me as Virginia Wesson! But instead,* she thought, gleefully, *he confirmed my own suspicions about Zarah being Lili! Poetic justice, that,* she gloated with the perverse pleasure of someone who has escaped doom by a mere hair's breadth.

# ❦ *26* ❦

### New York City

"*S*t. Luke's Hospital. Patient Information," singsonged the operator. A pause. Then, "The patient has improved. He is in stable condition."

There was a sharp intake of breath. "You sure?"

"That's what it says right here."

In the phone booth of the twenty-four-hour Market Diner, The Ghost hung up. Thought: *Time to get to work. Time to say, "Vaya con Dios, motherfucker!"*

Sammy was up bright and early. He couldn't wait to go back to St. Luke's and visit Aaron Kleinfelder. There were hundreds of questions he needed to ask.

*Won't Stephanie get a surprise when she calls!* he thought, smiling with pleasure.

He waited until eight before telephoning the hospital.

"I'm sorry," a nurse told him, "the patient is no longer here in ICU. He was moved to Room four-three-two."

Sammy sweet-talked her into transferring him to the fourth-floor nurses' station.

"How did you get this extension?" demanded a battleax of a nurse. "Visiting hours are from four 'til six!"

"But surely in extenua—"

"*No* exceptions!"

The line went dead.

Sighing, Sammy looked at the receiver, hung up, and checked his watch.

*Eight long hours to go . . .*

It was exactly four P.M. when the doctor in the white lab coat with the stethoscope dangling out of a pocket joined the crowd of visitors milling in the lobby. When an elevator *pinged*, everyone surged toward it.

"You first, doctor," a man said politely, stepping aside.

"Thank you."

Inside, the young doctor turned around and faced the front, all the while smiling that professional doctor smile—just what you'd expect of someone who cared for the diseased and the infirm.

When the elevator stopped on the fourth floor, the doctor said, "Excuse me," and got off.

The first elevator being too crowded, Sammy had to wait a few minutes for the next.

He was dandified to the nines. Wore a double-breasted silver-gray linen suit with a pink carnation stuck in his lapel. His white shirt was starched and his jaunty bow tie was yellow silk printed with little pink elephants, and there was a matching silk handkerchief sticking out of the breast pocket of his jacket. He was carrying a big bunch of carnations in florist's wrap in one hand and a bag of Mrs. Field's chocolate chip macadamia cookies in the other.

The doctor in the white lab coat walked briskly, like someone in charge with an official destination in mind. On both sides of the two-toned, green-floored corridor, the doors to the sickrooms were open, and friends and relatives of patients were arriving and filling vases with water and arranging bouquets and talking in hushed voices, while TV sets tuned to various afternoon talk shows spewed chatter and laughter and applause and commercials. From one of them came the *ding-ding-ding!* of a game show win, and from behind closed doors somewhere came the moans of a man in agony. At the nurses' station, a minor crisis preoccupied a huddle of staff: a female voice insisting, "But he isn't due another painkiller until six o'clock!"

From room 432, a perky voice issued forth from a TV set. "Did you ever want to give the gift of love? Hello. I'm Shanna Parker . . ."

Before going in, The Ghost took a quick look around. Stopped and waited maybe six or seven seconds to check the corridor both ways before slipping in through the open door and then closing it partway to shield what was going down.

On the TV, Shanna Parker was saying: ". . . as a CRY godparent, I get regular reports, photographs, and letters which keep me up to date . . . ," while The Ghost, looking around, was pleased to see it was a semi-private room. Only one of the two beds was occupied, the patient looking like a fat pasty cherub with gray frizzy hair. Despite the TV, he was sound asleep.

Not wanting to snuff the wrong patient, The Ghost approached the foot of the bed and checked the chart. KLEINFELDER, AARON.

"Say your prayers, motherfucker," The Ghost whispered, hanging the chart back on the bed. "You 'bout to depart this world."

The Ghost picked up a pillow from the empty bed, soundlessly drew the privacy curtain and, shielded from view, brought the pillow swiftly down over Aaron's face, holding it there with both hands.

Aaron Kleinfelder woke up in choking terror. He tried to scream, but the pillow swallowed all sound—just as it swallowed all light and all hearing and all oxygen. He thrashed about, his movements becoming weaker and weaker as his life ebbed until, after a short while, he gave one final twitch and lay still.

The Ghost removed the pillow and felt Aaron's neck for a pulse. Stood there looking down at the dead man and drew a deep breath, letting it out slowly and giving the corpse the kind of look one gives a piece of work well done—a painting, perhaps, or a piece of sculpture. *Killing's an art, too.*

On the TV, Shanna continued her tear-jerking pitch:

"It's such a wonderful reward to watch hunger turn into nutrition, despair into hope, and sickness into health! You'll be amazed by the changes you'll see. Just think! So little money . . . just pennies a day . . . can make such a world of difference . . ."

Still looking at Aaron Kleinfelder, The Ghost gave the TV an ironic kind of salute, and fluffed out the pillow, putting it back on the other bed and taking a red rose out of the lab coat's pocket and laying it on the pillow next to Aaron's head. Calling card in place, The Ghost strolled casually out, satisfaction showing through the professional smile.

With a flourish Sammy fished a carnation out of the bouquet. "Here's one for you . . ." he said, gallantly handing it to one of the nurses he passed. "And one for you . . ." He fished out another one, and gave it to an old lady using a walker.

They both looked surprised, but accepted the offering in the spirit in which it was intended.

Sammy walked jauntily on, glancing at the room numbers as he passed them. Seeing a doctor coming his way, he fished out another carnation and said, "Have a nice day."

The doctor took it and nodded and went on.

Which was how Sammy Kafka unknowingly gave The Ghost a flower.

# 27

## At Sea · Cannes · Nice

The remainder of the cruise was a countdown to Brazil. Corsica, Elba, Livorno, Portofino, San Remo, Monaco—all went past in a blur, and Stephanie couldn't shake the odd feeling that she would wake up at any moment and find herself in her own bed in New York, with reality reasserting itself, and Eduardo and Brazil—even the *Chrysalis* itself!—dissipating into the fog of all forgotten dreams.

She told Eduardo once, if she told him a thousand times, "I can't believe I'm really doing this!"

And he had smiled. "You will love Brazil," he predicted. "There is so much I cannot wait to show you."

"I want to see everything!" she declared.

"Everything," he murmured, kissing her deeply. "Everything and more . . ."

Stephanie still marveled at how easily she had breached the de Veigas' defenses. It seemed only yesterday that she had crashed the speedboat, and now here she was. Doted upon by Eduardo and his grandmother. Reluctantly tolerated by Ernesto, and even more marginally by Zarah. Sailing the blue Mediterranean aboard their megayacht. Preparing to accompany them to Brazil tomorrow.

*By all rights, I should be feeling triumphant,* she thought.

But in the deep of this starry, starry night, standing alone up here on deck, potent guilts and fears weighed heavily.

*It's not really me who's accompanying Eduardo to Brazil,* she thought. *It's Monica Williams . . .*

She stood there, her hair whipped back from her face by the wind, thinking how much simpler her mission would be if only she weren't so attracted to him.

*Eduardo, my darling, the last thing I ever dreamed would happen is our falling in love. But because we have, it's more important than ever for me to get to the bottom of this mystery—we can't have suspicions hanging over our lives like swords dangling from fragile threads. Don't you see, my love? Finding the truth is the only guarantee we have for lasting happiness. You do understand that, my darling, don't you?*

A faint whirring sound interrupted her thoughts, and she turned around. In the glow of the deck lights, she saw Zaza approach in her motorized wheelchair. She watched as the old lady maneuvered it expertly alongside, parked, and locked the brake. "I hope I am not disturbing you?" Zaza asked, peering up into her face.

Stephanie shook her head and fingered a length of hair back from her face. "No," she said, "of course not."

"You are a very nice young woman." Zaza smiled up at her. "I am so glad you decided to come to Brazil with us. I was right, you know. I sensed from the start that you would be good for Eduardo."

Stephanie smiled bleakly. "I wish I could be so sure."

"Ah! But I am."

Zaza sat in the chair as if on a throne. The tilt of her head, the regal profile, the way she rested her hands imperiously on the padded arms: she sat commandingly, as though by choice, and brought to mind a sage from decades past. "You come to this spot often, don't you?" she asked. "And always at night."

Stephanie turned to her in surprise. "You seem to be very well informed."

"I merely notice things." The old lady laughed softly. "The motor of this chair is very quiet. It permits me to ride around like a ghost. Besides," she sighed, "one finds that the older one gets, the less sleep one needs. So I roam these decks and corridors and observe things." Her eyes rested on Stephanie's face. "Did you know, I often come up here myself when I wish to think things over?"

Stephanie shook her head.

"It is a good spot for introspection."

"Yes," Stephanie agreed, "it is."

For a while, they both stared out at the dark sea, each preoccupied with thoughts of her own, and then Zaza worked her chair around until she had it parked facing Stephanie. "Liebchen," she said, reaching out and taking one of Stephanie's hands between both of hers, "if you are worried about Eduardo or Brazil, you needn't be. You love one already, and I am certain you will come to love the other as well."

Stephanie smiled wistfully. "You make it all sound so simple!"

"And it is!" Zaza said with a touch of exasperation. "You young people! Always complicating matters! Always making things seem so much more insurmountable than they really are! Wait until you get to be my age. Then you will discover that there are only three or four things in one's entire life that truly matter."

"Three or four?" Stephanie asked in quiet amusement. "That's all?"

"Yes, that is all. The rest is poppycock." Zaza paused and added in a quieter voice, "Well, if not exactly poppycock, then nevertheless, things which do not warrant one's attention, much less one's worry." She smiled and let go of Stephanie's hand. "Well, I must be off. You have a good night, Liebchen."

She put the wheelchair in reverse and rolled back a few feet.

"And try to get some sleep. If something is worrying you, remember: things always look different in the morning."

Stephanie smiled. "I'll keep that in mind," she promised.

Zaza gave a wave and rode off at a stately speed, the soft whirring of the wheelchair fading. Alone again, Stephanie turned and stared out at the sea again.

*Perhaps Zaza is right,* she thought. *Maybe things* will *look different in the morning.*

For right this minute, she knew that out there somewhere, beyond that dark horizon, Johnny was following this enormous, awesomely futuristic vessel.

*Following me.* She tightened her grip on the railing. *But not for long, Johnny Boy, not for long. Tomorrow we're on our way to Brazil, and you'll lose my trail. And then I'll have one less thing to worry about.*

Which still left about a baker's dozen.

The next day, Stephanie witnessed the silent, almost mysterious ease with which the de Veigas traveled, and she had the impression of a great unseen piece of machinery at work.

Returning to her suite after breakfast, she found her luggage already magically packed. Throughout her life, arranging for airline tickets and reservations, and packing her own luggage—in fact, the very act of seeing to these mundane details and minutiae—had always been an essential ritual; had, above all, been a comforting transition between leaving one place for another.

But now, with everything taken care of by unseen minions, she felt strangely detached and discombobulated. A disturbing mental image sprang to mind—an autumn leaf, delicate and brittle, at the whim and mercy of driving winds.

The idea of being that leaf did not appeal. Nevertheless, the unsettling image remained.

Stephanie felt even less in control when, half an hour later, Colonel Valerio came to collect her passport.

"I always get Immigration and Customs out of the way long before we board the jet," he explained. "That way, we can take off as soon as we board."

Stephanie was reluctant to hand over her passport because it represented her last link to freedom, but she had no choice but to comply.

Pocketing it, Colonel Valerio said, "Thank you, ma'am. Flight time is at fifteen hundred hours sharp."

Stephanie stared at him. She couldn't believe he'd actually said that.

"Ah!" she said, couching her sarcasm under layers of innocence. "You must mean three o'clock!"

His stony mask reflected no emotion—only twin fisheye miniatures of herself in his mirrored shades. "That's right, ma'am," he said. And spinning on his heel, he did a neat about-face and marched off.

"March two, three, four!" Stephanie murmured, sketching a mock salute behind his receding back. What was he? Some kind of machine?

She went up on deck. The *Chrysalis* was anchored a mile offshore. The sky was cloudless and the sun dazzled and the Maritime Alps were a purple haze. Gulls fluttered like confetti in the air.

She looked at her watch. It was nearly ten o'clock.

She tightened her lips thoughtfully. Between now and takeoff, she had five hours, and she would have to call Uncle Sammy in New York. She hadn't talked to him in nearly a week, and knowing him, he would be agonizing over her, thinking the worst.

But she couldn't telephone him from aboard the yacht; she wouldn't put it past Colonel Valerio to have bugged all the telephones. Nor would it be wise for her to go ashore expressly to use a public phone; that would arouse suspicions, for sure. So. She would have to think up something.

"There you are!" she heard Eduardo call.

Turning in the direction of his voice, Stephanie faced into the sun and raised one hand to shield her eyes. Eduardo was coming toward her, dressed in a white silk Versace shirt with the top three buttons undone and knife-creased white duck trousers and a brown belt from Hermès with a gold letter H for a buckle. On his feet were Roman legion-style sandals with a lot of brass hardware and thick brown leather straps that wound around the ankles. He had a canvas bag the color of oatmeal slung casually over his shoulder and was all smiles.

"I looked everywhere for you!" he exclaimed as he kissed her noisily on the lips.

Stephanie kissed him back and smiled. "You did?" she said, sounding pleased.

"Of course I did." He slung the bag off his shoulder and held it up. "Why would I have raided the changing rooms by the pool? Do you think matching turquoise bikinis will do?"

"Why?" she asked. "Are we going swimming?"

"Among other things," he said, nuzzling her nose with his.

"Oh? Things such as what?" Her eyes were bright and shiny and her teeth sparkled like pearls.

"Well, we are very close to Cannes," he said, pushing his body against hers, and their lips met again and all conversation ceased.

Eduardo had the launch drop them at Le Suquet, the lovely old fishing port with its small picturesque streets and bustling market. They had coffee at a quayside cafe and then walked along the Croisette, Cannes' glamorous beachfront with its fine tan beaches and majestic palm trees and white spun-sugar hotels—among them the world-famous Martinez-Concorde, the Majestic, and the Carlton.

As always, Stephanie found Eduardo to be the perfect guide. He seemed to know everything, and made an effort to point out all the sights. He took her to the rue Macé and the rue des Serbes, where they browsed around the antique shops, and then on to Alaska on the rue des Etats-Unis, where they bought the most delicious ice cream she had ever tasted—pistachio, peanut, and *marron glacé*. Licking their cones, they walked to La Californie, the hill at the other end of town, where kings, emirs, and billionaire businessmen owned secluded neo-Gothic castles. And, because no visit to Cannes is complete without it, they went to the Carlton pier, where they paid one hundred francs each for a mattress and sun umbrella, and, donning the turquoise swimsuits, splashed in the sea and played beachball with two delightful Australian children.

Watching Eduardo romping with them, Stephanie once again marveled at his adaptability, for he seemed equally at home here with the tots as he was talking with the local fishermen in the Old Port or dining in the formal splendor of a Michelin-starred restaurant.

*Every minute we spend together is so special,* she thought. *I wish this morning could last forever.* And she had to smile inwardly, for it was the same thought she had whenever they were together. *I wonder if he feels the same way?*

She hoped so.

After an hour at the beach, they changed back into their street clothes and went to La Palme d'Or, the restaurant in the Hôtel Martinez-Concorde. The dining room was Art Deco and the walls were lined with old movie stills. Eduardo ordered for them both. They had succulent baby lamb chops and sweet, thyme-flavored onion tarts and raspberries fresh from the Col de Bleine. It was one of the most delicious meals Stephanie had ever eaten. Even so, she was practically oblivious to the food: her attention was consumed by Eduardo, and bread and water would have tasted superb.

*I wonder,* she dared think. *What would a lifetime with him be like?*

Two o'clock rolled around and the maitre d' with the moustache and bald pate approached the table. "Monsieur," he murmured, "your car has arrived."

"Thank you," Eduardo said, discreetly transferring a concealed hundred-dollar bill from his palm into the man's hand. "Please tell my driver to wait."

The maitre d' gave a low bow. "With pleasure, monsieur," he said, and skimmed across the dining room, seemingly on a cushion of air. Eduardo smiled wryly across the table at Stephanie. She knew what that little smile meant.

Almost time to fly into the great unknown.

Returning his smile, she pushed back her chair. "Could you excuse me for a minute, Eduardo?" she said. "I've got to use the powder room."

Picking up her purse, she rose to her feet. Eduardo rose also, and didn't sit back down until she'd left the table. Knowing he was watching, she walked through the dining room with graceful slow steps, but when she left the restaurant and was out in the hotel lobby, where he could no longer see her, her gait quickened purposefully. She made a beeline for the nearest telephone booth.

She clutched the receiver with both hands and tapped her foot impatiently. Then, realizing she was hunched suspiciously over the phone, sneaking little sideways glances out of the corners of her eyes—*like someone acting extremely furtive!*—she forced herself to straighten her posture and raise her head. Turning half around, she glanced out at the vast lobby as she waited for the operator to connect her.

There was the usual hotel activity. Arrivals. Departures. Porters struggling with luggage. A young bellboy walking around, holding up a sign that read: M. FAYAD. A manager soothing the ruffled feathers of an outraged guest. A group of identically dressed Japanese businessmen surging out of an elevator. The requisite ill-behaved child. And a man seated in a chair, legs crossed, newspaper on his lap, staring directly over . . . at *her!*

Stephanie jerked and nearly dropped the receiver. Caught it with fumbling hands. She knew him! Christ, yes, she did! From Marbella! The aging gigolo who'd tried to warn her off approaching the *Chrysalis*. But what was he doing *here?* Following her? *Spying* on her? But for *whom?* And *why?*

Suddenly she was aware of a voice squawking something in her ear. Stephanie turned back around, holding the receiver close to her ear, struggling to listen even while she looked back over at—

—an empty chair. Folded newspaper on the seat. *Impossible!*

She blinked her eyes, stared.

*Where did he go?*

The operator cut in. "It's ringing."

"Thank you." Stephanie made one last eye-sweep of the lobby. But he wasn't there. Yet she *knew* she hadn't imagined him!

—and the distant rings were interrupted by a click and then Sammy's familiar voice said, *"Hel–*lo," in that curt way he had of answering the phone, and she felt the most immeasurably sweet, exquisite relief flooding through her.

"Uncle Sammy?" she breathed. "Oh, Uncle Sammy, thank God you're there!"

"Girlie? My God! I've been wracking my brains trying to come up with a way to contact you! Where *are* you?"

"Cannes. You know—"

But he cut her off. "Girlie, we have to talk! Something's come up! I told you about Aaron Kleinfelder? The man in the coma?"

"Uncle *Sam*my!" She shut her eyes momentarily in frustration. "I've only got a minute! I called so—"

"Girlie, *listen to me!*" It was the sharpest tone he had ever used with her. Any other time, it would have made her listen; right now, every second was precious. She had to get back to Eduardo before he came looking for her.

"Uncle *Sam*my! I don't have *time* to talk! I just wanted to tell you we're getting ready to fly to Brazil—"

"Girlie? Girlie—*will* you listen to me?" Sammy's voice took on an even harsher tone. "Aaron Kleinfelder is—"

"For God's sake, not *now!*" Her voice was a mixture of childish pleading and adult exasperation, and she kept glancing in the direction of the restaurant, half expecting to see Eduardo, scanning the lobby for her.

"Girlie, do you have any idea what you're mixed up in? No? Well, get ready. Aaron Kleinfelder *died* because he discovered this secret pro—"

Stephanie blinked. "He's . . . dead?" she murmured. "But I thought you just got through saying he was in a co—"

"He was," Sammy said, and quickly filled her in on how Aaron Kleinfelder had awakened from the coma, but had died soon after being transferred from ICU. "Girlie. Someone suffocated him. He was murdered."

"Murdered!" Her hands tightened around the receiver. "Uncle Sammy, a-are you sure?"

"Yes," he said wearily, "murdered. And the killer even left a calling card on his pillow. A nice fresh red rose. Can you believe it?"

"Oh, God!" She took a deep breath, put a hand on the wall of the phone booth, and rested her forehead against it. How she wished she had the luxury of time; how she wanted to discuss this in detail and get all of Uncle Sammy's input. But alas, time would not permit. She raised her head wearily. "Uncle Sammy," she sighed, "I really do have to run. I'll try to call again as soon as I get to Brazil—"

"For crying out *loud,* Girlie! Will you *listen* to me? And for heaven's sake: whatever you do, *don't . . . hang . . . up!* You must not—I repeat, *not!*—go anywhere with the de Veigas, especially not to Brazil! I know it sounds melodramatic, but Aaron Kleinfelder, Vinette Jones, *and* your grandfather were killed because of what they'd found out. So *please,* Girlie, *please!* Don't fool yourself into thinking you're not as expendable as they were—because you are!"

"Uncle Sammy, I—

"*Will* you hear me out? For God's sake, Girlie, what does it take to make you wake up? Do you think they won't hesitate to kill you, too?"

She sighed and shuddered. *Kill. Oh, Jesus.*

Sammy was saying, "Girlie, I want you to come back here—to New York. Right away. Take the next flight out of there. Then, once you're here, we can sit down and put our heads together. Surely between us we can think up a safer and saner way to approach this thing?" He paused a moment in order to gauge her reaction, and when none was forthcoming, he asked, "Girlie—did you hear me?"

"Yes," Stephanie sighed, "I heard you."

"Good. Then you'll do as I tell you, right? As soon as you hang up, you'll call the nearest airport? It's in Nice, I believe . . ."

But Stephanie was no longer listening to him. Something else had caught her attention—a bright flash of light glancing off the restaurant's glass door as it opened and swung shut again.

Instinctively, she shrank further into the shadows of the telephone booth, facing the wall and making herself as small and unobtrusive as possible. Then, holding her breath, she slowly turned her head and peered cautiously over her shoulder.

Eduardo! Looking around the lobby; searching for her, of course . . .

An involuntary groan, like a high-pitched mewl, escaped her lips. Swiftly she turned away, her expression stricken. *Shit!* she thought, staring accusingly at the receiver in her hand, as though it had been a snake she had been holding all this time. *Oh, shit!*

"Girlie!" Sammy's voice squawked from the earpiece, sounding suddenly inordinately loud. "Girlie? Girlie? Are you still there?"

Stephanie hesitated but for the merest fraction of a second. Then she quickly hung up, took a deep breath, and once again peered cautiously back over her shoulder.

Luck was with her! Eduardo was standing with his back to her. Facing in the opposite direction, away from her, cocking his arm to look at his watch—

Seizing the moment, she grabbed her purse and flew out of the phone booth, moistening her lips with the tip of her tongue, and forced a smile as she made a beeline toward him. In her path, a young couple holding hands let go of each other and broke in two as she rushed forward and past. And then there she was, standing directly behind him—and he still none the wiser!

She tapped him on the back. "Ahem!" she said. "Does it just stand there and look pretty, or does it move and speak?"

He turned around in surprise. "Where did you come from? I thought I looked everywhere."

She smiled smugly. "Didn't I tell you? I've got Houdini in my blood, on my mother's side." She laughed softly and slid an arm through his. "Well? Did you settle the lunch tab, or do we have to make a run for it?"

He smiled. "Everything is taken care of. But it is getting rather late. I'm afraid we had better get a move on."

Adroitly he steered her to the front entrance and into the back of a waiting Rolls Royce Silver Spur. She inhaled appreciatively. The car smelled very much like the inside of a very expensive, brand-new wallet.

"My. Oh, my." She ran her hands over the smooth parchment-colored glove leather. Then she looked over at Eduardo. "Tell me," she said. "Is it true that if you take care of the luxuries, the necessities take care of themselves?"

Eduardo laughed. "I certainly hope so!"

Unknown to them, they had company all the way to the airport.

It was a white Ford Escort, and it followed the Rolls from the moment it pulled away from the hotel. It stayed three cars behind the Rolls as it joined the eastbound traffic on the Croisette. And it followed at a distance as the Rolls took the airport turnoff in nearby Nice.

But the Rolls did not head to the passenger terminal. Instead, it took a service road which led directly to the hangars and maintenance facilities. There, it stopped in front of a chain-link gate.

Fifty feet behind it, the Escort slowed and pulled off to the side of the road. Its occupants watched as a uniformed armed guard approached the big car. After a brief exchange, he unlocked the gate and waved it smartly through.

The Rolls drove directly onto the tarmac, where it was dwarfed by the towering elevator fins of parked jetliners, before disappearing from view behind a hangar.

The chain-link gate swung shut again.

The Escort pulled away from the side of the road and drove up to the same gate and stopped. The guard approached it, but this time he gestured with unmistakable authority. "*Non, non! Cette entrée est strictement interdite aux personnes non-autorisées! Faites demi-tour tout de suite!*"

# ❦ 28 ❦

$\mathcal{T}$he Rolls stopped at a set of old-fashioned boarding stairs. When the driver helped Stephanie out, she found herself facing two jet engines that were so huge several people could have stood up inside them. Slowly, she raised her eyes and looked up past the giant swept-back wing at the rest of the plane. She was stunned. "Holy cow!" she said softly.

Eduardo, ducking out of the car behind her, looked concerned. "You are not afraid of flying, I hope?" he asked.

"What?" She turned to him. "No. That's not it at all. It just . . ." Words suddenly failed her.

"Yes?"

"Well, I . . . I expected a private jet," she said.

"This is a private jet," he replied.

She laughed softly. "This is a goddamn seven-forty-seven, Eduardo!"

He shrugged. "It may be a little bigger than most corporate jets, but it is private, I assure you. Now come." He cupped a hand under her elbow and led her up the boarding stairs.

The surprises were just beginning.

A beautiful flight attendant was waiting at the top. She wore a futuristic Claude Montana minidress made of metallic fibers and her blond hair was fashioned in an elaborate retro-sixties style. "Senhor de Veiga," she greeted warmly in a naturally smoky voice. "It is a pleasure to see you."

"The pleasure is mine, Camilla," Eduardo said.

The attendant smiled at Stephanie with that professional smile indigenous to attendants the world over. She said, "And you must be Ms. Williams."

"Yes." Stephanie nodded. "How do you do?"

"Welcome aboard. My name is Camilla. I am pleased to be of service."

Stephanie stared in wide-eyed amazement as she followed Camilla. The interior of the airplane was like none she had ever seen. The starboard side, along which they were walking aft, was one long, narrow corridor, like that on a train. Sliding doors led to spacious rooms which opened off to port.

Camilla showed them to a fantastic living room done in different shades of white with sleek, white-leather and chrome furniture and silk cushions and museum-quality Impressionist paintings attached to the white bulkheads. Stephanie recognized a Monet and a Pissarro and two incredible Vuillards. On a built-in sideboard was a three-foot-high bronze Degas dancer. *Any museum in the world would give its eyeteeth for any one of these treasures,* she thought.

Camilla said, "Everyone else is already aboard. Please strap yourselves in. We have received clearance from the tower to take off immediately."

Stephanie looked amazed. The *Chrysalis* she had been able to deal with—almost. But this?

As they strapped themselves into a white leather couch, the engines started up and the big jet began to taxi slowly toward the runway.

Stephanie felt as though she had left reality completely behind. And as the powerful engines revved up and the plane hurtled down the runway, she could only wonder what other surprises the future held in store.

Johnny Stone watched the de Veiga jet lift off and climb steeply up into the sky, where it banked to the south and got smaller and smaller until it was just a tiny flash of silver, and then that, too, was gone. He said, "Shit!" very softly, kicked the front tire of the little white Ford Escort, and struggled into the front passenger seat of the compact interior, knocking his kneecaps against the dashboard in the process. He said, "Shit!" once again and slammed the door shut. Puckered his lips and stared grimly out the windshield.

The aging Spanish gigolo he had hired in Marbella, as much for the man's battered cabin cruiser as his knowing his way around this part of the world, was in the driver's seat. He asked, "What do you want to do now?"

"Now?" Johnny made a gun out of the fingers of each hand and pointed the "barrels" across the airport. "I want you to drop me off at the passenger terminal," he said, and sat back.

Ernesto spent his airborne hours seeing to his far-flung business empire from the computerized command center aboard the jet, and Zarah preferred to remain secluded in her cabin during lengthy flights.

It was a cabin fit for a queen. Located on the top level of the hump-backed plane, directly behind the flight deck, it was reached by spiral stairs and was done up all in various tones of skin-flattering peach: the Edward Fields carpet with it sculpted butterfly motif; the king-sized bed with its padded, butterfly wing headboard; the ultramodern couch and two swivel chairs of pearlized peach leather. In addition, there was a built-in vanity with a round mirror framed by two elephant tusks, and a gimbaled lucite coffee table. On the bulkheads, a collection of voluptuous nudes by Boucher were spotlit by invisible lights.

A separate mirrored bathroom was complete with Jacuzzi and bidet, and there was a closet where Zarah kept a complete wardrobe of designer originals permanently onboard.

As the engines changed pitch and the jet reached its cruising altitude of twenty-eight thousand feet, Zarah was lounging on the bed. Wearing giant canary diamond solitaire earrings, a gold lamé turban, and yellow chiffon harem pajamas embroidered with gold thread. Her coco coral lips were pouted thoughtfully; her black onyx mascared eyes gleamed. All around her, spread out on the bed like toys, was her vast collection of jeweled butterfly brooches.

She loved playing with them, loved knowing their detailed histories and provenances, loved feeling their flawless workmanship between her fingers. Loved, even more, having to decide . . . which should she wear? So difficult having to choose. So endless the selection. There was the butterfly in profile with wings of diamonds and rubies and a body of teardrop pearls. *Once the Queen of Rumania's.* The spread-eagled butterfly completely encrusted with yellow-and-brown diamonds. *The deposed empress of Iran's.* A moth with wings of lapis-lazuli and a thorax of gold. *According to legend, Cleopatra's.* The malachite and jade one-winged butterfly, delicately hinged to become a two-winged locket when opened, with a tiny photograph of Alexandra Fedorovna in the left wing and Czar Nicholas II in the right. *The last Russian czarina's.* The butterfly by René Lalique, all delicate stylized Art Nouveau, fashioned of the palest rainbow enamels inset with tiny diamonds and even tinier sapphires. *The Philippine dictator's wife's.* The night-flying moth, made of matched mother-of-pearl shells and painted with miniature ladies and gentlemen from the French court. *Poor Marie Antoinette's.*

And so many more, dozens upon dozens . . . a queen's ransom.

Colonel Valerio, whom she had summoned immediately after takeoff, was standing near the door at parade rest, waiting. Still ignoring him, Zarah reached for the mother-of-pearl moth. *The ill-fated Marie Antoinette's.* Holding it up to the light and moving it about, she murmured, "Ah, how it shimmers! The way the patterns on its wings change to tableaux. Amazing, is it not, to think that something this beautiful could bring such exceedingly bad luck?"

Colonel Valerio did not reply, for he knew none was expected.

"But Monica Williams," Zarah continued, "does not need cursed jewels. The young woman makes her own hideous luck, wouldn't you agree, Colonel?"

Now he automatically snapped to attention. "Ma'am!" he said, realizing an answer was expected.

She tilted her head to one side, regarding the moth as she moved it this way and that. "I fear our Ms. Williams is becoming a serious liability,

Colonel." She frowned and put the moth down. "I have tried to warn her off, but alas. She would not listen."

Zarah raked the collection of winged insects across the peach spread, causing them to click and scratch like a horde of live beetles. Then, kneeling, she cupped her hands, scooped up a pile of the precious bijoux, and raised her arms high, like a priestess with a libation for the gods. She shut her lovely eyes.

"If worst comes to worst, Monica Williams must be taken care of," she said, giving Colonel Valerio a significant look.

And with that, she tilted her head far back, opened her fingers, and let the butterflies and moths drop.

Down they rained on her shoulders and breasts: rubies, diamonds, sapphires, emeralds, all giving the momentary illusion that they had come to life and were in flight. Zarah moaned in a kind of ecstasy and then they bounced and rolled and were once more still.

Colonel Valerio said, "I'll call New York and contact The Ghost. That way, we won't need to get involved ourselves."

Picking up a butterfly at random, Zarah perused it thoughtfully. "Do tell your Ghost not to be too hasty. I believe our Ms. Williams will not last long enough to require such radical measures. I want The Ghost in place merely . . . merely in case . . . as a precaution. You do understand?"

She smiled, and, humming to herself in an unearthly beautiful voice, plucked up another butterfly, and then another and another, until her hands shimmered with an exotic flock seemingly poised to take flight.

# ✽ *Book Three* ✽

# ETERNITY

## 1

### Rio de Janeiro, Brazil

The de Veiga jet had received clearance to deviate from the normal flight path. Now, bringing the 747 down to four thousand feet, the pilot put the big plane into a wide sweeping turn. Below, the dark blue of the South Atlantic became paler by degrees. Eduardo pointed, his finger tapping the window. "Rio will be coming up right there."

Stephanie leaned toward the Perspex. She could see the humpbacked coastal islands below, like emerald whales basking in the sun, and beyond them, the lushly vegetated volcanic mass of mainland. The pilot banked the plane to starboard and the wings dipped and, like magic, a whole panorama opened up.

There it was, spread out right below them. Rio in all its glory.

The breath caught in Stephanie's throat. "It's so beautiful!" she exclaimed.

"It is one of the most beautiful cities in the world," Eduardo agreed, nodding. He smiled. "To me it is the *most* beautiful."

And he pointed out all the familiar landmarks: Ipanema and Rodrigo de Freigas Lake and Corcovado Mountain with its giant statue of Christ on its peak and, off to the right, Copacabana and Sugar Loaf. Flotillas of sparkling white pleasure boats bobbed out in Guanabara Bay.

"See the racetrack below us?" he asked. "That is the Jocquie Club. I will take you there. And coming up is the Jardin Botânico. The royal palms around its perimeter are one hundred feet tall . . ."

Stephanie saw people sunning themselves around the rooftop swimming pools of the skyscrapers and bumper-to-bumper traffic on the wide thoroughfares which snaked around the curves of the sandy beaches. And then she caught sight of the other Rio—shantytowns massed on the steep hills and mountainsides all around. The profusion of slums was such that she was shocked, and suddenly the city lost some of its luster.

Stephanie said, "I've read about these shantytowns, and seen pictures of them. But good God! I had no idea they were *this* prevalent!"

"There are no simple solutions," he explained. "You must understand, Monica. Rio is huge. There are ten million people, and millions of them are very, very poor. Poverty here is more than just an enormous problem. It is a disease."

"All the more reason that something should be done about it," Stephanie murmured, staring numbly back down at the slums.

Then the plane executed a half circle and headed back out to sea in order to approach the International Airport on the Ilha do Governador from the east.

In no time at all they were on the ground and taxiing toward an out-of-the-way apron, where a limousine and a Jeep with a uniformed official from immigration and another from customs were waiting.

Eduardo unsnapped his seatbelt and stood up. "This is where we get off," he announced. Taking Stephanie's hand, he pulled her to her feet. "Welcome to Rio," he said huskily, drawing her close. He stared into her eyes. "I hope you will love it here as much as I."

She held his gaze. "I am sure I will," she said softly, wondering how things would work out. During the twelve-and-a-half-hour flight from Nice, Eduardo had outlined his plans for her. "The world headquarters of Grupo da Veiga is in São Paulo," he had explained. "My father is in charge of all operations there. But we have substantial holdings in Rio and need to maintain a large branch office there, which I head. That is where you will work also. I am certain you will find it very exciting."

Oh, if only she could be so certain! But then, she knew what he did not: that she was a fraud who had burst into his life with an ulterior motive.

"We'd better be going," he said. "My parents and Zaza are flying on to São Paulo. The sooner we bid them good-bye, the sooner they can be on their way."

In scant minutes, farewells were said, luggage transferred from plane to car, and immigration and customs—mere formalities for the de Veigas—observed. Then they were in the chauffeured limousine, heading into the city, a drive Stephanie would not soon forget.

She supposed it was due to the spectacular urban sights as well as Eduardo's regaling her with tales of the wonder she would find in this, his native country. Firing her interest was obviously of tantamount importance to him. She thought: *He wants so much for me to be happy here.*

"There is so much you will find fascinating," he went on, saying that of all the places in the world, next to Rio there was one he loved most: Recife.

Stephanie asked, "And where is that?"

"North of here, closer to the equator. It is an unspoiled colonial city on the Atlantic, built on a peninsula and various islands—all linked by bridges." He paused and declared, "We will go there together."

*As if I have no say in the matter,* Stephanie thought. But strangely enough, she felt no irritation. On the contrary, she loved traveling and couldn't wait to see everything.

Now they were riding along the heavily trafficked Avenida Infante

Don Henrique, alongside the wide expanse of sand that was the Flamengo beach. Stephanie saw tanned women in skimpy bikinis sunning themselves, and groups of athletic men in tiny briefs playing soccer and volleyball.

"From the looks of things," she mused, "I'd better buy myself a new bathing suit. I had no idea such skimpy ones were in!"

Eduardo laughed. "That's why they're called *fio dental*—dental floss."

She had to laugh, but then suddenly frowned. "Eduardo?" Her forehead creased. "Why's nobody in the water?"

He sighed. "Pollution," he said grimly. "Because of it none of the beaches surrounding Guanabara Bay are suitable for bathing."

"What a pity," Stephanie murmured. "It looks like such a wonderful beach."

"At least the ocean beaches are safe," he said, "and there are many of them. Rio has over fifty miles of beaches."

"Yes, but still . . ." She stared out at the accusingly empty body of water.

And then he brought up the Amazon: the greatest river on earth in the greatest jungle on earth, where the beauty was as breathtaking as the dangers were countless. Eduardo painted a picture of a land before time . . . of the Rio Negro, one of the Amazon's many tributaries, where there are no mosquitoes and the water is pitch-black from the rotten vegetation which kills the mosquito larvae . . . and the caimans, the South American crocodiles . . . and the electric eels and piranha . . . and the capybara, the largest rodent in the world, which can hold its breath underwater for eight minutes.

"Eduardo!" she protested. "When are we going to find the time to go to all these places? I thought I would be working—"

"And you shall," he soothed, "you shall. You see, Monica, Grupo da Veiga has an enormous pharmaceutical testing and manufacturing complex deep in the heart of the Amazon. It is called Sítto da Veiga, and every so often, we will have to fly up there on business."

They were on the Avenida des Naçoes Unidas, where traffic breezed right through the mountains by means of two long straight tunnels.

"Contrary to what some people believe," he went on, "I personally find nothing wrong with mixing business and pleasure." He smiled raffishly. "To me, they are one and the same."

He paused as the car entered the maw of the second tunnel.

"Ah," he said. "Now we are almost there." And as they burst back out into the blinding sunlight, he announced, "Here we are. In the *Zona Sul*, the South Zone. Look around you, Monica! We are in the travel-poster Rio de Janeiro."

Stephanie was alternately ducking her head and craning her neck.

This part of the city was affluent and sleekly modern. There were shops and sidewalk cafes and skimpily clad cariocas everywhere she looked.

*Eduardo's right*, Stephanie thought. *This is the very view I've seen on countless posters and postcards, in books and movies and brochures ... only, no photograph had ever quite done justice to the magnificent reality.*

"Well?" Eduardo asked. "What do you think?"

"I had no idea Copacabana was this *huge!* The beach goes on forever!"

"And adjacent to it is Ipanema, which is also enormous." He nodded. "I trust you will soon acquaint yourself with it, also. Now then. Would you like to drive around and sightsee a bit more, or would you rather go directly to your apartment?"

She turned from the window to stare at him. "*My* apartment? I . . . I don't understand."

He explained, "Actually, it is one of many buildings owned by Grupo da Veiga. In this one, we reserve a number of furnished apartments for visiting VIPs. The apartment is sitting there empty. Also, I should mention that you are welcome to live there for as long as you wish. Permanently, if you are so inclined."

*Permanently.* She was stunned. "I . . . I'd like to see it," she said.

Eduardo pressed a button which lowered the glass divider behind the driver's seat and gave the chauffeur instructions.

Stephanie sat back, staring out at the world's most famous beach. Once again, she felt curiously helpless, as if everything had already been decided for her and was happening in fast forward. She didn't know whether to feel gratitude or irritation. Was Eduardo uncommonly thoughtful, or did he have some ulterior motive? Abruptly she put that line of thought out of mind. *I mustn't be ungrateful. And, if he does have an ulterior motive, so do I.*

It was a penthouse duplex near the midpoint of Copacabana beach, with two terraces overlooking the ocean. The first floor consisted of a foyer, an enormous glass-walled living room, a separate dining room, a big Eurostyle kitchen, a powder room, and a separate maid's room. Wide spiral teak stairs curved gracefully from one end of the living room to three luxurious bedrooms upstairs, each with its own marble bathroom. The furniture was attractive and expensive, and there were beautiful framed lithographs on the walls.

A middle-aged woman with gray hair set in a tight permanent met them at the front door.

"This is Astrid, the housekeeper," Eduardo said. "She will help you get settled."

"How do you do, Ms. Williams?" Astrid's English was accented but fluent.

"Fine, thank you," Stephanie said, giving the woman a friendly hand-shake. *Eduardo didn't tell me about her.* She wondered what other sur-prises were in store.

A building porter arrived with Stephanie's luggage, and Astrid directed him upstairs. Then she turned to Stephanie again and switched ef-fortlessly from Portuguese back to English. "If you like, Ms. Williams, I can show you around."

"I'd be delighted!" Stephanie glanced at Eduardo. "You don't mind, do you?"

He smiled at her barely subdued excitement. "Of course not." He gestured. "I will make myself a drink and wait for you on the terrace."

Stephanie followed Astrid. Everywhere she looked, the apartment was immaculate and set up for perfect housekeeping—from the kitchen, which was stocked with every conceivable appliance and item of food, to the bathrooms, with their luxurious towels and imported soaps and perfumes and powders. Informal bouquets of fresh-cut flowers were in every room, and in the master bedroom, the sliding doors were open, the floor-length sheers billowing in the ocean breeze. Stephanie twitched them aside and went out.

Clutching the railing, she leaned over and looked straight down. Eduardo was standing directly below her on the other terrace, the wind ruffling his hair as he gazed out at the ocean, drink in hand.

*Eduardo. So handsome. So thoughtful. So irresistible.*

The tour completed, Stephanie thanked Astrid and complimented her on her housekeeping.

"I will now unpack your luggage," Astrid said, getting busy.

Stephanie went downstairs and joined Eduardo on the lower terrace. She came up silently behind him. "I really don't know what to say."

He turned around and leaned casually back against the railing. "Why should it be necessary to say anything?"

"*Why?*" She gestured toward the terrace doors, indicating the apart-ment. "Because the place is so big and lavish. But I won't need a full-time housekeeper—"

"Ahh," he grinned. "Actually you will. Your position at Grupo da Veiga will require you to do a certain amount of business entertaining. That is where Astrid comes in. She is very experienced at helping give cocktail parties and planning sit-down dinners. In time, I think you will find her indispensable." He raised one dark eyebrow in amusement. "You must learn to trust me, Monica."

"I *do*. But . . . this place!" She lifted her hands and then let them drop. "It must be outrageously expensive."

He laughed. "If it makes you feel any better, it can be deducted from your salary."

"Yes, but can I afford it?" She blushed slightly and looked away.

Then she took a deep breath, raised her head, and stared at him. "I don't mean to sound mercenary, Eduardo, but I don't even know *what* my salary will be, or what *position* I will fill. For that matter, I really don't know anything!"

He nodded. "I remember you telling me that you produced television commercials."

"Yes," Stephanie said, and thought, *Oh, God. Here I go again. How much larger is this web of lies going to have to get?*

"Grupo da Veiga," Eduardo explained, "consists of several individual industries. Unlike most of our competitors, we do not hire outside advertising agencies; we have an in-house division which produces all print and moving-picture ads. That is where you will work." He paused. "Does an annual starting salary of one hundred and fifty thousand American dollars sound satisfactory?"

Her eyes widened in surprise. "And what do I have to do for that?"

"You will be vice president in charge of moving-picture advertising." A slight grin began to form on his lips. "But you will not be required to make love to me if you do not wish to do so."

Her eyes gleamed like polished mirrors. "And if I wish to?" she asked huskily, holding his gaze.

His grin widened. "I would consider that to be a fringe benefit for us both."

She could feel a strong current of heat surging up inside her, and her mind flashed an image of his thrusting, muscular, naked body. Her voice quavered as she struggled to veer the conversation back to business. "How do you know I'm worth a hundred and fifty thousand a year?" she asked.

He smiled. "I am a firm believer in the sink-or-swim theory. Talent has a habit of rising to the top."

"And if I sink?"

Without taking his eyes off her, he put his glass on the ledge and pulled her close. "In that case," he said softly, "we will have to find something else for you to do."

# 2

*Rio de Janeiro, Brazil*

Grupo da Veiga was located in a pink-and-white mansion in the heart of the downtown "Centro" district. Casual passersby and tourists often mistook it for a consulate or a museum. Only a polished brass plaque by the front gate attested to its commercial function.

The security precautions were awesome. Armed guards were posted at the front gate, and two more stood to either side of the baronially scaled front doors. Stephanie suspected there were more guards inside.

Entering the building, she felt as if she'd stepped into another world. The palatial foyer contained priceless art and museum-quality furnishings. In the center of the room, a beautiful receptionist presided over a gleaming tulipwood *bureau plat,* its surface bare save for a multilined telephone.

After Stephanie introduced herself, the receptionist smiled and replied in perfect English, "I am pleased to make your acquaintance, Ms. Williams. Senhor de Veiga is expecting you." She gestured toward a grouping of antique chairs. "Please, have a seat?"

As the receptionist picked up the phone, Stephanie sat on one of the tapestried *fauteuils.*

After a few minutes, she saw Eduardo coming down the curving staircase. Rising to her feet and going to meet him halfway, she thought, *He looks somehow different . . . I wonder why . . .*

And then she realized what it was: this was the first time she'd seen him dressed for business, and his clothes certainly reinforced his already potent aura of power. Everything he wore seemed designed for one precise purpose: to exude confidence, authority, and raw power.

"Monica." With a smile, he took her hands in his and held them longer than was necessary. Then grinning disarmingly, he let go of her fingers and clapped his hands together in a businesslike fashion. "Now then," he said. "Are you ready for the grand tour?"

Astrid had waited until Stephanie had gone to work before placing the telephone call.

"Ms. Williams went to bed early and fell asleep immediately," she reported. "She neither received nor made any telephone calls, was up by six this morning, went jogging along the beach, showered, and had a breakfast of coffee, pineapple juice, and yogurt before leaving for work."

Colonel Valerio said, "Report in again tomorrow."

Astrid stared at the dead receiver in her hand. *And a nice day to you, too!*

The tour lasted the better part of an hour and a half, and Stephanie soon learned that the Rio branch of Grupo da Veiga was enormous. Their first stop was at the metallurgical division, then it was on to the chemical division, and the engineering department.

And so it went, from one division to the next. In the *florestais* section, Stephanie became acquainted with the products relating to lumber and pulp and paper, while in the *minerais* department, glass showcases displayed samples of the various ores and precious and semiprecious stones the company was mining.

But what fascinated Stephanie most was the genetics division, where actual samples of genetically engineered fruits, vegetables, and flowers were on display.

"Eduardo?" she asked softly. "Who is in charge of the genetics program?"

"Dr. Vassiltchikov."

Stephanie nodded. *I was afraid of that,* she thought. *God help us.*

"But enough of this," Eduardo said. "As you have probably noticed, I am leaving your department for last."

The advertising section was located on the second floor and consisted of an enfilade of nine high-ceilinged rooms. The windows overlooked the quiet, manicured grounds and except for the high rises poking up beyond the trees, it wasn't difficult to imagine oneself far from the hustle and bustle of the city.

When Eduardo showed Stephanie in, the entire staff gathered in the outermost office to meet her. Eduardo made the introductions.

"This is Rubens Montenegro . . . Senhor Montenegro is in charge of this entire department. You will report directly to him . . ."

*A tall, middle-aged aesthete with a trim gray beard and a professorial manner.*

And "Karolyn Gatto . . . Senhora Gatto is your counterpart for all print advertising. You will be working together quite closely on most campaigns."

*An earnest woman with gray hair wearing a high-necked blouse, gray suit, and no jewelry.*

And "Lia Cardoso, your personal assistant. Senhorita Cardoso speaks fluent English and is an excellent interpreter . . ."

*A perky young pixie with wide blue eyes, brown hair in a feather cut, and a bright ready smile.*

And "Amadeu Ricúpero ... Aloisio Fortes ... Maurício Carneiro ..."

Stephanie shook hands with everyone.

Eduardo looked at his watch and said, "I have some meetings scheduled. Senhorita Cardoso will show you to your office, and Senhor Montenegro will fill you in on your work."

And he was gone.

"You look slightly confused," Lia laughed. "I would be, too, meeting so many people at once. Come, I will show you your office."

It was large, with modern Italian furniture the yin to the grand, old-fashioned architecture's yang. There were several large-screen TV sets hooked up to video recorders. A large ceiling fan stirred the air with cool gentle currents, and the view out the floor-to-ceiling windows was lovely.

Lia said, "That is your desk over by the windows, and the drawing board and that computer are yours also. This desk here, by the door, is mine."

Stephanie looked around. "It's very nice."

"I hope you don't mind having to share it with me," Lia said, "but until the new addition is built, I'm afraid we'll be a little cramped for space."

"I think we'll get along fine," Stephanie assured her.

Stephanie walked over to her desk. *So far, so good,* she thought, trailing her fingertips across the polished rosewood surface. Thanks to Eduardo's tour, she had an overall picture of how the Rio branch functioned. She had her own desk in a large spacious office and her own bilingual assistant. *Now all I need to do is figure out my job.*

That first day flew by in a blur. There were invoices from television stations to sort through, new ad videos to sit through and critique, a lunch meeting with a video producer, storyboards of ads-in-the-works to approve. Stephanie found it fascinating, and was grateful for Lia's knowledge and constant good humor. "Quite honestly," she told her, "I don't know what I would do without you."

Lia laughed. "Oh, you'd make do," she said. "Look how you immediately saw how to cut that video ad by twenty seconds without losing its impact. You saved the company a million dollars already, and this is only your first day on the job! I think you're a natural!"

*No, Lia. I'm just a fraud who's slept with the boss.*

Fifteen minutes before quitting time, Lia fielded what must have been the fiftieth phone call of the day. After listening a moment, she said, "Monica, it's for you."

Sighing, Stephanie picked up her extension. "Monica Williams."

"How are things going, Ms. Williams?" It was Eduardo.

Simply hearing his voice made her heart give a leap. "Fine," she laughed, "if you count no major disasters as a good day!"

He laughed also. "Then I would say you've had a splendid day! Well? Are we still having dinner tonight? Or are you too tired?"

"Truthfully, I'm still jet-lagged, but I would *love* to have dinner."

"Good! I will pick you up at your apartment at seven."

Stephanie was humming to herself as she hung up.

Lia waited until Stephanie left for the day. Then she opened the middle drawer of her desk, removed the false bottom, and rewound the microcassette of the voice-activated tape recorder which was hooked up to Stephanie's telephone line. After listening to all the calls, she picked up her telephone and dialed a series of memorized digits.

A moment later, Colonel Valerio came on the line.

"This is Lia Cardoso," she began softly, and gave him a play-by-play rundown of Stephanie's first day at work. She ended by saying, "Senhor de Veiga invited Ms. Williams to dinner. He will pick her up at her apartment at seven o'clock. He did not say where they would dine."

"Very well. Continue to keep your eyes and ears open. I'll expect you to report in every day."

After she hung up, Lia reset the recorder, replaced the false bottom in the drawer, and went home, secure in the knowledge that her two incomes made her the highest paid administrative assistant in all Rio.

Stephanie wore a long-sleeved mini shift with horizontal tortoiseshell stripes in pink-and-peach sequins and sheer dark stockings and moderate black heels with straps around the ankles. She didn't wear a single piece of jewelry, not even a watch, and with her dark severe bangs and brightly applied makeup, Eduardo couldn't remember the last time a woman had looked quite so appealing.

And judging from the craned necks all around, apparently neither could the rest of the diners. Not that they weren't used to beautiful women, perfect bodies, and expensive clothes and jewels at the Petronius restaurant in Ipanema—it was just that Stephanie's very simplicity and her elegant carriage made her stand out in the crowd.

The maitre d' led them proudly to the choice table by the wall of windows overlooking the beach, and they were barely seated when a bottle of Dom Pérignon, compliments of the management, was brought over by a captain in formal attire.

"I'm impressed!" Stephanie whispered across the table. "You must be a big shot to have them falling all over themselves like this!"

"Me?" Eduardo held her gaze and shook his head. "I come here all the time, and I have never been treated like this!" He smiled. "It is not me who is causing the sensation, Monica. It is *you!*"

She laughed happily. "I knew this dress was cut too low!"

They ordered and went through the motions of eating, but their appetites were only for each other. Sublime though the food was, neither of them could have recalled a single dish afterward.

The concerned staff chalked up their appetites to *amor.*

Eduardo paid the check and tipped royally. Outside, the sky was black velvet and the wind had picked up and the southern stars were staging a show.

"Just for you," he murmured huskily.

"For *us!*" she corrected him, her eyes bright and dark at the same time. "Is it far to your apartment?"

"Only eight blocks in that direction." Eduardo gestured down the beach with his chin. "We can walk."

He took off his jacket and draped it over her shoulders, and they dashed hand-in-hand across the Avenida Viera Souto like the young lovers they were. Once on the other side, Stephanie held onto him as she took off her shoes and stockings, and then he held onto her while he took off his shoes and socks and rolled up his trouser legs. Then, shoes in hand, they slipped their arms around each other's waists and walked across the sand to the edge of the surf.

The salt air was heady, the water cold and tingly. Except for occasional couples, they had the beach to themselves. On their left, the row of high rises glittered like jewels, and up ahead, Sugar Loaf was drenched with floodlights.

"It's magic!" she whispered, pressing herself closer to him.

A larger wave dashed up, crashed against their calves, and made lacy phosphorescent swirls. He turned her to face him. "Monica."

They kissed, without grappling or groping, just standing there, suspended in time, in space, their arms loosely looped around each other, their lips touching and pecking, nibbling and tasting.

After a while, she drew her head back. "Mmm," she murmured, and intertwined her fingers in his and rested her head on his shoulder as they continued walking down the beach. They didn't speak until they reached his apartment.

It was atop the tallest building, penthouse and villa combined, a two-story, L-shaped structure with richly planted, cantilevered decks and walls of glass seemingly suspended above its own big rooftop pool. And the Atlantic was its front yard.

"Drink?" he asked as they came in.

She shook her head, put her arms around his neck, and pulled his head down to hers. For a while, their lips did all the talking, and then their hands joined in the conversation.

Slowly, teasingly, he unzipped the sequined shift and stepped back. It fell away like a glittering husk, and she drew a deep breath as her breasts leapt free, full and strong and proud, her nipples suddenly erect and jutting forward in the cool air.

"Eduardo!" she whispered. She could feel her legs trembling, the sticky wetness of her moist loins. Then, unable to contain herself, she attacked his shirt, tore frantically at the buttons, and raked her fingernails across his chest.

Suddenly his strong hands clamped around her wrists, and her talons stilled. "Not so fast!" he whispered, his eyes wide. "There is no rush . . ."

She stared at him as though hypnotized.

He smiled in understanding and reached out, his fingers featherlight as he traced the line of her cheekbones, the curve of her strong jaw. Then, cupping her face between his palms, his thumbs caressed the flushed smoothness of her cheeks.

"E . . . ed . . . uar . . . do . . ." she gasped.

"Ssssh . . ."

His thumbs smoothed back her cheeks, stroked the corners of her mouth. Almost chastely, he kissed her forehead, the tip of her nose, each eyelid in turn.

Her breasts heaved. This was driving her to madness! Utter madness! Why didn't he get on with—

His fingers abruptly entwined her hair and cruelly now, he pulled her head back. Her lips parted and her shriek became a cry as he brought his mouth down on hers.

Savage was his hunger, and savage was hers. Gone now was any vestige of restraint. He thrust a hand between her legs and her body arched as she tugged off his shirt and slammed her hips against his.

He was already hard. She could feel the trapped bulging ridge of his penis straining his trousers.

It only took seconds until he too was naked. His phallus slapped up against his belly and his testicles hung like luscious ripe fruits. A single vein pulsed along the length of the shaft.

For a moment they both stood there, breathing deeply, eyeing each other like sexual combatants. Then slowly, she sank down on a large ottoman, and lay there invitingly, legs spread wide, eyes glittering expectantly.

With excruciating slowness, he straddled her and his chest hovered over her breasts. Then he grabbed hold of her hips and lowered himself inside her.

She cried out at the quick sharp pain, and then a strange wild kind of wonder came into her eyes. "*Yes!*" she whispered. "Eduardo—*yes! Yes!*"

He started slowly, pushing himself in and then moving slowly half out, in again and half out again, penetrating the silky smooth secret at the heart of her womanhood. He could feel her tight muscles as he plunged more deeply, could feel the temperature inside her rise.

Slowly, he rotated himself inside her, then rocked against her, then rotated some more. And then, when he could stand it no longer, he rammed with primal ardor.

Her whispers turned into moans and the moans into screams as he began to ride her. Wildly she tossed her head from side to side, scissored her legs around his buttocks, and writhed and bucked in time to meet his every thrust. Her arms tightened around him and she drew his head down to her breasts. "Love me!" she moaned into his ear as he nibbled and sucked and thrust.

Her hips rose greedily to meet him, to impale her deeply upon his dagger of flesh. Faster, faster, he slammed into her, harder, harder!

Then her movements became even more frenetic and purposeful, and she was a burning bed of hot coals, a volcano, erupting and exploding and pouring fiery lava.

And then the explosions which had wracked her now rose up inside him in a torrent, and his own hot thick strength burst forth to merge with the flood of her juices.

"Monica!" he screamed, and his face contorted and he held on for dear life.

Then they collapsed, clinging to each other, their eyes glazed, their breathing raw and heavy. Slowly, the battering storms within them began to subside, like a great powerful flood receding, and they lay quietly, their breathing eventually returning to normal.

After a while, she raised her head and looked at him. "Wow!" she whispered. She contracted her vaginal muscles and smiled. She could feel him still inside her. Still warm. Still large. Still *hard*.

"That," he murmured, "wasn't at all bad for an appetizer . . ."

"Colonel, this is Astrid Bezerra."

It was the next morning. "Yes, Ms. Bezerra. Do you have anything to report?"

"Ms. Williams just left for the office. Last night, she came home from work at six-fifteen, showered and changed, and went to dinner with Senhor de Veiga at seven. She did not return until nearly two o'clock in the morning. She neither received nor made any telephone calls."

"I see."

"Good-bye—" she began.

But he had already hung up.

# ❦ *3* ❦

𝒮tephanie found working at Grupo da Veiga to be unlike anything she had ever known. Each day brought with it new challenges. There were ad campaigns and public relations films to think up for every division of the company. Thirty- and sixty-second ad spots to produce. Local talent to hire on a freelance basis. Products to familiarize herself with. No end of instant decisions to be made.

Yet to her surprise, Stephanie found it all highly stimulating and ultimately rewarding. There was no time for her to get bored. And increasingly, she became more and more grateful for her two godsends—Lia on the workfront and Astrid on the homefront. Stephanie didn't know how she would have managed without them.

Stephanie's driver was on the phone. "Colonel Valerio? This is Felipe Piva."

"Yes, Senhor Piva?"

"I thought you would like to know that every Monday, Wednesday, and Friday, Ms. Williams has me drop her off after work at the language school on Jose Inhares in Leblon. From there, she takes a taxi home after her lessons are over. I hope this information is of some use?"

"Yes, it is, Senhor Piva. An overtime bonus of twenty hours will be added to your paycheck."

"Thank you, Senhor! From myself and my family."

*My web is tightening around you, Ms. Williams.*

Stephanie checked in with Sammy at least once each week, and to play it safe, she only called him from the *Telerj,* the telephone company office on Avenida Nossa Senhora de Copacabana. It was open around the clock, and she could place operator-assisted international phone calls from a booth there at any hour of the day or night.

Invariably, the first words out of Sammy's mouth always were, "Is everything all right down there, Girlie?"

And on this particular late Wednesday evening, he used precisely those words.

"Everything's fine, Uncle Sammy," Stephanie assured him. "In fact, things couldn't be better."

"Good, good." He paused and sighed pointedly. "But I miss you, Girlie. Don't you have any idea how long you'll be down there?"

"No. That depends on when I get my security clearance so I can visit the various facilities and check them out. Right now, it looks like I might be stuck here for quite some time yet."

"Which reminds me," Sammy said. "Before he died, Aaron Kleinfelder gave me his CRY code and secret password. It could be that it hasn't been deleted from the computers yet."

Stephanie felt a thrill of excitement. "Wait a sec, I've got to get my address book out of my purse . . . okay, shoot."

Sammy said, "His ID number was oh-nine-nine, slash, three, cd— that's oh-nine-nine, slash, three, lower-case cd. His password was COOKIE. Got that?"

She read it back to him.

"Just remember what I told you about being careful," he cautioned. "I want you safe and sound—and in *one* piece!"

"Believe me, so do I. Listen, I need you to do me a favor—"

"Anything, my love! *Anything!*"

"Call the airlines and arrange to have Waldo flown down here, will you?"

"At once!" Sammy sounded positively delirious. "But that's not doing *you* a favor, Girlie. That's doing *me* the greatest favor in the world!"

By the second week, Stephanie was completely settled into her new life. Waldo's screechy arrival made all the difference, and home felt like home.

Astrid, understandably, was not all that keen about Waldo. "A parrot!" she exclaimed when Stephanie lugged the big cage in. "Bringing a parrot to Brazil is like . . ."

"Bringing coals to Newcastle," Stephanie completed for her. "I know." She smiled.

"Wal-*do!* Wal-*do!*" The big parrot was excitedly climbing the bars of the cage. "Waldo wants a crack-*er!* Eh-eh-eh-eh-eh!"

"You'll get your cracker," Stephanie promised soothingly, and stroked his beak. "Now just hush up."

"Steph!" Waldo screeched. "Steph! I love you, Steph!"

Inwardly, Stephanie cringed. With a sinking feeling, she thought, *That's all I need: being given away by a bird. Why didn't I anticipate this!*

"What is it saying!" Astrid asked curiously.

"Oh . . ." Stephanie murmured, "he's saying, 'Steph.' I think Stefan or Stephanie must have been the name of his previous owner."

Astrid nodded, and Stephanie was relieved both by her own quick thinking and the woman's ready acceptance of her excuse.

With that stumbling block out of the way, she decided to celebrate Waldo's arrival by inviting Eduardo over for dinner. She gave Astrid the night off, did the cooking herself, turned the lights down low, and popped a bottle of Dom Pérignon.

"To the two of us," Stephanie toasted.

Eduardo laughed. "It looks like there are three of us now," he said, already poking his finger fearlessly into the cage and finger-feeding Waldo one canapé after another.

Stephanie couldn't believe her eyes. Not only was Waldo on his best behavior, but he seemed to accept Eduardo instantly, and didn't once try to bite him! *Will miracles never cease?*

Colonel Valerio was saying, "And that is all, Ms. Bezerra? Nothing unusual has occurred? Nothing at all?"

"Well, now that you mention it, Colonel, there is one thing I find rather odd . . . It has to do with that infernal parrot Ms. Williams sent for."

"Yes?"

"Well, it talks nonstop. Only in English, of course. But I do find it rather strange that whenever it sees Ms. Williams, it tries to get her attention with one particular word."

"Oh? And what word would that be?"

" 'Steph.' The bird keeps shrieking that one word, 'Steph.' "

"And Ms. Williams responds to that?"

"*Sim.*"

"Did you inquire as to what the bird was actually saying?"

"I did. Her explanation was that it must have been the name of its previous owner."

*Silence.* Then: "Tell me, Ms. Bezerra. Does the bird try to get *your* attention—or anyone else's—by using that same word?"

Astrid didn't hesitate. "Never," she declared.

After a moment, Colonel Valerio said, "Hm . . . that is rather interesting."

*Your first mistake, Ms. Williams.*

"Stefan," Colonel Valerio said softly.

He was alone at the rifle range, his Pearson bow, with its adjustable flight wheel, fitted with a quiver of five compression-molded, carbon/fiberglass arrows tipped with one-and-one-eighth-inch steel razor broadheads. Sliding one into the bow, he extended his arm and pulled back on the string. Peering through the thirty-millimeter Aimpoint sight, he saw the sharp red dot centered on the target to which he'd stapled Stephanie's photograph. Letting go of the power release trigger, he launched.

At a velocity of 558 feet per second, the arrow ripped through the photo almost instantaneously. *Bull's-eye!*

Already drawing another arrow, he slid it into the bow, moved the sight a little to the right, put the electronic red dot on the second target, said "Stephanie," and launched. *Bull's-eye again!*

"Steffie . . . Stephan . . . Stefanie . . ." *Bull's-eye, bull's-eye, bull's-eye!*

In rapid succession, all five arrows he had launched hit true. Dead between the eyes.

Smiling, he lowered his bow and thought, *Hunting humans really is so gratifying. I'll take them over animals any day.*

"Good-bye, Ms. Williams," he said softly.

By the end of the third week, Stephanie had not only become acquainted with the geographics of Rio, but she had familiarized herself with all of Grupo da Veiga's old ads, and had come up with new campaigns for every division. More importantly, she had planned them with a specific strategy in mind—so that they might provide her with access to all of the company's various facilities.

It was high time she got back to sleuthing.

She decided, *I'll bring up my ideas at the next staff briefing.*

Lili sang. At the Quinta de Anastácio, the blue-and-white palácio on Ilha da Borboleta. In the majestic Sala de Hércules, with its pictorial blue-and-white rococo tilework, the voice that defied description soared up, past the giant rock crystal chandelier, to be absorbed by the flamboyantly painted, octagonally paneled high wooden ceiling. It drifted around the room like aural ectoplasm and spilled out, through the billowing antique lace curtains, to disappear into the cool of the Tropic of Capricorn night.

"Un Bel dì Vedremo" from *Madama Butterfly*. So heart-wrenchingly beautiful it made the angels weep.

"Come Scoglio" from *Così Fan Tutte*. Each note as dramatically gripping as it was technically dazzling.

"Où va la jeune Indoue?" from *Lakmé*. So delicate and haunting, the melody remained in the mind long after the last note had ceased.

And selections from *La Wally* by Catalin, *La Vestale* by Sontini, and *Medea* by Cherubini . . . all masterpieces destined to live forever.

Her head cocked to one side, Zarah listened closely to the recording of herself in another lifetime, another era. The *duchesse brisée* upon which she was lounging was angled across a corner, and her brow was furrowed, her attention absorbed by her own glorious voice. She held a fragrant rubrum lily, snipped of its pistils, and twirled it idly by its stem, occasionally pressing the waxy petals to her nose. Occasionally, she would nod to herself with satisfaction. No matter how idiosyncratic or difficult the role, she had sung each with a deceptive simplicity, her voice and technique so lyrical that it united music and poetry and made it one.

Ernesto was seated, facing her from behind a grand ormolu-mounted *bureau plat* angled across the far corner. A bronze lamp with a green silk shade illuminated the mesh-topped terrarium in front of him. It was filled with just-hatching yellow butterflies, and as he watched, more and more of them struggled out of their cocoons to try out their newfound wings. Before long, the entire glass box was aflutter, raising in his mind the image of a sunny kaleidoscope in which all the pieces of glass were one shade of vivid yellow or another. Ernesto was fascinated.

Colonel Valerio, standing in the shadows behind the *duchess brisée*, was waiting to report to Zarah. After a few minutes, she picked up the remote control and pressed the OFF button, shutting herself off in mid-aria.

The sudden silence was almost eerie.

She looked up at him. "Colonel?" she asked softly.

He stepped forward and cleared his throat. "You wanted to know about Ms. Williams, ma'am?"

"Yes." Zarah nodded and twirled the lily petals around her nose. "What news have you?"

"For the past three weeks," he said tonelessly, "Ms. Williams has spent each weekday in the Rio offices. She seems well-liked by her co-workers, and is doing quite well in her position. Judging by her notes and conversations, she has already come up with an entirely new advertising campaign."

"Indeed? Now then. What about her evenings and nights? How does our Ms. Williams spend those?"

Colonel Valerio said, "She spent the last three weekends at your son's apartment."

Zarah did not appear in the least bit surprised; she had expected as much. In fact, she would have been surprised if it had been otherwise.

Colonel Valerio glanced in Ernesto's direction and lowered his voice. "Ma'am? The Ghost has long since arrived and is awaiting word. Would you like Ms. Williams to be neutralized yet?"

Zarah compressed her lips thoughtfully and tapped the petals of the flower lightly against her mouth. Then she shook her head slowly. "I think it is a little early for that yet," she said softly, and her brilliant eyes suddenly changed color. She gestured across the room to the yellow blizzard in the terrarium. "Bring me one of those butterflies." Her voice had taken on an imperious mistress-to-servant tone.

Colonel Valerio strode across the carpet, bent down to speak to Ernesto, and came back with a specimen. He was holding it delicately by one of its wings; its other wing fluttered desperately in a futile effort to free itself.

Zarah dropped the rubrum lily and raised a slim, graceful hand. Pinching the fluttering wing between her fingertips, she took the butterfly from him and held it up, inspecting it closely. "Let us pretend this is Ms. Williams," she said, and gave Colonel Valerio a significant look.

"Ma'am." He inclined his head slightly.

"Like Ms. Williams, it is quite beautiful." A peculiar smile of satisfaction crossed her lips, and with slow deliberation, she tore off the fluttering wing, held it high, and let it drop as if it were the insignificant petal of a flower. Then, holding the insect by its thorax, she plucked off its other wing. She held this one high also, and let it drop, too.

The silence in the room seemed to intensify.

She paused dramatically and tossed the now wingless insect's tiny, twitching body at his feet. He stared down at it and frowned.

"Step on it!" she whispered.

He looked at her. Something bright and evil glowed in her eyes. Then, when he raised his boot, she held up a hand.

"Slow . . . ly, Colonel! Slow . . . ly . . . So that it *feels* the agony . . ."

She held her breath as Colonel Valerio's boot came down on the insect as if in slow motion, and the knowledge of her superior strength and power surged warmly through her blood.

*I will show Monica Williams!* she thought. *Oh, yes! I will play with her as if she, too, were nothing more consequential than a mere insect!*

Slowly Zarah raised her head. "Now do we understand each other, Colonel?"

The expatriate blues. They didn't hit often, but when they did, they could throw her for a loop.

Tonight, Stephanie put away the work she'd brought home from the office, considered watching an English-language video or reading a book, and then decided that either one would leave her feeling only that much antsier.

Restless, she went out on the second-floor terrace, arms outstretched, and rippled the foliage with her fingertips. It was a chilly night, but crystal clear and lovely—the kind of starry, starry night you wanted to share with somebody.

She leaned over the terrace railing and ruminated. She had nobody to talk to. Eduardo was in Buenos Aires on a business trip—so scratch that. Astrid was inside, and while their relationship was polite enough, they were far from friends—scratch that, too. She supposed she could call Lia, but something, and Stephanie didn't quite know what, held her back. Maybe because she didn't want to unburden herself to someone she worked with on a daily basis? Maybe. But that wasn't quite it, either.

And looking out at the dark ocean and the relentless white breakers rolling in, she thought: *I want to speak to some damn Yankees! I want to talk girl talk, or have a good gossip.*

There was only one thing she could do. Go to the *Telerj.*

She went inside, grabbed her coat, and sought out Astrid. "It's so nice out," she told the housekeeper, "that I think I'll go get some fresh air."

"Of course, Ms. Williams."

* * *

From a doorway across the street, Astrid Bezerra watched Stephanie enter the *Telerj*. The housekeeper smiled to herself. *So that's why Ms. Williams never uses the telephone at home!* she gloated with the smug satisfaction of one whose long shot has paid off. For it had been intuition, and intuition alone, which had made her follow the American woman.

*Fresh air indeed!* Astrid sniffed triumphantly, flagging down a cruising taxi so she'd be back in the apartment in plenty of time. *Yes,* she thought, *something very strange is going on.*

Astrid couldn't wait to call Colonel Valerio in the morning. She was aware that she had disobeyed his direct order by tailing Ms. Williams, but she wasn't worried. On the contrary—she was *glad* she had taken it upon herself to follow the American! *And Colonel Valerio will be just as pleased,* she thought. *I can't wait to tell him. Who knows? He might even reward me with a bonus.*

When Astrid spoke to Colonel Valerio the next morning, his reaction left her dumbfounded.

"Ms. Bezerra," he said icily, "in case you have forgotten, this is a team effort, and *I* am the head of this team. *I* call the shots. I strictly forbade you to tail Ms. Williams, for the express reason that it could blow your cover!"

Despite his being a hundred nautical miles away, Astrid found herself flushing.

"But . . ." she stammered. "I thought—"

"You are not paid to think!" he snapped. "Either you adhere to your orders, or you can go looking for employment elsewhere! Now, do I make myself clear?"

She sat there, stunned. "Very clear," she whispered.

When she hung up, Astrid was shaking. *"Bastardo!"* she spat.

Colonel Valerio had barely hung up on Astrid Bezerra when he dialed the number of a police captain in Rio.

"My friend," he said, "it has been a while since I could throw some extra work your way."

"I sure could use it, inflation being the way it is."

"Good. Then here is what I want you to do . . ."

When he hung up two minutes later, Colonel Valerio felt a warm glow of satisfaction. The next time Ms. Williams visited the *Telerj*, he would know the number she had called.

*Ms. Williams, Ms. Williams. You have made your second big mistake.*

He felt so good that he gathered up a stack of her photos, got his Pearson crossbow, and trekked out to the rifle range.

The arrows streaked toward their targets. *Whup! Whup! Whup!* Tearing Stephanie's photographs to shreds.

Stephanie and Eduardo had just reached her office, coming from a morning staff meeting. The door was open, and just inside it, Lia was seated at her desk, grabbing the ringing telephone, and answering brightly: "*Publicidade,* Cardoso. *Boa Tarde!*"

As Lia listened, the smile left her lips and the brightness went out of her voice. In its place was the sharp, strident sound of worry. "*Sim?* . . . *que!* . . ." She glanced out the door at Stephanie and Eduardo, her eyes expressing shock.

Stephanie went inside, mouthing, "What's the matter?"

Lia held up a finger, signaling for her to wait, and listened some more. Then she hung up the phone. For a moment she just sat there, speechless. "That was the police," she said finally. "Astrid Bezerra has met with an accident."

Stephanie was stunned. "Did they . . . did they say how bad it is?"

Lia shook her head. "Only that an ambulance has taken her to the hospital."

"Oh, God." Stephanie drew a deep breath, unconsciously squaring her shoulders in the process. "Well, I'd better be off and see how bad it is. Cancel the rest of my appointments today, will you, Lia?"

"You might run into language difficulties," Eduardo warned.

Stephanie was grateful for the suggestion. "Right," she said. "On second thought, Lia, you'd better come with me."

Eduardo shook his head. "*I'll* go with you," he decided, putting a hand on Stephanie's arm and adroitly steering her back out into the hall. "You will find I can be quite useful dealing with bureaucracies and cutting through red tape."

Lia watched Stephanie and Eduardo leave, then rose and walked around her desk and shut the door. She picked up the phone and punched the numbers swiftly.

"Yes." The harsh voice that answered belonged to Colonel Valerio.

Lia spoke softly. "This is Lia Cardoso in the Rio office, Colonel."

"Why yes, Senhorita. What can I do for you?"

"I thought you might be interested to know that at the staff briefing this morning, Ms. Williams's level-two security clearance was approved."

She could hear his harsh breathing in the phone. "I'm glad you brought it to my attention, Senhorita."

"I will call again the moment I learn anything else," Lia promised.

The dial tone sang loud and clear in Lia's ear.

*He frightens me,* she realized, not for the first time. *I don't trust him.* But he paid well. Very well.

Now that the call was out of the way, she was already feeling a little warmer and breathing a lot easier.

Until the next time.

*She is getting close. I can't allow her to get much closer.* Lili knew she would soon have to give the order. Even then, The Ghost would need time to make arrangements, to work his way to his target.

*Death!* How ironic, she thought, that death, the great equalizer, the very fate she refused to succumb to herself, should be something she looked forward to so eagerly—for someone else!

Ah, Ms. Williams's death would solve so many problems. Eduardo was spending altogether too much time with her. He had none left over for his own poor mother!

A smile crossed Lili's beautiful features. *But soon now, that will change. I will have him all to myself again,* mein schöner Mann, minha homem lindo, *and I will be rid of that meddling Monica Williams in the process! Then things will be as they have always been.*

But first, one other minor little detail. One more bit of icing on the cake. She would have to pass the word that Ms. Williams had to know what hit her. Oh, yes! She had to suffer. *Exquisitely.*

The old lady was nervous. Like an agitated ghost, she rode her motorized wheelchair through the *quinta*, whirring quietly through the hallways and large airy ground-floor rooms, the shady loggias and sun-dappled patios.

*I know what they are up to, Lili and the Colonel. Even Ernesto does not know the half of it. Why did I, of all people, have to ever hear this? I don't want to know these things! I don't want to be a silent partner to their criminal activities! Yet, I don't dare tell on them, either.*

*I'm damned if I do and damned if I don't.*

When the *quinta* walls proved too prisonlike, Zaza rode outdoors, along the smooth walkways that crisscrossed the island. But to no avail. *This entire island is one big prison. Oh, how I hate this place.*

## 4

The doctor came in, still in her bloodied surgical greens. She pulled off her surgical cap, shook free a head of gloriously thick chestnut hair, and shut the door. She looked over at Eduardo. "Senhor de Veiga?" Her voice was a rich, husky contralto which went well with her striking, classically chiseled features.

"*Sim.*" Eduardo rose.

"*O meu nome é* Dr. Amado," she said, taking his hand and shaking it briskly, almost like a man.

"*Fala inglês, doutor?*" he asked.

She nodded. "I did my internship in Miami," she replied in perfect, almost accentless English.

"This is Ms. Williams," he said, switching to English himself. "The reason I asked is because she does not speak Portuguese. She is Senhora Bezerra's employer."

Stephanie stepped forward, her eyes searching the doctor's face. "How is Astrid?" she asked anxiously. "Or is it too early to tell?"

Dr. Amado said sympathetically, "I am sorry, Ms. Williams. We did everything we could, but it was too late. Senhora Bezerra passed away without regaining consciousness."

Eduardo put his arm around Stephanie, but she shrank away from him and sank down on a chair, slack and open-mouthed, like a marionette whose strings had been cut. "W-what . . . kind of accident w-was it?"

Dr. Amado went behind her desk, pulled out her chair, and sat down wearily. She lit a cigarette and inhaled deeply, tilting her head back to aim the streamer of smoke at the ceiling. "Accident?" Her voice was soft, but there was no mistaking the anger in it. "What accident? Senhora Bezerra suffered from multiple stab wounds. She was mugged."

*Stab wounds.* Stephanie reached out for Eduardo's hand and clutched it like a lifeline. "But w-why would anyone have wanted to hurt her?"

"Why?" Dr. Amado dragged deep on the cigarette. "There are many reasons people kill each other, but no excuses." She shook her head. "More reasons than there are stars in the sky."

Stephanie drew a deep breath. "Did . . . she suffer much?"

Dr. Amado caught Eduardo signaling with his eyes. "No," she lied softly. "It was mercifully quick."

Stephanie nodded listlessly. She looked small and fragile.

Eduardo said, "I will have someone make the necessary arrangements. Our personnel department can pull Senhora Bezerra's file to see who to notify as her next-of-kin."

The doctor nodded. "That would be very helpful." She paused, then leaned across the desk. "Ms. Williams?"

"Yes?" There was no inflection in Stephanie's voice, only weariness.

"I know how difficult this must be for you. But perhaps you will find a little comfort in the fact that the *senhora* did not die alone."

Stephanie looked at her questioningly.

"There was a good samaritan," Dr. Amado explained. "A passerby the ambulance brought in with her. An American who intervened and tried to help, and who this very minute is being treated for stab wounds incurred in helping fight off the assailant."

Stephanie said, "I would like to go and thank him." She looked up at Eduardo. "It's the least we can do."

"The very least," he agreed, nodding. He looked at Dr. Amado. "If it is all right with you, doctor?"

"Of course." Dr. Amado permitted herself a small smile. "But don't be surprised when you discover that it is not a man, but a brave woman. I will take you to see her now."

She stubbed the cigarette out in a glass ashtray, pushed back her chair, and got to her feet, leading the way to a room three doors down. They went inside, where she signaled for Stephanie and Eduardo to wait by the door while she stuck her head between a drawn partition curtain. They heard her speaking to someone in Portuguese before switching to English, asking, "And how are you doing?"

"Feeling like a human pincushion, if you really wanna know the truth," a good-natured voice replied. "Tell me something, Doc. The way your colleague Dr. Frankenstein here is stitching me up, am I gonna end up looking like a monster?"

"I really don't think you have anything to worry about. Dr. Pinto is an excellent surgeon." Dr. Amado waited a moment before asking, "Are you up to having visitors?"

There was a groan. "Oh, *maaaaan!* Not the police again! How many times do I have to talk to them? I already told them everything I saw!"

"These are not the police; they are friends of the woman you tried to save." She twitched the privacy curtain open. "This is Ms. Williams and Senhor de Veiga."

The doctor's stepping aside gave Stephanie her first glimpse of the hero.

She certainly didn't look like the type who could defend herself, let alone indulge in heroics. She was in her twenties. A lithe, petite black woman with a style all her own. She had skin the color of pale mahogany and black hair sprouting like feathers up out of an embroidered silk head-band. Sitting up on the examining table, she wore a loose tunic dress made of a grayish Fortuny-type crinkle-pleat and tensed her legs as Dr. Pinto pushed the big needle though the ugly red gash on her upper left arm.

Stephanie stepped forward. "Hi!" she said brightly. "I hear you're quite the hero."

The black woman's face lit up. "Hey! You speak English—like a real American yet!"

"That's because I am one."

"Hot diggety dog!" The woman's eyes shone brightly. "Nice to meet a fellow countryman." She held out her good right hand. "My name's Barbaralynn Harris, but my friends all call me Barbie. Just like the doll." Her laughter was rich and infectious and bubbled up from deep in her throat. "I figure, now all I gotta do is find me a stud by the name of Ken and I'm all set!"

Stephanie took an immediate liking to Barbie. There was something genuine and earthy about her. She said, "The reason Eduardo and I dropped by, Barbie, was to thank you for what you did."

Barbie started to say something, then clicked her teeth together and tensed her legs. Stephanie cringed and averted her face as the needle went through the knife wound again. Barbie must have had twenty stitches on that arm already, and it looked as if she had another twenty or so coming.

Now that the needle was through, Barbie relaxed. "You and the lady that was mugged," she asked, "you related?"

Stephanie shook her head. "She worked for us. She was a very good woman."

Barbie's lips suddenly began to quiver. "I'm sorry I wasn't more help." Tears welled up in her eyes and she quickly turned her head away.

"Hey . . ." Stephanie said softly. She laid a hand gently on Barbie's good arm. "You got involved and tried to do something, and that's more than most people would have done! From what Dr. Amado tells us, you were incredibly brave."

Seeing how well Stephanie and Barbie were getting along, Dr. Amado said, "I will leave you to get acquainted. If you need me, I'll be in my of-fice."

After the doctor was gone, Stephanie asked, "I take it you're in Rio on vacation?"

Now that she had some distraction, Barbie was tensing less and less as Dr. Pinto stitched. "What I'm really doing is testing the waters," she explained. "Trying to see if I'd like living down here."

"Do you think you will?"

"It's still too early to tell. What happened, I was part of a nightclub act on a cruise ship, and when we put into Rio, I went ashore and it was like . . . I had this *revelation!*" Barbie's eyes shone with a fervent kind of intensity. "I saw so many black people here! And so many others of mixed races! After encountering the prejudice I had in the States, I thought: maybe I'd fit in better down here. So the ship sailed on without me, and here I am!"

"Did you find work yet?"

Barbie smiled. "I tried out for the *mulatas* shows at Oba-Oba and Pataforma One, but showgirls and dancers are a dime a dozen down here. I swear the competition's fiercer than in Vegas or Atlantic City! And it's even tougher when you don't speak the language. I did get an appointment to audition at Scala-Rio, the biggest club in town."

"How'd it go?"

"It didn't, because I never got to it," Barbie said grimly. "I was on my way there, and was just a few blocks away when I heard your friend's screams and . . ."

Stephanie watched as Dr. Pinto expertly tied the last suture. "For dancing," she told Barbie thoughtfully, "you need to move your arms as well as your legs."

"Not to mention showing them all off to advantage. I know," Barbie replied gloomily, "believe me I know."

She twisted her head in the opposite direction, looked down at her arm, and winced. Then she turned back to Stephanie and her tone brightened.

"But the doc said it'll heal fast. All I gotta do is make ends meet for another few weeks, watch I don't put on weight, and I'll be fine. By then, I'll have to find a job fast. Inflation the way it is down here, the price of everything just seems to keep doubling overnight."

"But without an income," mused Stephanie, "will you be able to hold out that long?"

"I'll manage!" A strange kind of pride came into Barbie's voice. Her fierce dignity tugged at Stephanie, who turned to Eduardo. "Can we, ah, talk for a moment?" she asked him quietly.

Outside in the hall, where the moans of agony and grunts of pain sounded like the language of some primitive pagan tribe, Stephanie shut the door to the room. "Eduardo," she said without preamble, "we have to do something."

"Such as?" he asked.

She put both hands on her hips. "Such as we've got to help her! If Barbie hadn't tried to save Astrid, she might have gotten that job. For certain, she'd be able to dance today. Now it'll be some weeks before she can. You saw that ugly slash in her arm."

"Yes, but she won't accept charity. You can tell she is too proud for that."

"No." Stephanie shook her head. "I'm thinking that for the time being, she could take over Astrid's position as my housekeeper. Just until she can find work dancing."

He stared at her. "You are joking, of course."

Determination gave her face a kind of blazing Amazonian strength. "I've never been more serious."

"But . . . she does not even speak Portuguese!" he countered.

"So? She'll do fine."

"But dealing with the shopping, the telephone and electric companies, caterers, part-time help, last-minute dinner parties—"

"—will come in handy for when she's on her own," Stephanie completed flatly.

"But . . . we do not know the first thing about her!"

"What do we need to know? I trust my instincts." She put a hand on his chest. "Please, Eduardo. She risked her life for Astrid! This is the least we can do!"

He stared at her with curiosity. "You want this quite badly, don't you?"

She nodded.

"Well, perhaps there is no harm in hiring her temporari—"

She threw her arms around him and kissed him noisily. "You won't be sorry," she promised huskily.

He smiled. "In that case, you can repay me with the pleasure of your company this weekend."

"But you enjoy that pleasure every weekend anyway! What makes this one so special?"

"Because it will be different. After what happened to Astrid, I think it would do us both some good to get out of the city. We will fly up to Ilha da Borboleta."

# 5

*Rio de Janeiro, Brazil*

*P*erhaps it was a case of misery loving company; they had, after all, met under the worst of possible circumstances. Or maybe it was because birds of a feather flocked together. Whatever the reason, Stephanie and Barbie took to each other like ducks to water. The fact that they both spoke the same language had more than a little to do with it, but it went far deeper than that: they were expatriates in a strange country, and female at that.

They were chattering like magpies before they left the hospital. Eduardo hopped a taxi back to the office, leaving his chauffeured limousine at Stephanie's disposal so she could accompany Barbie in safety and comfort to the inexpensive hotel in Santa Teresa where she was staying.

Stephanie didn't know when she'd had such pure, unadulterated, innocent *fun*. While the driver waited downstairs, she ran into the fleabag with her new friend and helped her pack and lug the cases, both of them laughing, caught up in the adventure of it all.

But Barbie kept expressing concern during the ride to Stephanie's apartment. She said, "I really appreciate what you're doing, Monica. But I promise, if this doesn't work out, I'm giving *myself* walking papers! No way am I gonna be a chain around your neck!"

After the car pulled up in front of the apartment building, Barbie got out slowly. She stared up at the luxury high rise in amazement. "Who-*eeee!*" she breathed. "And right on Copacabana beach!" She glanced across the car roof at Stephanie.

"God, Monica, you must be *loaded* to be able to afford this!"

"Don't be too impressed," Stephanie advised her dryly. "The apartment came with the job."

Barbie was floored by the apartment. "I've wondered what these oceanfront places were like," she marveled as Stephanie gave her a tour of the duplex.

They went outside on the lower terrace and watched the surf roll in.

"With a place like this," Barbie said, "no wonder you love it down here! I wouldn't want to go back to the States, either."

Her eyes hooded, Stephanie kept looking out at the ocean, wondering what Barbie would say if she told her how homesick she was.

"Come on, Barbie," she said. "Why don't we go inside. I'll check in with the office, and then I'll help you get unpacked."

"I'm late, I'm late!" Stephanie charged into the office the following morning wearing a white, black-trimmed Chanel jacket-dress, white tights with big black polka dots, and black-and-white patent leather shoes with gold coin buckles. On one lapel shone a gold doorknocker brooch, and she wore matching gold doorknocker clip-on earrings. "I'm late!" she called out again as she trotted, heels clicking, past Lia's desk, her briefcase held like a weapon in front of her. "I'm very, very late—"

Lia laughed. "For the first time ever! Slow down. Your calendar is clear until this afternoon."

Stephanie let her briefcase drop to the floor and blurted a laugh. "Then why am I running?"

Lia smiled. "You tell me. We even have time to enjoy our coffee."

Retrieving her briefcase, Stephanie went over to her desk. Behind her, Lia popped up from her swivel chair, picked up the silver tray she had already prepared, and carried it over to Stephanie's desk. The two of them had made it a habit to arrive in time to enjoy a ritual cup of fresh brew while going over the day's schedule.

Lia went about pouring two bone china cupfuls from the silver pot. "Did you see what arrived?" she asked, glancing at Stephanie. She set the pot down and picked up one cup by its saucer and held it out.

Stephanie dumped her briefcase and bag on her chair, took the coffee, and sipped on it gratefully as she looked around her desk. Yesterday afternoon's accumulation of mail, telephone messages, memorandums, and faxes were arranged in neat stacks. It couldn't be that.

Then it caught her eye. Right there in front of her. Precisely centered on the blotter, what at first appeared to be a silver plastic credit card, but which upon closer inspection was not.

Stephanie's heart gave a leap. It was her security clearance card—like the one she had watched Dr. Vassiltchikov use to unlock the door of the lab aboard the *Chrysalis!* She picked this one up and looked at it. The silver background had a large wide number 2 on it, and embossed along the bottom was her name, MONICA WILLIAMS, along with a twenty-digit row of letters and numbers. She turned it around and looked at the back. It was entirely covered with black magnetic tape.

Keeping her excitement subdued, Stephanie sipped her coffee with nonchalance and tossed the card back down. "Can't use this to go shopping anywhere, huh?" she murmured.

"No," Lia agreed, "I'm afraid not." She paused in the middle of stirring her coffee. "But with that security access card, you can do everything *but* shop. You better put it away immediately, and guard it as you would your wallet. Believe me, when one of those gets misplaced or stolen, it causes no end of difficulty with all the computer reprogramming that is required."

Stephanie put down her coffee, took the card, slipped it inside her wallet, and put her wallet back inside her bag. "There!" she smiled, giving the bag a few pats.

"Seriously, Monica. That card is your single most important document here at Grupo da Veiga. It can give or deny you access to any and all of our facilities. Your level-two clearance means you have access to anyplace but those requiring level one."

"Gotcha. Who has a level one, by the way?"

"Both Senhors de Veiga, Colonel Valerio, and perhaps five others."

"What have you got?"

"A level three. Oh, and carry yours on you at all times. If you forget it at home and travel to one of the facilities, they cannot make any exceptions. If you don't have it, you can't get in. Period."

"I see. I really had best guard it with my life."

"That's the idea." Lia deftly switched gears and poured them each a second cup. "Now, tell me all about your new housekeeper."

Stephanie shrugged. "What's there to tell? She's temporary, and I'll have to wait and see if she pans out."

Lia nodded. "If she doesn't, let me know. Grupo da Veiga maintains several VIP apartments around town for visiting dignitaries. They're empty half the time, but fully staffed. I'm sure I can get you a housekeeper from one of them if you need one."

"I'll keep that in mind. Thanks, Lia."

The phone rang and Lia answered. She said, "It's for you. Line three."

Stephanie punched a button and picked up the receiver. "Hello?"

Eduardo said, "It's me."

Stephanie glanced over at Lia, who was making a production of looking too busy to eavesdrop. She lowered her voice and said, "Yes, Senhor de Veiga?" Trying to sound crisp and formal and businesslike.

He chuckled softly, then cleared his throat. "The reason I called," he said, getting down to business, "is I have your memo in front of me. The one detailing your proposed visits to the various plants and facilities."

"Yes?" Stephanie was silent for a moment. "Is there a problem?"

"No, not that I can see. I was only wondering why you wanted to focus on genetics and charities and foundations first."

She couldn't very well say: *Because genetics is the logical place to search for the key to eternal youth, and charities and foundations piqued my interest because of its association with CRY.*

Glad she had thought her argument carefully through before she'd even written the memo, Stephanie now said, "It's the logical place to start. You see, genetics is not only exciting, since it's on the very cutting edge of technology, but in the long run it promises to yield the most radical benefits for all mankind. I think we can get incredible mileage out of the future by cashing in on it today." She paused. "Can you think of a better way to prove 'We're building better tomorrows'?"

She waited, but he did not speak.

"And the same goes for charity and foundations. That division, more than any other, will polish the entire de Veiga family of companies, give the greedily perceived big corporation an altruistic shine."

"Hmm," he murmured. " 'Family of companies.' I like that!"

*Thank you, Jesus!* she thought fervently.

"And you wish to start visiting the facilities on Monday?"

"It's time I got started." She paused, and a note of worry crept into her voice. "Is that inconvenient for any reason?"

"Oh no. No. You will have to fly out to Sítto da Veiga, of course, and plan to stay there for a few days."

"I'm hoping five days will be enough," Stephanie said.

"Good. We have gotten business out of the way, then. Now to more exciting things. I take it everything is still set for our weekend trip tomorrow? Or did you forget?"

"Forget?" Stephanie laughed. "How could I?"

"Good. To get an early start, we will leave directly from here at noon tomorrow. Bring your luggage in to work with you so we can go directly to the airport."

"That's a good idea. And Eduardo?"

"Yes?"

She lowered her voice. "I'm looking forward to it."

The call came that night, while Barbie was helping Stephanie pack for the weekend.

"I'll answer it," Stephanie said, expecting it to be Eduardo, and picked up the bedside extension. "Hello?"

There was only the rush of static.

Stephanie frowned at Barbie, who was standing there, a half-folded blouse in hand, waiting.

"Hello?" she said again. *"Hello?"*

Then a genderless voice hissed in her ear. *"Die!"* it said in English. *"Die, die, die!"*

And the phone went dead.

## ᔧ *6* ᔨ

*Ilha da Borboleta, Brazil*

As sleek and predatory as a shark, the silver executive helicopter raced its shadow north along the coast, barely skimming the tops of the emerald humps that were the coastal islands.

Inside, the aircraft was cushiony. Sound-proofed. And decorated like the chairman of the universe's conference room. All maroon glove-leather and matched burl veneers and custom-woven wool carpeting and executive-style leather swivel armchairs.

Aboard were a cockpit crew of two, plus a flight attendant, seven mobile telephones, and three fax machines.

"Don't tell me!" Stephanie had quipped as she and Eduardo boarded. "This is the only way to fly?"

"The only way to fly *there*," he'd explained. "The *ilha* does not have a landing strip, and the ocean is often too rough for amphibious planes."

Now, at three thousand feet, they approached the island from its easternmost tip and the pilot put the whirlybird into a wide, sweeping westward curve. "We're above it now," Eduardo said, pointing out the window.

Stephanie put her head next to the Perspex and looked down. From this high up, the shape of the island was clearly discernible. It really did look like its namesake, a butterfly. A closer inspection showed it to be green with verdant jungle and overgrown volcanic cliffs, and white with surrounding sugary sand beaches. In one of the two natural harbors, where the wings of the butterfly met and the land mass was thinnest, she saw a familiar shape riding the waves: the *Chrysalis*.

Then the chopper was coming down, giving the illusion that the Edenlike island was rising up to meet them. At first Stephanie thought it looked uninhabited. Then, suddenly, there it was, in a clearing surrounded by immaculate swaths of lawn, the two-storied *quinta* with its blue-and-white tiles and Moorish-style arches and columned loggias and weathered terra-cotta roofs. Fronted by a green pond with a horseshoe of balustrade-encircled grottoes and a cupolaed temple rising from its midst, and backed by the aquamarine rectangle of a swimming pool and scattered lawn furniture.

"God," Stephanie exclaimed softly as the helicopter skimmed the treetops and made a quick pass before whirling around and doubling back. "It's paradise!"

"Or as close to paradise as man could make it."

Having detected irony in Eduardo's tone, she glanced quickly at him, but his face was expressionless.

Now the helicopter slowed to a hover in the vicinity of the ornamental pond. The wash of its rotors sent quivers and ripples through the brackish water below, caused palm trunks to bend pliantly, fronds to shake, rattle, wave. Slowly the craft turned on its axis and descended. Stephanie felt a queasy lurch in the pit of her stomach, sure the craft was plummeting out of control. But a moment later it settled down on the grass, smooth as a feather on a down pillow. The whine of the engines decreased; the rotors began to slow.

The attendant was quick to open the cabin door and unfold the steps. Eduardo unbuckled his seat belt, stood, and stretched.

Stephanie followed suit. "You know something?" she said faintly. "I don't think I like helicopters. First, all that shaking . . . and then coming straight down . . . I'm not much for amusement park rides, I'm afraid."

As soon as they were outside, Stephanie saw two canopied golf carts headed their way.

"Let me guess," she said. "Ground transportation?"

Eduardo laughed. "That's right."

"Let's walk instead." She hooked an arm through his. "I need to get my equilibrium back."

They headed across the lawn. It was soft and springy underfoot, and as soon as they got far enough away from the petrol fumes of the helicopter, the air was fragrant with perfumes: bougainvillea and jasmine, passion flower and hibiscus. It was an Eden, with roses and clumps of birds of paradise rising regally from huge serrated leaves, and yellow guapuruvus, and lush moist ferns. But underlying it all, just beneath the flowery scents, was the faint but unmistakable odor of the tropics—of ever-present decay and life recycling, of the old constantly becoming mulch for the new.

Stephanie looked around as they skirted the stone coping of the pond, which was once again placid. To the left, along the treeline, she spied a guard with a shouldered rifle holding the leash of a German shepherd. And passing beneath a palm tree, she noticed a roaming video camera mounted thirty feet up the trunk. *This might be Eden,* she thought soberly, *but it's Eden without privacy. Big Brother's monitoring every move.*

They were approaching the house from the front. Mediterranean in style, it sprawled comfortably, constructed of brick, wood, and stucco. Its vine-clad façade had mellowed to a beautiful shade of fading yellow that went well with the antique blue-and-white tilework that clad the ground floor. Half the white shutters over various windows were closed, giving the house a torpid, deceptively sleepy look. Deferential royal palms swayed around it in the blossom-fragrant breeze.

They climbed weathered stone steps flanked by marble lions and were on the terrace when a large cloud of sapphire-blue butterflies fluttered toward them, enveloped them completely for a few seconds, and then were abruptly gone.

Stephanie whirled around to watch them disappear. She touched her face. "I could actually *feel* their wings tickling my skin," she whispered, wonder in her voice.

"*Morpho peleides,*" Eduardo murmured by reflex.

"What did you say?" She looked at him.

"*Morpho peleides.*" He smiled. "That is the name of that particular species. My father introduced them to this island."

He cupped a hand under her elbow, led her up a few more steps, and then they were in the cool shade of the arched gallery, where Colonel Valerio and a woman waited on either side of the open front door.

"Sir. Ma'am." Colonel Valerio stood stiffly at attention, his face a mirrored mask.

But the woman smiled with genuine pleasure and reached up and touched Eduardo's cheek gently. "Senhor!" she whispered.

She appeared to be in her late fifties and was strong and full-breasted, with the kind of poise that indicated an inner strength. Her graying red hair was pulled back into a loose knot and she wore her genealogy proudly on her face. Her complexion was the pale, milky skin of the Europeans, the shape of her head was from the local Indians, and her flat features were negroid, from long-ago ancestors who had come to Brazil as slaves. She wore a severely tailored black dress and had a diaphanous purple chiffon shawl wrapped around her shoulders like a stole, which she clutched together in front of her. Little garnets dangled from her ears.

"This is Joana," Eduardo explained to Stephanie. "She has run the household here at the *quinta* ever since I can remember. In many ways, she was like a nanny to me. Joana, I would like you to meet Ms. Monica Williams."

Stephanie stepped forward. "How do you do?" she said.

The woman smiled at her, politely speaking to Eduardo in heavily accented English instead of her native Portuguese. "Your parents and the doctor are still on the *Chrysalis,*" she told him. "They will be there for another hour or so."

Then she turned back to Stephanie. "And Mrs. Böhm asked me to personally convey her apologies for not being able to greet you herself. She is upstairs having her afternoon nap. She asks that you meet her in the Sala de Hércules at four o'clock for tea."

"Zaza seems to have taken quite a liking to you," Eduardo told Stephanie. His eyes added, *So have I,* and she felt a glow.

"In this house," Joana told Stephanie, "dinner is served at the traditional hour of ten. If you are hungry in the meantime, you have only to ring for a servant. Breakfast is usually served at eight in the morning, and lunch at noon." She paused and smiled. "Now then, if I might show you upstairs to your room? I'm sure you will want to freshen up."

Stephanie turned to Eduardo. "I'll see you later?"

"By the swimming pool in half an hour," he promised. "If you forgot your swimsuit, don't worry. There are plenty in the cabana."

Stephanie smiled at him and followed Joana into a vast center hall and up a magnificent curving staircase. On the *piano nobile,* the even grander second floor, they went down a wide gallery-corridor lined with windows on one side and stone-linteled doors on the other. The floor was bare, pale and smooth from daily scrubbings.

But what Stephanie found rather unsettling was that every twenty feet or so video cameras mounted near the ceiling panned slowly left to right, left to right, their cyclops eyes ever watchful, monitoring every movement, no doubt recording it on tape.

Joana stopped at a tall door, opened it, and stepped aside. "This is your room," she said pleasantly. "Your luggage is on its way up. If you need anything, anything at all, please do not hesitate to call. It really is no trouble." And with a friendly smile, she left.

Stephanie stood there for a moment, then walked inside and closed the door. She wandered around the room. It was quite grand in a country manor sort of way: perfectly proportioned, with a dado of splendid rococo tiles, carved wooden palmettes over the French doors, generously proportioned gilt chairs with rose silk upholstery, and scrubbed, bare wood floors. The carved four-poster bed was massive, like a room within a room, and was hung with its original tattered yellow silk hangings. The antique lace linen, Stephanie saw, was spotless: freshly laundered and in perfect condition.

She opened a door and discovered a luxurious old-fashioned bathroom. It had two pedestal sinks, a large Edwardian tub, and beautifully polished brass fixtures. Soaps, lotions, combs and brushes, towels, perfumes, robe: everything had been anticipated for a pleasant stay.

Closing that door, she crossed the bedroom and went out through one of the open French doors, finding herself on the second level of the broad gallery which banded the front of the house. Here the blazing sun was subdued, filtered by the clinging vines which, over the decades, had crept up the supporting columns and around the railings and eaves. The vista through this bower of dappled green was enchanting—she could look straight out over the terrace below to the cupolaed temple, reflected like some flooded relic from antiquity in the center of the green pond. Beyond it was the helicopter. As she watched, its rotors started up again for liftoff, and the wash of wind tore at the temple's reflection, scattering it like a million pieces of a watery jigsaw puzzle.

Hearing soft voices coming from within her room, she went back inside. A houseboy had brought up her two cases and a maid was already in the process of unpacking them. After exchanging pleasantries, Stephanie retired into the bathroom to freshen up.

Ten minutes later, she was outside. In her bikini. Eyes shut and luxuriating drowsily on a chaise by the pool.

She didn't know how long she'd been lazing there when a splash of cold water hit her like an icy shock. Letting out a yelp, she jumped to her feet. Eduardo was in the water, clinging to the edge of the pool and grinning up at her.

"That's mean!" she accused.

"I can be even meaner," he grinned, and she shrieked as he lunged and grabbed her by her right ankle.

"Eduardo!" she screamed. "Oh, don't! *Don't!* The water's too *cold—*"

And then he yanked her forward and she was cartwheeling through the air and belly flopping gracelessly into the water. When she surfaced, gasping and cursing, she spat a stream of water, smoothed her hair back, stuck her tongue out at him, and quickly ducked back under, swimming below the surface to the far end, Eduardo in hot pursuit.

Laughing and shrieking, she evaded him by feinting one way and then the other, crisscrossing the pool with quick even strokes.

"Ready to give up?" she shouted, breathless.

"Never!" he swore, and dove back under. When he came up too far away, she hooted with laughter and he ducked under like a porpoise again.

Abruptly she stopped swimming and looked around. He had disappeared. Where was he? She turned a circle in place, looking to see whether he had climbed out.

And then she *felt* him—sliding obscenely between her legs and crashing to the surface from directly below her. Grinning like the cat that swallowed the canary. "Let's do it in here," he suggested, pulling her close.

"Are you crazy?" She kicked herself away from him and karate-chopped a sheet of water at his face. "What is it about you and water, anyway? Every time we swim you get horny!"

He laughed. "Perhaps that's because I'm a Pisces. Besides, can I help it if you turn me on?"

"Well, you might as well forget about *that!* I've noticed that around here, even the trees have eyes." She tossed her head, changed position, and floated serenely on her back.

He swam in place beside her, unable to take his eyes off her breasts, which strained against the tight yellow fabric of her bikini top.

"I know places where the eyes in the trees are blind," he said.

"Oh?" She drifted lazily. "And where's that?"

"Where do you think? In the cabanas!"

She opened one eye and looked at him. "You're sure?"

He grinned.

Abruptly she lunged for the edge of the pool and climbed out. "Well?" she taunted, water sluicing off her. "What are you swimming around for?"

*Is there anything under the sun quite as earthshaking as sex in the afternoon?* Stephanie wondered happily as she breezed into the Sala de Hércules a full fifteen minutes early. Humming to herself, she drifted around the *sala,* admiring this and inspecting that. As elsewhere in the house, the furnishings were a tasteful mixture of the palatial and the colonial, mixing snobbish European grandeur with relaxed tropical comfort—*much like Eduardo embodied both the most patrician gentleman and the earthiest commoner,* she thought with a secret smile.

Hearing a familiar soft whir, Stephanie turned around. Zaza, regal as ever, was riding in through the doorway in her motorized wheelchair. Her head was bare, her gray hair carefully coiffed, and she was dressed in Queen Mother lavender. Her five-strand necklace was of sixteen-millimeter-pearls—genuine, not cultured—and teardrop pearls dangled from her ears. Rolling to a halt, she held out her arms, enveloping Stephanie in an invisible cloud of old-fashioned powders and sweet toilet water. "Monica."

Stephanie bent down and hugged her warmly. "Zaza."

The old lady held her at arm's length and raised her head. "I must confess I am quite upset with you." Her voice was gently reproving. "You should have visited sooner. You cannot know how I've yearned to see you in this boring place."

Stephanie laughed. "Oh, I'm sure you made do. I remember on the yacht, you were always quietly riding by . . . always watching." A hint of a frown crossed her face. "That's what's different about you! You don't have your binoculars."

Zaza waved a hand. "I tired of them, *Liebling.* Besides, I decided I really don't need them anymore. You see, as old as I am, people are beginning to get careless around me with their secrets. Thinking I am gaga, or half-blind, or not paying attention, they let down their guard. Truly, it becomes quite tiresome to see and overhear things one doesn't want to know . . . so why compound it with spying on people?" Then she smiled. "But enough of that. Come. Let us go over to the light so I can really *see* you."

Stephanie followed the wheelchair over to an open French door, where Zaza parked it neatly so that she faced into the room. She looked up at Stephanie. "Ah yes. Beautiful as ever." Then she looked a little concerned. "But you have gotten somewhat paler, I think?"

Stephanie stared at her in astonishment, surprised that she would notice. "To tell you the truth," she said, "I haven't been able to take much advantage of the sun yet."

"Then you must learn to make the time! I see I shall have to speak to Eduardo: he is obviously keeping you far too busy. Life, you know, is too short to spend it all working."

Stephanie smiled. "Don't worry so much. I've plenty of time ahead of me."

"Ah," Zaza said wistfully, "to be young again! To have the whole future ahead of one! Really, growing old is disgraceful—disgraceful!" Suddenly her voice dropped to a whisper. "But there is worse." She nodded sagely and sighed. "Far worse."

"Oh? And what would that be?"

"Why, *not* growing old, of course!" Zaza said, her watery eyes widening. "Stopping time. Keeping it standing still! What else *could* be worse?"

## 7

*S*tephanie was still digesting Zaza's comment when Joana entered carrying a tray with an elaborate antique silver tea service. Now that the air had cooled, the housekeeper had changed her diaphanous purple shawl for a black crocheted one held together in the front with a filigreed silver brooch. She looked over at Stephanie and Zaza as she put the tray down and smiled brightly. "Here you are! Would you like me to pour?"

Zaza waved a hand in disgust. "We are quite capable of doing it ourselves, thank you," she said crisply.

Joana smiled pleasantly and left.

"You see?" Zaza said, her eyes fixed on Stephanie's. "What did I tell you? I don't know why people think if one is confined to a wheelchair one must also be totally helpless!"

Zaza put the chair into gear and rode across the room to the tea table, Stephanie walking beside her.

"Sit there, on that chair," Zaza commanded, pointing to a yellow tufted armchair. "The sofa is too uncomfortable, and a chair can be easily moved about. Now go on. Do pour."

As she poured, Stephanie reflected that it wasn't tea on that tray so much as a meal: finger sandwiches, fruit muffins, pastries, slices of torte, nut-sprinkled cookies, and petit fours. The china was delicate: cups and saucers and plates so thin they were almost translucent. And the sterling seemed to weigh a ton.

They sipped their tea and indulged in idle conversation, and after a while, Zaza said, "It is so quiet in here. Why don't you put on some nice music? The stereo is over there, on that low bookcase."

Stephanie put her cup down, got up, and went across the room to the CD player. The shelves beneath it were filled with CDs, but she saw a stack of clear plastic cases beside the player. She picked them up and as she flipped hurriedly through them, felt a momentary shock. *Schneider à Paris . . . Schneider Recital I . . . Lili Schneider Airs d'Opéras Romantiques . . .* She flipped faster, as though driven by the Furies, *Schneider Opernarien . . . Lili Schneider Singt Lieder Aus Operetten . . .*

*If we wanted, we could listen to Lili morning, noon, and night!*

"Zaza?" she called across the room. "I don't know what to put on. What would you like to hear?"

"Anything, *Liebling*. It does not matter."

Stephanie fanned out the Schneider cases and said, "Eeny-meeny-miney-*mo.*" She put on the fourth one, *Opernarien,* and fiddled with the volume button. After a moment, the chords of a piano rang out, so startlingly rich and resonant that it was hard to believe the pianist was not actually in the room, playing live. And then came that voice, that unmatched, heavenly sweet voice which could only belong to one person—

"*No!*" Zaza cried out. "*No, no, no, no, no!* Turn that off at once! For heaven's sake, put on something else!"

Startled, Stephanie hit the OFF button and ejected the disc. She looked over at her. "What should I put on?"

"How about some Brahms? I love Brahms."

Stephanie rolled her eyes. Then why didn't you say so in the first place? she almost blurted, but checked herself in time. Her irritation at Zaza was, she realized, merely a reaction to her startling discovery of all the Schneider CDs. "Brahms coming right up," she called in what she hoped was a cheerful voice.

Crouching down, she scanned the CDs in the bookcase; they were all shelved in alphabetical order. Good, she thought. Good?

She popped back up. "Zaza! There must be fifty Brahms recordings here!"

Zaza held out a hand. "Come here, *Liebchen.*"

Stephanie went back over to her. "Yes?" she said.

Zaza took Stephanie's smooth soft hand between her own gnarled, dry fingers and pulled her closer. "Now listen, *Liebling,*" she whispered, her grip tightening, "and listen very, very carefully!"

The old lady's face underwent a sudden transformation: Gone was the watery sweetness in her eyes. Triumph, urgency, and a strange wild kind of excitement suddenly blazed from them instead.

It was such a radical change that Stephanie felt herself breaking out in goosebumps. And not only that. For the first time since meeting Zaza, she felt fear. Genuine fear. She took an instinctive step backward, but Zaza's fingers tightened like a vise. "You do not need to be frightened. I would never try to hurt you. *Never!*"

"No, of course you wouldn't!" Stephanie's voice sounded high-pitched, unnatural to her own ears; she attempted a smile, but it faltered.

Zaza said, "All I ask is that you listen!"

And against her will, Stephanie found herself being pulled even closer, with the old lady sitting up so straight and tall that Stephanie could actually feel her breath on her face.

Like a teacher hammering home a point, Zaza said very slowly: "My own favorite Brahms recording is Opus Sixty in C-minor, Quartet number three." Her eyes flared like icy blue flames.

The gnarled fingers squeezed even harder, and Stephanie clenched her teeth to keep from crying out.

"Do you think you can remember that?"

Stephanie watched the old lady's eyes. "Opus Sixty, C-minor, Quartet number three," she repeated with a tremor in her voice.

Zaza nodded. "Good. Now promise me you will never forget that." Her eyes searched Stephanie's wildly. *"Promise me!"* she hissed.

Stephanie wanted to wrench her hand away and flee, but for some inexplicable reason, she found herself unable to move. Outside, a cloud slid across the sun and the room went abruptly dim; ghastly shadows caused Zaza's cheek hollows to sink deeper and deeper, until her face looked like a skull.

"Repeat it!" the old lady insisted.

Stephanie's voice trembled. "Opus Sixty, C-minor, Quartet number three. But why is it so important?"

Zaza loosened her hand from Stephanie's. Almost expressionlessly, she said, "Who says it is important? Now go. Put it on."

Stephanie headed across the room, massaging some feeling into her numb hand as she walked. Then Zaza's voice stopped her.

"Monica!"

Stephanie thought, *Now what?* and turned around.

"Forget the Brahms," Zaza said wearily. "Put on Vivaldi. *The Four Seasons.*"

Stephanie thought: *Jesus H. Christ! Is she wigging out, or what?* But she found the Vivaldi and put it on.

When she turned around, Zarah and Ernesto were coming into the *sala.* He in the black slacks and puffy-sleeved, tight-waisted white silk shirt of the grand seigneur. She in retro-sixties, all Pucci-ed up: silk blouse worn out over helanca leggings—both in far-out pink-and-yellow Op Art patterns.

Now the sudden switch from Brahms to Vivaldi made sense to Stephanie. *Zaza is seated facing the open door,* she thought. *She must have seen them coming down the hall. For some reason, she doesn't want them alerted to what she's told me.*

"Hello, Mother." Zarah floated toward Zaza, leaned down, and kissed her forehead perfunctorily. "You don't mind if we join you for tea, do you?"

The old lady didn't look at all pleased. "In that case," she said cantankerously, "you had better ring Joana to bring another tray."

As Stephanie approached, Zarah was curling herself up, catlike, on

the couch. Sighing and saying, "Oh, darling, really! *The Four Seasons* has
become *such* a *cliché*. Don't you agree, Ms. Williams?"

And for the next hour, the conversation was stiff and formal.

It was stiff and formal again at dinner later that night. Dr. Vassiltchikov
joined them, and at ten o'clock, the six of them sat down around the lace-
draped table. The dining room had the ubiquitous blue-and-white tiled
dado, but the upper walls were white stucco hung with priceless tapestries,
and there were Baroque-framed overdoor paintings. Mirrors, strategically
hung at opposite ends of the room, reflected the Venetian chandelier and
its glowing tapers to infinity.

Ernesto presided from the head of the table and Zarah from the foot.
Stephanie and Eduardo sat side-by-side, she across from Zaza, he from Dr.
Vassiltchikov.

They had barely gotten seated when a young manservant went
around, snapping napkins open and placing them on everyone's lap.

Quail eggs in aspic with Beluga caviar were served first. One minuscule egg to a plate with a scant teaspoon of caviar each for Ernesto and
Zarah; four eggs to a plate along with frivolous heaping tablespoons of
caviar for the rest of them.

"Eduardo tells me you are working out extremely well at the office,
Ms. Williams," said Ernesto, ignoring his appetizer and sipping from a
glass of mineral water. "This morning, he filled me in on your proposed
advertising campaigns. I must confess: I find your ideas fascinating. I did
not realize you were so talented."

Stephanie searched his eyes for mockery, but found none. "I'm afraid
it isn't so much a matter of talent," she said, spooning up some caviar and
eating it. "It's more the ability of . . . of being able to identify what is
wrong with the existing ads."

"That in itself requires a certain talent, I should think."

"You're very kind, but I'd much rather you reserved judgment until
the ads have proven themselves."

"Talent *and* humility," observed Ernesto, toying with the stem of his
goblet and frowning at the intricate patterns cut into the heavy crystal,
"are unusual qualities by themselves, let alone as a pair." He raised his
eyes and looked at Stephanie with respect.

"I'll take that as a compliment," she said graciously, and laughed
lightly as she added, "But you might want to add frugality to the rest of
my virtues. After all, I'm a firm believer in getting maximum effect for
minimum costs." She picked up her champagne flute and sipped.

He said, "Then you really believe we can actually get better publicity
even if we cut—"

"Oh, let's *do* change this *dreary* subject!" Zarah interrupted testily.
They all looked at her.

"I find business discussions over dinner to be endlessly tedious!"

Ernesto snapped to. "Then we mustn't bore you any further, my dear," he said gallantly. "We bow to your wishes." And he decreed: "There will be no further talk of business while at this table!"

Carrot coriander soup was the next course. A cup each for Ernesto and Zarah; generous soup bowls for the rest of them.

Now Ernesto inquired how Stephanie liked Rio. He himself, he admitted, found the tourist aspect of the city quite tiresome; although culturally he preferred it to São Paulo. "Because of the opera, ballet, and museums," he said, "we maintain an apartment in Rio, although we use it only on very rare occasions anymore."

"I'm finding Rio quite enjoyable," Stephanie said. "It has so much energy and vitality that it reminds me of New York. But the poverty! It's distressing how much there is. I've never quite seen such a disparity between the wealthy and the poor."

"Poverty is very visible in Rio, yes." Ernesto nodded. "It is an enormous problem, and not only for the poor. Did you know, the *favelitos* there have actually begun invading luxury buildings under construction, and have simply taken them over? Imagine! Our engineering companies have had to resort to hiring armed patrols just to guard the construction sites!"

"Perhaps," Stephanie suggested, "the poor can't get decent housing any other way?"

"But what they are doing is criminal! And they are not invading 'decent' housing, as you put it. It is the luxury projects they are after!"

The servers whisked away the empty soup dishes and brought the main course. There were tournedos of beef sautéed with duck foie gras Périgourdine. Individual *galettes* of potato. Artichokes in a port sauce.

They had just begun eating when a bright flash of blue lit up the dark windows. Zarah dropped her fork with a clatter. "What was that!"

As if to reply, the rumble of nearby thunder filled the room, and a powerful gust of wind blasted in through the open windows, extinguishing the candles, causing the lace curtains to flap like sails, and sending heavy, smacking raindrops inside. The servers switched on the electric sconces and hurried from window to window, pulling the shutters to and fastening them.

Zarah looked down the table. "Ernesto!" she whispered, her voice suddenly filled with fear.

He smiled. "It is only a short tropical downpour," he soothed. "Otherwise, we would surely have been warned. Go on. Eat." He gestured with his knife and fork. "These tournedos are scrumpt—"

Another fork of lightning lit up the spaces between the shutter slats, making them look like hundreds of strips of flickering blue neon; another rumble, like a sonic boom, seemed to shake the house to its foundations.

Zarah put down her knife. "I am not hungry," she announced. She scraped back her chair, rose to her feet, and stood there, momentarily gnawing on a cocked knuckle. After a moment, her eyes grew huge and she lowered her hand. "Ernesto!" she said in horror. "What if this storm lasts through tomorrow, and the helicopter cannot—" She broke off in mid-sentence and stared down the table at him.

Ernesto was unfazed. "It will surely clear up tonight," he said, cutting himself another morsel of meat. "By tomorrow morning at the very latest."

But Zarah was not convinced. She turned, knocking over her chair, and ran out of the room, the clacking of her footsteps receding on the tiles. The younger of the two servers picked up her chair, pushed it back in, and cleared away her plates.

Now Dr. Vassiltchikov pushed back her chair, dropped her napkin on her plate, and got to her feet. She looked at Ernesto. "I will call Sítto da Veiga and have them fax us the weather satellite pictures," she said crisply, speaking her first words all evening. And with that, she marched briskly from the room.

Ernesto left immediately after. "Please excuse us," he said to Stephanie on his way out.

Stephanie sat there quietly, pushing her food around on her plate. She knew that Zarah's obvious panic at the storm and Dr. Vassiltchikov's concern with the weather pictures could mean only one thing. They were worried that their medication might be delayed. And she thought, *I wonder what would happen if it is?*

"As there are only the three of us," Zaza sighed, "I might as well go, also, and leave you two alone. Good night, my children." She held up her cheek for their kisses, put her chair in reverse, and turned around, riding out of the room with her customary stateliness.

"You must excuse my parents," Eduardo said apologetically. "This sort of thing happens very rarely."

"What's to excuse? It's their house. Besides, I wasn't very hungry anyway."

He smiled. "Neither am I." He gave her a peculiar look and then said, "Do you mind being outdoors in a storm like this?"

"Where are we going?"

He smiled secretively. "To a very, very special place," he said, "but to get there, we have to go on foot."

# 8

There was something Gothic and terrifyingly beautiful, almost supernatural, about being out in that storm. To Stephanie, it seemed Wagnerian, as if the gods were locked in battle. Amid this elemental chaos, with the wind shrieking like Valkyries and the rain lashing at their heavy rubber coats, it seemed appropriate that Eduardo should lead them away from the manicured part of the island to a muddy, overgrown path which twisted and turned through thick jungle shrubbery.

It was a menacing path, crowded with monstrous, Rousseaulike growth. Giant rubbery leaves, serrated spikes of green, and the tortured, skeletal arms of dead trees, choked with nameless vines, reaching out with clawlike fingers as though from some living nightmare. His flashlight and hers, piercing the blackness with their cones of light, seemed wholly inadequate, and what they lit up seemed to play cruel tricks upon the imagination, creating the monstrous out of the normal: rotted logs were ghastly creatures, leafless branches became giant spiders, and thick-coiled vines, poisonous snakes.

Eduardo turned around regularly to make sure she hadn't gotten lost. At one point, he stopped and played his flashlight at a paint-daubed stone, half-hidden by the overgrown path.

"When I was a child, I marked the way." He shouted to make himself heard above the drumming of the rain on the leaves and the incessant cracks of thunder. "In case you get lost, you can follow them back to the house."

She nodded. "But aren't we going to set off alarms or something?" she shouted back at him.

He shook his head. "Motion detectors and cameras are mounted all around the beach and the house, but not in this area. It is too overgrown, and falling branches or small animals would set them off continuously."

On they went, forks of lightning illuminating the boiling, rapidly moving storm clouds which seemed to scrape the vault of green overhead. It was, thought Stephanie, truly a night for the *Götterdämmerung*.

And, she soon discovered, the appropriate sets were all on hand, too.

The first indication of the bizarre was the ruins of a rough stone wall. It rose unexpectedly out of that foliage-choked wilderness to her right, and lit as it was—first caught in the sweeping beam of Stephanie's flashlight, and then in the flashes of lightning—she let out a cry.

For from the center of that wall protruded a face . . . a monstrous, three-dimensional face . . . a *live* face which *moved,* and which drooled water from the sides of its contorted mouth!

Eduardo had stopped to look back at her, and saw her standing there, hand to her throat, staring at that hideous face in horror.

"It's only a sculpture," he shouted, "a fountain."

*Only a fountain,* she thought shakily.

And suddenly, for fifty yards or so, the path was hemmed in on both sides by towering walls of rock. Eduardo stopped at midpoint to wash his flashlight beam first over one wall, then the other, his head tilted back to look up.

Stephanie did the same, squinting against the cold rain and brushing her drenched hair away from her face.

And then she saw it.

This was far more ghastly, more powerful and nightmare-inducing than the fountain! For these two facing walls of rock portrayed not purgatory but surely hell itself. And, like souls in torment, a multitude of grimacing stone heads cried out in silent three-dimensional agony. The expressions were so horrific they seemed like those of real petrified people, and the rivulets of rainwater, gushing like tears down the rock faces, seemed somehow appropriate.

Eduardo came up beside her. "I know it's not pretty," he shouted, "but it is quite dramatic. I call this place 'the Walls of Sighs.' What do you think?"

She lowered the flashlight. "They are . . . terrifying!"

"Would you rather we turned back?"

"No." She shook her head. "After coming this far, I might as well see what's at the end of the line."

Again they walked on, until finally, as though on cue, lightning zigzagged in the sky above and there it was, right in front of them. Yet another folly, this one the contrived ruins of a corniced stone wall built directly across the path. A central Gothic archway, flanked by the ruins—the contrived ruins—of monstrous caryatids, pierced it.

Stephanie followed Eduardo through the arch, to a kind of courtyard. Walled-in on three sides, the fourth wall was comprised of the steep, overgrown hillside before them, and set directly into it, like a mouth, was a small iron-reinforced door shrouded with vines. Above it, two Gothic-style windows, spaced widely apart, were watchful black eyes.

As Eduardo led the way to the door, she shouted, "Where does this lead? Into a cave?"

"Not really," he shouted in return and handed her his flashlight. While she held one in each hand, he began to attack the tenacious vines

clinging to the door. When they were loosened, they blew like giant
streamers of seaweed in the wind, and he grabbed the great iron handle of
the door. Struggling against the gusts of wind, he pulled it open.

"Go in!" he shouted.

Stephanie looked at him, then went slowly inside, cautiously playing
the flashlights' beams around.

She was in a low, narrow subterranean tunnel which sloped gently
down into the hillside. The floor was slippery, a gurgling wash of wet
stone, as were the walls. The ceiling was of wooden beams and boards,
much like in a mineshaft. With her lights, she tried to pierce the darkness
at the end of the tunnel, but it curved out of sight.

Eduardo came in, stamping his feet. Behind him, the wind slammed
the door shut with such force that debris drizzled down from between the
planks overhead.

Instantly, Stephanie raked the ceiling with swaths of light. She eyed it
with prudent distrust.

Eduardo took his flashlight from her. "You needn't worry," he assured her. "Structurally, it is quite sound."

His voice sounded loud and hollow, and she suddenly realized how
quiet it was in here. The storm seemed far away, shut out by tons of rock
and earth, and she could now differentiate between the various sounds:
the rapid babble of water flowing downhill, the symphony of wet plops,
as if an attic roof had sprung a thousand leaks, the rasp of her own
breathing and his. The combination of smells—of earthiness and stagnant
water—was repugnant. Suddenly she shivered. The tunnel was cold,
too—a good ten degrees cooler than it was outside.

She was about to lower her flashlight when she noticed a thick electrical cable and, at intervals along the wall, large, old-fashioned lightbulbs
screwed into fixtures behind rusted grilles. And there, practically beside
her, the light switch!

"Look!" she said, reaching out to flick the switch. "We can turn on
the lights!"

"*No!*" Eduardo bellowed, and leaped at her, tackling her with such
force that they both crashed against the opposite stone wall. Her flashlight fell from her hand, hit the stone floor with a dull thump, and rolled
back and forth in an arc. He let out a deep breath of relief. "I should
have warned you, but I forgot." He helped her regain her balance, plucked the flashlight up off the floor, and handed it back to her. Then he
moved the beam of light along the electrical cable.

"Do not touch any light switches, outlets, or wiring," he said. "The
electricity has never been cut off in here, and it's quite dangerous."

He looked around, spied a stick wedged behind a loose stone, and
picked it up. "Watch." He tossed the stick against the electrical cable.

The moment it made contact, a crackling web of thin, bright blue light danced along the cable.

"Good Lord!" she exclaimed. "That's an accident waiting to happen. Why haven't you gotten it fixed?"

"For one thing, no one comes here anymore except me. Everyone else seems to have forgotten about it." He led the way downhill through the tunnel. "During childhood this place was my playground, my very own secret castle. Here, by myself, I pretended to be a knight under siege, and a superhero rescuing miners buried under cave-ins, and the lone survivor of a starfleet battling vicious aliens." He laughed softly. "I had quite a vivid imagination."

"But you had to play here by yourself?" she asked. "Didn't you have *any* friends?"

"No," he said over his shoulder, his face bright in the wash from her flashlight. "Not when we were here, on the island."

Her heart went out to him. How awful to have had to grow up like that!

"At any rate," he said, "I was actually quite happy. But enough of that subject. I want you to guess where this tunnel leads."

"Down to a bomb shelter?" she ventured.

His laughter echoed, bounced off the stone walls. "Not quite."

Then they rounded another corner, and there it was. The last thing on earth she'd expected.

"A grotto!" she breathed, pushing past Eduardo into the large, high-ceilinged cave of a room. She uttered a squeal of delight as the soft spray from a fountain, activated when she stepped on a slab of marble, drizzled her from all sides.

Flashlight held straight out in front of her, she turned around and around in place. "Eduardo! There must be a hundred fountains!"

He smiled. "A hundred and seventy-five, to be exact. I counted them when I was eight."

Falling into a strange, reverential silence, she walked slowly around the central fountain and its dozens of thin jets of inward-arcing water. Her beam of light searched out the recesses of four alcoves, then the high dome above, so that the details of the grotto revealed itself in glorious bits and pieces.

It was unbelievable—unimaginable—this mollusk fantasy. Every square inch of the walls was intricately decorated with glass slag and mosaics of rare and beautiful shells! There were elaborate niches with shell-clad busts, pilasters encrusted with shells, composite figures of shell: fantastical parrots, human faces that recalled Archimbaldo's famous fruit and vegetable heads. And, inside each of four recessed alcoves, frolicking marine beasties with crustaceous breasts, ears of conch, beards of scallop.

"Oh, Eduardo," she cried, "it's heaven! Sheer heaven!" She lowered her flashlight and looked at him open-mouthed. "I had no idea places like this existed!"

He came toward her, the pressure-activated *jeux d'eau* drenching him with spray. "Actually," he explained, "this is a replica of a grotto the Margravine of Bayreuth had built."

"And those gruesome follies we passed?" she asked. "That fountain . . . those deformed caryatids and that . . . that wall with all the hideous faces?"

"Also replicas from Bayreuth."

Outside, lightning flashed, and for a few seconds the entire grotto was lit up in throbbing blue. Now Stephanie could see that the center of the dome was open to the sky; when morning came, it would allow daylight to pour in—not that she wanted to see it then; she imagined it would be at its most romantically magical by flickering candlelight.

She explored some more, studying the mollusk details in one of the recessed niches.

"Careful," Eduardo cautioned a bit anxiously at one point.

She looked beside her. The electrical cable was a mere six inches from her elbow and the condition of the wiring horrified her. It was worse in here than it was out in the tunnel.

She looked around and frowned. "If the wiring is in such rotten state," she asked thoughtfully, "how do the fountain pumps keep on working?"

"Simple. They are built directly atop an artesian well and do not require electricity."

"Mmm," she said, "clever."

And looking around, she added, "Do you know, I do believe this place is so utterly extraordinary that it's actually worth going past those hideous follies just to get here? It's almost as though the contrast between the ugly and the beautiful make the beautiful seem even more beautiful!"

He smiled. "I was hoping you would think that. Now then. We really should be getting back. If you wish, we can come here again tomorrow."

"I'd like that," she said, and suddenly yawned. "Now that you mentioned it, I do think I'm starting to fade." She kissed him lightly on the lips. "And after seeing this heavenly place, I can't think of anything I'd rather do than go to sleep. I know I'll enjoy the sweetest dreams I've ever had!"

But she didn't have sweet dreams. The storm raged on into the night, and she tossed and turned the whole time. Nightmare followed nightmare.

"I'll be waiting for you on the other side, Stephanie!" cackled the contorted stone face of Jed Savitt.

"If Lili had only shared her secret, I'd still have my entire life ahead of me!" moaned the chiseled stone face of Madame Balász.

"My own favorite Brahms recording is Opus Sixty in C-minor, Quartet number three. April Fools!" shrieked the face of Zaza in stone.

And Eduardo's sculpted stone face taunted, "Touch the wiring! Touch the wiring! Touch the—"

*Bang!* The explosive noise reached all the way down through her sleep and jerked her awake. Eyes snapping open, she uttered a sharp cry and sat bolt upright in bed. She was breathing heavily and felt drenched with sweat. For a moment, she looked around in fear, but the ghastly faces of her nightmare were gone.

She slumped against the headboard in relief. *I'm awake now,* she assured herself, *and everything's all right.*

She could hear the rain, driven by ferocious winds, still slashing at the French windows. But surely that wasn't what had awakened her? So what *had?*

*Bang!* The explosive noise, loud as a gunshot, came from just outside the French doors. For a heart-stopping instant, everything inside her froze. Then the noise came again and she recognized it. She chided herself with a soft, deprecatory laugh. *It's just a shutter which the wind has torn loose from its hook.*

Without bothering to switch on the lamp, she got out of bed and groped her way over to the French doors. She could see nothing, absolutely nothing. She felt for the door, opened it, and stepped out onto the verandah.

Rain blew at her with the velocity of hailstones, hitting sharp as needles against her bare skin. The wind had picked up considerably, and it was cold. Very cold. "Brrrrrr!" she cried. Shivering, she felt around for the flapping shutter and caught it. Groped for the hook and secured it to the wall. Then, teeth chattering, she rushed back inside, closed the door, felt her way over to the bed, and jumped underneath the warm dry covers.

But the darkness only seemed to mock—and with good reason, she thought. For how could she expect to solve a puzzle which underwent constant permutations, which grew ever more complicated, and to which so many major pieces were still missing?

Believing herself to be the only one awake, she was rudely startled by the soft taps on her door. It was Zaza.

"Did I awaken you?" the old lady asked in a hushed voice.

Stephanie shook her head. "I couldn't sleep."

Zaza rode into the room and said, "Neither could I." There was a silk blanket over her knees, dark and jewel-like, which did not go with her pale flowery nightdress, and she looked very sallow and very old, and for the first time, very much the invalid.

Stephanie asked, "Can I offer you something?"

Zaza shook her head, and there was something about the grim set of her face which Stephanie found peculiarly disturbing. She wondered to what she owed this visit, but she didn't want to rush the old lady.

Finally Zaza took a deep breath. "What I am about to tell you," she began slowly, "is not only for your own good, but for the good of us all."

Stephanie tried to lighten things up. "Warnings in the middle of stormy nights? How ominous!"

Zaza looked at her steadily. "Perhaps it does sound rather melodramatic," she conceded, "but be that as it may, this is no laughing matter." She shook her head and sighed. "I have come because it is my duty to be the bearer of unwelcome tidings."

"I gather," said Stephanie softly, "that you have come to warn me off?"

Zaza was not surprised by Stephanie's guess. "You are a very astute and clever young lady," she said. "I only hope you are as wise."

Stephanie held her gaze. "Why?" she asked quietly.

"Why? Because it is in the best interests of—"

"No, no, no," Stephanie said irritably. "What I'm asking is, *why,* specifically, should it be in everyone's best interests that I make myself scarce?" She raised her chin. "That is what you're suggesting I do, isn't it?"

Zaza did not beat around the bush. "Yes," she said simply.

"Then I think you owe it to me to at least tell me why. Perhaps if I knew the specifics of what I've done . . . or seen . . . I would feel more inclined to listen to your advice."

"Why must you be so stubborn!" the old lady hissed. "Can you not tell when something is in your own best interests?"

"But how can I possibly know that?"

Zaza's face went from sallow to white, and her lips tightened into a thin, hard line. She whispered shakily, "Good night, Ms. Williams, and farewell. I am afraid we have nothing more to say to one another."

Stephanie watched the old lady maneuver her wheelchair around and then she got up to let her out. The wheelchair whirred as she rode off.

With a sigh, Stephanie shut the door and leaned thoughtfully back against it. Try as she might, she couldn't make heads nor tails of Zaza's visit. Something had to have triggered it—but what? *Just what I need,* she thought sardonically as she went back to bed and turned off the light. *Yet another mystery . . .*

When she finally nodded off, she was no closer to solving it, and sleep was fitful, filled with more disturbing dreams and eerie faces of stone.

On her way down to breakfast, Stephanie decided to take Zaza aside and ask her outright about her middle-of-the-night visit. But that, she soon discovered, was easier said than done. The old lady did not show up for breakfast, nor did she come down for lunch. And in the afternoon, when the big executive helicopter came to fly them back to Rio, Zaza still hadn't put in an appearance.

# 9

*Rio de Janeiro ·
Ilha da Borboleta, Brazil*

"I'll miss you," Eduardo said, kissing her on the sidewalk while the chauffeur popped open the trunk and handed the doorman her weekend bags. "I hope you have a good flight to Sítto da Veiga." He gave her another kiss on the mouth, climbed back inside the Mercedes, and shut the door and waved.

She watched the big car nose out of the semicircular drive and merge into the traffic on the Avenida Atlantica.

When she got upstairs, Barbie opened the front door and hugged her like a long-lost friend. "Girl!" she exclaimed, "are you ever a sight for sore eyes! I was going crazy here without having anyone to speak English with!"

"Now, now," Stephanie laughed, "you'd better not let Waldo hear that."

As if on cue, from outside on the terrace came Waldo's squawking: "Steph! Steph! I love you, Steph!"

"God, but does that bird's shrieking ever travel! You can hear him all the way down on the *street!*" Barbie sighed dramatically. "Doesn't he ever shut up?"

"Never!" Stephanie replied cheerfully, and hurried into the living room and out to the terrace. *Yes,* she thought, *it feels damn good to be back—even if it's only for a night!*

Waldo was climbing excitedly all around the inside of the big cage, and when he saw her, he hung there upside-down, blurting, "I love you, Steph! Hi! Hi! Waldo wants a crack-ER! *Eh-eh-eh-eh-eh-eh-eh!*"

Stephanie made the cooing sounds which Waldo loved to hear and stroked his head gently with the tip of an index finger. He immediately settled down, half-closing his eyes and ruffling his chest feathers, the parrot equivalent of purring like a cat.

Barbie's voice drifted down from above. "Now, why isn't he sweet and quiet like that with me?"

Stephanie glanced up at the stepped-back bedroom terrace. "That's because you haven't learned how to talk to him yet, that's all."

"Oh, by the way," Barbie said, "Lia Cardoso called yesterday to tell me what you'd be needing for your trip to the Amazon. It won't be much.

I already packed everything she suggested in one suitcase. I left it open for you to stick any odds and ends into."

"Thank you," Stephanie said, marveling at how the efficient Astrid had been replaced by the just-as-efficient Barbie.

Barbie had one last question. "Are you gonna go out for dinner, or you wanna eat in tonight?"

"In," Stephanie replied without hesitation. "I want to make it an early night."

"How does vodka chicken and mashed potatoes sound? Say in an hour and a half?"

*Vodka chicken?*

"That sounds just fine," Stephanie said faintly. *At least,* she thought, *it gives me plenty of time to go to the* Telerj *and call Uncle Sammy.*

After giving the woman behind the desk Sammy's number in New York, Stephanie was directed to booth number seven. Once there, she picked up the telephone receiver and waited.

"*Hel*-lo!"

"Uncle Sammy?" Stephanie said.

"Girlie!" he exclaimed in pure delight, before his voice became reproachful. "Do you realize how long it's been since you last checked in with your poor old Uncle Sammy?"

Stephanie laughed and gave him a complete rundown of her weekend. He digested it in silence.

"I don't like the sound of it," he said once she had finished. "Why would the sweet old lady suddenly try to warn you off? You told me that she had taken quite a shine to you."

"Yes, but don't you see? Maybe that's why she took it upon herself to warn me," Stephanie replied. "For my own good."

He thought that over for a moment. "Perhaps," he conceded. "But I still don't like it, my darling. If you ask me, which I know you aren't, I think you should pack your bags and split."

"You know I can't do that! Not when I'm this close—"

"Girlie," he said mournfully. "I wish you would listen to reason."

"I'd like to. But right now I've got to follow my gut."

"Her gut! So now, heaven help us, she listens to her gut instead of to her poor old Uncle Sammy! What has the youth of this world come to?"

She had to smile. "Bye, Uncle Sammy," she said gently. "I'll call you again next week."

The man who had followed her on foot from her building to the *Telerj* had on a single-breasted, beige-and-cream woven linen suit from Armani, a tan linen shirt, and a blue silk tie. He easily had two thousand dollars on his back—not counting the big gold Rolex on his wrist.

He was over six feet tall with virile good looks. Jet hair, black eyebrows, penetrating dark eyes, hollow cheekbones, and a tan to die for. His grooming almost, but not quite, hid the hardness of his face.

He had the aura of a man only a fool would think of crossing.

While Stephanie made her call, he waited just inside the Telerj, ostensibly reading a folded-over *Jornal do Brasil*. But the moment she left, he tossed the paper aside and approached the operator who'd placed her call.

"*Polícia,*" he said, snapping open a leather wallet to display his badge. "*Inspetor* da Silva."

If the female operator wondered how a public servant could afford such expensive clothes, she gave no indication. Brazil's police were notorious for receiving payoffs.

"The woman who just left booth number seven," he said. "Who did she call?"

The operator knew better than to withhold the information. She consulted her records and read off the number, which he duly wrote down on an ostrich-covered notebook with a gold pen.

"I need to use a telephone," he said. "Official business."

"I'll need the number you wish to call."

He gave it to her. It was long distance, but within the State of Rio de Janeiro.

In his command center on Ilha da Borboleta, Colonel Valerio lounged back in his swivel chair, his boots on his desk.

"Thank you, *Inspetor,*" he was saying, staring at an eight-by-ten black-and-white glossy of Monica Williams's face. "The money will be delivered to you via our usual channels."

Colonel Valerio hung up and smiled.

*The Telerj: your third and final mistake, Ms. Williams.*

He snapped his fingers, and the technician on duty jumped up from where he was sitting, hurried over to the desk, and snapped to attention, barking, "*Sir!*"

Colonel Valerio tossed him the photo. "Feed this face into the computer and have it change her hair color and hair style. I want a printout of every conceivable combination."

"*Sir!*" The technician hurried off.

Colonel Valerio lowered his feet from the desk and picked up the notepad on which he'd jotted down the phone number which Monica Williams had called.

*New York City,* he thought. *How convenient. Just so happens one of my best ex-operatives opened a private detective agency there.*

Twenty minutes later, he had the man on the phone. "Listen, old buddy, I've got a job for you. I'm going to fax you a stack of computer-generated mug shots of a woman in various disguises. She goes by the name of Monica Williams, but I think it's an alias. She's been calling this number in Manhattan ... got a pen and paper handy?"

Stephanie was just letting herself in when the telephone rang. "I'll get it, Barbie," she called out, and snatched up the foyer extension. "Hello?" she said breathlessly.

The silence hummed.

"Hello?" she said again, feeling the first stirrings of fear. *"Hello?"*

*"Die!"* a voice suddenly hissed into her ear.

"Who is this?" she whispered.

*"Die!"* the voice hissed. *"Die, die, die!"*

She slammed down the receiver and recoiled. Her hands were shaking and her heart was thundering. She took a series of deep breaths to try and calm herself. *Maybe Uncle Sammy was right,* she thought.

At that moment, Barbie came bustling out from the kitchen. Wiping her hands on her apron, she announced brightly, "Dinner's ready! Get set for the best chicken south of the equator!"

# 10

*Rio de Janeiro · Sítto da Veiga, Brazil ·*
*New York City*

The Challenger 601–3A, Stephanie thought to herself as her driver pulled the car up beside the jet, trod the fine line between good taste and bad quite nicely; it was showy but not too showy, large but not huge. It didn't exactly whisper, but it didn't shout, either.

An attractive cabin attendant waited atop the fold-down steps. *"Bom dia*, Ms. Williams," she greeted, stepping aside. "Welcome aboard. My name is Gilda."

*"Bom dia,"* Stephanie returned with a smile.

Inside, the jet was all creamy leather, olive ashwood, and gleaming brass. Wide, hedonistically wide window seats faced each other across rounded macassar tables.

"Why don't you sit up front here?" Gilda suggested. "You will get less engine noise that way, and be less distracted. We will take off the instant the ambulances arrive."

"Ambulances!" exclaimed Stephanie, looking startled.

"Didn't you know? This is a fairy godmother flight!" Seeing Stephanie's puzzled expression, Gilda explained. "This aircraft is in the Fairy Godmother Program. It works like this. When we know we are going to fly a certain route and we have seats available, we call up a central number and give them our flight plan. They then check their computers to see if there is a child in medical need who has to be flown to a hospital that we can take along. If there is, the child and its guardians fly there for free."

"Why, that's wonderful!" Stephanie exclaimed.

"Yes." Gilda smiled. "We are quite proud of being part of the Fairy Godmother Program."

"Then there's a medical facility at Sítto da Veiga, I take it?"

Gilda nodded. "Quite a good one, from what I am told."

"You wouldn't happen to know who started the Fairy Godmother Program, would you?"

"Why, yes. It's run by CRY. You know—Children's Relief Year-Round? Any child who is not infected with a highly communicable disease and who requires urgent medical transportation is eligible for help under this program." Glancing out the window, she saw three ambulances pulling up. "There they are now."

Stephanie looked out the rectangular window and watched. From the first ambulance climbed a woman with a pinched face. She was holding a beautiful little girl clutching a doll. She appeared to be around three years old. From the second came a young couple with a slightly older boy on a stretcher. He was hooked up to an IV. And from the third, a uniformed nurse carried a portable Lucite incubator containing a terribly emaciated newborn baby.

In no time at all, Gilda had them inside and settled. The jet quickly taxied to its takeoff position, hurtled down the runway, and climbed steeply up through the clouds like a silver bird on a mission. Stephanie couldn't help but feel oddly disquieted, as if something wasn't quite right. And then she knew what it was.

Normally, the presence of children meant laughter and shouting and playing and crying. But these children were uncharacteristically subdued, abnormally quiet.

After the seat belt sign went off, she got up and went aft to visit them. The little boy just lay there, so weak all he could do was stare. The baby, obviously premature, seemed awfully small. But the little girl with the doll smiled bravely at her.

"Lourdes *está doente*," she declared, holding up her doll for Stephanie's inspection. "*Está de cabeça quebrada.*"

"What is she saying?" Stephanie asked Gilda.

"Rosa says her doll, Lourdes, is ill. That she has a broken head."

Stephanie smiled vacantly.

"You see, Rosa needs brain surgery, and she . . ." Gilda looked quickly away.

"Oh, the poor thing!"

With Gilda acting as interpreter, Stephanie spoke to the adults accompanying the children and asked about each child. What she heard would squeeze tears from a stone. "The doctors give her three months . . ."

And "This is our last hope. Everyone else has given up on him . . ."

And "It's a miracle she lived this many days; what is needed now is another miracle . . ."

Stephanie listened, her heart breaking.

She went back to her seat and stared unseeingly out the window.

Gilda smiled at Stephanie. "Please fasten your seat belt, Ms. Williams. We're making our final approach." She bent down and tapped the rectangular window. "There is Sítto da Veiga now."

Stephanie squinted out the window. A mile off the dipping port wing and two thousand feet down was what looked like a giant, light-refracting crystal pyramid rising up out of the emerald jungle. She marveled at its

size. Then, slipping on her sunglasses against the blinding glare, she saw
that it was a much bigger complex than her initial impression had led her
to believe.

Like spokes radiating outward from a central hub, six glass-enclosed
walkways connected six other geometrically shaped buildings with the
pyramid: a square, a trapezoid, a rectangle, a cone, a cylinder, and a
sphere—all sheathed with the same solar mirror energy cells. And up
ahead, cutting a clean white swath through the jungle, the airstrip—a
seven-thousand-foot-long runway.

There was a shudder as the landing gear was lowered and locked into
place, and then the ground rushed up and, moments later, the pilot set the
jet smoothly down. Stephanie felt herself thrust against her seat belt as the
plane braked; then they taxied slowly to where two glass-topped buses
waited.

As soon as the jet stopped rolling, the first bus pulled up alongside
and an accordionlike jetway was connected between the two conveyances.

Outside, the sweltering jungle was a steaming 101 degrees and the
humidity was 85 percent, but thanks to the accordion jetway, Stephanie
stepped from air-conditioned jet to air-conditioned bus without having to
take a single breath of fetid jungle air.

A man was waiting for her on the bus. "Ms. Williams?" he inquired,
getting to his feet.

"Yes?" She looked at him questioningly.

He extended his hand. "Welcome to Sítto da Veiga. I am Dr. Luiz
Medrado, the director of the facility."

She shook his hand. "Dr. Medrado," she repeated.

He was in his late thirties, she guessed, thin and sallow-
complexioned, and seemed all arms and legs. His wiry hair was prema-
turely gray and drawn back in a ponytail. He wore what looked like thin
green scrub clothes, the kind a surgeon wears into OR, and white plastic
sandals.

"You must excuse the way we dress here," he said, "but our sealed
high-tech environment requires it. Please, have a seat."

The bus door hissed shut. With a soft whir, it began to move.

"The engine's extremely quiet," Stephanie commented.

"That's because it's electric," he explained. "It works on batteries
which are charged overnight from electricity generated by the solar walls
of Sítto da Veiga."

Stephanie gazed out the domed roof at the approaching complex.
"This place is very impressive," she said. "And huge!"

He nodded. "It was an ambitious undertaking and cost in the neighborhood of three billion dollars. As you've probably gathered, the central
pyramid is the nerve center of the entire complex."

"Is its shape supposed to be significant?" she asked.

He laughed. "The pyramid was chosen because its geometric form is easy to prefabricate. Also, it made the most sense in this climate. With the equatorial sun almost directly overhead, all four sloping sides can simultaneously absorb solar power all day long."

"How long have you been involved with Sítto da Veiga?" she asked.

He allowed himself a modest smile. "Since its conception. I was part of the team which designed it."

Stephanie stared out as the dense jungle growth abruptly disappeared, replaced by incongruously mown lawn. And there, sprawling upon one hundred cleared acres, was the startling city of mirrors in all its splendor.

There was a jolt as the bus halted and the accordion tunnel unfolded itself, connecting the bus with the entrance to the complex.

"Here we are," Dr. Medrado said, launching himself off the bench. "Your luggage will be seen to by the staff, and will have to undergo decontamination—as will you and I, also."

The accordion tunnel led into a cool, three-story-tall, cone-shaped atrium. "This is our arrival and departure lounge," Dr. Medrado explained, gesturing around. "Also, this is the one building on the premises for which decontamination is not required."

He shepherded her to a door before which a young woman, also in green scrub clothes, sat behind a marble slab. She was leafing through a French *Vogue,* and looked up and smiled pleasantly as they approached.

"*Boa tarde,*" she said.

Returning her greeting, they walked past her and stopped at a brushed steel door. Dr. Medrado slid a plastic card into a slot beside it.

The door slid open noiselessly and they stepped through; behind them, it slid shut with a hiss. "It's airtight," he told her.

"But what about the air we breathe?" Stephanie wanted to know.

"It's filtered repeatedly and recycled. I should mention that each time you leave this airlock, you must be decontaminated again before you return."

He slipped his plastic card into another slot; another door slid open; they passed through and it hissed shut behind them. Now they were in a completely tiled room, where a heavyset woman in scrub greens was waiting.

"I shall turn you over to Margarida here. She will take you through there—" Dr. Medrado pointed to a swinging door marked with a female figure. "I will go through this one." He gestured to an identical door marked with a male figure.

"Please to come," Margarida said, and held open the door.

Stephanie went through it and Margarida followed. They were in another, smaller tiled cubicle.

"Please to undress. Put your handbag and all of your clothes, jewelry, and accessories in here." She indicated a wire basket. "All items will be cleaned appropriately."

Stephanie stripped down and waited.

Margarida picked up the basket and pushed it through a flapped hatch, opened a tempered glass door, and gestured Stephanie inside.

It was a small modular cubicle made of special heat-resistant glass.

Margarida said, "This is a steam bath, then comes foot bath and shower, and three more shower. All is timed automatically. You will stay in each until the treatment stops and the door to the next opens. Also, you are not to drink any of the water."

With that, the woman shut the door.

It was the kind of day that made a private eye want to throw in the towel—and hanker for the simpler, safer jungles of Cambodia or Nicaragua.

At breakfast, Myles Riley's fifteen-year-old daughter announced that she needed an abortion.

When he got to the office, his surly Morticia-haired secretary announced that her paycheck had bounced and that if it wasn't covered by the time the banks opened tomorrow morning, she'd quit. "Q-U-I-T quit."

He'd snatched the telephone messages from Morticia, and shut himself in his office and made a call.

"It's Riley," he said, when a woman picked up.

"I got what you want," she half-whispered.

"I'll meet you in the lobby of your building in twenty minutes."

"Unh-unh!" she told him. "I can't get away. Besides, someone might see us. You know O'Neal's Balloon at Sixty-third and Broadway?"

"Yeah," he said.

"Meet me there. Five-thirty, okay?"

"Yeah," he said.

"Got my money?"

"Yeah," he said again, tonelessly. And hung up.

# 11

*D*r. Medrado was giving Stephanie, dressed in green scrub clothes, the VIP tour of the facility. They began in the central ten-story pyramid where he showed her the administration department, a mini-mall shopping center, the thirty-room hotel, the book and microfilm library, restaurants, a video arcade, bank branch, the bar/cocktail lounge where there was nightly entertainment, and a two-hundred-seat movie theater.

"Now I know why it's called Sítto da Veiga," she said. "It really is a self-sustaining city!"

The next stop was the rectangular building, the four underground floors of which contained the hospital facilities.

"This is one of the best places on earth to get sick," the doctor told Stephanie. "We have the highest doctor per capita ratio in the world—plus all the latest in equipment. No expense has been spared."

The six above-ground floors of the rectangle contained a school, a gym, and one hundred compact but completely furnished apartments. There was also a large communal recreation room, a party room complete with kitchen, a daycare center, laundry and dry cleaner's, and a hermetically sealed, glassed-in sundeck complete with Jacuzzi and indoor pool.

The next stop was the seven-story cylinder. Going inside, Stephanie could only stare: the entire cylinder was a forest of vertical tubes sprouting plants. It was one huge, flourishing, vertical greenhouse!

"All vegetables, and all grown without a single grain of earth." Dr. Medrado proudly moved aside some leaves so he could show her.

She held up her hands. "But this must take massive upkeep!"

"On the contrary. What you are looking at is the farm of the future. Only three people work here, and they mainly harvest. All the rest is done by computer and robotics."

"A robot farm!" She shook her head slowly.

Next, they headed for the trapezoid-shaped building, which required that they once again return to the pyramid to take yet a different glassed-in tunnel.

Remembering all the security cameras on Ilha da Borboleta, and noticing the dearth of them here, Stephanie said, "I don't see any video cameras mounted anywhere. Isn't that a flaw in the security system?"

"No." Dr. Medrado shook his head. "Security is much tighter than it looks. We have a number of security devices, but the most important is our internal alarm system. There are electric eyes mounted in the walls of the labs and all the security-sensitive areas. They send out beams of light, which are invisible to the naked eye. The moment someone breaks a beam with a foot or an arm, the alarms sound. If you wander around at night, and happen across guards wearing red goggles, don't get spooked. They're just security guards doing their jobs while trying to step around the cobweb of beams without making the alarms shrill."

They had reached the trapezoid structure and conversation quickly veered away from security to pharmaceuticals. But, near the end of the tour, Stephanie did a double take—*was* that a bin of goggles with red lenses beside her? Infrareds? Quickly looking around to make sure no one was watching, her right hand darted out, reached into the bin, and snatched a set of goggles. She slipped them inside her pocket and looked around, hands in her pockets, lips slightly puckered. Cool as a cucumber.

"Now where are we off to?" she asked.

Dr. Medrado said, "The cube—that is, if you care to see the lab where we do the actual genetic engineering. Or are you getting tired?"

"Quite honestly, I am getting a bit bleary around the edges. We'll make it the last stop," she decided.

They came to the end of the glass tunnel, and another set of brushed steel doors. Stephanie studied the large yellow-and-black warning decals with more than a little apprehension. The one on the left read:

### CAUTION
**Biological Hazard**
Restricted Area
Authorized Personnel Only

And the one on the right:

### DANGER
**Carcinogenic Contaminants**
**Teratogenic Substances**
**In Use**

The facility director produced his plastic card, but Stephanie stayed his hand. "Wait," she said, and opened her purse. "Why don't we see if mine will work. This way we can see if I'll have to be escorted everywhere I go."

"By all means." He gestured at the card slot. "Be my guest."

She slipped her card into it and was rewarded by the blinking of a yellow light and the doors sliding apart. "Well, what do you know?"

"This," said Dr. Medrado, "is where we do our most important research."

"Which is?" Stephanie asked.

His voice was soft. "DNA research and gene-splicing."

She looked around and frowned. She had a gut feeling, an instinct that there was something sinister about this lab. They were at the far end of the room when she noticed the six doors. The one on the far left intrigued her especially. Its yellow-and-black decal warned:

TOP SECRET AREA
CAUTION
BIOLOGICAL AND RADIOACTIVE
AREA
Strictest Radiological and Genetic
Protocols Must Be Observed

"What's behind there?" she asked, pointing at it.

"That is our top-secret laboratory," Dr. Medrado said. "I'm afraid I can't take you in there."

Her pulse began to hum. "Then my key card wouldn't open it?"

"I'm afraid not. Even mine doesn't."

"I see," she said softly.

She felt something reach into her gut and twist. *Every instinct tells me I've got to get in there.*

And there was only one person who could unwittingly help. *Where's Eduardo when I need him?*

Myles Riley strolled into O'Neal's Balloon, glanced about, and scowled. He was wearing a light blue sport jacket, gray polyester slacks, and had his top shirt button open and his polyester tie loosened. The young dressed-for-success crowd depressed him, made him feel shopworn and every one of his forty-eight years. Reminded him that in the urban jungle prowled the fiercest animal of them all—singles.

Nancy Fleming had a little table way in the back where it was quiet. When she saw him, she lifted a hand and waggled her long fingers at him while continuing to sip her mimosa through a straw.

He glared around as he pulled out a chair and plopped himself down.

"You're late," she said around her straw.

"Yeah. Phone rang on my way out."

She shrugged, showing him she didn't much care and he twisted around, trying to catch the eye of a waiter or waitress.

Finally a waiter came and Riley ordered a draft beer for himself and pointed to Nancy's glass and held up one finger. They waited until the drinks came and he emptied a quarter of his mug in one long swallow. Then he put it down and licked the foam off his upper lip.

"Well?" he said.

She leaned across the table. She was wearing a cloyingly sweet perfume that made his nostrils itch and a pale gray linen jacket with the top two buttons undone, so that when she leaned forward the lapels parted strategically and he could see the swelling of her soft ripe freckled breasts. "I got what you wanted," she said. "Name, address, long-distance printout. The whole schmear." A steely look came into her eyes. "I think it's worth more 'n' a hundred's, what I think."

He looked at her levelly and shook his head. "No way. It's worth fifty, tops. I got the name and address on my own."

"Oh yeah?" She glared at him. "Then who is it, huh? You tell me."

"Kafka, Samuel I.," he said calmly. "Two-one-oh-seven Broadway."

Her expression changed. "Shit," she said, sitting back and adjusting her lapels and looking miffed. "How'd you find out?"

"Simple. I looked it up in the reverse directory."

She turned her glass slowly around in a circle. "Only cops are supposed to have access to those, you know."

He shrugged and took another swallow of beer. "So arrest me." His face was set and cold. "Seventy-five's as high as I'll go."

She lit a cigarette and drew in a mouthful of smoke. "Oh, all *right,*" she said truculently. "Seventy-five it is."

He reached for his wallet, counted out three twenties, a ten, and a five.

Her hand snatched for it.

"Unh-unh," he said, holding it just beyond her reach. "The printout, if you please."

"Oh, *Christ!*" She grabbed her bag, fished a folded piece of computer printout from it, and tossed it across the table at him. "There."

Taking his time, he slowly picked it up, unfolded it, and ignored everything but the itemized long-distance calls, which he scanned.

| | | | | | | | |
|---|---|---|---|---|---|---|---|
| 23 MAY 11:49 A | D | TO BUDAPEST | HU | 36 | 1 | 852200 |
| 25 MAY 03:02 A | E | TO SALZBURG | AU | 43 | 662 | 848511 |
| 27 MAY 02:16 P | D | TO MILAN | IT | 39 | 2801231 | |

"Well?" she demanded. "It's what you asked for, isn't it?"

"Yeah." He nodded. "It is." He tossed the money to her side of the table and refolded the printout and stuffed it into his breast pocket.

She smiled as she clicked her bag shut. "Now that we got business out of the way, what d'you say we have another drink? Maybe something to eat? Huh?"

He shook his head. "Not me. I gotta run." He finished his beer and pushed back his chair.

She glared. "Well, see if I'll help you out the next time," she sniffed.

He smiled knowingly. "'Course you will. With your tastes and what you make at the phone company, you need every extra penny you can get your grubby little hands on. Till next time, sweetums."

Lili floated. On a white air-filled lounge in the middle of the aquamarine pool. All in smart white. White one-piece swimsuit. White silk turban. White plastic wraparound sunglasses with mere razor-thin slits. Huge clunky white earrings and bracelets. Even her lips, fingernails, and toenails were painted pearlescent white to match.

From the edge of the pool, Colonel Valerio reported, "The man Ms. Williams has been calling is named Samuel I. Kafka."

Lili gazed unconcernedly up at the sky. "Kafka . . ." she murmured, "Kafka . . . The name sounds vaguely familiar. Should I know who he is?"

"I'm not sure, ma'am. My contact is investigating him right now."

"Let me know when you find out more." She moved her fingertips in languorous circles to create gentle ripples.

"Also, my contact faxed me copies of Mr. Kafka's long-distance telephone calls over the past couple of months."

"Indeed! How enterprising of you, Colonel! And where did our Mr. Kafka call?"

"One of the places was Budapest."

"Budapest!" She was suddenly sitting up straight, whipping off her wraparounds. She stared at him. "You're certain?"

"Yes, ma'am."

She sat very still, then released a long, quivering sigh. "Who did he call there?" Her voice was very soft.

"The Gellert Hotel. I talked to various people there, but no one at the switchboard remembered routing his call to a particular room. Nor was Monica Williams ever registered."

"Then perhaps it wasn't her he was calling. He could easily have been telephoning someone else who was staying there."

"Maybe," he drawled. "But somehow I don't think so."

"No," Lili said slowly, "nor do I." She lay back down and slipped her sunglasses back on. She thought, *I wonder if Judít Balász is still alive?* Not that it really mattered. *She would be a decrepit old woman. No one in their right mind would listen to her ramblings. And besides, she thinks I died in that fire in London . . .*

"And where else did Mr. Kafka call?"

"Salzburg."

"Enough," Lili said and lay absolutely still. She thought: *I haven't*

*been in contact with Detlef von Ohlendorf for over four decades. He too
believes I'm dead, so he couldn't have told anyone anything.*

But her arrhythmic heartbeat expressed her own doubts. Told her that
no matter how hard she tried to convince herself otherwise, she had everything to fear.

"You okay, ma'am?" Colonel Valerio asked.

She didn't answer. She could feel a great pressure starting to build up
inside her lungs. "And who specifically did Mr. Kafka call in Salzburg?"

"Once again, the number is a hotel. In this case, it was the Goldener
Hirsch."

"Don't tell me," she said sardonically. "They don't remember his call
at the switchboard, and no one has ever heard of Monica Williams."

"That's right, ma'am. She was never registered there." He paused and
added pointedly, "At least, not under that name."

"But you think she was there? Under an assumed identity? And that
it was she who he called?"

"Yes, ma'am, I do."

*And so do I,* she thought. *So do I . . .*

Lili eased the pressure in her lungs by letting out another long slow
breath and stared up at the sky. A huge tropical-cloud formation was
drifting toward her. For a while, she studied it. Such a strange shape it
was, an asymmetrical topiary of three overlapping gray-and-white busts
stacked one atop the other. The image did not tantalize or delight, but was
a menace. She could see the face of Judít Balász on the bottom one, and
Detlef von Ohlendorf on the one in the center, and she had the urge to
reach up and tear madly into it and shred it like cotton candy.

"Colonel . . .?" she asked slowly.

"Ma'am?"

Her voice was weary. "Did Mr. Kafka call anywhere else?"

"Yes, ma'am."

She steeled herself, stared at the top third of the cloud, at the bust
which was still faceless. She held her breath. *As long as it's not—*

"Milan," he said.

She had been expecting it; nevertheless, the word was a crushing
blow. She thought, *Slowly but surely, unseen enemies are closing ranks
around me.* But one question still remained to be answered: were Samuel
Kafka and Monica Williams working on their own? *Or were they part of
a greater, broader conspiracy?*

Lili forced herself to appear calm. "That will be all, Colonel," she
said dismissively. "I wish to be left alone now."

"Ma'am." Colonel Valerio spun around smartly and marched off.

Lili watched him go. The late afternoon shadows were lengthening,
and it was getting noticeably chilly, but she seemed unaware of the drop

in temperature. Still she floated in the center of that aquamarine pool, lost in deep thought.

*The Ghost is in place. All I must do to activate him is to give the word.*

A sudden fear rose inside her. She thought, *I only hope to God I didn't wait too long. Ms. Williams must be eliminated. And quickly.*

She used her hands to paddle to the edge of the pool and picked up a cellular telephone. She raised the antenna and pressed a sequence of numbers. "Colonel?"

There was a moment of silence, then static. "Ma'am?" His voice was a squawk.

Lili took a deep breath. "Activate The Ghost. I want Monica Williams eliminated. *Now!*"

# 12

After taking Stephanie to the geodesic dome, Dr. Medrado dropped her off at her fifth-floor quarters, where her decontaminated luggage awaited her.

The accommodations were compact but excellent—a pie slice of a room which reminded her of a large cabin aboard a first-class ship.

There was a wedge of closet to the left and a compact wedge of bathroom, with modular shower, to the right. Beyond this, the room widened, with a pair of two-seater couches facing each other across a low coffee table, the illusion of space the result of a wall of mirror behind each couch.

The sleeping area was directly beyond, and had a double bed, a built-in desk with a sleek adjustable chair, and a television with a video cassette recorder. A sweating ice bucket contained a bottle of chilled Dom Pérignon with a lavish white silk ribbon tied around its neck. She looked at the attached card. It read: *Wish I were here. Love, E.*

She smiled, touched by Eduardo's thoughtfulness. *I wish you were here, too,* she thought.

Her unpacking done, she took her travel kit of toiletries to the bathroom, slid the suitcase under the bed, and took the infrared goggles she had lifted from the security section out of her pocket. She deliberated over where to hide them and decided upon the back of the nightstand drawer. Pulling it open, she found a telephone directory, and a foldout map of the entire Sítto da Veiga complex. She left it out to study later.

The bedside telephone bleated and she picked it up on the first ring. A familiar voice said, "Well, how do you like Disneyworld?"

"Eduardo!" Her eyes were vivid and shiny. She was delighted to hear his voice. Despite all the distractions, she had found she missed his company sorely, and wished *he* had been the one showing her around.

"You know," he said, "you are hardly gone, and already I miss you."

She laughed happily. "And I miss *you*, too, dammit!" she said softly. "I've already begun counting the days until I'm back."

"I do not think that will be necessary. I am rearranging my schedule to try and fit in a quick visit there. I can't come for a day or two," he warned softly.

"I don't mind." A husky kind of intensity came into her voice. "Besides, the wait will only make it that much sweeter . . . for both of us . . ."

A knock on the door broke the magic spell. She turned and glanced quickly toward it. "Eduardo, I think somebody's at the door. I'd better go see who it is. Do you want to hold, or are you in a hurry?"

"Actually, I'm already late for a meeting. I will call you tonight?"

"I'd like that."

She smiled as she hung up, instinctively stopping by the mirror on her way to the door and self-consciously fluffing her hair with her fingers.

The knocks came again.

"I'm *coming*," she called out and went over and grasped the door handle. She was about to push down on it when caution intervened: the habits of New York City were hard to break. "Who is it?" she inquired.

"I have a delivery for Stephanie Merlin."

She let go of the door handle and jerked back, her hands flying to her mouth to stifle an inarticulate cry. *But I've told no one my real name!* she quailed inwardly. *I've covered my tracks completely* . . .

The door wobbled under a barrage of more insistent knocks.

"I'm . . . I'm sorry," she called out tremulously. "You must have the wrong room."

"Goddamn it," the voice growled. "Will you stop fooling around and open this damn door!"

The handle rattled. For a moment, she was frozen with indecision. *Go away!* she projected. *Leave me alone!*

Then swiftly, decisively, she stepped forward, wiped her hands on her green shirt, and took a deep breath. Before she could change her mind, she unlocked the door and yanked it open.

"*You!*" she gasped.

He shoved the door wider, pushed past her, and slipped inside, shutting it quickly behind him. "Surprised to see me?" he taunted, flashing her a grin so insolently cocky, and a wink so provokingly cheeky, that she was tempted to slap him across the face.

But shock had rendered her immobile. She watched in disbelieving affront as he inspected the room as if he owned the place. She gave a start as he whirled around, snapping his fingers in mock disappointment.

"Aw, shucks! I thought I was surprising you, and look at that! You were expecting me all along!"

He plucked the champagne bottle from the ice bucket.

A choking sense of outrage fast replaced her paralyzed shock. Furious now, she stalked after him, grabbed him by the arm, and twisted him around. "And what the *hell* do you think *you're* doing here?"

"Would you believe," said Johnny Stone, already picking the foil off the champagne cork with his thumbnail, "you asked the very question I was going to ask you?"

# 13

*Sítto da Veiga, Brazil · New York City*

$\mathscr{S}$tephanie had almost forgotten how maddeningly irritating Johnny could be. They were sitting across the coffee table from each other. She intractable. Rigidly erect with her arms folded in front of her chest. And yet there he was—utterly, irksomely, *impassively* at ease, without a tense muscle or care in the world.

"Shame to let good champagne go to waste," Johnny drawled.

The glass he had poured her remained untouched on the table. *I'd rather die of thirst,* she thought.

Having elicited no response, he merely shrugged, took a dip into his glass, and sighed contentedly.

"Ah!" he purred, settling back and putting his feet up on the table, "now this is the life. First-rate wine, three meals and a flop. *And* a bona fide Amazon to boot."

"Oh, cut the crap, Johnny!" she snapped sharply. "If you've got something to say, then why don't you just say it and then get your ass out of here! I'm not in the mood for your sadistic little games!"

As though he hadn't antagonized her enough, he gave a little yawn and held his glass directly under his nose, letting the bubbles fizz, pop, and tickle. "You don't suppose there's any more of this exceptional champagne," he murmured lazily. "I mean, you know how these hollow-bottomed bottles are. You always run out just when you think there's still half a bottle left."

She was flushed, almost crimson with rage. The weeks which had passed since their last run-in, on Capri, might as well have been yesterday. Johnny's inimitable talent for raising her hackles hadn't diminished a bit since then.

She fought to keep her voice under control. "I wouldn't worry about running out of champagne, Johnny, since that one glass is all you're going to have. Now, if you'll drink up and—"

"Champagne is made to be savored, not quaffed."

"Johnny, if you don't go now—this very instant!—you leave me no alternative but to call security."

"By all means." He flourished an unconcerned gesture toward the phone. "The number's triple nine, triple one. Shouldn't imagine Colonel

Klink's freelance foreign legion will take more than, oh . . . three minutes or so to get here?"

She iced him in silence, fingers drumming at her elbows. "Well?" she demanded.

"Call the Gestapo if you must," he said placidly. "No one's stopping you." He lifted one foot off the coffee table and crossed that leg casually over the other, settling back even more comfortably. "If you're hesitating because you're afraid I'll blow your cover, Ms. . . . er . . . Williams, is it, this time around? . . . I want to assure you that I'd never dream of doing such a thing." He winked slyly at her and smiled with subtle cunning.

The flush leached from her face. "You wouldn't *dare!*" she whispered.

His eyebrows rose with mock concern. "You suddenly look rather pale. Are you sure you're all right?"

"No, I'm not!" For one long, terrible moment she felt herself teetering on the edge of an epic volcanic eruption, and then the fight suddenly seeped out of her. She slumped back on the couch. "What is it you want from me, Johnny?" she asked wearily.

"Why, open lines of communication. I don't think that's too much to ask for, is it?"

"Open lines of communication?" she repeated blankly.

"As in you telling me what you've learned, and me telling you what I've learned."

"What *you've* learned!" She chortled derisively. "Don't make me laugh!"

He shrugged. "Have it your way then," he sighed. "Just don't come to me later and say, 'Why didn't you tell me?' "

She clenched her jaw in stubborn pride. If he thought she was going to say, "Tell me what?" he could wait till hell froze over.

"All I want to know," she demanded stiffly, "is how you knew to come *here,* to Sítto da Veiga."

"Whither goeth the de Veigas," he quoted, "there goeth I." He reached for the champagne and replenished his glass.

"Why don't you just take the bottle with you on your way out?" she suggested with saccharine sweetness. "In case you don't realize it, Johnny, I have work to do."

"Believe it or not, so do I. Be a shame to lose a job after only a month's work."

She gaped at him. "A *month?*" she whispered, so thrown for a loop that she actually gasped in disbelief. "You've been here an entire month?"

"Give or take a day or two, yes," he replied serenely, "I have."

Stephanie looked at him with peeved disgust. Just her luck to be out-maneuvered by the most unbearable, cocksure nuisance of them all.

"I gather this means you know your way around this place?"

"Every accessible nook and cranny." He smiled lazily and wiggled his toes as if he didn't have a care in the world. "Not to mention," he added, "some rather inaccessible ones."

Without realizing what she was doing, she sat forward, grabbed her glass, and chugalugged it in one long swallow.

"How do I know you're not just full of hot air?" she demanded, sitting back. "It could be you haven't learned anything of real value."

"Stephanie," he said, giving a deep sigh, "have I ever lied to you?"

"Well, not outrightly. But there've been times you've been guilty of the sin of omission."

"I guess you don't need my help. Maybe I *should* leave."

"I didn't say that," she said quickly.

"Does this mean you're calling a truce?"

"Well, perhaps an *uneasy* one," she said carefully, with obvious reluctance. She cleared her throat. "Since you're the expert on this place," she said, veering the conversation back on track, "how about you tell me what's going on around here?"

"Other than making a better tomato and producing a few pharmaceuticals?" he asked.

"You mean there's more? I just had the grand tour, and that's all I was shown."

"And face it, what you were shown's impressive." He paused. "But if you really want to be impressed, you should see their mice. That's where things get veeeeerrrry interesting."

"Their mice?"

He nodded. "And their guppies. And their rats."

She frowned. "I didn't see any of those," she said slowly. "Come to think of it, I didn't see a single animal."

"That's not surprising. Animal research is kept real nice and quiet."

"But why should you be privy to it? You can't tell me you just waltzed in here and bullshitted your way into an instant job?"

"In a nutshell, that's exactly what I did. You'd be amazed by the staff turnover they've got. Except for the scientific research staff, a lot of the other jobs are going begging. After a short time, most people find this place unbearably claustrophobic."

"I'm not surprised. Going without fresh air is enough to drive anyone batty." She tilted her head sideways and frowned. "What kind of a job did you fill?"

He grinned. "I'm, er, a fecal specialist."

"Excuse me?"

"I feed the critters and swab out their cages. If you want the official job title, it's assistant zoologist."

"You?" she sputtered. "A zoologist? How on earth did you ever pass muster? Surely they checked your references?"

He smiled. "That's one of the nice things about having a wide range of acquaintances."

"Ah, yes," she said, looking enlightened. "I'd almost forgotten. Your friends do run the gamut."

"Don't they?" he said cheerfully. "Anyway, one of my frat brothers is a zoologist in Maine. He owed me a big favor from way back when. Now he's returned it: for the time being, I'm him."

"Just so I know what to call you, what's his . . . *your* name?"

"Charles Conover," he told her. "And you might keep in mind that Charles Conover has access to the top-secret laboratories. Limited access, of course, since I'm always accompanied by Colonel Klink, Dr. Mengele, or, in their absence, my direct superior, Dr. Shirkant Jhanwar, head of zoology."

She gave him a strange look. "Dr. Mengele?"

"You know, the munchkin."

She giggled. "Oh, you must mean Dr. Vassiltchikov."

"Whose accent, did you notice," Johnny added, shooting her a significant look, "is not remotely Russian or Polish, as her name suggests, but pure German?"

"Hmm." Stephanie wasn't sure whether to be pleased by his knowledge, or irritated that he'd come by it before her. She looked at him narrowly. "*Was* she a Nazi?"

"I wouldn't doubt it." He smiled wryly.

She looked at him thoughtfully. "The animals," she said slowly. "They wouldn't happen to be kept in the building shaped like a cube?"

"The very one." He nodded. "Just beyond all those phony warning signs."

"Phony!" She stared at him. "Are you telling me there really *aren't* any biological or radioactive hazards behind those doors?"

"Biological, yes. But radioactive? No." He shook his head. "That's just a scare tactic. Those signs work better at keeping curious people at bay than fifty armed guards with drooling rottweilers."

"I can imagine." Stephanie sat back in thoughtful silence. "I suppose you've also found out in what areas, specifically, they're doing their animal research?"

"That I have."

"Johnny! You *are* a prince. So tell! Out with it!" Stephanie sat upright with excitement. Perhaps she didn't need to get into that lab, after all.

"Unh-unh." He shook his head adamantly and wagged a finger at her. "We share and share alike, remember? Now it's your turn to tell me what you've found out at your end. *Then* I'll continue where I left off."

* * *

Hearing her door buzzer sound, Eva Schenkein figured it had to be that nice old gentleman who lived down the hall—what was his name?—who liked to drop by regularly to see if she needed anything.

She couldn't remember Sammy Kafka's name for the life of her, but being in the early stage of Alzheimer's disease, she rarely knew her own.

The buzzer sounded again, and her cat was already at the front door, meowing loudly. Taking careful baby steps, she slowly shuffled her way to the door. After a struggle with the locks, Eva finally managed to get the door open. "Yes?" She stared up at the tall stranger.

"'Afternoon, ma'am," he said politely, breathing through his mouth. "My name's Myles Riley. I was wondering if I could take a moment of your time?"

She peered up at him, her slack jaw working. "Of course."

He slid the stack of pictures Colonel Valerio had faxed him out of the manila envelope he was carrying. "I was wondering if you could identify this woman," he said, holding the first one up.

She squinted at the picture of Stephanie with long curly dark hair and nodded. "Yep! Suki was one of Florenz's biggest stars. 'Course, she wasn't born Suki, that was just her stage name. Her real name was Beulah Stites, but it wasn't exactly a grabber, so Florenz made her change it."

Myles Riley felt a thrill of excitement. "Are you sure?"

"Of course I'm sure!" she cackled. "We were friends in the thirties!"

Riley's excitement faded as quickly as it had come. *She's nuts,* he thought, putting the picture on the bottom of the stack.

"And what about her?" he asked, just to make sure. "Do you know her?"

He was holding up another picture of Stephanie, this one with short blond hair.

Eva gummed her lips. "'Course I do. That's Nina Asch. She was real big in the forties. Saw all her movies." She nodded emphatically.

Riley put the stack of pictures away. "Thank you very much, ma'am. You . . . you were very helpful," he lied.

*Christ!* Riley thought, rolling his eyes as he made a beeline for the elevators. *What a waste of time!*

# 14

An hour had passed. The champagne was gone and they'd broken out a bottle of Pouilly-Fumé. Neither noticed its dry, assertive flavor, nor did it lift their sagging spirits. For a long while they brooded in silence.

Johnny was the first to break it. "Christ!" he exclaimed softly, shaking his head as though to clear it of cobwebs. "It's scary."

"Yes, it is." Stephanie nodded.

Their words hung in the still, artificial atmosphere of the room. Filtered air blew noiselessly down from the overhead grille, and the little built-in refrigerator kicked in and buzzed quietly.

It sounded unnaturally loud.

"You know something?" Johnny said softly. He was sitting hunched forward, forearms resting on his thighs, hands wrapped around his wineglass. "If I hadn't seen those animals for myself, I'd say you'd gone off the deep end." He raised his eyes and looked over at her.

Stephanie smiled with evident irony. "Believe me, I wish I had."

"Yeah. So do I." He stared morosely down into his glass.

"You've got to believe me, Johnny. Lili Schneider is alive and youthful and living as Zarah Böhm." Stephanie's face was sharp, judgmental, condemning. She paused and added bitterly, "I may not have concrete proof, but deep inside I *know* that's why Grandpa was murdered! Somehow he found out about it, and was silenced."

She half-expected him to argue; instead, he nodded wearily. "Makes sense," he said. "People've been killed for a hell of a lot less. But *immortality?*" He inhaled a sharp breath and let it out slowly. "Damn it, Stephanie! That's a tough one to swallow!"

"Swallow it, Johnny," she said quietly. "Didn't you just get through telling me about the dated metal ear tabs on the rats? Don't tell me you're suddenly changing your tune and rationalizing that they must have been dated wrong—or that it's all a big mistake, or part of some king-size scam?"

He lifted his glass and took a big swallow. "What about the caballero?" he asked.

"The caballero," she said severely, "happens to have a name. Eduardo."

"He a part of this?"

"No!" Stephanie snapped. She sat forward and set down her glass with a resounding bang. "I can't believe he is!" Then she sighed and slumped back limply. "At least," she said faintly, "I hope he's not. At this point, I'm really not sure about anything anymore."

"So other than that, I guess the one remaining question is, what's the secret formula? Genetics? Some rare jungle plant with amazing properties? A mythical well spewing forth the fountain of longevity?"

She frowned thoughtfully. "I told you that the medication arrives daily in a red thermoslike container. And is packed in what I think is liquid nitrogen."

"Right. And I told you that, like clockwork, one of those containers leaves the hospital here each and every day."

"Johnny . . ." Stephanie gave him a peculiar look. "Am I correct in assuming that the hospital here isn't exactly overcrowded?"

"You are. It's hardly ever used—except by the kids they fly in."

"The fairy godmother flights!" she said softly.

"Yeah. And they arrive day in and day out, like a scheduled airline." He stared at her and flinched as a terrible realization dawned. "Aw, shit!" he swore miserably. "Say it ain't so, Stephanie."

Stephanie felt the same outrage brewing in her as brewed in him, but for the time being, she fought it down. Right now she needed more information, had to assimilate it, and act upon it. There was time enough to come to grips with the entire nightmare later.

"Johnny." Her voice sounded strangled; she cleared her throat and coughed into a clenched fist. "As a rule, how many children are brought here each day?"

"At least one, but usually two or three."

She sighed deeply. "And as a rule, how many leave *alive?*"

"From what I've seen, they have a mortality rate of about . . . aw, no." He rubbed his face. "*Shit,* no . . ."

"Johnny?" She felt a stitch of fear under her heart and willed herself to look and sound composed and in control.

"One a day," he whispered hoarsely.

They stared at each other.

"I'm afraid we've found the magic ingredient of the fountain of youth," Stephanie said grimly. "Only it's not a fountain, nor is it derived from some rare exotic plant."

"At least that explains why there's a whole roomful of little coffins."

"*What!*" She sat up straight.

"Next to the hospital morgue," he explained. "There's a large storage area that looks like an undertaker's warehouse. When I first stumbled across it, I thought it strange that they were all child-sized coffins. There wasn't a single adult-sized one among them."

"You know something, Johnny? You might not have been so far off."
"How's that?"
"Having nicknamed the munchkin 'Dr. Mengele.' "
He shut his eyes.

"What I think," Stephanie said quietly, "is that she threw ethics to the wind and made a quantum leap beyond ewe cell injections and fresh placental implants."

"Yeah," Johnny said angrily. He gave an ugly laugh. "Quite a jump from ewe cells to human babies, if you ask me! Where did she train? Auschwitz?"

Stephanie felt her stomach contract. She grabbed her wineglass, tossed back what remained in it, and hoped it would do the trick and soothe.

*How stupid could I have been?* she railed silently. *Christ, everything suddenly seems so obvious. Why has it taken me so long to see it?*

With hindsight, so many things became crystal clear.

*For instance, why the de Veigas supported CRY so heavily. Of course they would. Where else could they find an endless supply of young children nobody wanted? Or would miss?*

A picture of the pathetic children on the airplane and their pain-filled eyes flashed through her mind. *And to think they all come here with such hope! To them, it's the place of last resort! How cruel to lead them on— and straight to their deaths!*

*Who would have thought that the secret to longevity was so simple? All it took was an inexhaustible supply of fresh cells or enzymes or young live organs—maybe a combination of all three—and Ernesto and Zarah needed only to lie back and enjoy their daily IVs.*

Stephanie reached for her purse and dug out her address book. "Later on, I've got to get to a computer," she told Johnny. And she thought, *I've got to see if Aaron Kleinfelder's code still provides access to CRY's files.* Then, before she could forget, she got out her plastic key card and slipped them both in her trouser pocket. That done, she got shakily to her feet and started for the door.

Johnny's voice stopped her. "Where are you going?"

She looked over at him. "Where do you think? The hospital, of course! Well?" she demanded. "What are you waiting for? Let's *go!*"

She offered up a silent prayer.

"God willing," she said huskily, "we might still be in time—before they sacrifice another kid!"

Myles Riley was seated on a barstool. He was on his third Manhattan, and his eyes kept straying toward the large flickering television set over the bar. The five o'clock news was on, and onscreen, a young brunette with an earnest expression was speaking into a microphone. He strained to hear above the rowdy noise of his fellow drinkers.

"Convicted serial killer Jed Savitt," the reporter was saying, "accused of murdering twenty-eight young women, is scheduled to die in the electric chair tonight at one-oh-five Eastern Standard Time. His last death sentence was stayed at the eleventh hour by the Supreme Court. Earlier today, Florida Governor Matthew Perrault turned down a plea for clemency. Unless the nation's highest court again stays tonight's execution, Savitt, thirty-five, will end his life here in the chair they call 'Old Sparky.'

"This past May, on the eve of Mr. Savitt's previously scheduled execution, the late Stephanie Merlin of the syndicated show 'Half Hour,' obtained an exclusive interview with the convicted killer. Here's a clip of part of that interview . . ."

The picture on the television changed to a familiar strawberry blond with widespread, pale topaz eyes. "Now then, Jed," she was saying, "you have one hour remaining before your scheduled execution . . ."

But Myles Riley was no longer listening. His drink forgotten, he tore open the manila envelope and yanked out the stack of computer-generated photographs. Keeping one eye on the television, he swiftly flipped through them until he came across one with a hairdo similar to the woman's onscreen.

On the television, the picture switched from the taped interview back to the reporter, who said, "Stephanie Merlin was killed several days after the taping of that interview when a gas explosion ripped through a Manhattan apartment."

"Killed my ass!" Riley murmured, gathering up the pictures and hurriedly stuffing them back inside the envelope.

Riley didn't wait until he got home; he used his AT&T calling card and placed a long-distance call from the first phone he could find. His hands were clammy and he could barely contain his triumphant excitement. It seemed to take forever for the call to go through.

"Security, Valerio," a voice said.

Riley took a deep breath. "Colonel? I've IDed the woman for you. She's a TV reporter who's allegedly dead. Only it seems she's very much alive. Name's Merlin. *Stephanie Merlin.*"

# 15

After he hung up on Myles Riley, Colonel Valerio wasted little time. He smoked a single cigarette, and by the time he stubbed it out in his ashtray, he had come up with a simple but workable last-minute strategy. *It's too late to rely on The Ghost*, he decided. *Besides, I like this way a lot better. If anyone deserves to stop Stephanie Merlin a.k.a. Monica Williams, it's me.*

This unforeseen development appealed mightily to his sense of sport—not to mention his efficient ruthlessness. He despised failure.

*I succeeded in having Carleton Merlin killed and making it look like suicide.* But relying on The Ghost had been a mistake. He realized that now. *The explosion that ripped through Merlin's apartment hadn't taken care of his granddaughter.*

Deep at heart, Colonel Valerio was a hunter and a tracker. He loved pitting his wits against a prey's, loved following a spoor and giving chase. Even more, he loved the thrill of a kill. Whether his prey was a deer, an elephant, or a man, the moment of the kill was what gave him the greatest satisfaction on earth.

First, he initiated step one. Calling the *quinta*, he spoke to Ernesto.

"Sir, it has just come to my attention that a cell of leftist terrorists are planning to attack this island," he said, playing on what he knew was the billionaire's greatest fear. "They want to take you prisoner and hold you hostage."

"Good God!" Ernesto gasped. "Are you certain of this?"

"Yes, sir. I strongly suggest that you, Dr. Vassiltchikov, Ms. Böhm, and her mother evacuate the premises at once. I will send Jeeps to pick you up at the house and drive you down to the *Chrysalis*. Make certain the entire household staff is evacuated as well."

"I see. Thank you, Colonel."

"Don't worry, sir. You will be on your way to São Paolo long before the fireworks start. I will call the yacht and tell the captain to be ready to cast off."

From the aft deck of the *Chrysalis*, Lili and Ernesto watched their island paradise receding into the distance. Before they went inside, Lili said, "It seems impossible that we wouldn't be safe there. Ilha da Borboleta has always been our refuge!" She stared at him.

Ernesto squeezed her hand reassuringly. "And it shall be once again. Don't worry. This could very well be a false alarm. But Colonel Valerio was right in evacuating us. It would be stupid to take chances."

Now that the yacht was gone and the entire household evacuated, Colonel Valerio initiated step two. By walkie-talkie, he ordered the entire security staff to leave their guard posts, lock the dogs in the kennels, and to gather in a formation in front of the security complex. Once they were lined up in neat military rows, he inspected his troops and then said, "Gentlemen, we are going to perform an evacuation drill. Within the hour, you will be ferried to the mainland by helicopter, where you will remain until you receive further word."

Forty-five minutes later, an armada of six jet helicopters skimmed low across the water to the island. As soon as they touched down, Colonel Valerio supervised the loading of his men aboard five of them.

He commandeered the sixth one for himself.

The fleet of five rose, one after the other, and took off for the mainland. Soon they were gone from sight. Only then did he tell his pilot to lift off.

"Where to, sir?" the pilot asked him.

"The airport in Vitoria," Colonel Valerio said. "I have a jet waiting there."

Within a minute the island was left behind. Twisting around in his seat, Colonel Valerio looked back at the emerald butterfly-shaped island.

Ilha da Borboleta was deserted, a ghost island from which all humans had been banished. Even the guard dogs were locked in their kennels. Only the kaleidoscope clouds of butterflies were allowed to flutter free.

Colonel Valerio nodded to himself. It would make the ultimate hunting preserve. And in a few more hours, he would have it stocked with his choice of prey.

## ❧ *16* ❧

*S*tephanie was leading the way, speed-walking like a determined exercise fanatic: her arms were bent and her hands clenched and her chin up as she practically flew down the glass tunnel to the pyramid.

"Christ almighty, Stephanie!" Johnny hissed. "Will you slow the hell down? How much attention are you trying to attract, anyway? I thought we were trying to blend in."

That stopped her in her tracks. "Right," she said, and waited for him to catch up. "Sorry. I wasn't thinking." She instinctively patted her right trouser pocket to make sure her address book and key card were still there; now would be a hell of a time to lose them.

They reached the central pyramid, from which all the other glass tunnels radiated in all directions. They continued walking until they finally found the one leading to the rectangular building. She looked down at her feet.

"These shoes," she pronounced, "weren't made for walking."

"Take heart. We're almost there."

As they reached the rectangular building, Stephanie saw that the exceptionally large lobby was second only to the pyramid as a hub of afterwork activity. She remembered that the hospital occupied the four subterranean floors; the six above-ground floors contained the school, gym, rec room, daycare center, enclosed sundeck, and family apartments.

She worked to keep her nervousness from showing, forced her movements to appear casual and unhurried. It wasn't easy, the lobby being so crowded. There were people everywhere. Gathered in gossipy little groups. Seated on benches under the potted trees. Watching their youngsters romp in the sandbox or climbing the jungle gym.

The eerie normalcy of the scene struck her as odd: this could have been any building in any city in the world—except for the green scrub clothes which even the youngest child was wearing.

She felt uncountable sets of eyes upon her and kept a bland expression frozen on her face. But intense worries gnawed at her. What if she and Johnny were stopped on their way down to the hospital? Or a security guard demanded to know what they were up to? Or she was recognized as a stranger and reported? God alone knew how protective these residents might be of their turf. Her heart was hammering, her stomach tied into excruciating knots. She told herself to calm down. Why should anyone take undue notice of her? Didn't she blend in? Wasn't she wearing the accepted uniform, right down to the accepted sandals? And wasn't she with Johnny, who'd been a recognized face around here for the past month?

"If I remember correctly, the elevators are over there," she said to Johnny, nodding toward them with her chin.

"I know a better way," he said. As they walked, Johnny looked around casually, saw no khaki-uniformed guards, and guided Stephanie to the far end of the lobby, where the fire stairs were located.

She frowned, confused by the signs posted on the door in several languages, including English: FIRE ESCAPE. ALARM WILL SOUND WHEN OPENED.

"Not to worry," he assured her smoothly. "Some of the medical staff use it when they don't want to wait for the elevators. The alarms have been cheated." He looked around once more. "Besides, the stairs aren't used nearly as much as the elevators."

"As long as you know what you're doing," Stephanie murmured.

The heavy metal door was conventional, and opened with a handle rather than a security card. Johnny glanced over his shoulder one last time before he swiftly tugged it open. Stephanie slipped inside first, noting that the latch had been taped over with duct tape. *So that's why the alarm won't sound,* she thought. Then Johnny followed her in and quickly closed the door.

Stephanie looked around. They were in a gray cinder-block stairwell; wide embossed black metal stairs led from the landing both up and down. Moving with the quick and quiet agility of an alley cat, Johnny descended the stairs, speaking softly so that his voice wouldn't echo.

"Pediatrics is on level four. Along with OR, post-op, intensive care, neurosurgical labs, neuroradiology, cardiology, pathology, and coffin storage, and—would you believe?—the morgue?"

Stephanie drew a sharp breath and leaned back against the cinder-block wall. Sick fear knotted her stomach, and for a moment, she felt completely sapped of energy. Neither of them spoke. In the silence, the second hand of a clock seemed to tick loudly, and then she realized it was the beating of her own heart.

She lowered her head slowly until her eyes met his. "We're wasting precious time," she said.

"I know."

Their eyes held. Neither seemed anxious to move on.

With a sigh, she pushed herself away from the wall and wearily trudged down the last flight of steps, brushing past Johnny, every step a major effort. At level four, she stopped and stared at the metal door and thought, *This is it. God only knows what we'll find.*

Breathing a silent prayer, she squared her shoulders and grasped hold of the cool door handle. Johnny was right behind her; she could feel his breath against the nape of her neck, raising the tiny hairs.

Carefully, silently, she inched open the door and peered out.

"See anybody?" Johnny whispered.

"No." She shook her head, inched the door further open, and nervously stuck her head out, quickly looking both ways. "Coast is clear," she said with immense relief.

"Good. Let's get going."

She opened the door wide. "Since you seem to know your way around here," she said, "you lead the way."

"Where do you want to go first?"

Stephanie didn't hesitate. "Pediatrics," she said.

The helicopter hung in the air just above the tarmac, lifted slightly, delicately adjusted itself, and then settled smoothly down on its skids beside the waiting Learjet. Colonel Valerio released his seat belt, unlatched the door, and leaped out of the helicopter. In a crouch, he ran over to the Lear and bounded up the steps. "Did you file the flight plan to Sítto da Veiga?" he demanded of the pilot as he ducked into the small, five-passenger jet.

"Yes, Colonel. We are cleared for immediate takeoff."

The retractable boarding steps were folded up, the door sealed, and even as Colonel Valerio was strapping himself into one of the gray leather seats, the sleek silver jet was already taxiing toward the takeoff runway.

Colonel Valerio's face was expressionless, though his mood bordered on euphoria. He couldn't have planned things better himself. *Stephanie Merlin's right where I want her. Trapped at Sítto da Veiga, the one place on earth from which there is no escape.*

*Soon,* Colonel Valerio thought as he watched the ground fall away and the earth tilt. *Soon she will be mine. And then I will bring her back to the island, to my private hunting preserve where she will be fair game.*

He smiled thinly to himself. *And then . . . what was it the Roman emperors used to say? Ah, yes. "Let the games begin."*

# 17

Eduardo snapped his gaze in from the glittering view of São Paulo and swiveled his chair back around to face the six men seated on the other side of the massive conference table. "I hate to disappoint you, gentlemen," Eduardo said.

Their smug expressions turned to shocked disbelief.

He looked from one of them to the other. "If you think a hostile takeover of Machado S.A. is such a good deal, then by all means." He spread his hands in a gesture. "Go ahead and do it. But I'm sorry, gentlemen; Grupo da Veiga will not get involved in any phase of it. Nor will I allow our banking division to help finance your project."

The men stared at each other, feeling outraged and mocked.

"My decision is final." Eduardo pushed back his chair, signifying that the meeting was over.

When he returned to the office he maintained on the penthouse floor, Mírtia, his secretary here, looked up. She said, "Senhor Machado arrived ten minutes ago. He and his two attorneys are waiting in the inner office."

Eduardo started past her when he stopped and said, "One more thing, Mírtia. Place a call to Sítto da Veiga. I want to speak to Ms. Monica Williams."

"I'll get on it right away."

"As soon as you have her on the line, buzz me. Otherwise, I don't want to be disturbed."

"Yes, sir."

Eduardo continued on into his office. "I'm sorry to have kept you waiting, gentlemen," he said to the three men.

"That is no problem," Jorge Machado, the older of the men, said. "It gave us the opportunity to read through the contracts once more."

"I take it you find everything satisfactory."

The old man looked at his lawyers, who nodded imperceptibly.

Eduardo didn't waste any time. "In that case, let me get my lawyers in here to witness the signing."

Eduardo took a seat and crossed his legs casually and made small talk. Neither his face nor his body language gave away the triumph he felt. By coming to him, the consortium had alerted him to Machado's real worth, and his own subsequent studies had borne their information out. By stringing them along, he had gotten them to do half the work for him. And by going behind their backs and cutting them out of the deal completely, he had not only saved a fortune and gained control of Machado, but even more important, he had no partners to answer to.

The men from the consortium had forgotten the cardinal rule of the de Veigas. They never went into partnership with anybody.

It was less than a half hour later when Senhor Machado and his attorneys left Eduardo's office. Then he pressed down on his intercom button. "Mírtia, have you tried to get hold of Ms. Williams?"

"Yes, sir," his secretary's disembodied voice replied. "She is not in her quarters, nor does anyone know where she is at the moment."

He sat back. "All right. Keep trying."

"Yes, sir."

The sleek silver Lear jet streaked high above the clouds. Colonel Valerio had pulled the curtains over the eight large portholes. He preferred to sit in the dark. It made it so much easier to concentrate on Stephanie Merlin without visual distraction. He didn't need to consult his watch to know how much flight time remained. One more hour.

The pain in his loins was almost unbearable.

In some ways, it was like most any hospital anywhere. It even smelled like hospitals the world over, that combination of alcohol and disinfectants.

What was *different*, however, was the lack of people. The waiting room was empty. A nurses' station was deserted. There was no receptionist. And where were the doctors? The patients?

It was positively eerie, this silence, overwhelmingly creepy, as though the world had suddenly been put on hold. Stephanie stayed close behind Johnny. She felt helpless and out of her element, and was unable to suppress the sensation that she, like Alice, had slid down a rabbit's hole and would find events were beyond her control.

The hallway seemed interminably long, lined by gray doors on both sides. Signs above some of them, which she would normally have found reassuring, only seemed to add to the surrealistic aspect of this place. ANGIOGRAPHY. In three languages. NEURORADIOLOGY. Also in three languages. Same with PATHOLOGY.

And still they didn't see a soul.

"What's this place staffed by?" Stephanie wanted to know. "Ghosts?"

Johnny didn't reply.

They turned a corner and headed down yet another high-gloss corridor. Although she wouldn't admit it in a million years, Stephanie was glad she had Johnny beside her as a guide. For without windows, or landmarks of any kind to refer to, these door-lined halls were a maze, while the dis-concerting silence was enough to make her skin crawl.

"*What was that?*" Her head whipped sideways and she stared at Johnny.

"Shhh." Whatever it was, Johnny had heard it too. He'd stopped walking and cocked his head to listen.

Then, from somewhere up ahead, they heard it again, as if someone were in great pain.

Johnny was hurrying now, heading toward the sound, and she was walking swiftly beside him to keep up. Every so often, just as they were sure they'd imagined the cry, it came again.

They turned a corner, and there was the sign, in Portuguese, French, and English: PEDIATRICS.

"It's coming from there, I think," Johnny said.

No longer considering any personal danger they might be in, Johnny pushed on the swinging door to Pediatrics with the flat of one hand and stepped aside. "Ladies first," he said.

Stephanie hesitated only fractionally. Her eyes met his, and then she hurried past him and he followed her inside.

Looking around, Stephanie could see that this was another small waiting room. Molded plastic chairs were lined up against the walls. And on one sat a weary-looking woman with a hand over her mouth, as though to hold in her sobs. Stephanie recognized her immediately. She had been on the fairy godmother flight. *The woman who'd accompanied Rosa, the brave little girl with the doll named Lourdes,* she remembered.

Then Stephanie realized that the woman was staring straight ahead. *Right at us . . . no—through us!* Stephanie glanced at Johnny. *Doesn't she see us?* she inquired with her eyes.

Johnny shrugged.

"Tell you what," Stephanie said, "this woman could use some com-pany. Stay with her while I check out these rooms."

First, Stephanie went over to the open door and looked in. She saw a large empty crib with mussed covers; the doll named Lourdes lay atop them.

Now for the closed doors. She knocked softly on the first one. Receiv-ing no reply, she opened it and looked inside. The light was off, but she could tell it was empty and unused.

She closed the door again and knocked on the one right next to it. She heard a man say, "*A pessoa à porta será o médico,*" and was surprised when it opened instantly. "*Sim?*"

The voice belonged to another familiar face from the plane. The man who, with his wife, accompanied the young boy who'd been brought aboard on the stretcher, hooked up to the IV.

Craning her neck to see past him, Stephanie caught the eye of his worried wife, who was seated on a chair beside the bed holding the hand of her four-year-old son. He was hooked up to another IV.

"*Desculpe me,*" Stephanie said guiltily, relying on the little Portuguese she had retained from her lessons and hoping it was the suitable response.

The man nodded and shut the door quietly.

The next door led into the toilet.

Now for the door directly on the other side. Stephanie rapped on it with her knuckles.

"*Sim?*" a woman's voice called out.

Stephanie opened it partway and looked in. It was the uniformed nurse who'd been on the plane; her charge, the emaciated, premature baby, had been transferred from the temporary incubator to a regular one.

"*Desculpe me,*" Stephanie murmured again, and quickly ducked back out and closed the door.

Now she tried the fifth and last door. That room, too, was empty.

When Stephanie returned, Johnny looked at her, eyebrows raised questioningly.

"We've found the children," Stephanie said. She paused and added, "At least, I can account for two out of three." She looked at the sobbing woman and then went over to her and squatted in front of her. "Senhora?" she said softly, taking the woman's hands. "Senhora!"

The woman sniffed, pulled one hand loose, and wiped her eyes.

Stephanie said, "*¿Fala inglês?*"

The woman shook her head.

Stephanie sighed. "*Eu não falo português,*" she said. Then she had a sudden inspiration. Remembering that if you didn't speak Portuguese, a knowledge of Spanish, although certainly no substitute, could come in handy, she turned to Johnny. "You wouldn't happen to speak any Spanish, would you?"

"Yes," he said. "A little bit."

"Go ahead, ask her in Spanish where her daughter is."

"*¿Dónde está la pequeña?*"

The woman frowned and Johnny repeated the sentence slowly.

"Ah." The woman nodded. "*Tem havido discussões em tôrno a uma nova operaçao.*"

Johnny frowned. "*Operação,*" he murmured to himself. ". . . *operação* . . ." Then he said, "Ah!" and clicked his fingers. "*Operaciones* in Spanish, *operação* in Portuguese."

"Which means *what?*" Stephanie asked urgently.

"The girl's in the operating room."

Stephanie felt suddenly sick.

"Johnny—" She found it difficult to speak. "We've got to get to the operating room. Now! *Before it's too late!*"

Before he could reply, Stephanie was already gone.

* * *

At six o'clock, Eduardo pressed down on his intercom and asked Mírtia to come into his office.

The door opened silently, and Mírtia stood in the doorway. "Senhor?" She had her dictation pad and pencil in hand.

He looked over at her and shook his head, then gave her a questioning look. "Did you keep trying to reach Ms. Williams?"

"Yes, Senhor. And I left countless messages."

"I see."

She stood there, waiting. "Is there anything else I can do?" she asked.

"Yes. Call down to the garage and tell the chauffeur to have my car waiting out front. Then call the pilot and tell him to have my plane ready for takeoff. I'm flying back to Rio."

Mírtia nodded. "I'll get on it right away."

Ten minutes later, Eduardo was in his limousine, heading to the airport. He tried to call Stephanie twice from the cellular car phone, but no one answered in her room. And an hour later, streaking northeast to Rio aboard his company jet, he tried calling her twice more. Still to no avail.

*She must have a thousand things to do,* he kept telling himself, but it didn't help. He was beginning to worry. *All afternoon long, I left messages for her to call me. Surely she's had the opportunity?*

It was all Stephanie could do to keep up with Johnny; he was literally racing down the corridor. Past him, at the far end, she could make out the signs above a pair of swinging doors. The sign both drew her and repelled.

Operating Rooms
**Salas de Operações**
Salles d'opération

They were moving so fast the doors to either side of them virtually flew past in a blur, and when they were halfway to the operating room—
—*Thunk!*—

Double doors, just ahead of them to the left, banged noisily open.

Stephanie froze in her tracks, unable to move, her body still poised in a run. Breathing had suddenly become impossible, and everything inside her had gone numb. Her circuits had shorted out, her systems shut down.

Then Johnny snatched her by the arm and jerked her into the nearest shallow doorway. Once he made sure she had flattened herself beside him inside the foot-deep niche, he slid his head cautiously around the doorway, just enough so he could get a glimpse of what was going on.

Three doors down the hall, rough voices cursed and laughed as a stainless-steel gurney rolled out of a room, presumably self-propelled, its rubber wheels squeaking on the linoleum. Just before it crashed into the opposite wall, two burly orderlies in green scrub suits chased after it; one caught it and spun it playfully to the left, expertly lining it up with the operating room doors at the far end of the hall.

The burlier of the two men bellowed something to the other, who uttered what was unmistakably a curse in Portuguese. Johnny gnashed his teeth with frustration.

The cursing man pushed his way back inside the swinging doors through which they had come, while the other looked up and down the corridor, waiting.

There was another bang on the doors, and again, they swung partly open. It was the second guy, pulling something heavy along behind him. The burly guy helped his partner pick up the other end and, together, they swung it aboard the gurney.

It was a small white coffin.

By this time, Stephanie, too, was leaning forward to look, and the sight of the small coffin caused her body to go rigid. With the chill of dead certainty, she knew precisely for whom that small coffin was intended, and she could only pray that there was still time to intervene.

Down the hall, the men whistled as they pushed the gurney along. There was a bang as they shoved it through the swinging doors to the operating rooms, and then the doors flapped shut.

Once again, the hall was shrouded in silence. Stephanie pushed herself away from the sheltering doorway and turned to Johnny. *Please, God,* she prayed. *Let us be in time.*

The Learjet was beginning its descent. Colonel Valerio could hear the engines in the rear change pitch, and could feel his ears begin to pop. He pulled the curtain over his porthole open. It was dark out now; night had fallen with that abrupt pitch-blackness with which it comes in the tropics. On the ends of the swept-back wingtips, the navigation lights blinked steadily, and below, as far as the eye could see, the jungle was one huge void. Except for what few scattered Indians remained, this entire region was uninhabited by humans.

His eyes searched the darkness far to the front of the plane, but it was still too soon. However, he knew it would not be long before he would be able to see the haze of light from Sítto da Veiga.

Another half-hour, and he would be there.

This time, Stephanie led the way. Slipping inside the OR door, she darted sideways and stayed in a low crouch in order to avoid being silhouetted against the bright hallway behind her. She was stock-still and poised, trembling, like a sprinter waiting for the starting gun to go off, her fingertips touching the white vinyl floor tiles.

After the bright fluorescents in the hall, the dim light in here was eerie, threatening, preternatural. Every nerve in her body seemed to twitch and thrum, and her heart pounded so fiercely that she had to strain to hear anything above it.

With heightened senses, she did a slow 360-degree eye sweep. Set into three of the walls were two doors each, but there was nothing to be seen of the burly orderlies, nor of the gurney they'd wheeled in. Perhaps, she thought, they had wheeled it into the scrub room, or one of the ancillary rooms between what she guessed must be three operating rooms? But all the windows set into the six doors were dark, save one—and coming from that one, she now thought she could hear the steady murmur of muffled voices.

Rising from her crouch, she held the door open for Johnny; after he slipped inside, she shut it soundlessly. As he glanced around, she whispered, "This looks like the OR receiving area."

"Figures." Johnny nodded and looked around.

Stephanie crossed silently to the door from which the bright light emanated. Flattening herself against the tiled wall beside it, she took a deep breath, assailed not so much by a sense of danger, as by the long chain of events which had brought her these many thousands of miles to this very spot, right here and now.

Slowly, she inched toward the reinforced glass and looked inside.

It was unmistakably an operating room, and under the harsh dazzle of the lights, a surgeon, appropriately gowned, capped, gloved, and masked, was bent over the operating table, assisted by a single nurse.

Stephanie's eyes involuntarily rested on the patient. Surprisingly, no part of the young girl's body was draped, and along her sternum, from neck to groin, a deep incision gaped.

Stephanie felt a wave of dizziness and battled against throwing up. *Oh, God!* she thought. The undersides of the clipped-back flaps of skin were yellowish with fat, and the open flesh itself seemed covered with an almost milky, cellophanelike membrane. Part of it had been cut through, and what she could glimpse beneath it looked like an abstract painting of purples and reds and pinks and silvers and blues.

Stephanie broke out in a cold sweat and quickly looked away. *I'm going to be sick,* she thought, feeling a smothering wave of dizziness.

She was glad when Johnny came and stood beside her.

"Looks normal enough," he whispered into her ear.

"I'm not so sure . . ." Stephanie said very softly. Then she heard the surgeon demand in English, "Syringe."

The nurse slapped one into his palm, and he held it up to the light.

Stephanie gasped. It was empty, but looked unbelievably huge. *What are they doing?* she wondered. *Taking blood?*

The surgeon said, "Now for the tricky part."

"Don't worry," the nurse said, her eyes, above the mask, sliding him a sideways look. "We've always got the two backups."

The surgeon laughed. "Yeah, but it doesn't look good if we need more than one a day."

Stephanie couldn't believe she could be hearing correctly. *This can't be happening,* she thought, instinctively reaching for the comfort of Johnny's hand. *They're mad! Certifiably mad!* She cringed as though she herself felt the stab of pain as the needle pierced the girl's open abdomen. Then the surgeon released a clip and tossed it into a discard pan.

Almost instantly, the syringe began to fill with a cloudy pale fluid.

"Perfect every time!" the nurse said admiringly. "I don't know how you do it."

The surgeon laughed. "You know what they say about practice." The syringe kept filling. "And didn't I tell you she'd make a great donor? Bet the other two wouldn't have had half the enzymes. There." Smoothly he pulled the syringe out; almost simultaneously, the EKG's sonarlike beeps became one long monotonous sound and the spiky green graphs traced a flat horizontal line.

Stephanie expected the surgeon and nurse to spring into immediate action like a crack drill team. Instead, the nurse reached casually back and flicked a switch, shutting the EKG monitor off. "Can't stand that damn noise," she said.

Time contracted into this one interminable, horrifying moment. Stephanie's eyes darted to Johnny, searching for an answer, but all he could do was stare helplessly back at her.

"Flasks," the surgeon said.

The nurse got a stainless-steel holder which kept two glass flasks secure.

And Stephanie suddenly remembered where she'd seen flasks identical to these. *That day on the* Chrysalis, *when I followed Lili, Ernesto, and Dr. Vassiltchikov to the ship's hospital, where the doctor had hooked them up to those robotic IVs.*

Carefully, the surgeon squirted exactly one hundred CCs of the fluid into each flask. On the operating table, Stephanie could see that the little girl's color had already changed to grayish blue. She thought: *How quickly life becomes death.*

"Procaine."

The nurse slapped a vial, then a syringe into the surgeon's palm. He drew precisely eighty CCs up into the syringe and squirted exactly forty into each flask.

"Magnesium."

The procedure was repeated.

"Now the mutated zygote, and we're done for the day."

She handed him a tiny bottle, and he used an eyedropper, adding a mere droplet into each flask. Then the nurse sealed them. As she worked, she said, "You know, I still keep wondering what this shit's for. Makes no sense to me. Like, it's gobbledygook."

"Maybe it is." He shrugged. "All I know is, losing our licenses to practice is the best thing ever happened to us. Who else pays five grand a day for twenty minutes' worth of work, no questions asked? No malpractice insurance to worry about? And Christ, everything around here's *free!* Now hurry up and sterilize those flasks and pack them in the carrying case so they can get outta here. Meanwhile, I'll sew her back up."

The nurse looked at him. "Didn't you forget something?"

"Like what?"

"Christ!" she hissed, rolling her eyes. "Will you get *with* it? She was supposed to have undergone *brain* surgery!"

"Oh, yeah." The surgeon laughed. "All right, hand me the razor. All I have to do is shave the top of her head, drill a hole in her skull, and saw part of it away with the craniotome. Two minutes, tops."

The nurse carried the flasks to one of the steel tables by the back wall. On it was various equipment, including the sterilizer.

It was then that Stephanie saw it. Right there, next to the sterilizer: the by-now-familiar red thermoslike container!

The memory of Eduardo's words burst through her mind like an electronic emission. *"On a trip through the Amazon, my mother and father caught a very rare and incurable opportunistic infection . . ."*

Even before the skull drilling began, Stephanie staggered away from the door. With a convulsive sob, she stumbled blindly across the white floor, hit the swinging doors running, and burst out into the hall, gasping for air. She slumped against the cool tile wall and wrapped her arms around her chest, rocking backward and forward.

But the oppressive, demonic weight of the horrors she had witnessed continued to rack her. *I didn't try to stop them!*

Hurried footsteps caught up with her.

"Stephanie?" It was Johnny. *"Steph!"*

At his familiar voice, her heaves died down. She raised her head and stared at him.

"Hey," Johnny said softly, taking her into his arms. "It's okay . . ."

"It's not!" she half-whispered. She was aware of her hysteria, felt smothered by helpless guilt and mounting rage.

Those fairy godmother flights! Oh, the *obscenity!* Her cheeks were streaked with wet rivulets and she could feel more silent tears forming, blurring her vision. Lives were not being saved here—they were being *taken!* And if she knew, then surely Eduardo knew also! He couldn't be blind to it . . . *could he?*

*Rare and incurable infection!*

His words burst inside her like a hideous pustule. How casually he'd said them! *My lover!* she spat mentally with a blaze of disgust and self-loathing. *How could I ever have let him touch me?*

A fresh flood of gut-wrenching tears burned down her face. She wanted to scream and scream and never stop screaming.

Day in, day out, they were murdering—just to stay young! That's what Dr. Vassiltchikov formulated! Some damned concoction which relied on enzymes from young donors to retard aging!

"Hey, Steph . . ." Johnny said softly, gently thumbing away her tears. "It's all right. We're going to make it all right—"

She stared daggers at him. *How could anybody make this right?*

Then, swiftly, her self-pity and hysteria converted into cold, calculating rage. She would destroy. Annihilate. Make the walls of da Veiga, like those of Jericho, come tumbling down!

With the same icy clarity with which she reached that decision, she knew the means were at her disposal. The two tools were right there, in her pocket.

Slowly, she reached in and pulled them out.

Her plastic key card and her address book. *My avenging swords.*

She wiped away her tears with the palms of her hands and then looked at Johnny. Her face shone like a polished blade of steel.

"You know your way around here," she said in a voice so softly flat, and so utterly emotionless and coldly sure of itself, that it chilled him to the bone. "I need to get to a computer. One that's hooked up to the mainframe. It has to be someplace where I can't be disturbed. Where nobody will be looking over my shoulder or asking any questions."

His heart swelled with a symphony of relief. *That's my Steph!* he thought. *I know that look. She's getting her old fight back!*

"Well?" she demanded coldly.

He frowned for a moment, and then snapped his fingers and grinned cockily. "I know just the place!"

"Then let's go, *now* for God's sake, take me there *now!*"

A mile away, the Learjet swooped out of the night and touched down on the runway like a screaming bird of prey.

Colonel Valerio had arrived.

## ❦ 18 ❦

"Whose office is this?" asked Stephanie in amazement, "God's?"

They stood alone inside the highest room of the entire complex—the tip of the pyramid which rose even higher to an exhilarating pinnacle far above them.

In the dark, it was like being in outer space. The three-quarter moon was a silversmith plating the spines, spandrels, and facets of the anodized aluminum gridwork with precious sterling and mysterious dark shadow, and outside, the other buildings glowed like platinum, adding to the moon garden fantasy. Stephanie felt the powerful illusion that she could reach up, up, up through the glass skin and pluck a handful of stars.

Then Johnny flipped on the lights and the spell was broken.

The enormous, cavernous space was empty except for two pieces of furniture. One was a gigantic ormolu-mounted tulipwood *bureau plat* which looked as if it should have been in Versailles, and the other was the chair behind it, a huge contoured blue leather executive throne.

"Well?" Stephanie demanded. "You still haven't answered my question."

"Which was what?" Johnny asked innocently.

"Whose office this is." She waited for a reply.

"Whose do you think?" he asked smugly.

She sighed. "Eduardo's."

He grinned. "But you must agree it's rather appropriate, don't you?"

Stephanie laughed harshly. *It is!* she thought with a blaze of righteous rage. *What better place to start dismantling this obscene empire than in Eduardo's office? He deserves what's coming as much as his parents.*

Johnny turned toward her. "Stop trying to blame yourself," he said quietly. "There was nothing we could have done down there. Oh, if we'd arrived a little sooner, we might have saved that one life—for now, at least. But as for the daily murders?" He shook his head. "All we'd have done was to dig our own premature graves."

She stared at him. He was right, she knew, but it wasn't much solace.

They had reached the desk. She stood there frowning down at it. It was entirely clear of everything except an opaque gray panel of glass which covered the entire surface and sloped gently upward: varying from half an inch to three inches in thickness. There was not so much as a pencil, a desk lamp, a keyboard, or a computer screen.

She whirled at Johnny. "I told you I needed a computer, dammit!"

"Take it easy . . ." he said. "Everybody at Sítto da Veiga knows about the caballero's computer. He's always showing it off."

She took a deep trembling breath and let it out slowly. "I'm sorry." She shut her eyes and raked a hand through her hair. "I guess my nerves are shot."

"They'll be right back on-line in a sec," he said and smiled. "Watch." He pushed the desk chair back, sat down, and felt along the edge of the glass panel. "It's here somewhere," he murmured. Then something flickered inside the glass and almost instantly, pulses of colored light spread out in a gridwork of fine glowing lines from the center in all directions: north, south, east, west.

And there it was!

She let out a cry of amazement. Whatever Johnny's fingers had touched had activated it! Unbelievable! The entire glass panel was one huge computer! Multicolored screen, televised keyboard—the works.

He wheeled the chair back, got up, and gestured for her to take a seat. "It's all yours."

She stared down at the awesome sight for a long moment, until it seemed less like a daunting amusement park novelty and more and more like a useful tool. Finally, she sat down gingerly and walked her chair to the edge of the desk. She studied the glowing surface, trying to figure it out. First, the keyboard. Except for its being electronic, with only glowing *pictures* of keys in various colors, it looked normal enough, except that there were two extra rows of instruction keys along the top.

So far so good. But where to begin?

She searched the keyboard and hesitantly pressed a button on the top row marked ACTIVATE. The blur of multicolored information streaking by abruptly ceased and went blank.

In a blink, large green letters filled the top half of the screen: *Oi! Alô!*

"Christ, no," Stephanie moaned. "A Portuguese-speaking computer's the last thing I need."

"Hmm." Johnny leaned forward over her shoulder. "Maybe you could try responding to it in English?" he mused.

"It's worth a try," she sighed.

Not quite sure how to touch-type on this futuristic gadget, she used her index finger to hunt and peck. She tapped the surface of the glass with her fingertips where the appropriate letters glowed to spell: HELLO.

In a blink of an eye her word disappeared and a reply literally exploded in cathode green:

388 *Judith Gould*

IS ENGLISH YOUR LANGUAGE OF CHOICE?

01 YES
02 NO
03 OTHER

SELECT ONE:

She searched the keyboard, then tapped:

01

The screen switched to:

HELLO
WE SHALL COMMUNICATE IN ENGLISH

"Do you believe this?" Stephanie said, turning her head to look up at Johnny. "It's un-fucking-believable!" Then: ENTER YOUR PERSONAL ACCESS NUMBER.

"Yeah. Next thing we know," Johnny said, "it's gonna ask you out on a date."

Stephanie ignored him. She was riffling through her address book to find the information Uncle Sammy had passed on to her. There it was. Aaron Kleinfelder's personal access code. *If it's still on file,* she thought.

She typed: 099/3cd.

She sat back, murmured, "Come on, come on . . ."

The screen then asked for her password, and she typed in COOKIE. And almost instantly, the screen changed again:

SELECT DESIRED PROGRAM OR
REFER TO MENU

Stephanie's eyes scanned the keys.

"There must be some way to bypass all this foreplay," she growled. She was about to press the MENU button when she had an idea. Poising her fingers above the keyboard for touch-typing, she quickly spelled out: CHILDREN'S RELIEF YEAR-ROUND.

"Now we'll soon see," she said. And suddenly the screen glowed as though a burst of green fireflies had hit—with no less than twenty-four categories of information concerning CRY.

"Fantastic," Johnny said. "What is this? The Ramanujan of computer programs?"

Stephanie sat there thoughtfully, wondering where to begin. This could go on and on to infinity, spiraling off into geometric details and recursive loops.

"Let's KISS. Stands for Keep It Simple, Sweetie," she said. "Otherwise, we'll be here for weeks."

"With the number of CRAYS they have here," Johnny said, "and the four sixteen-processor CRAY-Three supercomputers on order, I'd say it can hold billions—perhaps trillions—of pieces of information."

"Stop depressing me. Now then. Let's take a peek at the Board of Directors, shall we?" Stephanie typed: 01.

The number appeared on the screen, then it went blank, and then appeared a list of names.

"Yeow," said Johnny softly, and whistled. "Talk about heavy hitters!"

"And do you notice," Stephanie pointed out, "how Ernesto is nicely buried in the *middle* of all those names? Bet he could be chairman, but keeps turning it down to retain a nice low profile."

"Is it possible," Johnny said slowly, "that you've gotten even more cynical than you used to be?"

"Highly possible," she replied crisply, and made a mouth of thoughtful impatience. "This could go on for hours. It's time to cut through the shit. Pardon my French."

"And how do we do that?"

"Simple. Aaron Kleinfelder was looking for an orphanage-placed child who had allegedly disappeared into thin air. Probably," she added darkly, "she was brought here on one of those damn fairy godmother flights. Anyway, back to the menu."

"Great," Johnny said, leaning over her shoulder. "Now we're right back where we started."

"Not quite. I'll try CRY orphanages next." She scanned the list and typed in 12 for CRY orphanages. After several manipulations, she had managed to zero in on the CRY orphanage in Washington, D.C.

Stephanie stared at the screen thoughtfully.

"Doesn't it strike you as strange," Johnny said, "that Grupo da Veiga should be directly hooked up to CRY's computer system?"

"I wouldn't be surprised if Ernesto and Dr. Vassiltchikov initially set up CRY."

"In order to provide an endless stream of victims, you mean?"

"Exactly." She nodded.

"But one a day for ... when did it say it was founded?"

"Nineteen fifty-four."

"That's what? Which years? That makes ..." He frowned as he mentally calculated.

"Over fourteen thousand, six hundred deaths," Stephanie said.

"Jesus!"

"You can say that again." She stared at the screen some more and frowned.

"What's the problem?"

"I can't seem to remember Vinette Jones's daughter's name."

"Then try 'Parents of CRY-ORPH Persons.' "

"Looks like I'll have to." She typed in 1.010. Finally, after several more manipulations, she excitedly typed in Vinette Jones's name.

The reply blinked: REFER FILE CRY ORPH TS 10 NA CD 74830009944001.

Slowly, Stephanie typed exactly what was on the screen. There was a pause, and then the screen began to flash: ACCESS DENIED ENTER OPUS NUMBER.

Colonel Valerio's unannounced arrival at Sítto da Veiga's Security Section caused his staff to snap to. Passing one desk, he said, "Place a call to Ms. Monica Williams's quarters at once, but do not identify yourself. If she answers, apologize and say you have the wrong number and hang up."

"Sir!" The guard instantly grabbed his phone.

Passing another desk, he said, "I want all of Sítto da Veiga put on a quiet, general alert. No one is allowed to leave the premises. *No one.*"

"Sir, yes, sir!" barked the man at the desk.

Colonel Valerio ignored the rest of the men and strode directly to the fiber-optic wall map of Sítto da Veiga and stood there, hands clasped behind his back, studying the geometric floor plan of the entire premises.

After a minute, the guard on the telephone called out, "Colonel? I've let it ring eight times, sir. There is no reply."

Colonel Valerio turned to the man at the nearest desk.

"Sir!"

The Colonel's voice was even. "Call up Ms. Williams's security key code number on your computer."

"Yes, sir!" The man busily tapped away at his keyboard.

Colonel Valerio turned back to the glowing fiber-optic map. Pyramid, rectangle, square, sphere. In which was she? *I know you're here somewhere, Ms. Merlin,* he thought. *There is no way you can escape my electronic net.*

"Colonel, sir! I've called up her card number!"

Colonel Valerio kept his eyes on the fiber-optic wall map, silently congratulating himself on his foresight. Unknown to everyone but a handful of his senior security personnel, each plastic key card—including Ernesto's, Eduardo's, Dr. Vassiltchikov's, and Zarah's—had a microchip transmitter embedded in its magnetic strip.

"Punch the visual search mode and activate her transmitter," Colonel Valerio called out.

"Sir!" The man at the computer console tapped some keys. Almost instantly, a green dot glowed at the very epicenter of the pyramid.

Colonel Valerio felt the tension and excitement of imminent victory. "Zoom in on the pyramid and give me a three-dimensional picture."

More buttons were tapped, and as Colonel Valerio watched, it was as if a camera's zoom lens was activated in conjunction with a crane boom. With incredible speed and smooth elegance, the entire map of the complex tilted forty-five degrees, the buildings took on delicate, green three-dimensional gridwork forms, and everything surrounding the pyramid disappeared off the map until it was the only building left. A perfectly detailed cutaway, complete with spandrels, individual floors, elevators.

There she was. In Eduardo de Veiga's office.

Now only one question remained: Was she alone?

"Activate all transmitters of all personnel immediately," Colonel Valerio ordered.

The mostly deserted pyramid lit up with red lights—cleaning personnel or people working late. And, on the top floor, beside the green dot, glowed a single red one.

Colonel Valerio smiled. "Ah, now that is most interesting," he said, turning away. "She has someone with her."

"Opus number?" Johnny said softly. "What the *hell* is an opus number?"

Stephanie drew a deep breath. "It's a code of some sort," she said. "Un-huh."

"And," she said slowly, "I think I may have been told what it is."

He stared over at her. "You don't sound so sure."

She raked both hands back through her hair. "What I'm not so sure about is whether I remember it or not."

He continued to look at her. "You mean, someone *told* you a password and you forgot it?"

"At the time," she snapped, "I didn't know it *was* a password!"

"Sorry. Hey . . . don't be mad at me." He held up both hands placatingly.

"I'm not mad at you. Just let me think for a moment."

Stephanie shut her eyes and thought back to the weekend on Ilha da Borboleta. Was it possible it had been just this past weekend? It seemed so long ago. Part of another month. Another year. Another lifetime . . .

*Zaza and I had been alone in the Sala de Hércules having tea. It was after Eduardo and I swam and made love in the cabana.*

The brief memory stabbed like a pain, threatened to bring on tears. Swiftly she fast-forwarded the mental images.

*Back to the Sala de Hércules. Tea time, long before the storm. Zaza dressed all in Queen Mother lavender and huge pearls. I remember admir-*

*ing them. They were sixteen-millimeter genuine pearls. Four . . . no, five strands of them!*

The mental image became so clear that Stephanie could almost smell the old lady's fragrance of old-fashioned powders and sweet toilet waters.

*Joana had brought in the tea. An elaborate antique silver service.*

*Why don't you put on some nice music?* Zaza had said. *The stereo is over there . . .*

*I remember getting up. But what did I select? What did I play?*

She sat there, wracking her brains. Finally, she sighed and opened her eyes and slumped back in the big executive throne. "I can't remember!"

Colonel Valerio paced slowly back and forth in front of the huge fiber-optic pyramid. He was surprisingly calm. His spine was erect, and he was deep in thought. The dozen men in the security room were waiting for their orders. At last, Colonel Valerio turned to them.

"You, you, you, you, you, and you."

The six men he pointed to stepped forward and stood at attention.

"You will be the advance party. You are to go to the floor directly below the penthouse of the pyramid and secure the immediate area. You will seal off all the exits. If there are cleaning personnel around, you will *quietly* clear them out of the area. You will not draw attention to yourselves."

"Sir, yes, *sir!*" they bellowed in chorus.

"Good. Only when I give the order are you to ascend the stairs and take them prisoner. You will be armed, but you will not shoot."

Colonel Valerio selected a tall, scarred young man from among their ranks. "You, Queiroz."

The scarred man's chest puffed out proudly as he stepped forward. "Sir!"

"You're in charge. Now march 'em out."

Colonel Valerio stood there, watching them march from the room. *The net's tightening,* he thought with satisfaction. *Now for the hard part. Waiting to see precisely how much Ms. Merlin and her partner have learned.*

"Those ads are right," gloomed Stephanie with a frustrated sigh. "A mind *is* a terrible thing to waste. Oh, why *didn't* I pay more attention, dammit? The old lady spelled it all out for me! She laid out the *entire answer*—and what did I do? Let it slip my mind!" She looked at Johnny desperately. "Jog my memory, dear heart. Please, *please* jog it! Talk to me about *music,* Johnny!" she pleaded. "Discuss the four big Bs of classical music with me."

"The four big Bs? That a group I'm supposed to have heard of?"

"I meant Beethoven, Bach, Brahms, and Boccherini," she snapped impatiently.

"Aw, shit, Steph! You know my musical education stopped with Derek and the Dominoes!"

"Think Brahms!"

"Right, Brahms. Big bearded fellow."

"That's right. Now then, if you'll just reel off what he wrote, maybe it'll ring a bell."

"Well, now . . . let me think. A lot of gloomy symphonies and something called 'Schicksalslied.' The Song of Destiny. But my own favorite Brahms recording—"

"Say that again?" Stephanie whispered.

"I said, my own favorite Brahms recording—"

And as he said it, something began to stir in the depths of Stephanie's mind.

*Zaza's gnarled, dry fingers gripping her own smooth hand.*

The old lady was pulling her close, so close Stephanie could feel her breath on her face. She could almost hear her voice now, speaking very slowly, like a teacher hammering home a point. She remembered the gnarled fingers clutching her hand so tightly she'd all but cried aloud.

*"My own favorite Brahms recording is Opus Sixty in C-minor, Quartet number three."*

Startled, Stephanie sat up straight. "It's Opus Sixty, C-minor, Quartet number three," she repeated quickly, lest she forget it. "That's it, Johnny! THAT'S IT! Now, let's see what the computer says about *that*!"

And letting out a whoop of joy, she rolled herself up to the very edge of the desk and let her fingers do the tapping.

## ✺ *19* ✺

*C*olonel Valerio lazed back in his swivel chair, his eyes on his blank desktop monitor. It was a normal-size screen, but he couldn't care less. In fact, the ordinariness of it suited his purposes ideally. It didn't look like it was capable of doing much more than running off the simplest form letter or calling up crude graphics, but that was the beauty of it. Nobody took any notice of it, dismissing it out-of-hand as a piece of outmoded equipment.

When Colonel Valerio had explained his needs to the wild-haired computer whiz kid, he'd been pleasantly surprised. "What you're asking for, man, are two things. First, a built-in virus, which eats up the program, say, if one of three or four key people don't check in with it daily."

"What, exactly, do you mean by, it 'eats up the program'?"

"I mean, it literally eats itself up, man, until there's nothing left. It's like I said. If at least one of three or four key people don't punch in every twenty-four hours, the whole program comes under attack by the virus, and within ten hours—*kebang!* Every byte of information is gobbled up."

"In other words," Colonel Valerio had said, "it will be irretrievable?"

"Beyond even that, 'cause in order for something to be irretrievable, it first has to have existed. And once this virus automatically goes into effect—*bam!* There's no proof anything's *ever* been there."

Colonel Valerio had smiled. "And you guarantee that if the program disappears, no one will ever be able to . . . resurrect it?"

"Hell, Colonel, even *I* wouldn't be able to do that—and I can do most anything with these machines, you know?"

"I'll take your word for it."

"Now, for this other thing you asked about," the kid went on. "It's what we call a 'window,' or a 'trapdoor.' It's an object command which lets you get into the program while bypassing all the security keycheck programs. You following me?"

"Will I be able to watch on my screen what somebody else is doing on theirs?"

"Hey, you're talking to the expert, man! Sure you can do that, if we design it that way. It's simple. All you need is your own secret code, and so long as we put the trapdoor in, it's yours to come and go as you like."

Now Colonel Valerio sat forward and switched on his keyboard and monitor and tapped out the trapdoor command code. He had chosen an appropriate one: Eagle Eye One.

He used his fingers to hunt and peck: SEARCH DAT. LIMIT - EXEC ONE.

Exec One was the numero uno computer in the pyramid. He waited, and when the screen blinked again—*bingo!* He was tied in to Stephanie's vastly superior terminal in Eduardo's office. Was seeing exactly what she was seeing on *her* screen, that flashing message: ACCESS DENIED ENTER OPUS NUMBER.

He sat back and put his feet up on the desk and laced his hands behind his head and watched. Soon he'd know what she was up to.

Stephanie was cool, controlled. Getting more and more confident by the minute. She felt absolutely no nervousness and was breathing easily.

*Thanks to a little specially acquired knowledge,* she thought, giving Zaza a blessing.

"You want an opus number?" she murmured. "Well, try this on for size, big boy." With a flourish, she punched: 60. After a brief pause, the screen replied: ENTER KEY NUMBER. Stephanie typed in: C MINOR.

There was another short pause, then: ENTER QUARTET NUMBER.

"Three," Johnny reminded her. "The quartet number's oh-three."

The response was immediate: OPUS NUMBER CONFIRMED. PROCEED.

"I'll be damned!" Johnny crowed. "You did it! Whoo-*ee!*"

"It's still a little early to celebrate," she warned.

"Nah," he said. "My gal knows what she's doing."

"In that case, your gal's committed. Here goes." And slowly verbalizing the syllables aloud, Stephanie tapped out: JONES, VINETTE.

There was a long pause, then: SEARCHING PARAMS ANGEL FILE.

"Johnny?" She snapped a strange glance at him.

"What's the matter, babe?" He hurried around the desk and crouched by the side of her chair.

She pointed to the word *Angel* with a trembling finger. "That," she croaked hoarsely, a choking coming up inside her. "How . . . how *dare* they? God, the *arrogance!* The blasphemy!"

He puffed out his cheeks and released the air slowly. Then he reached for her hand and held it between both of his. Her flesh felt cold. He kissed her fingers quietly. "You can't let it eat at you," he said softly.

Her eyes filled with tears. "How can I help it? Elevating their victims to a kind of pseudoreligious sainthood and keeping them on file! It's *sick!*"

He didn't reply, just kept pressing her flesh, letting her know he shared her feelings.

"You know something?" she said softly. "If I'd known from the start what I was going to find . . ." She stared at him, eyes wide with confusion, and gave a kind of shrug. "I really don't know if I'd have kept at it."

"Bullshit." He shook his head adamantly. "I know you. You'd have been that much more rabid about chasing this down, that's all."

A weary little smile pushed through her face. "How well you know me, Johnny," she said. "You think maybe that's why we're always at each other's throats? Because we know each other so well?"

She tilted her head forward and looked down. "I don't know why, but sometimes, the ones we love most are the ones we end up hurting the worst."

He perked up. "Hey, this your way of saying you love me?"

"Oh, Johnny!" She tried to push him away.

But he had her smiling again, and she made a kissing motion with her mouth and suddenly the world was all right by him.

It was a moment before either of them realized the screen had switched to read: DECEASED CRY ORPH PERSONS.

"Damn! You do know how to distract a woman!" Stephanie quickly withdrew her hand from his and asked the computer for more information.

And almost instantly, a luminescent blur of vile green letters raced up the screen with impossible speed. When they stilled, it was three-quarters of the way into the Js:

### DECEASED CRY-ORPH PERSONS FILED BY ALPHABETICAL PARENTAL SURNAMES

| PARENT | OFFSPRING | DOD | CAUSE |
|---|---|---|---|
| JONES, Dennis & Marla | Alvin | 1/09/54 | H3 |
| JONES, Denyce | Raymond | 5/13/70 | R1 |
| JONES, Vinette | Jowanda | 8/23/90 | A0 |
| JONES, Wilma | Ida | 10/03/70 | B3 |
| JONG, Lee | Helen | 3/14/68 | S1 |

Johnny got up from his crouch and leaned over the tabletop. Running his finger down the CAUSE column, he said, "What the hell do these codes stand for?"

"Why don't we ask the computer?" Stephanie suggested, and typed in the appropriate question. The screen rearranged itself:

### ABBREVIATIONS OF CAUSES OF DEATH
A0  ALLERGIC REACTION
A1  ANEURYSM
B1  BACTERIAL INFECTION

B2   BLOOD CLOT
B3   BOTULISM
B4   BRAIN TUMOR
C1   CANDIDIASIS
C2   CARCINOMA
(CON'T)

"Hm," Stephanie said thoughtfully. "Jowanda's official cause of death is listed as A0. Allergic reaction." She glanced at Johnny. "Not that I believe it for an instant."

"Neither do I." He frowned. "So where do we go from here?"

"Well, how about we take a look-see at the chronological listing of deceased CRY-ORPH persons? Like, right around the time Jowanda died?"

She hit the CLEAR button, then typed in several commands.

Finally, there was that burst of blurring, scrambled letters unrolling faster than the eye could see. Then abruptly they stilled, and there it was:

### DECEASED CRY-ORPH PERSONS FILED CHRONOLOGICALLY BY DATE OF DEATH

| DOD | CRY-ORPH PERSON | AGE | CAUSE |
| --- | --- | --- | --- |
| 8/20/90 | Balas, Milhaela | 2.4 | D2 |
| 8/21/90 | Koen, Nelly | 1.8 | D2 |
| 8/22/90 | Ponomareva, Faina | 3.1 | L1 |
| 8/23/90 | Jones, Jowanda | 07 | A0 |
| 8/24/90 | Rica, Ulrike | 09 | D2 |
| (CONT) | | | |

"Do you see what I see?" Johnny asked as he scanned the column of dates.

"Be hard to miss." Stephanie nodded. "One a day."

"Yeah. They pop 'em like vitamins," Johnny replied.

"But there's something else. Those names. The kids are from all over the world."

"Yes, and I'd say that's one of the beauties of this setup. Correct me if I'm wrong, dear heart, but doesn't CRY sponsor villages and have orphanages or health clinics in sixty or seventy countries?"

"Everywhere from Angola to Zimbabwe, yes."

"So don't you see? As long as not too many kids die from any one place at any one time, who's going to suspect anything?"

"Us," she said solemnly.

"That's right," he agreed, "but we stumbled across it by accident."

She frowned thoughtfully. "If we want to shut this operation down for good, we're going to need hard evidence." For a moment, she drummed her fingernails on the tabletop screen, away from the televised keyboard. "Johnny . . .?" she said slowly.

"What?"

"I don't see a printer around here. Do you think the computer's sophisticated enough to tell us how to get a printout of all this?"

"Why don't you ask it?"

Stephanie poised her hands above the keyboard and typed: HOW DO I GET PRINTOUT OF OUR TRANSACTIONS?

There was a blink, the screen went blank, and the reply came slowly, as if laboriously hunt-and-pecked:

GOOD TRY, BUT YOU DON'T, MS. MERLIN. YOU AND YOUR FRIEND ARE COMPLETELY SURROUNDED. THERE IS NO ESCAPE. ADVISE YOU DON'T TRY ANY TRICKS OR MAKE SUDDEN MOVES.

Stephanie felt the skin on the back of her neck start to crawl. Very slowly, she turned and looked to her right, to the top of the curving stairs.

She caught her breath. Six armed guards each had an automatic weapon pointed at her and Johnny.

# ❧ 20 ❧

*T*hat evening, when he got home from São Paulo, the first thing Eduardo did was place another call to Sítto da Veiga. Monica's number rang and rang. Finally, he had an operator check to see if there was trouble on the line. There wasn't.

After he hung up, he loosened his tie, poured himself a generous snifter of Napoleon brandy, and went out onto the cantilevered deck overlooking his rooftop pool.

He gulped down his brandy and went inside and poured himself another hefty splash. *She's immersed in work,* he reasoned, going back outside. *Or she's discovering all the marvels in that Disneyworld of technological wonders.* In many ways, he knew, Sítto da Veiga was like a sophisticated amusement park for first-time visitors.

Then he laughed softly to himself. *What am I worried about, anyway? If anyone can take care of herself, it's Monica Williams.*

*I'll try her again first thing in the morning,* he decided. *If I still can't get hold of her then, I'll fly straight out there and pay her a surprise visit.*

Having come to that decision, he went to bed, secure in the knowledge that no harm could come to his girlfriend.

Before they left Sítto da Veiga, Colonel Valerio sent a man to Stephanie and Johnny's quarters to fetch appropriate travel clothes for each of them. The man returned with slacks and a dark sweater and tennis shoes for Stephanie, jeans and a sweatshirt and sneakers for Johnny.

*At least we get to change out of these damn scrub clothes,* Stephanie thought, while changing under the leering gaze of a guard.

Ten minutes later, their hands cuffed behind their backs, Stephanie Merlin and Johnny Stone were in the glass-topped bus, bound for the airstrip.

Five passengers boarded the Learjet for the return flight to Vitoria. Stephanie and Johnny, Colonel Valerio, and two of his men.

Stephanie and Johnny were seated apart. Neither was permitted to speak, but Stephanie found it difficult to hold her tongue. "Eduardo will make you pay for this!" she spat, raking Colonel Valerio with a lethal glare.

"I wouldn't be so sure," he told her with a serene smile.

Two hours later, when the jet landed at Vitoria, the five of them switched aircraft and boarded a waiting helicopter.

This flight to Ilha da Borboleta was vastly different from the one last week, when Stephanie had been with Eduardo. Then, she had come to the island as his willing guest. Now, she was returning as Colonel Valerio's prisoner. The helicopter even put down at a different location—the lit helipad at the security compound, on the far side of the island from the *quinta*.

Stephanie, Johnny, and Colonel Valerio were the only ones to get off. The two guards stayed onboard, and at a signal from Colonel Valerio, the helicopter instantly lifted off again, was briefly silhouetted against the three-quarter moon, and then disappeared into the night.

With its departure, the silence was unearthly. Except for the shrill of the insects and the sounds of distant surf, the island seemed strangely quiet, eerily desolate.

"I demand to call Eduardo," Stephanie said stubbornly.

"Then you'd better call at the top of your lungs," Colonel Valerio advised her grimly. "This entire island has been evacuated, and all lines of communication have been cut. The three of us are alone here."

Before she could register her disbelief, Colonel Valerio took her by one arm and Johnny by the other and force-marched them toward the dimly lit security building.

"I'm putting you in separate cells tonight," he told them. "And if I were you, I'd try to get a good night's sleep. You're going to need your strength tomorrow."

Johnny refused to give him the pleasure of asking why, and for once, even Stephanie was silent. Something told her she'd find out soon enough.

When Colonel Valerio had helped design the security complex, he had anticipated every contingency, right down to the potential necessity of a jail. Subsequently, two escape-proof cells had been built in the steamy, bug-infested basement of the barracks, at opposite ends of the building. Prisoners would be unable to communicate even by shouting.

Now Colonel Valerio shoved Stephanie and Johnny ahead of him, down a dark flight of narrow concrete stairs to the first cell. He unlocked Johnny's handcuffs and shoved him inside and slam-locked the door.

Johnny leapt at it in a last-ditch effort, but it was too late. The lock had clicked. With a cry of rage, he tried to reach his captor through the bars, but Colonel Valerio was out of reach and laughed softly. Ignoring Johnny's yells, he pushed Stephanie along a narrow, musty basement corridor to the other end of the building.

As he unlocked her cuffs, she surprised him by saying, "There's no need to push and shove, you know." And she entered the cell with all the dignity of a queen.

The barred door slammed shut behind her.

"Don't let the snakes and spiders bite," he taunted, and it was then that Stephanie saw the madness blazing out of his eyes. *Why didn't I see it sooner?* she wondered. *Why hasn't anybody?*

And then she knew. She had never seen him without his mirrored aviator shades before.

Colonel Valerio was feeling good. He was high with anticipation of the day to come, and he prepared for it by spending hours oiling and cleaning and fine-tuning his field gear.

He checked the string-to-cable connections of his Pearson Spoiler Cam bow and adjusted the flight wheel. He screwed on a Cobra VA-250 bow sight and the ArrowMax overdrive unit with its spring-wire arrow rest and Teflon sleeve.

He carefully selected fifteen arrows—five of graphite, each two-and-one-half times stiffer than aluminum, and nearly twice as strong and deadly; five of compression-molded graphite and fiberglass; and five lightweight shafts of a graphite and fiberglass laminate.

He chose his arrowheads and screwed them into the shafts. He'd selected evenly between conical broadheads, which were shaped like smooth bullets, but whose four one-and-one-quarter-inch blades opened on impact; octagonal-bladed one-and-one-eighth-inch steel knifepoint broadheads; and heavy-duty, moose-killing 140-grain chisel tips. He spent an additional hour lovingly sharpening and resharpening each blade until he could have shaved with it.

Finally satisfied, he packed a selection of arrows in the Hoyt quiver which he attached to his bow, and stored the others in a special hip quiver of his own design.

Next, he sharpened his hunting knife, chose his most comfortable pair of jungle boots, and checked the spikes he could strap onto the boots, as well as the military spec climbing belt: utilizing these, he could climb high and safe up any tree.

From his wall locker he chose the camouflage pattern which he knew would make him almost invisible in this jungle environment—gray-and-black Trebark of highly contrasting, ragged triangles. He also laid out matching camouflage shooting gloves and arm guards.

Finally, he packed a camouflage fanny pack with an extra pair of socks, dried beef jerky strips, candy bars, a spray can of Cutter's insect repellent, tubes of camouflage grease, and a box of matches in a waterproof case. Last but not least, he filled his canteen, added a water purification tablet out of habit, and was done. He was ready.

His gear was in order. His hunter's instincts were roused.

He stripped naked, showered, and hit the sack early. But he found he was still too wound up to sleep. The excitement of tomorrow's hunt electrified his blood. His temples throbbed with anticipation, and his penis was tumescent.

The scent of his quarry was strong in his nostrils.

*She is here, right here, locked up downstairs—she and that boyfriend of hers with the phony name and cocky attitude! What an unexpected bonus he is. Now my game preserve will be stocked with* two *human specimens instead of just one.*

His crazed eyes glowed silver in the dark.

He had it all planned. He'd release and stalk the woman first. The female of a species was always the most fun to track—even if she tended to be the easiest to nail. But when it came to males . . . now *there* was real sport!

*Mano a mano* . . . man against man.

Just thinking about it was enough to set him off. As he felt the torrent rise within him, he cried out helplessly and his seed burst forth.

Spent, he lay breathing heavily on his cot and then rolled over on his side and fell fast asleep.

## 21

As soon as Eduardo woke up, the first thing he did was place another telephone call to Sítto da Veiga. Once again, Monica's number rang and rang. Finally, he left another message with the main switchboard and then called his pilot to have a jet standing by, and his chauffeur to have his car brought around.

He showered, shaved, and dressed in record time. His housekeeper brought him a cup of coffee, and he sipped it while waiting restlessly for his car. Suddenly, he couldn't shake the premonition that something was terribly wrong.

He was on his second cup of coffee when the doorman rang to announce his car had arrived. Twice, he tried calling Monica from the Mercedes's cellular phone, but there was still no answer.

At the airport, the jet waiting on the tarmac was a medium-sized Sabreliner. By the time Eduardo hopped onboard, the pilot and copilot had already gone through the preflight check. Four minutes later, the sleek aircraft screamed down the runway and climbed steeply up into the cloud-banked sky. Heading northeast. To Sítto da Veiga.

The *Chrysalis* was cruising offshore, just out of sight of land. With Brazil's Atlantic coastline of 4,603 miles, it was easy for the high-speed yacht to virtually disappear during the night. Still, though neither radar nor sonar had picked up any vessels on their tail, Captain Falcão was taking no chances.

Lili and Ernesto felt safe so long as they remained on the move, even though they took threats of potential terrorism very seriously.

Zaza scoffed at these precautions. *If somebody wants to get us badly enough,* she opined, *they will.*

But she wisely kept this pessimistic view to herself. There was no need to frighten Zarah ... Lili ... any more than she already was. Besides which, Zaza was much too occupied with other matters to waste time worrying about terrorists: she was busy planning a luncheon.

At exactly eight-thirty that morning, she had her favorite steward hand-carry invitations to Lili's, Ernesto's, and Dr. Vassiltchikov's suites. Each thick, creamy vellum envelope had a pink rosebud pinned to its flap.

The thick Cartier cards inside were engraved with her name at the top; the rest she had handwritten in her spidery, though still elegant, old-fashioned script:

---

ZAZA BÖHM
*requests the pleasure of your company*
*for a special surprise announcement*
*at lunch this noon*
*in the Cabinet de la Méridienne*
*formal attire requested*

---

Ernesto thanked the steward, tore open the invitation, and scanned it. *Formal attire for lunch? Whoever heard of formal attire at noon?*

Lili sliced open her invitation with a malachite-handled letter opener which had once belonged to the last czarina of all the Russias.

She read the card and tapped it against the edge of her vanity table. A slight frown flitted across her face as she wondered what on earth to wear. It had to be something she'd never worn before: that went without saying—she never, *ever*, wore the same thing twice.

*How sweet of Zaza!* she thought. *And whatever can the surprise announcement be?*

It was just after 9:00 A.M. when Colonel Valerio brought Johnny's breakfast tray down to his cell.

The moment Johnny heard him coming, he rushed the steel bars and rattled them with all his might. "Listen, you bastard!" he snarled. "You've got no right to keep us locked up! You get us out of here—*now!*"

Colonel Valerio unhurriedly bent down and slid the tray under the bars of the cell. "You better eat, boy," he advised Johnny coldly. "You're gonna need all the energy you can get."

"Fuck you!" Johnny screamed. He kicked the tray and scrambled eggs, cereal, bread, milk, and coffee slopped all over the cell.

"You're gonna wish you'd eaten it," Colonel Valerio predicted calmly.

Hearing approaching footfalls, Stephanie hopped off the metal bunk and hurried to the bars of her cell. Her heart skipped a beat and she looked out hopefully. Perhaps it was Eduardo, come to rescue her and Johnny!

But her heart sank. It was Colonel Valerio with a breakfast tray.

"Morning, Ms. Merlin." His smile was mocking and his crazed eyes were hidden behind his mirrored shades. "Hope you found my hospitality to your liking?"

"How could I possibly not?" she asked facetiously.

"Glad to have been able to accommodate you. I take it the bugs and spiders didn't bother you too much?"

"Bother me!" She iced him with her eyes. "I *love* pets."

He stared at her for a long moment. It was as if he was seeing her, really seeing her, for the very first time. *Maybe stalking her will be more of a challenge than I initially thought,* he was thinking. *She's certainly got more spirit than I gave her credit for.*

She pondered: *Should I eat?* She remembered the old saying: *Nothing seems quite so bad when you've got something in your stomach.* She stooped down and started to pick up the tray when she let go of it and jerked her hands back. *What if the food's drugged?*

She started to get up—but forced herself to pick up the tray and carry it over to the cot. *You've got to eat,* she told herself.

She made herself pick up the piece of bread, nibbled it. Her throat felt dry. *He wouldn't dare drug me,* she thought. *He's only a sick bully out to scare me. He wouldn't dream of laying a finger on me. Eduardo would never allow it.*

And then a chilly thought made her go stone-cold inside: *What if Eduardo doesn't know what's going on? How can he help us then?*

In the Cabinet de la Méridienne, Zaza orchestrated every detail from her wheelchair. Part of her two-room suite, the Cabinet de la Méridienne and her adjoining bedchamber were the antithesis of everything the *Chrysalis* stood for: both rooms were perfect time capsules of the eighteenth century.

Now, in preparation for lunch, three fine gilt-wood fauteils were arranged around a beautifully set round table.

Zaza maneuvered her wheelchair to the table and cast her piercing perfectionist's eye around it. The damask cloth from Porthault had been ironed seamlessly, the damask napkins folded like bishops' miters. Four ormolu candlesticks with beeswax tapers waiting to be lit surrounded the large silver bowl filled with cut rubrum lilies. The heavy baroque cutlery, each piece perfectly balanced and made from a single block of silver, was spotless. And the plates . . .

Ah, the plates! She had selected her priceless hand-painted Sevres botanical plates, survivors of the famous "Salvandy Service," each a hand-painted, gold-rimmed work of art.

For Lili, she had chosen a plate depicting, appropriately, a rubrum lily and sprays of *Fleur-de-Veuve.*

For Ernesto, a plate rather more masculine, with dahlia blossoms and sprays of *Liseron des champs.*

For herself, her favorite—the plate depicting a cluster of bell-shaped *Campanulé à grosses fleurs,* so delicately lifelike she had often expected them to move as in a breeze.

And for Dr. Vassiltchikov, she had expressly selected the plate with the chrysanthemums: *autumn's flowers, hardy and rigid and stiff, suitable for funeral wreaths and graves.* Zaza nodded to herself. *Doubtlessly,* she thought, *Dr. Death will miss the point.*

"Is everything to your satisfaction, Senhora?" one of the young stewards inquired solicitously. "I have put the music you requested on the CD player. I will switch it on just before they arrive."

Zaza nodded, backed up the wheelchair, and rode over to the marble-topped gilt console. There, in two ormolu-mounted agate bowls, were still more clusters of pink-spotted rubrums. *Rubrums, Lili's favorite . . .*

And, under a dome of crystal, dessert. The meal itself would be the kind of calorie-light menu Lili and Ernesto favored. But for a celebration, there had to be something sweet. Zaza had had the chef bake a small but exceedingly rich torte; she herself had personally prepared the marzipan icing.

The torte looked beautiful. Zaza nodded to herself with satisfaction. Everything was perfect.

"Senhor de Veiga! Welcome back to Sítto da Veiga!"

"Have you seen Ms. Williams?"

"*Sim,* Senhor. She was here yes—"

"I don't care where she was yesterday. Where is she *now*?"

"I—I don't know, Senhor."

"Then find me someone who does. *Now!*"

"*Sim,* Senhor!"

"And get Dr. Medrado in here. *Imediatamente!*"

"Senhor de Veiga! To what do we owe the—"

"Dr. Medrado, I am in a hurry and a bad mood, so let's skip the formalities, shall we? I am looking for Ms. Williams."

"I was just told five minutes ago that she and a man left with Colonel Valerio yesterday evening."

"What do you mean, 'left'?"

"The Colonel had both of them in handcuffs."

"Handcuffs!"

"Yes, Senhor. Regrettably, it seems the charming Ms. Williams is not who she claims to be."

"Then perhaps, Dr. Medrado, you can enlighten me. Can *you* tell me who she is?"

"I'm afraid I am not privy to that information."

"I see. And under whose authority did Colonel Valerio arrest Ms. Williams?"

"I presume yours . . . or your father's."

"Tell me something, Dr. Medrado. Do you always let Colonel Valerio do as he wishes here? Does no one first check anything with you, or my father, or myself?"

"But the Colonel has been given unlimited authority—"

"The bounds of which he has obviously overstepped! I suggest you find out where Colonel Valerio took Ms. Williams."

"Yes, Senhor."

"You might begin by looking at the flight plan which was filed."

Stephanie heard the approaching sound of footsteps and the jingling of keys. She sat suddenly straighter and then, with a fresh surge of hope, jumped up from the cot and rushed to the bars of the cell, instinctively smoothing her hair with her hands. "Eduardo?" she called out.

And with a gasp, she took a reeling step backward.

"I told you I'd be back." The voice was Colonel Valerio's.

*But what was he wearing? And why was his face streaked like that? Where did he think he was? On a . . .*

"Battlefield?" she whispered aloud.

She instinctively drew back as he unlocked the cell door. He had changed into his gray-and-black Trebarks and his face was a distorted mask of camouflage grease. Instead of the mirrored aviator shades, he had on green ones, and beneath them, one cheekbone stood out like a shiny gray welt while the other receded like a concave black hollow, robbing his face of symmetry and all human form. Grayish-green field binoculars hung from around his neck, and he wore a web belt with a canteen. A quiver with arrows was strapped to his right thigh.

And slung over one shoulder was a futuristic crossbow the likes of which she had never seen.

The cell door slammed open. At the noise, she flinched involuntarily and backed against the wall. Her body was taut and quivering, her face pale and drawn. She felt her defiance shriveling, reducing her to a crumbling husk. She eyed him warily.

"Are . . . you going hunting?" she asked in a raw whisper as he approached. She swallowed to lubricate her dry throat.

"Yep," he said, and in two steps he was beside her, gripping her arm and yanking her out of the cell. "It's a great day for a hunt."

Her flesh was rising in goosebumps as he half-carried her along beside him. "But . . . I didn't think there were any animals here on Ilha da Borboleta! Only butterflies."

He stopped walking and turned to her and grinned.

And that was when Stephanie knew.

*I'm the prey.*

## 22

*I*t was all Stephanie could do to keep up with Colonel Valerio. Her right arm ached where his fingers were digging in, and her feet tripped on the stair risers, her left elbow banging the rough concrete wall and scraping open.

Then they were outside, in back of the security building. Stephanie blinked in the sudden daylight, abruptly slid on the moist dewy grass, and almost lost her balance.

She caught her breath. Under the overcast morning sky, a cloud of thousands upon thousands of silvery blue, black, and white butterflies swirled all around them.

"*Lysandras!*" she breathed softly, turning her head in amazement and remembering her suite aboard the *Chrysalis*. *Is this an omen?* she wondered. And as the *Lysandras* fluttered past, she saw, in the distance, kaleidoscopic clouds of other butterflies.

Stephanie looked around cautiously, her eyes taking in the military obstacle course equipment and the firing range. Her elbow throbbed where she'd scraped it on the wall. Twisting her arm around, she could see a bloody gash. She slid a glance at Colonel Valerio. He had unshouldered his bow and was staring at her. At least, she *thought* he was staring at her. With his green glasses on, it was hard to tell.

"First," he said almost laconically, "you gotta know the rules of the game. From your previous visit, you may be under the mistaken impression that this is Fantasy Island. Believe me, it's *not*. What this is, it's my private hunting preserve."

Stephanie stared at him. *This can't be happening,* she thought. *Dear God, please let me wake up—*

"The rules," he continued, barking as he got caught up in his monologue, "are so simple an idiot couldn't fail to understand them."

She cringed and nearly tumbled backward, resisting the urge to wipe his spittle off her face with the back of her hand. Bass drums were pounding in her ears and chest.

His nose was stuck right up to hers, and she could see twin wide-eyed reflections of herself in the lenses of his glasses. "When I tell you to, you are going to double-time down to the far end of the firing range, where you will *stop*."

*My God!* she was thinking. *He thinks this is some twisted sort of jungle boot camp! He's certifiable!*

Sweat trickled down his gray-and-black-streaked face, making the camouflage grease shine. "And the reason you will *stop,* is for a *demonstration.* This is just so you don't get the wrong *idea!* If you will look carefully, you will notice we are not *alone. Have* you noticed that? *Have you!"*

Her expression was confused and she found it difficult to think clearly. She could hear herself gasp and wheeze. It was as if all her energies were consumed merely trying to breathe. *Someone has put a vise around my chest and is crushing my rib cage into my lungs.*

"WELL? HAVE YOU!"

She stood there, swaying, forced herself to look down the length of the firing range. The target at the end of the range blurred, almost focused, blurred again. And then she saw. Oh-dear-sweet-Jesus, she saw!

She felt her cheeks draw in, her heart go cold.

Johnny . . . ?

She stifled a wet sob. What was he doing down there? Why didn't he move? She breathed raggedly. The drum pounding in her ears was splitting her skull now. *Why is he down there? Why is he just standing there?* Fear suddenly consumed her, threatened to overwhelm her; she shuddered violently. Colonel Valerio's drill sergeant voice snarled and barked, intruding upon the bass drum beating, beating, beating faster and faster inside her head. *Oh, Johnny,* she thought in bleak agony. *Oh God, Johnny . . .*

"You will double-time there and stand beside him! You will wait until I have launched *one* arrow. This is to demonstrate the power of my *bow.* Then, you will have precisely one half-hour's head start. *One half-hour."* He was yelling at the top of his lungs. Then, very quietly, enunciating every word very precisely, he said, "After that half-hour, I am coming after you. Am I making myself clear? Now get moving. *Double-time!"*

But she was frozen to the spot, her heart beating wildly. She knew she must move, must force her buckling legs to carry her down the length of the firing range.

He was selecting a broadhead, stringing it into his bow.

*Johnny!* she thought suddenly.

"No!" she cried, and then her legs moved and she was running as fast as she had ever run in her life, skidding on the wet grass—running toward Johnny—Johnny who would never just stand there! The monster must have tied him there. It was up to her to get him loose!

"Oh, Johnny," she rasped. "Oh, Johnny." He was tied to a stake, nylon ropes securing his arms, chest, belly, legs and ankles. "I'll get you loose!" she wheezed, tearing furiously at the rope. She looked back over her shoulder, saw Colonel Valerio in the distance, standing sideways, *aiming.*

"Johnny, Johnny—"

"Shhh!" he said, and smiled at her.

"These damn ropes won't give! The knots—"

"*Stephanie!*"

His sharp tone stopped her. She stared into his eyes. "Just want to tell you—" he began.

It came then, out of nowhere. She felt it rather than saw it. Silent as the wind, streaking past her, slamming into Johnny's shoulder. The impact jolted him, and he screamed, "Aaaargh!" and went limp.

The slim carbon shaft quivered like a riding crop, the razor-sharp broadhead buried deep in his right shoulder.

"*Johnny!*" she screamed.

He lifted his lolling head. "Just want to tell you I love you," he whispered. Then he slumped forward, held tight by the ropes.

Tears blurred her vision.

"Run!" he whispered. "Run, Steph! Get . . . away . . . from . . . him . . ."

She stood there, indecisive. Hesitant to leave him.

"Run . . ." he whispered, more weakly. "For me, Steph. For *us.* Run . . ."

She reached out, her fingertips brushing his face. "I love you, too, Johnny," she sobbed. The tears were pouring down her face.

"Run . . ." he repeated.

She kissed the top of his lolling head. Then she ran for her life.

# ☙ 23 ☙

## At Sea · Ilha da Borboleta, Brazil · Rio de Janeiro · Sítto da Veiga

*I*n his office aboard the *Chrysalis,* Ernesto started the workday by punching his personal code into the computer. First, he called up the previous day's mining extraction figures of de Veiga Metálicos. Next, he had a look at the closing prices of various metal commodity futures. Gold was +2.10, silver +3.1, and copper +4.6 on the Commodity Exchange, New York. Silver was +11.0 on the Chicago Board of Trade. And palladium was -.20, and platinum +6.70 on the New York Mercantile Exchange. All in all, not bad. No, not bad at all.

But in spite of the positive economic forecast, he waited to call up the foreign currency figures. He was more anxious to know what was happening on Ilha da Borboleta, and whether the terrorists had attempted to breach the island's defenses. Quite possibly it could merely have been a rumor. He dialed Colonel Valerio's number on the island, but he got no answer. Then he tried the main security number, and finally the *quinta.* There was no answer anywhere. *Perhaps Colonel Valerio and his men are battling the terrorists at this very moment.* The thought caused Ernesto to shudder. Quickly he reimmersed himself in the safer world of global high finance.

Unknown to him, there were no terrorists.

Also unknown to him, the mere act of having punched his personal code into the computer had disarmed the virus in the program for another twenty-four hours.

The virus he didn't even know existed.

On the *Chrysalis,* Lili went into the enormous climate-controlled walk-in closet adjoining her suite—a fifty-foot-long supermarket of the world's finest haute couture. Here, double tiers of electronically controlled drycleaner's racks were overloaded with hundreds, perhaps thousands, of hand-made outfits she had never once worn. All were carefully segregated by category, and further subcategorized by color.

Lili had custom-made mannequins of her body at the ateliers of all the world's greatest couturiers. And standing orders that they each whip up two $35,000 or $75,000 little somethings and air-express them to her each and every week.

Now she pressed the button and activated the electronic racks, and stopped at formal wear.

Oh, there were hundreds of immodest gowns, each vying to outglitter the other! Which should she wear? *Whom* should she wear? St. Laurent . . . Féraud . . . Kimijima . . . Valentino . . . ?

Then it caught her eye. The short strapless evening dress from Vera Wang, a silver-and-gold brocade fantasy with a wraparound infanta over-skirt. And the workmanship! The bodice and hems of both the short skirt and the cutaway overskirt were richly encrusted with crystal and cut-glass jewels and thousands of tiny seed pearls. With metallic stockings and front-ruffled, high-heeled slingbacks of gold silk, and her hair pulled tightly back into a chignon and diamond butterfly earrings, she would look ready for a photo session with Skrebneski.

Now that she'd decided upon what to wear, she softly sang to herself the opening lines from "Im chambre séparée" from *Der Opernball.* She would float through the rest of the morning, doing her exercises, getting a massage, lazing in the Jacuzzi, and leave herself at least an hour—no, an hour and a half!—to get dressed and put on her makeup.

She sang happily, gloriously, all for her own benefit:

> *Geh'n wir in's chambre séparée*
> *Ach, zu dem süssen tête à tête . . .*

Miraculously, now that she had her vanity to feed, she had completely forgotten about the threat of terrorists.

On Ilha da Borboleta, Johnny wasn't moving. Still tied to the stake, his head hung forward with his chin against his chest. His face was ashen from shock, and his sweatshirt blotched with blood from the shoulder wound. The brown graphite arrow with its streamlined orange tail still protruded, but no longer quivered.

With an effort, Johnny opened his eyes and then shut them again. His body felt exhausted from the impact of the blade, and the pain was excruciating when he made the slightest move. He had no choice: *I have to keep still if I don't want to pass out.*

He tried to lift his head to look up the range to see if the Colonel was still there, but everything swam before his eyes. His entire body felt as if it were on fire.

*Run, Steph!* he willed her silently. *You've got the brains to stop him.*

"And I'm just useless," he whispered and then mercifully passed out.

In her bedroom adjoining the Cabinet de la Méridienne, Zaza dismissed the maid who had helped her dress. Then she rode to the full-length mirror to study herself. She nodded with satisfaction. The dove gray dinner suit she'd finally decided upon, with shoes to match and a white silk blouse, was appropriate and tasteful for the occasion. So was the fact that she wore absolutely no jewelry, excepting her slim gold watch.

She lifted her wrist and looked at it now. *I still have two hours to wait,* she thought.

In Rio de Janeiro, The Ghost had decided upon the modus operandi. It was simple to the point of ingenious. It would not even require a weapon. All there was left to do now was to wait for Ms. Monica Williams to return from her trip.

She would be welcomed back with a beautiful red rose.

Red, the color of blood.

In her laboratory aboard the *Chrysalis,* Dr. Vassiltchikov was sitting in front of her computer, which was directly linked by satellite to one of the CRAY supercomputers at Sítto da Veiga. At the moment, she was analyzing a single protein of a DNA molecule, a numerical sequence which took up the entire screen of the monitor.

There had to be a way to clone this sequence, or, better yet, create it artificially!

She sighed to herself. The problem was, the entire DNA molecule was composed of three billion of these data bases. Just to peripherally study the entire strand, even with the help of the supercomputers, would take a person an entire lifetime.

She never failed to marvel at how huge that infinitesimal strand of life was. So tiny, and yet the key to life itself.

Not for the first time, she felt a pang of regret. *If only I'd submitted myself to the treatments. I'd still have a lifetime . . . perhaps many lifetimes . . . to continue my research.* But it was too late to begin them now. Aging could be arrested, yes. But the clock could not be turned back.

*I couldn't bear to be old forever.*

*I'd rather die.*

In Sítto da Veiga, Eduardo was listening to Luiz Medrado, who told him that Colonel Valerio's pilot had filed a flight plan for Vitoria. That was when Eduardo knew the Colonel must have taken his prisoners to Ilha da Borboleta.

Commandeering the nearest telephone, Eduardo called the security compound on the island, but the call did not go through.

"I am sorry, Senhor, but we are having trouble on the line," the operator told him.

Next, he tried Colonel Valerio's private number, and it was the same story.

Finally, when the telephone at the *quinta* was also out of order, he called the *Chrysalis* and talked to his father. "Is Colonel Valerio aboard?" Eduardo asked without preamble.

His father replied, "No, he and his men remained behind when we evacuated the island."

"You evacuated it! What in heaven's name for?"

His father explained about Colonel Valerio's warning of a possible terrorist attack. "The Colonel is holding down the fort," Ernesto assured him.

"I see," Eduardo said dryly, and did.

*Terrorists?* he thought grimly. *And Colonel Valerio has the time to jet to Sítto da Veiga and back?* He had to hand it to the ex-CIA man. *It's as good a way as any to have the island evacuated.*

"I hope you're not thinking of flying there," Ernesto told his son. "Whatever is happening on Ilha da Borboleta right now could well be dangerous."

Eduardo thought, *More dangerous than you think.*

Fifteen minutes later, he was airborne again.

He hoped to God he would be in time.

# ❦ *24* ❦

*S*he was trapped in the jungle of her nightmares, in a carnivorous landscape by Max Ernst. Stephanie soon realized she couldn't keep plunging blindly through this dense overgrowth of *oititeiro* trees and bamboo groves and cascading tree ferns. Disturbing cloud after cloud of butterflies and sending them swirling high into the sky to give away her position, was *not* the way to survive. And if she continued like this, she would get lost—was, in truth, *already* lost—and could easily end up running around in circles, making herself an easy target for Colonel Valerio, so he could pick her off real quick and neat.

She felt the heat of anger rise within her. *If he wants to kill me, then he'll have to work for it, the bastard!*

She slowed her panicked flight, forced herself to stop. She needed to rest. To take time out to think.

How stupid, blundering like a stampeding elephant, leaving behind a track a child could follow! *Why don't I send up flares to announce my whereabouts?* And it had been sheer folly to take off running without any sense of direction. She needed to formulate a plan.

Now then. Her foremost priority must be to get over to the other side of the island. Yes. There she would at least be familiar with some of the territory.

And once there? What would she do then? Where would she hide?

Suddenly, the memory of the place pierced her consciousness. *Of course! Why didn't I think of it right away?* For there *was* a place where she knew the terrain—a place Colonel Valerio might actually be unfamiliar with! Where there were no video cameras, no alarms.

She recalled Eduardo saying, *No one comes here anymore except me. Everyone else seems to have forgotten about it . . .*

Yes, but had Colonel Valerio?

There was only one way to find out.

Colonel Valerio was in his element.

He was proud to belong among a killer elite. One either had it in one's blood or one didn't. He considered it a great gift. A talent.

He sat on the ground in the shade, leaning back against the security

building. Taking it easy. Giving the woman the half-hour lead he'd promised her. From the looks of it, she'd need every minute.

He chuckled to himself. Hell, the way she'd gone thrashing into the
jungle, you could see the trees moving half a mile away! The dumb bitch.
She'd leave a trail HelenfuckingKeller could have followed.

He peered over the tops of his shades, looked down to the end of the
firing range at her boyfriend. The dumb fuck.

Pity to've had to mar him. But the wound wasn't lethal, not if it was
seen to in time. *I'll get my chance to hunt him yet.* But using him as a
demonstration had been sheer inspiration. Had brought the bitch to her
senses. Gotten her on the run.

He glanced at the nonreflective dial of his wristwatch. Thirty minutes
had passed. Time to get a move on.

Stephanie had clamped a lid on her panic, had calmed down enough to
think clearly, positively, creatively. Now she knew what she had to do.
Yes.

*Do the unexpected.*

*Take your cues from him, blend into the background the way he does.
Do as the chameleon—disappear in plain sight.*

Savagely, she tore at the elastic crew neck of her dark sweater. The
cotton/wool blend cut into the soft flesh of her fingers, resisting her efforts
to tear. *Oh, for a pocketknife,* she thought yearningly.

She gave the crew neck a particularly fierce tug and then, with a triumphant ripping sound, rent it loose from around her neck.

She slipped the elastic crew neck around her head, using it as a head-
band. A positive first step.

Squatting down, she dug her fingers into the dank dark earth.
Quickly, she scooped up a handful of the rich black soil and spat on it.
She needed mud. Moist, sticky mud.

*Change your colors and your spots. Do as the chameleon, and disap-
pear in plain sight.*

She smeared the mud liberally over her face, slathering the front and
back of her neck, scooped up more mud and spat on it and rubbed it into
her white tennis shoes. *He'll be looking for a pale complexion,* she reminded herself. *Make certain no pink skin shows.*

Then she stood up and looked around. She found what she wanted
right away and pushed her way slowly, cautiously, through the dense
vegetation to the bush with large, serrated waxy leaves. She selected
carefully, instinctively parting the outer branches and snapping off inside leaves, where what she'd done wouldn't be immediately noticeable.

Some of the leaves she stuck into her headband, a few inside her torn neckline, some more inside her waistband. There. Now she would blend in better with her surroundings.

*Let him search for a panicked woman on the run,* she thought. *It won't be me.*

Suddenly she felt a chill.

A silent, startled flock of butterflies swirled around her, enveloped her in a cloud, and was gone.

Stephanie knew what must have sent them into flight.

He was coming.

Twenty-five thousand feet above the Amazon, the copilot of the Sabreliner made his way aft and stopped at Eduardo's seat. "I'm afraid I've got some bad news, Senhor," he said quietly.

Eduardo looked up at him. "What is it?"

"We're flying directly into a strong headwind. It's going to change our ETA."

Eduardo sighed. "How much is it going to slow us down?"

"By at least half an hour, Senhor."

"Damn." Eduardo shut his eyes. He thought, *Monica, Monica, I'm on my way . . .*

For the time being, at least, Stephanie thought she had lost him.

A breeze had sprung up, rippling the leaves of the vine-strangled jacarandas and *oititeiros* and *Bertholletia* trees. She moved with the speed of the breeze, barely visible among the wild hibiscus and tree ferns and stands of bamboo.

Stephanie heard only the rustling of leaves, an occasional slithering in the underbrush, and her own tense breathing and quiet footsteps. She tried to guess how long she'd been on the move now, but she had no idea. It hadn't occurred to her to check the time when she'd first started running. All she knew was that it seemed like hours.

Then the trees and vegetation ended so abruptly that she almost blundered out onto the manicured lawn. She barely stopped herself in time. She parted the branches carefully and peered out.

There it was, just on the other side of the placid green pond with its cupolaed temple. The *quinta* with its arches and loggias and blue-and-white tiles and orange roofs.

"*Hey! Merlin!*"

Everything inside her went numb. The *bastard!* He'd been waiting here! Expecting her to be lured by the deceptive safety and familiarity of the *quinta!* Even as she reeled instinctively backward, she caught sight of him. He was crouched in front of a shrub near the pond, blending in almost perfectly with its branches. His bow was raised, an arrow poised—

*And me lined up in his sights! Shit!*

She dove hard to the left, twisting diagonally through the air the same instant he launched, and the breath whooshed out of her as she hit the ground and rolled. She'd heard the arrow whistle, felt its slipstream brushing past her face. Then it thudded noisily into a tree—*ca-RACK!*—blasting pieces of bark and splinters in all directions.

*Jee-sus!* she thought, staring up at it. And even as she turned back to him and saw him unhurriedly stringing another arrow into his bow, she caught sight of the white-daubed stone beside her. *The stone!* she thought jubilantly. *One of the stones Eduardo painted as a child. One of the stones that show the way to the grotto!*

Swiftly, she rolled over several more times, disappeared from Colonel Valerio's scope, and melted back into the jungle. Following the stones to the one place she thought of as *her* turf.

# 25

## At Sea

Zaza glowed. It was impossible to miss it. She was in one of her rare and special hostess moods. Chatty, charming, amusing, hospitable, full of joie de vivre. She delighted in dragging out the mystery, giving no clue as to what her surprise announcement might be. Meanwhile, the sense of mystery added spice and fascination and anticipation to the lunch, brought brightness to the eye and flushes to the cheeks. Lili and Ernesto basked in the old lady's effervescent attentions, while two handsome young white-gloved stewards served minute portions of grilled squid, white Belgian asparagus, and spinach with raisins and pine nuts.

And adding to the perfection of this *tableau vivant,* Lili Schneider's superb renditions of the lesser-known works of Mozart played in the background: "Vorrei Spiegarvi, Oh Dio!"; "Exsultate, Jubilate"; "L'Amerò Sarò Constante . . ."

How effortlessly the vocal flourishes seemed to climb and plunge and rise and caress, only to climb ever higher, again! Like chimeras, they sifted through the conversation and the laughter, these glorious bursts of song.

Zaza waited until the lunch plates were cleared, the dessert plates laid, and the torte was set on the table.

"None for me," said Lili automatically.

"Nor me." Ernesto shook his head, waved away his plate.

*"Lieblings!"* Zaza cried. "I insist you try the dessert! Just a mere *sliver—"*

She showed them just how tiny a sliver by parting her thumb and forefinger.

"To *celebrate!"* she added, raising her water glass to her lips, its facets catching the candlelight and flashing rainbows over the walls and ceiling and her face. She looked over its rim. "I instructed the chef myself, you know. And iced it personally."

"Not *Mandeltorte!"* Lili exclaimed softly.

"Yes!" Zaza cried, her eyes, warm with a distant memory, holding Lili's. "Your favorite . . . the way I used to make it for you long ago."

Lili laughed with delight. "And how can I refuse?" She nodded her head nostalgically. "But Zaza! You have not told us *what* we are celebrating."

Zaza dismissed the stewards. In the background, the song now intoned, *Basta, vincesti . . . Ah non Lasciarmi, no.*

Impulsively, Lili began to sing with it, making it a duet of mellifluous, identical voices:

*Basta, vincesti; eccoti il foglio.*
*Vedi quanto t'adoro ancora, ingrato.*
*Con un tuo squardo solo . . .*

Zaza clasped her hands to her breasts. "Ach! Your voice is still so divine! Look, Lili, look!" She sniffed and wiped her eyes. "It's brought tears to my eyes!"

Lili stopped singing, smiled, and reached across the table, covering Zaza's hand with her own. "It is sweet of you to say so, Zaza, but it is untrue. Unfortunately, my voice is no longer divine. No." She shook her head. "It has become rusty . . . corroded at the edges."

She frowned slightly and turned to Dr. Vassiltchikov.

"It is bizarre," Lili murmured, "that the voice should change while the body hardly does. Why should that be?"

But Zaza tapped her water glass with a spoon, bringing silence to the table. "No more talk of these matters. It is time for my announcement."

"Yes!" Eagerly Lili sat forward, her eyes bright with anticipation. "Do tell us!"

"Ah, but first. Ernesto, hand me that candle." Zaza gestured at the candlestick nearest to him.

He half stood as he wrenched the lit taper out of the ormolu holder and leaned across the table and handed it to her. Zaza smiled her thanks, lit the single candle in the center of the torte, then handed the candle back to Ernesto. "There. You can put it back now."

Ernesto twisted it into the candlestick and sat back down, but he leaned forward expectantly. All eyes were on Zaza.

The moment stretched, the suspense grew. From the hidden speakers Lili's flawless voice rose in an expressive *andante,* coloring the silence with vivid shades of sound. The flickering candlelight shimmered richly on the gilt boiserie, turned the carvings to voluptuous curves of liquid gold.

"Oh, do stop looking so confused!" Zaza said finally. "Today is my birthday. There. Now you know. And don't look at me as if I've lost my mind," she said crisply in reply to Lili's strange expression. "I'm not referring to the *day* I was born, but to today, the day I am *reborn!*"

Three sets of eyes stared at her.

Zaza's face brightened in amusement. "Really, *Lieblings!* Do none of you understand?"

Her eyes skipped from Lili to Ernesto, and finally rested on Dr. Vassiltchikov.

"I see that I shall have to explain." She smiled. *"Lieblings,* I have decided to join you! *Now* do you understand?"

"You'll join us . . .?" Lili was bewildered.

"Yes. Old and decrepit I may be, but I have decided that I do not wish to wither further and die."

"I cannot believe this!" Lili stared at her. "I always thought you were so—"

Zaza held up a hand. "Please. I was never as close to my earthly demise as I am now. That factor has certainly helped me see things in an entirely new light."

"Then you really have decided!" Lili breathed, clapping her hands together in excitement and pressing her steepled fingers against her quivering lips. Her eyes swam moistly. "You really are serious about joining our longevity program!"

"Yes." Zaza nodded firmly, then looked around questioningly. "That is, of course, if you are still willing to have me."

"Willing?" Lili's tears burst from a dam of sheer happiness. "You don't know how *glad* you've made me! *Du hast keine Ahnung!"*

Dr. Vassiltchikov's eyes were little more than slits, and when she spoke, a harshness crept into her voice. "You know, of course, that we cannot turn back the clock?"

"Of course I know that!" Zaza said testily. "I don't expect to turn nineteen and get out of this wheelchair and start ballroom dancing!"

"And you will have to change many of your habits," Dr. Vassiltchikov continued sternly. "That means no alcohol. A reduced diet." She made a point of frowning at the torte.

"This is my last cake, so you might as well let me enjoy it," said Zaza. "Now then. I am going to make my wish."

She sat perfectly still, shut her eyes, and smiled serenely. Then her eyes blinked open, she bent forward, and blew out the candle.

She said, "Now that you know what we are celebrating, you must all join me and have a bite of my *Mandeltorte."* She picked up the sterling cake server, cut four minuscule wedges, and waited for Lili and Ernesto and Dr. Vassiltchikov to pass her their plates.

Resting her elbow on the table and her chin on her hand, Lili kept staring at Zaza through eyes blurred with tears. "Oh, I'm so happy!" she kept repeating. "So happy!"

"And so am I, *Liebling,* so am I. Now, shall we see if my *Mandeltorte* is still up to par?"

"I haven't eaten cake in years," Lili whispered, carefully dabbing her eyes dry with a corner of her napkin.

"Next year, I shall celebrate with a candle in a tiny salad," Zaza said. "That is"—she slid Dr. Vassiltchikov an amused glance—"if I'm permitted even that. Now eat! *Schmeck es! Wir müssen es Kosten!"* She picked up her fork, cut a tiny bite, and speared it on the long narrow tines. "Well?" Zaza raised her fork in a toast. "To eternity," she proposed.

"To eternity!" the three others chorused, and popped cake into their mouths.

Zaza watched them chew. "How is it?"

"*Sehr gut.*" Dr. Vassiltchikov nodded approvingly.

"*Prima!*" Lili pronounced, rolling her eyes in ecstasy. "Heaven." She speared another small piece and chewed it slowly, savoring the sweetness. She gestured at Zaza's plate with her fork. "You haven't tried yours yet!" she scolded.

Abruptly Dr. Vassiltchikov jerked straight upright. "*Aber der Nachgeschmack!*" she croaked. "The aftertaste!" Her fork slipped from between her fingers and clattered loudly on her plate. She raised her hand to her neck. "My throat!" she whispered in horror. "It . . . it is burning! And closing!" She tried to push herself to her feet, but suddenly there was no strength in her arms or her spine. Weakly she slumped back into her chair, perspiration beading her forehead.

Instant realization dawned.

Uttering a strangled cry, Lili dropped her fork and swept her plate aside, sending it flying from the table to shatter on the parquet. Putting a hand around her neck, she stared across the table at Zaza. "*Die Mandeln!*" she whispered in horror. "*Oh, Du Lieber Gott!* The almonds!" Her voice rose in a tremolo. "The almonds," she wailed, "the bitter almonds!"

"Cyanide!" Dr. Vassiltchikov rasped, her face tightening. "She's poisoned us!" She was seized with a sudden spasm and convulsed in her chair. "And I . . . gave it to her . . . years ago . . . as I gave it to . . . all of you . . . in case . . . in case . . . in—" She couldn't continue. Her ancient face was turning blue, and she fell abruptly sideways, overturned her chair, and hit the floor with a thud. Her body convulsed and twitched and was still.

"Zaza!" Lili whispered hoarsely.

Suddenly Ernesto began to laugh.

Lili whipped her head in his direction. "What . . . is . . . so . . . funny . . .?" She was finding it difficult to speak. The burning sensation she felt in her throat was unbearable.

"We're dying," he gasped, struggling for oxygen even as he laughed. "Don't you . . . see? The only people ever . . . to taste of . . . of youth eternal . . . and . . . we're dying!" His laughter turned into gargling hacks and he reached out to touch Lili, but everything blurred and went black. Slumping limply forward, he pitched head-first onto the table. Plates jumped, glasses fell over, and the candles sputtered and went out, trailing black wisps of waxy-smelling smoke.

Lili was struggling to breathe. "*Warum?*" she whimpered, the hand around her throat tightening. Her eyes searched Zaza's. *"Warum?* For God's sake, *why?"*

Zaza's face was full of tender love and infinite sadness. The charade of the past hour had drained her completely, and she felt so weary . . . so terribly, terribly tired. "Because of the children," she said softly. "Because of the thousands you have sacrificed in the past, and the many thousands which would have been sacrificed in the future."

Lili could hardly see through the mist that was enveloping her. "I . . . only . . . wanted . . . to live . . . forever!" she cried, and then the mist thickened all around her.

Zaza put her face in her hands. In the background, accompanied by the beguiling clarinets and oboes, the French horns and cellos and shimmering violins, swirled that voice so pure in timbre, so silvery in radiance, that it was no wonder all the angels in heaven were weeping.

But it was only after the recording automatically stopped that Zaza realized it was not the angels she heard weeping. It was herself.

# 26

Stephanie crashed through the giant rubbery leaves, dense branches, and choking vines like a stampeding elephant. Melting into the jungle was a luxury she could no longer afford. Speed was of the essence. She had to make it to the grotto.

She ran as fast as she could, arms extended, thrashing aside the leaves and branches. Her heaving chest burned with the exertion, her breath rasped harshly. Keeping her eyes peeled for the paint-daubed stones, she missed seeing the clutch of gnarled roots until it was too late and—

—For Christ's sake, *no*—

—went flying.

The belly landing knocked the air out of her lungs, made her aware of the stitch in her side. Sheathed in a film of sweat, now that she'd stopped running, she felt a chill.

*Was that a sound?* She swung her head around, looked fearfully over her shoulder, back the way she had come. She strained to listen, but all she could hear was the hammering of her heart.

She pushed herself to her feet. "Get with it, Steph!" she urged herself, hearing the whine of fear in her voice. "Get your ass in gear!"

She took several deep lungfuls of air and ran on. She couldn't see or hear him, but an instinct borne of survival told her that he was out there.

The grotto was her only hope.

Colonel Valerio was like liquid, gliding smoothly along on a silent cushion of air, as though a barely noticeable human-shaped cutout of the jungle itself was on the move, constantly arranging and rearranging itself, now completely lost to the eye, now glimpsed almost briefly, but already gone.

Snapped branches and torn ragged leaves pointed out the way. At one point, he stopped for a moment and stood looking down, tapping a half-hidden paint-daubed stone with the toe of his boot. His camouflaged face hid his smile. He moved a couple of yards and stopped again. There was another one, like an overgrown highway marker. Hell, she was making it *real* easy, not even bothering to get off the marked trail.

*Yeah, but where did it lead?* he wondered. This part of the island, which had been left to its own devices and let grow wild, was new to him. Since it wasn't part of the patrolled perimeter and far enough from both the *quinta* and the beaches not to interfere with security, he'd never explored it. Now he wished he had.

As he continued on, he instinctively slowed his speed and proceeded with extra deliberation. He thought: *A little caution never hurt.*

Not that it mattered much in the long run. As far as he was concerned, she was already history.

The Sabreliner dropped out of the low, sullen sea of clouds, which blanketed the sky above Vitoria. Even before the jet came to a complete standstill, Eduardo had the door open. He leaped out and dashed over to the helicopter, and the moment he'd climbed in, it lifted off and rose into the sky, climbing until it hugged the undersides of the low dense clouds.

*Thirty minutes,* Eduardo thought. *All I need is thirty minutes . . .*

Suddenly a flash of lightning lit the humidity-laden clouds, and before the thunder rumbled, the downpour began.

The pilot turned to Eduardo. "Weather doesn't look so good," he shouted above the din of the rotors.

Eduardo's voice was grim. "Just keep flying."

The downpour began just as Stephanie slewed around a switchback; flayed by the rainy torrent and the rising wind, she was already drenched to her skin when she reached the halfway point. There it was on the right, the first gruesome landmark: the ruined stone wall with its giant stone face drooling water. Its hideous arrogance only served to remind her of her pursuer. She thought, *If Colonel Valerio were a statue, this is what he'd look like.*

On she ran, grasping at the air in front of her to clear branches out of her way. Then abruptly the foliage ended. She slid to a stop and shielded her eyes with a raised forearm, squinting against the rain in an effort to see into the distance. Her breathing sounded ragged and uneven, and her lungs ached. But this was no time for rest. She had to keep going. For in front of her loomed the most dangerous stretch of all—the straight path through the two towering walls of cliff. The Walls of Sighs, Eduardo had called them.

*Only fifty yards,* she told herself. *Only fifty yards . . .*

But fifty yards of straight path, with no brush to hide behind, nothing to provide refuge.

Fear gave her the impetus to move.

Clenching both fists, she burst into a high-kicking fifty-yard dash. Keeping her head up and her slitted eyes straight ahead, she ignored those faces of petrified torment. Her legs pistoned. Her chest pumped like a bellows. Fifty yards was soon reduced to thirty, then twenty, fifteen, ten, five—

A stone gave way under her right heel, her ankle twisted, and down she went.

For a moment, she just lay there, winded, elbow and knees scraped, hands cut and bleeding, her twisted ankle sending messages of excruciating pain. Shaking her head to clear it, she raised her eyes to the safety of dense jungle foliage taunting her from a mere five yards away.

She tried to kneel, and let out a yelp. God, that ankle hurt! Looking around, she spied a sturdy, yardlong stick lying not three feet from her.

A serendipitous find.

Reaching out, she grabbed it and used it for leverage to thrust herself to her feet, where she swayed unsurely. She steadied herself and glanced back over her shoulder.

A cry rose in her throat but never made it past her shocked vocal cords. She could barely make out the rain-blurred shadow of a man, but there he was, standing at the entrance to the two cliffs.

Her mind replayed the moment the arrow had whistled past her, slamming into Johnny's shoulder. Even now, she could hear the thump of the impact.

"Noooo!" Her cry rose from deep within her gut and set her body into motion without conscious thought.

Using the stick for leverage, she swung herself in swift limping arcs. Her twisted right ankle sent knifelike stabs through her legs, but she almost welcomed the pain. It proved she was alive.

Five yards. Then four, three, two, one—*safety!* Back she crashed into the dense jungle, lost to his sight. Once again, her allies were the branches twisted in strange embraces, the labyrinth of menacing bracken, the monster brush and malevolent leaves which whipped her face and drew blood.

But each step extracted an almost unendurable pain which shot through her ankle.

But she would not stop, could not stop! She was no longer guided by her mind, but by a survival instinct as old as time itself. She was driven by adrenaline and fear.

Colonel Valerio found himself walking slowly, head tilted back in amazement as he stared first up at one cliff face, and then the other. *Christ,* he thought, *what is this fucking place?*

In fact, he'd become so distracted and mesmerized by the ugliness that at first he'd actually missed seeing Stephanie.

Then, when he did notice her, she'd been limping off into the jungle, and it was too late to line her up in his sights. Her limp had not gone unnoticed.

*So she's hurt,* he thought with smirking satisfaction. *Serves the bitch right.*

Then he stood still, hands on his hips. Something was wrong. He was right on her tail, and it wouldn't be long before he'd catch up with her. Normally, that should have aroused his hunter's instincts. Instead, he felt peculiarly wary. Then he realized why.

*She's luring me somewhere!* he thought. *Why else would she leave such a crude trail for me to follow?*

Suddenly Colonel Valerio had had enough. There had been moments when he'd felt a reluctant admiration for Stephanie Merlin's spirit and inventiveness. Not anymore.

Ignoring the stone faces, he marched purposefully past the cliffs and then pushed his way into the dense green jungle. He wasn't about to let a woman play games with him. *Shit, no. Time I showed her who's the boss.*

Had Stephanie known Colonel Valerio's suspicions that she was luring him somewhere, she would have been the first to deny it. In truth, she couldn't have given a plausible explanation for why the grotto was the one place she believed would afford her protection. Yet that was precisely where her instincts were guiding her.

She came across the next folly even sooner than she had expected— the stone wall with the Gothic archway.

*At last!* she thought with a flood of exhilaration and relief. *I'm almost there now.* She remembered that through that arch was a kind of large courtyard—and a door set into the hillside.

The nearness of it made her move faster. She was almost home free. At her refuge.

Suddenly she wondered what she would do once she reached it.

# 27

*I*n the wind-buffeted helicopter, Eduardo sat forward in his seat, wiped at the fogged-up windshield with his sleeve, and peered down through the momentarily cleared arc left by the windshield wiper. Almost instantly, the windshield was obscured by exploding splats and streaky rivulets. He waited for the metronomic rubber to clear another arc, and peered down again.

*There!* A hundred feet below! Ilha da Borboleta.

It was all he could do not to let out a whoop of triumph.

"Stay at this altitude and fly to the far side of the island!" he yelled at the pilot, and pointed southwest. "I'll tell you where to land."

The pilot glanced sideways at him. "Sure hope you know what you're doing."

Stephanie clawed the tenacious vines loose from the iron-reinforced door, adrenaline blessing her with a physical strength she didn't know she possessed. Finally she wrenched the last vine loose, and it joined the others blowing in the wind like thick streamers of kelp.

She grabbed the great rusted handle and tugged. At first, the buffeting wind and rusted hinges offered resistance; then it creaked open. Holding onto the heavy door with her left hand, she used her makeshift crutch to swing herself inside. Once she was in, the wind slammed the door shut behind her.

The darkness was intense, blacker than any night. She'd have to progress by touch—but keep clear of the lethal electrical wiring.

*Whup!*

Outside, something hit the door with such explosive force she heard the wood crack and shake under the impact; so lethal, it pierced the door and pelted her with splinters. Around the arrowhead, thin shafts of daylight thrust into the darkness.

*Shit!* Stephanie thought. *He's right behind me!*

And even before the thought registered, she was already staggering with terror and haste downhill along the wet, slippery wash of stone.

Outside, standing under the Gothic arch, Colonel Valerio lowered his bow and smiled.

*That was just to let you know I'm right behind you,* he projected silently. *In case you're feeling too sure of yourself . . .*

He was tempted to hurry across the courtyard to see where the door led, but all in good time. *There's no great rush,* he told himself. *She's not going anywhere.*

"Here!" Eduardo shouted. "Put down right here!"

The pilot nodded, and with the agility of a juggler, dropped the helicopter toward the undulating ground, adjusting the descent as they went. Gray became pale green and pale green turned emerald. Then, with a shudder, the skids touched down and the trembling sense of airborne fragility was exchanged for the solid comfort of terra firma.

"Shut down and wait for me here," Eduardo yelled. "I don't know how long I'll be."

"Hey, Meeeeerliiiin . . ." Colonel Valerio's taunt rose on the rush of chill air which swept through the curving tunnel. Then there was an abrupt slam and the door to the hillside cut off the cross-draft and the wind was stilled. "Hey, Meeeeerliiiin . . ." Without the rushing of the wind his voice came louder, echoed endlessly in the stony confines.

Stephanie froze. She could feel everything inside her knot up and cramp. His derisive voice vibrated through her, buffeted her like a physical blow, caused a tremor which raised her hairs and sent ripples crawling along her flesh. Her teeth were clenched with determination, as though to stifle any cries, and she tightened her grip on her makeshift crutch. Swallowing the sudden onset of nausea, she steadied herself and forced herself to continue moving. *One step at a time,* she thought, swiftly swinging herself along on her crutch.

But even as she sped up her crutch swing on the downhill-graded curve of tunnel, his voice never seemed far behind, unnerving her, imbuing him with power.

"You gotta make things hard for yourself, don't you, Merlin?" He sounded cool and confident, totally in control. She could hear his boots squeak and squelch wetly.

She rounded another corner, and now the darkness paled and became deep blue. Rain sounded loud again, the rushing and splashing of water constant. A cool, eerily whistling wind blew past her, chilling her with its ghostly tendrils.

Then she turned one last corner, and there it was. The grotto.

Now what?

"MOOOOONIIIIICAAAAA!"

Eduardo raced through the *quinta*, throwing open doors and bellowing her name at the top of his lungs.

Through the dining room and loggias and Sala de Hércules he sped, then up the graceful stairs, which he took three at a time. From one wing of the mansion to the other he searched, but only silence greeted him—the empty, mocking silence of a house which has been deserted.

He leaped down the stairs and back outside, dashing from the terraces down to the lawn. He turned several full circles in place, his impatient eyes desperately seeking some clue, some inspiration. *They have to be around here somewhere,* he thought.

The grotto! If she managed to escape, that's where she would be headed! And something inside him scoffed, *Yes, but what if she didn't escape? What if you're wasting precious time?*

He turned another hesitant circle. For once in his life, he was indecisive.

*Jump back in the helicopter, check out the security compound? Or head straight into the jungle for the grotto?*

His instincts told him to head for the grotto. He started out for it as fast as his legs could carry him.

This was not the grotto of her dreams. It had lost its magic and gained a malevolent edge. In the rainy column of bluish daylight which poured in from the open dome overhead, the grotto seemed smaller now, more confining. And the mosaics and shell-clad busts were no longer extravagant and fantastical, but soulless monuments created from discarded carapaces—art crafted from death.

And then his voice came again, closer than ever. "Hey, Merlin! Are you ready?"

Stephanie looked around in desperation, tense as an overwound spring. Her face was taut, ashen, pinched. The sheen of rain and perspiration sleeked her skin; jittery nerves churned up bile in her stomach.

There had to be someplace she could hide. But where could she—

—there! That recessed niche was the darkest; it would afford the most protection. Instinctively, she drew toward it. As she slid into its shadows, she realized it was the very niche Eduardo had cautioned her about when she'd nearly touched the frayed electrical wiring. She looked at the live cord now, shrank away from it, flattened herself in the shadows.

Steadily, inexorably, Colonel Valerio's voice came louder: "Might as well give yourself up, Merlin. You're dead meat anyway. They've hired a professional assassin to get you. So why fight it?"

*Professional assassin?*

Her breathing sounded coarse and ragged. Her heartbeat was explosive. There was no way out, she knew. She was cornered like a rat . . .

"They hired the same one I got to lay those explosives in your grandpappy's apartment. That place was blown to kingdom come. So you're a lot better off with me. Least there'll be something left to bury." His laughter echoed, bounced off one wall and then another.

Stephanie's mind reeled, struggled to absorb the staggering information—

—and then he came into view. The Pearson Spoiler bow was at his side, an arrow already in its drawstring. Light from the open dome caught the knifelike edge of the arrowhead, glinted like a sharp blue flame.

"Whoa!" He had stepped on the marble slab which activated the fountains and was being sprayed from all sides. "I'll be damned!"

Stephanie had trouble breathing, felt the spring within her being wound tighter, tighter, then even tighter yet.

Slowly he began to walk the circumference of the grotto. Raised his bow as he came up on the first niche, and aimed. Lowered the bow and moved on to the next niche, where he repeated his aim.

Stephanie half lowered her eyelids and willed herself small, unimportant, *invisible*.

Boots squelching, Colonel Valerio waded around in an inch of stagnant water and came up on the third niche. "Won't do you any good to hide," he said.

His arrowhead swept the shadowed recesses of the mosaics, left to right. He stepped back slowly and lowered the bow.

Stephanie clenched her teeth hard to keep from making noise. She felt fear—raw, primordial, and paralyzing. She knew she was defeated.

"That's right," he went on, slowly turning to the fourth and last niche now. "Wanna do you myself. I like it. Just like your grandpappy. Guess who arranged to have him gotten rid of?"

Everything inside her went stone-cold with rage. *He* arranged to have Grandpa killed? He had arranged it, the bastard?

Almost unthinkingly, she reached out with a trembling hand, her fingers like a flattened spider creeping across the sharp edges of shell toward the exposed, frayed electrical wiring. She squinted in the dark, trying to find an unfrayed section.

Impossible. She couldn't see well enough. She'd just have to take her chances.

Water, electricity . . . electricity, water . . .

She poised her fingers to grab the wire—*did* grab hold of it—and just as the expected jolt of electricity never came, Colonel Valerio snapped in her direction—face, bow, arrow, and all.

Stephanie yanked hard, heard the wire snap and the live electricity buzzing faintly. She called out, "Yo! Valerio!"

He crouched forward, eyes agleam behind the bow.

"Here," she said. "Catch!" And she tossed him the electrical cable.

Wide-eyed with surprise, Colonel Valerio threw his bow arm up in front of him, but it was too late. The cable lashed him, and for an instant, he and his Pearson Spoiler bow were sheathed in a crackling web of bright blue light which danced all around his body and along his arms and legs.

And the grotto resounded with his hideous bellow. And then the snaking cable fell and hit the puddle he was standing in.

Instantly, the water hissed and crackled and churned. Steam rose from its surface.

Stephanie turned away and clapped her hands over her ears. She could not bear to watch his electrocution, could not stand hearing the deadly hisses and crackles and his high-pitched screams. She had a sickening vision of Jed Savitt's face on Colonel Valerio's body, of Valerio shuddering in an electric chair.

Behind her, arms flailing and body jerking, Colonel Valerio fell onto his back, where he thrashed wildly about while his screams rose even higher in pitch. Then his skin turned lobster red, his eyes bulged, he went abruptly rigid, seemed to levitate, and finally went limp and was still.

The sudden silence was unnerving.

After a while, Stephanie lowered her hands from her ears and slowly turned to look. He was sprawled in the water, his face frozen in tortured agony, his bulging eyes staring up at the rain coming down on him through the open dome.

She began to tremble, and wrapped her arms around herself. Her teeth were chattering and it felt as though the temperature had suddenly dropped to freezing.

"Monica!" From far away in the tunnel, she was aware of someone calling her.

Carefully avoiding the wet areas, she picked her way around the grotto and, like a zombie holding itself together, walked into the darkness of the tunnel. Still shaking uncontrollably and crying softly.

# 28

*T*he rain had stopped, and it was dark by the time they left the hospital in Vitoria. The doctor had wanted to keep Johnny overnight for observation, but Johnny, being Johnny, wouldn't hear of it. He was determined to see the day through. "Way I figure it, today can't get any worse—right?" And the brilliant he-man grin he'd flashed made Stephanie's heart ache.

She knew exactly what he was up to. *Doing a John Wayne number to one-up Eduardo,* she thought sardonically. *On the other hand, after what he's been through, he's entitled to a little posturing.*

He came out of the hospital, his arm in a sling and a showoff swagger in his step, then promptly fell asleep in the car. Stephanie hated waking him up for the helicopter ride, but she knew his pride would be irreparably wounded if he didn't board on his own two feet.

Throughout the flight to the *Chrysalis,* she sat beside him and held his hand. Kept holding it and murmured encouraging sweet nothings even long after he fell asleep.

Exhausted as she was by her own ordeal, she couldn't shut her eyes. She was thinking of her conversation with Eduardo at the hospital while they'd waited for Johnny to be sewn up. She had told him who she really was, that she'd been working undercover to do a story on the de Veiga empire, that Colonel Valerio had discovered she was an imposter and had come after her, and that Johnny was an old boyfriend who had followed her out of concern. She couldn't bear to tell Eduardo more, deciding that he would have to discover the truth about his parents on his own.

Now, Eduardo stood up and leaned over the seat in front of theirs. After watching them for a while, he came around and crouched down beside her. "You really love him, don't you?" he asked softly.

Stephanie slowly turned her head sideways on the headrest and stared at him. "Funny, isn't it?" she whispered, "that it should take a crisis for me to realize it?"

"Not really," he said. "Sometimes a tragedy makes one see things in a totally new light."

She nodded. "Not that I know why I'd ever want to put up with him." She turned her head in the other direction and regarded Johnny fondly. "Johnny Stone," she said, "is one ornery, smug, self-centered, unbearable, conceited, superior, chauvinistic—" Catching herself, she stopped and laughed softly. "Just listen to me! I sound like—"

"A wife?" Eduardo said gently.

She whipped her head around and stared at him.

"If you ask me," Eduardo said, "he is a very lucky man. I should be feeling envious."

She looked into his face: he who was also so proud, and so determined, not to show his hurt. "Do you?" she asked. "Feel envy?"

"Yes," he admitted. "How could I not?" He forced a smile. "But I think I can keep it under control."

It was just the kind of smile Johnny would have come up with, and she felt a painful swelling tightness rise up inside her. Somehow, she'd always known this moment would come. And yet, she still wasn't ready for it. Hurting Eduardo was the last thing she had wanted.

"I'm sorry about the way things turned out, Eduardo," she said huskily. Tears had sprung into her eyes, blurring her vision, but she managed to blink them back.

"I am sorry, too," he replied quietly. He was blinking his own eyes in a valiant attempt to hold back tears.

She reached out and touched his arm. "You do believe me when I say I really thought I was in love with you?"

He smiled and nodded. "Yes," he said, "I believe you." Then he stood up and looked down at her. After a moment, he leaned forward and chastely kissed her cheek.

No matter how hard she tried, the tears started rolling now.

They made the rest of the flight in silence. And when they landed aboard the *Chrysalis,* a whole new can of worms awaited.

"Grandmother!" Eduardo knocked on the door.

They could all hear the CD player blaring away inside—Lili Schneider singing the part of the Marschallin in *Der Rosenkavalier.* He knocked again and glanced at Stephanie and Johnny. Still no one came to the door.

Eduardo rattled the gilded handle. It was locked. He banged on the door with his fist. "Grandmother!" he shouted. "It is me. Eduardo."

Abruptly the CD player was turned off. Eduardo was about to knock again when Stephanie put a hand on his and stayed it. "I think I hear her coming," she said.

They both listened. The faint but unmistakable whir of the wheelchair could be heard approaching the other side of the door. The lock tumblers clicked, and the old lady opened the door partway. She was sitting forward in her wheelchair, peering suspiciously out into the corridor. Her face was red, and her eyes swollen. "Who is with you?" she demanded in an abrupt tone of voice.

"Monica Williams, who is not really Monica Williams at all, and a friend of hers, whom Colonel Valerio wounded."

The old lady's eyes searched her grandson's face.

"The Colonel is dead," Eduardo replied to her unasked question. "He tried to kill Monica—I mean, Stephanie—but she killed him first."

Zaza did not look at all surprised. "A resourceful young lady." She nodded her approval. "Listen, my darling. I will move my chair back, and the three of you may slip inside. But no one else. Is that clear?"

"Yes." His voice was puzzled. "Of course."

She rode backward a few feet, and Eduardo was the first one inside, followed by Johnny and then Stephanie. Stephanie shut the door and Zaza rode forward and locked it.

Suddenly a strangled cry rose from Eduardo's throat, and they all turned in his direction.

*"Meu Deus!"* he whispered, and rushed over to the dining table. He stood there, looking around in shock, and then slowly sank to his knees beside his mother's chair. "Mother!" he sobbed softly, lifting her icy hands and putting them to his lips. "Oh, God! Mother—"

Stephanie's hands scrabbled to her lips. "Oh, my God." She shut her eyes and quickly pressed her face into Johnny's good shoulder. One glimpse had been enough to know they were all dead.

Taking a deep breath, Stephanie drew away from Johnny and crossed over to Eduardo. Dropping to her knees, she put an arm around him. "Oh, Eduardo," she moaned softly. "I'm so sorry."

He put his head into his mother's lap and keened quietly. His grief pulled at Stephanie's heartstrings, but above his sobs she thought she could hear the laughter of the gods, a triumphant, exultant roar at the folly of mere mortals who tried to taste of the cup of life everlasting.

When finally Eduardo raised his head, his face was contorted and quivering, a mask losing its form. Tears streamed down his cheeks. Then he looked away, sniffed, wiped his eyes, and pulled himself together. When he turned back around, he gave Stephanie a little nod, acknowledging her comfort and thanking her and telling her he was all right now.

She looked at him a moment longer, then rose, squeezed his shoulder affectionately, and went to stand beside Johnny, who put his good arm around her waist. When Eduardo got to his feet, he had drawn an obscuring veil over his emotions. He looked at his grandmother stonily. "What happened?" he wanted to know.

Zaza rode over to her grandson and looked up at him. "They are dead," she said simply.

"Yes, but—*how?*" he demanded, staring at her. *"Why?"*

"Why?" The watery, wise old eyes studied him and the seconds ticked silently by. Time elongated, and it seemed she might never speak. Then she sat up straighter and shook her head. "Eduardo, *menino,*" she said, her voice gently reproving, her expression reprimanding. "How can you be so innocent? How could you have been so naive, and never suspect?"

Zaza sat straight and tall, imperially sure in her quiet strength. She had already shed her tears in private, and if Stephanie hadn't known better, she would never have guessed the old lady was in mourning.

At Zaza's suggestion, the four of them had distanced themselves from the gruesome *tableau morte* and had moved into the adjoining bedroom. Eduardo was seated on a *duchesse brisée,* head down, hands clasped between spread legs. Johnny reclined on the alcove bed, and Stephanie sat perched on its edge. If she looked beyond Zaza, she could see out the half-open door and glimpse Lili in profile, her neck still arched over the back of the chair.

Stephanie lifted her delicate glass and took a swallow, tasted liquid gold flavored with bitters sliding smoothly down her throat, warming her insides. Zaza said, "Cistercian monks. They make the very best liqueurs, you know. Their vows of silence, celibacy, and poverty leave them with no pleasure but that of the palate. Is it any wonder they take such care with fermentation?" She smiled tolerantly. "I know what you must be thinking: that I am quite mad."

For the last couple of hours she had regaled them with a great variety of subjects which, bit by bit, helped Stephanie fill in the missing pieces of the Schneider puzzle. How Lili, during a concert tour of South America in 1948, had met Ernesto and fallen hopelessly in love with the tycoon—and vice versa. That Zaza herself was really Lili's inseparable sister, Louisette, and had been masquerading as her mother after having steadfastly refused to participate in Dr. Vassiltchikov's youth treatments. And she told how, during a visit to Hitler's lair on the Obersalzberg, the Führer himself had introduced Lili to Dr. Vassiltchikov.

"I don't think you're mad," Stephanie said softly.

Zaza smiled, but sadly. "Perhaps you do not. But your friend Mr. Stone does not know quite what to think. And Eduardo's eyes. Such scepticism they reveal! Not that I blame you, *menino.*"

Giving a bark of a laugh, Eduardo jumped to his feet and stalked about the room. Then he faced the wall, raised a fist, and banged it angrily on the boiserie. "Dammit, Grandmother!" He raked a hand through his hair as he spun around. "Do you take me for such an idiot that you think I will fall for that . . . that fairy tale?"

Zaza's eyes flashed impatient anger: "Open your eyes to what goes on around you," she said coldly. "Oh, Ernesto and Lili were clever, I give them that. But did you *never* wonder why neither your father nor your mother ever visibly aged in nearly three decades?"

Eduardo struggled to find a plausible explanation. "They . . . they took good care of themselves. They had their physical regimens. The diets and facials. Cosmetic surgery—"

Zaza sighed. "You are grasping at straws. Lili only underwent two operations in her entire life. An appendectomy in nineteen twenty-two; then plastic surgery to change her appearance in nineteen fifty. Yes, Eduardo: in nineteen fifty! Forty-three years ago!"

He stood there in stunned silence.

The old lady went on quietly but mercilessly: "And did you ever ask yourself what was in that medication they took every day?"

"Of course not. Why should I? They needed it because of that illness they contracted in the Ama—"

"Illness!" Zaza cut him off. "They were as healthy as horses! The only times they became ill were when the medication was late in arriving. That is also when they panicked, because without their daily doses, they would have died." And then she told him about the age-retarding medication and the sacrifice of children it required.

Eduardo's head was spinning. "This is all so staggering to believe!"

"Believe it," said Stephanie quietly.

Eduardo started to whirl on her, but then he deflated like a punctured balloon. He sank back down on a chair and held his head in his hands. "Suddenly I do not know what to believe anymore!" he said quietly.

Zaza's voice gentled. "I understand your being upset and confused."

"But . . . thousands of *children?*" Eduardo shook his head. The world had become a Pandora's box, full of ills and ugliness. "It is unbelievable!"

Stephanie looked at him and said, "When Colonel Valerio caught us, Johnny and I were in your office at Sítto da Veiga. We used your own computer to break into a top-secret file. It's called the OPUS file and lists every child they ever murdered—one each day—along with a purported, 'official' cause of death." She paused. "Eduardo, they set up CRY to use the orphanages as a source for children. If you don't believe me, you can use any computer and see it for yourself. Zaza knows the code. She gave it to me last weekend, on the island." Finally, she told him about her grandfather's biography, his death and Pham's, and Vinette Jones's and the others. She told why she had really entered the de Veigas's world.

Eduardo listened to her bleakly. He looked struck, mortally wounded.

Stephanie turned to Zaza. "Who was Dr. Vassiltchikov?"

"Frau Doktor's real name was Klara Henschel. She was in charge of the Führer's pet undertaking, Project Methuselah. Naturally, since he dreamed of a Reich which was to last a thousand years, he wanted to be around to enjoy it."

"Good Lord."

Zaza noticed that their glasses were empty. "Some more liqueur?" she asked.

"Thank you." Stephanie picked up the bottle and refilled Eduardo's and Johnny's glasses. Holding the bottle up, she looked at Zaza questioningly.

The old lady shook her head. "Not yet, thank you."

Eduardo tossed his drink down in a single swallow. Then he leaned forward, gripping his empty glass until his knuckles were white. His body seemed weighed down by an enormous burden, yet at the same time, it seemed ready to spring into manic action. Stephanie's heart went out to him. She could only begin to imagine what he was going through.

"It all began on that fateful first visit to the Obersalzberg," Zaza explained with a sigh. "I was there, and so was Dr. Vassilt—Dr. Henschel, as she was known at the time. At first, she and Lili did not get along at all. But then at dinner, everything suddenly changed. Lili learned that the doctor's specialty was gerontological research, and the doctor learned about our poor, dead, Liselotte having been a geromorph. The doctor and Lili became utterly fascinated with each other. It was only natural, I suppose. Ever since Liselotte's premature aging, Lili could not bear the idea of growing old and dying. She became obsessed with remaining young forever. As for the doctor, the opportunity to study a geromorph's sister was manna from heaven. That weekend, the doctor took samples of Lili's blood, and afterward, they kept in touch—Lili, from wherever she might be touring, and the doctor from the Forschungs Institut für Geriatrie—the research institute in Badgastein, of which she was director. Incidentally, the institute never lacked for human guinea pigs. Himmler provided it with all the humans the doctor required."

Her audience of three listened in stunned silence.

"And there you have it," Zaza said quietly. "As the years passed, the doctor made great strides in her research, but before she could make her breakthrough, the war ended. But she was no fool. She had long since spirited money and valuables to South America. Toward the end, she destroyed all the institute's records, and had all her human guinea pigs and the entire staff put to death. She left absolutely no trace."

The old lady paused to sort out her thoughts, and continued.

"Naturally, she kept in touch with Lili. The next time they met was in nineteen forty-eight, during Lili's South American concert tour—when Lili fell in love with Ernesto. Then, in nineteen fifty, the doctor finally made a breakthrough and summoned Lili, and Lili confided in Ernesto. He, being in love with her, and having unlimited financial resources at his disposal, was the ideal partner. So he helped Lili fake her death— murdering Sir Kenneth and some poor anonymous woman in the process."

Eduardo's head ached. "My *parents!*" he burst out, horrified. "Dear God, my *own* flesh and blood did this! How do I *live* with that?"

It was all Zaza could do not to look away from his tortured gaze, his haunted, tormented face. "Perhaps it will make it easier for you," she said, "if you know they were not really your flesh and blood. How could they be? Lili had been barren, and Ernesto's sperm was infertile."

*"What?"* Eduardo jerked as though she had slapped him.

"Another irony," Zaza said. "Their sterility was a direct result of Dr. Vassiltchikov's youth-prolonging treatments."

Eduardo could no longer sit still. He got up and prowled back and forth, his face reflecting the agony of a man whose entire world had collapsed. Finally he stopped in front of Zaza. "If what you say is true, then who am I?" he demanded quietly. "Did I lose my identity as well as my parents?"

The old lady looked at him. "In my heart, you will always be my grandson, just as in the eyes of the world, you are still the son of your mother and of your father."

Eduardo swore softly. "I do not *care* what I am in the eyes of others! I need to know for myself who I really am!"

Zaza's soft face was the essence of compassion. She reached up to touch Eduardo, but he jerked away from her touch.

She let her hand drop. "You were one of their so-called 'angels,' " she said quietly. "One of the orphaned children they had chosen to sacrifice."

He looked stunned, taking first one step backward, then another, and another. "But why didn't they chop *me* up or whatever it is they did to the others? What made *me* so special?"

"They wanted a child, and you were the most beautiful child they had ever laid eyes upon."

"And another child took my place and died in my stead?"

"Yes."

Eduardo was beyond feeling any pain. There was only disgust and loathing and a hatred more powerful than any he had ever experienced. He no longer seemed to know who to strike out at, the living or the dead.

There was a long, drawn-out silence.

"So what do we tell the world?" It was the first time Johnny had spoken, and they all turned to look at him.

"Why not the truth?" Eduardo suggested with a cynical laugh. "The world has a right to know the kind of monsters my so-called parents were. Besides, they are dead. Scandal can no longer hurt them."

*"No."* Zaza's spine went rigid with determination. "The world must never, ever know of this."

"Then who will seek justice for all those children?"

"No one," the old lady said flatly. "No one."

Eduardo started to protest, but something in Zaza's face stopped him.

She said, "Are you so selfishly concerned with your own pain, that you *still* do not comprehend the enormous implications of Dr. Vassiltchikov's work?"

"I am beginning to," Eduardo said.

Her eyes stared coldly at him. "This is perhaps the most lethal knowledge the world could be given. If it were known that eternal youth is ever possible, can you imagine the rush that knowledge would create to duplicate the results—ethics be damned! This entire planet would become a world of cannibals, the old, in effect, eating the young. Religion, ethics, morals—the very sanctity of life itself would be threatened!"

Eduardo stared at her silently.

"Your grandmother is right," Johnny said quietly. "If people found out that the key to longevity lies in their fellow human beings, the result would be catastrophic. Babies could well be bred to be killed, like chickens at a poultry farm."

"So we just forget those thousands of children? Is that it?"

"No," said Zaza, "but we make certain the children of the future are protected from the fiendish fate these have suffered."

Eduardo sat there, his face pale, two bright, livid spots burning on his high, prominent cheekbones. After a while, he sighed. "I suppose you are right," he said grudgingly.

"I know I am," Zaza said. "It is up to us to make certain this will never happen again." She looked around. "We *are* all in agreement, then?"

Stephanie and Johnny nodded, and finally Eduardo nodded also.

"*Gut,*" Zaza said. "At least that is settled." She glanced around again. "Do any of you have any other questions?"

Stephanie nodded; something was still bothering her. She said, "When I was in Rio, I kept getting anonymous phone calls. All the person kept whispering was, 'Die!' Do you know anything about that?"

Zaza said, "That, *Liebling,* was me."

"*You!*" Stephanie stared at her. "But . . . *why?*"

"I wanted to save your life," Zaza explained. "When I overheard Lili and Colonel Valerio plotting your death, I hoped I could frighten you away."

"You scared me half to death!"

Zaza nodded. "That was the idea," she sighed. "But I should have known better than to think I could frighten you so easily."

Stephanie frowned. "What I can't understand is, if you were trying to frighten me away, then why did you give me the OPUS number?"

"That was my alternate plan. If I couldn't chase you away for your own good, the least I could do was help you accomplish your goal."

Stephanie was astounded. "You knew all along who I was?"

"No. Not *who* you were. But I had a good idea what it was you were after."

"But how did you know I wasn't going to misuse what I might discover?"

"I didn't. I had to trust my instincts. After all these years, I have learned to judge character quite well, you know. I knew from the start that your search was selfless. I would never have encouraged Eduardo to pursue you, otherwise."

Stephanie could only sit there in amazement, trying to digest it all.

Zaza said, "At least, now you know why I poisoned my own sister, her lover, and that fiendish doctor. I feel remorse and sadness, yes. But even more, I feel immense guilt. Not for killing them; I should have done that long ago. What I will never forgive myself for is having let the horror continue for all these decades."

"It's all over now," Stephanie said softly. "You must stop blaming yourself."

Zaza looked shocked. "My dear, I am as guilty as they are! My love for my sister led me to condone it. I fully understood the horror, but allowed it to happen. I am by far the guiltiest of all."

There was a long silence.

"And now," Zaza said, "I think I will have a drink. All this talking has left my throat feeling parched."

Stephanie reached for the bottle of tangerine liqueur.

"No, thank you." The old lady shook her head. "I myself am not particularly fond of that liqueur." She put her wheelchair in gear and rode over to the *table en chiffoniére,* which held the drinks tray. Lifting a decanter, she unstoppered it and poured herself a small glassful. Then she stoppered it again.

"What is that?" Stephanie asked.

"This?" Zaza held up her glass. "An almond liqueur."

"I've never tasted that. Could I try some?"

Zaza smiled. "I fear you would not like it. It really is an acquired taste." Then she lifted the drink as though in a toast. "To the natural order of things," she said. "To life and to death—and eternity be damned!" Then she raised the glass to her lips and drained it.

"*Noooooooooo!*" There was a guttural bellowing roar as sudden comprehension dawned on Eduardo. He leaped from his chair and lunged at Zaza, knocking the glass out of her hand. It flew to the parquet and shattered, but it was too late. The glass was already empty.

Zaza convulsed. "Forgive me, *menino,*" she whispered, and then she clutched her throat and a vast shudder distorted her face.

"Grandmother," Eduardo whispered. "Oh, Grandmother. Please, do not leave me alone!"

Zaza lowered her hand and gripped his arm tightly. The pain was gone from her face, and she looked serenely at peace. Her voice was raspy but soft. "Do not be afraid of death, my child," she said, "for what is more beautiful than eternal peace?"

# ~ 29 ~

*S*tephanie had never been so glad to see a city as when the *Chrysalis* steamed into Rio the following morning. She couldn't help but think of the yacht as a ship of the dead. Knowing the four bodies were stored in the onboard morgue chilled her. She couldn't wait to get off.

"I just talked to Eduardo," she told Johnny when she came out on deck as the yacht was getting ready to dock. "The official story being handed out is food poisoning."

"Think the authorities'll swallow it?"

"The de Veiga billions say they will. Half the government's probably been on the payroll sometime or other."

"Right," he said. "I keep forgetting. They practically own the country."

"Also, Eduardo thinks it's just as well we don't attend the funeral, and understands why we want to fly home as soon as possible."

She came up beside him and leaned her head gently against his good shoulder and smiled at shore. "A courier's already on his way from Sítto da Veiga with our passports, which Colonel Valerio had appropriated. Someone will bring them to the apartment. Now all that's left for me to do is go there and pack, and then it's *arrivederci*, Rio."

"Dock and fly," he teased. "Depriving me of the Girl from Ipanema, too."

She elbowed him in the side. "I catch you staring at one of those little chickies in their *fio dentals*, you'll have *both* arms in a sling."

The *Chrysalis* was now a hundred yards from the quay, lined up lengthwise with it. The underwater thrusters slowly moved the giant yacht sideways toward it.

"The marvels of technology," Johnny muttered. "Whatever happened to tugboats?"

"Didn't you hear? They went the way of LPs."

"And telexes," he said. "Speaking of which, while you pack, there are a few things I need to do, too. We'll meet at the apartment later, 'kay?"

"And where are you off to?" she demanded.

"Seeing to our airline tickets," he said. "You know, supersaver, super-discount coach? Plus, there's a few other personal odds and ends I've got to take care of."

"My, my, but you're a whirlwind of activity," she remarked dryly. "You must be making a speedy recovery."

"What can I tell you? Can't have my girl saddled with a chain around her neck, right?"

The *Chrysalis* nudged sideways against the quay, protected by rows of giant, sausage-shaped, white foam fenders. Within moments, the big yacht was secured and the blue-carpeted gangplank bridged ship with shore.

Stephanie waited to get off until the police and morgue attendants had boarded. Then she disembarked.

Eduardo caught up with her before she was halfway down the gangplank. "Stephanie!" He sounded breathless from running.

She stopped and turned around, one hand poised on the railing.

His eyes were moist and implacably sad. "I do not want us to part like this," he said in a low, tortured voice. "Not after what we have shared . . . and been through together."

She stared at him wordlessly, a pain wrenching her gut. It was all she could do to keep from crying.

He said, "If it is all right with you, when your passport arrives I will deliver it personally to the apartment. We deserve to say our good-byes the way they should be said."

Stephanie nodded. "If you're sure," she said softly. "Although it looks like you'll have your hands full here."

His smile was fleeting, sad, and wistful. "Nevertheless, I would never forgive myself if I did not drop by. I do not want you to remember me by what happened on the island and onboard this yacht. What we shared was much more than that."

She looked deep into his dark eyes. "Yes," she said huskily, "it was."

"I am glad you feel that way." He glanced past her, down at the quay, and cringed. It was especially busy, with police cars parked this way and that, ambulances and limousines waiting, a crowd of onlookers and reporters held at bay. "How quickly the vultures smell blood," he murmured. Then he drew his gaze back in and looked at her questioningly. "What will you do once you get back to New York?"

"What will I do?" She turned and stared off into the distance, at the white high-rise buildings packed like stacked sugar cubes at the feet of the humpbacked emerald hills covered with *favelas*. A faraway look came into her eyes. "I'll try to pick up where I left off," she said softly. "I'll try to be my old self again."

On the way to the apartment, Stephanie first had her driver stop àt Grupo da Veiga's pink-and-white mansion in the Centro district. She told him to wait while she hurried inside to her office. She cleared out her desk of personal items and put them in two shopping bags she found in the closet.

*I'm glad Lia's not in,* she thought. *I hate farewells. There's something so final about them.*

Stephanie felt a twinge of guilt. She also hated disappearing like a thief into the night. The least a co-worker deserved was a personal note of thanks. She nodded to herself and quickly scribbled one to Lia. She decided that when Eduardo came by the apartment later, she would recommend he promote her assistant to the position she herself was vacating.

*Lia will make a good replacement,* Stephanie thought. *And the promotion will be the best good-bye present I could give her.*

Leaving the note on Lia's desk, she weighed it down with a paperweight and lugged the two shopping bags of personal things out to the limousine.

Stephanie unlocked the penthouse door. The terrace doors in the living room were open, and a sudden cross-draft rushed through the apartment, banging the door shut behind her.

"Hel-lo-oooo?" she called out, putting the shopping bags down. "Barbie? Waldo? Anybody home?"

Silence.

For an instant, the quiet made her feel an irrational trickle of fear. And then a familiar voice squawked, "Steph! Steph! I love you, Steph!"

Stephanie smiled. *Good old Waldo,* she thought, dropping her keys on the foyer table. She went through the living room, pushed aside the billowing floor-length sheers, and stepped out through the open sliding doors. She could see Waldo's cage at the far end of the lushly planted terrace. Smiling, she headed toward it, past the tooth-edged Japanese aucubas and the thriving kentia palms and potted citrus trees.

Her clicking heels slowed on the terra-cotta tiles as she neared the cage, a frown suddenly marring her features, her nerves inexplicably quivering. Something was not quite right. Waldo should have been climbing the bars excitedly. Should have been ruffling his feathers and preening.

"Hiiiii . . . hiiiii . . ." Waldo's strident, ear-piercing screech continued even as Stephanie reached the cage.

Suddenly she clapped a hand over her mouth, stifling the low, strangled moan which rose from deep inside. Her stomach lurched and she felt weak and dizzy; a giant bass drum seemed to pound relentlessly in her ears.

For there at the bottom of the cage was her pet parrot—her Waldo— lying motionless on his back, his stiff legs straight up in the air.

The trickle of fear she had felt when she had first come into the apartment had swelled to icy, full-blown terror. Her legs wobbled, seemed to want to give out from under her.

"Waldo wants a crack-er! Wal-do wants a crack-er!"

She spun around, stood there swaying uncertainly. If Waldo was dead, where was his voice coming from?

"I love you, Steph! Eh-eh-eh-eh-eh-eh-eh!"

His voice was coming from *there*—behind that thicket of palms!

Every instinct told her to get away from here! To run—*flee!*

She quailed outwardly. It was as if someone had clamped a strip of steel around her chest and was inexorably tightening it, trying to crush her. Air. Why couldn't she get enough air?

"Steph! Steph! I love you, Steph!"

*Flee! Run! Get off this terrace, out of this apartment.*

No. First she had to find out where his voice was coming from! *I have to see for myself,* she thought. She found her legs and stumbled past the palm fronds.

She uttered another involuntary cry. A tape recorder! Waldo's words and squawks and screeches were coming from a cassette recorder! Heedless of the razor-edged palms, she lunged at the cassette player and punched frantically at all the buttons until she hit STOP.

Suddenly silence: now she could only hear the distant sounds of normalcy, of life going on as usual. The faint hissing of car tires on the *avenida* below. The muted crashing of the surf. The cries and laughter of children playing volleyball on the beach across the street. And fear. The pounding of her heartbeat, the jackhammering of her pulse: above all, she could hear her own fear. Smell her own fear.

And then that feeling: *I'm being watched!*

The hairs on the nape of her neck and on her arms tingled and rose. She went rigid; her listening sharpened, filtering out the white background noise of cars and surf and laughter. *I'm not alone, I'm not . . . me and poor dead Waldo and . . . who else? What else?* Cautiously, slowly, her terrorized eyes searched the thickets of foliage all around, the bougainvillea-clad windscreens at either end of the terrace, the purplish-black shadows, the stepped-back terrace above . . .

*I'm forgetting something . . . something important I should be remembering.*

Fronds rustled behind her, whispered in the air. Shadows quivered, stretched—

She whirled around, holding her breath. It was only the ocean breeze. Beyond the balcony, the deep blue Atlantic filled her vision, stretched away to infinity until it became an indistinguishable haze where water met sky.

And then it hit her with numbing force—*Colonel Valerio's taunt*—and her heart lurched. Sweat seeped from under her armpits, beaded on her forehead, prickled down along her spine.

*Even if you were to escape . . . you're dead meat . . . they've hired a professional assassin to get you . . . the same one I got to lay those explosives in your grandpappy's apartment . . .*

The memory of those terrible words exploded in her brain, sent her mind whirling. Instantly, she thought of Pham, Vinette Jones, Aaron Kleinfelder, and—

Astrid Bezzera!

The realization stunned her like a physical blow. She could hear the strident sob rise within her. How foolish could she have been, dismissing Astrid's murder as the act of an anonymous thief!

There was a menacing air of claustrophobia about the terrace now, the sense of being trapped in a cage.

Get out of here!

She forced herself to think clearly. No. She must not run. She must use the telephone! *Yes!* She must call the police. Now she turned and ran, blundering through the potted jungle, slipping on the terra-cotta tiles, fighting her way through the billowing sheers which impeded her like gossamer ghosts. Wrenched them aside—

There! The extension phone on the end table! She lunged at it, snatched the receiver, banged it against her ear.

What? No dial tone?

Desperately she tapped the cradle with her fingers. Still no sound! A high-pitched chirrup rose from her throat.

A chime rang, pierced through her like an electric shock. The doorbell! *Oh, God!* She made a faint mewling sound, dropped the receiver, looked around in panic. *He's here! The assassin's here! He's coming to kill me!*

"Girl!"

Stephanie whirled around, her heart soaring at the familiar voice. It was Barbie, her one and only friend, coming down the spiral stairs. The rush of relief enveloped her in a torrent.

"Oh, Barbie!" Stephanie sobbed. "Oh, thank God! Am I glad to see you!"

"What's the matter?" She frowned at Stephanie and touched her face. "Why, you're as pale as a ghost! And you're shaking all over!"

Stephanie nodded. "Someone . . . someone's trying to kill me!"

Barbie's voice was calm. "Now, why would anybody want to do something like that? Nice lady like you—"

The doorbell chimed again, and Stephanie's entire body jerked convulsively at the sound.

"You expecting someone?" Barbie looked at her questioningly and started toward the foyer.

*"No!"* Stephanie half screamed. She grabbed Barbie by the arm and yanked her back. "Don't let him in! Don't!"

The doorbell kept ringing, long and short two-tone bursts of sound.

"What am I going to do?" Stephanie moaned. "I've got to get out of here! And there's only the front door!"

"I know!" Barbie said. "There's always the terrace of the building next door! The only thing separating it from this one is the windscreen. There's a ledge you can use to step around it." Barbie took her by the hand and pulled her back outside to the terrace. "Now, just be nice and calm," she advised. "No one's going to hurt you while I'm here."

Barbie's inanely soothing voice worked its magic and calmed her somewhat. Now they could no longer hear the chiming doorbell and the sudden fury of a pounding fist on the door and the muted shouts coming from the other side of it.

Stephanie looked gratefully at Barbie. *No one's going to kill me while I'm with her,* she thought. *Assassins don't want eyewitnesses.*

Barbie hurried her across the terrace to the opaque windscreen. Bougainvillea, loaded with cascades of pink and magenta blossoms, covered it completely.

Barbie showed her the narrow concrete ledge. "You've only got five feet to go. Now, just hop up there and hold tight to the windscreen. There's nothing to be afraid of. Just try not to look down."

Stephanie eyed the ledge with misgiving. It suddenly seemed incredibly narrow. *That can't be wide enough,* she thought with a sinking feeling. "I-I can't get up there," she said uncertainly. "It doesn't look safe."

"Just kick your shoes off," Barbie said cheerfully, "and upsy-daisy."

Stephanie hesitated, wishing there was some other way to escape the apartment.

"Hurry up," Barbie urged, glancing back at the open glass doors and billowing sheers.

"All right," Stephanie said hoarsely. She slipped out of her shoes, took a deep breath to stifle her fears, and held onto the wobbly frame of the windscreen. Gingerly she climbed up onto the ledge.

"You're doing fine," Barbie assured her. "And you don't need to worry. I'll be right next to you the whole way."

Nodding uneasily, Stephanie carefully inched her way sideways along the ledge. The sounds of traffic coming from below sounded louder; the ocean wind seemed stronger. She felt cold and clammy and aware of the twelve stories which dropped away like a sheer cliff. Gripping the windscreen and clenching her teeth, she moved another few inches, and then a few more. *Perhaps it's not that difficult after all,* she thought.

The next instant, a chunk of concrete gave way, and she screamed in horror as she dangled twelve stories in midair.

# 30

"*S*tephanie?" Eduardo's voice was loud and sharp. He leaned on the doorbell and kept pounding. "Stephanie! Stephanie, *open up!*"

He knew she was in; he'd asked the doorman when he'd arrived. But after she hadn't responded to the house phone, the doorman, knowing the de Veigas owned the penthouse, had let Eduardo go on up, anyway. *Why isn't she opening up?* he wondered. *I know she wants to see me, and she needs her passport.*

He hammered on the door again. A neighbor, disturbed by the racket, opened her door, cast him a disapproving look, and scolded.

"Ste ... pha ... nie!" He pounded again. "O ... *pen up!*"

Eduardo stopped for a moment, ear to the door, listening.

Still nothing. He couldn't understand it. She was expecting him.

Murder, violence, suicide—if, after all that, somebody hurt Stephanie now, he would never be able to forgive himself ...

He was about to ride back down and get the passkey from the concierge when he thought he heard something. No, not something—

*Screams!*

Heedless to the prying neighbor, he put his ear against the door again and listened. They *were* screams, very faint and distant, but definitely coming from inside the apartment! *Probably from one of the terraces!*

"Call the police!" he shouted at the inquisitive neighbor. "Tell them to hurry!" When the woman didn't move, he screamed: "*Polícia!*"

That got her moving. Her head ducked back inside her apartment; the door slammed.

He backed as far from Stephanie's door as he could, and with all the speed he could summon, hit it running. The door shook and creaked under the impact, but held. He repeated the maneuver, ramming it lower.

This time, the lock disintegrated and wood splintered; the door crashed open against the wall, and a cross-draft, pungent with sea air, swept out into the hall. Carried along by the momentum, Eduardo hit the floor, rolled over, and scrambled to his feet. He looked around frantically, trying to decide in which direction he should head.

And then the screams penetrated his thoughts, caused his body to jerk. They were coming from out on the terrace somewhere.

Fast as his legs could carry him, Eduardo dashed across the room and wrenched the sheers aside, hoping he would be in time.

"For Christ's sake, *help* me! I'm going to fall!"

Stephanie hung from the windscreen, kicking her legs in a desperate, futile attempt to find purchase. Already, she could feel her grip weakening, her hands tiring. "Help me!" she cried hoarsely. "Barbie, please help me!"

Barbie grinned, her black eyes bright as she lazily held out a beautiful red long-stemmed rose.

"*Grab me!*" Stephanie screamed. "*For God's sake, Barbie, pull me up! I can't hang on much longer!*"

Barbie reached out and stroked Stephanie's face gently with the velvety rose petals. "Ever hear of The Ghost?" she asked softly, as though they had all the time in the world.

Stephanie tried to focus on Barbie's words. *Who the hell's The Ghost?* she thought furiously. *And why doesn't she just grab me and pull me to safety?*

As though reading her mind, Barbie said, "The Ghost is the best assassin in the world. The Ghost was hired to kill you." Her voice dropped to a taunt. "And you know what?"

"Please, help me, Barbie . . ." Stephanie whispered. She was becoming exhausted, could feel her fingers loosening and gravity inexorably pulling her down.

"My name's not Barbie," she shrieked. "My name's Shanel, and you're the only person on earth know's Shanel is The Ghost!" She slapped Stephanie's face hard with the rose. "And now, it's time to fulfill my contract!"

"Nooooo!" Stephanie sobbed.

The thorny rose whistled through the air like a whip and stung Stephanie's face again. Then Shanel began to pry her fingers loose.

"No," Stephanie sobbed. She felt Shanel tugging at her hands, yanking them loose. She clutched her handhold grimly, squeezed her eyes shut.

"Good-bye," Shanel said, "and good riddance. Now die bitch, die!"

Johnny was getting out of a cab in front of the apartment building when the screams coming from above drew his attention. Leaning his head back, he looked up to the top of the building and then moaned. Even from twelve floors below, he could see Stephanie dangling in midair—knew it was Stephanie! He started to race into the building, moving as he had never moved in his life. But even before he reached the entrance he could hear the blood-curdling screams gaining in volume. The next instant, two bodies, clutched together in a grotesque embrace of death, came hurtling down.

He watched in horror as they crashed into the roof of the cab with such force that the roof caved in and the safety glass burst out in a shower of pellets.

On the twelfth floor, only moments earlier, Stephanie had struggled to hang on, fighting Shanel's relentless hands with everything she had. Stephanie had never seen such obdurate single-mindedness in her life, and she had the urge to hang on by one hand and use the other to fight the assassin off, but she resisted. Instead, she gripped the windscreen even tighter as Shanel yanked furiously at her hands.

"Let *go!*" Shanel hissed. "I'll break your fuckin' fingers if I have to!"

The fury of the attack rocked Stephanie's body from side to side. Her feet and knees scraped across the sharp rough concrete. Stephanie cringed as the torture continued, trying to resist the fists pounding on her fingers. "Stop it! Stop it!" she heard herself groaning, not knowing how much longer she could hold up to this kind of punishment—

—when Eduardo appeared, a knight in shining armor gilded by the bright sun. He hesitated only momentarily to get his bearings. Shanel, hearing his bellow of rage, let go of Stephanie's hands and turned to face her new adversary. But already, Eduardo was hurling himself toward Shanel in a flying tackle and caught her around the thighs.

Shanel let out a mortal bray of fury and lost her balance. That, together with Eduardo's momentum, was too great to interfere with the laws of gravity. Stephanie screamed as he and Shanel went somersaulting over the railing, embracing each other like obscene lovers as they hurtled past her and tumbled down, down to the faraway ground below, their echoing screams fading until she heard a report like a gunshot.

Then there was silence.

Everything inside Stephanie seemed to contract. "No!" she screamed with a dry, aching throat. "Eduardo! Eduardo!" And it seemed that her limbs were tearing themselves from her hands, and that her muscles and bones and cartilage were stretched to the point of snapping.

She thought: *But I don't want to die! I'm not ready to die yet!*

"S-t-e-e-p-h-a-a-n-i-i-e-e . . ."

From above the sounds of traffic drifting up from below, she could hear Johnny's bellow rising. Could it really be him?

"Hang on!" he yelled.

Her heart pounded wildly with hope. It *was* Johnny! *If only I can hold on a moment longer . . . and then another moment . . . and then another . . .*

Her eyes filled with tears. It was getting more and more difficult not to let go. Her hands were slick with sweat, her fingers and wrists and arms totally numb. It was a miracle her grip hadn't loosened already.

*All I have to do is hang on a moment longer,* she told herself.

That moment stretched into another moment, and that moment into eternity.

The memory of Johnny's voice was all that kept her clinging there, fighting to keep her tenuous grip on life. Battling to survive. *For Johnny.*

Suddenly she could hang on no longer.

Stephanie screamed, "Nooooo!"

And then her hands loosened and she let go.

The rest happened so quickly and unexpectedly she was barely aware of it. Johnny's hand clamped around her right wrist and he pulled her to safety. Once he had her on the terrace, his strong arms closed around her. Holding her tightly, he kissed her all over her face, saying, "I love you, Steph. God, how I love you, my darling! It's all right now. Nobody's ever going to hurt you again . . . ever . . ."

She listened to his soft, soothing words, and suddenly, she realized that the nightmare was over and they were together.

Twenty-four hours had passed since Eduardo's death. With no one left to perform the daily task of checking in with Grupo da Veiga's sophisticated computer system, the virus which had lain dormant for all these years suddenly activated itself.

Unnoticed, it raced throughout the tentacles of the far-flung system, crisscrossing the world through telephone cables and fiber-optic lines and satellite transmissions. It jumped from mainframe to supercomputer and on to individual terminals and programs. But only once it had spread to every corner of the de Veiga empire and had settled into every program and disc did it kick in and carry out its manifest destiny.

Around the world, the entire de Veiga empire began to unravel and self-consume.

The virus spread like wildfire.

Within the hour, the entire de Veiga-developed Fleet Wing Airlines Reservations System (FWARS) used by six international and ten national carriers—not to mention over twenty-six thousand travel agencies around the world—spat out garbage and then went dead.

The result was chaos at every major airport on earth.

Passengers were stranded, scheduled flights suddenly no longer existed, and crew manifests disappeared, never to be retrieved. The computerized car rental and hotel reservations systems, which were subdivisions of FWARS, went next.

Within three hours, the entire FWARS system itself ceased to exist. It was as though it had been swallowed up by a black hole.

At each de Veiga factory, the computerized robotics went berserk, performing their jobs with ever-increasing and unstoppable speed—*faster,*

*faster, faster!*—until, one after the other, the complex, state-of-the-art machines ceased to function.

In France, Groupe Byi S.A., the country's third largest insurance company, a de Veiga-controlled corporation, electronically lost track of three billion dollars in investments—not to mention one and a half million subscribers.

Funds and information which were lost forever.

All electronic transactions on the Hong Kong and Frankfurt stock exchanges, which had been designed by one of the de Veiga subsidiaries, ceased to function, and then the system itself vanished without trace.

Leaving nothing but useless hardware.

At Sítto da Veiga, the computer-run artificial environment broke down. The automatic plant sprinkler systems created a flood while the temperature and humidity levels rose to such great levels that the computers themselves burned out and the residents fled outdoors. Then there was a tremendous explosion, the entire glass city seemed to rock, and the complex shattered and was flattened to its foundations.

Stephanie and Johnny watched the picture postcard view of Rio de Janeiro drop away and tilt as the Varig 747 climbed steeply into the sky.

"Think you're gonna miss Rio?" Johnny asked.

Stephanie turned away from the window. "Johnny," she said with patient resignation, "after the past five days of police and government investigation and interrogation, do you think I give a hoot if I never see a photo of Sugar Loaf again?"

"They say time heals all wounds."

"Maybe," she sighed. "But it'll be a cold day in hell before these heal, I'll tell you that."

"Well, there are two things that might make you feel a little better," he told her.

"Really?" She sounded unconvinced.

"First of all, there's the matter of your resurrection . . . or your resurfacing."

"I know." She sighed gloomily. "I've been giving it quite a lot of thought."

"Well, think no more. The minute we land at JFK, every major newspaper and television reporter will be gathered for a press conference."

"Oh, no," she groaned. "Tell me it's not so, Johnny," she begged.

He smiled. "As the song goes, 'Don't worry, be happy.' You don't need to say a word about longevity or CRY or genetics. We've got eight and a half hours before we land in New York, and that gives both our